STRAIGHT UP   CHASER   LAST ROUND

TWISTED FOX SERIES

BOOKS 3 - 5

CHARITY FERRELL

Straight Up

Lincoln

THERE'S ROCK BOTTOM, and then there's the underbelly of rock bottom.

My underbelly?

Getting arrested and going to federal prison.

Today, I'm being released from the hellhole.

With my chin held high, I salute the guard and exit the place where I've been held hostage for two years.

There's no stronger high than freedom.

No drug.

No booze.

No sex.

Nothing.

Everything I took for granted in the past I'm grateful for.

Hello, fucking freedom.

It feels damn good, being released from prison for a crime I didn't commit.

———

I'VE BEEN HUMBLED like a motherfucker.

I went from owning a million-dollar penthouse to sleeping in a prison cell to crashing in my brother's guest bedroom.

From being the VP of a million-dollar empire to broke.

The feds took possession of nearly everything with my name on it.

Underbelly of rock bottom.

It's been a long-ass day. After leaving the prison, I was treated to a steak and lobster dinner, courtesy of my mother.

"I read that people like a nice, big meal after being released from incarceration," was what she declared.

I replied with a forced smile and enjoyed the meal.

Who turns down a steak and lobster dinner?

I didn't have the heart to tell her that all this guy wanted straight out of prison was solitude, peace and quiet. One more luxury I'd taken for granted.

After showering, I slide into the king-size bed—the silky sheets yet another relic of my old life—and snatch my phone. Just as I plug it into the charger, a text comes through.

Unknown number: It's Isla. Can we talk?

My blood boils, and my grip tightens around the phone.

How'd she get my number?

I had my brother, Archer, change it, so I could have a fresh start when I was released.

Cursing, I delete the text, toss my phone onto the floor, and sigh as I soak in the silence.

Had it not been for Isla, I might not have been incarcerated.

Had it not been for Isla, my father might not be in a prison cell, awaiting his own freedom.

CHAPTER ONE

Cassidy

"HAVE YOU LOST YOUR FUCKING MIND?"

Since I'm walking out of the county jail, my brother's question isn't a shocker. Barefoot with my heels in my hands, I hop down the concrete steps one at a time. Call me classy.

Don't judge.

Get Arrested wasn't on last night's bingo card.

Kyle leans against his Jeep with crossed arms and a deep scowl. I gulp back the dread of the interrogation he'll deliver on our drive back to my sorority house.

"Yes, you've definitely lost your mind," he adds when I fail to answer.

I squeeze my forehead to ease my pounding skull while facing him. "Can you not be so loud?"

My head throbs.

My body aches.

My heart is wounded.

Everything hurts.

A drove of emotions kicked through me while I sat in the jail cell, waiting to be bailed out.

Sadness. Anger. Abandonment.

Last night was supposed to be a parade of romance while celebrating six months with my boyfriend, Quinton.

Correction: *ex-boyfriend* after he deserted my ass.

What great taste I have.

Fall for a man who bails when the cuffs come out.

Instead, my night ended with me incarcerated and him walking free.

"What?" Kyle shouts.

I wince.

He raises his voice. "You don't want me to be loud?"

I roll my eyes, yank the door open, and hop into the passenger seat while Kyle slides into the driver's side.

"Thanks for bailing me out," I grumble. Frustrating or not, I have to respect the man who rescued me from jail.

He shakes his head and starts the Jeep. "You're not goddamn welcome."

"I should've called Rex." I jerk the seat belt across my body. "He wouldn't have freaked out like this." My younger brother would've arrived with an iced coffee and offered me a high five.

"Had I not been able to pull strings, I'm sure you would've."

Facts.

Kyle is a cop, and with his help, I hoped for a speedier release.

Which happened.

I chose less jail time over an iced caramel macchiato.

Proof I don't always make stupid decisions.

Kyle runs a hand through his dark hair. "You ready to face Mom and Dad?"

"Hell to the no." I pin my gaze on him. "Which is why, dear brother, you're keeping your mouth shut about this little adventure."

I'm twenty-one. My parents don't need to be filled in on every component of my life. There are things a lady should keep private and all.

"Too late. The university called to inform them of your expulsion." A heavy sigh leaves him. "Hell of a wake-up call for Mom."

The fuck?

"They can do that?" I shriek. "Don't they have, like … a HIPAA for criminal records?"

His lips twitch as he fights back a smile. "You lose confidentiality when you break the law."

"Remind me to write to the attorney general about that bullshit."

"I have more news." He offers me a pitying glance.

"This is all a prank, and I'm on some reality show?"

"You wish." He snorts. "Our next stop is your little sorority house to pick up your shit since they're evicting you."

My lips tremble. "How can they do that? What happened to innocent until proven guilty?"

When it rains, it apparently pours and kicks you out of college.

I'm throwing out humor. It's who I am.

On the inside? I'm choking back the urge to vomit.

The urge to break down in tears.

This arrest will ruin every life plan of mine: college, law school, becoming a successful attorney.

One mistake.

All aspirations shattered.

"This is ridiculous," I snap, tossing my bag on the floorboard.

"You broke the rules—broke *the law*."

I didn't break shit. I cried to the officers, claiming my innocence, but someone had to take the fall. That someone ended up being me. With tearful eyes, I begged Quinton to confess. He refused, and his lie resulted in my arrest. The asshole didn't even bother to bail me out either.

"Oh, like Becky didn't break the law, forcing us to take ecstasy during rush," I scoff. "Or when Sam drunkenly smashed a cop car's windows? Neither were booted."

Kyle shakes his head. "You should've taken tips from Becky and Sam on how not to get kicked out then."

I slump in my seat. "I'm fucked."

He nods. "You're fucked."

Expelled.

Kicked out.

Criminal.

All for a crime I didn't commit.

CHAPTER TWO

Cassidy

One Month Later

ONE BAD DATE destroyed my future.

Booted me from my sorority.

Granted me with a criminal record.

My present-day life, ladies and gentlemen.

Following my arrest, my world became a shitshow. My mom sobbed. My father threatened to ship me off to military school. I reminded him that wasn't possible since I was an adult.

What was possible?

Him cutting me off.

Which was what he did after my little *I'm an adult* remark.

"You're a college expellee and irresponsible," he said after breaking the news that he'd no longer support me.

They did at least foot the attorney bill that helped drag me out of the mess Quinton had thrown me into. My punishment ended in probation and community service.

Word of advice: don't listen to the sugary pop songs.

Bad boys are never good for you.

After collecting my belongings from the sorority house, I moved in with my older sister, Sierra, in our hometown of Blue Beech, Iowa. News travels fast in small towns, so it didn't take long for my arrest to hit the gossip mill. Everywhere I went, I was asked about my jail stay.

"What did you do?"

"Are you a drug addict?"

"Were you, like, dealing with the Mafia?"

Like, no, Karen. I was put in a crappy situation and screwed myself.

No hot Mafia heroes here.

I decided it was time to leave my old life behind. The problem was, I was on probation, and I couldn't legally venture too far. Sierra stepped in and found me a job. I used my savings to rent a one-bedroom apartment in Anchor Ridge, two towns over from Blue Beech. Even with the short distance, there's a relief, walking into a coffee shop without being known as the troublesome daughter of Blue Beech's mayor.

Now, I'm just the customer who orders a deathly amount of espresso shots in her coffee. One employee actually wished me well in the next life, claiming no one could survive that much caffeine. Taking that as a challenge, I ordered an extra shot the next day.

All of that led me to my new job at the sports bar, Twisted Fox. Maliki's—Sierra's boyfriend—best friends own the place, and they agreed to hire me. My first shift is tonight, so I'm dealing with a ball of nerves in my stomach the best way I know how—by drinking two vanilla lattes and cramming four mini Snickers bars into my mouth on the drive there.

I walk into the crowded bar, and Finn, the bouncer, jerks his head in greeting. Casually dressed patrons with beers in their hands yell at the display of mounted TVs—a different sport on each screen. A long wooden bar is stretched along the back, a mirrored wall behind it, throwing back the reflections of the happenings in the building.

The sweet aroma of fried bar food trails with each step I take toward the employees-only door in the back, following the directions I was given. Venturing down a short hall, I knock on Cohen's office door.

The co-owner answers and waves me into the room. Since Cohen is Maliki's best friend, I've met him a few times. Last weekend, Sierra dragged me to his birthday party and introduced me to my new coworkers.

We briefly chat before he passes me a stack of forms to complete. Twenty minutes later, I return to the front of the bar in search of Georgia—my trainer for the night and Cohen's younger sister.

I do a sweep of the bar and spot Georgia waving me over in a similar fashion as her brother did.

"Hey, girl!" she shouts.

I wade through the crowd, dodging a group of guys arguing over a sports call while women yell at them to grow up, and join Georgia and her friends at the pub table.

"Hey." I pull out the stool and plop down next to her before exchanging hellos with her friends—Lola, Grace, and Silas—all people I met at the party.

While they make conversation around us, Georgia guides me through the employee handbook and training packet. I've never waitressed before, but the job seems simple enough. I'm a people person. I got this.

Georgia claps when we're finished. "You ready?"

"I think so." I twist my watch and do another scan of the room.

That's when my gaze lands on the man behind the bar, and all background commotion fades. A black shirt, sleeves rolled up and cuffed at the elbows, reveals his muscular frame. Biting into my lip, I drink him in as if he were the cocktail he's pouring into a glass, a bachelorette party cheering him on in the process. He's older—my guess, five to six years on me. Thick raven-black hair is trimmed short on the edge and longer on top. I play with my fingers, wishing I could run them over the scruffy stubble stretching along his cheeks and strong chin.

The woman's eyes light up with as much desire as mine as he slides the glass to her.

It's him.

The type of man I shouldn't want.

The type of man who is nothing but heartache and criminal records.

Dear heavenly father, please forgive me. I want to sin with this man.

"Who is he?" I point at my future boy toy. "I want him for breakfast, lunch, and dinner."

The table falls silent while all focus moves in the direction of the guy I'm nearly drooling after. The mood has shifted, and everyone's eyes avoid me.

"You might be eating those meals through a straw if you keep staring at Archer like that in front of Georgia," Silas says.

"Archer?" I shake my head and look away from my new man crush.

No wonder everyone is shooting me death glares. They think I'm referring to Georgia's boyfriend.

"Not him," I clarify before I'm fired or stabbed. "We met at the barbecue. I'm talking about the guy next to him." Mentally, I slap my forehead and inhale a sharp breath.

Dear heavenly father, it's me again. Please do not let that guy be one of the other girl's boyfriends.

That'd be just my luck.

"Lincoln?" Silas asks, cocking his head to the side while staring at me. "Archer's brother?"

My muscles relax, as a drink hasn't been thrown in my face. "If that's the man next to him, then yes. Is he single? Can I have him? What's his favorite breakfast, so I can make it for him on our morning after?"

Everyone laughs while I do the same.

"Be careful, newbie." Silas scratches his cheek. "We have a strict *no relationship between employees* rule around here. Too much drama."

I glance at Georgia, raising a brow. "Aren't you and Archer dating? They both work here."

"They're the exception," Lola states matter-of-factly.

I smile, perking up. "Maybe I can be the exception too."

Although I have no pull around here. Georgia has the advantage of dating the co-owner. Pretty sure they make the rules but don't have to follow them. Maybe I can have the benefit of nepotism on my side, and Archer will allow his brother and me to fraternize.

Instead of replying, Georgia checks her watch and stands. "All right. Time to get this training party started."

Georgia reminds me of myself. She's quirky and a ball of energy, and everyone loves her.

I slide off my stool and am on her heels as she gives me a tour of the bar and introduces me to the employees I haven't met.

Oh shit.

Here we go.

My heart freezes and then pounds when we stop at the bar. The new closeness provides me with a better look at Lincoln, a better look at every physical feature I find attractive.

I know; I know. Boys get me in trouble.

Literally.

Something about this man is different.

Maybe it's my being on a strict no-guys diet and my weakness is standing in front of me.

Maybe it's that the only *eye candy* I had for months was Blue Beech eye candy, and that shit hasn't changed since middle school.

A little flirting won't hurt, and it'll keep me entertained in this new, boring life of mine.

"You met Archer." Georgia's sugary-sweet voice snaps me back into reality. "And this is Lincoln. They're our bartenders for the night."

I display my flirtiest smile, hoping it's not overkill.

He returns the smile; it's friendly, easygoing, nowhere near as desperate as mine.

Dammit.

"Hi, I'm Cassidy." I step in closer. "Your future wife."

I was voted Most Outspoken in my senior class.

Talk to a crowded room? No problem.

Meet new people? Sign me up.

My lack of shyness and wit is why my parents said I'd make a great attorney.

Thanks for ruining that, asshole ex.

I went from studying the law to breaking it.

Georgia snorts behind me as I level my attention on Lincoln. He throws his head back and laughs. It's deep, rumbling, masculine—my new favorite sound.

"You working here?" He tilts his head forward and smiles. It's a smile that nearly buckles my knees. "Are you even old enough to legally buy a drink?"

Hot and a smart-ass.

One point for Lincoln.

This will be fun.

"Obviously," I fire back. "Or they wouldn't have hired me."

"I stand corrected." He winks. "I'm the fun bartender." He jerks his head toward Archer. "He's not."

Archer gives him a warning glare.

Lincoln shrugs with a smirk.

I grin harder.

Archer murders our flirting when he says, "You go train away, baby," to his girlfriend. He slaps her ass with a towel and kisses her.

I'd place my hand over my chest and moan *aww* had he not thrown off my flirting with his brother.

With a silent groan, I shuffle away from the bar on Georgia's heels, forcing myself not to check if Lincoln is watching me.

"So … why aren't you working at Maliki's bar?" Georgia asks.

I expected that question. Maliki owns the Down Home Pub in Blue Beech. It'd make sense if I needed a job, he'd give me one. He offered, but I declined.

"I got into some trouble." I mentally curse myself at the admission and backtrack to what I planned to say. "And we decided I needed to get out of town for a while."

I decided.

My mother claimed it was a terrible idea. My father swore I'd fall into more trouble, working at a bar.

Georgia perks up, fanning strands of thick brown hair out of her eyes. "What kind of trouble?"

"Just stupid stuff that got me kicked out of college." I wince, wishing I hadn't said that either.

"Oh, I'm going to get that story out of you some time." She laughs and swats my shoulder.

I'm grateful she doesn't push for more.

———

WAITRESSING ISN'T AS easy as it looks.

Twisted Fox's crowd has nearly doubled since the start of my training, and as the night grows later, the customers grow needier.

More handsy.

Ruder.

Drunker.

After shadowing Georgia for an hour, she gave me two tables of my own to serve. All of them are easy two-tops, but hey, I'll take it. She instructed me to tell Finn if anyone gave me trouble. As a girl who attended frat parties like they were her second major, my creep meter is legit. I can spot a dude who's contemplating catching a feel or slipping a roofie in seconds.

"You bitch!"

Whipping around at the comment, I spot Georgia across the room with a man standing in front of her.

He pulls his shirt out, his face wild and inebriation bleeding through him, and inspects a red stain. "You ruined my shirt!"

"You okay, Georgia?" I yell, a chill snaking up my spine.

Creep meter is losing its shit over here.

She nods, giving me a thumbs-up, and talks to the guy. When he grabs her ass, I dash in their direction. Her tray crashes to the floor, and he stumbles when she shoves him.

"What the fuck?" Archer screams, jumping over the bar like a damn hyena and storming toward them.

Oh shit.

My throat turns dry as I witness the fiasco along with everyone else in the bar. Not one TV is getting an ounce of attention at the moment. Not one drink is being sipped. This is now tonight's show, and it's better than any *Real Housewives* reunion.

"Archer, no!" Georgia yells at her boyfriend.

"Fuck that shit," Archer roars. "Move, Georgia." He levels his gaze on the asshole and tightens his fist.

The murderous glare on his masculine face has me convinced the drunk dude isn't leaving in one piece tonight.

"He's drunk," Georgia pleads. "Let Finn kick him out."

"Nah," Archer says, spit flying from his mouth. "I'll take the trash out myself."

I cover my mouth to conceal my chuckle.

Good comeback there, Archer.

Lincoln appears at his brother's side. "I got this." It's a failed attempt to ease his brother.

"Oh, look," the jerk mocks. "The assholes are coming to her rescue."

I throw my arms up.

Dude deserves at least one punch from Archer.

"Georgia," Archer yells, advancing toward the man, "goddamnit, move."

My attention flicks to Georgia when she calls out my name and asks me to round up Asshole's friends.

I nod and scramble toward their table. "Seriously, grab your friend and get out of here before he gets his ass handed to him." As much as I'd love to witness Archer teaching him a lesson, it can't happen here.

With a string of curses and glares, they down their drinks and stand. I snort when one mutters, "Chad is done being invited to guys' night. Dude is a fucking hothead."

We're too slow to save the day. Archer circles around Georgia to kick Chad's ass, and she attempts to block him. It all becomes a blur of movements and shit-talking, and in the end, Georgia falls and smacks her head on the ground.

CHAPTER THREE

Lincoln

IT HAPPENED FASTER than when I'd come the night I lost my virginity.

Two pumps, and I had been apologizing to my unsatisfied date.

Two seconds, and Archer attempted to kill the guy who had grabbed Georgia's ass.

The problem was, he hadn't planned on her jumping in to stop him.

I stand out of the way as the ambulance wheels an unconscious Georgia out on the stretcher. With flaring nostrils and not a word to anyone, Cohen rushes out of the bar behind them. Archer sprints out seconds later.

The instigator and his friends fled the scene at the mention of cops. When the cops and EMTs arrived, everyone turned silent, so there were no distractions as they took care of Georgia. An uncomfortable silence—something I'd never heard in Twisted Fox— hung in the air as people pleaded for Georgia to *just open her eyes.*

Terror took residence on my brother's face, regret flashing alongside it, and I cracked my knuckles. Everything would change after tonight.

How much? I'm not sure yet.

"You okay to keep the bar covered?" Silas asks, chewing on a toothpick while eyeing the bar—customers staring at each other in question, unsure if they should return to screaming at ref calls or go home.

Archer being gone leaves me slinging drinks solo. Not that I mind. Even if he'd tried to stay, I'd have forced him to go be with Georgia. Half the bar cleared out after the cops arrived, so it's manageable. Even if it wasn't, I'd lie.

"I got this," I answer with a nod.

"Appreciate it, man." He slaps me on the back. "Prepare to be there for your brother."

That's the understatement of the motherfucking year.

Whatever happens tonight, my brother will never be the same.

I nod again in uncertainty.

"You know my number if you need anything," Silas adds. "Finn will wait until close to leave, so someone will still be working the door."

I check my watch. "It's only an hour before close."

"You think she'll be okay?" He jerks his head toward Cassidy, who's headed in our direction.

The new girl was living in my head rent-free all night before the shitshow happened. She sprinkled flirtation with every drink order she called out to me, making it impossible not to laugh. In my short breaks, I eyed the men watching her strut through the bar, sleek and almost catlike. Her wavy blond hair feathered over her shoulders with each step she took, and it never took long for her petite frame to get lost in the sea of crammed tables.

"You good with working without help?" Silas asks her.

"Definitely." She shoots me an amused smile. "If I have any questions, I'll ask my man here." Her attention returns to Silas. "You going to the hospital?"

Silas plays with the toothpick in his mouth. "Yeah."

Cassidy snags the pencil behind her ear and shoves it into her apron. "Will you keep us updated on her condition?"

"I got you." He salutes us and leaves.

A flush creeps up Cassidy's cheeks as she rests her elbows on the bar and smirks. "Looks like it's just you and me."

I offer a polite smile. "Looks like it."

"We'll make a damn great team." She holds out her hand for a high five.

I high-five her with as much enthusiasm as a dude who just tested positive for the clap. It's out of character for me to be uptight, but tonight, concern pours through me. Hell, I'd take a curable STD over what happened to Georgia. Archer doesn't cope well with loss, people getting hurt, or when he seems responsible for something bad happening. If Georgia's condition is critical, it'll gut him. Turning the TVs back on, I hope the rest of the night flies by.

"Yo! Bartender!" a yellow-polo-sporting frat boy yells a few barstools down from us. "How about a drink on the house for that mood killer?"

"What an asshole," Cassidy says, not bothering to lower her voice. "Poison his drink … or at least spit in it."

Frat Boy shoots her a glare.

She smirks in response.

Even though all I want to do is kick him out, I yank a glass from the stack and pour him a beer *on the house*.

The cheapest shit we carry.

The kind that delivers a hell of a hangover.

I hate fuckers who take advantage of vulnerable situations.

Asshole mutters a, "Thank you," and his friends blurt their *free drink* requests at me.

This will be one long hour.

In what seems like every five minutes, I check my phone for any updates on Georgia, and before I know it, it's closing time.

"Last call!" I shout.

Customers guzzle down their drinks and finish their games of pool. The free-drink-loving frat boys are in the corner, throwing out desperate last shots at convincing a group of women to go to their place for round two. The man in front of me asks me to find his wife's name in his phone and calls for a ride home.

A typical closing night at Twisted Fox.

Different situations but always the same characters.

Finn waits to leave until the bar clears out, and while he's walking out the door, Cassidy reminds him to send her updates. I kill the TVs —what I always do first when closing—but the silence is needed more tonight than ever.

Dirty glasses and beer bottles clank together as Cassidy collects and tosses them into the garbage. Just like with Archer leaving me, Georgia's rush to the hospital left Cassidy alone for the night.

"If you want to go, I'll finish up," I say, dumping the contents of a red food basket into the trash before stacking it on top of the others.

She doesn't need to feel obligated to stay and close shop with a stranger.

"I'm good." She strolls to the next table. "It's my job."

My throat tightens.

Would she be okay if she knew who I was?

Where I've been?

My past?

My money is on no.

There's an automatic assumption when it comes to people like me.

An automatic notion that criminals are not to be trusted.

"Any updates on Georgia?"

Her question jerks me from my *woe is me* thoughts, and I cringe, remembering Cohen's latest text.

The good news? Georgia is doing well.

Bad news? Archer left the hospital, hasn't returned, and isn't answering his phone.

I clear my throat. "She's stable. They think it's a concussion." I scrub a hand over my face, adding a deep pressure with the tips of my fingers.

"Then why do you look so stressed?" She tilts her head to the side. A strand of blond hair tucked behind her ear falls free.

"Archer is MIA."

Whoa.

I retreat a step.

I'm a private person, never one to air out my family's business.

"What do you mean, MIA?" She stops cleaning and focuses on me. "Why isn't he there with her?"

"That's the question of the century." Holding in my aggravation over my brother's dumbass actions is a struggle.

"No offense, but that's messed up."

It is.

We've only known each other a few hours, but within that time, I've learned that Cassidy isn't a bullshitter. When shit with my brother blows over—which it'd better, or I'll kick his ass—she'll be a hoot to work with.

"He has issues," I say, snatching the disinfectant from underneath the bar and spraying the top down.

"They always do."

I set the bottle down and stare at her from across the bar. "What's that mean?"

"All hot guys have issues." She levels her deep hazel eyes on me, and I wish the lights were brighter so I had a better view of her. "So, what's yours, big guy?"

I quickly glance away in guilt. "Who says I have one?"

Shit, and who says I only have one?

I could write an entire damn novel on mine.

"Like I said, all hot guys have issues."

I point at her with the towel. "Don't let Georgia hear you call Archer hot."

She laughs. It's feminine, indulgent—a sound I wouldn't mind having as my ringtone. "Considering Archer is MIA, I'm sure she'd rather me call him worse." She clicks her tongue along the roof of her mouth. "So ... your issues?"

My stomach twists, and I hold up my hands. "No issues here."

"Mm-hmm." She strokes her chin, and her eyes meet mine. "I have an idea. When we're finished here, we'll embark on Operation Find Archer and Kick His Ass."

Relief settles through me at the subject change. I chuckle. "How about this? You'll go home, and *I'll* go hunt my brother down and kick his ass."

It'll be a hard enough job to get Archer to talk to me. If I have someone with me? No dice.

She shakes her head. "You'll need backup—like Batman and Robin."

"I show up with you, shit will get worse."

She sighs. "Geesh, you and your bro are serious buzzkills."

"My brother is." I shove my thumb into my chest. "Not me. I told you, I'm the fun one."

"Does the fun one have a girlfriend?"

I'm rendered speechless for a moment. I pause to study her, zooming in on the way she waits in anticipation—licking her lips, a smile twitching at them.

"I don't," I croak. Nor do I want or need one.

I got involved with a woman who fucked my entire world up.

"Perfect." The word slowly slips from her bubblegum-pink lips. "What's your breakfast of choice?"

I raise a brow.

"I need to know what to cook the morning after our first sleepover," she replies like *duh*.

I scratch my cheek. "You're pretty blunt for a girl."

"Girls can't be blunt?" Her eyes, brimming with mischief and challenge, meet mine. "If you don't like a blunt woman, this is where I retract my breakfast offer."

"Nah, I'm good with it." I share her grin, mine cockier. "I actually like it."

Resting her pink-manicured hand over her Twisted Fox tee, she pouts. "Are you going to ask if I have a boyfriend?"

I hesitate, my voice turning strained. "I think me asking that is dangerous."

If I don't know, I can convince myself she's taken and off-limits. Technically, she is off-limits. There's a *no fraternizing* policy here—which no one obviously takes seriously—and Cassidy is my brother's employee. Not only that, but she's also younger than my usual taste.

At least, I think that's what my problem was. Back then, as hard as I tried, there was no connecting with women my age. Maybe it was the chicks in my circle, in my world, but I never found anything in common with them. Cassidy, on the other hand, is proving every *she's too young for you* theory wrong.

There's this electricity between us that's zapping me to life.

"Why is that dangerous?" She makes a *hmm* noise in the back of her throat.

"You're trouble." It's a statement. A fact. A motherfucking warning to myself.

She rests her hands on her hips. "What's wrong with trouble?"

I gulp. "Trouble leads to more trouble."

I know that from too much experience.

CHAPTER FOUR

Cassidy

"TROUBLE LEADS TO MORE TROUBLE."

If that's not the understatement of my life.

Trouble finds me and then becomes a domino effect.

If I ever became a reality star on *The Real Housewives*, I'd make that my tagline.

After Lincoln calls me trouble, he hastily shifts our conversation a different route. While cleaning, we talk about customer reactions to tonight's disaster. Lincoln muffles out laughter at my jokes here and there, but my commentary isn't where his head is.

It's on his brother.

There's nothing sexier than a man who cares about others. That attraction is deeper now that I've had my fill of dating one of the most selfish men on earth.

Good-bye, self-absorbed men.

Hello, selfless ones.

Lincoln offers to walk me out when we're finished cleaning. "From now on, park in the employee lot in the back. You don't need to be walking through a parking lot where drunk people might linger. We always walk the female employees out after their night shifts."

I salute him, a sense of security hitting me. "Got it."

This man could tell me never to eat chocolate again, and I'd do it. *Okay, maybe I'd do it for a month.*

A girl has to have her s'mores frapps in the fall.

The wind whines around us while we walk side by side, our strides coordinated. My skinny frame next to his muscular one. There's a sense of safety as I walk with this man. With another bite of the wind, I catch a whiff of his cologne—masculine, subtle, and expensive.

We stop at my car, the parking lot light shining over us.

I tug my keys from my purse. "What's your last name?"

He pauses and averts his gaze. "Why do you ask?"

"Just curious."

A flicker of anguish flashes across his face, and he forces a smile. "You plan to cyberstalk me when you get home?"

"Damn straight."

He shakes his head. "Nope, not letting you in on my secrets yet."

"Yet?" I raise a brow. "Does that mean there will be a time when you do?"

"Get in your car, trouble."

He chuckles and tips his chin toward my shiny red BMW coupe—another item my parents let me keep after the snip-snip of my financials. I unlock my car, and he opens the door, stepping to the side to allow me room to slide in. I start my car, rubbing my freezing hands together, and curse myself for not remote-starting it earlier.

"Good night, trouble." He peeks through the door. "Drive safe."

"Good night, Lincoln."

He offers me one last smile, gently shuts the door, and waits until I leave the parking lot before returning to the bar. I replay our conversations in my head on the ten-minute drive to my duplex. After parking, I grab my bag and scramble into my apartment.

Noise flows through my neighbor's walls. The closest we've been to a conversation is when he screams at his video games at three in the morning and I bang on the wall.

I check my phone for Georgia updates and then shower, savoring the steaming water pelting at my sore muscles. Tipping my head back, I groan as my real-life problems evade my thoughts. Work was a temporary reprieve from them.

A reprieve from Quinton.

Stepping out of the shower, I dry off. My skin crawls when my phone beeps with a text.

Quinton: Quit ignoring me. We need to talk.

I stopped blocking his number when he found other ways to contact me. He'd randomly show up where I was or call me from different numbers, and once, he even had some rando kid deliver a letter like we were in the Cold War and I was his wife, waiting at home for him. Answering his calls is easier than dealing with his weird alternatives.

I stab my fingers against the screen like I want to stab him.

Me: We've talked plenty.

Quinton: I don't trust you.

Me: I don't trust you. We're even.

Quinton: Don't make me fuck up your world.

You already have.

CHAPTER FIVE

Lincoln

A WEEK HAS PASSED since Georgia's fall.

A week that I've been covering for my pain-in-the-ass brother.

His absence has created a major disruption at the bar. I'm the only one who knows where he is, and I've refused to share that information, crowning me as the most hated coworker.

Out of guilt, I'm covering his shifts. It's not like I have shit else to do anyway. Working helps me pass the time, clears my mind from the bullshit, and it's better than sitting at home alone since Archer and I live together.

"Your brother pull his head out of his ass yet?"

I stop counting inventory at the sound of Cassidy's voice and sweep my gaze over the bar. Cassidy's marching in my direction, her hips swaying from side to side with each step. With me covering for Archer and her filling in for Georgia while she recovers from a concussion, we've been working together all week. Like with working, being around her keeps my mind off my problems.

"Hello. Good afternoon to you too," I say instead of answering her question—the same one she asks daily.

She wrinkles her nose. "I'm up for kidnapping his ass ... wherever he is ..." She leaves the rest of her sentence hanging.

"Hmm …"

On the outside, I'm acting cool.

Inside, agitation speeds through me.

Archer's actions have been putting me through hell. I'm trying to be understanding, but it's hard when everyone around is pointing out what an idiot he is.

"If only someone—*say, you*—knew where we could find him." Her oval-shaped eyes sharpen as she glares at me.

I ignore her comment, not even bothering to *hmm* this time.

Too bad Cassidy isn't one to steer clear of sensitive subjects.

"What's his deal?" She ties back her glossy blond hair in a high ponytail. "Can't you force him to do the right thing or tell Georgia where he is, so the girl can rip him a new one? She at least deserves that."

"Archer is … complicated." Defending him makes my jaw twitch. He doesn't deserve it.

"How about you *uncomplicate* the situation, force him to pull up his big-boy panties, and face Georgia?"

I scrub a hand over my face. "You have siblings?"

"A sister. Two brothers." She pauses and holds up a finger. "Shit, three brothers. I recently found out about a secret half brother that my dad hid for fifteen years. And now, my brother is marrying his sister."

I cock my head to the side, replaying her words. "Jesus. That sounds messy."

"Yep." Her red nails make a *tap, tap* against the bar, and her voice turns stern, almost parent-like. "I know complicated, and if one of those siblings was acting as if they were still in Pampers, I'd make them face the consequences of their actions."

"Your parents still together after the whole *secret baby* thing?" I'm still processing what she told me *and* desperate to turn the conversation away from Archer.

"Nope. They tried, but it was hopeless." She props an elbow on the bar. "Not that I blame my mother for leaving him. If I found out my husband did what my father did, I'd file those divorce papers in a heartbeat." She smirks. "If I didn't kill him so he no longer had a heartbeat."

I can't help but chuckle.

Apparently, I find homicidal innuendos made by tiny blondes funny.

"What about you?" she asks. "Your parents still together? Any other siblings?"

My mouth turns dry, and I gulp in an attempt to fix it.

I shouldn't have asked her any family questions.

Should've known those questions always circle back.

"It's just Archer and me," I reply, a pain in the back of my throat. "And my father … he's dead."

My chest tightens in surprise at my revelation. While I'm not as closed off as Archer, I don't openly talk about his death. It's a sore subject for me. I'm not sure when it won't be.

Her face falls in apology. "Lincoln, I'm so sorry. I shouldn't have asked."

He died in prison shortly after I was released. He died somewhere he shouldn't have. Sure, maybe he deserved his place of residence for his actions, but no one should die there.

That's why I fought so hard to prevent it.

And failed.

It nearly killed me when I got the call.

Slaughtered my mother.

Crushed Archer, even with their strained relationship.

Lucky for him, he had Georgia at his side.

Me? I had no one.

I clear my throat, shaking my head. "Nah, it's cool. I asked. You asked back. No biggie."

"You get to work with the cool bartender today, ladies and gents!"

Our attention shifts to Silas as he saunters across the bar. His leather jacket and shredded jeans break the dress code per our employee handbook, but from what I've discovered about Silas, he's the epitome of a man who gives no fucks.

I was him once.

Parties. Drugs. Booze. Sex.

I lived my life day to day and traveled to exotic locations on a whim, and rules were only for those who couldn't afford to break them. A slice of that changed after my grandfather's death. That was when I stepped up in our family business since Archer refused to. Within a year, I went from a highly educated trust-fund kid to the VP of a multimillion-dollar empire.

How did that *give no fucks* attitude evaporate from my body?

When my father started committing felonies and leaving me to cover up his crimes.

"I beg to differ," Cassidy argues, wagging a finger at him. "Linc is the coolest-slash-best-slash-hottest bartender here."

Her compliment wipes out the sorrowful thoughts of losing my father.

Not that they won't resurface later.

"That's my girl." I hold my arm across the bar.

She grins and high-fives me.

Silas jerks his jacket off his shoulders and peers at Cassidy. "I'll let you have that one because Maliki would kick my ass if I ever touched you."

She scrunches up her face. "You're not letting me have *anything*." She pats his chest. "No offense, pretty boy, but only one bartender has my heart." Blowing a kiss, she turns and strolls toward the employee entrance.

My gaze is trained on her, her curves, the pep in her step as she walks.

"Safe to say, she likes you, man," Silas comments, his lips curving into an amused smile.

I don't look away from Cassidy until she disappears through the door. "She's young."

"Twenty-one isn't that young," he scoffs. "What are you, twenty-six?"

I nod.

"Five years ain't shit. Which means you're using *age* as an excuse, and I have the best solution for that."

I raise a brow.

"Telling Cohen to schedule you and Blondie together."

"Girls are the last thing I need to worry about."

What do I need to worry about?

Getting my life in order, moving into my own place, and adjusting to this new world.

I'll never be the same man I once was.

SPORTS AND SHOUTING customers consume my environment as I sling drinks—a margarita here, a shot there, a beer here. I went from ordering drinks to serving them. Don't get me wrong. I'm thankful as fuck for the job. My only experience upon being hired was that I'd drunk a whole lot of liquor.

Bartending isn't my passion. Making small talk with people isn't my jam. Hearing people whine about their problems like I'm a damn therapist is hell. I came from the corporate world, and in the corporate world, we told people to shut the fuck up when they whined about their problems.

What was once my passion?

Business. Finance. A salary with six numbers.

That was the name of my game.

Until that game ended and I was the loser.

"Silas. Oh, Silas," Cassidy sings out at the end of the night. "I volunteer as tribute to take over your closing duties."

Silas stops collecting trash. "Seriously?"

All night, as I poured drinks and ignored people bitching, I thought about Cassidy. The girl, she's getting to me.

Whether it's platonic or sexual attraction, I want to spend all my time with her.

I want to learn everything about her, every single damn tidbit I can.

I want all of that ... while also desperate she doesn't learn about the real me. As much as I don't want it to happen, it will eventually. My past hasn't been a secret, given everyone knows me as Archer's brother.

They all know my story.

Do they judge me for it?

I'd bet every damn dollar in my bank account that some did at the beginning.

Now, not so much. They invite me into their homes, they allow me in the bar's cash, and I've never given them a reason to worry.

Cassidy eagerly nods. "Seriously."

Silas peers over at me. "You cool with that?"

I shrug, striving to appear casual. "Sure. Whatever."

Cassidy helping means I'll leave later, and even though I'm as exhausted as people are after Thanksgiving dinner, I'd rather spend time with her than sleep.

"Cool." He snatches his jacket, and when Cassidy turns around, he elbows me playfully.

I shove him away.

"Catch you guys later!" Silas salutes us before leaving.

"Who volunteers for extra work?" I ask on my way to lock the door behind Silas.

"It's better than going home to an empty apartment," Cassidy replies with a shrug.

"I feel you on that. It's the same with Archer being gone."

"Another reason to drag his ass home." She clears a table of two drinks before spraying it down with cleaner and wiping it.

"Me doing that equals working less … which means less time you get to spend with me."

The towel falls from her hand. "He can come home *for Georgia*, and you can still work. Dude probably needs time to clear that stubborn head of his and grovel at Georgia's feet. I suggest he take classes on how to be a good boyfriend."

I bite back the urge to ask if she's ever been in a serious relationship. For someone who thinks she's Dr. Phil, has she even dealt with real-life problems yet?

"If you understood Archer and his past, you'd think differently," I reply.

She cocks her hip against the bar and levels her hazel beauties on me. "Tell me about it then."

Well, shit.

Not where I was going with that statement.

I thought it'd shut her up about my brother.

"Archer, he …" I clear my throat while searching for the right words. "He sees himself as the Grim Reaper. He thinks it's safer for Georgia to stay away from him. In his weird-ass head, he's punishing himself, not her, for what happened."

"He might think that, but Georgia is being punished in the process."

Returning to the bar, I snatch the universal remote and power off the TVs. "Trust me, I tried explaining that, but he's hardheaded."

So are all of us Callahans.

It's why my brother and father could hardly stand to be around each other.

"What about you? What would you do in that situation?"

I draw in a deep breath as her question sinks into my blood, pulling out honesty. "I wouldn't run." My response is a sellout to my brother—me agreeing with everyone but him.

A satisfied smile stretches along her lips. "Good. You weren't lying when you said you were the cool one."

I match her grin. "Told you so."

We make small talk while finishing up cleaning, and I learn:

She was voted Miss Teen Blue Beech, to which I replied, "That sounds like the honkiest shit I've ever heard." That resulted in a napkin being thrown in my direction.

The night she found out about her father's affair, she lit every birthday present he'd ever given her on fire.

She lost her virginity on prom night but lied about it because she didn't want to seem like a cliché.

What do I share with her?

I graduated with a finance degree from Stanford.

I used to lie about being allergic to shellfish, so I wouldn't have to eat nasty-ass caviar because my parents served it on the regular.

Before prison, I embarrassingly didn't know how to work a washer and dryer.

"Do you live around here?" I ask while we walk to our cars, leaves slashing along the concrete.

She nods, unlocking her car. "Like, ten minutes away. What about you?"

"About twenty." I fail to mention the reason I'm crashing with my brother. That the feds took nearly everything with my name on it, not caring if I had two nickels to rub together.

"I'll have to come see it sometime." Standing on her tiptoes, she smacks a kiss to my cheek and flashes me a playful grin. "You can give me a tour."

As she leaves, I glide my finger over my cheek, feeling the heat of where her lips were.

I grin like the damn Grinch.

———

"GEORGIA," I greet when she walks into the bar.

Georgia narrows her eyes in my direction. "Unless you're here to tell me where the hell your bastard of a brother is, I'm not speaking to you."

She's the CEO of my haters club—not that I blame her.

I'm also waiting for her to castrate me, per her threats.

As much as I want to defer the topic away from Archer, I can't. He called last night and asked for a favor. I drove to his hiding place—our grandparents' lake home—and prayed he decided to get his shit together. No such luck.

All the little prick did was hand me an envelope to give to Georgia. When I questioned what it was, he wouldn't tell me. I had an urge to open it on the way home, but I didn't. My brother might have thrown me smack dab in the middle of his mess, but I'm trying to distance myself from the situation.

And a mystery envelope isn't my damn business.

She stares at the envelope as if it's tainted when I pull it out and offer it to her. "What Archer needs to do is grow some balls, face me, and tell me why he left."

Facts.

I thrust the envelope closer. "Archer doesn't always do what he needs to do. You know this."

"What's his plan then?" Cassidy asks, leaning back in her stool and crossing her arms, always joining in conversations that have nothing to do with her. "He's just never coming back?"

"I think that's his plan," I reply even though I'm as clueless as she is.

Cassidy's eyes widen, and her voice rises a hitch. "What about you? Are you leaving too?"

I shrug, the thought forming a rock of dread in my stomach. "I have no idea." I thrust the envelope further toward Georgia. "Now, take the envelope."

"What's in it?" she asks with a glare.

"He didn't say. Only asked me to give it to you." I hold up my hands. "Don't shoot the messenger."

She snatches it from me and stares in my direction while ripping it open. All eyes are on her as she reads what's inside. I silently pray it's an apology letter.

"You've got to be kidding me," she hisses. "Tell me where he is."

I shake my head, my stomach churning at the anger in her eyes. It's more intense than it was before. "No can do, babe."

"Goddammit, Lincoln!" she shrieks, tossing the letter onto the pub table. "Forget your stupid loyalty for one damn minute and tell me where he is." She flicks the letter away. "He's trying to sign over the bar to me."

"What?" I blurt.

She jerks her head toward the letter. "Read it."

With nearly shaking hands, I read the letter, my throat constricting as I take in every word in his handwriting. He's signed over his cut of the bar—fifty percent—to her. I shut my eyes in pain. Not because I'll lose my job, but because my brother is sacrificing his dream. After our grandfather's death, he turned his back on the millionaire lifestyle we'd grown up in. As soon as he had the perfect opportunity, he quit the company. Owning a bar is all he's ever wanted.

This bar, like Georgia, brought him happiness and peace he hadn't had in a while.

That's it.

This has to stop before he ruins his life.

I slam down the letter. "He's at our grandparents' lake house."

"Address, please," Georgia replies, her face unreadable.

I give her a *really* look.

"Directions," she demands.

"Fine, fine." My face falls slack. "But don't say I'm the one who gave it to you."

A hint of regret slivers through me before I brush it away. Archer can be pissed at me all he wants, but I'm not allowing him to fuck over his life.

Deal with your problems, Archer.

Cassidy chuckles, wearing a proud smile on her face. She's elated that I finally caved. "There's no way you're getting out of this one." She stands and slaps my arm. "Think of it as your good deed of the day."

I fight back a smile, her comment downsizing my tension. "Listen, youngster, don't you have some frat boy's heart to break or Barbies to play with?"

I'm unsure if our relationship is big brother, little sister or sexual tension we play off as humor. Most of the time, I'd put my money on it being the latter, but it's weird for me. I've never gone for chicks younger than me.

The problem is, we work together, and the timing sucks.

Cassidy flips me off. "Don't you need to go find your vitamins to keep your bones strong and pick up your Viagra from the pharmacy?"

I laugh, turning my attention to Georgia. "Georgia, since you might be the new co-owner, fire her ass."

Cassidy throws her head back. "Lincoln, dear, the chances of you being fired are much higher than mine since you're related to the devilish heartbreaker."

"He's going to kick my ass for this," I tell Georgia, rubbing my forehead in stress. "So, be happy that I like you."

"Just tell him I went through Lincoln's phone and gave it to you," Cassidy comments with a *give no shits, I'll piss off my boss* attitude.

Chick has balls of steel.

"I'll text you the address," I inform Georgia.

She replies with a pleased smile.

"You okay to drive?" Cassidy asks. "I can take you if you want?"

"She wants a front seat to the shitshow," I add.

"Rude." Cassidy shoots a glare in my direction. "I *also* want to make sure she's cool to drive."

"I'm fine," Georgia replies. "They told me to wait forty-eight hours before driving, and it's been a week. I haven't felt dizzy at all. All I need is for you to cover my shift tonight."

Cassidy points at her. "I got you. Good luck!"

Georgia dashes out of the bar, and I already feel bad for the wrath Archer will face if she goes to my grandparents'. I yank my phone from my pocket to give him a heads-up but then shove it back in place. I'll let this one be a surprise.

"Are you sure you're okay working a double?" I ask Cassidy.

She worked through lunch and the mid-dinner rush and was clocking out when Georgia arrived. I planned to pull a double to fill in for my jackass brother. Plus, I need the cash. The money is decent here, but it's nothing like what I made before.

It's not like I don't have *any* money. Call it foul, but my mother created a bank account to transfer my funds so I didn't lose everything.

"I have nothing better to do," Cassidy replies.

"That makes two of us."

Her phone chimes, and she rummages through her bag, searching for it. My eyes are on her when she reads whatever is on the screen. She stills, her face paling, and seconds later, as if someone snapped her out of a haze, she frantically shoves the rest of her shit into her bag. In the process, she drops her phone. When she ducks down to retrieve it, the bar conceals her.

"Everything okay?" I ask, standing on my tiptoes in an attempt to see her over the bar.

"Yep." She comes back into view, blowing strands of hair from her face. "Georgia's shift doesn't start for, what, another ten minutes? I need to run home really quick, and then I'll be right back."

"Cassidy." I circle the bar, my brow wrinkling.

"Gotta go." She rushes out the door.

My throat constricts as my intuition tells me something's wrong.

CHAPTER SIX

Cassidy

RULE NUMBER ONE IN RELATIONSHIPS: don't date the biggest drug dealer on campus.

In my defense, it's not like I knew Quinton was one when we started dating. We met at a frat party and immediately clicked. He became the perfect boyfriend—polite, never made me question his character, and decent in bed. His Mercedes, his wining and dining, and the gifts were never a red flag because he came from money. His family owns Landing Holdings, a large commercial real estate and investment firm.

Turned out, all that wining and dining wasn't on his parents' dime. It was funded from profits from selling drugs. When his car was in the shop, he borrowed mine while I was in class. Too bad I didn't know *borrow* was code for drug runs. We got pulled over on the drive to dinner—me in the driver's seat. The cop claimed there'd been a familiar make and model in a drug hot spot.

Knowing I had nothing to hide, I wasn't worried when they demanded to search my car.

Key word: *I*. I had nothing to hide.

Turned out, my boyfriend did.

And asshole had hidden it in my trunk.

I should've known something was wrong when Quinton told me not to pull over and make a run for it, like I'd graduated from sorority girl to Grand Theft Auto pro. I stupidly thought he was joking, and he cursed under his breath when I followed the law.

He muttered a quick, "Thank fuck," when the officer approached my window.

That followed with an, "Oh shit," when the other officer appeared.

As the cops searched my car, Rat Bastard stared at me straight in the face and said, "I don't know what kind of shit you're into, Cassidy, but not cool." His attention slid to the officer. "Those aren't my drugs. Can I call a friend to pick me up?"

The officer, who'd been cool with him the entire time while eyeing me skeptically, said, "Of course, man."

Then ... they did the man hug.

Yes, my drug-dealing boyfriend did a bro hug with a cop.

A cop who then instructed me to turn around before slapping handcuffs on my wrists.

I cursed at Quinton.

Screamed.

Called him countless names.

But he didn't budge.

I sat in the back of the cop car, careful not to touch anything. The stench of rotten eggs and french fries along with the sound of AC/DC tortured me during the ride.

Quinton's betrayal shocked me.

My trust in people was a reality check.

Never to be repaired.

Not only did Quinton ruin my future, but he also ruined my insight on life.

On people.

Quinton called after Kyle bailed me out.

Over and over again.

Threatening me with a creative variety of things he'd do if I even muttered his name to authorities—slit my throat with barbed wire, cut my mother's uterus out, catch my house on fire.

You know, all normal things a man you dated should say.

I might've been ignorant enough to fall for the wrong guy—the *bad boy*—but I refuse to be stupid enough to cross him. I'll stay in line and keep my mouth shut until he leaves me the hell alone.

It's been a week since he graced me with a text. That changed ten minutes ago when he messaged me with a selfie of him sitting in *my living room*, blindsiding and scaring the shit out of me. Dude was even holding my favorite teddy bear. He's not supposed to know where I live, where to stalk me.

It's fall, but I'm sweating when I step out of my car. Dread accompanies each step I take toward my apartment. With shaking hands, I shove the key into the lock, only to realize it's unlocked.

Did he pick the lock?

Kill my landlord to get one himself?

I inhale a deep breath, terrified of what I'm about to walk into. Quinton is waiting for me on the couch. His arms are sprawled out along the back, and a Rolex dangles from one wrist as if he were a king awaiting his peasants.

Or prey, in my case.

I slam the door shut and toss my bag onto the floor. "Breaking and entering is against the law. Keep committing crimes, and I'll eventually turn your ass in."

You see, sometimes, I'm not the wisest with my mouth. I might be smart enough not to rat on Quinton, but that doesn't also apply to my sarcasm. He can't have both.

He drops an arm to rub the hard line of his jaw, and his lips curve into a sinister smile. "Say you'll turn my ass in again, and that sweet mouth of yours will be toothless."

Well then.

Not trying to have falsies before thirty.

I shut my mouth and curl my arms around myself. "What do you want, Quinton?"

Licking his lips, he eyes me up and down, his predatory expression stronger. "You look good, babe."

Ugh, vomit.

"And you look gross and criminal."

Again, this damn mouth.

When he rises to his feet, my back straightens, and the hair on the back of my neck stands, but I quickly fix myself. He advances toward me, needing to only take a few steps before he's inches away, tipping his head down to stare at me.

Don't let the psycho know he affects you.

I hold out my palm in warning. "Don't."

"Why?" He smirks. "I thought you liked compliments."

Yes, when I didn't know you were a damn monster.

Now, you make my skin crawl.

I retreat a step, my back hitting the wall. "What do you want?"

He doesn't move closer. "Just want to make sure we're still on the same page."

"Still on the same page." I gulp.

He eases closer, slow and wolfish, and caresses my cheek, causing me to flinch. His hand is smooth, yet there's a greasy coat over it. His breath, a deep cinnamon, hits my skin. "Good. Keep it that way."

I swat his hand away.

A hard chuckle releases from his chest before he turns and leaves.

As soon as the door clicks behind him, I snatch my teddy, which now feels corrupted, and throw it at the door.

How did he know where I lived?

I need to buy a baseball bat, just in case.

———

"EVERYTHING GOOD?"

I expected this, yet I hoped Lincoln wouldn't ask that when I returned to the bar. He had seen me when I read Quinton's text and witnessed the sheer panic on my face.

After Quinton left, I hurriedly locked the door and opened a meditation app my mother had been pestering me to try. Five minutes into forced reflection, my mind wasn't shutting off, so I quit.

Meditation isn't what'll work for me tonight.

I need vodka, or a Xanax, or a distraction.

Working will be good for me.

Nodding, I join Lincoln behind the bar and yank a bottle of vodka from the glass shelf. "Of course."

I snatch a shot glass, pour myself a double, and knock it back, relishing the burn as it seeps down my throat, hoping it'll bring a dose of forgetfulness later. His eyes are pinned on me as I set the glass down and wipe my mouth with the back of my hand like a lady.

"You sure?" He wrinkles his brows, his gaze shooting from the glass and back to me.

I give him a nervous smile while I consider pouring another shot. Too bad I'm on the job and I don't want to get fired. "Positive."

No one will find out about Quinton's visit.

It'll be my and my stupid tormentor's little secret.

Among many.

He reaches out, running his hand over my arm, as worry flashes along his features. "If you need anything, I'm here. You know that, right?"

If it were any other time, I would revel in his touch. Now, I can't keep my mind straight because all I'm thinking about is Quinton.

I tap his wrist. "You getting soft on me, Callahan?"

"Hell no." He snorts.

I do a sweep of the bar, noticing the growing crowd, and know soon, there won't be much time for conversation. "Did Georgia find Archer?"

"Sure did." He smirks. "Archer texted me, bitching about not giving him a heads-up."

"Good girl." I smile, a real one this time, as I think about Georgia barging in on Archer. "Tell him it's time to rip off the Band-Aid."

"Trust me, I did. Who knows if he'll listen, though?"

"Make sure to keep me updated." I pat him on the back.

He groans. "Hard pass on keeping you updated with my brother's love life."

I mock his groan. "Fine, I'll be texting *you* for updates."

"Too bad you don't have my number."

"Too bad I do." I dance in place, Quinton temporarily dissipating from my thoughts. This is what I needed. "You're just lucky I haven't sent you nudes yet." I pause and press a finger to my mouth. "Or does that make you *unlucky*?"

He scrubs his hand over his face, peeking at me through the spaces between his fingers. "How'd you get my number, you little stalker?"

"There's a spreadsheet in the employee room in case we need someone to cover our shift."

"Remind me to have Archer change that."

"Pretty sure Archer has bigger concerns at the moment than me knowing your number."

"Nope." He presses his hand to his chest, feigning defensiveness. "That's a serious violation of privacy."

This is how it is with Lincoln.

I spend time with him, and all my frustrations fade.

I shove him at the same time I say, "Shut it. Who else will I call when I'm lonely at night?"

"Fine. *Only* if I'm the last resort ... *and* you tell me what's going on in that pretty head of yours."

———

"YOU WANT to talk about what's been on your mind tonight?" Lincoln studies me as we walk out of the bar.

I blow out a ragged breath when we reach my car. As hard as I tried to act normal while working tonight, a sudden chill would rush down my spine at times. I'd anticipate Quinton standing behind me. My throat thickened when I checked my phone, in fear I'd find another text from him.

If he knows where I live, surely, he knows where I work.

I shift from one foot to the other. "Have you ever loved someone you shouldn't?"

I'm disgusted with myself at times.

Disgusted that I thought Quinton was a nice person.

That I allowed someone so shitty to take a piece of my heart.

Lincoln's mood changes at my mood-changing question. "I don't know if I've ever *loved* someone I shouldn't, but I've been involved with someone I shouldn't have been."

"Sounds scandalous." I perk up in curiosity. "Details, please."

He cups my chin in his hand, sending ripples of goose bumps over my skin. "I'll give you details when you tell me what made you run out of the bar as if it were on fire."

Our eyes meet under the streetlight.

His full of questions.

Mine filled with answers he won't get.

I place my hand over his. "Looks like I'll get those details another time."

CHAPTER SEVEN

Lincoln

"THANK FUCK you got your head out of your ass," I tell Archer over the Bluetooth in my car.

The news of him and Georgia making up is the best I've heard all day.

Hell, all month.

I brake at a stoplight and tap my fingers along the smooth leather of the steering wheel. The feds might've seized the bulk of my assets, but I'm also not a complete dumbass. I got smart before they put their grimy hands on everything. Archer packed up my belongings and stored them at his place, and my grandparents purchased my Porsche, which they gifted back when I was released.

"How'd it happen?"

Jesus, I sound like Cassidy, wanting all the relationship gossip.

This is my life now—questioning my brother about his love life since mine is in the tank.

"None of your business," he grumbles with a huff.

I chuckle. "Happy for you, bro."

"As bad as I want to kick your ass, thanks for telling Georgia where I was; it really cemented reality into me that I needed to stop acting stupid. I'm a grown-ass man who shouldn't run away from his problems."

"Damn straight. I'm on my way to Mom's. You coming home?"

"Nah, I think Georgia and I are crashing here again tonight."

"You kids have fun."

The light turns green, and I whip into the local coffee shop's parking lot. I order an iced coffee for myself and some fancy shit for my mother. Just as I'm about to turn onto the intersection, a flash of blond hair catches my attention. Slowing down, I peruse the group of people picking up litter off the side of the road and pull over.

Rolling down the window, I stick my head out for a better view.

No fucking way.

It's her.

I'd know that body and hair anywhere.

It belongs to the woman I can't stop thinking about.

I cup my hand over my mouth and yell, "Yo! Did you get a new job?"

Cassidy veers to face me, stunned, and mutters, "You've got to be kidding me."

Not that I hear her. I'm just decent at reading lips.

She shuffles toward me as if I were a dreaded stepparent she had to spend the weekend with, wearing plastic gloves and carrying a trash bag along with a picker.

When she reaches me, she stabs at loose strands of hair falling from her hair tie.

I lean farther out the window, sticking my head out like a turtle from his shell. "If you need more hours at the bar, I can ask Archer." There's no stopping my lips from twitching into a smirk.

"Shove it," she grumbles, chewing on her plump lower lip. "This is my community service."

"Community service?" I shift my car into park. "What do you have community service for?"

This woman grows more interesting by the hour.

Her gaze drops to the ground, and she kicks at the tiny rocks in the gravel. "I don't want to talk about it."

"I do." I want to know every damn detail.

She moves from one foot to the other. "Too bad it isn't happening."

I frown. "How many hours did you get?"

"I have one more day. Saturday morning. Then, thank the Lord, I'm finished."

"Hey! Excuse me!"

At the gravelly, smoke-cured voice, our attention swings to the middle-aged woman stomping in our direction. A neon-orange vest is draped across her shoulders, and a clipboard is gripped in her hands.

"No talking to men in cars like some hooker!" she yells, snapping her fingers. "Get over here before I report you for breaking guidelines!" She releases a final huff while glaring at Cassidy.

"Ugh," Cassidy groans, rolling her eyes before shooting me an apologetic smile. "Thanks for stopping and talking shit. It's always a pleasure."

"Anytime, Cass." I wink.

"Looks like I'm not the only stalker in this relationship of ours." She winks back more dramatically, holds up her trash picker, and walks away.

———

"TACO TUESDAY, BABY!" Silas calls out, slamming his palm on the bar and pointing at Cassidy. "You coming?"

"Sounds tempting," Cassidy replies, biting into her lower lip before locking eyes with me. "Lincoln, are *you* attending Taco Tuesday?"

"Of course he is," Georgia answers for me. "No one misses Taco Tuesday. It's one of the rare nights the entire crew has off."

Cassidy takes a sip of her vodka cranberry. She sometimes has a drink before going home after an early shift. "I'll be there."

"Awesome!" Silas whistles. "See you there. Bring your appetite for some guac."

"You mean, for queso," Georgia corrects.

"Jesus. I need to talk to Cohen about how he raised you," Silas disputes. "Guac is where it's at."

The two then start arguing about which is better, their passion as strong as those who argue over politics.

"It's guac," I state to Cassidy, out of their conversation. "Definitely guac, but it has to be good guac."

"Nope." Cassidy shakes her head while scrunching up her nose. "Queso is delish. Smooth white cheese you dip a tortilla chip in. *Mmm*. Queso has never let me down. Guac, on the other hand? I've had people completely destroy guac."

"You taste my guac, and I guarantee, you'll never think about queso again."

A woman I dated pushed me to take a cooking class with her in Spain, where I learned all the inside tips on making the perfect guacamole.

She raises a brow. "Does that mean you're making guac tonight?"

"Considering we're going to a restaurant, it might be rude to crack mine out at the table."

"Hmm …" She taps her chin. "Looks like you'll need to make me dinner one night, so I can taste your guac."

"I'll think about it."

"Eh, I'll let you *think* you'll think about it, but you're doing it. Until then, don't you dare bail on me tonight, or I'm kicking your ass."

"Hmm …" I tap my chin the same way she did. "I'll think about it."

"Like with the guac, there's no *thinking* about it. We're the newbies of the group, so we must stick together." She pouts. "I like having you around so I don't feel left out."

The feeling is mutual.

The group—Archer, Cohen, Finn, Silas, Georgia, Grace, and Lola —has been tight for years. It's not that they exclude new people; it's just hard not to feel like the odd one out. You don't have the history, know the inside jokes or shit that happened years ago, like they do.

"I'll be there," I reply.

She claps her hands and squeals. "It's a date."

I shake my head. "It's not a date."

"Oh, it's a date, babe."

———

TACO TUESDAY IS BEING HELD at La Mesa.

It's the only taco joint in Anchor Ridge. From a guy who's wined and dined all over the world, I have to say, La Mesa has some damn good tacos.

Are they the best I've tasted? Nah.

Are they better than tacos I've paid double for? Hell yeah.

Our table is nearly full when Archer, Georgia, and I arrive. I sweep my gaze over the faces, in search of the one I've been looking forward to seeing.

The one with cute freckles that dust over her nose and cheekbones when she doesn't wear makeup.

The one whose smile can light up a damn bar.

The one who's given me a reason to smile nearly every damn day—something that was once forced.

That face isn't present.

Georgia and Archer take their seats while I nudge myself into a chair near the end of the table. The only one with an empty seat next to it. An empty seat that had better be occupied with Cassidy's ass soon, or she'll be hearing from me in the form of endless texts. She can't break our newbie pact.

Just as I'm easing my phone from my pocket to text her, I hear Lola say, "Damn, Cassidy! You look hot."

My gaze shoots to Cassidy as she struts toward us.

Lola isn't lying.

Cassidy is breathtaking.

A black sweater revealing a hint of cleavage and tight black jeans.

Tousled blond curls.

Ruby-red lips.

There's something about red lipstick.

Something about a girl you know who's trouble, rocking red lipstick.

I'm so fucked.

She greets everyone, a slight shyness in her tone, and doesn't hesitate to plop down next to me.

As soon as her ass hits the seat, I lean into her, inhaling her sweet floral perfume. "Nice of you to finally show … *late.*"

She swats at my shoulder. "Oh, shush, Callahan. No one has ordered, and I couldn't get my mother off the phone. She thinks I'm going to some huge party even though I insisted countless times that it was just dinner."

I cock my head to the side. "Why's she so worried?"

"She doesn't want me hanging around the wrong crowd."

"Did you used to hang out with the wrong crowd?" The community service and sudden move are enough that I shouldn't need to ask that question.

"A little, yes."

"Good thing you found me because I'm the best crowd." I theatrically push my chest out.

She laughs, rolling her eyes. "So damn cocky."

We're interrupted when the server stops to take our order. Everyone makes small talk as we wait for our food, and my stomach grumbles at the mouthwatering smell of fresh tortillas. My mouth waters each time a waiter passes us with a sizzling plate of fajitas, going straight to another table.

Everyone is here, including Cohen's very pregnant girlfriend Jamie, and his son, Noah. Jamie, a doctor, isn't around as much as the other girls, but I have great respect for her. She's stepped up as a mother figure for Noah—even in the tough situation of Cohen being her sister's ex.

"How's it at the love-rekindled shack?" Cassidy asks when our food arrives, and we dig in.

Archer crashes with Georgia most nights, but they make appearances at our penthouse. It's funny at times—my brooding brother dating the spunkiest, loudest, and most outgoing person I've met in my life.

"As much as I'm glad they're back together and that my brother is happy, love can be gross." I bite into my carnitas and groan at how much more delicious it gets with each chomp.

"If you ever want a break, you can stay at my place." Her lips tilt into a smirk. "My bed is *always* open."

I chuckle, shaking my head, and decide to change the subject before taking her up on that offer. "You have community service tomorrow, right?"

"Ugh." She throws her head back and groans. "Yes. The last day of hell awaits me."

"Is it an all-day thing?"

"Nope, just until noon."

"Picking up trash again?"

"Unfortunately."

I bite back the urge to ask what she did to earn community service. This isn't the time or the place to ask. I know from experience, from when I've had someone blurt out questions regarding my past in front of people, it's not a good time. It's humiliating—something I'd never want Cassidy to experience around me.

The woman eating a quesadilla while dancing in her seat is becoming one of my closest friends. And if I dig deep into my soul for answers I've shoved away, just like I'm biting back that urge to ask questions … I know there's the urge to have more with her.

CHAPTER EIGHT

Cassidy

MY COMMUNITY SERVICE OPTIONS SUCKED.

It's not like in the movies, where you get a simple task of painting a wall or washing a car, and then when you arrive, a hot guy is working. You bond, fall in love, and live happily ever after. No, my type of community service isn't Hallmark movie–worthy.

Mine is picking up litter.

The guy I'm working with? Said I was cute for a girl with a small ass.

I check my watch for the thousandth time and sigh in relief.

My work here is done, ladies and gentlemen.

I'm ripping the latex gloves off my hands when a car similar to Lincoln's parks on the curb next to me. The window rolls down, and sure enough, Lincoln is perched up in the driver's side, staring at me with interest.

How can he afford such an expensive car?

A Porsche this nice isn't something a regular paycheck can purchase, especially one on a bartender's salary. Hell, even with my parents' money, they don't roll around in vehicles that cost six figures. He and Archer have high-end rides, never seem to be in need of cash, and even though they don't walk around in expensive clothes, theirs aren't cheap.

I know quality clothing, and they wear quality clothing.

Maybe they come from money.

And that's how he can afford such luxury.

It's hard for me not to be curious about these things anymore. Quinton came from money, so I never questioned how he afforded his Mercedes, the five-hundred-dollar meals, and Tiffany jewelry. It turns out, most of it was probably purchased with money he'd earned selling drugs to my fellow coeds.

Lincoln's voice snaps me out of my questioning haze. "You finished yet, my little criminal?" The midnight-blue baseball hat he's wearing covers his ebony-black hair and shields half his face.

As I step closer, a gust of wind whips around, pushing the masculine scent of him mingled with the tropical air freshener in his car toward me.

"All done." I toss the gloves into my trash bag. "What are you doing?"

Not going to lie, him being here is mortifying. It was the same the last time. There is nothing worse—okay, other than being arrested because you dated a criminal—than the guy you're crushing on seeing you picking up trash, looking like the so-called convict you hate. And it's not like I dressed up for the occasion in my old jeans and ill-fitting sweatshirt.

He shifts the car into park and relaxes in the leather seat. "I was in the neighborhood and figured you needed lunch after a hard day's work."

I need lunch, a shower, and then a shot of vodka.

With the sun shining in my eyes, I lower my hand over my brows to get a better view of him. "Your treat?"

"My treat, you little hellion."

I half-shrug. "Sounds good to me."

Whistling, he jerks his thumb toward his passenger seat, and I hear the click of the doors unlocking. I make a pit stop to check out with Helga, the monster in charge of community service.

On my first day, she asked if I was ready to get whipped into shape and said, "Helga doesn't like slackers. Helga sends slackers back to jail. Don't piss off Helga."

I'm pretty sure I pissed her off as I snorted to hold in my laughter.

After tossing the bag into the trash, I stop at my car to grab my purse and pour sanitizer into my hands on my walk to Lincoln's car.

"Okay, it smells like my first piña colada in here," I say, scrunching up my nose as I slide into the passenger seat and inspect the car. "I took you for more of a woodsy-scent kinda man."

He playfully glares at me. "My mom gives my car fresheners to me, and what the hell is wrong with piña colada? You get in my car, and it's like a mini vacation to the Caribbean."

"Nothing is wrong with piña coladas ... if you're a fifteen-year-old girl getting her first drink." There's no holding back my smile.

This.

This is why I love hanging out with Lincoln.

As soon as I saw him, my thoughts weren't stuck on hating community service, or losing my future, or my crazy-ass ex. His presence eases my mind and soul.

There's no better company than this man.

"Keep insulting my air freshener taste, and *my treat* for lunch will be a cup of water and three french fries."

"Fine," I groan. "For the sake of my stomach, I shall stay quiet ... *for now.* Once I'm fed, I can't make any promises." Shifting to grab the seat belt, I buckle up. "Where to?"

"Anything you're in the mood for?"

I spent my morning picking up trash, cigarette butts, and a few used condoms—*who the fuck tosses condoms on the side of the road?*—so I'm in need of a reward, like a nice steak and lobster.

But as great as that sounds, I'm not a brat who expects people to buy her expensive meals, so I say, "Surprise me."

Anchor Ridge is a small town, known for its local restaurants, shops, and bars. With the exception of Burger King, McDonald's, and Starbucks, there aren't many chains. My choices are limited, and since I haven't ventured out much, I don't have an answer that doesn't involve an Egg McMuffin.

Lincoln nods. "I got you."

I'm updated on Georgia and Archer's love situation while he drives out of Anchor Ridge and along the outskirts of town, closer to the city. He flicks his turn signal and cuts the wheel into the parking lot of a quaint yellow home that's been converted into a restaurant. A bright pink-and-yellow sign reads, *Yellow Peep*.

"Have you been here before?"

I shake my head. "Nope." I've heard of it, and it's definitely no McDonald's. In alarm, I glance down, inspecting myself, and tug at the hem of my sweatshirt. "I don't think I'm okay to go into a place like this."

He scratches his cheek. "I'm not catching your drift."

I throw my hand down, gesturing to my homely appearance. "Uh, I look like someone who was picking up trash on the side of the road. *Literally.*"

"Babe"—his voice is stern, but his eyes are soft—"picking up trash or not, you're fucking gorgeous. I wouldn't think twice about walking in there with you."

I blush—like seriously blush—in a way I've never blushed before. "Stop lying."

"Not lying. You look damn good." He kills the ignition. "Now, let's get you fed. You deserve a good meal after today's contribution to society."

He steps out of the car, opens my door, and extends his hand. I grab it, the warmth of his large hand burying mine underneath it, and we walk into the restaurant.

Hand in hand, like we're a couple.

A relaxed ambiance collides with us the moment we enter through the doors. A man in the corner is playing piano as people sit at white-clothed tables—some with mimosa flutes in their hands, some with waters, and some with coffees. No one is dressed like me—no freaking one. Sure, there are some casual diners, but no one underdressed, who was picking up condoms ten minutes ago.

As much as I want to haul ass out of here, Lincoln's words ring through my thoughts, crashing through my insecurities.

Fuck it. I'm starving.

Who cares?

It's not like I'm interested in anyone but the man who already told me he gave no fucks about what I was wearing.

We stop at the hostess stand, where menus are stacked up with a basket of rolled silverware placed beside them. The girl behind the counter, complete in a white button-up shirt and black slacks, greets us before leading the way to our table in the corner of the room.

"I'm going to wash my hands," I tell Lincoln before scurrying to the restroom and returning minutes later. Lowering myself onto the chair, I set my eyes on him. "You so planned this, didn't you?"

He unrolls the cloth napkin and drapes it over his lap while I do the same. "What do you mean?"

"You planned to find me finishing community service, so you could take me to lunch *because* you love hanging out with me."

He shoots me an amused smile. "What can I say? You're cool ... like a little sister."

I cringe at those words.

Little sister.

That's the furthest from what I want him to see me as.

"Oh God, never call me your little sister again." I rub my forehead with the heel of my hand. "That'd mean you're like my big brother ... and no way in hell can I say I'm sexually attracted to my brother."

As if with perfect timing, the waitress approaches our table at the same time those words leave my mouth. The way her eyes widen, her jaw drops open, and her gaze pings back and forth between me and Lincoln confirms she heard my little comment. My head spins, and swear to God, I'm tempted to dash out of this place. I might be able to handle looking like a hot mess, but our waitress thinking I want to bang my brother, that's where I draw the line.

I cast a quick glance at Lincoln, who doesn't look fazed by my comment. In fact, he only appears entertained at my awkwardness.

"Hello," the waitress chirps, gaining control of her thoughts. She's my age, and fingers crossed, she realizes it was a sarcastic statement. "I'm Taylor. Can I start you off with something to drink?"

I quickly peruse the drink menu and order a mimosa while Lincoln asks for an ice water. Taylor scurries off to grab our drinks, and Lincoln's eyes level on me, humor shining in them.

"Should we make it clear that I'm not your brother?" he asks with a raised brow.

"I'm sure that would be *more* awkward." My cheeks redden.

He smirks.

"All right, here ya go," Taylor says, dropping off our drinks.

"Thank you," I say. At the same time, Lincoln replies with, "My girl here wants to make it clear that I'm not her brother."

I freeze, mid–mimosa grab, and want to drown myself with the liquid.

No, he didn't.

Taylor stares at Lincoln. I'm unsure if it's in captivation or if she's speechless at what he said. I'm leaning a bit toward captivation, though. When she took our drink orders, she was so flustered that she barely looked him in the eye. Now that she is, she's realizing she likes what she sees.

I set my drink down.

He wants to have some fun? Let's have some fun.

I shift my attention to Taylor, and mischief barrels through my belly. "You see, I *don't* want him to see me as a little sister, though."

Taylor nods, catching my drift, and sweeps her long black hair off her shoulder as her gaze leaves the guy I wish hadn't just said I was like a sister to him.

"Ah, I get it now," Taylor says, her voice no longer timid, her tone now confident. "He's dumb if he doesn't see you as more because you're gorgeous."

Yes.

A girl's girl.

I like her.

Taylor's gaze nervously slides back to Lincoln. "And if you're paying the bill, don't use that against me with my tip, please."

Lincoln holds both hands up. "I'll be tipping you more for your honesty."

A rush of relief leaves her. No doubt, she didn't plan on that little outburst. "Thank you. Now, what can I get you?"

Our conversation turns more professional as she rattles off the lunch specials. We order, and she shoots me a smile before scurrying away.

"I can't believe you did that," I comment, wrapping my fingers around the stem of my glass.

"And I can't believe you did that," he replies.

"Touché." I smile. "You wanted to make things awkward, and I needed to up the ante."

"You sure did." He takes a long gulp of his water. "You working tonight?"

"Nope." I moan at the first sip of the sugary mimosa. It's been a while since I've had one. I tend to save them for days I'm nursing massive hangovers or for weddings. "We both have the night off."

"How'd you know I have the night off?" He tilts his head to the side and chews on his lower lip.

"The schedule."

He waggles his finger at me. "My little stalker, you."

"You love it."

"Any big plans tonight?"

I ignore the chatter around us and focus on Lincoln. "Possibly."

"Like what?"

"Sex." I lick the rim of my glass in a failed attempt to appear seductive. *Yeah, I most likely look like a baby licking a toy.* "Lots and lots of sex."

Unfortunately, my response doesn't choke him up as I hoped. Lincoln is hard to rile up, to my surprise, and my humor never shocks him.

He scoffs, "Bullshit. My money is on you staying home, watching cartoons, and cuddling with a stuffed animal you've had since you were two."

"It sounds like you're speaking from experience." I crack a smile and tap his hand. "Is that what you were doing at twenty-one, Grandpa Bartender? When did you finally break up with your baby blanket?"

He chuckles. "Nah, you got it all wrong, babe."

"I bet it was Ninja Turtles ... am I right?"

He stays quiet, fighting back a grin.

"Oh my God!" I cover my mouth to hold in a shriek of laughter. "I'm so right."

"Wrong." He plucks an ice cube from his water and flicks it at me. "My baby blanket—which I haven't used in years, *thank you*—was Mickey Mouse."

I thrum my fingers along the edge of the table, engrossed in this conversation like it's a revelation as deep as how the world will end. "Do you still have it?"

He swipes his palm over his chin. "My mom probably does."

"Ask her because I'd love to give it to our kiddos when the time comes."

He throws his head back and laughs. "What am I going to do with you?"

"Marry me. Knock me up. Whatever you'd like." I chug my mimosa and motion toward him with it. "But not anal. I don't do anal, prewarning."

Call Taylor the CEO of poor timing because it's at *anal* when she returns with our plates.

"Uh …" she mutters, searching for the right words before quickly placing our plates in front of us.

This time, Lincoln is the one covering his mouth to contain his laughter.

CHAPTER NINE

Lincoln

DAMN, does it feel good, having the night off.

As much as I love the mental interruption the bar provides, a break is nice. A grip of disappointment squeezes at my core, though. I'm home alone with no plans and no one to make plans with. Archer is working, and my bet is, he'll go to Georgia's when he gets off.

Before my life fell apart, I had friends.

By the dozens.

Friends I partied with, traveled with, acted like spoiled rich kids with.

Fake-ass friends—most of them dropping me like flies when news broke.

A few were at my side during litigation, but after I was locked up, they were ghosts. No letters. No visits. No calls.

After my release, my mother threw me a *welcome home* party. Some of those *friends* came. I said my hellos, but just as they'd done to me, I wanted nothing to do with them. Hell, I hardly want anything to do with the old life I once had.

Loyalty—it's a big damn deal to me.

If you're not loyal, if I can't trust you, then there's the fucking door.

I've kept my mouth shut to remain loyal.

Got time for staying loyal.

If I say I have your back, I have your back.

I'm channel-surfing when my phone rings.

Cassidy.

"Hello?" I answer.

"Hi, handsome," she says, her voice casual as if this were a daily occurrence for us. "Whatcha doing?"

I scratch my neck, savoring the sound of her voice. It flows like an expensive ink, and I could soak up every drop. Cassidy's voice doesn't match her appearance, doesn't match your typical sorority girl.

"Not much," I reply. "Just chilling."

"By yourself?"

"Why?"

She's so nosy, and for some damn reason, I love it.

"Answer the question, Mr. Complicated."

"Yes"—I chuckle—"I'm alone."

"That's my good future husband."

The call ends.

The fuck?

Pulling the phone away, I stare at it in confusion. Just as I'm about to call her back to see if we lost connection, a FaceTime call comes through.

Cassidy.

I accept the call, and a zoomed-in Cassidy pops up on my screen—her face makeup-free, her blond hair swept back into a messy bun with stray pieces hanging loose around her eyes, and a knotted tie-dye headband pushed at the top.

"What movie do you want to watch?" When she shifts to make herself comfortable, her upholstered headboard comes into view.

I raise a brow. "Huh?"

"What's tonight's movie of choice?" She adjusts the collar on her silk pink-and-white striped pajama top. "Do you have Netflix?"

"Yes." I stare at her, blinking.

"Coolio." She leans forward, positions the phone so she's hands-free but still in view, and grabs her remote. "What are you in the mood for? Action? Comedy?" She glances away from the TV and shoots me an amused smile. "Me personally? Romance is the name of my game."

"Babe," I breathe out, "you need to clue me in here."

She plays with the remote in her hand. "Both of us are home, solo. Might as well watch a movie … hang out."

"Hmm … from what I remember, you said you'd be having *lots and lots* of sex tonight."

Nausea permeates in my stomach at her sleeping with a random guy who doesn't deserve her. That nausea morphs into satisfaction that she's not with a guy tonight.

No, she's with me.

Virtually.

But I'll take it.

I'll take any extra time I can have with her.

She scoffs, "You're dumber than I thought if you believed that."

I knew she was fucking with me.

The thing is, I love fucking with her right back.

"You have six seconds to decide before I take matters into my own hands," she says, breaking me out of my thoughts. "And trust me, it'll either be a serial killer doc, a cheesy romance, or some tiger people's drama."

I kick my bare feet up on the concrete coffee table. "You plan to come over?"

She shakes her head. "We're watching a movie via FaceTime."

There's no, *Do you want to?*

Cassidy—my new bossy best-friend-slash-coworker—has no problem telling me what *my* plans are for the night.

"Ah, is this what the cool kids do these days?" Observing my surroundings, I search for the perfect phone stand and decide on a leather pillow. Snagging the pillow, I settle it on the coffee table and balance the phone against it—a setup similar to Cassidy's.

"Nope. We typically Netflix and chill. Netflix and chill is when—"

Not wanting to hear about her Netflix-and-chilling with anyone, I talk over her, "I know what Netflix and chill is. I'm not *that* old. You pick the movie. I'm down for whatever."

"Let me grab my movie snacks."

Movie snacks?

"I wish you had given your boy a warning, so I could've grabbed some movie snacks."

"Joke's on you. Everyone should have movie snacks on hand at all times. Next time you go to the store, I'm tagging along to make sure you're loaded with the good stuff." Blowing me a kiss, she jumps off the bed, providing a short glimpse of her in her short pajama shorts, and disappears from the camera's view.

I train my eyes on the screen, not wanting to miss a second of our conversation. Minutes later, she returns with a bowl of popcorn, movie-theater snack boxes, and a Coke. My mouth waters, practically tasting the buttery popcorn.

She darts a quick glance in my direction, as if double-checking I'm still with her, and settles her snacks onto the bed. Sliding back onto the bed, she fluffs out a pillow and makes herself comfortable.

"Want a virtual kernel?" She holds the bowl toward the phone.

"Funny." My stomach grumbles like a chain saw. "You're making me hungry."

"Be better prepared in the future." She pops a kernel in her mouth and shoots me a sly grin.

I frown in disapproval. "Give me a heads-up next time."

"I love that you're agreeing this will happen again." She winks before tearing open a box of Junior Mints and tossing one into her mouth.

"Pause and let me see what I can wrangle from the kitchen." I drop my feet and groan as I stand.

"Wrangle? What are you, a cowboy going to hunt for his next meal?"

I flip her off before heading into the kitchen in search of snacks. Since Archer and I prefer takeout to cooking, I don't get my hopes up on matching Cassidy's snack game. Rummaging through the cabinet and fridge, I return to the living room with a bag of pretzels, a beer, and a box of Thin Mints.

How the living hell my brother managed to have Girl Scout cookies is beyond me.

I plop down on the couch at the same time I rip open the pretzels. "Choose our movie."

She nods, chewing the popcorn in her mouth, and rattles off some romance movie title.

Suppressing a groan, I type it into the search bar. "Got it."

"All right," she says, simulating a game show host's voice, "one, two, three, hit start."

We hit the button on our remotes at the same time, and the movie starts. Instead of watching the movie, I stare at Cassidy—all creeper-style but also justifying it as this is what she wanted. I soak up her surroundings, of the small area I can see of her bedroom.

"It sucks you're over there," Cassidy says, sliding the popcorn bowl onto her nightstand before tugging a white blanket up her chest. "We could snuggle." She *snuggles* into the blanket, into the bed, the same way I'd want to with her.

It does suck that we can't.

It's also good for us that we can't.

My heart quickens at the thought of her in my arms, but instead of agreeing, I say, "Eh, I don't know. I'm putting my money on you not only being a bed hog but also a snorer."

I joke.

It's in my nature.

My defense mechanism without sounding defensive.

Humor is what steers me away from conversations, from honesty I'm too scared to admit.

She wiggles her finger in a *come-hither* motion. "Come and see for yourself then."

I repeatedly shake my head. "Trouble, trouble, trouble."

Our attention returns to the movie, and every so often, one of us will comment about it. Mostly Cassidy, who has no problem telling movie characters they're being stupid. Even though romance movies aren't typically my jam, it's not terrible.

After a long spread of no Cassidy comments, I glance over to find her sleeping. Her mouth is somewhat open, her chest dropping in and out slowly, and the box of Junior Mints is gripped in her hand. I hesitate, unsure of what to do, but decide to keep watching the movie.

If she wakes up, she'll know I didn't bail on her.

She's still crashed out when the movie ends.

Whispering, "Good night," and hoping the mints don't spill all over her bed, I hang up.

And just like that, I had my first virtual … date … hangout … with Cassidy.

———

"I'M THROWING Archer a surprise birthday party," Georgia announces while walking into the bar.

Georgia and I have gotten along since day one. She and Archer … well, *Archer* was in the midst of denying his feelings for Georgia then. She flirted with me, resulting in my brother wanting to kill me. I knew he liked her, so I told her to keep doing it until he got his head out of his ass. When our father died, I called Georgia to be there with Archer. She was who he needed.

Even in the small amount of time we've known each other, I can depend on Georgia.

I respect Georgia.

I hope to God my brother never fucks up the good thing he has.

I snort. "Yeah, he won't be happy about that."

"Yes, he will," she answers with certainty as if there'd never been a truer fact.

Archer and surprise parties go together like the Pope and a strip club. My brother would probably choose to have his balls tugged off than attend a party solely for himself. Although, now that Georgia is in the picture, he's changing. The dude is becoming more of a social man. And given the hell he put Georgia through when he was working through his issues, he's nearly bowing down to her.

He won't love the surprise party, but he'll enjoy it for the sake of his relationship.

He'll enjoy it because his girlfriend threw it for him.

I chuckle, shaking my head. "You and my brother being total opposites yet also obsessed with each other would confuse the smartest dude on the planet."

"Opposites attract." She taps her finger against the side of her mouth. "Sometimes."

I cock my head to the side. "What's that supposed to mean?"

"Sometimes, cut from the same cloth attracts each other too." She offers me a bemused smile. "Like you and Cassidy."

It's a struggle, hiding my bullshit. "There's no *me and Cassidy* unless you're referring to our friendship."

"Yeah, okay." Sarcasm covers her tone. "Anyway, I'll give you time to come to terms with your liking her. Your grandparents offered the lake house for our little soiree. So, it'll be an overnight thing. Be there, or I'm shaving your head next time I sleep over."

A sinking feeling sets in my stomach. "You sure that's a good idea?"

Concern etches along her face. "Do you not think so?"

Archer doesn't mind the lake house.

He goes there all the time to clear his head.

Me? That's who I'm worried about.

There are too many memories there.

Regret rushes into me like a scorned ex as I remember what took place there.

But like I tell my brother, you have to face your shit, not run away from it.

"Nah, it's cool." I gulp. "He'd rather have it there than at some club."

The worry on her face dissolves, and she claps her hands before releasing a squeal. "I invited the crew, and hopefully, everyone can come."

I nod. "Let me know if you need me to do anything."

"You're the best." She blows me a kiss before scurrying away at the same time Cassidy comes into view.

"Gotta say, babe"—I shake my head in exaggerated disappointment—"you suck as a movie-watching partner."

My thoughts retrace to last night and how she made it seem less lonely, made me feel as if I had someone, a friend other than my brother. Someone I can call anytime, who I can ask to hang out, and who enjoys my company as much as I enjoy theirs. I'm damn grateful for this woman squeezing her way into my life.

She twists her ponytail around three fingers and laughs. "Look, a girl can be tired after picking up trash all morning. You didn't catch me at my movie-watching peak."

"And you say I'm old. You didn't even make it past midnight."

"Had you been there with me, I would've stayed awake *all* night."

I confine a laugh into a snort.

"Will you be in attendance at your brother's birthday party, old man?"

I nod. "Yep. You?"

"Georgia invited me, so I'm considering it." She grins. "It'll be a good time to show you how great my night-owl movie-watching skills are."

"My sidekick had better show up." I click my tongue against the roof of my mouth. "Can't leave me hanging as the odd one out."

"I'll be there. I'm Batman. You're Robin. Sidekicks forever."

"Whoa, whoa. I'm Batman. You're Robin."

I shake my head and snort. "I'm Batman."

She throws her arm out, signaling to her body. "Green isn't my color. It washes me out. Therefore, I can't be Robin."

"Too bad. You're *my* sidekick."

She rolls her eyes. "First, you're *my* sidekick. Second, here soon, I'll be moving my way up to the love of your life."

I cover my face to conceal a snort. "Swear to God, you and your craziness will be the death of me."

"Craziness? You haven't seen anything yet. Just wait until you get me in the bedroom."

The glass in my hand slips through my fingers and shatters on the floor. The thought of having Cassidy, of kissing Cassidy, of sliding into her warmth, into a pussy that'd probably be the best I've ever had, sends my heart into overdrive.

I am so screwed with this woman.

————

NO MATTER how much time has passed, a grim cloud will always be over my head when I visit the lake. What was once an enjoyable hangout for me is now nothing but a pitiful reminder of who I lost.

"Don't worry about hiding," Lola says, walking into the cabin with Silas trailing her. "The surprise is ruined. There will be no shocking gasps from Archer when he walks in."

Grace sighs, her hand covering her mouth. "What?"

"We parked down the street for this," Finn adds. "And it's fucking chilly outside."

Silas scoffs, "Dumbass. Did you honestly think Archer would hang out in the car, *blindfolded*, for hours? A hundo he *maybe* lasted ten minutes before he tore the damn thing off."

Lola shakes her head in disapproval. "What a pain in the ass."

Silas drapes his tattooed arm over her shoulders. "Don't act like you wouldn't do the same."

"Wrong. I enjoy being blindfolded." Tilting her head back, she peers up at Silas with a teasing smile. "I'd keep it on *all* night."

"What am I going to do with you?" He drags her against his chest and wrinkles his hand through her midnight-black strands before she smacks his hand away and smooths down her hair.

Silas and Lola are best friends.

Or so they say.

Something I've observed about my brother's circle is, people are in love with each other.

Archer and Georgia are obviously now dating.

Silas and Lola act like an old couple.

Finn acts as if he's Grace's bodyguard, her protector, and keeps a constant eye on her. While she stares at him with stars in her eyes.

Way more than friendship between them.

Briefly, I consider their viewpoint of Cassidy and me. They've made comments about us dating and being into each other.

Speaking of Cassidy, she declined my offer for a ride here and rode with Lola and Silas instead. She mentioned something along the lines of finding new friends. Which I get. Working so much, she doesn't get out much. Neither Grace nor Lola work at the bar, but they hang out at Twisted Fox like it's their second job, and she spends time with them during her breaks.

Everyone's attention shifts to the front door when it flies open.

Forgetting what Lola said, we yell, "Surprise!"

False alarm.

Instead of the birthday boy coming into view, it's my mother and grandparents. I smile, appreciative that Georgia included them. My mom has gone through hell the past few years, and with my father gone, she's lonely. When Archer and I were younger, we hardly spent time with our parents. Now, I check on my mother a few times a week, have dinner with her, watch movies—anything to get her mind off her loss.

"Wrong person." My mother's brown eyes widen with concern about ruining the surprise. "Although I'm sure Archer won't be upset about missing the surprise part." She struts into the house, and her heels clack against the wood floor. A Prada bag hangs off her shoulder, and she's wearing a white pantsuit.

To a lake house.

Josephine Callahan doesn't do casual.

Hell, I'm not sure she even owns a pair of jeans.

Designer pantsuits and dresses are her fashion choice.

Behind her are my grandparents, walking hand in hand.

"Although I did enjoy a greeting like that." My grandmother—barely wrinkled with the help of Botox—scrunches her face as she grins.

The room erupts in laughter.

Cassidy lifts on her tiptoes next to me and whispers, "Is that your mom?"

I nod at the same time my mother reaches us. Cassidy retreats a step, allowing my mom room to wrap her arms around me in a hug and smack a kiss to my cheek.

Before the *incident*, my mother wasn't a hugger.

Kissing cheeks was more of a formality than maternal.

My father's death changed her.

Changed her outlook on life and she tapped into her inner self.

Same shit with me.

"Okay, you're absolutely gorgeous," Cassidy blurts out.

My mother beams at the compliment, her pearly veneers showing.

I hold in a chuckle and gesture to Cassidy. "Mom, this is Cassidy. Cassidy, this is my mother, Josephine."

"Oh, I like her. Are you two ...?" She signals back and forth between us.

"Not yet," Cassidy answers before I can. "Your son is quite stubborn."

My mother offers me a nod of encouragement as Lola calls Cassidy over.

Cassidy holds out her hand toward my mother. "It's really nice meeting you. I can't wait for us to shop for my wedding dress when the day comes."

My mother squeezes her hand once and then twice while grinning at her.

Just like how those maternal instincts kicked in, my mother has started asking when I'll settle down, when I'll find a nice girl like Georgia, when I'll stop wanting the *bachelor* lifestyle. I don't live the bachelor lifestyle. I'm living the survival lifestyle—working my ass off, fighting my demons, and not wanting to punch the world in its face every time I think about how it's fucked me.

That isn't me being a whiny bitch either. I'll accept responsibility for what I've done and the choices I've made, but there are people in high places who hate me. And they brought me down.

"Why haven't you asked her out?" my mother rushes out as if she's been holding on to it like a breath underwater. "She's better suited for you than ... others you've dated."

A fucking Kit Kat bar would be better suited for me than the women I've dated ... well, was involved with because *dating* is a heavy term. A term I've never used with a woman—nor have I had to with the type of women who found their way, sneaking into my bed.

I scratch my cheek, averting my gaze to the opposite end of the room—to where Cassidy is talking to Lola and pouring herself a drink. Talking about the women I've *dated* is the last talkfest I want to have with my mother. The situation, the women I was involved with, is awkward enough.

I clear my throat, hoping to dispose of the uneasiness. "We're just friends. She's young and—"

"Honey, honey," she interrupts. "She isn't that young. And so what if she's a few years behind you? She's full of life, and she obviously likes you … and from the way you've been staring since she walked away, I'd say the feeling is mutual. She reminds me of Georgia. Look how good she is for Archer."

"Georgia and Archer are different." I slip my hands into my jean pockets. "Archer has his life together, and his past isn't as fucked up as mine."

My mother's fair-tinted face falls while she captures my hand in hers. "I'm sorry for what happened, but in order to be happy, you have to move on from the past. We're suffering the same pain—in different ways but still similar. I want you to rise above it more than I want it for myself. All it takes for you is a reason, an incentive, a realization that not everyone will judge you for your past."

"I know; I know." The thought still sends nausea through my stomach.

Thankfully, Archer and Georgia walk in, interrupting our conversation. The surprise is delayed this time, happening a good minute after they come into view, and everyone cracks up in laughter. Archer, not appearing one bit surprised, thanks everyone for coming.

Georgia ordered a taco bar that I picked up on my way to the lake, and Lola brought enough drinks to last us a week. We eat, drink, and celebrate my brother's birthday.

As the sunset transitions into darkness, I say good-bye to my mother and grandparents and walk outside. I accept the bite of the wind as I stroll down the wooden dock and settle myself on the edge. Shutting my eyes, I soak up the silence and absorb the semblance of my surroundings. There's something about the lake, the rhythmic echo of the water, that lends a hand to your psyche and relaxes you.

Yet at the same time, the solitude of the water forces you to remember.

The two-story home, complete with a wraparound porch and wall-to-wall windows, has been in the Callahan family since my grandfather bought it in his thirties. It's been renovated a few dozen times by my mother, whose interior style is a revolving door of changes.

After my grandfather's death, the home was passed down to my father. It was supposed to keep that same course—the home being passed down from generation to generation. Too bad that didn't last. The feds wanted it, and before they managed to get their grimy hands on one of my favorite childhood destinations, my mother's parents stepped in and purchased it from my father. That way, it could stay in the family, and we wouldn't lose yet another thing. The lake house is modest compared to our other family homes, but it was my grandfather's pride and joy. We'd already annihilated the business he'd built from the ground up; we couldn't lose the lake house too.

"Hey, party of one out here."

I glance back to find Cassidy stopping behind me.

"Can I join you?"

I pat the space next to me. "Sure."

If it were anyone else, even Archer, who'd asked that question, I'd have told them I needed alone time. But not with Cassidy. I'll never decline a second with her. Like the serenity of the lake, she's practically a sedative for me. And this isn't about me being codependent with a girl; it's about being around someone who shines so fucking bright that I can't help but be zapped with her energy.

About a woman I can sit here with, not say a word, and she'd understand.

Or I could ramble off about the most random shit, and she'd understand.

Or I could ask her to leave, and she'd also understand.

Cassidy is understanding, and in the world of the rich and felons, that isn't a common trait.

She plops down next to me, our shoulders brushing as she settles herself. "This is gorgeous." With a sigh, she leans back on her elbows and lifts her head, studying the open sky. "I could stay out here all night and take in the stillness of this place."

"This is where my father's ashes were spread." The words, unrelenting, spill from my lips like a waterfall.

Fuck!

Regret seeps up my throat.

I should've kept that to myself.

Way to morbid the night up, Linc.

"Oh." Dead air passes before her voice softens, and she stretches out her arm to rest her hand over mine. "That has to be hard."

That's an understatement.

It ripped me apart.

I was close with my father.

After graduating college, I took over the VP position at Callahan Holdings since Archer refused to. My father and I worked together every day and got along great, and then he hired Phil, his longtime friend. His shady friend who had too many ideas but not enough sense.

That friend convinced my father he could avoid repercussions from breaking the law because he was rich and had a company to stand behind. I warned him, threatened the friend, begged my father day after day to stop. It generated a wire of tension between us that was never uncut. He was breaking the law, and all I could do was sit back and watch the fire spread, praying to the good man above that my father would come to his senses. Archer, not giving a shit about family loyalty, resigned the moment he found out.

Me? I stayed. Callahan Holdings had been ingrained in our blood, and I'd never turn my back on blood.

Then I also went to prison with my father and Phil.

"He died while serving time in prison." Another unstoppable confession.

"What?" There's no stammer in her tone.

"He was in prison, had a heart attack, and died."

She shifts to face me, and under the brilliance of the light seeping from the front porch, I spot the curiosity swimming in her eyes. I wait for the endless questions, but they don't come. Cassidy, my mind-reading confidant, understands I'm here to reflect upon my past, my father, and not confess the wrongdoings of a man who's no longer with us.

"It's nice he can rest somewhere so peaceful ... so pretty."

I nod. "It is."

I never perceived it that way, but Cassidy has a point. My father loved the lake; it was his resting place, so it only makes sense it's where he was finally laid to rest. Criminal or not, he deserved a proper goodbye, a proper place for his soul to reside.

Cassidy, the girl who never stops talking and bullshitting, sits silently next to me. Eventually, she rests her head on the crook of my shoulder, and I wrap my arm around her back, tugging her closer to me, nearly on my lap.

"You cold?" I ask, peering down as she rubs her hand over her goose bump–covered arm.

"A little," she whispers.

I tighten my grip on her, hoping to transfer a sliver of my body heat, and run my hand up and down her arm—similar to what she was doing. Her skin is soft, smooth like the organic apples my mom overpays for. When the goose bumps don't disappear, and she shivers, I slowly pull away, already missing her warmth, and stand.

I hold out my hand, and there's no hesitation before she takes it, allowing me to pull her to her feet. Only inches separate us. Our breaths meet, and my heart thrashes against my chest in uncertainty of what's to come.

She licks her lips.

I do the same.

The desire of this woman cuts through my veins, as if it's begging to be let free.

I inhale a deep breath.

No, I can't ruin our friendship.

I lower my voice, swiping flyaway strands of hair from her eyes. "My sidekick."

"Your sidekick," she whispers.

Without thinking, without considering the repercussions of such a reckless move, I bow my head and rest my forehead against hers.

"Lincoln." She says my name in a shaky breath.

Her voice. That tone. It ruins me.

It's the push that leads me to drop my lips to hers.

She kisses me back, her lips plump and soft.

As we kiss, it's as if she's breathing life back into me.

Yet also casting a calmness alongside it.

When she opens her mouth, sliding her tongue along the seam of my lips, reality shatters through me.

My head spins when I break our connection, retreat a step, and catch my breath. "Shit, Cass. I'm so sorry."

This time, she's caressing my arm while appearing unfazed by my pulling away. "No, it's fine." A hint of a smile crosses her face. "In fact, I'm down to do it again."

I hesitate.

That urge that caused me to kiss her moments ago resurfaces.

My mouth already misses the taste of hers.

"Yo! Party ditchers!" Finn calls out into the night from the back porch. "Get your asses in here!"

And just like that, Finn saves us from ruining our friendship.

"I'm going to punch him," Cassidy grumbles. "In the balls. Then the kneecaps. Then the balls again for good measure."

I chuckle, and my hand is sweaty when I grab hers. I wait for her reaction—whether she'll tug away, try to kiss me again, or ask about the kiss. With a sigh, she squeezes my hand, and I lead her back into the house, where everyone, except Georgia and Archer, are in the living room. Drinks are in their hands, and some trivia show is playing on the TV, all of them screaming answers at the contestant.

"We thought you guys had gotten lost out there," Finn says, falling down on the couch next to Grace.

"Prepare to have mosquito bites out the ass," Lola comments, shuddering as she peers back at us from the front of the couch. "Those things are brutal around here."

Finn slides his hands together. "I don't know about y'all, but I'm exhausted. The birthday boy has retired to his bedroom, and that means we can crash at any time." He does a once-over of the room.

I peer over at Cassidy and drop her hand. "You staying the night?"

A sleepover was Georgia's plan. It's a four-bedroom, providing plenty of room for everyone. Archer and I are crashing in our bedrooms, which leaves the master and guest bedroom.

Cassidy nods. "Sure am."

"What are the sleeping arrangements?" I ask everyone.

Lola yawns, stretching out her arms. "Grace and I are crashing in the master." She shoots a glance at Cassidy. "We can squeeze your tiny butt in there if you want?"

Cassidy laughs. "That might be a little too uncomfortable. I'll take the couch. No biggie."

"Eh, I'm taking the couch," Finn says. "Silas and I flipped for the guest room, and I lost."

"You can have my bed, Cassidy," Silas offers. "I'll crash on the floor." He winks at her, sending a streak of jealousy through my blood.

"Nah, take my bed," I interrupt. "It's more comfortable than the guest bed, and I'll crash on the floor."

"You don't have to do that," Cassidy replies, biting into her lower lip—a lip that I now know the taste of.

For someone who's talked plenty of shit about being in my bed, she sure seems shy about it now.

"The floor is comfortable," I add. "I like sleeping on it."

She rolls her eyes. "You are such a liar."

"Punish me for my lying by taking my bed then." I smile. "You know I'm the perfect gentleman."

"Okay," she dramatically groans. "But don't say it's my fault when you're sore from sleeping on the floor."

CHAPTER TEN

Cassidy

"OH MY GOD, you're such a bullshitter," I say, laughing when Lincoln drops down to pull out a bed from the couch in his bedroom.

He smirks. "What?"

"You were acting like such a gentleman, offering to give me your bed and sleep on the floor, when in actuality, you have a damn pullout bed."

"Hey, I'm giving you my bed, aren't I?" He places his hand over his heart. "I'd say that's a damn good gentleman. I could be making *you* sleep on the pullout, which isn't nearly as comfortable as my Tempur-Pedic."

"I can take the pullout." I hate inconveniencing people.

"No, you'll take my bed." He shakes his head. "There's no changing my mind."

Dropping my overnight bag onto the carpet, I size up his bedroom. "This is cute."

It screams *I played lacrosse, come from money, and haven't been here since my high school years* with its plaid wallpaper, black furniture, and blue bedding.

He raises a brow. "Cute?"

"Definitely an adolescent teen's bedroom."

He advances the few steps to the closet and gathers sheets and a blanket. "No judging. I didn't stay here much growing up." He stops, a flash of regret on his features, and scratches his scruffy cheek. "I didn't spend much time with my family back then, so my mother didn't bother renovating rooms that weren't being used."

"Why didn't you hang out with your family?"

Even though my family could have a two-part special on *Dr. Phil*, we're close. My mother held mandatory dinners, and I regularly came home from college on the weekends. My parents' marriage might've been messy, but my mother made sure to build a strong support system within my siblings.

I stroll around the bedroom, as if I were in a museum, and inspect everything. Grabbing a framed photo, I hold it up. "Is this your dad?"

His face is unreadable as he nods and stares at the photo. "Yeah."

I eye the man's features. "He and Archer are spitting images of each other."

"Yeah, they were nearly twins."

Unlike Lincoln, Archer has broad shoulders, thick hair that reaches his neck, and a wide face. Lincoln is slimmer with short hair, and while they both sport facial hair, Lincoln's is cleaner cut. The similarities between his father and him are limited. While Archer took after their father, Lincoln resembles more of his mother.

I gulp, setting the photo down, and snag another of him in a tuxedo. His arm is wrapped around a girl, who is sporting a frilly, gaudy-as-hell pink dress.

"Girlfriend?" I jerk my head toward the photo.

"Prom date."

"Did you bang her?"

He cracks a smile. "None of your business."

"Secrets don't make friends, Callahan, and if I recall correctly, that's what you keep saying we are. *Friends*. So … let a friend know."

He shakes his head. "It was prom. I was a stupid teenager. So, yes."

I love that he's honest with me. After what happened with Quinton, honesty and trust are my biggest turn-ons. Quinton did a lot of fucked-up things to me, and the biggest takeaway from it was, trust is an important component of a relationship.

Well, behind not dating a criminal.

The next photo I pick up is of Lincoln in a lacrosse uniform. *Shocker.*

"You were hot." I smile. "I so would've dated you in high school."

He stops in the middle of making up his bed and wrinkles his nose. "Only in high school?"

"Shut up." I return the photo to the dresser. "You know I'd date you so hard *right now*. And don't bother saying the same because I know if I were old, *like you*, you'd date me so hard."

"But unfortunately, you're too young for me."

"And you're too dumb for me for saying that."

He winces. "Ouch."

My chest tightens, but I'm strong enough to maintain a straight face. We're joking, being good ole buddies, ole pals, but it pains me every time he mentions our age difference, when he calls me too young. It's not like he's Hugh Hefner and I just graduated from high school. Yes, there's a *slight* age difference but nothing too out of the ordinary. Hell, Georgia is years behind Archer.

That heartache of the topic hits harder now that we've kissed. I had known kissing him would be exciting, but it was more than I'd expected. It was perfection. Never before had just a kiss dragged out emotions so strong, a need so heavy, a compulsion to want to have everything with a man. Him kissing me verifies he feels the same way, but in true Callahan boy fashion, he's hiding.

Now, he's acting as if it never happened. Since we're in a house full of people and I'm not sure where the conversation would lead, I decide to save it for later. If he says the wrong thing, it's not like I can storm out of here and leave. Walking home or asking Grace to leave in the middle of the night aren't options.

There's a time and a place to talk with the guy I'm falling for. A time and a place to bring up the kiss. My stomach sinks at the realization that he might think said kiss was a mistake.

Kneeling, I unzip my overnight bag and yank my pajamas from it before snagging my toothbrush. "I'm going to change and get ready for bed."

He salutes me as I stroll into the adjoined bathroom. With a large glass shower and a blue rug, it doesn't provide as much character as his bedroom does. Walking out in a silky camisole and plaid pants—I packed casually but still kept a hint of sexiness—I find Lincoln changed into a white tee and gray sweats. I blush, taking him in, before noticing the candy pile on the bed.

"What's this?"

Lincoln glances up at me. "Movies and snacks until we crash out … until *you* crash out."

And just like that, the tension over our kiss unbinds.

Temporarily washes itself out of my thoughts at him remembering our movie night.

"Sounds like a plan to me." It's hard to contain my happiness as I plop down on the bed, stomach first, and allow my feet to dangle off the end as I inspect the candy selection. "AirHeads, Starbursts, Nerds, Junior Mints. Jesus, you hooked a girl up." Rolling over, I bring myself up and rest my back against the headboard. "You planned for this, didn't you?"

"I might've made a pit stop on the way here." He snatches the pillow on the pullout and fluffs it out. "You're my sidekick, remember? We gotta look out for each other."

I cock my head to the side. "How'd you know I'd be in your bedroom?"

"That I had no idea. I figured we'd hang out in the living room, but this is better."

"Oh, really? Why's that?"

"No one can jack our snacks."

"Good point." I snatch the Nerds, open the box, and pour the mini candies into my mouth. "I've had alcohol, and now, I'm about to sugar binge. I'm either going to be up all night like a crackhead or crash out in twenty minutes. There's no in-between."

"Hmm …" He taps the side of his mouth. "What was it you said before? If I were with you, you'd stay up all night?"

Ugh, I hate when my words come back to bite me in the ass.

"Who said that?" I look from one side of the room to the other. "I don't know who said that. You got the wrong girl, buddy."

Marching toward me, he plucks the AirHeads box off the bed,

opens it, and grabs a blue one. "I say, you put your candy where your mouth is."

"What does that even mean?" I stare at him with raised brows.

"I have no idea actually. It sounded much better in my head." He chomps off the end of the AirHeads.

"I sure hope so."

He collapses next to me on the bed and stretches out his legs. "What are we watching tonight?"

"I chose last time." I chew on my lower lip. "It's your turn, *but* I have a few rules."

"Rules suck, but throw them at me."

"No unrealistic action movies. Otherwise, prepare to hear me bitch about how it's not physically possible for a forty-year-old with a dad bod to beat up three ninjas and sixteen gun-bearing men and then get away with the millions in cash from jumping building to building in a Corvette."

"Babe," he groans. "Nearly all action movies are unrealistic."

"I guess that means all action movies are vetoed."

He chuckles and points at me with his wrapper. "I see what you did there."

"What?" I shrug innocently.

He shakes his head and lounges next to me. My breathing stalls at us being so close *in a bed* while the touch of his lips still lingers on mine. He allows me to choose the movie, and this go-around, I choose a romantic comedy. We make ourselves comfortable, selecting our movie snacks, and watch the movie.

As I do, thoughts of our kiss return.

Thoughts of how broken his face was when he confessed what he'd been thinking about while sitting on the lake dock, his feet dangling where his father's ashes had been spread. As we stood, as he warmed me up in his arms, there was a spark—a spark that had been heating me from the moment our eyes met—and I saw desire flicker through like a flame.

There was a connection unlike anything I'd shared with someone before.

Not much time passes before my eyes are heavy and I'm fighting to keep them open. We haven't even hit midway through the movie before I cave in to sleep.

I talk a lot of shit for a girl who can't stay awake for an entire movie.

———

I WAKE up in an unfamiliar bed with a familiar scent.

A scent I wish I could bottle up and keep forever.

Moaning as my body slides along the expensive, chilly sheets, I rise to find the room Lincoln-free.

No Lincoln, but plenty of memories of our kiss last night. My spine tingles at the recollection. I cast a glance at the pullout bed, wondering if he slept there or in bed with me. We could've slept together. Granted, there was no intimacy happening, but it was *kind of* a date, right?

Lincoln could have pulled a move on me last night. He could've kept kissing me, laid me down on the dock, and I would've been down for whatever he wanted. He could've brought me into his bedroom and put the moves on me. I would've gone down on him, ridden his cock, done anything he wanted. Coming from a sorority girl whose men consisted of frat guys, it's what I'd expect from a sleepover with a guy.

But Lincoln isn't just any guy.

He isn't a stupid kid or a guy who only wants one thing from me.

He's so much more.

And I'm terrified he'll never want those things … because I do.

And it's not just sex I want from him. I want his friendship … his heart … so that way, I can give him mine in return. I can trust Lincoln with my heart, just as he can trust me with his.

I slide out of bed, brush my teeth, wash my face, and am bunching my hair into a ponytail as I walk downstairs to where I hear commotion. Everyone is in the kitchen, the smell of bacon wafting in the air, and Silas is at the stove with multiple pans in front of him.

My stomach growls, pleading to balance the sugar I binged last night with a supplemental meal.

"Morning, sunshine!" Lincoln greets, and a trail of hellos and mornings follows from the group. "How'd you sleep?"

His smile is bright as he stands in the kitchen, his fingers wrapped around a coffee mug, wearing the same sweats he wore last night. Gray sweats are where it's at, ladies. Don't think I wasn't looking in that waist area for a sneak peek of what Lincoln has to offer.

"Good," I reply around a yawn.

"My bed is pretty damn comfortable, eh?" He winks.

I roll my eyes. "Joke's on you though because I'll be demanding to sleep there every time I'm here."

"You two will be dating soon," Lola states with a tone of certainty. "I doubt there will be an issue with you being in his bed."

Lincoln swiftly looks away at her statement and stops our playful conversation.

If only I could read what's dancing through his mind.

We eat breakfast—this is the moment I realize Silas is amazing in the kitchen—and drink the mimosas Georgia whipped up.

After hanging out for a few hours, the lake house starts clearing out. Those few hours, I got a different Lincoln from last night, from the one who had greeted me this morning. Lola's comment had changed his attitude toward me, and even though he sat at my side as we ate, he didn't mention the kiss. Nor does he as we say good-bye.

And so, I wait for the perfect time to bring it up ... along with other questions.

CHAPTER ELEVEN

Lincoln

"YOU TWO ARE ADORABLE," Grace singsongs, answering the door in an *Alice in Wonderland* costume.

It's two nights after Halloween, and she's throwing a costume party with Georgia. Since Halloween is one of the busiest nights at Twisted Fox, we all had to work, so we're celebrating now. What I'm learning from Archer and his friends is, they like to celebrate shit and party. They're different *parties* than what I'm used to.

They have kid-friendly pool parties at Maliki's, Cohen's best friend.

Birthday dinners for each of them.

Barbecues at Cohen's.

They're tight-knit, *who's bringing what food* parties.

"Look at you two, all matchy-matchy," Georgia shouts, coming into view with a mixed drink in her hand. "I am obsessed with it."

Georgia has to be the most supportive person I've ever met, everyone's biggest cheerleader. I've never known a friendlier soul. A sarcastic-as-fuck but kind soul.

Had I not overheard her and Archer bickering earlier, her Bride of Chucky costume would've been a surprise. I nearly spat out my water when Archer appeared in the living room in his Chucky costume—complete with the spiky orange wig, striped shirt, and overalls that

were a good three inches above his ankles. He put his foot down when
it came to makeup, only allowing Georgia to make one face scar.

"It had to have been planned," Grace says. "It's adorable."

"We didn't plan it," I argue.

"Um, we *so* planned it," Cassidy corrects, bumping her hip into
mine. "In fact, Georgia, it was all your future brother-in-law's idea."

Georgia's face lights up at Cassidy's comment. Archer hasn't
popped the question yet, but everyone knows it's coming. The other
day, when I caught a ride with him, a jeweler's card was in the
cupholder. No doubt, he'll have something custom-made and hit it
out of the ballpark. He loves spoiling Georgia.

"Batman and Robin! Hell yes!" Finn calls out. "Or should I say,
Batwoman and Robin?" He stomps our way in his Mad Hatter
costume—one that matches Grace's Alice costume.

The couple of costumes are a trend, I see.

One Cassidy and I also followed with our Batwoman and Robin
getups. Last night, Cassidy instructed me to pick her up for the party
and informed me she had my costume. I scoffed and stated I wasn't
wearing a costume, let alone allowing her to dress me up as some Ken
doll.

When I arrived at her house tonight, she greeted me, wearing a
black faux leather dress that landed inches above her knees and
showcased her tanned legs. My mouth nearly dropped to the floor, and
my dick hardened as I took in her thigh-high black boots that brought
her closer to my height.

While I urged my dick to calm itself at the view of her, she shoved
the Robin costume into my chest and directed me to the bathroom.
Compared to her, I don't look nearly as hot in my costume … in my
goddamn tights.

Yep. She dressed me in fucking tights.

A green-and-red jumpsuit, complete with a foam utility belt and
cape. The polyester is scratchy, and my nuts screamed at me when I
shoved them into the jumpsuit. To top it off, my black mask won't
stop falling off the side of my face.

I look like a damn joke.

But Cassidy told me to do it, so I did.

Call it friendship-whipped.

"Hey!" Noah, Cohen's son, shouts when we walk into the living room. He's on the couch with a caramel apple on a plate sitting on his lap.

Next to him is a very pregnant, looking close to bursting, Jamie, dressed as Jessie the Yodeling Cowgirl—I know who this is because my cellie's daughter was obsessed with *Toy Story*—and Cohen, dressed as Woody.

"I was Batman last year. This year, I'm Buzz Lightyear!" With carefulness, Noah settles his plate on the coffee table and jumps off the couch to show off his Buzz space suit—lifting one foot, then the other, and then spinning around fashion show–style.

Cassidy laughs and drops to one knee, so she's at his level. "That's awesome! I bet your Batman costume was way cooler than mine."

Noah's face lights up as he eats up her attention.

Tugging on my mask, I stare at them, devouring the scene. She's talking to Noah, giving him her full attention, and my breathing catches in my throat. Never have I been turned on by seeing a woman with a child, but watching Cassidy and the way she throws her head back laughing while talking to him is hot.

"What's up, big man?" Silas asks, slapping me on the back—knocking me out of my Cassidy trance.

I burst into laughter as I turn to him. "Dude, what the hell are you wearing?"

And I thought my costume was bad.

"What?" Silas grunts, his lips parting into a grin. "Don't be jealous of my ensemble." He performs a move similar to what Noah did.

"I'm far from jealous." I shake my head, feeling embarrassed for him.

"Lola," Silas shouts, wrapping his hands around his mouth. "Lincoln is talking crap about my costume!"

Silas's leaf-covered romper makes sense when I see Lola wearing a matching dress. At least Cassidy didn't decide for us to be Adam and Eve. A jumpsuit was pushing it. My ass will never be in a romper. I don't care how much Cassidy begs me.

Lola smooths her hands down her long black hair before playfully flipping me off. "Don't be jealous that Silas can show off his legs."

I snort. "Silas can definitely be the romper-wearer of our group."

"I'm going to miss this," Grace whines, peering over at Georgia and plopping down cross-legged on the floor. "Miss us hanging out here, drinking wine, gossiping, and watching reruns of *Schitt's Creek*."

Georgia, who's sitting on Archer's lap in a chair, peers at Grace with sad eyes. "You can come over anytime you want for wine time *or* just move in with us."

"Whoa," Archer grunts behind her. "Where's she going to sleep? The couch?"

"No, we'll add a bedroom to the penthouse," Georgia replies.

"Yeah, that'll be easy to do on the top floor of a building," I comment.

Grace's shoulders droop. "It's fine. I'll just move in with my parents or something."

"Why?" Cassidy asks, shooting a glance to Jamie. "Did you sell the place?"

Jamie rented out the townhouse to the girls after moving in with Cohen.

"Nope," Jamie answers. "It's all *love's* fault."

Cassidy's head tilts to the side in question.

"Here soon, Georgia is going to move in with Archer," Grace explains before narrowing her eyes at Lola. "And *my other* best friend won't fill in the roomie role."

"Uh, I can't just break my lease." Lola stares at her with apology. "If I had an open room, I'd so give it to you."

"I told you, I won't move out until we find you another roommate," Georgia says.

"I can move in," Cassidy says. Her cheeks redden as all attention turns to her. "I mean, if that's okay with you? I live alone but am down for having a roommate."

Grace's face lights up. "Really?"

Cassidy nods repeatedly. "Really."

Grace squeals before jumping to her feet and hugging Cassidy. "Yay! Georgia moves out next week, and then the room is all yours.

Tell me what you can afford rent-wise, and we'll work something out."

"Shit, Grace would let you move in for free," Finn inputs.

"See! There you go!" Georgia throws out her arms. "Everything worked out, and you don't have to move back in with your parents."

"This calls for a toast," Finn announces. "Everyone, to the kitchen!"

Cohen stands, holding his hand out to Jamie, and pulls her up while she groans. Cassidy loops her arm around mine, and we follow everyone to the kitchen. Finn and Lola start passing out drinks.

"All right," Finn calls out, "grab your beers, your wine"—he stops to glance at Noah and Jamie—"your Capri Sun and seltzer water and hold them in the air."

Noah's grin takes over his entire face at being included and raises his arm as high as he can.

Finn lifts his beer. "To friendships, to roommates, to Halloween. May we always celebrate our holidays together—even if it's days later —and always have each other's backs."

"Hell yeah," Silas says.

At the same time, everyone else shouts, "Cheers!"

"Georgia is moving in, huh?" Cassidy asks as everyone starts conversing. "Looks like you'll be third-wheeling all the time."

I shrug. "I don't mind. Archer is happier when Georgia is around. A plus for me. Georgia also doesn't mind making coffee runs. Another plus."

Georgia brings life into my brother, is a blast, and even helps when I'm feeling down. I'm happy my brother has found a great partner.

"Just wait until we start dating and I move in with you." Cassidy winks, gently elbowing me. "We can go on all the coffee runs together."

I chuckle. After the kiss, our jokes hit differently. I can see it in her face when I make an innuendo, and I'm sure she sees it in mine. There's now an underlying realization that it's not just *joking*. It's more.

"If you agree to coffee runs, tell Grace she's losing her roommate now, and you can sleep on the couch."

She rolls her eyes. "Your bed or no new roommate."

"Charades time!" Grace yells. "Let's get teams together."

Grabbing our drinks, we return to the living room, where we play charades until everyone is yawning. A few years ago, I'd have called something like this lame—it's something I'd have laughed at—but not anymore. I actually enjoy this shit.

In the past, my idea of good times with friends was expensive clubs, traveling abroad, or snorting lines.

"You need a ride home?" I ask Cassidy as the townhome starts clearing out.

"Obviously." She smacks my arm. "You picked me up. You're responsible for getting me home."

"Like your babysitter."

"I was thinking more along the lines of *like your date*."

Her words smack into me like a train. If you looked up the definition of *date* in the dictionary, it'd be what I've done tonight—drove to her house, picked her up, and attended a party together. Sure, during the drive, I told myself I was picking up a friend, but it's growing harder and harder to keep up with that lie.

Neither of us has mentioned our three-second kiss at Archer's party —shocking, considering Cassidy loves talking about everything, especially conversations I'd kill to avoid. You don't kiss people unless you're attracted to them or have feelings for them. If she asks me why I kissed her, I'd have to admit to both of those reasons.

I say my good-byes while Cassidy gives out hugs and tells Jamie that she can't wait to meet her little girl.

By the time we're walking to my car, our masks are off, and her cape is balled up in her hands. As soon as she slides into the passenger seat, she starts a series of yawns.

"Ugh," she moans around another yawn. "I could sleep for nine straight days and still be exhausted."

I crank up the heat and our seat warmers. "You been partying too hard?"

She works all the time, but she could be fitting in clubs and parties in her spare time. If she does, she never talks about it.

She shakes her head, rubbing at her eyes. "Just haven't been sleeping well."

"Why not?"

"Maybe it's the apartment ... living alone ..." She tips her head down and studies her red nails. "At first, it was nice. Now, it's just ... weird sometimes."

She's not telling me everything. I know when Cassidy is holding back.

"Why? Your neighbor giving you a bad vibe?"

"No, not at all," she rushes out. "All my life, I've been surrounded by people, and now, I'm not. It's different, is all." Perking up in her seat, she releases a ragged breath. "We made a pretty good Batwoman and Robin tonight, huh?"

I chuckle. "Gotta say, with the exception of Buzz Lightyear, we had the best costumes tonight."

"Team Batwoman and Robin for the win." She holds out her fist, and I bump mine against it before she pulls the seat belt across her body. "Now, this superhero needs her beauty sleep."

"Aye aye, boss."

I shift the car into drive, and it's a short ride to her duplex. Without a word, I unbuckle my seat belt, step out of the car, and open Cassidy's door—all date-style even though this isn't a date, right? My hand finds the base of her back when she steps out, and as we stroll side by side to her unit.

During the drive home, worry followed me with every mile over her comment about not sleeping well. I could be reading too much into it, but there has to be a reason. At times, I've slept terribly, but it's always been because of underlying issues. I'm almost tempted to invite her to my place and give her my bed while I take the couch.

My hand doesn't leave her back until we walk into her apartment, and she starts flipping on the lights. Her apartment is small and doesn't display much of her character. A deep red sectional rests against the living room wall with furry white pillows scattered along it. There's miscellaneous pink and feminine wall art. Across the room is the kitchen and an area where a pub table sits.

Cassidy shoves away a few pillows, collapses onto the couch, and eyeballs me, her gaze sharp and searching. "All right, Callahan, are we ever going to talk about our kiss, or shall we act like it never happened?" Her tone is clear—no bullshit, no beating around the bush.

My chest seizes with pain, and I force a laugh while attempting to calm my mind. "I was hoping we'd act like it never happened."

She sucks in a breath, disappointment clouding her features. "That sure makes a girl feel good."

I tug at the neck of my costume, wishing I could kick my own ass for kissing her. Not that there was no attraction or that I didn't want to do more. No, I wanted to drag her to my bedroom and do more than watch TV and eat snacks. I wanted *her* to be my snack, wanted the movie to be the background noise while I fucked her in every position possible, and then I wanted to feed her breakfast in bed the next morning.

Unfortunately, my dumbass has only managed to complicate our friendship.

"My answer has nothing to do with you and everything to do with me," I grind out, more disgusted with myself with each word of bullshit I deliver. With the time I've had, you'd think I'd have come up with a better reason for shutting us down.

She cringes as if she'd been slapped in the face. "That's a pretty crappy reason, by the way. I'll take *bullshit* for three hundred dollars."

I throw up my arms before allowing them to fall to my sides. "Cass, right now, you're pretty much my best friend." I swallow hard at my confession, at me putting all my honesty out there. "I don't want to fuck that up because we kissed. I don't … I don't want to *lose you*." My voice breaks with the last two words the same way my soul would if our friendship turned sour.

Even before my life changed, I never had fun with someone like I do with her. I never bantered, had witty conversations, found someone I could vocally spar with like I have with her. I never thought about someone so damn much. And I don't want to lose her.

She blinks at me. "Why would that mess things up?"

"Kissing leads to feelings." I rest my back against the door and pinch the bridge of my nose. "Feelings lead to problems, fallouts, *hate*."

Every relationship—scratch that—every hookup I've had has ended in messiness.

She's quiet for a moment, as if digesting my words. "Kissing can also lead to better." She raises a brow and licks that plump bottom lip of hers. "*Hotter* things."

Fuck.

I need to abort mission before this friendship of ours takes a leap into something not platonic ... into something we both crave but shouldn't. Continuing this conversation can only result in two outcomes: us kissing again—most likely *hotter*, as she said—or me pushing her away, resulting in her hating me. The weight of guilt presses against my chest, making it difficult for me to breathe as I mentally rifle through my options.

Fixing my gaze on the woman I'm falling for, I take long strides across the room and stop abruptly in front of her. My neck strains as I stare down at her. Her gaze meets mine, her eyelids fluttering.

I clear my throat, wanting to be as straightforward as possible. "Those *hotter things* come with risks."

She nods. "I'm aware."

"They can ruin us."

"They won't."

"They will ruin you with any other man."

"I won't ever need another man when I have you."

Her response is my undoing.

Her confession deviates my train of thought, turning them from alarmed to desire. We hardly drank at the party tonight, so we can't blame this on liquor tomorrow. This won't be a night of fun we can pretend to forget in the morning. What happens in the next five minutes will solidify our relationship.

I gulp before asking, "When you talk about us getting married, about us being together, you're joking, right?"

At first, it was fun and games for me.

Flirting here and there.

But somewhere along the way, it shifted into more than that.

She chews on her bottom lip. "Yes and no."

Not the response I was searching for.

My voice turns weak yet rugged simultaneously. "That's not a clear answer."

Before I make any move, we need to be on the same page. I need to know where her head is. Maybe she's looking for casual. I'm unsure if that'd be a relief or torment for me. If she says she's joking, it would kill the thoughts in my head about her that shouldn't be taking residence.

"I mean ..." She hums softly, as if searching for the appropriate words. "Yes, I joke about it—have since day one at Twisted Fox. In the beginning, it was innocent flirting, but the more time we spend together, the harder my heart races, and the more I like you, Lincoln." She sighs, averting her gaze to the other side of the room and away from me. "Like really, really like you."

Tension and lust carry through the air.

Heat spreads through my chest. I look at the ground before letting my gaze return to her face.

To the flushed face that's done nothing but consume my mind.

"Tell me you feel it too, Linc," she whispers.

My head spins. "I do."

"Then do something about it."

She stands, as if in mutual understanding that this is happening. I catch her chin between my thumb and forefinger, caressing it as our gazes meet. Hers eager. Mine gentle.

"I've wanted this for so long," I say.

She squeezes her eyes shut. "Me too."

That's when I claim her lips.

My claim is demanding and impulsive—a drink we've slowly sipped that we're ready to fully consume. Her tongue darts into my mouth, colliding with mine, and we devour each other. Our lips meshed as one.

I'm catching up on breaths as she breaks away. "My bedroom. Right now."

Yeah, I have no argument against that.

Interlacing our hands, she leads me down the short hallway, through a doorway, and flicks on the light. Before I'm given the chance to look around, her lips are back on mine.

While keeping our connection, I guide her to the bed before slowly pulling away, already missing the feel of her lips on mine. "I want to see you. *All* of you."

I retreat a step as she stands before me, intense emotion filling my lungs, and she slips me a sinful smirk before gesturing to her outfit.

"Unzip me."

That's when I realize we're still in our costumes. I was so consumed by her that I forgot I was trying to seduce a woman while wearing a damn Robin outfit.

Yeah, this shit definitely needs to come off before it becomes a mood killer.

As bad as I'm aching to unzip her dress and touch every inch of her, I need this damn thing off first. The room is quiet with the exception of our breathing—heavy and layered with need—and she watches in interest as I hastily kick off my shoes and undress. Flinging the costume across the room, I stand in front of her, wearing only boxer briefs. There's no missing my rock-hard cock, standing at attention, confirming that all it wants is her.

Since we started developing a connection, Cassidy has been the only woman on my mind as I jerked off, stroking myself as I imagined it was her hand instead of mine.

I haven't touched another woman.

Kissed another woman.

Thought about another damn woman.

Cassidy has overtaken me.

And I wouldn't want it any other way.

Her lips are swollen from our earlier kiss, and she swipes her tongue along the bottom one as her eyes level on my erection.

That's for you.

All for you.

"My turn," she croaks. "But I need a little help." Turning around, she slides her hair off her shoulder and stares over it at me.

I gladly accept the invitation, advancing toward her, and I stop so close that my cock brushes along her leg, causing her to shiver. I shove the zipper down, listening to the loud *zip*, and the dress pools at her feet, giving me the best damn view ever. Cassidy wearing only a black lace thong and matching bra. Her ass cheeks perky.

She gasps when I deliver a quick smack to each globe before cupping both, loving how they fill my hands to perfection.

"Your ass is amazing," I whisper into her ear, slowly licking along the lobe.

Pressing my lips to her shoulder, I inch her bra strap down. A light hiss releases through her lips when I suck hard on her skin. It'll most likely leave a hickey, and my dick stirs at the thought of marking her. Of making her mine.

"Climb on the bed," I say, releasing her and taking a step back.

She nods and doesn't glance back as she does, that plump ass sticking in the air. She slowly arches her back, causing her ass to jiggle, and swear to God, I'm about to come all over her white rug. Unable to stop myself, I wrap my hand around my cock and slowly stroke it as she flips onto her back and rises. Pushing her elbows out, she leans back on them to stare at me, raising a brow in question.

I take in the sight of her, my gaze traveling up and down her body, soaking up her smooth skin, her curves, and the way her breasts bounce with every sharp breath she inhales.

No more.

There's no more holding back.

Desire permeates through me like a drug.

"I could watch you do that all night," she says, drawing my attention back to her face.

I smirk. "Or we could do better things." Dropping my hand from my cock, I join her on the bed, slightly crawling over top of her, putting all my weight on my forearms to hold myself up.

I tilt my head down, and she offers a gentle smile before reaching around, gripping the back of my neck, and dragging my mouth to meet hers. This kiss is slower than the others as we soak up what the other enjoys, as our tongues tangle in a web of our attraction to one another.

She gasps when I pull away and then shudders as I rain kisses down her chest, along the cup of her bra, before directing her to rise so

I can unsnap the band. As she stretches out her arms, I gently slide off the fabric, revealing more of her beauty.

To reveal the body of a woman I'm falling into a deep pit of lust with.

To reveal every inch of the woman I want to keep forever.

My mouth waters as I lick a circle around her nipple before sucking hard, feeling it harden between my lips.

Raising my arm, I push my weight onto the other while sliding down her body. She rubs her toned legs together in anticipation while I toy with the slim string of her panties with my pointer finger. Without warning, I jerk them down her legs, causing her to lift them, before I fling the thin material across the room.

I press my erection against her thigh as I slip a finger through her soaked folds.

Up and down.

Up and down.

Torturously, as she writhes underneath my touch, waiting for me to push my finger inside, to relieve her, to play with her pussy until she's crying out my name.

"Please," she breathes out. "Give me more."

Her pleas.

Jesus.

She could ask me to do anything in that voice of hers, and I'd do it in a heartbeat. Using my elbow, I lever it between her thigh to open her wider before shoving three thick fingers inside her. She's tight, her warmth wrapping around my fingers like a harness, and I swiftly pull out, not wanting to hurt her.

With how tight she is, I'm not sure she can handle my cock, but I want to take things slow. I want to play with her longer, for days, which means I don't want her to be too sore for me. This time, I slip two fingers into her, the pad of my thumb traveling to her clit, slowly moving it in circles.

"Oh, wow," she moans, rotating her hips, swiveling them to meet my strokes.

I've spent hours sitting around and wishing for this moment, longing to have Cassidy moaning as I touched her begging pussy, and it's better than what I imagined.

Wetter.

Hotter.

Louder.

Needing more, I plant a kiss on her belly button, shifting so I'm kneeling between her legs, open her folds and lower my head.

Only to have her grab my hair, nearly ripping it from my scalp, and stop me.

Having my hair gripped? Normal.

But it's usually as the girl is about to get off on my tongue.

Not before. Never before.

"Whoa," she rushes out.

I lift my face, resting my chin above her clit while pushing my palms up the inside of her thighs, and stare up at her in question.

"I don't ..." She hesitates, her cheeks turning pink. "I don't do that."

"Do what?"

She gestures to where I am. "Faces down there."

There's no containing my snort to her explanation. "You've never been eaten out before?"

"I tried it once for maybe two seconds but stopped ..." She shakes her head. "It's weird. I feel too ... on display."

"That's the point. You put your pretty pussy on display for me, and I fucking worship it."

A wave of satisfaction charges through me that no other man has gotten her off with his face between her thighs.

Her face is unreadable as she stares down and studies me. As badly as I want to taste her, if she doesn't want it, I'll pull back and go another route to please her. No matter what, Cassidy needs to feel comfortable with me.

Her pleasure is what I'm thriving for.

I couldn't give two fucks about mine—even though eating her out would make my damn year.

I squeeze her thighs. "Do you trust me?"

She nods. "I trust you."

"If you don't like it, tell me to stop."

"I guess I have to try everything once."

"That's my girl."

I slide my body down, lower my head, and suck on her clit.

I'll prove to her there's nothing she'll enjoy more than my tongue in her pussy.

Well, other than when I fill her with my cock.

CHAPTER TWELVE

Cassidy

MY BACK BUCKS off the bed when Lincoln's lips suction around my clit.

Jesus Christ.

My heart thunders in my chest, a jolt of electricity passing through like a storm, as I peek down at the man having a snack between my legs. I'm consumed with not only my need for him but also slight premature embarrassment.

I stress about my OB/GYN—*who's a woman*—inspecting my lady parts.

How am I supposed to be chill when it's the man I've wanted for months down there, seeing me so up close and personal?

Are vaginas even pretty?

I've never been one of those women who sits in front of a mirror and examines her kitty. It's always been a strange concept to me. It's not like I'm a virgin and I've never been touched there. It's just typically sex that unfolds in the same trail of events—making out, five seconds of finger foreplay, and then sex. Never have I been with a man wanting as much foreplay as Lincoln.

Also, never have I wanted foreplay as much as I want with Lincoln.

My muscles are quivering, my body tingling with need for this man. At this point, I'll allow him to do anything, stick his face anywhere, to get relief from the pleasure streaming through me, begging to be released.

Those other guys?

They never kissed me like that.

Never touched me like this.

Never made my body burn hot.

Never made me want to push away all my boundaries.

My ribs tighten as I spread my thighs more, providing plenty of room for him to have his way with me.

Chills cover my naked body when his mouth leaves my clit, and his skilled tongue slides through my folds, sending a rush of shivers through my body. I inhale a deep breath, unsure what to expect. This is the moment when I made the last guy stop.

It felt too personal.

Too intimate.

Which is funny because I was getting intimate with the guy.

As I brace myself, Lincoln shoves the tip of his tongue inside me. My back shoots off the bed as a desire I've never experienced courses through my blood.

Lincoln licks.

He sucks.

I'm on fire.

This is what the hell I've been missing?

How was I so stupid not to want this?

I arch my back and release a moan.

Who am I kidding?

No way would it have felt like *this* with any other man.

Bursts of pleasure ride through me as I gasp. "This feels amazing."

He doesn't lift his head, but he does raise his voice as he says, "Do you like that?" against my core.

The room grows hot when he shoves a thick finger inside me and then another in addition to his tongue.

My breaths knock from my lungs in harsh pants, nearly fracturing my ribs, as I try not to come yet. As badly as I want to drag this out for as long as possible, I'm dying for a release. Delving my hand into his thick hair, I grip it tight. Not to stop him this time, but to hold his mouth there as I ride his face.

My hips buck against his mouth as he gives me everything I need and more.

When he plays with my clit, a wave of pleasure rockets through me.

It's over.

I'm coming on his mouth with no regrets of allowing this to happen.

As I whisper his name, I already know I want this to happen again.

And again and again.

I'm catching my breath when he pulls away, his lips and chin wet from my juices. He uses his tongue to scoop up the excess on his bottom lip. His grin is cocky, and his face is patterned with the same lust that's overtaking me.

I throw my arm across the bed and point at my nightstand. "Condom in there. Get inside of me before I die, please and thank you." I can't wait for him to fill me to my core and thrust inside me.

He shakes his head. "We're not having sex yet."

I wince. "What?"

"We're not having sex yet."

With the exception of his panting and his erection brushing against my leg, you'd think he wasn't fazed by my nakedness or what we did.

"I heard you loud and clear." My tone grows aggravated because, dammit, I want that large cock inside me. "*Why?* I'm not a virgin, nor will I get crazy emotionally attached, if that's what you're worried about." Okay, the second statement is somewhat of a lie. I'm already pretty emotionally attached to this man.

"Not what I'm worried about at all." He rests his palms on the sides of my face, and his chest rubs against mine as he pulls himself forward, up my body. "I'm more worried about myself getting emotionally attached." He says the last statement so softly underneath his breath that I'm questioning if those words left his mouth.

Stroking my cheek, he peers down at me with an expression I've never seen from him before—an expression I've never witnessed from anyone—a mixture of arousal, concentration, yet also contentment. A smirk is on his face as he dips his head down and places a quick kiss on my lips, where I briefly taste myself.

He just pleasured me in endless ways, hasn't received any for himself, but appears content. Lincoln looks as if he's on top of the world after eating me out, not even concerned about me returning the favor.

I rise up onto my elbows, our faces only inches apart. "Come on. You seriously just gave me an incredible orgasm. It's not fair for the favor not to be returned."

His lips brush against my nose before he pulls back. "First, my mouth on your pussy wasn't only a favor to you. Babe, it was a favor *to me*. You know how many times I've watched you, wondering how sweet your pussy tastes? How many times I've watched you lick the rim of your glass, wishing I could do the same to your clit?" He shakes his head. "Jesus, fuck, Cassidy. You handed me everything that's been on my mind for months." He smirks. "And I love that I proved it wasn't weird. I love that you trusted me enough to give me the honor."

"So give me the honor of getting you off," I argue with a pout.

He moans when I reach for his cock and run the tips of my fingers along the massive length. I eye it, my mouth watering, and wonder how well it'd fit inside me. It's the largest I've ever seen, and that's coming from a girl who watches porn on the regular to get herself off.

He draws back, away from my reach, causing me to frown. "How about you lie there, looking hot as fuck and all orgasmed out by yours truly?" He wraps his hand around his cock and starts jerking himself off. "That's all I need from you."

I groan, throwing my head back like a toddler close to a tantrum. "How's that fun? I let you go down on me, so it's only fair I get to do the same."

"Small steps, baby." His breathing turns ragged as his gaze moves down my body in appreciation.

"Small steps is licking and sucking on my vagina?"

"Damn straight."

He loses himself in his strokes, his pace growing, and I'm invigorated at the view of him jacking off in front of me. He inches closer, and I wait for my perfect opportunity. He grunts when I reach out and wrap my hand around his, joining him in pleasuring himself. He throws his head back, savoring the moment, and I take that weakness as an advantage for me.

Dropping my hand, I grip both his shoulders and push him onto my bed, back down. I climb over him in seconds, slide my hair over my shoulder, and say, "Trust me," before sucking the head of his cock.

"Jesus, fuck," Lincoln hisses, rotating his hips.

I work him with my mouth and fingers, tasting the saltiness of his cock as pre-cum leaks from the tip. His fingers find their way to my hair, and he runs them through the strands.

"Shit, I'm close," he hisses.

I peer up at him to find his eyes shut at the same time I swallow his cum.

"Fuck," he groans, coming down from his orgasm high. "That was … holy shit."

Licking up and down his erection, I clean him up, worshipping his cock. "I'm glad you enjoyed it."

———

ORAL SEX WITH LINCOLN …

There's nothing like it.

Nothing hotter.

I can't even imagine how actual sex will be with him.

We're in my bathroom, naked and cleaning ourselves up—along with taking off the Halloween makeup. When I saw myself in the mirror, I was horrified. Runny mascara, smeared lipstick, and patches of glitter described my face.

A silence hangs in the air, but it's comfortable. I'm riding off the high of being with Lincoln, and exhaustion is starting to sink in from my orgasm and giving my all while sucking Lincoln's cock. My goal was to get him off faster than any other woman who'd had her mouth on his dick.

Walking back into the bedroom, I open my dresser to snag my

pajamas as Lincoln stands in the doorway, still naked. He retrieves his boxers from the floor and pulls them up his legs.

There's a question riding on the tip of my tongue that I'm nervous to ask. I say it while pulling the shirt over my head, so he can't see the hesitation on my face. "Are you staying over?" I sound somewhat muffled when the cotton rubs against my lips.

"Cass, I just had my mouth between your legs," he replies with a hint of amusement in his voice. "You think I'm going to walk out of here ten minutes later? Abso-fucking-lutely not."

My body relaxes as I yank the shorts up my legs and tighten the string around my waist. Not only is it amazing that he's staying but I also know I'll sleep better with him at my side. There will be no Quinton fears when I'm in Lincoln's arms.

When Lincoln slides into bed with me, it's comfortable. Without hesitation, he wraps his strong arm around me and drags me into him, my back pressing against his chest.

Lying in his arms, I've never felt safer. At the point when I thought I was done with relationships, done with men, when my trust was the lowest it'd ever been, he stepped into my life and changed that.

For the first time in what seems like forever, I fall to sleep without fear.

Without wondering if someone will be sneaking in my house.

I fall asleep in the arms of a man I know is perfect for me.

And a man I'm afraid of losing.

CHAPTER THIRTEEN

Lincoln

MY FIRST MORNING waking up with Cassidy.

We're lying in her bed, side by side, having our own form of pillow talk. It's been endless conversation since we woke up, our limbs tangled together like lost ropes and the heat of the other's body a comfort. I fell asleep with Cassidy in my arms and woke up the same way—fucking heaven. As she slept, I stared down at her, not muttering a sound, and admired the woman who'd been stealing my heart little by little, day by day.

If someone had told me before the party that this was where I'd end up this morning, I would've told them to shut the fuck up. No way did I think I'd finish the night with my tongue between Cassidy's legs, tasting her sweet pussy, and then wrapping her in my arms.

What led us here?

Hours upon hours of conversation.

Random phone calls and movie nights.

A bond stronger than a diamond, shaped from friendship to intimacy.

Sense of humors blended together like an expensive painting.

Never has a woman understood, gotten me, or matched my personality better.

I inhale a series of deep breaths as Cassidy curls up closer, her chest nearly pressing into mine, and I drape my arm over her waist.

She sighs, resting her chin on my forearm to stare at me. "Remember when I asked what your favorite breakfast was all the time?"

I chuckle at the memory. "Oh, I remember."

I always laughed and blew off the question, claiming she was crazy. Her interest wasn't only on breakfast either. Over the course of us knowing each other, we revealed our front-runners of everything— breakfast, lunch, TV shows, movies, sexual positions.

If Cassidy was curious about something, she asked.

The same went for me.

She smirks before dropping a kiss to my arm. "I have maple, strawberry, apple butter, and raspberry."

I raise a brow in question.

"Pancakes are your favorite breakfast, *but* you never revealed your favorite syrup, so I bought a variety pack for when this morning came."

My gaze lingers on her, as I'm mesmerized that she took the time to do such a thing. "All this time, I assumed you were fucking with me."

"In the beginning, it was more of a flirt-buddy situation. I had recently been screwed over, so I wasn't looking for a relationship. Guys were the last thing I was worried about … what I planned not to be worried about until you bulldozed your way into my life."

"Until I did? Babe, we know you came barreling into Twisted Fox, ready to set my world on fire." I squeeze her waist. "And who screwed you over?"

My mind wanders back to the day she asked if I'd ever loved someone I shouldn't. A gloominess shadowed her that week, an anguish when she walked into work, and whenever I asked if everything was okay, she blew me off.

Her face falls, a twinge of sorrow tilting into her mood, and her lips press together in a tight grimace. "Just a guy I dated."

"What did he do to screw you over?"

If this were anyone else, if past relationship problems were introduced, I'd throw my clothes on and duck out. The thing is, this isn't anyone else. It's Cassidy, and we talk about everything. The difference between her and anyone else is that I want to know every detail of her life.

Our conversations have been endless, but they've never deviated out of small talk. We've never ventured into our pasts, old relationships, or why we were both in trouble with the law. Hell, she doesn't even know I've been in trouble with the law. But after last night, we need to drag our demons to the light and fight them together.

She bends her knees and then straightens them before releasing a harsh sigh. "He was a lying jerk who really messed with my head … with everything I thought was real." She shuts her eyes, a pained expression crossing her features. "Before him, I was softer. I trusted people, and I was happier. I saw life differently. The old me, she was friends with everyone and never questioned allowing anyone in. Now, I have major trust problems." She levels her gaze on me. "Prewarning."

I gulp, a heaviness pinning my body to the bed. "Looks like I'd better prove myself then."

Drawing her arm out from underneath the blanket, she reaches up and traces the line of my jaw with her finger, running it along my facial hair. "Just never lie to me, okay?" Her tone softens. "And if I ever confide in you, then that needs to stay between us."

"You can always trust me." I curl my fingers around her wrist and pull her hand to my lips, kissing it. "I'll never betray you."

"I was arrested." That soft tone diverts into coolness with her confession.

It's not much of a confession to me—no new insight into Cassidy. Since she was serving community service, I figured she'd been in trouble. Most likely nothing too serious, given she was sentenced to pick up trash on the side of the street and not time served.

I stay quiet while waiting to see if she'll provide more.

I won't push.

Won't throw out question after question.

This is her truth to tell me on her time and in her own way.

Her gaze darts from one side of the room to the other, and when she speaks, my breathing grows a little easier.

She trusts me.

She wouldn't be opening up like this if she didn't.

"I dated a guy in college and let him borrow my car while his was in the shop. What I didn't know was he sold drugs as a hobby and was using my car to do said drug dealing in. We got pulled over, he said the drugs in the car weren't his, and I had to take the fall for it." She holds up her hand. "They weren't, FYI. I experimented with some uppers in my sorority house, yes, but they were never my thing. I like to be in control too much. Anyway, he walked free. I was arrested and charged with a misdemeanor."

I grind my teeth, hoping she doesn't feel my body tensing. "The guy, where is he now? That fucking bastard shouldn't get away with what he did."

She bites into her lip. "I'm not sure. I just want to move on from him. It happened, I did my time, and now, I'm only looking forward."

"If you ever want to speak out, to turn him in, I'll be by your side, you hear me?"

"Thank you." She shivers in my arms. "And please don't say anything to your brother, Cohen, anyone. You're the first person I've shared the full story with. My brother is a cop, and he, along with others, have been up my ass to give them more information."

"You can always trust me to keep your secrets."

As much as I hate that she won't turn the asshole in, I have to respect her decision. She knows what's best for her, more than anyone.

"I know. That's why I'm opening up to you." She shuts her eyes, inhaling a ragged breath before loosening her muscles. Her tone turns playful as she asks, "How about those pancakes, huh? I know I said I'd make your favorite breakfast and all, but don't judge if they're burned. I'm not the best in the kitchen."

"I'll be your right-hand man. We'll make them together."

Sliding out of bed, I hold my hand out. Taking it, I drape her over my shoulder, hearing her laughter as I walk us to the kitchen. Somehow, before the pancake mix even leaves the box, she ends up spread out on the pub table with my mouth between her legs.

Playing with Cassidy will be fun.

The heartbreak that might come after? Not so much.

CHAPTER FOURTEEN

Cassidy

"WHAT ARE you up to after this?" Lincoln asks, coming up behind me and wrapping his strong arms around my waist as I clock out in the employee room. "We can head to your place and have some fun."

I squirm in his hold as he rains kisses along my neck. "We are in our place of employment, young man." Laughing, I pull away from him.

He groans, "I know; I know."

Two days have passed since the Halloween party. The next morning, after pancakes, we agreed to keep quiet about us hooking up. Witnessing everyone, myself included, in Georgia and Archer's love life was a warning to keep private until we're ready to talk about it. I don't want to start my *whatever this is* with Lincoln alongside everyone asking questions and invading our privacy before we even have the opportunity to form a healthy relationship.

Another reason is fear.

What if things don't work out with Lincoln?

What if we try something more serious than being friends and end up hating each other?

What if he isn't as much into me as he said?

Quinton really messed with my head.

I'm scared to put everything out there, only for Lincoln to break things off later and make me look like an idiot.

I shove my wallet into my purse. "Jamie gave birth to baby Fox, so I'm stopping by the hospital to give her the adorable onesie I bought and to meet her. Want to tag along?"

He rubs his chin as if in deep thought. "Sure."

"Don't act too enthused now."

Placing his hands together, he holds them to his heart and mocks my voice. "Oh my God, yes! I want to bring all the baby gifts with you."

I click my tongue against the roof of my mouth and point at him. "That's more like it, Callahan."

"Your car or mine?"

"Mine."

"Your place or mine later?"

"Mine, considering neither your brother nor Georgia can know about us yet."

A flicker of disappointment flashes over his features when he says, "Okay."

Lincoln remote-starts his car to warm it up, and before we get in, I grab the baby gift from my back seat. On our way to the hospital, we make a Starbucks pit stop, where he gives me a quick peck on the lips before handing over my iced caramel mocha.

I gotta give it to the man. He knows how to turn on the romance in and out of the bedroom. Well … the *foreplay* in the bedroom since we've yet to have sex. Every time I try, he says we're not ready yet.

When we walk into the hospital waiting room, we find Georgia and Archer sitting next to each other. "Hey, guys!" I flick my wrist in a wave.

Georgia smiles, returns the wave, and then whispers into Archer's ear. Archer nods in greeting, nearly all his attention on his girlfriend, while Lincoln and I take the chairs across from them.

With my insecurities creeping in, I wrinkle my nose while fighting back a frown. When someone whispers, I automatically assume it's about me. Blame it on growing up, competing in stupid beauty pageants, and living in a sorority house full of competition and toxicity. You only whisper if you're gossiping about someone.

"I hate when people whisper around me," I tell Lincoln, my throat tightening.

"Get used to it around those two." Lincoln dips his head down, his mouth moving to my ear, and talks softly, so only I can hear him, "Plus, my hearing is impeccable. Georgia is betting him orgasms that something will happen between us."

I lean into him, my insecurities morphing into eagerness. "Really?"

He grins. "Really."

"Looks like Archer will owe her some orgasms."

"Yeah ... when you decide you want to tell them."

Before I can ask how he truly feels about us waiting to share with our coworkers and friends that we're oral buddies, Silas and Lola walk into the waiting room.

Silas gestures from Georgia to Archer. "When you two have a baby, you'd better hope it has your personality, Georgia."

Georgia grabs Archer's chin and playfully moves it from side to side. "Why? You know he has a shining personality."

"Only for you, babe," Archer says, winking at Georgia.

I look over at Lincoln with a smirk and smack his thigh. "I think our baby will have a combination of our personalities."

"Your baby?" Silas asks. "What did I miss?"

Lincoln shakes his head and stretches out his legs.

"Hypothetical baby," I say.

"There will be no babies," Lincoln corrects, still shaking his head while fighting back a smile.

"I mean, first comes marriage," I say before peering over to Georgia. "You'll be such a good sister-in-law, Georgia."

Georgia laughs, and we stop when Cohen walks into the waiting room. I've never seen a happier man.

"You ready to meet my daughter?"

Before standing, I look over at Lincoln and whisper, "In order for us to have babies, you have to have sex with me first."

"We'll have to work on that then, won't we?" He winks.

———

ISABELLA FOX HAS to be the cutest baby I've ever seen with her peach fuzz and wrinkled forehead.

"Do you want kids?" I ask Lincoln as I run a finger over her soft cheek.

I gulp back the regret of asking him that question.

It's something I've never thought twice about, but after finding out Kyle's girlfriend can't have babies, I've learned to be more sensitive. It's a conversation I now tread lightly on. Sometimes, the answer is more complicated than yes or no. But this is Lincoln, and with Lincoln, I've tried to be as transparent as I can be. Plus, I'm super curious about his answer.

"I do," Lincoln replies, leveling his strong gaze on me. "There was a time when I thought it wasn't an option, but someday—*in the future*—I do. What about you?"

"I do … *in the future*." I sigh and lower my gaze to Isabella. "For a while, I questioned myself. As a little girl, I dreamed about being a mother, but after everything fell apart with my parents, I told myself I'd been fed a lie. Marriage, love, kids, family—it all seemed like something that wouldn't work, you know?"

His eyes don't leave mine. "What made you change your mind?"

"I realized my parents shouldn't be my only influence on my outlook on love. I witnessed my brothers and sister find love. Kyle with a woman who hated him. Maliki and Sierra, who did nothing but fight for years. And Rex with his best friend. There's hope out there for me." I stare at him, unblinking. "Like I told everyone, I think our baby will have a combination of our personalities. Hopefully, he or she will have my sense of humor."

He chuckles, shaking his head.

I hold out my hand and fake inspect it. "I can't wait to see the ring you propose with."

"One from a candy machine, of course."

I bump his shoulder with mine. "Where are we getting dinner after this?"

"Wherever you want."

I perk up. "And then can I be your midnight snack?"

"I've created a monster out of you, haven't I?"

"Sure have."

I'm falling in love with this man, and the fear he isn't falling as hard feels like a brick to my chest every time I think about it.

───────

I OFFICIALLY HAVE A ROOMMATE.

The townhouse is larger and nicer than the apartment I moved out of, and the rent is the same price since I'm only paying half with Grace. My brothers and Maliki helped me move all day today. Lincoln had offered, but I didn't want him to call off work at the bar.

Grace struts into the living room with a sparkly gift bag in her hand. "To my new roommate." Her strawberry-blond curls are in braids down each side of her head, and her pajamas are floral print.

I smile, grabbing it from her while sitting on the couch, and she plops down on the other side. "Aw, you didn't have to get me anything."

"You saved me from moving back in with my parents." She gestures to the bag. "I owe you, like, fifty of those."

I laugh, tugging at the tissue paper. "You couldn't swing rent by yourself?"

They say it's rude to ask about finances, but I'm genuinely curious. Grace teaches in an upscale private school, her father is a judge, and she never seems pressed for money. The few hundred I'm paying in rent doesn't seem like it'd be enough to push her out of the townhome.

"It's not about the money." Grace rests her hands in her lap, all proper and ladylike. "I don't like to live alone."

"I get that." I tried it, and it wasn't all sunshine and rainbows.

But then again, I also have a crazy ex who keeps popping up, adamant on scaring the shit out of me.

I tear the rest of the tissue paper out of the bag to find a box inside. Opening it, I find a mug with my name scrawled across it in pink glitter and a cartoon figure of my face.

"It was an inside thing with Georgia and me," Grace explains. "Nearly all of our mugs had our names on them."

I smile, holding up the mug. "Thank you. I really appreciate it."

When I was expelled from college, I lost contact with most of my friends. Some of them because they looked down on me for being arrested. Others were too busy, which I understood. I've been invited to parties on campus by some of my former sorority sisters, but it seems too weird to go back there. I also don't want to risk running into Quinton.

Grace stands. "You have the mug. Now, we make the roomie hot chocolate."

"The roomie hot chocolate?"

"Yep." She jerks her head toward the kitchen. "Come on. You're going to love it."

I follow her into the kitchen, and she opens a cabinet and pulls out a matching mug with her face and name. She sets it on the counter before gathering the ingredients, consisting of milk, hot chocolate, whipped cream vodka, and marshmallow vodka.

"Do you need any help?"

"I got it," she replies, warming the milk.

We make small talk while she prepares the hot chocolate, pours it into our mugs, and hands one to me.

"Will this get me drunk?" I ask, moving the mug in circles, watching the chocolate swish in the cup.

I'm not a lightweight drinker, but the amount of vodka Grace poured in might have me hugging the porcelain throne if I get too crazy. It was so strange, seeing someone who appears so put together and proper pouring an exuberant amount of vodka in hot chocolate.

"Possibly." She grins before holding her mug up in a *cheers* gesture. "To being roommates."

I smile and bump my mug against hers. "To being roommates." Taking a sip, I moan. "This is officially my favorite hot chocolate. I'm going to insist they start selling it at the bar."

"Georgia tried, but Archer and Cohen vetoed the idea, calling it too complicated to make. They also didn't think it'd be too popular in a sports bar, so we just drink it when we're here."

We walk to the living room and plop down on the couch.

"Roommate task number two," Grace says. "We find a new show to binge."

We go through the options, finding one neither of us has seen, and promise not to watch an episode without the other. Grace—the shy and conservative Grace—is beaming with a personality I've never witnessed from her before.

As we're in episode three, my phone beeps with a text.

Lincoln: You all moved in?

I grin while replying.

Me: All moved in.

"Uh-oh, who's the guy?" Grace singsongs.

I drop my phone into my lap to look at her. "Huh?"

She gestures toward the phone. "The one you're grinning at while texting."

"Oh, it's just Lincoln, asking if I got moved in okay."

"You and he …?"

"We're, uh …" I hesitate, running my fingers through the fur of the throw pillow next to me.

"Don't worry." Grace taps my hand playing with the pillow. "Anything we talk about stays between us. I promise."

"We're just"—I shrug—"hanging out … seeing where things go."

She nods, playing with her braid. "Lincoln is a nice guy. You two are good for each other."

The corners of my mouth turn up at her response, and a sense of relief hits me. "I think so too."

"And just like when Archer was dating Georgia while she lived here, he's welcome to hang out here whenever."

My smile grows.

I peer at my phone still in my lap when another text comes through.

Lincoln: Want some company when I get off? You can give me a tour of your bedroom.

I grab the phone to answer.

Me: You won't be exhausted?

Lincoln: Nah. I'll leave a little early and let Archer clean up. He owes me that.

Me: I'll be here.

Lincoln: See you in a bit.

Had Grace not said anything about him being welcome here, I would've questioned asking him to come over so late. I know Archer used to stay over with Georgia all the time because Grace would sometimes call him her second roommate. I think the more people there are around, the more Grace is happy. She seems to be a people person who doesn't like being alone.

I relax into the couch, sipping spiked hot chocolate while bonding with my new roommate, and wait for my man to get off work.

———

LINCOLN: **You awake?**

My grin takes over nearly my entire face.

Call me desperate, but I've stayed up to see if he forgot about me.

Me: Awake and waiting for you to get here.

Lincoln: I'll be on my way in 10.

Me: See you soon.

Jumping out of bed, I dart to the bathroom and inspect myself in the mirror. Pulling my hair into a ponytail, I check my teeth before strolling into the living room. Grace went to bed a few hours ago, and I don't want to wake her.

Lincoln texts when he's outside, and I scurry to the door, unlocking it, then stepping to the side to allow him room to come in. A dark beanie covers his head, and a black coat is tight over his muscles.

He wastes no time before ducking his head down to press his lips against mine. "Hey, babe."

"Hi." I peek up at him, blinking, as an abrupt wave of shyness hits me.

"Let's see this bedroom of yours."

He tosses his overnight bag over his shoulder and interlaces our fingers, and I lead him to my new bedroom. The room is a decent size

—larger than my old apartment and bedroom at the sorority house, but not as big as the one I had growing up. As the daughter of the town's mayor, I lived somewhat of a privileged life.

After pushing my queen-size bed in, there wasn't much room for more furniture. A simple white nightstand sits next to one side of the bed, and I have a standing mirror against a wall along with my desk.

Breaking away, I jerk my thumb toward his bag. "A little overeager there with the overnight bag, huh?"

He chuckles, slightly holding up the bag. "Eh, I figured you'd need assistance with testing out your new bedroom."

"Fine." I dramatically groan while fighting back a smile. "For testing purposes, I'll allow it."

To be honest, I'd have been disappointed had he not planned to spend the night since that's what he's done the past few nights.

I wonder where Georgia and Archer think he's staying.

Do they even keep tabs on him like that?

Lincoln drops his bag onto the floor and does a once-over of the room. "This is cute, babe."

"Thank you." I shut the door behind us. "Hopefully, I can see yours soon."

"You can come over anytime you want." Wandering into the room, he takes a seat on the edge of my bed, over the white duvet cover. He leans forward, resting his elbows on his knees, and focuses on me. "Cass, you know I always want to be honest with you."

I freeze, my pulse thrumming in uneasiness. "Good." I clear my throat and lower my voice. "I want you to always be honest with me."

Surely, he wouldn't have packed an overnight bag if he planned to bail on me tonight?

Unless he just changed his mind at the last minute.

There's a brief stillness, a lapse of time where he gathers his words. "There's something I need to tell you."

I clasp my hands together, hold them to the front of my body, and for some reason, prepare for the worst. "Okay …"

"I'm a felon."

The three words are a fist crushing my soul.

The memories of what happened with Quinton crawl through my thoughts.

No.

Just when I thought Lincoln was different, he tells me that.

"What did you do to … become a felon?" My last word is practically squeaked out.

"Aiding and abetting."

"Aiding and abetting for what?"

"Money laundering."

I'm quiet, digesting his words.

It all reminds me too much of Quinton.

Law breaking.

Secrets.

"You're mad," he says, his voice soft. "I get it. That's why I tried to keep my distance."

I inhale a steeling breath before answering, "Why didn't you tell me?"

"Being a felon isn't something I go around bragging about."

"We've spent enough time together for you to tell me."

A blend of irritation yet also understanding seeps through me. I get him keeping it from me when we were friends, but I opened up to him, so he should've done the same with me. I told him about my arrest and Quinton. That was a big step for me.

"That's why I wanted to start tonight by talking to you about this. I don't want any secrets between us, and from your reaction, I can see it's a big deal for you. I'm a felon. I was in prison. And if you're not comfortable with that, I understand."

"Wow." I slump down on the bed next to him and blow out a downward breath. "Prison."

"Prison," he repeats, mirroring my breath. "If it makes you feel any better, I *technically* didn't commit the crime."

I imagine most people would snort and roll their eyes at his declaration, his plea of innocence, but knowing the situation I was in, it's believable. I once wanted to be heard, said the words that I didn't commit the crime, and was mocked and ignored. I'd never do that before hearing someone out.

I swallow before speaking, "Okay."

He turns to face me, our eyes locking, and his face is pained. "I know it's stereotypical for criminals to say that, but hear me out." He shakes out his hands. "My crime was not turning my father in for corruption. I was the VP of the company he was laundering money through, and I kept my mouth shut, so I was brought down with him." He drapes his hand over mine. "You're the first person I've really talked about this with."

I battle with my internal emotions.

Back and forth.

Right and wrong.

Good guy or bad guy.

I'm not sure how much silence passes before he says, "Do you want me to go?"

Pulling away, he levels his palm on the bed to pull himself up, but I stop him.

"No, please don't," I whisper.

Prison was Lincoln's past, not his future.

He's done nothing to convince me otherwise. If he were doing shady shit, there'd be too many inconsistencies, people would be talking at the bar, and no way would Maliki and Sierra let me be around him.

Unlike Quinton, Lincoln is admitting to his wrongdoings.

Unlike Quinton, Lincoln took the fall, even when he hadn't committed the crime.

He's nothing like Quinton.

He's the man I wanted Quinton to be.

"Stay." I grab his hand and place it back over mine. "Always stay."

The initial shock has dissipated, reality bleeding through in its place. No way will I lose him over something like this.

His tense shoulders slump, releasing pressure, and he kisses my forehead. "I'll always stay ... for as long as you'll have me."

And just like that, I know this is a man I can trust.

This is a loyal man who I can tell my secrets to and who will keep my secrets.

But what happens if I'm not ready to tell him all of mine yet?

What happens if he wants me to be as open with him as he was with me tonight?

I'm not sure that's possible if I want to protect us.

Knowing how Lincoln is, if he finds out Quinton is messing with me, he'll intervene. If he's a felon, it'll send him right back to prison. Lincoln isn't getting in trouble over Quinton's dumbass. I'll handle his stalking on my own.

CHAPTER FIFTEEN

Lincoln

"HAVE FUN AT YOUR DINNER, BABE," I tell Cassidy as we walk to our cars. "And drive safe."

With a smile, I do a quick scan of the employee parking lot, making sure the coast is clear since we're still keeping our relationship a secret. I press my lips against hers and wrap my arms around her waist, somewhat pushing her against the car. My hips grind into hers while I release a groan. My heart speeds at the taste of her when my tongue slides into her mouth.

I had the day off at the bar, but Cassidy worked the mid-shift, so I stopped for lunch and hung out with her.

She releases harsh breaths when I pull away. "I don't want to be late."

"Nope." I smack a kiss to her forehead.

"I'll be texting and calling," she says, "so make sure you're available at all times."

"Aren't I always available to you at all times?"

"Good point." She stands on her tiptoes to present me with another kiss, wiggles her fingers into a wave, and gets into her car.

Puffing out cold air, I rush to mine, rubbing my hands together to create warmth. Neither one of us remembered to turn our auto-starts on, so our cars are freezing. Sitting in my running car, I wait for Cassidy to reverse out of her spot and leave. It's what I do every time.

Last night, I spilled my truth to her, gave her every component of myself. I told her about my father acquiring the family business after my grandfather's passing and how he'd started committing crimes. It was petty shit at first, but the more he got away with, the more he pushed his limits. Why? I'm still clueless. We had plenty of money, never needed for anything, but for some reason, my dad wanted more. I confessed all the feelings that'd rushed through my body when the feds showed up at my front door and how I'd wanted to jump out of the bathroom window the day I was sentenced to time in a federal penitentiary.

That night, on the drive to Cassidy's, my nerves had been on fire, uncertain of how she'd feel about my admission, about my dark past. She wasn't jumping for joy, but she handled it better than how most people would. She heard me out, was calm and rational, and in the end, she told me to make myself comfortable in her bed.

We didn't have sex, didn't hook up.

We lay in bed, talking about our pasts before falling asleep in each other's arms.

That night, as I lay in her bed, it cemented that I'd done the right thing.

That I was falling for and opening up to the only person who understood me like I needed to be understood. I'm not sure what it is about her, but the scorned parts of our hearts seem to be fitting together perfectly like a puzzle.

A horn blares through the parking lot from her car, causing me to jump out of mine, and I rush over to her. Reaching her car, I find her sitting in the driver's seat with her forehead pressed against the steering wheel. I knock on the window, and she slowly lifts her head as I gawk at her.

Opening the door, I drape my arm along the top of it and lean in toward her. "You honked?"

She smacks her palm against the steering wheel. "My car won't start."

I gesture for her to get out and take her spot. I tinker with the car, trying all the ideas I can come up with to get it to start, but nothing. It doesn't help that she's moving from foot to foot, shivering, while watching me try to fix something I know nothing about.

I'm a numbers guy who doesn't know much about auto shit. A reminder to brush up on those skills because it doesn't impress the girl you're falling for if you don't know shit about how to fix her car.

"If all else fails, you Google it," I say. "Let me grab my phone and try to fix the issue. If we can't, you can get it towed to a shop. There's one right around the corner."

She checks her watch as disappointment clouds her features. "Ugh, I'll call a tow truck and ask Rex or Sierra to come get me."

Tonight is one of her family dinners. If she calls one of her siblings, they'll miss a portion of the dinner, having to drive here and then back.

I scratch my cheek. "If you need a ride, I'm not doing anything."

"It's over thirty minutes away." She shakes her head. "I can't ask you to do that."

"I could use a good drive."

———

I PEER over at Cassidy after parking in her mother's circular drive. "If you need a ride back, text me."

"I can have someone drive me home." She grips the door handle, slightly opening it, but stops, whipping around to face me. "Unless you want to come in and stay? I told them my car was on crack and a friend was giving me a ride. No one will mind." She fidgets with her bracelet, as if she's nervous I'll say no … or that it'll be weird because everything we are is so up in the air.

A friend.

For reasons unknown, my skin crawls at the term.

No, we're more than friends.

She gave me so much shit all the times I said we were *just friends*, but now that we're on the journey to change that, she's holding back. Things get trickier when I notice Maliki's black Camaro parked in front of us.

Does he know about Cassidy and me?

What he does know is my history, where I was months ago, and plenty of negative stories are circulating about me. Sure, he's been cool with me at parties and the bar, but me possibly dating Cassidy is a different level of simple friendliness.

I have a record.

Automatically, that makes some assume I can't be trusted.

Cassidy pouts her plump lower lip and steeples her hands in a begging motion. "Come on. Be my sidekick tonight, Robin."

I chuckle.

Robin.

That term doesn't make my skin crawl as much.

"Fine," I theatrically groan as if she were asking me to cut a vein or some shit.

Cassidy grins. "You da best, Callahan."

I cut my car's engine and survey the two-story brick home. It's the nicest in the neighborhood, but in my old life, it'd have been considered small.

My old world was full of superficial assholes.

"Is this where you lived, growing up?" I ask her.

She nods. "For as long as I can remember."

We step out of the car and walk stride for stride into the house. A commotion erupts as soon as the door shuts behind us—talking and laughing. We take a quick right, leading us into the dining room with a massively long table lined with people down each side, drinks in front of them. In the middle sits a variety of food bowls and plates.

"Everyone," Cassidy announces, "this is Lincoln. We work together, and since my car decided it was done being my friend, he was kind enough to give me a ride."

We work together.

I gulp.

Is working together worse than saying we're friends?

Hell yes, it is.

An older version of Cassidy and Sierra stands and immediately wraps Cassidy into a tight hug. "I've missed you so much, honey."

"Mom," Cassidy says, squeezing her, moving side to side, "you saw me the other day."

"Yes, but I miss my kids *every day.*"

When they pull away, Cassidy runs her hand along my arm. "Lincoln, this is my mother, Nancy."

From the stories I've been told and her appearance, Nancy is the opposite of my mother—your classic homemaker.

I suck in a startled breath when Nancy hugs me next, slapping my back a few times. "It's so nice to meet you, and I appreciate you giving her a ride. Our family dinners mean so much to us."

"Are you kidding me?" someone says when Nancy pulls away.

All attention shifts to a man at the table, sporting an officer uniform and a cold glare slapped straight in my direction.

Cop.

Criminal.

Bad combo.

"Cass," he says, his voice harsher but his eyes not leaving me, "a word."

"Nope," Cassidy chirps as if the mood in the room hasn't shifted into darker territory. "Whatever it is can wait until later." A frown of dismay briefly crosses her face before she forces a smile while also shooting daggers at the guy.

She knows what he's pissed about.

Everyone's attention hops between the three of us, watching the show with curiosity.

"Cassidy," he grinds out, slamming his napkin onto the table.

I open my mouth, prepared to tell him if he has an issue with me, to take it up with me, not Cassidy. I'll leave if I'm not welcome. Cassidy shouldn't have to fight that fight for me.

The blonde next to him smacks his arm and shoots him a glare stronger than the one Officer Jackass is giving me, but he pays no attention.

"Kyle," Nancy warns, her tone stern but her voice light and sweet, "we are having dinner. You can talk to your sister later."

Cassidy delivers a smug look at him.

From the conversations I've had with Cassidy, I've learned she's close with her mother. She was the only child living at home when her father's affair came to light. She was the largest shoulder and support system for Nancy. After hearing the stories, I imagined her family to be like a *Jerry Springer* drama, but all I'm getting is *Brady Bunch* vibes.

Except for Officer Pissed Off, of course.

"Everyone, have a seat." Nancy throws her arm out toward the open chairs at the end of the table.

As I survey the table, I halt when my gaze meets Maliki's. My throat constricts at the warning clouding his features. Just as I suspected, he's suspicious of me hanging around with Cassidy. I've gained friendships with most of the guys in my brother's circle, but since Maliki lives in a different town and owns his own bar, he doesn't come around as frequently as the others. Meaning he hasn't had as much time to realize I'm not a bad person.

Next to Maliki is Sierra, Cassidy's older sister. Even though it hasn't been brought up around her when I've been around, I wouldn't doubt her knowing my story. But unlike her fiancé, her lips are curled into an inviting smile.

"Have a seat, guys," Sierra says, pulling out the open chair next to her. "Mom made rib eye, roasted rosemary potatoes, and her famous sweet corn. I'm starving, and I will die if we don't eat soon."

My gaze darts up and down the table as everyone waits for us to take our seats. Cassidy squeezes into the seat next to Sierra. As I take the chair next to her, I quickly glance at the officer—*Kyle*. Chills speed down my spine, the dread of him interrogating me already causing my stomach to curl.

"I'm Rex," the guy across from me says. "Sup, dude?"

Rex is sporting a black leather jacket and a cross necklace. From what Cassidy has said, he's the cool brother.

A mousy, dark-haired girl shyly waves at me. "I'm Carolina, Rex's better half."

Next to Rex is Trey, a guy around the same age as Cassidy. From what Cass has told me, he's the half brother no one knew about until recently. He says hello with a simple chin jerk in my direction.

Chloe, the woman who smacked Kyle, introduces herself before elbowing Kyle to do the same. "I'm Chloe, this guy's—who's actually nice, I promise—girlfriend."

Kyle snorts.

"Quit acting like a little prick," she hisses underneath her breath to him.

"Don't," he says before his dark scowl returns to me. "Kyle."

At least he doesn't introduce himself as *Officer.*

It's annoying when people do that shit.

"Sweetie, do you know what's wrong with your car?" Nancy asks Cassidy as I drape the cloth napkin over my lap. "Did you tell your father, so he can get it looked at?"

Cassidy shakes her head. "I'm for sure not calling him. I'll get it figured out."

"I'll get it looked at for you," Kyle says.

"It's at the bar, but I'm going to have it towed," Cassidy informs.

"Send me the bill for the repairs," Rex adds.

"Now, let's get you some drinks," Chloe comments, her voice overeager, as if she's compensating for her boyfriend. "We have sweet tea, lemonade, water, or I can grab a soda from the kitchen?"

"Lemonade," Cassidy replies before peeking over at me. "My mom's lemonade is to die for."

"Lemonade for me too," I reply with a smile.

Our drinks are poured, and we devour Nancy's rib eye.

———

"NOT TO SOUND LIKE AN ASSHOLE," Maliki says, sitting next to me on the living room sofa, prepared to most likely sound like an asshole, "but I'm not sure if you two are good or bad for each other."

After dinner, Nancy brought out the dessert. And when I say she brought out the dessert, good ole Nance brought her dessert game. There was a chocolate cake, a cherry pie, and cupcakes. All made from scratch. I'm so full that I could not eat for another week, and I still wouldn't be hungry.

Maliki reminds me of my brother. He is closed off, isn't much of a conversationalist, owns a bar, and is dating a woman the complete opposite of him. Sierra is outgoing, pushes people's buttons, and loud. She and Cassidy share similar personalities.

I bite my tongue, holding back the urge to tell him I couldn't care less what he's sure of. Instead, I cock my head to the side and mutter, "Why do you say that?"

He grips his beer in his fist. "Cassidy tends to have a type … *trouble*, and no offense, dude, but you're trouble."

Here it goes. My past haunting me again.

I want to be trouble and tell Maliki to fuck himself and stay out of our business.

A criminal record shouldn't automatically label me.

"I *was* trouble," I grind out. That's a lie. I didn't break the law. I *knew* someone was breaking the law, and my silence bit me in the ass.

He drains his beer. "Told you, not trying to be an asshole. I get it, man. Your situation was fucked up, and not many people would do what you did for your family. I respect your loyalty. I'm only mentioning it because her cop brother *and* parents, who recently had to deal with her legal troubles with her ex, might not be as understanding."

I slug down my lemonade. I've kept it strictly nonalcoholic tonight.

"Are you going to tell them?" I croak out.

Fear creeps into me like a shady snake at the thought of losing Cassidy because her family doesn't approve of me. Losing her would be a slit to the heart.

"Not my business to tell." Maliki levels his gaze on me. "All I'm saying is, if you haven't told her your past, you should. Not only is one brother a cop but Rex can also hack into anything. Give the guy your first name, and in five minutes, he can provide every digital move you and your family have made your entire lives. Cassidy is a good girl— sarcastic and mouthy as shit, like her sister, but she has a heart of gold. Don't fuck her over."

Our conversation is interrupted by the sound of Cassidy arguing with someone in the other room.

"He's a fucking criminal, Cassidy," Kyle roars from down the hallway.

He managed to keep things casual the rest of dinner but didn't mutter a word in my direction or glance at me again. I had no doubts that he was waiting for the perfect moment to get Cassidy alone to warn her about me.

"Oh shit," Maliki says, shaking his head. "And here we go."

I stand and head in the direction of their voices.

"How do you know that?" Cassidy asks.

"Everyone knows who the Callahans are," Kyle replies. "They were all over the news!"

"You don't know the entire story," Cassidy argues.

"What don't I know?" Kyle's voice rises. "He was in prison. Did he tell you that?"

"He did."

I reach the doorway of the room they're in to find her facing off with Kyle, her arms crossed.

"And in case you forgot, I was also arrested," Cassidy adds.

Kyle shakes his head. "Big difference. You didn't go to goddamn prison."

"White-collar prison," Rex corrects, and my gaze tears across the room to find him sitting in the corner, watching the show in front of him. "Dude, you know that's two different things. He didn't fucking murder someone."

Rex, I fucking like you.

"Prison is prison," Kyle snaps.

"I'm not having this conversation with you," Cassidy says.

Kyle crosses his arms, mirroring her stance. "Do you want me to call Dad, so you can have that conversation with him instead? We can let him know you're hanging out with convicts."

"Oh, don't try to bullshit me." Cassidy snorts. "You wouldn't call Dad if your dick was on fire and he had the last glass of water to put it out."

Rex scoffs, shaking his head. "That was a good one, sis."

Having had enough, I place my knuckles against the door, tapping lightly to make my appearance known. This isn't how I wanted to meet the fam, but I'm not going to sit back and allow Cassidy to take the heat for my actions.

"Don't give her shit," I say, leveling my eyes on Kyle. "Yes, I'm a felon. Yes, I was in prison. My father had committed a crime, and I'd refused to snitch on him. Call me whatever you want for it, but I'd do it again if I had to. My past will not hurt your sister in any way. I'm not trouble. I work at the bar, keep my nose clean, and that's it."

Kyle looks at me, shocked, as if he expected me to sit back and allow Cassidy to fight my battles.

"I can vouch for him," Maliki says behind me, and I'm not sure when the hell he arrived, but I'll take his support. "He's Archer's brother. Dude has kept it real with me since the day he was released. I met him a few times before he was locked up. He's a good guy." He shrugs, sipping on his beer. "We all know our past shouldn't come back to bite us in the ass."

Kyle runs his hands through his hair. "Fine, whatever." He looks at me, and in the same tone he used with Cassidy, he says to me, "A quick word."

I nod. "Sure."

Kyle waves me out of the room and down a hallway, so we're alone. We land in a bedroom, and he shuts the door behind us.

"I wasn't trying to be a dick," he automatically says.

I chuckle. "You failed at that."

"I'm just ... worried about my little sister, you know?" He strokes his jaw. "The last thing she needs is to fall into trouble again. She might've managed to end up with community service last time, but she has a record now, which could result in a harsher punishment."

"I swear to you, I have nothing but your sister's best interests." I silently pray he can see the honesty in my eyes, the deep care I have for Cassidy, and that he'll trust me with her. "I get wanting to protect your sister, but I won't get her in any trouble."

"What are you?" He blinks. "Dating? Friends?"

I feel stupid when I say, "I have no idea actually."

He nods as if he understands that complicated time in figuring out what you are with another person. "Look, I'm giving you the benefit of the doubt because I know your family was good until all that shit went down. I've met Archer, and he seems like a cool-ass dude. Just don't get my sister in trouble."

"That's the last thing I ever want to do."

"Sorry for the interrogation, bro."

"Nah, it's cool. Thanks for hearing me out and giving me a chance, instead of letting my past define who I am."

"If it makes you feel any better, Cassidy has never brought a guy home since high school, so she must really like you. She seems happier than she's been in months. Don't break her heart."

———

"DID you enjoy meeting your future in-laws?" Cassidy asks when we get back to her place.

I nod and smile, both of them overexaggerated. "Oh, yes, I definitely enjoyed it. I don't think it could've gone any better."

She laughs, shaking her head. "Of course, my brother had to know you've been in trouble with the law."

I slump down on her bed. "It was all over the news. I tend to be more shocked when people don't know or don't recognize my last name."

It's humiliating when I see the recognition cross people's faces when they figure out who I am.

What I am.

It's no secret that Cassidy deserves better than someone with a record, but if she's okay with it, then why would I run away from my own happiness?

I want that life—the life that Archer, Cohen, and Maliki have. A relationship. Another half. Someone to come home to. Someone to be my everything and vice versa. Never have I wanted a relationship before. Never has someone slid into my life, into my head, and—dare I say it—into *my heart*.

Cassidy joins me on the bed, perky and ready for conversation. "Other than that, what'd you think?"

"They're cool. Your mom is a kick-ass cook."

She smiles with pride. "My mom is a kick-ass everything."

I shift to face her, leaning in, and kiss her cheek. "Just like her daughter."

She smiles harder before it slips. "What are we?"

Now, if that question doesn't nearly knock me on the ass. It's not the turn I expected this conversation to take so quickly. It is the turn we need to take though because there's nothing worse than not knowing where you stand with somebody—with someone you want to stand next to, love, and be with.

"What do you mean?" I choke out.

For people who like to talk about everything, we've done a poor job of broaching serious topics. It's almost as if dragging out the complicated questions will change something and ruin us.

Nervousness covers her face as she plays with her hands. "I mean, my sister asked me what we were tonight, and I had no idea what to tell her."

My chest tightens. "I guess we'd better clear that up then, huh?"

She raises her gaze, her eyes searching mine. "We should definitely clear that up."

My heart turns in my chest. "I'm whatever you want me to be."

I want to be her everything.

I want her to want every piece of me for the rest of our lives.

Some might say having feelings so strong with someone you've known for only a few months can't be real. Some might say that there needs to be a longer period to truly fall for someone, but I've spent enough time with Cassidy to know who she is, to know how my day brightens when she's around and how my mind constantly wanders to her when she's not.

"Hmm … anything I want you to be." She scoots in closer, nearly on my lap. "I'd say my husband, my baby daddy, the man obsessed with me."

I chuckle. "Give us some time, and I can be all of those things, baby."

She chews on her lower lip, excitement and nervousness prevalent in her expression. "I'm scared, though."

I raise a brow. "Scared of what?"

"Scared to take the leap with you, to hand myself over to someone and then end up broken. My feelings for you are stronger than what they were with my ex, and what he did tore me apart. If things ended badly between us, it'd kill me, Lincoln."

I stretch out my legs and nod in understanding. "That's why I didn't jump right into having a physical relationship with you." It's something we could've easily done from the beginning, that could've also ended messy. "I wanted to be certain I was comfortable enough for more than sex so that I wouldn't hurt you. And that time wasn't to realize how much I liked you; it was if I'd be good for you, if I'd be able to make you happy … and keep you happy."

"I appreciate that, and I think we both needed that time before jumping into something. My parents' marriage was a complete joke. High school sweethearts. She invested everything into them, only for him to have an affair and completely screw her over. I don't want that to be me."

"I give you my word that I'll never screw you over. Do you hear me? We're alike in so many ways. We both are big on loyalty and honesty. I went to prison for having someone's back. I promise, I'd do the same for you. And I have concerns too."

She blinks at me. "Like what?"

"You recently got out of a bad relationship. Are you sure you're ready for another?" Just as scared as she is that I'll hurt her, I'm scared of putting myself out there too.

"Do you plan on us having a bad relationship?" She furrows her brows.

"Fuck no."

"Then why would I hold my ex's actions against you? Our relationship will be a clean slate."

I shudder. "Other than those few things, which we've now settled, you got anything else?"

She shakes her head before releasing a deep sigh. "I've got nothing."

My confidence beams. "So then, take something."

With that, she grins, crawling into my lap, her weight distributing to my body. Her lips crash into mine, making me come alive, and without hesitation, I dip my tongue into her mouth.

Tasting her and the sweet desserts we devoured after dinner.

Tasting what I keep wanting and wanting and wanting.

My heart thrashes against my chest as I reach around and grip the back of her neck, feeding more of her to me. Kissing Cassidy is a rush I've never experienced. As a man who's had his fair share of women, I've never had these emotions climb through me with just kissing.

The want.

The need.

The urge to give her all of me.

I want to grab Cassidy in my arms and make her mine.

Keep her underneath me while we forget our problems.

I grunt when she grinds into me, her jeans rough against mine, and my cock hardens with every movement. She yelps when I curl my hands around her waist, then turn and ease her onto her back, her hair fanning over the pillow. Luckily, she didn't make her bed this morning, so there's no messing with undoing the bedding to make her comfortable.

I draw back, smacking my palm to the mattress to hold myself up, and stare down at Cassidy. Her chest heaves in and out as she peers at me in expectation, in challenge, as if saying, *What are you going to do with me?*

Slicing my hand up the bed and between her legs, I jerk her thighs open before sliding between them, making enough room for my heavy body. I tip my head down, kissing her, before lowering my mouth to her neck and sucking on the sensitive skin.

"Stop teasing me," she groans. "We've done plenty of foreplay. It's time to get to the main event."

I chuckle. "There's never too much foreplay, baby." My sex game has always been to pleasure the woman first, so that's what I need to make sure I do with Cassidy.

With a strength that surprises me, she hooks her leg around my waist and attempts to flip me over on my back.

Stopping her, I shake my head. "Oh no, baby. Nice try."

She frowns. "I'm going to bite you in the neck and possibly stab you if you don't get me naked soon."

"Oh, I like it kinky, babe." I click my tongue against the roof of my mouth. "And since you were such a good girl today, I'll give you what you need. Let's get you naked."

She glares up at me. "Let's get *us* naked."

"I like the way you think."

Giving her what she wants—what we both need—I hurriedly undress, and she does the same. This isn't how I expected our first time to go, but she's right; we've been waiting for this for what seems like months. Within a few breaths, we're naked, in the same position we were before—her underneath me, me situated between her legs.

Reaching down, I massage my hand between her pussy lips, separating them with my fingers, before slipping down the bed. Her legs tremble when my face reaches her core. I bend my neck and suck on her clit, sliding my tongue between her folds.

I could eat Cassidy for every meal and still be hungry for her.

"More," she moans, writhing underneath me. "I need more."

"I can do that," I reply with a sly smile, moving back up her body.

I take my cock, gripping it, and slide it against her opening.

Back and forth through her soaked slit.

Back and forth before I dive into heaven.

She moans, her back coming off the bed. "Mmm ... I like that ... *more.*"

"Jesus, you sure are needy." I slide down and take one long, straight lick against her slit.

"Needy for your cock," she gasps.

"Tell me you want it," I say, flicking her clit before sliding two fingers inside her. "Tell me how bad you want my cock."

"So bad," she moans. "I want your cock so bad, Lincoln. I want to feel your big cock inside me, filling me up in every way."

Her words are my undoing.

"Condom?" I rasp out.

"Nightstand." She points toward it. "Second drawer."

I stretch across the bed, my erection pressing up against her thigh, and she raises her hips, moaning as she grinds against it.

Fuck, she's killing me.

I jerk the drawer open, finding a box of condoms, and pluck one out. Ripping the wrapper open with my teeth, I pull out the condom and slip it down my cock. Cassidy pulls at my ass in the process, dragging me to her, nearly using all of her strength to push my cock inside her.

I laugh, loving how strong her need is for me.

When I slide inside her slick warmth, I suck in a breath. "Jesus, you're tight as fuck," I hiss.

"It's been a while," she says, a shyness overcoming her.

"It's been a while for you?" I work my jaw from side to side. "All I've done since I've been released is yank it in the shower. Baby, I'm about to be born again into sex."

Not going to lie; I've been nervous about having sex with her. It's not that I don't know how to use my dick or that I worry I won't pleasure her, but it's been a minute since my dick dipped into a pussy. And it's been *never* since it's had anything as sweet as her. My fear is, I'll thrust into her and blow my load, becoming a disappointment and embarrassing myself.

Our breathing is harsh as I pump into her. I claim her, rotating my hips from side to side as she writhes underneath me. Her pussy convulses before tightening around my dick, and she says my name when she comes. Her body shakes as her orgasm shatters through her.

"Say it again," I growl. "Say whose cock just got you off."

"Lincoln."

"Yes, baby," I groan, thrusting into her, trying to control my pace, but now that she's gotten off, now that I know her cum is alongside my dick, I can't take it any longer.

Sweat is dripping off my chest, onto her stomach. Raising her legs into the air, I hitch them over my shoulders, wrapping my arms around them, and pound into her.

A few pumps later, I bust inside the condom and collapse on top of her—out of breath, out of energy, out of fucks to give on why it's not a good idea to be with her.

Us together is a damn good idea if you ask me.

CHAPTER SIXTEEN

Cassidy

LINCOLN STARES at me as I'm drying off my hair, fresh from a shared shower. "What are you up to today?"

Last night, we had hot sex.

This morning, we had slow sex—nearly lovemaking.

Then we had slippery, frantic sex in the shower.

"Going shopping with Georgia." Goose bumps cover my arms as I reach for my tee. "She wants to girlie up your place."

I laugh to myself, wondering how Archer will love that. Better yet, he seems to let Georgia do whatever she wants, so he'll probably just shake his head and move on if it makes her happy.

In the same move I pictured Archer doing, Lincoln laughs and shakes his head. "Oh shit."

I nod. "Yep, be scared."

He drops his towel, grabbing for his pants, and my gaze shoots straight to his cock—the one that was inside me while he slammed me against the wet shower wall, our bodies melding into one. Grace was at work, so I moaned while he whispered how good it felt to be inside me.

"I'll see you at work tonight?" He pulls his pants to his waist, buckling them.

"You'll see me at work tonight. Are we having a sleepover at your place or mine?"

"Hmm … wherever you want." He plants a kiss against my lips. *Finally.*

Finally, we had sex, and it was perfection.

More than what I'd imagined it would be.

This man was made for me.

He's open, honest, great with his tongue, and he cares about pleasing me in the bedroom. A rare gem in a sea of men with two pumps, who think foreplay is a clit flick before setting off for the finale of sticking their cock inside me.

I'm certain, when he leaves here today, he won't call his buddies and brag about hooking up with me. He won't play mind games, ignore my texts, and call the other girls he's talking to and say, *Sorry, babe, I fell asleep.*

Lincoln is the real deal.

Our relationship is the real deal.

I don't care if he's a felon because that's not what defines him. He's a good man, the man I can see myself spending the rest of my life with, the man I hope whose emotions are just as strong.

———

"YOU KNOW ABOUT LINCOLN'S … legal problems, right?" I ask Georgia, sitting across from her at the food court in the mall.

We came. We shopped. She bought furry pink pillows, a pink-chandelier canvas print, and rose-gold candleholders. I cannot wait to see them matched with Archer's home. I haven't been there yet, but from what Georgia's told me, its Pinterest board would be labeled *Make My Home As Masculine As Possible with No Character.*

Georgia nods, sipping her açaí smoothie—something I've never had, but she talked me into trying it, saying Jamie got her obsessed with them. "I do. What do you know?"

"What do you know?" She's not giving me details until she finds out what Lincoln has confided in me. I respect that.

She's the first person I've brought Lincoln's record up with. I can't exactly talk to my siblings about it, and I don't have many friends. Plus, with her being Archer's girlfriend and living with Lincoln, there's no doubt she knows about his past.

"He was in prison …" I bite on my straw.

There's no hesitation before she jumps into her response, and it's with such certainty that you'd think she was telling me a fact about herself. "That pretty much sums it up. Lincoln is a man of a different character—a *good* man. One of the most loyal men you'll ever meet— like Limon to Pablo Escobar loyal. When Archer was acting up, he did everything in his power to set him straight—before and after the bar incident—and has been a great role model as far as helping Archer withdraw from his past mistakes." Her eyes settle on me. "*Prison, felon*—they're scary words, I know, but you can't bundle the terms, bundle the people who've had those titles, as if they were one. Lincoln didn't commit a violent crime. He loved his dad enough to cover for them, to say, *I have your back, no matter what happens*, and because of that, his father received less time. In ways, I respect him for it."

I nod repeatedly. "Me too."

Loyalty is an honorable trait, and yes, some might say that integrity changes when it's for illegal activity, but I don't agree.

"You know," she goes on, "I'm surprised he opened up to you. He's never talked about it with me or even Archer, last I heard. That has to be a hard thing to open up about."

"He told me some secrets. I told him some. He's easy to talk with."

"Are you two …? *Have you* two …?"

There's no holding back my smile. "Last night was the first time."

She literally squeals. "How was it?"

I sink in the chair as if all emotions of happiness were weighing me down. "Amazing. Perfection. I've had sex before, but it's different with him. Lincoln is unlike any guy I've ever been with."

"Swear to God, it runs in the Callahan blood. Prewarning: what also runs in the Callahan blood is …" She pauses. "Although I'm not so sure that's Lincoln. The guy isn't as distant as Archer is, and Lincoln seems to have more sense to him. You definitely got the less difficult brother. While Archer is a loner, someone who keeps everything to

himself before it eats him up, Lincoln hides his pain behind a smile.
I'm not sure which is worse."

"I guess we'll see. He's the only man to have ever opened up to me
like that, and coming from a broken home, where my father kept
secrets like pets, it means so much to me."

"He's never brought another woman around us. Shoot, I've never
even heard of him dating, hooking up, texting. He's not looking for a
quick screw. He's looking for a future with someone."

We leave lunch at the food court and return to our shopping
adventures. When we're finished, Georgia's car is full, so she calls
Archer to come meet us and to fill his car with her purchases.

"We'll drop off the stuff, and you can surprise Lincoln," she says
on our drive over.

Too bad I'm in for a surprise from hell when I get there.

CHAPTER SEVENTEEN

Lincoln

SHE'S the last person I expect to see when I answer the door.

The last person I want to see.

If I had a choice to see her or Satan, I'd choose the Devil.

I grind my teeth while asking, "How the fuck do you know where I live?"

She stands in the doorway, a Chanel bag draped over her shoulder —a bag *I* bought her—and her blond hair is cut shorter than before. She winces at my greeting before straightening her stance. "Everyone knows where Archer lives. It's no secret."

With how I've ignored her phone calls and the last words I said to her, she'd be dumb if she expected me to talk to her.

"Better yet," I growl out, "why are you here?"

She pulls on the strap of her bag. "Can we talk?"

Leaning against the doorframe, I release a huff. "What do you want, Isla?" I shoot her a venomous glare. "Can't you put two and two together and realize that me ignoring your calls means I don't want to talk to you?"

She releases a humph before shoving her way into the penthouse. I might be an ass, might tell her to get fucked, but I can't push her back. I don't put my hands on women. At the same time she enters the living room and I'm about to slam the door shut, I hear voices coming down the hall.

Recognizable voices.

Just as I'm gripping Isla's hand to pull her into my bedroom, the door swings open. My heart sinks into my stomach when Georgia, Archer, *and* Cassidy walk in.

You've got to be shitting me.

I have to be the chairman of bad timing.

The three of them halt in their steps, their eyes shooting from Isla to me. Archer, the only one who knows Isla, glares at me without blinking. His hands knot into fists, and I gulp, waiting for him to kick her out of his place. My gaze swings from him to Cassidy. Her hand is pressed against her throat as she anchors her attention on Isla before shifting to stare at me, pain and anger in her eyes.

"Who are you?" Cassidy asks. "His mom?"

Georgia snorts.

The fact that Cassidy can say that with a straight face is impressive, considering she's met my mother and she knows Isla clearly isn't her.

"No, I'm not his mother," Isla snarls.

If there's one way to piss off Isla, it's mentioning her age. She might not be my mother, but she is the same age.

"Oh." Cassidy smirks. "My bad. Who are you then?" Sarcasm seeps through her words, but there's no hiding the hurt in her eyes.

With heat burning along her cheeks, Isla turns to me and ignores Cassidy. "Can we talk in private?"

"Nah, I'm good." I shove my hands into my jean pockets. "I think our time here is over."

Not only am I pissed she's here but I'm also infuriated by her timing. The day after Cassidy and I slept together, she finds another woman at my house. I understand her anger. I'd share the same hurt and irritation.

"We haven't discussed anything during my time here, Lincoln." A flash of desperation crosses Isla's Botoxed face. "I'm not leaving until you talk to me."

Motherfucker.

With a jerk of my head, I direct her to my bedroom, not having the heart to look at Cassidy. It's a dick move, but I'm not sure what else to do. I'm not sure what Isla would have started saying if we'd stood there any longer. All I can do now is hear what Isla has to say and then kick her ass out.

"Why are you punishing me for the actions of someone else?" Isla snaps as soon as I slam my bedroom door shut behind us.

I scoff, memories of what happened shooting through me like a drug, and it's a struggle to keep my voice low. "You mean, the actions of *your husband*? Surprise, sweetheart, they go hand in hand."

"And what he did was *out of my hands*. If I could've done something—"

"You're right. I should've kept *my hands* to myself. And that's on me, and considering I don't want your husband meddling in my family's life again, you need to leave. And never come back."

She reaches for me, desperate and pleading. "Lincoln, please. I miss you."

I slam my eyes shut. Not because her words hurt or that I miss her. I'm reliving the stupidity of crossing the line with her. It's not that I ever thought I was in love with Isla. We fucked. Plain and simple. Neither of us exchanged love devotions. She'd go home to her husband, and I'd go out and party. Then a few days later, we'd do it again.

It was an unhealthy cycle that lasted a year until all hell broke loose.

Until my stupidity of screwing a married woman blew up in my face.

"You need to go," I snarl, holding back the urge to yell. Stalking to my bedroom door, I jerk it open. "And don't come back. Quit calling. Forget I exist."

"This isn't how it's supposed to be," she whispers, wisping slanted bangs out of her eyes.

"We were never supposed to be." The words come out croaked, and I swing my arm out, begging her to leave.

This time, she listens. Isla struts out of my bedroom, not paying Georgia or Cassidy one glance, and leaves. As soon as the door shuts behind her, I pull at the roots of my hair and groan.

Glancing at Cassidy, I take a deep breath to prevent my voice from shaking. "That wasn't what it looked like."

Georgia kicks her leg out, glaring at me. "Then explain what it was."

"That's none of your business." The response comes out before I can stop it.

Georgia winces at my words. "Okay, rude. Go be a dick somewhere else, please, before I spit in your favorite ice cream."

I've never been an ass to Georgia. She's like a little sister to me, but Isla's visit has fire burning through my veins, and I want to breathe them out, get her out of my system.

Not wanting to have this conversation in front of Georgia—aka the gossip queen—I charge into my bedroom with a load of guilt, hoping Cassidy is behind me.

She is.

"Nice room," she comments, slipping inside before crossing her arms and glaring at my bed in disgust. "Were you just banging her in that bed? I don't think I should sit down on it."

The thought makes my stomach crawl. Isla is nothing but a reminder of my past, of every mistake my father and I made. She's a reminder that I was a stupid guy with no morals who thought his actions had no consequences.

"She means nothing," I grit out.

"Sex must've sucked then, huh?" She rests against the wall as if she truly believes my bed has some sexually transmitted disease.

"If there's anything you won't ever have to worry about, it's me sleeping with her."

"*Have you* slept with her before?"

Do I give her honesty? Do I lie?

Because it's Cassidy, because I always want her to be up-front with me, I nod.

"Interesting." She stretches the word out. "Looks like you had no problem giving older a chance before younger. And from the big-ass rock on her finger, it seems you've also tried them *married.*" A snarl leaves her, disgust on her face—a reminder of how often she's told me she despises cheaters and homewreckers since they're what broke up her family.

I bite my tongue from asking how she's certain Isla was married when we were together. My canines dig into my defense, knowing that she'll most likely ask me to clarify what Isla was when we started sleeping together. And Cassidy is right. From the very first time I met Isla, she's had a ring on her finger. It's fucked up, I'm well aware.

Wanting to change the subject, I clear my throat and say, "Did you figure out what was wrong with your car?"

She nods.

"If you need a ride anywhere, call me Cab Callahan."

She's not agreeing with the convo change being a good idea. "I can call you Homewrecker Callahan or The Man Who Had Another Woman in His Bedroom After Dicking Me Down Callahan. Those might be better for the situation we're currently in."

Right as I hold out my hand to explain myself, her phone dings.

Ignore it. Ignore it.

She doesn't.

Instead, she digs into her pocket, and horror flashes on her face as she reads whatever is on her screen.

"Cassidy ..." I drawl out her name as she pales.

"I have to go," she stammers, attempting to shove the phone in her pocket. Her hand trembles, making it difficult, and the phone drops to the floor. "Shit!"

I reach out, prepared to repo her phone to see what suddenly worked her up, but she beats me to it. This time, she grips it in her hand, not bothering to put it away.

"Cassidy," I whisper, "what happened?"

Her eyes are crestfallen as she spares me a quick glance. "Nothing, really, I gotta go."

Without another word and before I can stop her, Cassidy sprints out of my bedroom.

CHAPTER EIGHTEEN

Cassidy

MY HEART IS RACING SO hard that I'm waiting to have a heart attack.

Me moving in with Grace was supposed to prevent this.

What the hell?

Thankful Grace isn't home, I charge into my bedroom, my upper lip snarling, and hold back the urge to punch the man sitting on my bed. "What the fuck do you want, Quinton?"

He chose the wrong day to mess with me. I already walked in on the man I'm falling for with another woman in his bedroom. I'm not in the mood to deal with a crazy-ass ex in mine. I'm mouthy to begin with, and today has pushed all my limits. Chances are, I'll be taking my anger with Lincoln out on Quinton, and it won't be pretty.

Quinton slides his hand over his smooth chin. "You moved in with a judge's daughter, huh?"

I blink at him. "What?"

"Your new roommate's father is a judge." A cruel smirk curls at his lips.

That's why he's here?

To question me about Grace's father?

Dude needs to find a real job because he has too much time on his hands.

I pull in a deep breath to calm myself. "I didn't give her a questionnaire before moving in."

His smirk widens. "Oh, how I miss that mouth of yours."

I hold in the urge to dramatically make a vomiting noise. I don't want him to miss anything about me. I don't want him to even think about me.

I remain in my bedroom doorway, maintaining a safe distance between us. "Look, Quinton, I don't care what you're doing. Keep committing crimes. Don't. I don't give a shit. I got into trouble because you're a coward, but I've moved on."

His back straightens, his smirk dropping faster than his loyalty to me. "Coward?" he huffs. "I'm no goddamn coward."

I imitate his huff. "Who puts drugs in their girlfriend's car, and then when said car gets searched, claims the drugs aren't his? You made me take the fall *for your crime*. I rode off in a cop car, and you drove away in your brother's Mercedes. That, my regrettable ex-boyfriend, is a coward. Be lucky I don't rat you out."

"Why didn't you snitch on me then?"

"I don't want your wrath, *obviously*. I was stupid enough to date you, and now, I want nothing to do with you."

"I'm the one who decides when I'm done with someone. Not the other way around."

I snort. "Think again. I'd never touch a loser like you again, who lives off daddy's money but wants the high of playing drug dealer for a few years."

Wrong words.

I know my mouth has gotten me in trouble again when he jumps up from the bed. His face reddens in fury as he snatches my elbow and jerks me into my bedroom. I gasp as his hand moves to my throat, and I'm slammed against the wall.

"I will end you." Quinton hisses in my face. His grip tightens before he suddenly pulls back, his hands slapping the wall on each side of my head.

I draw in a shaky breath in an attempt to calm myself that does nothing but that. "Don't be stupid, Quinton. It's not smart, breaking into a judge's daughter's house. It might lead to you getting in trouble."

The reality of my words dawns on him.

He drops an arm but doesn't pull away. "You fucking cunt."

I brace myself for another chokeslam or slap or something, but he takes a step back.

"Fuck you, Cassidy."

"Get out of my house."

———

ME AND MY BIG MOUTH.

That's what I think as I wince and stand in front of the mirror, examining the large bruise around my neck. Arguing with Quinton was stupid, but I couldn't stop myself. Cringing, I carefully pull a sweatshirt over my head, drag the hood up, and tighten it. That way, if Grace comes home, she won't see anything out of the ordinary.

Except that I'm walking around, looking like a damn Eskimo.

If she sees what Quinton did, she'll tell Sierra. Grace might be my roommate, but she's been friends with my sister longer. Grace is also a nice person. She'd reach out to someone out of concern for me. To prevent that from happening, I'll be hiding out until this bruise fades.

As I make myself comfortable in my bed, I look through my phone.

Lincoln has called and texted numerous times, and I've ignored every one of them. Afraid that he'll come over if I don't, I text him back.

Me: Sorry, I have a headache. Can I talk to you later?
Lincoln: Are you sure everything is okay?
Me: It's fine. I'm just going to nap.
Lincoln: Talk when you wake up?
Me: Of course.

So much has happened today.

Lincoln and the random woman who he no doubt has history

with. Quinton making a visit and physically assaulting me. The day had started as a fairy tale and ended as a nightmare.

———

THROUGHOUT THE NIGHT, I sleep like shit.

The next morning, I wake up to find more texts from Lincoln.

I shut my eyes.

The day after we had sex, the day after we discussed our issues with trust, everything falls apart.

My phone rings, and it's Georgia. She's also texted a few times, asking if everything is okay. I've blown her off by replying with smiley face emojis.

"Hey, girl! Taco Tuesday is at our place tonight! Consider it a housewarming-slash-margarita party."

I chuckle. "I'm sure Archer is loving a party at his house."

"Well, it's *our* house now, and if I say we shall party, then we shall party." She laughs. "Plus, he's so happy I finally moved in that he'd let me throw a hundred parties. The fun starts at seven. Come with an empty stomach."

"I wish I could," I say around a groan. "But I have a killer migraine, and I think the move exhausted me. Sorry, but I'm going to sit this one out."

"Okay, but if you change your mind, you know where to come! Let's catch up this weekend, okay?"

"Sounds good."

Opening my nightstand drawer, I grab two ibuprofens and wash them down with water. As I surf through different Netflix options, my phone beeps with a text.

Lincoln: You coming over?

I sigh, debating on my response. He texted a few times earlier, asking me to let him explain himself. I briefly replied, saying I'd talk to him about it later.

Twenty questions had been on my tongue when I walked in and saw some random woman with Lincoln, but then Quinton texted me a picture of him sprawled out on my bed. My throat burning, my stomach churning, I knew I needed to get out of there. Not only because I was worried about being sick, but I also needed to get to my house before Grace did, so I could kick Quinton out.

Yes, my heart had sunk into the pit of my stomach when I saw Lincoln with that woman, especially it being the day after he and I finally had sex. But right now, I'm not in the mood to go back and forth. All I want to do is stay in bed, binge-watch a sappy show, and sleep. We'll discuss his stupid behavior another time.

Me: No, staying in for the night.

Lincoln: Come on. I need my sidekick.

Me: Sorry.

As bad as I want to go and take my mind off everything, I'm in pain, and there's no hiding my bruise yet. If someone bumps into me, if someone touches me in the wrong place, I'll wince.

Quinton wasn't like that when we dated. Yes, after thinking back, I remember the few times he was sketchy, but I didn't think he was dealing drugs.

Not only did I not want them to go to the police, but I also didn't want them to beg me to tell on him, nor did I want them to assume I was involved with his little side business. Knowing my parents, they would've freaked out and tried to stick me in rehab.

Lincoln: Everything okay?

Me: I'm just tired.

Lincoln: See you tomorrow?

Me: See you tomorrow.

I'm not sure if that's true.

CHAPTER NINETEEN

Lincoln

"YOU'RE NOT on the schedule tonight," I say when Johnna, one of the bar's waitresses, walks in.

Johnna shoves a notebook in her apron. "Cassidy asked me to cover for her."

Dread pools through me.

I planned to talk to Cassidy tonight about what had happened. With the anger I'd had when Isla was there, surely, Cassidy had to know there is nothing between us. Not one emotion in my body feels anything but disdain for Isla. I was ready to explain everything to Cassidy, but then her phone rang. The mood in the room hadn't been fucking rainbows, but whatever she'd read on her phone spooked her.

Since she left, I've texted her a few times. When I received no response, I expected to see her at Georgia's party. That didn't work out, just like my plan to talk to her tonight. Cassidy has never opted out of our get-togethers, and now, she's calling off work. My stomach unsettles, and I'm tempted to pour myself a shot to soothe my anxiety.

I fish my phone from my pocket and text her.

Me: You okay?

She replies minutes later.

Cassidy: Yes. I have a migraine and want to rest.

Me: You want me to bring you something when I get off?

The temptation to ask if she needs company hits me. I've picked up countless shifts for people, and someone could return the favor.

Cassidy: Thanks, but I'm fine.

Disappointment shatters through me. I want to be that guy for her, the one she calls when she has a migraine, who she calls when she's bored, whose name she moans when I'm inside her.

That damn guy.

I want to be everything for her.

Even though I shouldn't.

Unease drives through my blood as I text her back.

Me: Let me know if you change your mind.

Another text comes through, and that disappointment from earlier soars because it's not Cassidy.

Isla: Can we talk?

I clench my hand around my phone. Just seeing her name gives me the urge to throw it.

Me: Nope. Go talk to your husband.

Getting wrapped up in Isla was a mistake. Just like all the other women before her. She was crazy, but her husband? Dude was even fucking crazier when he found out we were sleeping together. I was young and dumb. Still, after it ended, I realized that wasn't an excuse for sleeping with a married woman. In my defense, she told me they were separated and in the process of a divorce.

Turned out, that was a lie.

With a curse, I block her number.

The rest of the night, my mind is on Cassidy.

I check my phone periodically, hoping she changed her mind.

Hoping she reached out.

Said something.

But it doesn't happen.

———

ARCHER GLANCES up when I knock on his open office door. Setting his pen down, he stares at me in expectation as I stand in the doorway.

I rest my shoulder against the doorframe. "Did Cassidy give a reason she called off tonight?"

He shakes his head. "Nah, she talked to Cohen."

Cohen is on baby leave, and I'd feel horrible for waking him. As bad as I'm trying to fight it off, all night, there's been a heaviness in my stomach that something is wrong with Cassidy. When she read whatever was on her phone, that light she carries around like a fucking pet dimmed.

I rub the back of my neck, hoping to relieve the tension. "If you can ask next time you talk to Cohen and let me know, that'd be great."

Archer lifts his chin, anchoring all his attention on me. "What's the deal between you and her?"

"We're"—I hesitate, wondering if I should tell him the truth even though Cassidy asked to wait—"friends."

Tenting his hands together, he levels them on his desk, his voice turning stern. "I know what *faking* being friends is. Georgia and I did it for years."

"Wrong." My voice wavers as I continue, "You and Georgia fake hated each other. I've never disliked Cassidy, and we don't pretend shit."

Okay, the last statement is a lie.

We do pretend that we don't have feelings for each other.

He nods, staying quiet.

His silence pisses me off.

I point at his phone next to him. "Can you ask Georgia if she's heard from her?" I'd text her myself, but like with Cohen, it's late, and I don't want to wake anyone up.

Archer blows out a ragged sigh. "Look, bro, Cassidy might not be the girl for you."

I pull in a breath, trying not to flip my shit on him.

How fucking dare he.

"The hell are you talking about?" I snarl. My stomach twists.

My brother, the number one person in my life, is telling me the only damn woman who's ever made me feel something might not be the one for me.

He's insinuating that the woman I'm falling for isn't for me.

Bull-fucking-shit.

Realizing he's hit a nerve, Archer lowers his voice. "She's on probation for a drug charge."

"And I was recently released from prison. What's your point?"

CHAPTER TWENTY

Cassidy

ONE OF THE most miserable feelings in the world is not being able to sleep.

Two days have passed since Quinton's chokeslam visit, and I've turned into an insomniac. Even with shutting and locking my bedroom door, the panic that he can barge in at any time haunts me, becoming a real-life nightmare since I can't actually manage to sleep to have a nightmare. Attempting to sleep has become as much of a pain in the ass as Quinton.

I dreaded calling off work but had no choice. No way could I wear my Twisted Fox employee shirt without my bruise being on display. Luckily, Johnna took my shift with no questions asked.

It's three in the morning, and I've been bingeing *Shameless* episodes. Just as I hit the remote button that tells Netflix, *Yes, I have no life and am still watching*, my phone vibrates on my nightstand. My back goes straight. Quinton has instilled a fear in me that rises whenever it goes off. I stretch across the bed to retrieve it and see Lincoln's name flashing across the screen.

My body relaxes … and then my stomach clenches as I ignore the call. When you're a romantic at heart, a guy you're falling for calling in the wee hours of the night is goals. But tonight, there's nothing but anxiety.

Anxiety he'll sense something is wrong.

Shoot, he definitely knows something is off, considering he's calling me in the middle of the night.

A text comes through seconds later.

Lincoln: Just tell me you're okay, Cass. Text me, call me, email me, tell Georgia, whatever. I need to know nothing is wrong.

I bite into my cheek as I read his text, so many raw emotions running through my head. My fingers itch to text him back. My heart yearns to call him and hear his voice—to make me forget about Quinton.

Me: I'm okay.

I owe him a response. He's been there for me. If our situation were reversed, if he'd avoided me this long, I'd blow his phone up *and* show up at his place.

I should tell him what's going on, but I can't. If I tell anyone Quinton is my stalker, they'll want me to go to the police. All that will do is provoke him further. Quinton is stupid and just wasting his time tormenting me. All I want to do is move on from him. It'd be in his best interest to leave me alone, so I can forget he exists.

Too bad all he's done is left reminders.

The texts.

My throbbing neck.

The ugly-ass bruise painting my skin.

He's texted me a few times, apologizing for his manic behavior, to which I replied with middle-finger emojis.

My thoughts are broken by my phone ringing again.

Lincoln.

"Are you ignoring me because of Isla?" he rushes out as soon as I answer, as if he's worried that he'll only get a second to speak.

Yes, I'm pissed about Isla, is what I want to scream.

Ask how dare he.

Mainly, I want to yell to release all the frustration from the past few days.

I exhale a stressed sigh. "I'm sure you'd be upset if you found some rando guy at my house *the day after* we had sex."

"Fair point." He blows out a breath. "I'm sorry, Cassidy. She showed up out of the blue. I want nothing to do with her. I've ignored her for months."

"Who is she?"

The truth test.

Let's see how much honesty Lincoln will give me.

"Can I come over? Explain myself?"

His question blindsides me as chills chase up my back. As I run his question through my mind again, my blood warms. If there's anything that'd make me feel safe, that'd give me a sense of security, it'd be Lincoln.

And fuck you, Quinton, for ruining this moment, when this perfect man wants to come be with me, to comfort me. You've ruined it by scarring me.

"Yeah," I breathe out. "You can."

"I'll be there in ten."

———

NOT WANTING TO WAKE GRACE, Lincoln texts me when he's outside. Tightening the strings around my hoodie, I check myself in the mirror before walking out of the bedroom.

There's no way I can pull this off. Lincoln will know that something is wrong. My heart thuds louder and louder as I tiptoe down the hall, uncertain of how the rest of the night will go. Inviting him here was dangerous. No doubt Lincoln will question me over my wardrobe choice. Before answering, I turn down the thermostat. If I make it the damn Arctic Circle in here, I can use that as my excuse.

Sorry, Grace.

Taking a reassuring breath, I swing the door open to find Lincoln standing before me. It's dark, and I can't see much, but there's no missing his body language.

Lowering his head, he reaches out and rubs the exposed skin of my cheek. "Thank you for letting me come over."

I chew on my lower lip as shivers barrel over my skin. Every part of me wants more of him.

"Come in," I croak, stepping to the side to allow him room.

Shutting the door behind us, he follows me down the hall to my bedroom.

Sitting on the edge of my bed, I wait for Lincoln to speak.

He shuts my bedroom door, and his eyebrows squish together as he studies me. "What's with the sweatshirt?"

Of course that's the first thing he notices.

I play with the strings of my shirt and glance away from him; my goal is to avoid all eye contact. "Grace likes to keep it cold in here."

"Bullshit. Georgia used to complain about how warm she kept it when they were roommates." He eyes me skeptically.

"Maybe she's had a change of thermostat heart." In need of a new subject, I tap the space next to me before slapping my hand against my knee. "You wanted to explain yourself?"

I hope my tone isn't bitchy, but regret rushes through my thoughts. I knew Lincoln would be suspicious of the hoodie. If we don't talk about another subject, that conversation will stray back to what I'm wearing. The problem is, I don't know if I can deter him from it all night.

Lincoln runs his hands through his thick hair before plopping down next to me, his leg brushing against mine. "You not showing up to Georgia's party or to work tonight scared the shit out of me." Shifting, he looks at me, the expression on his face brimming with exhaustion and concern. "I'm not sure if you're avoiding me because of what happened, but I can't ..." His voice drifts as he searches for the right words ... or the balls to say what is already on his mind. "I can't lose you, Cassidy. I can't lose you over a stupid miscommunication."

My mouth falls open, all thoughts of Quinton temporarily pausing.

"I can't lose you."

As if I wasn't hot enough in this hoodie, his admission sends a shot of warmth through my blood.

How long does it take the air conditioner to freeze this place up?

He squeezes his eyes shut. "That's why I'm here ... to make sure you don't hate me." Slowly opening them, he locks his heavy gaze on mine. "And if you do, then my next mission is to convince you not to."

Just when I thought this damn man couldn't be perfect enough, he has to show up and allow those words to fall out of his mouth. Never in my life have I experienced a man like this—a man who doesn't prioritize hanging with his frat boys over me, a man who's worried I'm upset and stresses about it, a man who has done nothing yet still wants to prove himself.

"I won't lie and say it didn't catch me off guard. It crushed my soul when I walked in to find you with her."

He doesn't break eye contact. "It was fucked up, I know."

"Had I not shown up, I would've never known about her."

"There's nothing to know about her. She means nothing to me."

"But she did once. I saw the hurt on her face when she left." It was the same raw emotion I'd feel if I lost Lincoln.

"Isla and I were *sex*. Nothing more." He signals back and forth between us. "You and me? That's not us. I want so much more than sex with you."

"How did you even get involved with her? It's not like you went to school together."

"She was one of my mother's best friends."

"Oh, wow."

"Back then, I had trouble connecting with women my age—"

"Or younger women, it seems."

He nods. "Fresh outta high school, I started dating one of my mother's friends. It was a short fling, and I guess word got out that I liked"—he clears his throat—"cougars. After graduating college, I got involved with Isla."

"While she was married?"

"She told me she was separated from her husband."

"Did it last long?"

"Almost a year."

"Wow. So, it wasn't just a *fling*. That's a long-ass time."

"On and off for a year, depending on where I was in my life."

"What happened when things broke off?"

"Her husband found out, and then I went to prison. She tried visiting a few times, but I refused. I want nothing to do with her. Her husband is the one who put my family in prison."

"What?"

He nods. "He found out about the affair and became dead set on bringing my family down. I guess there were whispers about fraudulent shit. That, or Isla fed him information after I broke things off with her. I'm not sure."

I like that he's telling me the truth.

"So, she really means nothing to you?"

"Absolutely nothing." His eyes soften. "You're the only woman who means something to me like that. You're the only woman I want to be with, Cass."

We're inches away from each other. Emotions high. My hormones on overdrive. Our eye contact is firm. It's dangerous, given my bruising. I've never connected with anyone like this before.

Unable to stop myself, I scoot closer to him, erasing any distance between us, and stare up at him.

With a slight hesitation, I brush my lips against his. With him, there's no hesitation. As soon as our mouths meet, he slides his tongue into my mouth.

As our lips tangle together, there's a raw emotion that didn't exist during our last kiss. This kiss, we're allowing every emotion toward the other to take the frontline, feeding it to the other.

He brackets his hands around my waist and tugs me onto his lap. There's a slight pain in the movement, but I ignore it. Tilting my hips forward, I rock against him, his cock hardening underneath me, causing me to grind on his lap.

"Cass," he groans, pulling back, resulting in an annoyed huff from me. "We need to talk about us more."

"Kiss first, talk later."

"Cass." This time, he says my name in more of a warning.

"Linc," I mock. "Just a minute. Give me a minute of kissing."

"Fine," he says, feigning annoyance. "We can have some fun before we go into the deep parts."

"Mmm ... deep parts." I grin.

"Jesus, babe. We have to get your mind out of the gutter."

"The gutter is the best place for the mind to be." I go in for another kiss, thankful he's giving in to our desires.

We start slow before it turns frantic, and he's lowering me onto my back.

"We need to get this damn sweatshirt off," he says, hovering over me.

Since his lips are on mine, I don't process his words. I'm so wrapped up in him, forgetting my real life, and I lift my arms to assist him. When I tip my head back, he rains kisses over my cheek while slowly drawing the hoodie over my body. I gasp in pain, knocking me out of my Lincoln haze, and reality smacks into me harder than my need for this man.

"What the fuck?"

I freeze at his tone.

He's staring at my neck in fury as I lie underneath him, wearing only a sports bra. Quinton's damage is on full display.

CHAPTER TWENTY-ONE

Lincoln

ANGER COILS THROUGH ME, tightening around my veins, like a snake as I stare down at her.

Cassidy's eyes are glossy with humiliation and panic. She rubs them, an attempt to blur away the evidence, before looking around the room in panic. She quickly tries to grab the hoodie from the floor, but it's out of her reach. In order to grab it, she'd have to get out of bed.

I glare at her neck as if it were my worst enemy, silently begging for answers while processing what I'm seeing. The skin is bruised, a fusion of black and purple, and swear to God, I see a damn handprint pressed against the dark colors.

"Cassidy," I grit out. "What the hell happened?"

"It's nothing," she rushes out, crossing her arms over her chest in an X motion.

"Bullshit," I snarl. "Someone put their goddamn hands on you. There's a handprint around your throat." I pull back to examine her further, my eyes hardening with every second. "Who did this to you?"

She stays silent.

"Cass, you're scaring me here."

"Just stop, okay." She swats at me, and taking the hint, I draw back, so I'm no longer above her. Pulling herself up, she wraps the blanket tightly around her, as if a shield to her secrets. "You know what? It's late. You should probably go."

I flinch. "Whoa. How did we go from that to you kicking me out?"

She uses her arm to cover her eyes, to cover her tears. "I can't talk about it."

Reaching out, I gently pull her arm away from her face and use the pad of my thumb to brush away a tear. "Baby, if there's anyone you can talk to, it's me." I fight for my voice to be soft and nurturing, but there's no unclenching my jaw. I'm holding in my anger to comfort her.

She shakes her head, sobbing. "It doesn't matter."

"It does fucking matter," I grind out, and I hate that a hint of my softness disappears to make way for anger. "Give me a name. Who hurt you?"

She stares at the ceiling. "Some guy."

"Give me that guy's information, so I can go rip his fucking head off."

"I can't," she cries out, shutting her eyes as pools of tears resurface. The floodgates finally break, and tears for days fall down her cheeks like a rainstorm. "Please, just drop it. I haven't been sleeping. *Please.* Tonight, I don't want to talk about it. All I want to do is get some rest."

"Okay," I say gently, scooting in closer and staring down at her. "Have you been icing it?"

She slowly nods.

"Are you in pain?"

"No," she chokes out. "I took ibuprofen a few hours ago."

"Do you need more?" I rush out. "Something to drink?"

I have to push back my anger to care for her. It's late, she's exhausted, and right now, what she needs is sleep.

She rubs her forehead with the heel of her hand. "Really, all I want to do is lie down and sleep."

"Do you want me to go or stay?"

"Stay," she whispers, her body going stiff in alarm. "Please ... please stay."

"All right." I slide off the bed, stand, and pull my tee over my head.

"And please hand me my hoodie." Desperation covers her tone.

"Cass, you were burning up in here. The secret is out. You're already in pain. At least don't make yourself sweat to death."

She nods.

I kick off my pants but leave on my boxer briefs. After carefully climbing into bed, I stare over at her. "Light on or off?"

She hesitates, and from the look in her eyes, I know she's been sleeping with the light on. She's been in fear of this happening again. She snuggles into my side, being careful not to hit the bruise.

"I'd pull you into my arms, but I don't want to hurt you," I whisper.

She shifts closer. "Please. Being in your arms is what I need."

I drape my arm over her waist, my lips brushing along her ear. "Get some sleep. I'm right here. Always."

———

I WANT to wring a motherfucker's neck.

Wring his neck and then his hands, so he can never put them on a woman again.

I don't give two fucks if it ruins my life.

Someone put his hands on the woman I'm falling in love with.

He deserves to be ripped to shreds with mine.

With my arm cradled around Cassidy's waist, as if shielding her from any more harm, I shut my eyes. It's a game I've been playing for hours now—since her breathing became steady and a slight snore slipped through her lips.

I came over last night with the intent to lay out everything and explain Isla. As soon as I walked through the door and saw her dressed as if she were about to climb Mount Everest, I knew something was off. The thoughts of her wardrobe dissipated some when her lips hit mine … and then the shitshow started. Nothing mattered anymore—not Isla, not my problems, nothing—when I saw the bruise on her neck.

My blood ran cold.

And then hot with fury.

Somehow, someway, I need to convince Cassidy to open up about what happened. It won't be easy. The more time we spend together, the more I'm learning that Cassidy's been keeping slices of her life from me. I'm falling for this woman whose secrets I need to know.

My attention shoots to the floor when the hallway light flips on, the light shining through the bottom crack of the door meeting the carpet, and there's movement on the other side. Footsteps, quiet and soft. I slip out of bed, careful not to wake Cassidy, and tiptoe out of the bedroom, gently shutting the door behind me.

Grace is in the kitchen, a green turtleneck on, warming up a bagel in the toaster oven. She gasps, her hand pressing into her chest when she notices me. "Jesus, Lincoln. You scared me for a sec."

I smile gently. "Sorry about that."

She tips her head down the hall. "You two *finally* opened your eyes and realized you liked each other, huh?"

I pinch the bridge of my nose. "Something like that."

"I'm happy for you two. I swear, just in the short time she's been here, all she does is talk about you." She turns to open the fridge and grabs the cream cheese before snagging a knife from a drawer.

I pull out a barstool from underneath the island, take a seat, and clasp my hands together. "Have you noticed anything weird going on with her? Anyone coming over? Her being worried at night?"

"No." She shakes her head in hesitation as if checking she hadn't missed anything. "Not that I can think of. We don't see each other much since our schedules are the opposite. Why? Did something happen?"

I rub my temples, debating on how to answer. Blasting Cassidy's information would be an untrustworthy move, but Grace needs to know.

What if the guy comes back?

He could hurt her too.

Grace stares at me in question, a bagel in one hand and knife in the other.

"Nah, she just bailed on Georgia's party and work last night." I shrug. "Just worried me, is all." After I talk to Cassidy, I'll insist she tell Grace.

"I'll let you know if anything catches my attention." She spreads cream cheese over her bagel before holding it up. "Want one?"

"I'm good." I have no appetite.

"There's plenty of food here if you get hungry." She takes in the sight of me. "Although it appears you need sleep more than anything at the moment. Did you keep each other up that late?" A suggestive smile takes over her face. "I do have to say thank you for not being loud. Your brother and Georgia tended to make it known when they were ... *you know.*"

"Trust me, I know."

"Ah, forgot she's your new roomie."

I chuckle. "I plan to get some shut-eye here in a bit. Just wanted to say hi."

"Make yourself at home in the meantime, okay?" She finishes off her bagel and then grabs her bag. "I'm off to teach children."

When Grace is out of sight, I tip my head down and rest my forehead against the granite countertop. The chill pressing against my skin is a relief to my impending headache. The girl I'm falling in love with is going through something. The last thing I want to do is create more stress, but whoever did that to her needs to suffer the consequences for it. She needs to go to the cops, file a report, get a restraining order. If I don't find him and break his neck first.

That should be enough of a consequence for him.

Eh, maybe he needs a little castration too.

I grind my jaw, just thinking about it again.

Convincing Cassidy to turn him in will be one hell of a struggle.

With a stressed sigh, I stand, fill up a glass of water, and chug it down. I refill it and carry it to Cassidy's room for when she wakes.

Sliding back into her bed should be perfect, the best damn moment in the world, but there's that heavy secret looming over us now. I sink into her mattress, my body growing heavy, and finally shut my eyes, giving in to sleep.

THE BRIGHT SUN shining through Cassidy's window wakes me.

That'll be the only damn thing that's bright this morning. I'm preparing for the worst. No way can I sit back and not question Cassidy about who hurt her. No way can I not demand she turn him in.

She was petrified when her bruise was exposed, and it rotted me to the core that she'd been in pain for who knows how long. My guess is, since the day she skipped Georgia's party.

I'm unsure of how late we slept in, but rest was long overdue for us both.

When I peer down, I find her awake and squinting up at me in question.

"Good morning," I whisper, my throat dry.

She offers a sleepy smile. "Morning."

"How'd you sleep?"

"Good." She yawns. "Thanks to our spooning."

How bad has she been sleeping lately?

It appeared to have been days' worth of exhaustion on her face last night.

"Are you ready to talk about it?" I didn't mean for the words to release from my tongue so early. I'd planned to ease my way in and get her to crack without throwing out pressure.

"Nope." There isn't a moment of hesitation in her response.

"Too bad." I lift myself, causing her to do the same along with me. Scooting up the bed, we rest our backs against the headboard and stare ahead. "It needs to be talked about."

"I beg to differ." She pulls the blanket up her body, making sure there's no way for me to catch a glimpse of her bruising. "Subject change."

"Cass—"

"Please." Her voice breaks. "Please don't tell anyone about this."

"I won't tell anyone."

She bows her head. "Thank you."

"Because you will."

Her body tenses, her shoulder stiff against mine. "No, I won't."

My nostrils flare, and like last night, I'm struggling to constrain my anger. "What's your plan then, huh? To just let this guy get away with hurting you?"

Was it random?

Did someone come here?

How did this happen to her?

"It was one time," she mutters with no certainty in her voice.

It's a lie to not only me but also to herself.

"Who did it?" That seems to be the question of the motherfucking year ... that I'll never get the answer to.

"It. Doesn't. Matter," she grits out each word with a huff as if spitting out bad meat.

"You need to go to the cops."

She snorts. "Please, no. This isn't what I want to talk about first thing in the morning."

"If you wait too long, the bruising will fade, and you won't have a case." Shit like this needs to be reported fast. "What if he hurts someone else?"

Cassidy might not care about protecting herself, but she has a big enough heart that she'd be concerned about the guy doing it to another woman.

"I don't want a case," she snaps. "I want it to fade and to forget about it."

My heart squeezes in my chest.

This isn't the Cassidy I know.

"You can ask me a thousand ways to Sunday, and it won't happen," she continues. "This is a part of myself that I'd like to keep private, and I hope you respect that."

I cast a glance in her direction and shift to get a better look at her. The blanket is being used to conceal the damage as if she doesn't want me to be reminded of how bad it is.

As if she doesn't want *either* of us to be reminded of how bad it is.

Is she protecting him or herself?

"Are you shitting me?" I snap. "This isn't me being overbearing or nosy. Someone *assaulted* you, and he needs to face the consequences for his actions."

Her voice turns almost robotic. "It happened. It's over. I'm almost healed. Time to move on."

"Time to move on?" I huff out. "Time for you to get out of bed, and we'll march our asses right into the police station."

"I'm not going to the police. The guy who did this ..." She pauses to gesture to her chest, slight sniffles releasing from her, and I know her well enough to know she's holding back her pain, her hurt, her tears. "He's the reason I was arrested ... the reason I got kicked out of college, out of my sorority, why I had community service. He's already done enough to fuck up my life. I'm not trying to give him another reason to do more damage."

"He won't fuck anything up. I promise. I'll be here every night. I'll be your personal bodyguard—whatever you need for you to be safe. Whoever that guy is, I swear, you won't have to worry about him any longer."

She's silent.

Another trait I'm learning about Cassidy is her stubbornness.

"Cass—"

Frantically, with shaking arms, she jumps out of bed, as if it were on fire, and her voice cracks. "Discussion over."

I raise my voice. "Discussion not fucking over. I got your back, Cass. Whatever you need, I'm here."

"Just stop!" she screams, stabbing her finger in my direction. "I am done talking about this. You will not tell anyone, do you hear me?" There's a mix of panic, anger, and determination in her tone. "If you do, I swear to God, I'll never speak to you again." Her eyes finally meet mine, her gaze a mirror of her tone, and she claps her hands over her hips.

There is no changing her mind. She's hell-bent on protecting this asshole.

I clear my throat, prepared to say either she goes to the police or I tell her family, but I stop myself.

What do I do?

Keep quiet, so I don't lose her?

Go behind her back and tell someone, only to lose her?

Not to mention, no way in hell am I leaving her alone here.

Throwing one leg and then the other off the bed, I stand. She doesn't say anything, only waits for my next move.

I hold her gaze, praying she's the one who changes her mind.

Nothing.

Heat burns at her cheeks.

My eyes flash to her chest. The bruise is on full display now that the blanket isn't there acting as a protector. My blood boils while endless thoughts of self-doubt and uneasiness flicker through my mind.

"Fine," I finally say, defeated. "I won't say anything." I hate myself as the words climb out of my mouth—with force and pressure.

With regret.

Her body softens, a weight dragged off her shoulders, and for a moment, I'm proud of myself for unwinding that tension. Then I remember what I did, what I said, and how I shouldn't get any recognition for that because I agreed to keep this a secret between us.

"Thank you," she whispers, stepping closer and wrapping her arms around my waist.

I bow my head, kissing her hair, and feel like a fucking coward.

———

LOYALTY.

It's a hard drug for me.

A problematic drug for me.

I could do what I've done all my life—be loyal and keep my mouth shut.

After helping Cassidy undress and get into the shower, I step out of the bathroom and grab my phone from her bedroom.

I call Archer, and when he answers, I say, "Hey, I need someone to cover for me tonight at the bar."

"Dude," he grunts, "a little late notice. You can't call in this late and expect it to be okay."

"Something came up."

"What's that something?"

"I can't talk about it."

"Yeah, sorry, but I'm not letting you have the night off so you can spend time with a girl."

I clench my hand around the phone.

Now's not the time to mess with me, brother.

"Oh, says the guy who went MIA for nearly a fucking week, and I covered for you," I snap, attempting to keep my voice low in case Cassidy gets out of the shower soon.

"That was different." Agitation spreads along his words. "You can go to Cassidy's after."

"I don't want her alone."

"What?" That agitation alters into concern.

I lower my voice. "I came to her house last night since she was ignoring my calls."

"That probably has something to do with Isla's ass showing up at our place."

Pausing, I look from one side of the living room to the other before deciding to change my mind. With quick steps, I walk outside and shut the patio door behind me. What I'm about to do goes against everything I stand for, but I care about Cassidy too much. I have to tell someone before it eats away at me.

I tighten the phone against my face. "That, and she has a big-ass bruise around her neck after being assaulted."

"What the fuck?" Archer yells into the phone.

"Yeah, tell me about it. Now, do you understand why I'm not leaving her?" I kick at the grass with the same force I'd like to kick her assaulter's ass.

"Is she going to the cops?"

"She refuses to." My answer is a reminder of what I'm hiding for her. It's also a reminder of what I'm not really hiding and how I'm deceiving her by telling Archer this.

"Wait until her family finds out. No way will they let that slide. I'm surprised they haven't shown up on her doorstep yet."

"She hasn't told them, and my guess is, she won't."

"The fuck? I can't keep something like that from Maliki. He's one of my closest friends."

"I know." I blow out a ragged breath. "I know."

"Look"—his tone turns serious—"you need to tell them. Ditch your loyalty for a moment and think about Cassidy's well-being. What if the guy shows up again and does worse than what he did before?"

I scrub a hand over my forehead—an attempt to ease the regret, guilt, and headache pounding through. "I don't know. Taking care of her is my biggest priority at the moment. Just find someone to cover my shift for me."

Subconsciously, I'm not sure if I'm telling my brother this because I need someone to confide in or because I know he'll tell someone he shouldn't.

CHAPTER TWENTY-TWO

Cassidy

FOR THE PAST FEW DAYS, I've been through hell ... and then back after Lincoln showed up.

I'm not sure what I was thinking when I invited him over. In the back of my mind, I knew the bruise would come to light, knew he'd see it, but his comfort was what I needed as a Band-Aid to cover my pain.

Lincoln understands keeping secrets. I trust him, and even though it'll kill him, I know my secret is safe with him.

Will he constantly pester me to turn Quinton in? Absolutely.

Will he go behind my back and do it himself? No.

I've put him in a tough situation, made him go against what he thinks is right, and for him doing this for me, I'll forever be grateful.

Lincoln is in the shower when the doorbell rings. He told me he left the door unlocked and to run in there if there was danger. The poor guy has been scared to leave my side since he arrived last night.

Since I'm not expecting visitors and the last thing I want to do is talk to someone, I ignore the doorbell. If it's important, they'll call or text. If it's for Grace, she's at work, so they'll have to come back later anyway.

I prop my feet up on the coffee table, and the doorbell rings again.

And again.

And again.

Then my phone rings.

The hell?

Lincoln, who apparently has the ears of a moth, walks out of the bathroom, now freshly showered. His hair is dripping wet, and he's wearing black sweats and a tee. "Is that the doorbell?"

It rings again.

"Yes," I groan. "That's the doorbell."

"I got it."

Commotion erupts as soon as he answers the door, a hurricane storming into the living room, a rush of frantic voices taking in the space.

"Let me see it!" Rex, a man who rarely yells, does as soon as he comes into my view. His voice cracks when he continues, "I am going to kill whoever it was!"

"Babe," Carolina says, her tone sharp as she shoots me a despaired look.

"No!" he shouts. "I am going to kill whoever put his hands on her!"

The room falls silent. I stifle back a scream of dread. My leg muscles tighten, begging for me to flee, but I can't move.

I cannot speak or move.

No words are coming to me.

No excuse to justify why I'm hiding this.

I shoot a panicked glance to Lincoln, tears automatically approaching as a whimper leaves me.

That's all I can manage.

A damn whimper as I cover my mouth.

He told them.

He lied to me.

Betrayed me.

Now, my entire family is standing in my living room, staring at me and waiting for answers.

Shock and pain reside in Lincoln's eyes. He stands inches away from me, fists clenched, as we wait for whatever scene is about to unfold.

Rex's hands are shaking. He went through a similar situation with Carolina's ex giving her hell, and he knows the damage that can be done when someone decides they're not finished with you yet. Next to him stands Carolina, a deep concern etched along her forehead.

Kyle stands next to Rex, his face reddened with fury. My mother scurries over to me, nearly tripping over the rug, and collapses on the couch a few inches to my right. Panic fills her voice as he says my name over and over again, tears in her eyes.

"You think I can't hack into your shit and get answers in seconds?" Rex asks. "Who did this to you?" His attention briefly flicks to Kyle. "Wasn't there a guy in her car when she was arrested? Who was it?"

Them not even considering it's Lincoln confirms they heard the news from him.

Kyle shakes his head. "The guy wasn't in the police report." He throws his arm out toward me. "And this one here won't budge on providing a name."

"It doesn't matter," I cry out. "It's over with."

Lincoln curses underneath his breath at my response, but I don't glance over at him.

I can't.

Even though I should, so he could see the hurt and betrayal flowing through me.

I'm thankful that I'm wearing the hoodie. It's been off and on today, depending on my mood. Whenever I get up to use the bathroom, I see myself in the mirror and put it back on. Then as I get warm, I take it off.

Rex steps forward. "It does matter! Someone beat you up!"

"Calm down," Carolina tells him. "You guys can't just barge in here and demand answers."

"Damn straight we can," Kyle inputs.

"I get it, protective brothers and all," Chloe says, coming into view, and I want to die that nearly everyone I'm close with is here to witness my embarrassment. "It's hard for women to open up to their brothers.

How about this? You guys chill in the living room and let us girls talk, okay?"

Before anyone answers, Maliki and Sierra walk through the door, their eyes shooting straight to me. Sierra's cheeks are red, and Maliki's fists are clenched.

"Bedroom. Now," Sierra demands.

I nod and hop off the couch, but before I can go to my bedroom, I whip around to face Lincoln.

"You told them," I cry out in despair.

"Did you expect him not to?" Rex asks. "I'd fucking hate the dude if he didn't."

Lincoln shakes his head, torture and guilt clouding his features. "I told Archer, and he must've told them." He gulps, taking a step closer to me. "I'm sorry, Cassidy, but we both know this is what needed to happen."

"Screw you," I hiss, tears approaching. "I trusted you!"

His eyes water. "I know." He bows his head. "I know."

"Archer told Cohen, who told Maliki," Sierra explains. "Archer was unsure what to do about an employee being in possible danger, so he asked Cohen. He told Cohen not to tell Maliki, but Cohen felt he couldn't hide something like that from his best friend."

"I'm going to kill my brother," Lincoln grits out, his eyes not leaving me.

"You should've told us," Maliki says.

"I just found out last night!" Lincoln screams, throwing up his arms. "I've been trying to talk her into going to the police and giving her time to process, not barging in and complicating shit for her. This has already messed with her head enough, and no offense, but she doesn't need people screaming at her while she's recovering. I planned to try to talk it out with her again today. She needs time, like some victims do."

Everyone is shocked into silence at Lincoln's response, no one expecting those words to leave him.

He thought he was going to change my mind.

Wow. Is that why he stayed here with me—to try to talk me into turning Quinton in?

Sierra gently grabs my elbow. "Your bedroom. Now."

I nod, turning my back on the man whose betrayal hurts deeper than Quinton's, and everyone with a vagina follows me into my bedroom.

"Let me see," Sierra demands, taking the lead, her tone as sharp as Rex's. "I'm not going to yell, but I need to see."

While taking a seat on the bed, my mother snivels, her eyes glued to me like her favorite soap opera.

With a heavy breath, I pull my sweatshirt over my head.

"I'm going to kill the bastard myself," Sierra hisses.

"Just ..." I shake my head. "It's over."

"Is it, though?" Carolina asks. "How do you know he won't come back and do the same ... or worse? From my experience, it's not over until the guy is set straight or is scared enough to leave you alone."

"I think it's time you talk about what happened," my mother says. "Or I'm involving your father."

"Or we have Rex hack into your shit and find out everything," Sierra chimes in.

"Invasion of privacy much?" I huff out.

"I'll take you being safe over you being angry with me," my mother replies.

CHAPTER TWENTY-THREE

Lincoln

THIRTY MINUTES HAVE PASSED since Cassidy went to her bedroom to spill her secrets … or at least since she left the room with people attempting to get her to spill her secrets.

Thirty minutes of me pacing, of Rex cursing every three seconds, and of Kyle saying he's going to strangle the guy nonstop.

Cassidy is a tough nut to crack.

Doesn't give in easily.

And I've never seen such determination from someone who's breaking inside.

I wouldn't be surprised if they were in there for hours, begging her to talk to them, to give them anything to get the man who hurt her in trouble.

She's a victim.

But Cassidy won't admit that part yet.

We freeze when Sierra comes into view, her attention shooting straight to me. "She wants to talk to you." Her face is unreadable, and she doesn't disclose a word more.

The other women stand behind her.

I nod, shoving my hands into my pockets, and walk around them.

When I enter the bedroom, Cassidy is on the bed, her shoulders curled over her chest. When she raises her head, her face is red and puffy, tearstained, and I rush over to her.

"Baby," I whisper, collapsing to my knees in front of her. I want to console her, hold her, wipe away every single tear, and make sure she never feels pain like this again.

Not only physical pain torments Cassidy.

It's emotional pain.

Tearing her apart.

And I hate it.

She jerks away from me. "How dare you."

She's cold.

Hostile.

Taking out the anger on me that she should be taking out on someone else.

I can take it, though.

I'm strong.

I'll take every emotion she needs to release.

"I ..." I stutter for the right words, but there are none that'll bring her comfort, none that'll convince her that I didn't tell Archer about her out of malice. But in reality, I know my brother. In the back of my mind, I knew he couldn't keep that information to himself, not when it came to a woman being in trouble. I had him do my dirty work, hoping I wouldn't have that guilt bearing down on my shoulders. "I didn't know he'd tell."

She sucks in a sob as she glares down at me. "Bullshit. You knew exactly what would happen. You think he'd keep his mouth shut about that? You know how much I trusted you, telling you that, but it turns out, you're just as bad as them."

"You can trust me," I croak out, my hands and voice pleading.

"Please leave."

I slam my eyes shut. "Cass—"

She shakes her head, sniffling back tears. "Get out, Lincoln."

———

I LEFT.

I left because she needed space, and with her family there, I knew she was safe.

I left because I'm going to get answers.

For years, I've kept my mouth shut for those I love, to protect them.

For my father.

For my grandfather's company.

I've kept so many damn secrets that I could get lost in them.

It was different with Cassidy.

Someone hurt her.

She's not committing crimes.

I went to prison for protecting my father.

I'd go to prison to protect her too.

If she won't tell me what is going on, I'll figure it out myself.

I know just the person to ask for help.

It's also the last person who'd ever want to help me.

———

LOUIS BERBAN.

Iowa's district attorney.

The main force behind putting my father and me in prison.

Isla's husband.

No one was looking into my father until Louis found out I was sleeping with his wife.

It was bullshit since I thought they were separated. When he found out, all hell broke loose. The first thing he did was tell my mother that I was sleeping with her friend, a woman her age, which broke her heart. He also made it a point to disclose that Isla wasn't the first friend of my mother's I'd *spent time in bed with.*

Him going to my mother caused friction between us. It gave her more trust issues than she already had. I never went looking for older women. It'd just … happened.

"I thought I'd never see your face again."

I stare at Louis from the doorway of his office. He sits behind his massive cherry-wood desk with built-in bookshelves behind him, shelves filled with law books and family photos.

It was risky, barging into his office and asking his secretary to speak to him. I figured he'd send security out to escort me off the premises, but surprisingly, he told her to send me in.

Pushing his black-rimmed glasses up his nose, he waits for me to speak.

"Trust me," I say, "I never wanted to see yours again."

"Why are you here?" He flicks his Montblanc pen in his hand before sliding it into the pocket of his suit jacket. "To beat me up now that you're free? To keep sleeping with my wife? What?"

Should I tell him his wife is still visiting me?

Considering I need a favor from him, I keep that tidbit of information to myself. I'll make it clear to Isla to leave me the fuck alone or her husband will be hearing from me. For once, I need the law on my side.

I venture deeper into his office, stopping in front of his desk, and stand tall. "I need a favor."

He snorts. "Why would I do *you* any favors?"

"Do me a favor, and I won't fuck your wife again." I step closer, leveling my eyes on him. "How's that sound?"

It's an asshole move, but my attitude needs to match his.

Berban can't lock me up for dicking down his wife. Not that I would, but threats seem to work well. It's what he did to me for months before locking me up.

His dark brows knit together. "You walk into my office, talk about fucking my wife, and want a favor from me? Did they beat the sense out of you in prison or something?"

"You scratch my back, and I'll scratch yours. Or rather, I'll leave your wife alone."

Not that I'd touch Isla with a ten-foot pole, but she's Louis's weakness. Dude loves her more than he loves anything.

He leans back in his leather chair, crossing his arms. "What can I help you with, Callahan?"

"I have a friend who's in trouble."

He keeps staring, not muttering a word.

"And I need help figuring out how to get her out of trouble."

"What do you want me to do?"

I gesture to his computer. "Look up her record. There's a guy who's messing with her."

His back straightens. "Define *messing with her*."

"She's bruised up." I make a circling motion around my chest. "My guess is, from a guy she was arrested with. His name isn't in the police report, but I'm hoping your report has additional information you can give me."

"What's her name?" He pounds a finger onto the keyboard.

"Cassidy Lane."

He freezes. "Lane ... as in the daughter of the mayor of Blue Beech?"

"I think so."

I knew Cassidy's father was the mayor of their town, but she doesn't talk about him much.

Surprisingly, Louis types on his computer, moving his mouse as he reads the screen. "Hmm ... she only has one charge. A drug misdemeanor. It appears she was pulled over, and there were drugs in the car. Not enough to consider distribution, but it was pretty damn close."

"What else?" That information is shit I could've easily googled or had Rex hack to find.

"That's about it. Police report said she was pulled over with her boyfriend. She denied the drugs being hers, but the boyfriend said they didn't belong to him either. It was her car, so it became her charge. When they asked where she got them, she wouldn't answer any questions. She was bailed out six hours later, put on probation since it was a first-time offense, and sentenced to community service." He shrugs. "Not much there for you."

"The boyfriend." I hastily point at the computer. "Does it give a name?"

He squints at the screen. "A man by the name of Quinton ..." He pauses, recognition dawning on him. "Landing. Quinton Landing."

"Well, fuck me," I mutter.

He nods. "That might be a problem for you, huh?"

"Could be, but at this point, I don't care."

In the Iowa investment industry, Landing Holdings was the biggest competitor to Callahan Holdings. As Callahan Holdings began to spiral, Landing rushed in to poach our clients, giving them the notion they could get in trouble by allowing *criminals* to work with their money. They painted us as people who couldn't be trusted. That we stole money from our clients and would be spending the rest of our lives in jail. The Landing family is as conniving as they come.

Now, I need to figure out if Quinton is the one who hurt Cassidy.

Time to hunt him down.

I attended private school with his older brother, so I can always start there.

"Can you pull up his address for me?" I ask Louis.

He looks at me as if I grew a horn out of my head. "No."

"Come on."

He shakes his head.

"You put me in prison … give a man a little favor now."

"I've told you all I can." Even after everything that's happened, there's a hint of remorse on his face.

CHAPTER TWENTY-FOUR

Cassidy

IT TOOK me forever to convince my family to leave.

Correction: *most* of my family to leave.

Sierra and Maliki have stayed, wanting to *hang out* for a while.

Code word for: babysit me.

While in my bedroom with my mom and the girls, I revealed my bruise but held my ground. I'm not telling them who did it or providing any details.

It's my story to tell.

And I'll tell it when I'm ready.

If I'm ever ready.

They tried and finally gave up—at least on getting a name. When I asked them to have Lincoln come into my bedroom and talk, I wasn't sure what I was going to say.

Betrayal had sunk its claws into my thoughts. None of this would have happened—my entire family wouldn't have shown up like a circus—had he not told someone. A light of hope had begun to surface that day, positive thoughts of forgetting about Quinton approaching, and my future with Lincoln was all I was looking toward. And then Rex had barged through the door like a madman, dissipating all that confidence.

Because of Lincoln, they know.

Because of Lincoln, my family sees me as dishonest, as weak, as someone who needs to be watched.

Johnna is covering my shift at Twisted Fox again tonight. Cohen was understanding when I texted and told him. It's time for me to come up with a plan. As much as I love working at the bar and living in Anchor Ridge, what happens now?

Now that people know what happened to me.

I don't want to be known as Cassidy Lane, the girl who was abused, needs saving, and couldn't hold her own against some jerk.

I'm in the living room, staring at the TV yet not processing anything happening on the show. Maliki and Sierra are in the kitchen, whispering and warming up frozen pizzas. My head rises, my gaze shooting toward the entry, when the front door opens.

Grace appears, strutting into the house, wearing a wool jacket, pencil skirt, and kitten heels. She smiles at me, dimples popping out along her fair cheeks, and drops her computer bag to the floor before relaxing in the chair next to the couch.

"Hey, babe," she says. "You have the night off again?"

I stare at her, blinking, struggling to get a read on her. "Do you know?"

"Know what?" She genuinely looks confused, which confuses me because I was under the impression that the group told each other everything.

Gripping the hem of my sweatshirt with my hands nearly trembling, I drag it up to reveal my bruise. It happens without thought, as if my brain told my body I could trust Grace.

Or maybe I'm sick of hiding it.

She gasps, her mouth falling open, her eyes wide. "Oh my God! Who did that to you?"

"An ex." My voice is fainter than a whisper as the truth releases from my lips for the first time, and I shove the sweatshirt back down.

And just like that, Grace is the first person I've muttered those words to. I'm not going into specifics and telling her it was Quinton, but it's more than what I've given anyone else. I'm not sure if it's because there's an ease, a comfortableness, with Grace or because I finally want to talk about it so I can stop thinking about it incessantly.

All her attention is on me, her forehead creasing in concern. "Did you call the cops?" She jumps up from her seat. "Do you need anything? Ice? A drink?"

I was worried about telling Grace this for two reasons: one being that she might think it's unsafe to be my roommate and the other being that her father is a judge and she might ask him to step in.

"I thought I could trust Lincoln, but he ran his mouth. So, my family knows." I blow out a breath. "I'm surprised the news hasn't hit you because I'm pretty sure Georgia knows."

Her face softens, and a genuine smile that's meant to be helpful and comforting spreads along her lips. "It's a personal matter. Yes, we're a tight-knit group, but if one of us confides in another, that secret stays with that person. Georgia wouldn't tell your story, wouldn't disclose your secrets, unless she knew it was okay with you for her to do so. Just like I won't mention this to anyone unless you're comfortable with it."

"If only Lincoln had followed that same structure."

"I'm sure it sucked for him to break your trust." She sighs. "But what happened to you is serious. Someone physically assaulted you … and it's scary. Trust me, I know. But are you protected now? Will they come back and continue messing with you? Violence tends to lead to more violence."

"I know; I know."

"I'm sure Lincoln was trying to protect you because he cares about you."

———

WE'RE in the living room, munching on cauliflower pizza, when the front door opens again, and Lincoln stalks into the living room.

He's called and texted a few times, but I've ignored them. Uncertainty of where we're at has stopped me every time. I trusted him, and he proved I'd been stupid in doing that. Maybe he didn't plan on Archer telling my family, but he still went behind my back and told Archer. What I had shown Lincoln, told him, was supposed to stay between him and me.

Not Lincoln, me, and my entire family.

If the tables were turned, I'm not sure what I'd do either. *If one of my friends or family were hurt, would I keep that secret or reach out to someone in concern?*

Everyone goes quiet, Sierra even pausing the show we're watching, when Lincoln comes to a halt in front of me.

"Is it Quinton?" he asks, staring down at me, not sparing a glance in anyone else's direction. "Is he the one who hurt you?"

A sudden coldness hits my core.

How does he know Quinton?

All attention plasters to me.

"That's none of your business," I grit out, clenching my fists, my nails digging into the sensitive skin of my palms.

"Quinton?" Sierra asks. "Quinton who?"

"No one!" I shout. "Just some stupid guy I hung out with at school."

"Quinton Landing," Lincoln says, his voice firm. "The guy you were with the night you were arrested. The guy who went free while you didn't. Is *he* the one who put his hands on you?"

Why would he do that?

Say his name in front of everyone.

In seconds, my sister and Grace will be looking up Quinton Landing. Sierra will examine every social profile of his before sending the information to my brothers.

Lincoln won't sit back and allow me to remain silent.

I slap my hand onto the couch before standing. "Can we talk in private?"

He nods.

I walk around the coffee table, all eyes on me, and Lincoln follows me to my bedroom.

Whipping around, I face him, a deep scowl on my face. "Why would you do that?"

"Do what?" He raises a brow, and my outrage heightens that he'd ask *do what*, as if he didn't just barge in here.

"Go and say his name in front of everyone." I shake my head, grimacing. "How'd you even find out about Quinton?"

When I dated Quinton, I didn't talk about him with my family. Sure, I briefly mentioned I went on a few dates with a guy, but I tended to be more private, knowing how they like to get involved. I was in college, living the life, and wanted to keep that life to myself for as long as I could.

"Why wouldn't I say his name?" Lincoln asks. "Is he the guy who did that to you?"

I bite into my lower lip.

"It was him, wasn't it?"

I'm not much of a liar.

There's a difference between lying and hiding information from someone.

As Lincoln stares at me, his eyes filled with concern, I can't lie to his face.

I bow my head and nod, a flight of embarrassment soaring through me, though relief also treads behind it.

"Please, Cass, please turn him in," he begs, his voice nearly breaking.

"Just ..." I blow out an uneasy breath. "Give me a day to digest everything, okay? I hadn't planned for this to happen today. I'm bruised up." I move my gaze to him, narrowing my eyes. "I'm very upset with you, and I need to let my mind rest for a minute before I do anything."

His stare is pained in my direction. "I don't want you staying here alone."

"Grace—"

He keeps talking. "Grace won't be able to do anything if Quinton comes back to mess with you."

I nod in agreement. Nor would I want to put Grace in that situation. I feel bad enough that Quinton came here, and all night, I've waited for her to ask if it's safe to stay here. Grace doesn't like being alone; she checks that the alarm is set numerous times before going to bed at night. There's a history there that I haven't felt comfortable enough to ask about yet.

"Trust me, no one in my family will leave me alone right now. Even though I wish they would for a moment." My shoulders slump. "Quinton hasn't returned in days. He came over, we fought, and it happened. He freaked out as soon as he realized what he'd done."

"If no one can stay with you, you call me, okay?"

As much as I want to tell him I'd prefer it was him staying at my side, I don't.

I don't because I'm still so angry with him.

"Okay," I whisper.

"Promise not to ignore me."

"I'm not making that promise," I say. "I'm angry with you, Lincoln. Pissed off beyond belief that you went behind my back."

"Hate me if you want, but at least I'll know you're safe." He takes my hand in his, careful at first, waiting to see if I'll pull away, and when I don't, he uses it to pull me into his hold. "If it takes you hating me to keep you safe, then I guess the heartache and pain I'm experiencing is worth it because your safety is the most important thing to me. Not my heart, not my feelings. *You*."

I shake in his arms and choke back a sob.

What do I do?

I can't forgive him. I trusted him, and he broke my heart.

CHAPTER TWENTY-FIVE

Lincoln

"WHAT DID you do to make Georgia not hate you anymore?" I ask Archer, sipping on my coffee and narrowing my eyes at him. "I still can't believe you said something to Cohen."

Sleep was like a blocked-off street to me last night. All I thought about was Cassidy.

Is she safe?

Will Quinton hurt her again?

Will she ever forgive me?

With our talk after I returned to her house, mentioning Quinton, I don't think she hates me. I'm scared that she won't trust me any longer, and if you can't trust someone fully, can you be with them? I don't want to have a half-assed relationship with someone who is on the fence on whether they can share their deepest secrets with me.

I'd been tested, and I failed.

I failed and told my brother what I'd said I wouldn't.

Somehow, someway, I need to earn her trust back while also fighting for her to go against Quinton.

In the end, do I regret telling my brother? No.

Because it might convince Cassidy to turn Quinton in.

There's a stronger pulling force alongside me now.

Archer gapes at me. "Dude, don't try it. You knew I'd tell him."

I scrub a hand over my face, not admitting that he's right.

"And as far as the Georgia hating me question, I'm not sure how she doesn't hate me." He chuckles. "My advice is to do everything in your power to make things right and earn her trust back."

"It's hard to earn back her trust when all I can think about is that motherfucker hurting her."

"Don't get yourself in trouble, brother. You've already gone to prison once."

I shift in my seat. "What would you do if someone did that to Georgia?"

He delivers a dark look at the thought. "Rip their head off and feed it to them through a straw."

That's how my brother understands feelings. You ask how he'd feel if it happened to someone he loved. Otherwise, the dude is cold as the Arctic.

"Exactly," I deadpan. "You can't expect me to sit back and forget about it. I want to rip his head off and feed it to him through a spoon … it'd be more hands-on."

Archer holds up a finger. "A. I don't have a criminal record." He holds up another. "B. I'm in love with Georgia. Are you in love with Cassidy?"

I stay quiet.

Am I in love with Cassidy?

It's an internal battle.

I've never been *in love* with anyone. Or so I thought.

But what is love? Is there a specific destination, a specific rhythm your heart follows until a light dings inside your head that says, *Hey dumbass, you love this person?*

How do you know you love someone when love is an invisible thing?

"Think about it," he says, interrupting my thoughts. "Think about the risk and your feelings for her. And then do whatever you need to do to protect her."

———

WHAT I'M ABOUT to do will create the opposite of convincing Cassidy not to hate me.

But hey, if I already started off by disappointing her in this situation, might as well keep adding to the list that'll only lead me deeper into the hole of her possibly never speaking to me again.

"I have some information," I tell Maliki and Rex.

Not only did sleep evade me last night, but I also spent most of the time looking up Quinton. From what it appears on his Instagram, dude is a prick who regularly uses hashtags like #richkids, #getlikeme, #bejealous. His feed is full of photos of him and his frat brothers in their loafers and button-ups, lined up with beers in their hands, and sporting Gucci belts. I had to pour myself a drink out of embarrassment for him.

Hopefully, it'll change to #iscurrentlyincarcerated next.

Before leaving Cassidy's, I put Rex's and Kyle's numbers into my phone. We've shared a few texts here and there, but I asked to get together, so I could give them everything I know about Quinton. Kyle is a police officer, and from what I've heard, Rex is our generation's Kevin Mitnick—only without the criminal charges.

That's what led me to Rex's kick-ass house, and I'm not that easily impressed when it comes to real estate. The guy has everything teched out. I could spend all day asking him questions.

"Whatcha got, bro?" Rex asks.

"The guy who hit her is Quinton Landing. He's also the guy who was in her car the night she was arrested. He got to walk free. She obviously didn't." I suck in a deep breath. "A while back, she told me her ex was the biggest drug dealer on campus, to which she didn't know, and he borrowed her car. That's why there were drugs in it. If you put two and two together, Quinton's face lights up in guilt every damn time."

"Landing." Rex snaps his fingers, searching for words. "Name sounds familiar."

"From Landing Holdings?" Kyle asks.

I nod. "I'm going to pay him a visit. Is Cassidy still at Sierra's?"

Maliki texted me last night, letting me know that Cassidy was crashing with them.

"She is, but last I heard, she plans to stay at her place tonight," Rex replies with a hint of disapproval. "We're going to make sure one of us is there with her at all times."

Oh boy, Cass will love that.

"Let's rewind back to your previous statement," Kyle says. "It's not smart for you to *pay him a visit*. You're fresh out of prison, and the last thing you need is to go back."

It's a struggle not to smile at his comment. His concern over me returning to prison means he doesn't see me as a threat to his sister. If he did, he wouldn't give two shits about me being locked up again because it'd mean I'd be away from Cassidy.

"And here we thought you didn't like him," Rex says to his brother with a smirk.

Kyle shoots me an apologetic smile. "Sorry, dude. I was worried about my sister."

"Nah, it's cool," I reply. "I'd probably do the same if I had a sister."

"Do you know this Quinton guy?" Rex asks.

"Not personally," I reply. "I looked at his social media, know his brother and family, but that's it. I wanted to make sure I gave you guys his name, so you're as updated as I am." I turn my attention to Kyle. "You have connections to look into him, to possibly get him arrested even if Cass doesn't go to the cops. That's your job." I direct my gaze to Rex. "Your job is to try to find whatever shit you can on him ... and to get me an address."

———

REX SCORED me the address I was looking for in ten minutes. They weren't lying. Dude has skills. Without waiting for them, I got in my car, plugged the address into my GPS, and was on my way.

Thirty minutes later, I'm pulling into a neighborhood I've frequented enough that I know the gate code. Apparently, they don't change that shit for years. I drive past million-dollar house after million-dollar house and cut a right before parking across the street from a two-story red-brick home.

It seems too expensive for a college student, so it might be his family's home, or he could live off-campus. I'm sure the guy would rather be in a home like this than some stinky frat house. Not sure if this is where he's at, and wanting more information, I snatch my phone from the cupholder to call Rex and confirm this is Quinton's current address. I stop after unlocking my screen when a silver Benz pulls into the drive.

The driver's door opens, and a man in a fitted black suit steps out.

A man I recognize.

I do the same, slamming my door shut behind me, and unlike him, I'm in a black jacket and jeans when I move toward him.

The guy, as if sensing my presence, turns around, squinting in my direction. "Lincoln Callahan?" He cocks his head to the side, attempting to appear casual, but there's no missing the way his shoulders straighten. "What's up, man?"

That's right.

Be nervous because your family shit-talked mine to death.

Without bothering with small talk, I say, "Where's Quinton, Christopher?"

He sniffs, his face overconfident. "What do you want with my brother?"

I clench my hands. "I want him to stop putting his hands on women."

The air goes quiet, leaves blowing across the drive and over our feet.

"The fuck are you talking about?" Christopher asks, that overconfidence slipping away like the clients he poached from us.

"He hurt a woman, choked her, and she has the evidence." A tone of certainty and warning is clear with my response.

"What?" he hisses. "Is she going to the cops?"

"She's considering it."

"What's her name?" he stutters, his Ivy League education not strong enough to have trained him for this conversation.

"You'll find out when she files the police report against him."

I stop myself from disclosing Quinton's drug dealing. It'd be stupid to talk to Christopher because he'll call his brother to give him a heads-up as soon as I leave here.

Before I turn around to leave, Christopher, with a voice brimming with snark, says, "Might want to be careful. You wouldn't want to go back to prison, would you?"

This smug motherfucker.

"I've already been there once," I sneer at him, my lips curling into a cold smile. "What's another sentence? Especially if it's punishment for beating the shit out of the guy who put his hands on my girlfriend."

That smugness falls to the ground along with the leaves. "I'll talk to my brother."

Without a word, I turn around and return to my car. He stands in his drive, watching me, before hastily shoving his hand into his pocket and dragging out his phone.

I do the same and dial Rex's number as soon as I return to my car. "That's his brother's address. I need Quinton's campus addy."

"On it."

Just in case Christopher gets slick and calls the police for my trespassing, I drive off, and Rex has a new address for me as I'm pulling out of the neighborhood.

"Text it to me," I demand.

"You're not doing this alone," Rex argues. "We don't want you to get in any more trouble."

"I got this. You just go to Cassidy in case Quinton tries to get to her."

CHAPTER TWENTY-SIX

Cassidy

"HEY, SIS," Rex says over the phone. "I need to come over. My Wi-Fi is down, and I have some work to do."

Even though he can't see me, I roll my eyes. "You're going to make a thirty-minute drive to my house to use Wi-Fi when you can go to any coffee shop or to another sibling's—who all live much closer to you, by the way? Seems legit and not at all suspicious."

He chuckles. "Someone needs to be there with you. Maliki has to go into work, so I'm clocking in."

Clocking in.

I hate that I'm like a job to them.

"Look, I'm fine here on my own," I say, chugging the rest of my water. "Plus, Grace is here, so I won't be alone when Maliki and Sierra leave. Problem solved. Go fake need Wi-Fi somewhere else."

"The Wi-Fi is down everywhere else."

He hangs up, and ten minutes later, there's a knock on the door. I answer it to find Carolina and Rex standing in the doorway. Since he lives a good half hour away, no way was he sitting at home, struggling to connect to Wi-Fi.

"Oh, look," Sierra says, gasping dramatically. "What a surprise."

"Shush," I grumble, shooting her a dirty look. "You knew the *surprise* was coming."

Carolina gives me a hug hello, and then Sierra gives me a hug good-bye. She tells me to call or text if I need anything.

"If you're going to play babysitter, at least order some pizza," I tell Rex as we make our way into the living room.

He chuckles. "I can do that in exchange for the Wi-Fi."

"Oh, yes, the Wi-Fi."

―――――

"CAN I say something without you being pissed at me?" Rex asks.

Grace, Carolina, and he are all in the living room with me as we watch TV and devouring slices of greasy, cheesy pizza.

"Depends on what it is you say." I pop a pepperoni into my mouth.

"You shouldn't be mad at Lincoln," he says matter-of-factly. "You know that, right?"

I point at him with my slice of pizza. "Yep, that definitely pisses me off."

It's a topic I've battled with myself over. Since I kicked Lincoln out, I've done nothing but think about our argument, think about how I asked him to leave with such sorrow filling my heart. I've thought about what I'd do in a situation like that, whether it be the person I'm falling in love with, a close friend, or a sibling.

How hard would it be to keep something like that from others?

To know they could be in trouble but wouldn't do anything about it?

To know that something worse could happen?

"Come on," he says with a chuckle. "Hear me out first."

My brother is brilliant, one of the smartest men I know, and his problem-solving skills are out of this world. He also has a heart of gold. At the beginning, his and Carolina's relationship had some bumps in the road because she was keeping secrets from him—the same way I did with Lincoln.

"Fine," I mutter. "Let me hear it."

"Our situation was similar but not similar."

I scoff, "Uh, that's not a great way to start because it doesn't make any sense."

He sets his plate to the side, scoots to the edge of the couch, and rests his elbows on his knees, pinning his attention on me. "I was worried about Carolina and looked through her phone ... and hacked into her ex's shit ... all to protect her." A glimpse of frustration flashes along his face at the memory, and Carolina scoots in closer to him, squeezing his knee. "When you care about someone that much, you care about their safety more than them possibly being mad at you. Had Lincoln not gone to someone, had he not wanted you to go to the cops, I'd be questioning his feelings for you. At least talk to him, and please, for the love of God, go to the cops."

His words are another punch in the reality face for me.

Would I have questioned Lincoln's actions later if Quinton were to come back and do more damage or if he decided he wanted me to permanently go away, so he wouldn't worry about me tattling on him?

And had I forced Lincoln to keep that secret, how bad would it have torn him up inside if Quinton were to take things more serious?

I sigh. "I know ... I'm just coming to terms with everything."

"Have you thought any more about going to the cops?" Rex asks, an expectant look on his face.

I stay quiet and slowly shake my head.

"When my ex threatened me with a sex tape, I was terrified to go to the cops," Carolina starts but then hesitates when all eyes fall on her. "I was scared of retribution from him, but I knew it was what I had to do. I had to do it for me, so I'd no longer live in fear and also to protect other women he might hurt in the future." Her eyes are wide as she focuses on me. "It's scary, I know, but you'll feel better. I had a longer timeframe to do it since most of my proof was digital, but it's not that easy with you. When your bruises fade, the chances of him getting the punishment he deserves will also fade. I'll go with you. I'll be by your side if you want someone who's experienced it."

Carolina, my brother's sweet best friend turned girlfriend. They're opposites of each other—her quiet and reserved, him loud and outgoing.

"Me too," Grace says. "Whatever you need from me, I'm there."

Their support means everything to me.

It's a comfort to know I have women at my side who understand what I'm going through and are offering to help. And Carolina and Lincoln are right about Quinton having the power to hurt another woman if he gets away with what he did to me. Or what if he sells drugs to someone and they OD?

I play with my hands in my lap. "I'll think about it." Standing, I force a smile. "I need to use the bathroom."

Moving toward my bedroom, I dig my phone from my pocket and call Lincoln.

He doesn't answer.

CHAPTER TWENTY-SEVEN

Lincoln

"YOU TOUCH HER AGAIN, and I'll kill you."

Growing up, I got along with most people, so I wasn't involved in many fights. That changed when I went to prison. There, you have to prove yourself, prove you can't be messed with. Prison is where I established my fight experience.

Tonight's fight isn't to prove myself.

It's to prove that Cassidy can't be messed with. Quinton needs to know that if he pays Cass another visit, there will be hell to pay.

On the drive to Quinton's campus apartment, my mind raced with reminders of Rex and Kyle telling me to wait for them and Archer warning me to stay out of trouble. Going back to prison isn't something I want, but if it's for Cassidy, I'll do it.

The new address Rex provided was correct. No one spared me a look as I took the stairs to the fifth floor, knocked on the apartment door, and asked if he was Quinton. The moment he said yes, I gripped him around his scrawny throat, dragged him through the entryway, and threw him against the wall—similar to what it appeared he'd done with Cassidy.

He yelled, "What the hell?" at the same time I kicked the door shut with my shoe, blocking out as much noise as I could.

He cries out when I draw back my fist and punch him. My fist stings when it connects with his jawbone, a throb shooting up my veins. He slides down the wall and slumps to the tiled floor like a crumpled pile of laundry.

I kneel down to his level, inches from him, spit flying from my lips as I snarl, "Go near her again, and I'll kill you."

It's not an empty threat.

Cassidy's bruise will haunt me until the day I die. I'd do anything in my power to prevent any harm or hurt to Cassidy.

"Fine, whatever," he groans, his head falling against the floor, small sprinkles of blood next to him. "She isn't worth this shit." He nearly rolls into the fetal position, in fear of another strike from me. Sweat lines his forehead. Blood, alongside slobber, drips from his mouth.

I bend my knee back, gearing to give him a swift kick to the ribs, but he cowers, staring up at me in alarm.

"Hurt me any worse, and I'll make sure you go back to prison." His eyes are panicked, his words sputtered. "Don't think I don't know who you are, Lincoln Callahan."

I scoff, my hand sore and shaking. "Go to the cops? How about we go now, huh? We can explain why I beat the shit out of you." I deliver a mocking smile. "It'll be fun."

He spits at my feet.

"Stay away from her." I bend at the knee, my face in his. "Her brother is a cop. I have connections from being *locked up*, and we've hacked into your shit. Mess with her again, and you'll regret it. Your daddy won't be able to get you out of that mess with your drug-dealing ways."

I shoot him a cold smile full of warning before nudging his knee with the toe of my shoe. I spent less than ten minutes with the asshole, but hopefully, I've knocked some sense into him. As I'm walking out, I rub my hand down the outside of my pants, wiping away Quinton's blood.

I'm practically bouncing on my toes from the adrenaline while returning to my car. Quinton didn't put up much of a fight and backed down in seconds. If he's scared of me, then he'll stay away from Cass.

As I slide into the driver's seat and pluck my phone from my pocket, I find a missed call from Cassidy. My palms sweat as I stare at her name, my heart pounding harder than it did when I was punching Quinton, and I don't waste a second before calling her back.

"Hey," I breathe out into the speaker when she answers.

"Hi," she replies, her tone timid and shy.

There's a brief silence as I wait for her to speak, unsure of where to go with this conversation.

"I've decided to go to the cops," she finally says. "I'm going to turn Quinton in."

For her to tell me that, I feel a relief stronger at this moment than I did the day I was released from prison. I want Cass to get her justice more than I wanted mine.

Quinton will look real pretty when they bring him in beat up.

"Will you go with me?" she asks.

Her asking me this means so much. It hands a piece of the trust she lost from me back, giving me another chance to prove to her that I'll be by her side, that I'm always here for her.

"Of course," I reply.

She shouldn't even have to wonder if I'd go with her.

"Will you …" She hesitates, and I hear her heavy breathing. "Will you stay with me tonight?"

"I'll be there in twenty." I need to run home, shower, and then be back at my girl's side.

CHAPTER TWENTY-EIGHT

Cassidy

I'M DOING the right thing.

Those are the five words I've been singing to myself like a lullaby song on repeat in a newborn's room.

"I'm scared," I tell Lincoln as I change into my pajamas.

I called and asked him to come over.

He did.

If I dig deep inside myself, if I claw into my heart, I have no doubt I can trust Lincoln. Am I still upset over him telling Archer? Yes. But I'd much rather have a man more worried about my safety than pacifying me.

His arrival shocked everyone in the living room. I hadn't told them that I invited him over, nor had I told them that I'd decided to go to the police. I needed to know that Lincoln had my back, would be by my side, before I made any declarations. Lincoln made small talk with everyone as we all yawned like we'd been on no-sleep binges.

Ten minutes ago, Grace went to bed, and after confirming Lincoln was staying with me fifteen times, Rex and Carolina went home. It's nice, knowing I have so many people who care about my well-being. I should've known I wasn't so alone earlier.

"Scared of Quinton?" Lincoln asks, stopping to stare at me from across the room.

I nod. "After my arrest, he threatened me, my family, to do things to us. I'm terrified he'll retaliate."

Lincoln peels off his shirt, revealing his six-pack. "He seems more bark than bite."

"How do you know?" I raise a brow, eyeing him up and down—not only in curiosity, but also because, damn, he's hot. Even in situations like this, I'm still attracted to him in every sense.

He blows out a breath. "Honesty is the best policy, right?"

"Honesty is the best policy."

"Your brothers and I ..." He rubs at his forehead. "We tracked Quinton down."

"Why am I not surprised?" I mutter.

"Quinton's family owns a competing business to my family's. After my father's and my arrests, his family went and poached all of our clients, forcing us to shut the company down. As soon as I found out the name, I knew who it was."

"So, you'd met him before?"

"Before tonight? No. But I know his brother. We went to school together."

"Whoa, what do you mean, before tonight?"

"I paid him a visit ... told him to leave you alone."

That's when my eyes travel to his hands. I noticed a few scratches on one but didn't pay it too much mind because there's already enough stuff on *my mind*. Now, it makes sense. "Is that what the messed-up fists are from?"

There isn't one inch of shame on his features. "Possibly."

"Lincoln"—I release a heavy sigh and sink down on my bed—"I don't want you getting in trouble over me."

"Cass," he says, his voice soft-spoken. "I'll never stop standing up for the woman I'm falling in love with."

Good thing I'm sitting because this is the moment I'd fall on my face.

Our conversation comes to a halt.

My brain, though?

It spirals, spinning with countless emotions and questions.

I'm not sure how I'm looking at him, but as he peers at me, panic sets over his features.

He blows out a deep breath, a labored breath, and falls to his knees in front of me. "Cass, I know we've been on the fence, but when I saw what happened to you, it killed my soul."

I stare at him, bewildered.

He continues speaking, continues warming my heart, confirming that this won't be the end of us and that I can still be happy. "Your pain caused me pain. Is there a possibility I can get in trouble for kicking his ass? Maybe. But I'll take those consequences if that means he'll stay away from you." He abruptly stops, his face nervous and frenzied as he eyeballs me. He grabs my hand in his, massaging the top of it, and softens his voice. "When it comes down to it, yes, I'm falling in love with you. I didn't go into this thinking that, and it's only been a couple of months since we started hanging out, so it might be considered early, but you feel what you feel, you know? I've never felt this way with anyone, and from what I guess, it's love because it's surreal to me."

Oh.

My.

Freaking.

God.

Did he say that?

I wish I could rewind that moment and listen to it over and over again. All my awareness is on us, on our connection, on our emotions toward each other. I squeeze his hand, my heart jumping in my chest, thankful for *finally* some happiness and some damn good news. Lincoln has been my savior, and I'm so happy I found a man who knows how to handle me, how to care for me, how to love me. And in part, I'm going to do the same for him.

Dropping his hand, I reach down, and with shaking hands, I cup his chin. Tears fall down my cheeks, my feelings for him finally being thrown out in their truth.

I taste the salt of my tears as I say, "I'm falling in love with you too. I'm sorry for being angry with you … for keeping the Quinton thing

... the bruise from you." My words are all flowing into nearly one, as I'm frantic and scared that I won't be able to express all my feelings before this moment is over. "I was just in shock, but I love you."

His hand blankets mine over his face, shaking over my shaking ones, as we pour out our truths like the drinks we serve.

Straight up.

No bullshit.

All honesty.

Me and him.

I sniffle back the tears. Unlike what they've been lately, these ones are from relief, from happiness, from the excitement of being loved. He nuzzles his face in my palm, his rough scruff rubbing against the sensitive skin. We relax against each other. It's as if a tension bubble had been popped.

When he pulls away, our eyes meet, and he reaches out, his thumb abrasive as he wipes away my tears. "I love you, Cassidy."

I gulp, nodding, and blurt out, "I love you, Lincoln."

———

IT'S the ass crack of dawn when my doorbell rings.

And rings.

And rings.

Oh God, here we go again.

Last night started in hell and ended in heaven. After Lincoln and I finally broke down and explored our emotions before throwing them out to the other, the night relaxed. When he asked to see my neck, to see how it was healing, there was no hesitation this time. He stared at it, anguish in his eyes as if he wished he could heal it with them.

We lay in bed that night, his finger running along the bare skin of my thigh, and talked for hours—about anything and everything.

Lincoln slips on a pair of sweats, throws on a hoodie, and says, "I got it," before leaving the bedroom.

"Oh, man, do I have some fucking news for you," I hear Rex say from the other room.

I hurriedly dress and join them in the living room, where Rex is standing with a stack of papers tucked underneath his armpit. Grace is on the couch, staring at him in curiosity, while we all await his early morning pop-in information.

"Quinton, your little ex," Rex starts, his gaze darting to me. "The guy has quite the drug setup going on. Not only is it him and a few friends, but there are dirty cops on his team as well." He snatches the stapled papers from his arm and throws them down onto the coffee table. "You gotta read this shit."

So much dawns on me.

Quinton being comfortable with one officer and then uneasy when the other showed up.

Him doing the bro hug with the officer.

He'd been working with the first one who approached my car.

"We need to do something about this," Rex says.

"I know a way." Lincoln grabs the stack of papers. "I'll be back."

He smacks a kiss to my cheek and leaves without providing any additional information.

CHAPTER TWENTY-NINE

Lincoln

THIS TIME, I don't bother going to his office.

I go straight to the source and pray he doesn't call the cops on me.

Isla answers the door, wearing a pink silk robe. "Lincoln?"

"Where's Louis?" I rush out. "I need to speak to him."

"What?" she stutters, a string of disappointment crossing her features that I'm not there for her.

"I need to speak to your husband."

She stares at me, speechless.

It's a plus for me that their doorway is massive enough to fit a semi, and I duck around her before rushing inside their home, marble flooring underneath my squeaky sneakers. Louis is sitting in the kitchen, a full breakfast plate in front of him and the paper in his hands, all old-school style.

He frowns when I come into his view. "Jesus, why do I keep seeing you?"

I'm sure the man your wife had an affair with isn't what you want to see before starting your day.

I hold up Rex's papers. "I have a case for you."

He puts the paper down and picks up his coffee. "If it's about the assault, you need to take that up with the police. We don't deal with small crimes like that."

"Is a massive drug operation on a college campus a big enough crime for you?"

He pauses mid-sip of his coffee. "Go on."

I slam the folder down on the table in front of him, causing his coffee cup to rattle. "It's all right here. Texts, voicemails, the guys involved. My guy managed to speak to a man who used to work for them. When he told them he wanted out, they beat the shit out of him. If you can grant him immunity, he'll tell you everything you need to know from the dirty cops they're paying off, to their connections, to where they're buying and making the drugs." I blow out a breath before going on. "Cassidy, the woman he assaulted, is filing a police report against him today. Her brother is a police officer with Blue Beech PD. His thoughts are, as soon as they talk to Cassidy, they'll go pick Quinton up for questioning. That means, he'll basically be delivered to you."

He gawks at me. "How do I know this is factual evidence?"

"I know I'm not the guy you want to trust, but this is worth looking into." I gesture to the documents, the ones I read during stoplights on my drive here. "You think I had time to forge these? That I'd make this shit up?"

He pays the evidence a quick glance, a *this is a joke* glance. "I'll look through it."

"That's all I'm asking. And there are some dirty cops in there you might want to look into as well."

That piques his interest, and he starts thumbing through the papers.

"Do with it what you please. I have to get back to my girl."

Isla gasps as I walk by her, and I don't glance back once.

CHAPTER THIRTY

Cassidy

"YOU'RE the bravest person I know," Lincoln tells me on our way into the police station.

It's scary.

More terrifying than the one I was actually taken to when I was arrested.

The drive here was filled with me battling with myself. Me coming here would be a clear *fuck you* to Quinton, and that scared the shit out of me. I remembered his intimidation, all the threats he'd put against my family and me, and I silently prayed that they were all empty.

Surely, he wouldn't be that dumb.

Not to mention, Quinton isn't a hardened criminal who likes to get his hands dirty. We went for couples pedicures on the regular.

I'm brave because I have a great support system. Brave because I have my family and friends with me. Some of them have stayed outside, not wanting to overwhelm me—Grace, Georgia, Lola, Carolina, Chloe, and Rex.

We take small steps into the station. Kyle, my mother, Sierra, and Lincoln all at my side, forming a line of protection with me. All eyes turn to us at the sound of the door shutting, and the first officer I see is him—the one who was chummy with Quinton and arrested me instead. Fear spirals up my spine, and if my hands weren't clasped with Lincoln's and my mother's, I'd be out the door, running and changing my mind.

Kyle shakes his head, muttering a curse underneath his breath, knowing he's the dirty one since I described him to a T on the drive here. It's one thing my brother hates—dirty cops. He plays by the rule book as best as he can, treats everyone with respect, and doesn't use having a badge to his advantage.

When I make it to the front counter, I clear my throat before saying, "I'd like to report an assault."

The woman nods and asks me to follow her before calling for a man to come with us. A heavier-set officer steps up and waddles his way toward us, gulping down a coffee on his way.

This is it.

There's no going back.

We cram into a small, chilly room. I take the chair across from the officers, my mom occupying the one next to me and Lincoln collapsing into the one on my other side. Everyone else stands behind me, and a sense of comfort settles through my body at the feel of Sierra's hands clasping my shoulders, a gentle squeeze of assurance that she's here for me.

The officers are kind as I speak and don't seem frustrated as I slowly ease into the story of what happened the night Quinton came to my house and put his hands on me. My mother cries, short sobs coming from her, but I stay strong. Not one tear drips down my face. A few times, my voice nearly breaks, but I suck in deep breaths to stop it.

I am strong.

I got this.

He will go down for touching me.

Goose bumps rush up my arms when I ease the sweater off my shoulders, revealing a cotton cami and the bruise. The woman officer snaps photos from dozens of angles and has me sign my statement before sliding a restraining order across the table. After I fill it out, they tell me they'll be in contact.

As I walk out of the station, a heavy weight the size of an elephant drops off my shoulders.

CHAPTER THIRTY-ONE

Lincoln

"I DON'T KNOW how welcome you are here."

My attention shoots to Archer's line of vision at his aggressive tone. He's gripping a towel in his hand and shooting daggers at Louis, who's walking in our direction, wearing determination and an expensive suit, sticking out like a sore thumb in the bar.

"Not here to see you," Louis deadpans.

"It's cool," I tell Archer, stalking over to them.

Archer stares at me like I've lost my mind before understanding dawns on him. I filled him in on Cassidy and Quinton's situation—not giving him all the details because I know Cassidy wants some specifics kept between us.

I jerk my head toward the end of the bar. Louis nods, his strides long as he meets me.

"What's up?"

This has to be good news, right?

He wouldn't pay me a visit for the fuck of it.

"You handed me some useful information," he says with a nod of certainty and appreciation.

"I know," I reply, wanting to get to the point. "Now, are you going to do something about it?"

He has to.

Quinton needs to go down for his crimes.

He was arrested shortly after Cassidy made her statement, but it didn't take long for his attorney to show up, and he was bailed out in an hour. The power of having money and people in high places. Quinton's issue now is that he has Louis against him, and this motherfucker likes to bring criminals down. He's a fighter, and he has been featured in documentaries about how many cases he's won and how well he convinces jurors that criminals need to go down for their crimes. He doesn't fuck around, and that's exactly who we need on our side to take Quinton down.

"Already started," Louis replies. "We've tracked him, and we know he's been bailed out. We've kept it hush-hush, not going to his attorney, until we find out what cops he's working with." He taps his hand against the bar. "Just wanted to keep you updated."

With Kyle's connections, he's informed us on everything Quinton related the best he can. Cassidy's restraining order is active, and we make sure she's not alone. She calls us overbearing, but we're not giving Quinton any chance to retaliate.

"I appreciate that." I tilt my head in his direction. "How about a drink on the house?"

Louis shakes his head. "Not interested in having a drink poured by the man who was sleeping with my wife."

Louis is the most straight-to-the-point, no-bullshit man I've met in my life.

With that, he turns and walks out of the bar.

———

IT'S Cassidy's first night back at work.

It seems like it's been forever since she's been here, and I've missed her. I've been waiting in anticipation to see her walk through those doors.

I've missed all the jokes she added to her drink orders, missed our closing times together, missed walking her out. Most of all, I've missed just spending time with her, hearing her laugh, seeing her smile.

I'm so damn pussy-whipped.

So damn Cassidy-whipped.

She's been hanging out with Georgia, Lola, and Grace today. Even though there isn't one of us guys with them, I have no doubt that with the four of them, they'd kick Quinton's ass if he tried to pull anything.

She wanted her bruise to completely heal before returning. Our close friends know what happened, but she doesn't want other employees or customers to see any signs of the bruise.

I've stayed at her house, in her bed, every night since the evening before she reported Quinton. We've ordered takeout, binge-watched TV shows, and talked.

You know what we've also done?

We've exchanged *I love you*s as if they were simple hellos since the night we tore out our hearts and gifted them to the other. That night, sitting on her bed, is really the first time the words fell from my mouth. The Callahan household wasn't one to express themselves. We didn't share hugs and *I love you*s. With the exception of my mother a few times, Cassidy is the only other person I've said those words to. Hell, she's probably the only other person who will have my heart enough for me to do so. She owns every piece of me in so many ways.

All eyes are on her when she struts into the bar as if nothing has changed, and she didn't spend days in her own personal Quinton hell.

That's right.

My girl is strong as hell.

A fighter.

"Welcome back, Cassidy," Cohen calls out. "We're glad you're here."

Archer nods and echoes Cohen. "Welcome back."

I grin, a smile I can't contain creasing my face, and a pleasant hum warms my blood. She wastes no time in circling the bar, heading straight in my direction, and kissing me on the lips. There are no gasps of shock. It's no surprise to our friends. Even though we haven't come out and told people we were dating, from the way we've been around each other, from my sleepovers and protectiveness of her, they'd be stupid if they didn't know.

"Back to reality," I say against her lips before pressing mine against them again.

"Back to reality," Cassidy says. "Only now, it's better."

I raise a brow. "Oh yeah?"

"Yeah, because now, people can know we're in love with each other …" She stops and winks. "And that someday, you're going to be my baby daddy."

CHAPTER THIRTY-TWO

Cassidy

TACO TUESDAY IS EXACTLY what I need for my first night out.

My bruise is healed, but sometimes, as I'm getting dressed or in the shower, I peek down at my neck, expecting the reminder of Quinton's abuse. At times, I feel like the journey I've taken on since my arrest has been the one intended to make me a stronger woman. Even with my father's infidelities, my parents did everything they could to create a perfect *unicorns and rainbows* life for me.

Quinton prepared me for the real world and taught me how it's not always perfect, not always safe, and not always the way you want it to be.

It also led me to the man who stole my heart and protected it through that journey.

Tonight's dinner is being thrown at the Callahan-slash-Georgia penthouse. The last and only time I've been here was the day I walked in on Lincoln and Isla whispering like two kids on the playground, and as everyone knows, I hate whispering.

I expected my stomach to turn, for nausea to swarm my body, but when I walk in and see my friends, I smile.

Smile because, like Lincoln, I've found something real—authentic friendships I know will last over time. No matter what happens, no matter if I get in trouble, no matter if I try to run and hide, they'll have my back.

I rode with Grace. She hasn't stayed at the house much and doesn't mention where she's been sleeping. I'm worried her absence has something to do with me. Maybe she's worried Quinton could come back to finish me off and hurt her in the process.

The aroma of fresh-baked tortillas, quesadillas, and tacos smacks into my nostrils as I take a look around. There's no stopping me from laughing when I see the décor Georgia bought the day we went shopping. That day seems like an eternity ago after all the events that took place.

"Hey, girl, hey!" Georgia says, wrapping me up in a hug and leading me into the kitchen, where Silas and Archer are.

Silas is cooking while Archer is standing next to him, talking with a beer in his hand.

"Cassidy," Archer says as Georgia grips his shoulder, leaning into his side. "How have you been?"

I smile, happy that he asked. "Good ... better."

"I'm glad you're okay. I'm happy for you and my brother." He blows out a breath, and his face softens into an expression I've never seen him wear before. "I'm sorry for going behind your guys' backs and telling Cohen. I was in shock, unsure of what to do. As an employer, I know shit that happens out of work might not be my business, but also as an employer, I care about my employees—even with as standoffish as I am. I also know how much you mean to my brother, and if someone was hurting you, I wasn't sure how much further they'd go. So, I called Cohen to ask for advice, knowing that he'd call Maliki because that's the kind of guy he is."

"It's okay," I reply with all honesty. "You did the right thing."

Silas whips around, a spatula in his hand. "Does this mean you and baby Callahan are together?"

"It sure damn does," Lincoln says loud and clear as he enters the kitchen. With swift steps, he comes up behind me, wraps his strong arms around my waist, and places a gentle kiss on my ear. "Hi, baby."

"I'm swooning," Georgia says. "Seriously swooning."

Same, Georgia. Same.

A blush caresses my cheeks as everyone stares at us.

This is what I originally wanted from Lincoln.

This is what I wanted all those times I joked around with Lincoln but never thought I'd get.

His hands on me.

His mouth on me.

Him claiming me in front of everyone, making me feel wanted, making me feel like I could get a man who wouldn't turn his back on me.

Silas grins. "I like it. Another couple breaking through our *only friends* rule." He shakes his head. "Now, we're waiting on Grace and Finn."

"And then you and Lola," Georgia adds.

"Nah, Lola and I will be the only two who stick to the *just friends* pact."

"I wasn't aware we'd made a pact," Georgia replies.

"No, we did. In the beginning, Cohen said things were to stay strictly platonic between us and you and your friends." He shrugs. "Cohen made the rules, and we were supposed to follow them."

"Yeah, well, too bad Cohen doesn't make our rules," Georgia says with a frown. "And I'm going to kick his ass for telling you that."

"And speak of the devil," Silas calls out when Cohen, Jamie, and baby Isabella walk into the room.

Cohen has his tiny daughter wrapped in his arms, her head resting on his shoulder as he holds her tight.

My mind wanders to when Lincoln will be a father—how he'll hold our baby, how he'll love it, how we'll be as parents.

Whoa, getting way ahead of yourself there, Cass.

I can't help it. I want everything with him.

"What devil are we speaking of here?" Jamie asks, running her hand along Isabella's back as she sleeps.

"Your other half telling his friends that my friends and I are off-limits," Georgia says, resting her hand on her hip. "The audacity."

"I think he's learned his lesson on saying relationships are *off-limits*," Jamie says with a twinkle in her eyes as she stares up at her fiancé. "We broke the ultimate *off-limits* rule."

"True that," Silas says. "The baby mama's sister. That's on a whole different level."

Cohen narrows his eyes at Silas. "A particular situation, thank you very much."

He seems to be protective of Jamie and their relationship, but from what I've heard, it was hard in the beginning, so I don't blame him.

"Are the tacos ready?" Finn asks, walking in with Noah hanging off his back.

"Just about," Silas calls over.

I help Georgia along with Lola and Grace, who join us from the living room, set all the toppings for the tacos and quesadillas out on the massive kitchen island.

We eat. We drink. We play games.

Everyone, at least once, comments with how happy they are for Lincoln and me.

It's a great night to start my new life.

———

"MY FIRST TIME IN YOUR BED," I say to Lincoln, lounging against his headboard, moving my legs up and down his smooth sheets.

He was having a conversation with Archer, and out of exhaustion, I ventured to his room, undressed, and slipped into bed.

"About damn time," he says, shutting the door behind him. "I've been waiting for this day for what seems like forever."

"Oh, really?" I smile before giggling—the giggling is a result of too many margaritas since in sober life, I am not a giggler. "What were you waiting for?" Another damn giggle.

Ugh, I'm going to hate my giggling self in the morning.

He nods toward the bed. "To fuck you on those sheets. To screw you from behind and have you mask your moans with my pillow." He licks his lips, and I can imagine they taste like margarita salt since I convinced him to drink one with me. "To hold you when we're finished making love, and then in the morning, I'll make *your* favorite breakfast—Belgian waffles and scrambled eggs."

"What are you waiting for then?" My eyes flutter in his direction —another side effect of the damn liquor—and I slowly crawl across the bed on my hands and knees to where he's standing at the foot.

He hisses when my face comes into line with his waist, and I tug at his belt buckle.

I waste no time unzipping his pants and taking his cock out. Draping it along my palm, I rub a finger up and down the skin as it jerks in my hand.

"Oh," I say, wrapping my hand tightly around his cock and slowly stroking him. "This cock brings me so much pleasure."

His legs go straight, his body stiffening as I increase my pace. "And you bring it more pleasure."

Being with Lincoln is sex I've never experienced.

His touch is a different breed of intimacy.

When I glance up at him, his eyes are glued to my hand, to our connection, and I want to provide a better view. His knees buckle when I slip my fingers down his cock to make room for my mouth.

I stare up at him, watching his face and the changes it makes.

The way it forms an O when I suck on the head.

The way his mouth drops open as a gasp escapes it when I swirl my tongue around his balls.

The way he rasps, "Jesus Christ, Cass," from his throat.

"I'm close," he hisses. "Turn around, get on your hands and knees, and stick your ass in the air."

Anticipation showers through me as I do what he said. He climbs onto the bed behind me and places his palm to the base of my back, pushing me down to my stomach, and lifts up my legs. I gasp when he tears my pajama shorts and panties down my legs, and he tosses them over his shoulder as I peer back at him.

Bending over me, he grips my hips, tight and firm, and hauls me back up to my knees. Holding me in place as he stretches across the bed, he opens a drawer in the nightstand and plucks out a condom. I bite back the urge to ask why he has condoms in his drawer because he didn't ask me about the condoms I had in my nightstand.

Did he wonder the same thing when he got one from my nightstand?

Shoving his pants down his waist, not even bothering to take them off, he slips two fingers inside me.

"You're already soaked for me, baby," he practically growls.

"Always," I whisper, nearly panting for him.

Without warning, he thrusts inside me.

I hiss before releasing a long moan, taking in his large size, and hope Georgia and Archer are no longer in the living room. He lifts my shirt with one hand, holding it away from my waist, while lowering the other around my body to play with my clit.

He pounds into me.

I fuck him right back.

It's been too long since he's been inside me, and for once, I couldn't give two fucks about foreplay. The only playing I want is him inside me for as long as he can last.

Our harsh breathing occupies the room, the only sounds coming from us as we get each other off. My body swells with pressure, with intimacy, with love, and just as I'm about to scream out my release, his large palm grips the back of my head, shoving my face into the pillow.

Just like he wanted to.

My orgasm rips through me, just as strong as the first night we had sex, and he holds me tight as he finishes himself off, our flesh smacking together and making its own rhythm.

He groans out my name and slaps my ass as he comes inside the condom.

CHAPTER THIRTY-THREE

Lincoln

"DOES this mean we'll be new roomies?" Georgia asks the next morning.

Somehow, I got suckered into making *everybody* breakfast. Well, *buying* everybody breakfast because the first Belgian waffle I tried was an absolute fail. So, I told everyone to get dressed, and we're sitting at a table at Yellow Peep to get our waffles.

As soon as we sat down, I was reminded of Cassidy and me coming here after her community service—the day she thought she didn't look *dressed* to come into a restaurant like this when she didn't even realize how damn beautiful she was.

She is.

Inside and out.

"Oh my God." I hear from Cassidy, and at the same time, she covers her face.

I glance up to find the same waitress, Taylor, who helped us before, standing at the front of our table, a bright smile on her face.

Her smile broadens when she notices Cassidy and me, and she gestures to us with her pencil. "From the looks of it, I'm hoping this means you no longer see her as your little sister?"

Cassidy adds her other hand to cover her face as she groans.

Georgia snorts, her attention bobbing between Taylor and us. "What?"

"Nothing," Cassidy and I answer at the same time as she uncovers her face.

"Nope," Georgia says, shaking her head. "As soon as we give our drink orders, we're going to need that story."

"They came in a while back," Taylor chirps, apparently ready to answer for us. "And they were going back and forth about him seeing her as a little sister, and she was upset because she didn't want to say she was attracted to someone who saw her as a sibling ... something along those lines."

"I can't believe she told them that," Cassidy hisses so only I can hear.

Appeased with the answer, Georgia orders a mimosa with Cassidy doing the same. Archer and I opt for coffee and water, and Taylor scurries her tattletale self off to get our beverages.

Georgia straightens her napkin in her lap and leans into us. "Now, back to the conversation we were having prior to finding out you used to think of her as a little sister." Her gaze whips to me.

Archer grunts before mocking his girlfriend's voice. "Yes, totally. We don't need to discuss new roommates as a couple at all."

She turns to pat his chest with her palm. "That's right, baby."

Archer shakes his head and laughs, pinning his attention on Cassidy and me. "I'm just fucking with you. It's only fair to let my brother's girlfriend move in since I already moved Georgia in. Cassidy, you're welcome whenever."

Cassidy smiles at the invite before it collapses into a frown. "I don't think I can do that to Grace, though."

Georgia nods, wisping strands of hair out of her face that fell from the pigtail buns on the top of her head. "Yeah, I felt horrible too. I almost didn't do it, and that's why I waited until you agreed to move in because I didn't want to leave her alone."

Cassidy rubs the back of her neck, and I do the same, feeling a wire of tension up my neck. "If I do, will she have to move in with her parents?"

Georgia nods. "Probably."

"What's the deal with that?" I cut in. "What if we tell her we'll spring for rent until she finds another roommate? Problem solved."

I love the thought of Cassidy moving in with me, the thought of us calling the same place home and going to bed together every night.

Taylor delivers our drinks, all her attention on Cassidy and me, like she's waiting for me to drop to one knee and propose or some shit. It's as if we're the new couple she's fangirling over. It could be a compliment, but I hate attention on me, and from the way Cassidy tenses every time it happens, it's the same for her.

Georgia shakes her head, and with certainty, she says, "Grace won't stay somewhere overnight without another person there."

I cock my head to the side. "Why?"

"Not my story to tell," Georgia replies, not making eye contact with anyone and instead focusing on her mimosa. "But there's a reason I didn't agree to move until she had another roommate."

"I get that."

Cass and I have spent a lot of time with Grace since we've been hanging out at their house so much. Lately, she's been acting strange. Cassidy has noticed it too.

Is she worried that Cassidy will move out?

Hell, does Cass even want to move in with me?

I shake my head, remembering the smile she had when Archer invited her before the dread of leaving Grace clutched at her thoughts.

"It's cool," I say. "We're good where we're at, and Grace doesn't seem to mind me hanging out there." I reach under the table and squeeze Cassidy's thigh. "We have plenty of time to move in together."

"And who knows? The penthouse might be completely open for you two," Georgia says.

That catches my attention, and I focus on the couple across the table from us. "What?"

"We *maybe* found a second home—"

"A second home?" I blurt out. "A second home for what?"

"For us to hang out in ..." Georgia says before trailing off, as if she lost her train of thought.

"How did we go from you saying *let's be roommates* to you saying you're moving out?"

"Technically, we don't close on the house for another month," Georgia says. "Plus, Archer isn't selling the penthouse. He wants to keep both, and it's good news for you. When we move out, you guys will have the place to yourselves."

I stare at them, blinking, while processing the news that I wish Archer had given me. We're supposed to tell each other everything, especially something as big as this.

"The penthouse is yours to stay in for as long as you'd like," Archer says. "Georgia just keeps on girlie-ing up shit, so I figured we needed our own place for that."

The discussion has changed from Cassidy moving in with us to Georgia and Archer moving out. It'll be weird, not having them there with me, but I understand their reasoning. If I had the option to have a place with Cassidy solo or with roommates, I'd for sure take a place for just the two of us.

Now, I just need to figure out when we can make that leap in our relationship.

CHAPTER THIRTY-FOUR

Cassidy

I WALK into the kitchen to find Grace grading papers, notebooks spread out along the table and her laptop to the side. "Hey, girl."

She grins up at me, shutting her computer. "How did last night go? The first night at the boyfriend's?"

"It was ..." I'm no doubt beaming like those love-drunk yuppies in movies. "Amazing."

"Aw, yay! I'm so happy for you, Cass. You really deserve it. I think you're a great match." Her voice is genuine and soft, and if I were ever to cast an angel in a movie, it'd be her with that tone, her strawberry-blond hair, and her fair skin.

She stayed with her parents last night because I'd given her a heads-up that I was staying the night with Lincoln. He'd asked me to since it was something we'd never done before, and he said he wanted his sheets and bedroom to smell like me.

Hell, I wanted his sheets and his bedroom to smell like me to ward off any middle-aged women who might try to become his cougar.

Although I was unsure of how deep her not wanting to stay home alone was until breakfast this morning, I'd known she wasn't a fan, known she was always nervous at night, but I'd thought it was similar to me—a girl who had always been surrounded by company and wasn't used to being alone. After seeing the uneasiness on Georgia's face when Lincoln asked why, I know it's something deeper than that.

The nervousness on her face matches the nervousness on mine after Quinton's visit. Something similar happened with her, I'm sure of it, but what I'm not sure of is how to start a conversation about it.

Or if I even should.

I pull out the chair across from her, and my voice becomes hesitant as I take a seat. "Is there something wrong?" I lean back against the seat and take her in, wanting to make sure I don't miss her reaction to my question. "Are you unhappy about Lincoln spending so much time here?"

She stares at me with intent, her hand resting against her chest. "Oh, absolutely not. Why would you think that?"

"You've just seemed … off lately."

She flicks at the corner of a paper. "Is it that noticeable?"

So, there is something.

"Kind of." I stare at her, determined to help with whatever she's struggling with, to be a friend like she was with me during my Quinton issues. "I don't want to overstep any boundaries, but does it have anything to do with me? If so, I want to be able to fix whatever it is. I want you to be happy and comfortable."

She shrinks in her chair before nodding. "I have been nervous about you moving out now that you and Lincoln are together." Her words become more rushed. "Not that I'd blame you. I'd probably want to do the same with the man I love, so I wouldn't take any offense to it. That doesn't mean it hasn't crossed my mind more often than it probably should."

I'm happy she's not upset about Lincoln crashing with us, but my heart breaks that the thought has been haunting her.

"You don't need to worry about me moving out," I say, reaching forward and squeezing her hand. From the fear on her face, that won't be happening unless she finds someone or says she's okay with living alone.

She sits up straighter in her chair, as if my words were connected to a chain that lifted her back up. "You know, I don't care if Lincoln moves in here. It'd actually—and no offense because I love you being here and want to keep you forever—be nice, also having a guy with us, you know? Two girls living alone can be scary at times."

I love the sound of that.

Although I'm not sure how much Lincoln will love it.

I know he likes the penthouse, but after Georgia and Archer's news at breakfast, he might feel a little differently.

Grace turns quiet, her breathing hitching, and as she plays with her hands, I know there's more than what she's telling me.

"Grace," I say softly, "we're roommates. You can talk to me, you know that? Just like you kept my trust, I'll always do the same with you."

She blows out a breath and glances around the room as if she's worried someone is hiding in the shadows. "I haven't told anyone this, but I was dating the principal at our school."

"Oh." I'd tell her that's great, but from the expression on her face, it's not.

"He's married." She bows her head in shame.

"Oh."

"I didn't know that, though," she blurts. "He's new. It's his first year, and I guess his wife was still packing up their belongings and everything before moving out here after he got the job. He didn't tell me that he was married. He said he'd *been* married, but that he and his wife had recently divorced." She holds in a sob that becomes a sniffle. "I didn't think much of it, and then, the other day, his wife showed up at the school to surprise him … after we messed around in his office." She covers her face. "It's humiliating and heartbreaking."

"Oh my God, why didn't you tell me?" I feel bad because she was at my side during this Quinton mess when she was going through her own issues.

"You were dealing with something way more serious."

"I'll talk to Lincoln, see what he thinks, but no matter what, you don't have to worry about losing me as a roommate." I switch to the seat next to her. "Now, come on. Let's make some roomie hot chocolate and Netflix it up."

———

"I TALKED TO GRACE."

Lincoln peers over at me, and I'm almost positive my sentence came out in somewhat of a slur. We might've had one too many hot chocolates, but they were putting Grace's mind at ease. What the guy had done was messed up, and from the few details she gave me throughout the night, she was really falling for him.

Which is weird because I thought Finn held the key to her heart. As bad as I wanted to ask what happened with that, I didn't want to bring it up, in fear there were bad memories there as well. Maybe Finn turned her down, or maybe they just flirted, but that was it. Although I would have put my money on the two of them being the next to date.

Heck, I would've put my money on them dating before Lincoln and me when I first started working at the bar.

"You did, did you, drunkie?" Lincoln asks with a laugh.

I nod, swaying as I walk toward him. "And I can't move out. You and I are staying here." My words come out in short blasts as if I were slamming my foot on and off the gas pedal of my mouth.

Lincoln nods. "I figured that'd be the case, and it's cool. We can keep doing what we've been doing. It works for us."

"She offered for you to move in … said it'd make her feel safer, *and* I definitely feel the same."

He stares at me from my bed, scratching his jaw. "I mean, I'm cool with that. As long as I get to be with you, I'm happy."

"Yes, but our apartment is definitely no Archer penthouse."

"I don't give a shit about that. All I care about is having you and a bed. Nothing else matters."

———

IT'S the day before Lincoln's birthday.

And good thing I questioned him dozens of times because he didn't give me a birthday reminder. Tomorrow, we're going to celebrate with our friends, but today, I have something special for him.

At least, I hope he sees it as special.

I told him we were taking a trip to Blue Beech, and he was excited even though the last dinner was a hot mess.

My mother is throwing him a birthday dinner. After the initial shitshow of when Kyle questioned me about him being a convict, everyone seems to be getting along now. In fact, Lincoln now texts my brothers on the regular, like they're friends, which makes me happy. I love my brothers, and for them to like the guy I'm dating is a big deal.

My mother is also a Lincoln fan, which is why, when we walk in, there's a birthday feast laid out on the table—all of Lincoln's favorite foods. It's what she does for our birthdays along with fixing two birthday cakes—one for everyone else and then a personal one for the birthday person.

Everyone yells, "Happy Birthday!"

My mother scurries around the table and gives him a tight hug, singing the "Happy Birthday" song to him. Lincoln laughs, shaking his head, and hugs her back.

"Wow, looks like you've sure won her over," I say with a laugh.

Lincoln winks at me when they pull apart. "Like mother, like daughter."

Just as we're about to sit down, Lincoln's phone rings in his pocket. Dragging it out, he looks at the screen before holding it up.

"Let me take this real quick," he says, walking out of the room.

I'm taking a seat and pulling my chair in when Lincoln returns with a bright smile on his face. As he holds the phone in the air, he's practically dancing.

"I have good news," he says as if it's an announcement.

"What's up?" Rex asks.

Lincoln points at me with his phone. "And, babe, you should be receiving a call soon, but I can't keep this from you. Louis wasn't supposed to tell me, but he thinks you should know."

I frown at *Louis* even though I shouldn't. I appreciate all the help he's given with Quinton, but I hate that he's connected to Isla. It makes me uneasy because all I remember is the look of heartbreak she gave when Lincoln told her to leave.

She loves my boyfriend.

Therefore, I don't like her.

Lincoln sets his phone down before sliding his hands together. "First, they have Quinton in custody."

"Hell yes," Kyle says while Chloe squeals, shimmying in her chair.

Quinton hasn't sent a text or made an unwanted visit since his arrest.

"With the evidence they have, he should be facing some time," Lincoln continues. "I don't know all the details yet, but we did it." He walks around the table and stops to high-five Rex. "And secondly ..." He pauses, going quiet while taking the seat next to me. Wrapping his arm around my shoulders, he beams down in my direction. "Cass, Louis plans to expunge your record."

"What?" I gasp.

He nods, and Kyle jumps out of his chair, knocking his fists in the air.

"Holy shit!" Rex shouts. "That's fucking awesome."

My heart batters against my chest, and I repeat, "What?" because I have no other words.

For so long, I've accepted being a criminal. Having that misdemeanor was a part of me, forever who I would be. That might change now.

Lincoln nods. "Yep, say good-bye to your record."

Tears are in my mother's eyes. "That means ... that means you can go back to school, get a degree, go back to do whatever you want."

"Best damn birthday present ever," Lincoln says, smashing a kiss to my forehead.

———

WE'RE STILL RIDING the high of Quinton going down and me losing my record when we get back to the townhome. We talked on the way home, and Lincoln decided he wanted to move in with us.

Best day ever, seriously.

I'm ecstatic for us to take the next step in our relationship.

All the lights, except for the hallway bathroom, are off when we walk in, which is strange because Grace's car is parked in the drive. She rarely leaves the lights off. The girl sleeps with a night-light and has one in every room.

Lincoln glances at me, his brow raised in concern. "You think everything is okay?"

No.

Dread soars through me. "I hope so." I take small steps to the bathroom and knock on the door. "Grace?"

Sniffles come from the other side of the door, but no response from her.

My hand is trembling when I knock again. "Are you okay?"

Again, silence and sniffles.

"Just go in," Lincoln whispers, motioning toward the door.

I nod, hoping she doesn't see this as an invasion of privacy. Lincoln stands to the side, out of view of the bathroom, so they can't see each other. I play with the door handle, tinkering it from side to side to see if she'll tell me to stop, but nothing. Slowly, I open it, sliding between the crack, and shut it, my back pressing against the door.

Grace is crouched down on the floor, back to the tub, tears in her eyes, and … a pregnancy test in her hand.

"I'm pregnant," she croaks out, her hands shaking.

Oh my God.

CHAPTER THIRTY-FIVE

Lincoln

Three Weeks Later

"I'M GOING to miss working with you," I tell Cassidy.

"Oh, stop." She swats at my arm. "I'll still be there on the weekends, and don't think I won't be sitting at the end of the bar, studying it up while you're working."

"You promise?"

"I absolutely promise."

I chuckle. "Nothing like studying for law school in a bar."

"Studying for the bar while in a bar," she singsongs. "If I ever write an autobiography when I'm some famous attorney, I shall make that the title."

Cass is going back to school. It's online for now until she figures out where she wants to go or even if she wants to attend somewhere where she'd have to live on campus. She's made it clear to her mother that she's not going back to her old college because there are too many Quinton memories.

"I don't want the old typical college life," she told her mom.

I was worried she didn't want to go because of me, because we now lived together, because she thought we couldn't make it if she was gone. I didn't want her to give up on her future. She swore up and down that wasn't the case.

She's even changed the route of what kind of law she wants to practice. Before everything with Quinton went down, her plan was to go into law and become a defense attorney because that was where the money was.

Now? She wants to become a prosecutor to take down people like Quinton.

I'm so damn proud of her.

Before she was expelled, she was a few years back from earning her bachelor's degree, so law school is still far down the road, but she can do it. She's a fighter, and when she has her mind set on something, it gets done.

She climbs across the bed and into my lap, wrapping her arms around my neck. "I'm so happy I found you. So happy and thankful for our love."

I brush my thumb over her cheek. "Me too, baby. Me too." I shut my eyes. "I'd probably be living in a ball of sorrow had you not skipped your way into my life and told me we'd be sleeping together eventually."

She saved me.

Showed me what love was.

Hell, she showed me that love actually existed.

I'd be a skeptic, someone who called it a joke, had Cassidy Lane not come into my life.

She throws her head back and laughs. "All those times I said we'd sleep together sure caught your attention, huh?"

"It sure did." I open my eyes, meeting hers, and smile. "And what else was it you always said? That we'd sleep together and have all the babies?"

"Oh, yes, that was definitely another subject that was regularly brought up."

Another subject that I can't wait to happen.

She bows her head to kiss me.

I kiss her back. "I love you." *More than you'll ever know.*

"And I love you," she says, raining kisses along my cheek. "I can't wait to be your wifey and have little Lincolns running around." Lacing our fingers together, she squeezes my hand. "What's your favorite love song?"

That's one we haven't touched on for me, surprisingly.

"Hmm ..." I tap the side of my chin as if contemplating the question strongly. Not that I listen to *love songs* on the regular. I go with the first thought. "Umm ... '*Next To Me*' by Imagine Dragons. Why?"

"Just preplanning what song we dance to first at our wedding."

I chuckle before kissing her hard.

I love this woman.

She loves me.

Straight up.

No bullshit.

We got this.

Chaser

CHAPTER ONE

Grace

I'M SUING TROJAN.

Ninety-eight percent effective, my ass.

Ten tests.

Each one positive.

The only time I want my period, she decides to go on hiatus.

Stupid thing always had bad timing—prom night, spring breaks, recovering from a bad breakup.

I stare at the white stick I'm holding with tears rolling down my cheeks.

Two thin pink lines.

Two reminders of what I did.

How could I have been so stupid?

I slept with a man I should've never slept with.

Trusted and fell for a man who was nothing but a heartless, lying asshole.

I'm unsure of how long I've been sitting here, slumped against the tub with the cold tiles hitting the backs of my thighs. I pull my knees to my chest and stare at the truth, wishing I had the power to change it.

A knock on the door breaks me away from my thoughts of regret.

Tensing, I grip the stick, and my breath is heavy, as if I'd run a 10K.

Like that'll ever happen.

"Grace," Cassidy, my roommate, calls from the other side.

Wiping my snotty nose with my arm, I open my mouth to answer, but no words come. A faint whimper is my only response.

She knocks again. "Are you okay?"

Hell no.

I'm pregnant … and terrified.

My overpriced Catholic high school was on to something in their abstinence sex-ed classes when they forced us to watch those childbirth videos. It scarred me for life. Sure, eventually, I planned to marry and have kids. My plan was to at least be prepared and have a partner to share this moment with.

The door slowly opens at my lack of response, and Cassidy slips inside the bathroom. She shuts the door, resting her back against it, and sighs. Concern is etched along her face as our gazes meet.

I sluggishly hold up the stick as if I were seven and Santa had brought me the wrong Barbie for Christmas. "I'm pregnant."

My heart races at my confession.

It's the first time those words have left my mouth.

The first time my secret has been given permission to break into reality.

It'll become my new world, a regular phrase in my vocabulary for the next nine months. Although as my belly grows, that'll be the only evidence people need. Deep down, I know dreading becoming a mother is terrible. I'm a teacher, for Christ's sake. I'm supposed to adore the little rascals, but just because I enjoy children doesn't mean I'm ready to become a single mother. I'll be nursing a baby while nursing my broken heart.

Her soft voice cuts me away from my thoughts. "Is it his?"

I nod. "Unfortunately."

My family is going to kill me.

I'm going to kill him.

The man who swore he was falling in love with me but lied.

The man I wish I could take back ever touching.

The man I thought was different.

CHAPTER TWO

Finn

"YOU ASSHOLE!" a drunken idiot yells, the stench of his beer and nacho breath hitting me in the face.

Gripping the back of his shirt, I smirk. "An asshole who's kicking you out."

He grunts and stumbles forward as I forcefully guide him through the bar and outside to the parking lot. I release him, and he turns to flip me off, nearly tripping on his feet. Shaking my head, I chuckle and wait for his ride to pick him up. His friends shove him into the back seat, cursing him for ruining their night, and I wave good-bye before returning to the bar.

Another night, another shift of tossing drunk idiots out of Twisted Fox—the bar where I work. I'm the bouncer, ID checker, and the man who handles any bullshit from customers.

Two guys shove their IDs at me as soon as I'm back at the door, and I step aside, allowing them entry.

There's no stopping a huge-ass grin from taking over my face when the next group comes into view.

I whistle. "There are my favorite girls."

That's not some bullshit compliment babbled with the hopes of getting laid at the end of the night—a popular move among guys in my line of work. Being a bouncer at bars and clubs gives sway with the ladies.

The compliment is the truth.

The nights are always better when they're here.

What's also the truth? They're off-limits to me.

Georgia, the snarkiest and shortest, is at the front of the line. "Hey, Finney," she says, playfully smacking my stomach.

Behind her is Lola, who winks, and then Cassidy wiggles her fingers in a wave before blowing me a kiss.

I love this group of girls, but no matter what, I have a number one, and tonight, she's at the end of the line.

Save the best for last.

Grace Mitchell.

The only person I'm terrified to love.

The only woman I'm not supposed to crave like I do.

This woman has somehow slipped underneath my skin, rooting her innocence there, and no matter how hard I fight my feelings for her, there's no winning.

She's all I'll ever want and everything I don't deserve.

An alarm rings through me as I look at her, yet she won't do the same with me. Her customary smile—that polite, sweet, and lopsided yet cute-as-fuck grin—is nonexistent and replaced with a deep depth of worry. She walks at a slow pace, and her shoulders are slumped as if being held down by a deep burden.

What the fuck?

This isn't my Grace.

I stop her before she passes me. "Damn, babe, bad day?"

"Bad week," she mutters, fidgeting with the strap of her designer handbag.

Just as I'm about to ask why, Georgia says, "Let's grab our table before my favorite is stolen."

Cassidy laughs. "Your favorite, meaning the one closest to your man?"

"Damn straight." Georgia smirks at her. "Don't act like it's not close to *your* boyfriend too."

Lola gestures toward their usual table. "Silas is already saving it for us."

Neglecting my job and not giving a shit—*sorry, bosses* (aka my friends who won't fire me)—I follow them to the table. On my way, I direct another employee to take my place. The girls slide out their stools, plopping down one by one. As soon as Grace's ass hits her seat, she bows her head, her strawberry-blond hair creating a wall of curls around her face.

My gut twists from seeing her like this. Squeezing between her and Georgia, I tip my head and whisper in Grace's ear, "What happened?"

"Nothing," she rushes out.

Georgia slaps her hand on the table. "All right, give me your margarita orders."

Everyone blurts out their flavor but Grace.

"Just a water for me," she replies, her voice soft.

"No margarita?" Georgia asks, raising a brow.

Margarita nights are a weekly tradition for them. Not only that, but it's also her go-to when she's having a shit day.

"I wish," Grace replies before slapping a hand over her mouth and shutting her eyes. She quickly changes her tone. "I work in the morning."

Lola checks her watch. "Babe, you look like you've had a hell of a day. Have a drink, scarf down some greasy bar food, and don't give a shit about calories. Consider it a serotonin booster." She winks at her. "Trust me, I'm a pro at this stuff."

Grace drops her hand to her stomach. "Maybe another time."

"Whoa," Silas says from the stool next to Lola. "You knocked up or something?"

Leave it to Silas to ask a stupid-ass question like that.

No one laughs.

The table goes silent with the exception of Cassidy breaking out in a fit of coughs. Grace chews on her upper lip as I edge in closer to her. I wait for her to deny it, to tell Silas he's ridiculous, to laugh it off.

She doesn't.

As corny as it sounds, my heart stops. Hell, my entire world stops.

The sounds of customers yelling at sports calls on the TVs and mindless chatter surrounding me fade. Squeezing my eyes shut, I pray this is a bad nightmare, that I drank too much last night and I'm hallucinating, or this is some prank. Everyone's reactions tell me my wish isn't coming true.

It could be considered selfish of me to not want to hear Grace is pregnant. For years, I've carried a deep fear of losing her. Her being pregnant with another man's baby is step one of that looming reality—of my upcoming loss of the woman I never want to disappear from my life.

My world, my happiness will never be the same.

CHAPTER THREE

Grace

ONE THING my parents loved about me while I was growing up was I almost always told the truth. No matter how much a lie was on the tip of my tongue, it never slipped.

Did you participate in senior skip day? Yes.

Did you attend a party instead of going to Georgia's after prom? Sure did.

Did you cheer on Lola to put a laxative in your ex's drink after he took your virginity and then cheated? Unfortunately, yes, and by the way, he's threatening to sue.

That's why I can't look my friends in the face and deny being pregnant.

Was I that obvious?

I hadn't bailed tonight in hopes it'd take my mind off being knocked up. With the exception of work, I hadn't left my house since accepting the results of the tests. I had anxiety that someone would know my secret as soon as they saw me.

Or as soon as I declined a margarita, apparently.

All eyes are on me.

God, if you're listening, please open up the floor and swallow me whole.

I'm not sure how long it takes before I draw in a nervous breath and nod. I shut my eyes to block out their reactions, afraid of what they'll be. A crowded bar isn't where I planned to spill the beans, but at least it's over with.

Another name off my list.

Friends. Check.

The others, like my family and the baby's father, won't be as easy.

And unfortunately, I can't have a margarita with those either.

"Who's the father?" Finn asks, his voice pained and cracking with each word.

Yeah, I'd rather give up margs for the rest of my life before explaining that tonight.

Out of everyone, his reaction is what I've been worried about the most. As much as I like the other guys, I don't care about their opinions. The girls will support me one hundred percent—there's no question.

I could lie and say IVF, but my friends would call bullshit, knowing I'd never keep something like that a secret. Nor can I say I turned into the next Virgin Mary and got prego without having intercourse.

My head spins, a myriad of excuses flashing through my thoughts, but I'm unable to grasp one.

I clear my throat. "I don't want to talk about that."

Questions fly from people's mouths, but Lola shoots her hand up, stopping them.

"She'll talk about it when she's ready," she says, smiling in my direction before sending Finn a *shut the hell up* glare.

That's Lola—always the first to speak up and the first to shut people down.

"Do your parents know?" Georgia asks.

"Not yet," I croak, my throat sore.

Georgia shifts in her stool, her hand falling over mine and squeezing it. "Do you want me to go with you when you tell them? I mean, I'm down for being a second mom."

This is why I love my friends. Along with my older sister, Faith, they will be the strength I need to get through this and prove I'm not alone.

I can't muster the courage to turn and look at Finn. From his tense muscles and his heavy breathing, I'm scared of witnessing the disappointment I know is written on his face.

The anger.

And possible disgust.

Even though he and I have never overstepped our friendship line, we share an emotional intimacy that we deny it to everyone. We've surpassed friendship. When I met Finn, I didn't expect us to develop the connection we have. I never anticipated this man, who was the complete opposite of me, to steal my heart, taking it little by little with every conversation until he owned every inch of it. And since neither of us planned our relationship to grow as it has, we're terrified to admit our feelings to each other, so we've been playing pretend for years.

I'm in love with Finn. If there were anyone I'd want to be the father of my baby, it'd be him. In my dreams, if I could have my life any way I wanted, I'd be with Finn. I've had those feelings for years, but sometimes, you can't always have what you want.

After longing for Finn while witnessing endless women flirt with him at the bar, I stupidly attempted to move on. I threw myself into a relationship even though my heart belonged to someone else. I wanted to find happiness without the fear of cutting myself open and confessing my feelings to Finn, scared of being shut down, of hearing I wasn't his type.

I'm in love with him, my best friend, and it's too bad the other man's heart also belongs to someone else. He was running from his problems, his responsibilities, and used me. Unfortunately, I found that out too late.

And that man, ladies and gentlemen, is the father of my baby.

CHAPTER FOUR

Finn

THE FIRST THING I do at closing is march behind the bar, snag a bottle of whiskey, and pour myself a double.

Pregnant.

Grace is fucking pregnant.

I had no idea she was even dating someone, and from her reaction when I asked who the father was, the dick had probably fucked her over. Unless it was a one-night stand and she doesn't know who the father is, but for as long as I've known Grace, I can't see that being the answer.

My goal is to drink away the reality until it's no longer fresh in my mind. I'm using the liquor to cope with the pain of losing her. I cringe, thinking of some underserving asshole touching her, kissing her, doing everything I've wanted to do for years.

"You good, man?" Silas comes up behind me and slaps me on the back.

It's all fun and games, joking about someone being pregnant, until it's the girl you're in love with.

When Grace confirmed she was pregnant, Silas looked straight at me, knowing it'd hit me the hardest. I knotted my hands into fists, nausea crawling up my throat, wishing I hadn't followed them to their table. That's what I get for being a shit employee and not minding my damn business.

After her pregnancy news broke, I got back to work. My head was spinning, and I needed to clear it. I shot quick glances to their table throughout the night, watching her drink water and pretend to laugh. Her face was tired when she left the bar, and before she walked out, I smacked a quick kiss on her forehead and reminded her I would always be there for her, no matter what.

This is just another reminder that Grace and I were never meant to be together. I'm not sure how it happened, but I've connected with her more than anyone in our small group. We get along, share stories, and spend every minute we can together. I should've known something was up because we've started drifting apart for the past few months. Now, I know why.

"All good," I clip, taking another drink to drown out my lie.

He snatches the bottle from me. "Don't bullshit me."

"Would you be pissed if you found out Lola was pregnant?"

He looks away. "I don't know."

"Bullshit." I mock the tone he used with me. "You would."

He sighs. "Let me drive you home."

Before he can stop me, I pluck the bottle from his hand and take a long draw. Passing it back nearly empty, I gulp. "Let's go."

This is my hell. All these years, I've convinced myself that Grace is too good for me, but I've always turned a blind eye to what would happen if I never made my move. What would happen if another man had bigger balls than me and asked her out.

In the back of my mind, I stupidly believed we'd stay friends forever and nothing would ever change. Sure, we've gone on dates— neither one of us staying celibate, *obviously*—but nothing ever turned serious.

We shut the bar down, and as soon as I fall into his passenger seat, I text Grace.

Me: You okay?

Since she wakes up early for her job, I don't expect a response back until morning. I'm shocked when three bubbles pop up on the screen, and a text comes through.

Grace. Yes. Just tired.
Me: I'm here for you. Don't forget that, okay?
Grace: I know.
Me: Always. Get some rest.
Grace: *heart emoji*

My heart stings, and I tip my head back, regret eating at me.
Why did I wait?
It's too late now.
All I can do now is be there for her.

No matter what happens, no matter how much it kills me inside, I'll always be at her side for as long as she needs me. Rain or shine, day or night, until she moves on with a man who isn't too chickenshit to let her all the way in.

"Try not to think about it," Silas says, parking in front of my condo. "Block that shit out because there's nothing you can do now." He taps the center console. "Go to bed because you look like shit."

"Rest?" I snort. "Doubt that'll happen." Clutching the door handle, I nod toward him. "Thanks for the ride, man."

"Anytime."

I take two steps at a time, surprised I can even walk, and it takes me a few attempts to open the door. Slamming the door behind me, I dart to the kitchen for the vodka bottle stashed in the top cabinet before plopping down on the couch in the living room. I take a shot of vodka at the same time I grab the remote with my free hand. Groaning, I toss the remote on the floor, not in the mood for background noise. It'll be me, silence, and my broken heart tonight.

I stupidly thought Grace and I would have a chance someday.

When I had my shit together, when I was more than a bouncer in a bar, when I could provide her with the life she'd always been given.

Waiting is for fools.

What a goddamn mistake that was.

Now, I'm paying for it.

CHAPTER FIVE

Grace

I HAVEN'T HAD a good night's sleep since I was thirteen, but last night was the worst I'd had since moving out of my parents' home.

I'm yawning on my way to the kitchen when there's a knock on the door. Making a detour, I check the peephole before answering it. Finn stands in front of me, his eyes heavy-lidded and his ashen-brown hair disheveled.

Apparently, I'm not the only one suffering from a lack of sleep.

A green smoothie is gripped in one of his hands, and in the other is a brown bag, both items sporting the logo of my favorite breakfast café. I stare at him, blinking, shocked he's even awake. He works late and tends to sleep in until noon. Just like he never expects a text from me past eleven, I never expect one from him until lunch.

He fakes a smile and holds up the bag. "I thought you could use a good breakfast this morning."

I return the smile—mine not fraudulent. It's the first real one I've had in days.

"I can't believe you're up this early," I say, motioning for him to come inside.

"Neither can I." Walking in, he follows me to the kitchen, hands me the smoothie, and settles the bag onto the counter before rubbing his eyes. "I couldn't sleep."

"Why?"

He shrugs. "Probably the same reason you couldn't." His eyes widen, and his next words are rushed. "I didn't mean for that to make me sound like a rude asshole."

I'm not offended by his honesty. You take one look at me and know I'm lacking sleep. Circles that I was too exhausted to cover up with makeup are under my eyes. My pink dress is one that's shoved in the back of my closet, only used for *I'm feeling bloated* days.

"Finn"—I sigh—"please don't worry about me. I got this. I'm a big girl."

"Don't worry about you?" He throws his arms in the air in frustration. "All I'm going to do is worry about you. Will the father be in the picture?"

"I … I haven't told him yet."

That's on today's … or tomorrow's … or next year's … or never's to-do list.

He rubs at his brows, but his stare doesn't slip away from me. "Why?"

"Right now, I don't even want to look at him."

He moves his hand, his face reddening. "Did he hurt you?"

Only emotionally.

"No," I reply. "It's nothing like that."

"Has hell frozen over?"

I turn around at Cassidy's voice as she joins us in the kitchen.

Another person who normally doesn't wake up this early.

Her blonde hair is a mess, and she's sporting one of her boyfriend's tees.

"Finn, what are you doing up?" she asks, her gaze from Finn to me before stopping on him. "Please tell me you slept over."

"Nah." Finn shakes his head. "I just brought Grace breakfast before work."

Cassidy's attention shifts to me, giving my appearance a once-over. "Don't take this the wrong way, babe, but I think you're due for a sick day. I'll take one with you."

"I'm down for a sick day," Finn says.

"Me fucking too," Lincoln, Cassidy's boyfriend, says, coming into view.

Looks like this is a breakfast party.

I want my non-prego peace-and-quiet mornings back.

As much as a relief taking the day off would be, it's too late for that. Plus, I have decisions I need to make, and one of them requires me showing up to work.

I blow out a breath. "I can't call in sick thirty minutes before I'm supposed to be there."

"You know, you can quit if you want," Lincoln says, shoving his hands into the pockets of his sweats. "We're good to cover rent."

Since Lincoln was with Cassidy the night she came into the bathroom and nearly lives with us, he was the second person to find out about my pregnancy. Like Cassidy, he kept his word on keeping it a secret. Also like Cassidy, he knows who the father is.

"Why would you quit your job?" Finn asks.

Lincoln and Cassidy exchange a look.

"Just … stress," I rush out, not exactly lying to him.

Being there, being around *him*, will be stressful.

He nods, although there's still a question in his eyes. He'll wait for the answer until we're alone. One thing I appreciate about Finn is that he never puts me on the spot and always makes sure I'm comfortable.

We make small talk before Finn grabs my breakfast bag and walks me to my Mercedes coupe. Our pace is quick and hurried. I set my purse into the passenger seat, rest the cup in the holder, and turn back to look at him.

He fixes his gaze on me as if attempting to crack answers without asking questions.

Endeavoring to *read me* without making me uncomfortable.

Reaching out, he brushes away a strand of my hair waving in the wind. "Don't forget, you need anything, and I'm here."

"I know." I bow my head. "I know."

He hugs me good-bye.

Finn and I share two types of hugs.

Our friendly ones—him casually throwing his arm over my shoulders in a playful manner.

And our deep ones—him blanketing me in his arms, as if he's my protector, and holding me tight.

Today's is a deep one.

And as I'm bundled in his arms, I wish it would last forever.

———

I WALK into Sunset Hill Preparatory with a slow pace, my throat tightening with doubt.

I've taught third grade here for two years. It's an elite school with tuition costing nearly as much as an Ivy League.

I wave at Rachelle, the secretary, as I enter the office and hope my voice doesn't sound scratchy. "Morning! Is Principal Long in his office?"

Is this the right place to do this?

Probably not, but I don't want to meet him in private anywhere.

The less time with him, the better.

He also can't make a scene here.

So, the school it is.

She grins from ear to ear at his name. "Sure is!"

Rachelle is a big fan of the principal.

Most at Sunset Hill are—staff, parents, students.

The man succeeds at faking it.

My hand trembles when I knock on the door. I'm close to changing my mind, to flee, when he yells for me to come in.

"You can do this," I whisper to myself, avoiding Rachelle's gaze, worried she'll notice my nervousness.

I'm proud of myself when I open the door and step inside. I glance back at the door, debating on whether to shut it. It's something I was always hesitant about in the past—closing us in and people speculating we were up to no good. This moment is similar ... although something different will be happening this time.

Sitting behind the mahogany desk is a man I once adored yet now think is trash. He looks the part in his black suit and fun tie; his brown hair is curly yet controlled simultaneously.

A flash of shock quickly passes over his features at the sight of me.

He smirks and jerks his head toward the door—a silent demand to shut it, and I do. "And here I thought you were done with me." Leaning forward, he steeples his hands and rests them over a stack of paperwork on the desk.

Gone is the nice-guy front he delivered for months.

Why is it always the quiet, polite ones who end up being the most deceitful?

As much as I've frowned upon players, at least they're open about their intentions.

I raise my chin. "I am."

"Why are you here then?" The satisfaction in his tone confirms he assumes this is me running back to him.

He licks his lips while eyeing me in expectation.

Here goes.

"I'm pregnant." I'm proud of how sharp my tone is—no stuttering, no doubt.

The smirk he was carrying drops faster than his morals. "Motherfucker." His face pales as he slides his chair out from the desk and stands. "This can't be happening."

"I don't expect anything from you," I rush out, nearly pleading. "You can sign over your rights, and I'll raise the baby on my own."

I swallow at the thought of doing it alone, but as terrifying as single motherhood sounds, I'll take that over having Gavin in my life.

He rubs the back of his neck. "No, that's not what I want."

Wait, what?

Not what I expected.

"You know what you're saying, right?" My words come out slow, as if I were speaking to one of my students.

He nods. "I do."

"You'd have to come clean to your wife." I squeeze my eyes shut at the last word.

It's a hidden detail of his life.

A label he kept in the dark.

There was no ring. No photos. No social media.

All I had was his word ... or lack thereof.

I assumed he didn't have a wife since he never made it clear he did.

"Not exactly." He clicks his tongue against the roof of his mouth while circling the desk to come closer.

I grimace as he draws near. "I'm confused."

"My wife ..." He clears his throat and stands tall in front of me, the sage tones in his cologne hitting my nose. "She's also pregnant."

I swing my hand back, prepared to punch him, but hold back.

This motherfucking asshole.

Curse words aren't a regular in my vocabulary.

Since I'm around children all day, I've trained myself to use kid-friendly language.

But this ... this calls for profanity.

And a quick kick in the balls if being fired wasn't a consequence.

"Did you ..." I retreat a step and signal between us, begging tears not to surface. "When did *you know?*"

When we had sex?

Exchanged love devotions?

Had sleepovers at his temporary condo?

He tugs at his ear, his eyes leveled on mine and lips pinched together. "That doesn't matter. If she finds out I cheated, our prenup will be null and void. No way in hell am I giving her half of the money my family worked their asses off for." The disdain on his face disintegrates, his mood changing, and he smiles. "I want to be with you, Grace. I love *you*, not her."

Reaching out, he attempts to take my hand, but I swat his away.

Snarling, I shove my finger in his face. "Don't. Don't you dare. You no longer get to touch me. You lost that privilege when you failed to tell me you were married."

Gavin recently relocated to Anchor Ridge, Iowa, from California to take the job as principal here. His wife wanted his children to finish out the semester at their old school and decided to join him later. Temporarily, he rented a small condo while waiting for them. Not once did he mention a wife, so I never questioned it.

Along with most of the staff, I found out about his family when his wife showed up at the school to surprise him. As I dropped my bagel to the floor while processing what was happening, the warning signs I'd missed became clear. The times he had taken calls in different rooms with hushed whispers and how he'd hardly mentioned his life in California.

His mouth falls slack at my rejection. "There is something between us."

This time, when he takes a step closer, I don't move as if frozen in place. Reaching out, he runs his soft palm over my face, and I tremble.

"We were falling in love, remember? Those feelings aren't something that can just be thrown away … forgotten."

Him lowering his hand to swipe a finger along my top lip snaps me back into reality, and he stumbles back when I push his chest.

"Maybe, but I'd never be with a married man," I hiss.

"What if I was no longer married?" He shakes his head. "Let me figure out a way to get out of this marriage without it being messy. Then, we can be together and have a perfect life."

"No way. I shouldn't have even told you I'm pregnant."

He raises a brow. "Why did you?"

"I'm a good person, and keeping something like this from someone would be wrong. But I forgot it's you—a manipulative jerk. Go be with your wife or don't be—I don't care. Anything that was ever between us is over."

He snarls, pointing to my stomach. The man changes moods as much as he lies. "That's my unborn child, which means I have rights as a father. I don't intend to give those up."

My stomach clenches.

I was trying to do the right thing, but it's backfired in my face. Since he's such a shitty person, I thought he'd want nothing to do with this baby.

"You want rights?" I ask. "Go tell your wife because sooner or later, those rights will result in her knowing about us."

He goes quiet.

I snort. "That's what I thought."

With that, I open the door and walk out.

CHAPTER SIX

Finn

THE RINGING PHONE wakes me up, and I groan when reading the name across the screen.

The past twenty-four hours since finding out Grace is pregnant have been a roller coaster of emotions. I'm still trying to get my head on straight, and now, I'll have the added stress of this call. But like always, I answer.

I answer out of fear of what will happen if I don't. "Hello?"

"Hey, son." His chipper tone should be a relief, but all it tells me is, he's about to ask for money.

I pinch the bridge of my nose. "What's going on?"

"Oh, nothing," he drawls out his response as if preparing himself to break the news. "My car broke down, and I can't afford to fix it."

Just as I thought.

Saving money is nearly impossible because I'm always handing it out like candy. I'm not a selfish man, and I'm always down to lend a helping hand to those down on their luck. My issue is supporting someone who blows through their Social Security checks on booze and drugs and then comes to me when he can't pay his bills.

"Take it to the shop." I shut my eyes, hating myself for enabling him. "Have them call me. I'll either go there or pay it over the phone."

He grunts. "I'll come by and pick up the money. It'll be easier that way."

"No." My voice turns stern. "We do it my way, or it doesn't get paid."

"Fine," he grumbles. "You always make it difficult when it could be easy and save you the trouble."

It's a trick I've fallen victim to countless times. Me handing him money in these situations, resulting in him conveniently *losing it* or having an excuse of how he had to pay for something else. The man once claimed the hundred-dollar bill I'd once given him blew away in the wind like it was a damn kite. It's been this way for as long as I can remember, and I don't expect it to change anytime soon.

――――――

TACO TUESDAY IS my favorite day of the week.

As someone who grew up with no family, what drags me out of a sour mood is my friends. For once in this fucked-up life of mine, I'm not lonely 24/7. I have people who care about me, who I care about, relationships that weren't created to see what someone could get out of me.

I met Cohen while we worked at a club in the city together. Over the years, we built a tight circle, consisting of Cohen, Silas, Archer, Maliki, and myself. After we met, Cohen introduced us to his sister, Georgia, and her friends, Lola and Grace. Later, Cassidy and Lincoln started working at the bar, and our group was complete.

Meeting Grace changed my life. I'd never met anyone like her. She had the smile of purity, an angelic voice, but her personality was what drew me in. There was no doubt she was high maintenance, someone who had come from money, but she had no problem casually hanging out with us at barbecues and shooting the shit. She was a breath of fresh air.

I won't lie. In the beginning, I judged her for her privileged life—her Mercedes and the way she talked like she hung out in country clubs during her summers—but she proved my ass wrong.

Taco Tuesday is being held at Archer, Georgia, and Lincoln's penthouse. Technically, it's pretty much Lincoln's because Archer and Georgia recently bought another home that's more Georgia's style. Not that he stays there much either since he practically lives at Cassidy and Grace's.

I press my palm to my heart when I walk in and see Grace sitting on the couch, surrounded by our friends. She turns, her eyes meeting mine, and shoots me a sweet grin.

That damn smile.

My favorite fucking view.

I could live with that being the only sight I see for the rest of my life, and I'd be one happy man. The penthouse is an open floor plan, so I see everyone scattered throughout the place. On my way to Grace, I wave to people in the kitchen and high-five Cohen's son, Noah. After saying hi to everyone, I plop down next to Grace on the couch. I squeeze Grace's thigh—a silent question that she's okay—and she nods.

"The margaritas are ready!" Georgia shouts, walking into the living room, a frozen drink in each hand, and she hands one over to Grace. "And a virgin one for my girl, so you're not left out."

Grace laughs while taking it from her.

"What's *a virgin one* mean?" Noah asks, scrunching his brows.

"It means ..." Jamie—Cohen's girlfriend/baby mama—says before pausing, searching for the right words.

"It means it doesn't have alcohol in it," Georgia says, using her free hand to ruffle his brown hair.

Noah perks up. "Does that mean when I drink chocolate milk, I'm drinking virgin chocolate milk?"

"Oh my God," Jamie says, facepalming. "That is not where he needs to go with this."

"And what about milkshakes?" Noah goes on. "Are they virgin milkshakes?"

"I'm going to kill all of you," Jamie says, using her finger to gesture to us. "All of you will be drinking virgin margaritas during our Taco Tuesday nights." She peers at Grace and winks. "Get ready for those questions in five years."

Grace's face pales, and I give her thigh another squeeze.

Every minute I can, I want to make sure she's comfortable. She's venturing into a rough journey, and I'll be there for her every step she'll allow me.

Even if it hurts because I wish I were the father, that I'd stepped up and told her my feelings. Now, all I can do is be a support system, a friend, a man who wishes she were his.

———

I DON'T GET a moment alone with Grace until after dinner.

With the exception of the few minutes we had before being interrupted at her townhouse, we haven't had a full conversation since her pregnancy news broke.

We're back on the couch after stuffing ourselves with tacos and guac.

There are so many questions I want to ask, yet so many I don't want to know the answers to.

Tell me about how it happened, but I don't want to know that you had sex with another man. Explain how you kept a relationship from me, but also don't tell me shit about him.

I might not know the dude, but I hate him.

I've done a decent job of playing it cool tonight, but finally, I can release the anxiousness that's been eating away at me. My attention is fixed on her, not taking in any of the motions or conversations around us. Her hair is pulled up, exposing her slim neck. I shut my eyes, remembering the first time I saw her. As weird as it sounds, the color of her hair reminded me of fruit—a mixture of apricot and strawberries.

She changed from her work clothes—her teacher outfits, as I call them—and she's wearing striped overalls. They're not Farmer Ben overalls—more along the lines of what you'd see a celebrity sporting on the front page of a magazine. It fits her skinny frame, the cream color and blue stripes beautiful against her sun-kissed skin.

"How are you feeling?" I ask, blowing out a stressed breath.

She sighs, avoiding eye contact. "I told the father."

"And?" My heart races.

Do I even want to know?

Her answer could make or break us.

If she got together with the baby daddy, would he want me around?

Or would he see me as a threat?

If the roles were reversed, I know I would.

Anyone who watches Grace and me together knows that we're not just friends, no matter how much we lie to each other about it.

She plays with her hands in her lap. "He wants to be in the baby's life."

Fuck, this stings.

"Is that what you want?"

"Not exactly. I mean ... yes ... but no."

I scratch my head. "What do you mean?"

Moments of silence pass as she chews into her cheek.

Her hands stop, and she looks forward. "He's married."

My mouth drops open.

Not what I expected.

This motherfucker.

Her shoulders slump. "Married ... with children ... and another one on the way."

Anger swells inside me, but I draw in steady breaths to hold myself back from acting on it. I thought I had questions before, but this? This is an entirely different field.

She eyes me nervously. "I didn't know he was married. He hid it from me."

Scrubbing a hand over my face, I appear as stressed as her. "What are you going to do?" I wrap my arm around her shoulders, drawing her into my side. "Are you sure you don't want to take me up on the offer of kicking his ass?"

At this point, if I knew who the bastard was, I'd do it without asking. It'd feel damn good to smash my fist into a man's face who lied, played, and knocked up the most important woman in my life.

She relaxes into my hold. "No, it'll only make the situation worse."

"Did he tell his wife?"

"As of yesterday, nope."

"He thinks he can hide it from her?"

This dude has some serious balls.

"I have no idea." She frowns. "My guess is, he wants to be in the baby's life because he wants to keep me."

I grind my teeth.

"But I think he'll chicken out when it's time to tell his wife, and then the baby and I will be on our own." Her eyes squeeze shut.

I carefully take her hand in mine. "You're strong, and you won't be on your own. You have me. You have our friends."

A tear falls down her cheek, and she bows her head. "My sister lost so many friends after she had my niece. It changes things."

"What's wrong, babe?" Georgia asks, taking a seat on the floor at Grace's feet and crossing her legs.

As much as our friends bring joy into my life, they have terrible timing. They have no problem with interrupting conversations and calling people out.

Grace swipes the tear from her rosy cheek. "I'm just thinking about doing it all alone if the dad doesn't want to be in the picture."

"Um, you have me," Georgia counters.

"And *me* in the next room," Cassidy chimes in, walking toward us with the group following behind her.

"You have *all of us*," Lola adds. "Every step of the way, we'll be there for you. I'm totally up for Lamaze class, and we all know Georgia is the queen of positivity. She'll be at your side every step of the way, holding your hand through labor. We can take turns being the baby daddy, and one day, you'll find a man ready to step up and take over our job."

"I'm down for playing baby daddy for a few days," Silas says, pointing at Grace with his beer.

Grace's mood doesn't improve. "That's if I'm alive when my parents find out."

"It's the twenty-first century. We're in new times," Cohen says. "Even if they're upset at first, they'll get over it because they love you."

Georgia reaches up and squeezes Grace's knee. "We got this, babe."

———

"YOU KNOW, I was thinking about something," Silas says.

He and I, along with Georgia and Archer, who are in the kitchen, are the only ones left in the penthouse. It wasn't long after our conversation with Grace not going on her journey alone that she went home.

I snort. "That's fucking scary."

"I have the perfect plan for Grace and her baby."

"Not taking any advice from the guy who suggested we have an adults-only baby shower at the club."

He rolls his eyes before pointing at me. "You step up and be the dad."

I should've known better than to take a drink before he spoke because as soon as the words leave his mouth, I'm choking on my beer. Dribbles scatter along my shirt as I gawk at him. Silas is the jokester of the group, and I expect a sarcastic smirk on his face. There isn't.

"I can't tell if you're joking or serious," I grunt, wiping my palm down my shirt.

He chuckles. "Eh, kind of both. Although leaning more toward serious."

"For someone who doesn't drink, you sure say some drunk-person bullshit."

"The least you can do is act like it in front of her parents. The poor girl looked stressed as fuck when she mentioned them."

I shift in my seat. "And what? Be a dad for a day?"

"Go with her, introduce yourself as the dad, and then later, she can say you broke up." He delivers a self-satisfied smirk. "*Or*, better yet, maybe this is the moment you've been waiting for. Have a relationship with her and be fucking happy."

I chug the rest of my beer. "You're nuts, dude."

"Are you honestly going to lie and deny you want to be with her?"

My jaw clenches at his truth. "Oh, like you haven't wanted a relationship with Lola for years and not done shit about it?"

He leans back in his chair, slouching some, and I know my words hit a nerve. "Lola and I would never work. We're too much alike."

"Grace and I are too different."

"Keep lying to yourself, dude, and be fucking miserable for the rest of your life." He holds his bottle of water in a cheers gesture before standing and walking away.

As I get in my car and leave, Silas's comment sticks with me.

CHAPTER SEVEN

Grace

I'M NOT sure what's worse.

Finding out your boyfriend is trash or morning sickness.

Screw you both.

You're already going through enough during pregnancy—hormone changes, weight gain, peeing your pants on occasion. Why throw *get sick every morning* into the mix? Give us a break on something.

My sister complained about morning sickness during her pregnancy, and I passed it off, thinking it was normal. I sincerely apologize to anyone who's ever had someone downplay the hell.

It's brutal.

Disgusting.

Resting my head on the toilet, I groan.

This isn't how my mid-twenties was supposed to go.

After rinsing my mouth and brushing my teeth three times, I shower and get ready for work. Another day of avoiding my baby daddy at every turn.

IF I'M EVER LATE, call the cops.

Nothing good comes out of tardiness.

Shoot, my late period proved that further.

Growing up, I was taught if you're not early, you're late. As the daughter of a judge, I grew up with manners that were expected to be on display and rules that were never to be broken. It's not that my parents are jerks. It's just that they're strict, and they have had expectations of us since childhood.

College. Job. Marriage. Children.

In that order.

My sister performed well.

Me? Apparently, I'm rearranging those expectations.

I'm at my desk thirty minutes early, grading papers and sipping on seltzer water before my class starts. At times, especially now, I appreciate silence before the chaos that begins with children shuffling into the room.

"Wow, babe, you look gorgeous today."

I straighten in my chair, a chill shooting up my spine.

That voice.

His presence now is so different than what it was when we met … when he was charming me. Gone is the phony compassion and sweetness, now replaced with arrogance. For someone whose life could change if I confessed the truth, he sure has some balls.

Knocking on the door with his knuckles, Gavin stands in the doorway. "Pregnancy shines on you."

My head pounds as Gavin shuts the door and strolls toward me, a smirk on his face. Nausea thicker than my morning sickness creeps up my throat.

How'd I allow him to fool me?

Infatuation is blinding, ladies and gents.

"Screw you," I hiss, dropping my pen.

He places his hand over his chest. "Aw, you used to appreciate my compliments."

"*Used to* being the key words. Now, they make my skin crawl because I know they're coming from a married man." I scowl while pointing at the door. "Get out."

"I'm the principal." He scrubs a hand over his smooth jaw and smirks. "My job is to ensure you're doing yours and there are no issues."

"My only issue is you."

"Now, now, is that any way to talk to your superior?" He stops in front of me, his palms falling to my desk, and bends so we're eye level. A combination of his spearmint breath and strong cologne floats between us.

I snort—convinced if I don't entertain him, he'll leave.

"Or better yet, the father of your child?"

My face burns, and I hold myself back from slapping him in the face. "Don't say that to taunt me."

He draws nearer, our faces only inches apart. "The truth taunts you?"

"*You* taunt me." It's a struggle to stop my voice from wavering. "Your asshole attitude taunts me. Being around you taunts me."

Typically, I don't resort to insults, but he deserves it. Gavin lied, made me fall for him, all while knowing it'd all come crashing down. He didn't care that I was playing victim to his lies while he was having fun.

He was a pro at it. The man excelled at hiding what he wanted, so my bet is, I'm not the first affair he's had. I was stupid. In today's day and age, you're supposed to cyberstalk potential new love interests— look through every Instagram photo, see how cute their exes dress, and discover their political views.

The problem was that Gavin declared social media a waste of time, but I also trusted him. We worked together, and the school is strict on background checks. It wasn't like I could ask around since we agreed to keep our relationship private for a while. I was scared of it ending before things got serious and there'd be talk around the school.

It ending too soon was my fear.

Not him being married.

I grip the edge of my desk, pushing my chair out, and stand. "Out of my room."

His back straightens as he pulls away, standing tall and slender in front of me. "Oh, come on, Grace." He approaches me. "I told you, I'm leaving my wife, but for now, let's go back to the way it was.

Remember how good we were?" He shuts his eyes as if the memories are so good, but all they do is haunt me.

I shove him away. "All I remember is that you're a cheating jerk."

"Forgive me." He presses his hands into a praying motion. "I saw you, I wanted you, but I knew if you found out I was married, you'd want nothing to do with me."

"You think?" I scoff.

He opens his mouth, most likely to spew more lies, but a group of children barreling into the classroom interrupts him. Pulling away, he says, "Have a great day, Miss Mitchell. Until next time."

———

"YOU LOOK like someone ran over Mr. Bubbles," my sister, Faith, says when I enter her kitchen.

Her signature candle—honeydew melon—is lit in the center of the granite island, a relaxation to my anxiety. The irritation from Gavin's morning visit stayed with me. All day, I stared at the door, waiting for him to make another pop-in.

Brian, her husband, chuckles. "Grace would probably kill someone if they ran over Mr. Bubbles."

Mr. Bubbles is the stuffed rabbit I carried around until I was ten and still have to this day. There's something about safekeeping childhood objects. My plan was to pass him down to my children. Looks like that time is coming sooner than I thought.

"I'm pregnant," I blurt out, unable to hold my secret in any longer.

Faith and I share everything. Keeping information from her is hard.

"I'm sorry, but did you just say you're *pregnant?*" Faith gapes at me as if waiting for me to tell her I'm joking.

I clear my throat. "I'm pregnant."

As nervous as I was to tell her, a rush of relief settles through me now that she finally knows. Her support will mean so much to me during this journey, and she's the closest person to me who's been pregnant.

"Whoa," Brian says, his tone subdued.

"Is this a good or bad *I'm pregnant*?" Faith stares at me in expectation. "Because you most definitely don't look like I did when I found out I was pregnant."

Chewing on my lower lip, I walk to the fridge, jerk it open, snag a bottle of water, and chug half of it.

All eyes are on me. The knife that was in Faith's hand while she chopped onions sits on the counter, and Brian is no longer holding his phone.

"I don't know if I want to answer that." I slump back against the fridge. "I don't want to say something negative and have my baby pick up bad vibes, yet I don't want to say good because I'm freaking the heck out."

"Who's the father?" she asks.

God, I hate that question.

I squeeze the bottle tight, wishing it were Gavin's balls. "I don't want to talk about it."

Her gaze is glued to me. "Is it one of the guys you and Georgia always hang out with?"

"No." I shut my eyes. "It's someone I work with."

"Why the long face then?"

Even though I just drained a bottle of water, my mouth turns dry. "It recently came to light that he's married—"

"Oh fuck," Brian says.

"And he's also expecting another child with said wife." My stomach revolts at the confession.

"Holy shit," Faith hisses, tapping her French-manicured nails along the counter. "Good luck explaining that one to Mom and Dad."

Brian points his beer at me. "Please make sure we're in attendance."

Faith playfully smacks the side of Brian's head.

"Who knows?" I drag out a stool and collapse onto it. "Maybe it won't be so bad."

"I have an idea," Brian says. "Buy your mom a Chanel bag and slide the ultrasound picture in there." He cracks a cocky smile. "No one can be pissed when they've been gifted an expensive-ass handbag."

I rub my forehead. "Chanel won't drown out an unwed pregnancy."

Brian snorts. "Surely, your parents don't believe you don't have sex."

Faith shoots me a smile. "Grace is an angel in their eyes."

"They thought the same thing about you." I wiggle my finger in her direction.

"Angel, my ass," Brian mutters, finishing off his beer.

"It was you who corrupted me." She points him in the direction of the chilled wine on the counter. "Now, pour me a glass of that, so I can help my sister come up with a plan."

Brian salutes her before doing as she said.

"Drink in front of the pregnant woman," I mutter. "That'll sure make me feel better."

"Hey, my best ideas come when I've had a few glasses," Faith says. "All I'm saying is that Mom and Dad will find out sooner or later. You can't exactly hide being pregnant."

I tap the corner of my mouth before pointing at her. "What if I go on a long vacation when I start showing?"

"Then what?" Faith grabs the glass of red wine from Brian. "Are you going to tell them you randomly found a newborn?"

"She might be going somewhere with this," Brian says. "Go to Bermuda and bring them another grandchild as a souvenir."

I use both hands to flip each one of them off.

"What about you get a boyfriend and have him become the baby daddy?" Faith suggests.

"Those few sips of wine must've hit you hard if you think I can just date someone, and he'll step up as the father. Who wants to date a fat, randomly knocked-up woman?"

Faith swirls a strand of her hair—the same color as mine—around her finger, deep in thought. "You could always rent a baby daddy."

"Rent a what?" I stutter.

"Have a guy pretend to be the dad for the time being, introduce him to Mom and Dad, and then say you broke up," she explains as if it were the most logical advice she'd ever given.

I scrunch my nose. "You're out of your mind."

"Am I, though?" She empties her glass, pours herself another, and opens the fridge.

"Funny," I grumble when she pulls out a juice box and slides it to me.

She smiles. "Think about it."

———

"HEY, BABE," Cassidy says when I enter our living room.

She and Lincoln are snuggled on the couch. *Schitt's Creek* is playing on the TV—most likely an episode we've seen twenty times. Two empty wineglasses, an empty pizza box, and a bag of Doritos are on the coffee table.

Why does it seem like everyone is drinking when I can't?

Jamie owns the two-bedroom townhome. After she moved in with Cohen, Georgia and I rented it from her. Not too long later, Georgia and Archer got their heads out of their butts and finally started dating. As much as I was happy for her, I was devastated when she broke the news of them living together. She promised not to move out until I found another roommate, knowing I'd rather burn my earlobes off than live alone.

Luckily, Cassidy overheard us talking about it and offered to move in. She lived alone in a small apartment, and like me, she didn't like being alone. A new fear surfaced of losing another roommate when she and Lincoln started dating. Even though they could stay in Archer's empty penthouse, they chose to stay here, so I wouldn't have to live by myself.

As great as it is, having them here, another worry has hit me since finding out about the pregnancy. Cassidy might've said she was okay with being in the next room over and helping with the baby, but eventually, when she's up all night, listening to the baby crying, she might change her mind and leave.

She pauses the show, sits up, and snags the Doritos. "How'd it go with your sister? Did you break the baby news?"

I nod, dropping my bag to the floor, and relax on the bright red chair across from them.

"What'd she say?" She chomps on a chip.

I blow out an upward breath. "Her genius advice was to rent a baby daddy."

Lincoln snorts, sweeping Cassidy's blonde hair off her shoulder before draping his arm over it. "That might be a lucrative business actually."

My shoulders slump. "Yes, but I can't afford to rent a baby daddy for eighteen years."

Cassidy licks cheese off her fingers. "Hopefully, you'll find someone to be a great dad by that time."

"I have a good idea," Lincoln says, kicking his feet onto the table. "What about Finn?"

I blankly stare at him. "What about him?"

"Have him be the baby daddy," Lincoln explains.

I wish.

I'd do anything for Finn to be the father instead of Gavin.

Cassidy perks up. "That's actually a really good idea." She kisses Lincoln's cheek. "Look at you, being all smart, baby."

Lincoln smiles with pride before smacking a kiss against Cassidy's lips.

I shake my head. "I can't ask him to do that."

"Why?" Cassidy asks. "I bet you twenty bucks he'd totally say yes."

CHAPTER EIGHT

Finn

NOT MUCH RELAXES ME.

I play the role of the opposite—the laid-back guy who cracks jokes and doesn't have a care in the world. I'm a good pretender—always have been. I tricked my teachers into thinking my dad worked so much that he wasn't able to attend any conferences or events. I convinced child services that I didn't stay home alone all night because my father was out, not giving a shit about his son.

I'm a survivor, and what better way to survive than to act like you don't give a shit?

At least tonight, being with friends will clear my mind from my dad's bullshit. The day after I paid for his car repairs, he called and needed money for his electric bill. He claimed it had to be paid in two hours or they'd shut it off.

It's his normal MO. He asks for shit last minute to create urgency of getting what he wants. You can't say, *Let me call you back in a few hours*, or question him because if you wait too long, there's always the dreaded reconnection fee.

Reconnection fees have fucked me more than any ex-girlfriend.

Like the dumbass I always am, I paid it while he bitched in the background on how dare I lecture where he spends his money.

"Less on drugs, more on bills," is what I'd said.

Only the guys know about my father, and out of respect for me, they've always kept it hush-hush around others. Grace discovering the trash I grew up as terrifies me. Her family is structured—wealthy and stand-up people. Not only that, but if her father has a good memory, he'd warn her about me.

It's the main reason that has stopped me from making her mine. There's too much against us to make it work, and now, her being pregnant with another man's baby only adds fuel to that messy fire.

The gang is already there when I walk into Cohen's backyard. Our group tends to get together as often as we can. Cohen has a kick-ass yard, where we grill out, play cornhole, and celebrate special occasions if the weather isn't shitty.

As if on autopilot, I immediately scan the yard for Grace. I don't care what the occasion is; Grace is always the first person on my mind. She's sitting at a table with Georgia, Lola, Cassidy, Lincoln, and Silas, and before I reach them, I pause and smile, watching her from across the yard.

My favorite is when she doesn't know I'm watching or that she's on display for anyone. Laid-back Grace is the best Grace. It's a heavenly sight when she puts her guard down. Her playful behavior tears through that daily polished appearance. Just like my bliss is when I'm with our friends, it's also when the true Grace shines.

Her strawberry-blonde hair is pulled back from her face with two thick braids entwined along her forehead. Her plump lips are a soft pink, and a white silk top falls off one shoulder. Looking at Grace, you'd see her fitting into a puzzle with a man sporting loafers and a thousand-dollar polo. Not me—a man who doesn't give a shit what the label on his shirt says, who has a few tats and overgrown stubble on his cheeks.

We're not supposed to fit.

Yet we perfectly click.

For a moment, I forget how shit has changed for us, how we'll never be the same even though I'd pay for our friendship to never change course.

When her eyes meet mine, I stroll toward her.

A light brush of wind hits my cheeks when I stop behind her chair.

"Hey you," I say, wrapping my arms around her shoulders.

Her body relaxes against my touch, and a smile tugs at her lips when she tips her head back to peer at me. "Hi."

I give her shoulders a slight squeeze before pulling back and taking the chair next to her. It's open as if everyone knew next to her is always my spot.

I clasp my hands together and focus on her. "How are you feeling?"

She sighs. "I'm feeling okay … just working and silently asking God why he made wine bad for pregnant women." Her cheeks turn rosy as she scrunches up her face. "Why can't wine be like vitamins? A daily prenatal glass of wine."

I chuckle before tipping my head toward Silas. "Make Grace a kick-ass nonalcoholic drink."

Silas isn't a drinker, so he's mastered the skill of concocting nonalcoholic drinks some would prefer over the real thing.

"I've already tried. Her pregnant taste buds think all of them suck," Silas replies, shrugging.

"I'm picky," Grace mutters.

My attention returns to her. "Other than the no-liquor inconvenience, how are *you* doing?"

"Shitty," Lincoln answers for her, bringing it to my attention that everyone's eyes are on us. "She needs a baby daddy. Any suggestions on where she can get one?"

"Seriously?" Grace narrows her eyes at him.

My gut twists, and I hate him for even mentioning that idea. "I can't help with that, babe, but if there's anything else you need—"

"You can help with it," Cassidy interrupts, leaning forward from across the table. "Do you have plans for the next six or seven months?"

I raise a brow, knowing where she's going with this but hoping I'm wrong.

Cassidy gestures to Grace, who's giving her a *shut up* signal by slicing her hand against her throat. "She needs a baby daddy, and, Finn, I think you're the man for the job."

"Don't listen to them," Grace rushes out. "They've been lucky enough to have alcohol, and they have lost their senses."

"Come on, Finn," Georgia cuts in. "Grace is nervous about telling her parents she's pregnant on top of there being no father. She hates disappointing people. I'd paint a beard on myself and stuff some socks into my pants to make it appear like I had a cock, but they already know me."

Grace does a sweeping gesture toward everyone at the table. "I am killing all of you."

"Look," Lincoln says, his eyes on me, "it's not like you have anything better to do. Everyone is coupled up, except Silas and you, and I doubt Grace wants Silas playing baby daddy."

Silas slaps his hand over his heart. "That's rude, asshole."

Lincoln shrugs. "It'll be a little awkward when you later become Lola's baby daddy."

Silas smirks at Lola, grabbing her chair and dragging it closer to his. "I'll take that."

Lola ruffles her hand through his thick hair. "In your dreams."

"Every damn night, baby." Silas slaps a kiss to her cheek, only inches from her lips.

"Back to the topic at hand," Cassidy says, her tone serious. "You game to play baby daddy, Finn?"

"You don't have to listen to them." Grace's voice is panicked.

"You should definitely listen to us," Georgia corrects.

All eyes are on me.

Everyone is quiet.

Including Grace.

As I peek at her, I read every emotion on her face.

There's fear.

I'm not sure which is stronger, though—fear of me rejecting the idea or fear of disappointing her family, who mean the world to her. She's not begging me to say no, not walking away, only staring ahead and waiting for my response.

"All right." I grab Lincoln's beer and chug it. "Why not?"

CHAPTER NINE

GRACE

Grace

"WHY NOT?"

The words replay through my brain as if stuck.

Did Finn just agree to ... play my baby daddy?

Pretty much said challenge accepted to our friends?

Excitement buzzes through the air, our friends ecstatic over Finn agreeing to their crazy idea. Their elation and throwing out ideas of creating the perfect relationship deflect attention away from me—thank God. It gives me time to process the situation.

I refuse to peek at Finn, but I feel his stare pinned on me, searching for my reaction. Rather than ask me questions, Finn captures my hand and links our fingers together. He settles them on his knee—a silent reminder, assuring me that everything will be okay.

With perfect timing, Cohen interrupts the conversation.

"Food is ready!" he shouts, heading in our direction.

In one hand is a plate of burgers and steaks, and the other has hot dogs and chicken. Behind him, Jamie carries Isabella in her arms and Noah grips bags of chips.

Nausea curls at my stomach. Pulling away from Finn, I cover my mouth, gagging, doing everything to hold in the urge to vomit.

Yet another reason to knee Gavin in the balls.

Not only do I get morning sickness, but certain foods also make me hurl.

Cohen places the plates on the table, and I can't stop myself from wincing and pushing back in my chair. The last thing I want to do is decorate tonight's dinner with my vomit.

Finn scoots in closer. "Everything okay?"

I gulp, another attempt to not puke, and shyly peek over at him. "The baby isn't a fan of meat."

He nods in understanding. "What is the baby a fan of?"

"Cupcakes … deviled eggs …" I scrunch up my nose in embarrassment. "Bagels dipped in taco sauce."

How I came up with that combo, I have no idea.

"That should be easy." He slaps his hand on the table and pulls himself to his feet. "I'll raid Cohen's kitchen, and if all else fails, we'll order something."

I grab his arm before gagging again, the wind pushing the odor toward me, making it stronger. "I don't want to be a pain. I'll hold my breath and snack on chips."

"Sorry, guys," Finn says, standing tall as if making an announcement. "I forgot to tell you, I'm trying the whole meatless thing."

This time, I cover my mouth to mask a snort. Our friends' reactions are similar to mine. Finn's favorite meal is a juicy steak and veggies.

"Dude, you brought half the meat," Lincoln says.

"It was my turn to bring it," Finn says. "I'm not going to try to push my new lifestyle onto you."

Silas shrugs, suspiciously eyeing Finn before lifting his chin in his direction. "More for me then. Now, let's eat up."

"Feel free to raid the pantry," Jamie says while Cohen pulls out a chair and motions for her to sit.

"Thanks," he says, giving her a thumbs-up. He runs a finger along my arm, and I shiver. "Grace, I need some help."

Resting his palm against the base of my back, he veers me toward the house.

"Thank you for the save," I whisper, bumping my shoulder against his. Once again, he's saving my ass.

He bumps me back. "You know I always got your back, Mitchell."

It's a short walk to the back door, and we head into the kitchen. My heart thrashes into my chest now that we're alone and I'm no longer consumed with trying not to puke. Us being alone most likely means one of us will broach the subject of what he agreed to do.

He turns, resting his back against the fridge, and crosses his arms. "I figured you needed a minute … and also that you didn't want to barf on everyone."

I shuffle my sandals along the floor. "I wasn't expecting that."

"That makes two of us, but given our friends, it shouldn't be much of a surprise."

"You don't have to do it, you know?"

Our friends can be pushy, and he was put on the spot.

If Finn fakes being my baby daddy, that'll momentarily stop him from dating someone else.

"Grace, look at me." His tone is stern.

I slowly lift my chin, our gazes meeting. Mine is giving off a *scared shitless* vibe. His is intense and concerned.

"Will it help you?"

I slowly nod. "It will."

"Then I'm game. Whatever you need, I'm here." He pauses to hold up a finger. "As long as you're okay with it. This is your decision, not our friends'."

"It's better than renting someone." I crack a forced smile.

"What?" He flinches. "You were going to *rent a dude*?"

"Negative. It was my sister's advice."

"Don't listen to your sister anymore. Whatever you need, I'm here." He pushes himself off the fridge. "Now, let's get you some *baby in your belly*–approved dinner."

———

TIMES I'VE BEEN JEALOUS:

  1. Meeting one of Finn's flings.

2. Being ten and my mean cousin getting the Barbie
   Dreamhouse that I wanted from Santa.
3. Seeing Instagram models eat sixteen hot dogs and not gain
   a pound.

I rarely envy people, but at times, it sneaks up on me.

Today, it's snuck up on me like heartburn.

Sitting in my chair, I watch Finn play cornhole with Noah. They're on the same team—something not many adults like to do because they tend to lose when they're with the kid. But Finn? Finn never minds. He cheers Noah on every turn and high-fives him whether he misses or not.

A knot of regret forms in my gut, and the macaroni Finn made me earlier threatens to come up.

I wish I were pregnant with Finn's baby.

What I'd give for the role we'll soon be playing to be my reality.

Watching him, I know he'd be a better father than Gavin. I also love him, not Gavin. But it's too late for that now.

I'm used goods.

A woman pregnant by a married man.

"There you go!" Finn shouts after Noah throws the sack into the hole, lifting him up in the air.

Noah bursts into a fit of laughter.

That right there is a man I imagined being pregnant with.

Someone who doesn't mind forgoing their favorite meal to have boxed mac and cheese with me. A man who doesn't mind losing as long as a kid is happy.

Finn might tell people he doesn't deserve a woman like me, but he's wrong.

I don't deserve a man like him.

———

I WAKE up in a pool of sweat, every muscle in my body tight.

I'm in bed but in a state of terror and unaware of my

surroundings. My heart pummels against my chest so hard that I wait for it to burst from my body.

I dart up from my bed, pushing my back against the headboard, and pull my knees to my chest. My hair is soaked, and I swat it away from my eyes as tears fall down my cheeks. Sucking in deep breaths, I attempt to calm myself, to stay quiet so I don't wake anyone.

It's been a while since I've had a nightmare ... especially one as realistic as the one I just had. They tend to make appearances when I'm stressed, feeling lost, struggling to cope with my reality.

What's more stressful than being knocked up by a man you can't stand?

My nightstand lamp shines next to me—a dim light so I'm still able to sleep at night—and I rock back and forth as if I were preparing to cradle the baby I'll soon have.

"Breathe in, breathe out," I repeat between sobs.

My lungs only knock harder against my chest, my breathing more panicked, the fear of suffocation rising through me. With shaking hands, I snatch my phone from my nightstand so hard that the charger falls off the wall.

I bite back a scream while calling Faith and cry her name into the phone when she answers.

"Another one?" Her voice is sleepy yet alert at the same time.

"Another one," I sob.

"Stay on the phone with me until you calm down, okay?"

I love my sister. There will never be another person who understands this bad side of me, this fear that is stuck to my core and will never be released, a flaw so deep that it's with me forever.

She stays with me on the phone—some time spent talking, some crying, and some in silence.

I don't hang up.

She waits until I'm sleeping to end the call.

CHAPTER TEN

Finn

"THERE'S THE BABY DADDY!" Silas shouts, his hand cupped over his mouth when I walk into Twisted Fox.

I flip him off while joining him at the pub table. "Real funny, asshole."

"You really doing this?" He stares at me with humor on his face.

I gulp. "I think so."

I haven't talked with Grace much since the whole *agreeing to be the fake baby daddy* thing. We didn't have much privacy at Cohen's. Last night, I texted and asked what she needed of me. Tomorrow, my role as her baby daddy will start, and I'm scared shitless.

Silas plants his elbow on the table and stares at me. "How do you feel about it?"

I suck in a breath. "It'll be ... weird."

"Nah, you and Grace are practically dating anyway." He snatches a fry from his red basket of food and tosses it into his mouth. "It won't be any different."

"Except I'm meeting her family ... her father, the *judge*."

"Oh fuck, I forgot about that."

At times, I forget who Grace's dad is, too, but then randomly, it'll creep back up—my past surfacing through the stained cracks. It's a reminder that no matter what, I'll always be my father's son. I was once on the same path as the man who puts me through the wringer daily. Not the drug part, but the *not getting my shit together and thinking rules don't apply to me* part. Thank God I dragged myself out of that life. That doesn't mean I haven't made mistakes that have come back to bite me in the ass.

"It's not like I can go back on my word now."

"Dude, I doubt he'll even remember you." He gestures to his basket. "A fry for your thoughts?"

I shake my head, my stomach roiling. "Let's hope he doesn't remember me."

I'm tight with all the guys in our circle, but Silas and I are the closest. Especially lately with everyone else being coupled up. We're two single guys who act like we're dating women we aren't.

We both have our secrets.

Shady pasts we've kept from people so they don't look at us differently.

"Want to do something tomorrow?" He pushes his basket up the table. "Watch the game? Have beers? Whatever to get you prepared for your new role?"

"Can't." I snatch up a fry. "Baby-daddy duties start tomorrow."

He smirks. "Which is?"

"Meeting the sister."

––––––––

I DID some crazy shit in my early teens.

Blame it on lack of parental guidance.

Hating the world.

Rebelling as much as I could.

Not that I ever got in trouble.

There was no grounding for me because that would have meant my father would have to parent—something John Duke had no time for.

But what I'm doing with Grace?

It takes the cake.

I wipe my sweaty hands down my jeans as I walk up her porch stairs and knock on the front door. It swings open, and Grace stands in front of me. A worried smile stains her pink lips as she nervously waves me inside. As soon as she shuts the door behind me, I pull her into a tight hug—an assurance that everything will go smoothly today.

"Day one of us fake dating and acting like I knocked you up," I say, cracking a smile as we pull away.

She slowly nods. "At least I don't have to lie yet since my sister already knows we're faking."

I bite into my tongue, holding back from saying, *What if we don't fake it?*

If someone were to ask me what my dream life was, it wouldn't be riches, mansions, or an endless supply of women. It'd be a life with Grace—her in my bed, wearing the diamond ring I picked out, and having our children.

I do a sweeping gesture down her body. "I'd like to throw out that my fake baby mama looks hot as hell today."

No matter what Grace wears, she always looks fucking adorable. Her style changes from day to day, but she usually sports loose-fitting dresses or casual clothes when it's just our friends and us. Today, she's chosen a yellow sundress that hangs loose off one shoulder and ends inches from her ankles, showing off glittery sandals. Her hair is in another crown braid—her signature style—and the only makeup she's wearing is a light-pink shimmer over her eyes.

She blushes. "You clean up pretty well yourself."

I dragged Silas and Lola out shopping this morning to help me dress the part of Grace's boyfriend. My usual casual tee has been traded out for a black collared button-down. Grace only brought a few guys around us before we became close, and none of them resembled me. Not that I want to look like them either.

You can bet your ass, you'll never catch me sporting khaki shorts with creases in the middle and a sweater draped over my neck.

No fucking thank you.

A moment of awkwardness passes—something that hasn't happened in our relationship in years but seems to have become the regular since her pregnancy news broke.

I study her for a moment, double-checking she's not too stressed, and I check my watch. "You ready to go?"

She nods. "As ready as I'll ever be."

Leaving the house, I guide her to my Challenger, open the passenger door, and wait until she slides in before joining her.

During the drive, my mind scrambles.

How will we end this game?

When will we know it's time to pull the plug?

How deep will it wound our relationship when we stop playing pretend?

It's too late to back out now.

———

I SHIFT my car into park and turn in my seat to peer at Grace. "You nervous?"

Hell, my nerves might be climbing higher than hers.

It's not every day you fake being a woman's baby daddy—especially when you wish it were true.

I'd do anything for this woman to be mine, but I was too chickenshit to take my shot.

"A little," she replies, fidgeting with a charm on her bracelet. "How strong will the interrogation be?"

"My sister is nice but can be overprotective." She unbuckles her seat belt. "Now's your chance to back out. Speak now or forever hold your peace."

"No backing out, babe. I'm here for as long as you need me."

Her shoulders relax. "You're too good to me."

No, you're too good for me.

I reach over my console and capture her hand in mine, running my finger along her soft skin. "We got this, babe. We've made a badass team for years. It was about time we stepped our game up to see what else we could do."

She repeatedly nods as if my pep talk is convincing her. "You're right. We got this."

I kiss the top of her hand before releasing her and cut the engine.

Grace's sister's neighborhood is exactly what I expected. A gated entrance; a large, grassy lawn, manicured to perfection; and a home that could be featured in a magazine.

It's a far cry from where I came from.

I wasn't the rich kid in school.

I wasn't even the middle-class kid.

I was the dirt-poor boy whose hand-me-downs stank of cigarette smoke and whose father showed up to one of my football games, drunk off his ass, demanding I give him money for *all the shit he's done for me*. Rich kids mocked me until they realized I'd beat their asses. After a few punches to their faces, the jerks' shit-talking lessened. That didn't mean they still didn't look down on me.

Facial expressions always speak louder than words.

Grace adjusts her dress, inhales a steady breath, and steps out of the car. I do the same and am by her side. The scent of fresh-cut grass follows us up the driveway to the bright red front door surrounded by potted plants.

Without bothering to knock, Grace walks us in.

"Hello," she calls out while entering the expansive entryway.

There's shiplap—shiplap everywhere.

I only know what damn shiplap is because Grace and Georgia used to force me to watch some HGTV shit, and every damn homeowner wanted their walls covered in the shit.

Apparently, Grace's sister fits that bill as well.

"In the kitchen!" someone out of view yells.

My attention shifts to the stairs as Raven, Grace's niece, comes barreling down the stairs.

"Aunt Grace!" she yells, stomping down each step. "You brought Finn! He's my friend!"

Raven tags along with Grace sometimes, especially when Noah is involved. They've become good friends, and it gives Noah someone to play with. During our last trip to a ski lodge for Noah's birthday, she told me she asks her parents for a little brother or sister daily. I'm sure having a cousin will help too.

I grin. "I sure am."

I'm good with kids—at least, that's what people tell me. Hell, half the time, I'd rather sit and chat with a kiddo than an adult.

Raven's red-hued pigtails bounce in the air as she hops on her feet. "Maybe we can play games later?"

"Maybe." Grace plays with her braid, twirling it around her fingers.

Grace squeezes Raven's shoulder. "Let's see what your mom is up to."

"Oh, she's just making dinner," Raven says, throwing her hand up as if it were no big deal while we meander down a hallway. "She's making me dino nuggets, though, because it's what I want."

Grace laughs. "You're going to end up turning into a dino nugget."

"Hey now," I say, winking at Raven. "Dino nuggets are pretty darn good."

She squeals, clapping her hands, her walk turning into a skip. "See, Mommy! Finn loves dino nuggets too!"

Reaching the kitchen, we stop. The smell of garlic smacks me in the face as I do a quick once-over of my surroundings. It's a big-ass kitchen with more shiplap, stainless steel appliances, and baby-blue cabinets. It's a kitchen you'd normally find in a farmhouse, not a home like this.

"Hey, guys!"

My gaze shifts to the island, where a spitting image of Grace stands —only taller and with more blond in her hair. She smiles at us while slicing a knife through a tomato on the cutting board.

Grace steps to my side, somewhat in front of me as if she were my bodyguard. "Finn, this is my sister, Faith."

With the knife still in her hand, Faith waves at me, tomato juice slipping onto the counter. "Hi, Finn." She shoots a mischievous look to Grace. "We've heard so much about you. You sounded too good to be true, so Brian and I had a bet that you weren't real."

"Really?" Grace grumbles with a scowl.

"He's real, Mommy!" Raven jumps up and down and points at me. "He buys me ice cream too!"

"Yes, she always raves about the ice cream you get her," a guy says, walking into the kitchen, holding a bottle of wine. "Can I get you something to drink, Finn? A juice box for you, Grace?"

Grace rolls her eyes. "You should really go on the road since your jokes are so original. I'm sure no pregnant girl has heard that one before." She motions toward the guy. "This is my brother-in-law, Brian."

The guy dramatically bows. "Thank you. I always knew you appreciated my jokes."

I expected something different—snobbery or an upturned nose—but these people seem as laid-back as our friends.

Sure, the size of their home, the large rock on Faith's finger, and the expensive bottle of wine Brian is opening scream money, but their personalities scream cool.

"Beer?" Brian asks. "Jack and Diet? We have a full bar, so anything you want, I can grab you."

"I'll have a water." I don't want Grace to feel like the odd one out of drinking.

"I'll take one of those juice boxes ..." Grace pauses. "Actually, why don't you grab the juicer and make me some fresh OJ, Brian?"

"Why don't you drink Raven's sugar-free shit?" He smirks.

"Daddy said a bad word!" Raven says with a scowl.

"Finn, I hope eggplant parmigiana is okay with you," Faith says. "Meat makes Grace sick, so we're trying an alternative."

Grace pulls out a stool under the island, and I grab her hand, helping her jump up onto it.

Gripping the back of the stool, I reply, "That's fine with me."

And now, we get ready for our baby daddy game to start.

CHAPTER ELEVEN

Grace

"I LIKE HIM," Faith says when we're alone. "Like, really like him and could totally smack you for not getting knocked up by him." She shoves my shoulder. "I swear, for someone who's so damn smart, you fail in the dating department."

We're outside on the patio after dinner. We ate outside, and the fresh air helped calm my nerves. No one brought up the game Finn and I are playing. Most likely because Raven was with us, and that girl is the definition of the game Telephone. Never say anything in front of her you don't want our entire family to find out about.

Finn had to take a phone call, and Brian left to grab Faith another glass of wine.

I lean in closer, lowering my voice in case Finn comes back. "We are *friends*. That's it."

"Mm-hmm." Sarcasm coats her tone.

I don't know why I was nervous about Finn meeting Faith and Brian. They get along with nearly everyone. While I helped Faith with dinner, Finn and Brian made small talk. It was comfortable, and I wish I hadn't realized I could've had this sooner before getting involved with Gavin. We could've had this if we weren't too terrified of commitment with each other.

Gavin has never met my family.

I've never met his … for obvious reasons I now know.

Now, after discovering the real Gavin, I know Faith would've probably hated him.

It's different with Finn—the stakes are higher.

We're not just friends anymore.

Us playing pretend will create more attachment to each other.

It's a dangerous game we're playing—the game of *everything we've ever wanted.*

And no doubt, our feelings will grow as this plays out. I'll discover what it's like to be his girlfriend, but eventually, he'll pull away at the end, and I'll be left broken. I need to start preparing myself for when that day comes.

"Now, it's planning time," Faith says, snapping me out of my thoughts.

I raise a brow. "What do you mean?"

She flips her long hair over her slender shoulder. "Mom and Dad will ask questions—*lots* of them. They'll drill you on every detail, so you need to be prepared. You and Finn need to be on the same page— how you met, how you got pregnant—"

"That one is fairly obvious," I interrupt.

She swats my shoulder. "You know what I mean. They'll ask Finn how he plans to support you and the baby, if he's ready to become a father, why he didn't pop the question before knocking you up—all that personal shit."

The thought of my father's interrogation sends a chill up my spine.

"Jesus," I hiss. "Did they cross-examine Brian like that?"

She shakes her head. "Brian and I were married, though. Dad had already interrogated him when we started dating. Our pregnancy wasn't a shocker … wasn't with a man they'd never even heard of." She levels her eyes on me, her expression turning stern. "Therefore, tie those loose ends before they unravel in front of Mom and Dad."

"I guess we'll"—I scrunch up my nose—"tie stuff up."

I haven't even planned on when I'm telling my parents, and I'm already stressed.

I have to train myself on being a better liar before I enter that rabbit hole.

"You need a clear, concise plan," Faith continues. "That starts with you moving in together."

I picked the perfect time to take a sip of water and spit it out at her words. "Excuse me?"

Her face is serious. "You are dating, having a baby, but not living together? That screams suspicious."

"I'll blame it on them not wanting me to move in with a guy before marriage."

"You're knocked up. They'll at least expect that."

"Easier said than done. I live in a two-bedroom and have a roommate I can't exactly kick out."

"Share a room with Finn then." She throws out the suggestion so casually as if it were sharing ice cream, not a bed.

"You've had too much wine." I snatch her glass and set it out of her reach. "You're cut off."

She stands up from her chair enough to confiscate her glass from me. "Think about it, okay?" She chugs it. "It'll make your story much more believable. Mom and Dad will believe the relationship is serious and that you didn't get knocked up by some rando."

She makes a point there.

My parents will immediately think Finn and I aren't serious if we're living separately and we haven't met each other's parents, therefore not taking our *relationship* to the next level.

"We'll lie about living together." My mouth grows dry at the thought of another lie, and I wish I could yell for Brian to pour me a glass too. "There. Problem solved."

"You're racking up the lies there, dear sister." She shifts in her chair, relaxing against the back. "On another note, while you're hiding from Mom and Dad, where are you going to crash when Lincoln and Cassidy work at night? You either need to come clean to them soon, sleep here, or be alone." All playfulness in her tone has vanished. "If they find out Finn works late nights at the bar, they won't believe you live together. They know you'd never be with someone who couldn't be with you at night."

Crap.

She has a point.

A big freaking point.

I thought I was figuring it out, and then she had to throw a wrench in that plan.

"He works at night, and I can't ask him to quit his job," I say, my voice strained. I grip the arms of my chair. "Not to mention, I can't ask my roommates to move out."

She stares at me intently. "You said before that Lincoln and Cassidy have another place, but they haven't moved out because they don't want to bail on you. Can you ask them to stay there until you get stuff figured out? You also need to talk to them about plans for when you have the baby. Will the baby sleep in your room?"

"I hate when you ask all the questions," I grumble.

"That's what a big sister is for." She brushes her hand along my arm. "Look, everything will be okay."

"All right, sorry about that," Finn says, strolling toward us and sliding his phone into his pocket.

He arrives at the same time Brian returns with a beer in one hand.

I offer Finn a smile that fails to reach my eyes. "Totally fine."

Faith locks her fingers together and rests them on the table. "Finn, how do you feel about moving in with Grace?"

Finn stops mid-step.

CHAPTER TWELVE

Finn

THERE WERE things I expected from meeting Grace's sister.

Questions regarding my job.

Asking if I was good at faking being someone's boyfriend.

What I'd do when the charade was over.

None of those questions came to the surface.

What I got instead was ...

"How do you feel about moving in with Grace?"

Faith said it casually as if she asked me if I wanted dessert.

"What?" I stutter, my mouth dropping open.

The idea never occurred to me. I assumed Grace and I were only playing our game around her parents, but moving in together? That makes it more real. It'd be more than faking it. We'd be *living* it.

All eyes are on me.

Grace's panicked.

Faith's in expectation.

Brian's unsurprised.

"You don't ... you don't have to do that," Grace rushes out. "As you can see, my sister loves wine, and it's made her come up with crazy ideas."

Faith holds up a finger. "Your first statement is true. The second isn't crazy." She waves her hands toward the table. "Take a few breaths. I'm sure my question was a shocker, but now, let's talk about it."

"Okay," I drawl out. "Let's, uh … talk about it."

"You don't have to do this," Grace says as soon as I sit back down.

"Our parents will expect you to be living together," Faith says, and I'm figuring out now why she became an attorney. "It's something they'll expect. If you're not married, it'd at least show that there's a commitment somewhere."

"This is all new to us," I croak. "We're pretty much playing it as we go."

My head scrambles.

Could I do that?

Live with her and not want her more?

Play house before jumping ship and acting like it never happened?

"Are you going to keep working at Twisted Fox?" Faith asks, clearly in charge of the conversation.

"Jesus, Faith." Grace releases an exasperated breath. "The only interrogation Finn expects is from our parents, not you."

Faith shakes her head. "Mom and Dad will never believe you're dating if he's not there with you at night."

Grace's face pales. "Finn can't exactly move his work schedule around. People don't go barhopping in the morning."

"What if you had another job, Finn?" Brian asks, looking me straight in the eye.

I hold his eye contact. "What do you mean?"

He leans back in his chair, gripping the neck of his beer. "You can work at Luxury Imports."

Luxury Imports is a chain of dealerships that specializes in selling high-end and hard-to-find luxury cars. You nearly need a black card to test-drive a car there. I've never been inside, but Archer purchased his car from them. Pretty sure Lincoln did too.

I bend my neck forward to hide the shock on my face. "Man, I can't ask you to do that."

"You didn't ask. I offered." There's no hesitation in Brian's tone— no, *my wife is making me do this*. No, the dude is genuinely offering me a job at one of the largest chains of car dealerships in the state.

As much as I'd love to take the offer, I can't.

"My best friends own the bar I work in," I say, raising my chin. "I can't up and leave them."

"What about working at the bar only a few nights a week and supplementing that income by working at my place? I have a few different positions that I think you'd be perfect for." He smiles. "Your pick."

Silence passes over the table.

"How about this?" Brian finally says, knocking his knuckles against the table. "I'll pay double what you make at the bar, and you won't have to work nights. You'll get benefits, a 401(k), all that good stuff. I know you don't want to let your friends down, but this is a great opportunity for you."

I hide my shaking hands under the table. "What about when Grace and I break off"—I refuse to glance at her—"whatever this is?"

Brian sits up straight. "You'll still have a job for as long as you like. I think you'll be a good fit. Trust me, I wouldn't have offered if I'd thought you'd be a shit employee."

———

GRACE'S VOICE is frantic as soon as we get into my car. "Don't feel obligated to take that job, Finn. I know tonight was a lot, and I hadn't planned on any of that going down. I'd figured they'd have questions, but I had no idea. I swear, I had no part in it."

I place my hand over her trembling one.

"Are you mad?" she asks at my silence.

I sag against the seat. "I didn't earn it."

I don't like favors.

They always come with a price, an *I did this for you.*

Blame it on a father who throws every damn thing in your face—*I made sure you were fed, I bought you clothes to cover your back, I gave you a roof to sleep under.* Every time my father did me a favor, it was thrown in my face.

That's why I never ask for help.

Why, sometimes, my pride bites me in the ass.

"Finn," Grace says, her voice softening, "sometimes opportunities come as luck. You're putting your life on hold for me. You deserve this. You've earned it. It's not easy to land a job at Luxury Imports. It's not your typical car dealership. It's a big deal."

"And what about the *moving in with you* thing?"

CHAPTER THIRTEEN

Grace

SILENCE IS in the air while Finn walks me to my front door.

I turn to look at him and fiddle with the keys in my hand. "Cass and Lincoln are home. Unless you want to be interrogated by them next, I wouldn't suggest you come in."

We only spent a few hours at Faith's, but Finn appears as if he's been through the wringer.

It's the same with me.

Topics came up that I hadn't expected.

My life has become a spinning wheel of answers to endless questions.

He scratches his cheek. "Text me later?"

I nod. "Thank you so much for doing this, Finn. It means a lot."

"Grace, anything you need, I'm here. Good night."

He pecks a kiss to my forehead and waits for me to walk inside before returning to his car. As I drop my keys on the entry table, thoughts of how much my life is changing hit me.

I enter the living room to find Cassidy and Lincoln on the couch, snuggled as usual and watching TV. Our living room is where we spend most of our free time. Cassidy and Lincoln are homebodies, like me. We binge-watch shows, eat junk food, and have our friends over for game nights. It's on the smaller side, but the open floor plan is great for entertaining.

Cassidy raises her head from Lincoln's chest and sits up. "How'd it go, babe?"

Collapsing onto a chair, I rub my forehead. "I'm done with questions for tonight … or heck, even the next year."

She laughs. "All right, I'll wait until the morning to drill you on how well Finn played the boyfriend role."

"Not only did they tell him to move in with me but they also want him to work for Luxury Imports."

Cassidy and Lincoln stay quiet, staring while waiting for an explanation.

I give them what they want. "They think it'll be more believable to my parents."

"What did Finn say?" Lincoln asks, stroking his jaw.

"He's hesitant about the job because he doesn't want to bail on Cohen and Archer after he's worked for them for so long." I stop myself from slapping a hand over my mouth.

Archer is Lincoln's brother, and I'd feel terrible if he told Archer about Finn's job offer before Finn had a chance to talk to him. I gulp before remembering this is Lincoln, and he's one of the most trustworthy people I know.

"Is it better pay?" Cassidy asks.

I nod.

Lincoln settles his gaze on me. "I guarantee you, if Finn tells them it's a better opportunity, they'll be happy for him."

He's right. Our circle of friends is supportive of each other, no matter what. We will step up and do anything to help because we're like family.

"I promise I'm not saying this to stress you out," Cassidy starts.

"You saying something isn't meant to stress me out will definitely stress me out," I interrupt.

She laughs. "Well then, prepare to be stressed for a minute." Her voice turns gentle as she stares at me. "What will you and Finn do after the baby is born … after you're finished convincing your parents that he's the dad?"

I hate that question because I have no idea how to answer it.

Will we stay friends?

Will we have a fake breakup plan?

"I haven't thought that far ahead." I narrow my gaze on her. "You guys are the ones who came up with the genius plan. I guess you can come up with post-baby plans too."

"You two could"—Cassidy hesitates as if trying to come up with the right words—"stay together."

"Oh, come on," I sing out, dropping back my head.

"What?" She perks up. "I'm sure Finn would be okay with that plan."

A knot ties in my belly. "Have you seen the girls Finn has dated? They're the opposite of me. We're friends. That's it."

"No, I actually haven't," she replies. "In all the time that I've known Finn, I've never seen him with another woman other than you … and our friends, of course."

The air starts to grow heavy.

My breathing grows ragged.

She's right.

Finn stopped bringing girls to our social gatherings years ago.

He doesn't entertain women who flirt with him at the bar, but I'm also not stupid. Just because he doesn't flirt with them in front of me doesn't mean he's abstained from sex. I find it as more of a respect thing for me.

"Same," Lincoln inputs, twirling a strand of Cassidy's blond hair around his finger. "Nor have I heard him even mention another woman."

"You two have sexual chemistry off the charts," Cassidy adds, nodding with certainty. "Try it. What do you have to lose?"

"Um, our friendship," I say like *duh.*

"Cass and I were scared of that too," Lincoln says, shooting Cassidy a flirtatious grin. "When we got our heads out of our asses and took the risk, it was worth it." Throwing his arm around Cassidy's shoulders, he drags her closer to him and kisses the slant of her jaw. "It's what happened with all our friends. Take that damn risk, Grace.

You only have one life, and trust me, shit can change in an instant." He snaps his fingers. "I know that from experience."

"I'll think about it."

Apprehension and fear gather within me. Lincoln and Cassidy take the hint that I've had enough talk, and our conversation gears toward a *drunken idiot at the bar* story. The conversation of Finn moving in doesn't arise again. I'm not sure if it's them giving me a mental break or if they're upset with me. I make a mental note to ask when my nerves aren't on fire.

It's not long until I tread down the hallway and into my bedroom. I pull my phone from my bag to find a good-night text from Finn.

As I slide into bed, my brain goes through memories of Finn.

Other than my father, he's been the most reliable man in my life. When he says he'll be there, he'll be there.

I trust Finn with my life … but can I trust him with my heart?

CHAPTER FOURTEEN

Finn

MY EYES ARE heavy as I walk into Twisted Fox.

I spent my night thinking about Brian's job offer. I'd made it clear to everyone at dinner last night that I wouldn't make any decisions until I talked to my friends.

As soon as Cohen and Archer decided to open Twisted Fox, they offered me a job. I've worked in bars for as long as I've legally been able to.

Okay, that's a lie.

I *helped* in one before I was even legally able to get my license. My father was a frequent patron at a local bar, and since I was the one always picking him up, the owner hired me to pick up trash and miscellaneous bullshit while I was waiting on my dad to have *just one more*.

I think the owner felt sorry for me and didn't want me at home with no supervision that young. He paid me under the table. It wasn't much, but it paid for my food and the school supplies my father was too broke to buy me. It also paid for the times he held out his hand, asking for every penny I had to make my contribution to the bills.

When I turned twenty-one, I started legally working in bars since it was quick money. It stuck, and I've stayed with it since. Working in bars is what led me to my friends, and I'll always be thankful for that.

Cohen is one of the kindest dudes I know. He's had it rough, practically raising his sister and then becoming a single dad. The baby mama dipped on him right after giving birth, and then years later, he started hanging out with her younger sister. Some drama happened, but now, they're happy.

I rub the back of my neck before knocking on Cohen's office door. The door is open, but he's my boss, so I respect his privacy and wait for him to let me in.

Cohen looks away from his phone and toward the doorway. "Hey, man."

I rock back on my heels. "Can I talk to you and Archer real quick?"

"Sure." His brows draw together as he sets his phone down and stands. "We'll go to his office because he'll bitch if he has to come to mine."

I chuckle. "Fact."

As much as we love Archer, the dude has to be the crankiest son of a bitch I've ever met—and I grew up around addicts. He's not a people person, but that doesn't mean he doesn't have a big heart.

We walk the few steps to Archer's office, and unlike Cohen's, the door is shut. There's never an open invitation into Archer's world.

"Just a minute," Georgia yells from the other side after I knock.

I cast a glance to Cohen, who's pulling at his hair.

"They're having relationship talks in there," he says.

I paste on a smile. "That's definitely what they're doing."

Neither of us is convinced that's what's happening behind Archer's closed door.

The door flies open, and Georgia walks out, straightening out her skirt.

"Really?" Cohen grumbles.

"What?" Georgia asks, her cheeks red. "We were discussing the schedule."

I snort.

Cohen motions toward the hallway. "Go home and read the Bible."

She smirks and waves good-bye.

Archer reclines in his chair, his large stature making the desk appear small. He eyes us suspiciously as if we're coming to him with a problem. He prefers to pour drinks and handle business, not deal with employee drama.

Cohen does a sweeping gesture of the room, pinching his lips together. "Dude, do whatever you want *under your own roof.* Not here."

Archer's mood is unreadable. "I expect the same rules to apply to you and Jamie then." A flicker of a self-satisfied smile briefly flashes along his lips.

Cohen flips him off.

"To what do I owe the pleasure?" Archer asks, getting straight to the point.

Cohen casts a glance my way.

"I was offered a job," I say before stopping and holding up a finger. "Not that I was looking. Grace's brother-in-law offered me a position at his company since I'll be there for the whole"—I hesitate, my mouth turning dry as I search for the right explanation—"pregnancy thing."

My attention moves back and forth between Archer and Cohen.

Cohen is the first to speak. "So, is this a full-time thing?" He raises a brow. "I thought it was playing pretend in front of her parents?"

I suck in a breath. "Honestly, I have no idea. Grace is having issues with the baby's father, and I don't want her to go through this alone. If she needs someone to help play dad for a minute, I'm game."

Cohen nods. "Understandable."

"That's how the job offer came to life," I tell them. "They want me to be with her at night since Cassidy and Lincoln sometimes work late."

"If it's a better opportunity for you, take it," Archer inputs. "If the job fucking sucks, you're welcome back here at any time. Don't feel obligated to stay here. I don't want to hold you back from a good thing."

"Agreed." Cohen slaps me on the back. "Congrats, man."

I smile. "Thank you."

"One question, though," Cohen says before I leave the room. "Do you have to wear a suit?"

Archer snorts. "Oh God, are you going to start wearing fucking loafers, Finn?"

This time, I'm the one flipping Archer off … and then I direct it to Cohen. "Both of you, fuck off."

Cohen laughs. "We're going to miss you, and your ass had still better come hang out here."

"That'll never change."

———

I PULL the business card from my wallet and stare at it.

Never did I think I'd ever have a job opportunity like this.

I was born into a white-trash family, to addicts, to nothing but scum. They're all labels I've heard my entire life. At first, it hurt to hear the truth, but as time went on, I started agreeing with them.

Meth addicts.

Thieves.

Deceitful.

Those words described the few family members I knew of.

I dial the number, a hard swallow with each digit.

"Brian," I say when he answers, "it's Finn. Grace's—"

"I know who you are," Brian says with a deep chuckle, his voice matching the millionaires you see in business movies.

"I'll take the job." I say this with deep confidence, so he doesn't regret the offer.

That strong tone lowers. "Thank you."

He's thanking me?

I shake my head even though he can't see me. "No, thank you."

"It means a lot to Faith and me that we'll have someone there for Grace. When can you start?"

"Whenever you need me."

"Tomorrow?"

"Tomorrow works."
My life is changing more and more each day.

CHAPTER FIFTEEN

Finn

I'VE NEVER FELT SO out of place in my life.

Never felt like a damn poser.

It was a forty-five-minute drive to the dealership since no one in Anchor Ridge has the bank account to purchase a vehicle that costs as much as some people's homes. I felt poor as fuck as I parked in the parking lot filled with cars I'd never seen before.

As soon as I walked into the dealership this morning, my surroundings screamed wealth. Every wall was made of shiny glass. Range Rovers, Bentleys, a Lamborghini, and Mercedes decorated the showroom floor. There was an entire bar with expensive waters, champagne, and snacks in the corner. Nothing like I'd ever witnessed.

Brian greeted me, his bright smile wide, to give me a tour and go through all my employee shit. My mouth dropped open when he disclosed not only my pay but also the commission I'd receive from selling these high-end cars.

From the whispers, I learned it was uncommon for the VP of the company to pay so much attention to a new employee who hadn't proven himself worthy of selling one car.

"Whose dick did he suck to get this job?"

"Nepotism at its fucking finest. I'm sure it's a cousin, friend, sister's boyfriend. Dude isn't even wearing an expensive suit."

All comments I heard in the background.

Unfortunately, unlike my job at Twisted Fox, I can't throw an asshole out for talking shit. This will take some adjusting.

At least Tim, the guy training me, is cool, but he caught on that Brian and I had a personal relationship. Unless he wanted to lose his job, he had to be nice to me.

Something else I'm not used to is early mornings. I chugged a coffee on my drive before chasing it with an energy drink and am still struggling to keep my eyes open. It didn't help that I had been awake until four this morning since I worked a shift last night.

What a dumbass move to tell him I could start today.

"All right, man," Tim said. "You ready to learn about some badass cars? Another perk of the job? We get to test-drive them."

————

"WANT TO GRAB LUNCH?" Brian asks, poking his head into Tim's office and interrupting him schooling me on the differences between Mercedes models. "Celebrate your new job?"

A rip of guilt presses through me as I shake my head. "I appreciate the offer, but I'm bringing Grace lunch."

I've never done that before since our sleeping schedules were opposite. But things have changed now, as we're not only friends, and I want to see her. The school she teaches at isn't far from here, and it'll be nice to surprise her.

I also need a break from the dealership, and no doubt if I have lunch with Brian, there will be work talk. Grace is always a breath of fresh air … like a damn Prozac when I'm having a hard time. She's an optimist, always seeing the glass as half-full—the opposite of me.

We make a good team.

She keeps me positive.

I keep her from dealing with shitty situations by herself.

Not wanting to feel like a jackass, I add, "Tomorrow?"

He smiles and nods. "You did a good job today. Tim said you're catching on well."

———

I TEXT Grace as soon as I get in my car.

Me: Can I bring my baby mama some lunch?

It's not until I hit send that I realize I didn't put *fake* in front of *baby mama*.

It's the first time there's no reference to it being fake when it comes to us dating or her being pregnant with "my" baby.

My phone beeps with a reply minutes later.

Grace: I'd love that. Lunch break starts in 10.

Me: Craving anything specific?

Grace: Surprise me.

Me: Be there soon.

I drive to her favorite bistro she likes when we're closer to the city, order our sandwiches, and rush to my car. The faster I get there, the more time I can spend with her before our breaks get cut off. I pull into the school's parking lot, kill the engine, and jump out of the car.

The sun peeks through the clouds, and I pass benches spread along the walkway and rows of pine trees while heading toward the brick building. Today isn't the first time I've been to Sunset Hill. I came once when Grace was hosting a charity auction and another time when she needed help bringing in supplies for the new school year.

Light classical music plays when I enter the administration office.

"Hey there," a woman behind the desk greets, setting her coffee cup down. Her lips are dark red with a slight smudge on the corner.

"Hi," I reply, holding up the sandwich bag. "I'm here to visit Grace Mitchell."

I'm not sure if I should've said her full name or Miss Mitchell. Mitchell is a common name, and this isn't a student I'm talking to.

She grins, tapping her finger toward a clipboard on the desk. "Sign in here, please. I need your driver's license. We'll get you a name tag, sweetie." She picks up the phone. "Hey, Miss Mitchell. You have a guest here to see you." She wiggles her fingers in giddiness, and I automatically like her.

Setting the bag and drinks down, I jerk my wallet from my pants and hand her my license.

I grab the pencil to sign my name when I hear a harsh voice say, "Miss Mitchell, huh?"

I scribble my name down before looking up to find a man walking in my direction. His gaze is stony as he stands next to the secretary.

He scowls at me. "Are you her brother? Relative?"

I chuckle, offering an amused smile. There's nothing better than ruining a guy's attempt at being an asshole by not taking the bait. "Nah, definitely not her brother."

His back straightens. "What are you to her then?"

"Finn!" Georgia says, exiting a room and heading in our direction. She motions to the bag. "I hope you brought me something too."

Georgia is the school counselor at Sunset Hill.

"Shit, sorry," I reply, feeling like an asshole for forgetting her.

"Rude." Her voice is playful. "Next time, I'll be sure to text my order."

I salute her. "I got you."

The man clears his voice. "You never answered the question as to who you are."

Georgia moves in closer. The playfulness in her tone changes to disgust. "That's none of your business."

The secretary gapes at them.

"I'm the principal," the man grinds out. "Everything that happens here is my business."

Before anyone can throw out a response to this asshole, the door opens, and Grace walks in, looking her gorgeous self.

Grace is beautiful.

Period.

No exceptions.

She's gorgeous when she's dressed in her sexy-as-fuck teacher clothes.

When she's wearing loose clothes, overalls, or those long dresses she likes to wear.

When she's sporting sweats with a runny red nose, and I bring her chicken soup when she's sick.

She grins brightly. "Hey, Finn."

"A new friend?"

Her shoulders tighten, and her gaze swings to the man.

"An *old* friend," Georgia corrects snidely. "More than that actually."

Grace gestures to the guy. "Finn, this is Principal Long."

I lift my chin, and it kills me to say, "Nice to meet you, man."

I'm not sure how much power this dude has, but I plan on lunch visits with Grace to become a regular thing. I can't have him giving us a hard time.

"Pleasure." The snarl on his face confirms it's not.

I clench my jaw.

Grace is running her fingers through her hair.

Georgia is practically snarling at the man.

"We're having lunch," Grace tells Georgia, breaking the awkward tension. "Want to join us?"

She shakes her head. "Archer and I are having a Zoom lunch." She winks. "It appears we both have lunch dates."

"This isn't a place for dates," Principal Long scolds.

"Is that your boyfriend, Miss Mitchell?"

I spin on my heels to find a little girl sitting in the chair in the corner of the room. Her bright pink bookbag is settled on her lap, and she's sending a gap-toothed smile at Grace.

Everyone looks at Grace for an answer.

CHAPTER SIXTEEN

Grace

"IS THAT YOUR BOYFRIEND?"

Lizzy, the questioner, is the pigtailed girl in the corner, waiting on a parent to pick her up. She was my student last year and a nosy one. With Gavin's hostile questioning, I'm not sure if anyone noticed her.

Everyone is staring at me in expectation. All of them wanting me to share my personal life as if it were a job requirement. Georgia and Finn already know the situation. Rachelle, the secretary, who appeared lost during Gavin's questioning, shifts excitedly in her chair, awaiting her chance to share today's gossip in the teachers' lounge later. Gavin's grinding his teeth, and from the spiteful expression on his face, I'm positive he'll bug me about this later.

Deciding to ignore the question, I settle my attention on Finn. "We can eat in my room."

I'm done pleasing people with information.

Gavin is my superior, but I don't owe him any details of my personal life. He lost that privilege when I found out he was a married prick. Finn and I do need to chat about how we'll define our relationship to others.

I didn't expect Finn to bring me lunch, and I was giddy when I read his text.

Gavin clicks his tongue against the roof of his mouth. "We don't recommend guests for lunch. Next time, I suggest you make dinner plans."

Unsure of what to say, I pay a quick glance to Finn. He folds his arms across his chest, and his hands are clenched.

"Says the guy whose *family* visits him on the regular," Georgia fires back.

Gavin's eyes are cold when he shoots me a quick stare before he turns, walks into his office, and slams the door shut.

Rachelle stares at us, speechless.

Gavin needs to stop behaving like a child if he doesn't want the entire school to know he knocked me up.

Georgia winks at me.

The day after everone finding out about my pregnancy, I broke down and told her about Gavin. There was no way she'd allow me to keep it from her. We've been best friends for over a decade, and we have always confided in each other. Now, anytime she's around Gavin, she gives him shit.

"Let's go," I tell Finn.

Finn shoots Georgia and Rachelle a wave and follows me into the hallway. We pass banner- and poster-covered walls while heading toward my classroom. When we pass a line of fourth graders, they snicker and point to Finn.

"What's the principal's issue?" Finn asks when we walk inside the classroom. "Does he like you, or is he just a dick in general?"

"Just a dick in general," I reply.

He rubs at his lip as if questioning whether he should call me out on my bullshit. Finn is a pro at reading me. Eventually, I'll have to tell Finn the truth, but today, I want to have lunch with him and forget about Gavin.

"This is cute," he says, taking in my classroom. "It screams Grace."

Finn helped me move all my supplies in, but he hasn't seen it since I started for the year. A large bulletin board is decorated with positivity quotes and art displays, and I have posters covering the walls.

I've wanted to be a teacher since grade school. Some kids might have grown out of that phase but not me. My parents weren't excited at first, being their occupations pay more than a teacher's salary. There also isn't room for advancement unless I obtain a higher degree and become a professor.

My father is a judge, and my mother's a professor. Faith is an attorney. Even though this wasn't the career they hoped for me, they're supportive of my job. They've never once made me feel like my job isn't as important as theirs.

Finn grips the edge of a desk and starts to drag it toward mine, but I stop him. I smile and take the one next to him. He scoots his closer to mine.

"I like your new look," I tell him.

I wanted to punch Gavin just for ruining my moment of eye-screwing Finn when I walked into the office. I love Finn in every look, but him dressed up, looking like he's ready to take care of business, is hot. Although I prefer his casual look—because it's him—it's nice to see him mix it up. He's like me now, having different business and fun clothes.

He grins, pulling at the collar of his blue button-up. "I'm trying to fit the part of a man who sells hundred-thousand-dollar cars."

"You fit the part, and you are, no doubt, the hottest car dealer there."

He wipes his thumb over his jaw. "When I sell my first car, I'm taking you out for a kick-ass dinner." He jerks his thumb toward my belly. "And buying whatever you need for the little one."

My heart warms at his comment.

Butterflies swarm in my stomach.

He's not lying.

Finn would do anything for me … or my baby.

My cheeks are heated when I point at the bag. "What's on the menu?"

He grins, holding up the bag. "Bistro Bella."

"Mmm. My favorite."

My stomach growls when he pulls out two sandwiches and settles one on my desk. Next comes a bag of Cheetos and a Sprite.

All my favorites.

"How's your day going?" he asks as I unwrap my egglant and ranch sub. He hasn't touched his food yet. All his attention is on me.

I shrug, ripping open the Cheetos. "Same ole, same ole."

"How are you feeling?"

"Let's just say, pregnancy is not a fun party."

He chuckles, opening his veggie sub. He's kept meat away from me since the day I told him it made me nauseas.

"How's the first day at the new j-o-b."

"It's, uh … different."

Different.

Not good.

Not bad.

Indifferent.

I smear my finger through a ranch glob on the wrapper. "If you don't like it, don't stay there. I didn't expect you to take that job."

"What do you expect from me?"

His question startles me.

"I didn't mean to sound like an asshole." He reaches out and caresses my arm. "It's me genuinely asking what you need from me to make you happy during this. Whatever it is, it's yours."

I take a giant bite of my sandwich, hoping to swallow it along with my emotions. I sniffle and frown. These damn pregnancy hormones are getting the best of me. I cry at nearly everything these days.

Cheerios commercials.

When I chose the wrong color for my manicure.

When Snooki got arrested during a *Jersey Shore* rerun.

I take a sip of my Sprite. "I want you to do whatever you're comfortable with."

"I'm comfortable with whatever. You call the shots." He pops a Cheetos in his mouth.

"I shouldn't call the shots when you're the one doing me a favor."

"Like you haven't done me favors throughout the years? You're one of my closest friends, Grace. If you need something as simple as that—"

"Simple?" I shake my head. "What I'm asking from you isn't simple. I'm asking you to lie and pretty much put your life on hold."

He drops his sandwich to give me his full attention. "Babe, if lying is what you need from me, I'll lie all the way to hell. Tell me what a normal baby daddy does, and I'm there."

———————

"SWEAR TO GOD, if Gavin keeps this shit up, I'm hiding mice in his office ... or at least giving him a swift kick in the balls," Georgia says. "You could easily get him fired for what he did."

It's the end of the school day, and we stopped by our favorite smoothie place before going home. With everything going on and her no longer being my roommate, it's harder for us to catch up.

Georgia and I met in middle school when she transferred, and I was her tour guide. She was the quirkiness to my shyness. Since Cohen practically raised her, she spent a lot of time at my house while he was working to support them. Lola joined our group during our junior year. Like Georgia, she was a transfer. I'd turned a guy down at a party who was giving me a hard time, and Lola jumped in to set him straight. Since then, the three of us have referred to ourselves as The Three Musketeers. My life would be boring and lonelier if it wasn't for them.

I shake my head. "They'd most likely fire us both. Damage control would be easier if everyone involved was gone."

I shudder at the thought of losing my job. I love it at Sunset Hill. I was there first, so if anyone needs to go, it should be Gavin. I'm not sure if the school board would look at it that way, though.

"That's messed up." Georgia pulls her brown curls that are blowing in the wind into a ponytail. "You should tell his wife."

"Trust me, I've thought about it." *Too many times.* "But what good would it do?"

"Get his ass in trouble, is the good it'd do. Make his wife leave him and take half his shit." She points at me with her cup. "If he pulls that shit again, threaten to tell his wife ... or better yet, *I will.* Don't let him ruin the good thing you have with Finn."

I blow out a breath. "What do you mean, good thing?"

"Finn is an amazing man," she says with such certainty it's as if she's stating her blood type.

"He is … but …" I trail off, unsure of how to explain my feelings about the situation.

She raises a brow. "But what?"

"It's not like we have a real relationship … or that he's actually the father of the baby. In the end, he'll leave, and I'll be a single mother."

It's scary, doing it alone, but I've come to terms that it'll be my new life. At least on the bright side, there will be no baby-name fights. I try to rid those thoughts, knowing I'll still have my family and friends.

"Why can't it be real?" she asks. "Finn might not be the biological father, but you two have liked each other for years. Look how he's stepping up. I'm sure he'd be okay with being the dad—"

"He's *playing* the dad. It's a role." I keep reminding myself this so the hurt won't be so deep when he leaves.

Her face softens. "It's not a role to him. He's doing things where you don't have audiences to act in front of. Give him a chance."

"Not only am I pregnant"—I glance down as shame hits my cheek —"but I'm also weird." A sour taste forms in my mouth, and I push my smoothie away as nausea creeps in. This subject always makes me want to puke … and hide.

Georgia holds up a finger. "First of all, you're not weird. Weird is choosing Nick Carter over Justin Timberlake or thinking *Sister Wives* isn't creepy." She signals toward me. "You, my best friend, are not weird."

"You were my roommate." I bite into my lower lip. "You know how I am."

It's a reason I wanted to kill Faith when she mentioned Finn moving in with me. Other than the nightmare the other night, I haven't had many incidents lately.

She reaches across the table and presses her hand over mine. "You went through something that was fucked up, and you have PTSD. It's common, and Finn would understand. He cares about you. I mean, would any random man sign up to put his life on hold like this?"

I release a heavy sigh. "I know; I know."

A smile plays at her lips. "Now, make him yours and stop being afraid."

CHAPTER SEVENTEEN

Finn

AS BAD AS I want to turn my phone off, I can't.

I'm always nervous something will happen.

My dad's name flashes across my phone for what seems like the hundredth time. Since he's already left three voicemails, I know what he wants, but I'm at work. He'll have to wait until I get off. I won't risk this job to deal with his messes.

He's shown up to Twisted Fox countless times when I haven't answered his calls. He's made scenes, asked for free liquor, and once started a fight with a man over a game of pool. The less he knows about my life, the better. Otherwise, he never fails to make his existence known when he wants something. No way am I risking that embarrassment here.

Hell, he'd probably come in drunk, asking to test-drive a BMW.

I wait until my lunch break to return his call.

"Quit blowing up my phone while I'm working," I hiss as soon as he answers.

"At work?" he huffs. "It's too damn early for you to be at work. I called, and they said you weren't there. Not to mention, you never go into work during the day." He lowers his voice, forcing it to sound sad. "Why are you lying to your own flesh and blood?"

"I got a new job—a day job."

"Ah, where?"

"None of your business."

"That's rude." He releases another huff, and knowing him, he's scowling. "As your father, I should know. What if there's an emergency?"

I sink deeper into the seat of my car and tip my head back, resting it against the headrest. "Do what you always do. Leave messages, and I'll get back with you. Most of the time, your *emergencies* don't constitute as *emergencies.*"

"Me going hungry isn't an emergency?"

His response sends a fire through my blood. "You're not going hungry. I bought groceries for you earlier this week."

"I need something new. I can't make food all the time." He pauses as if searching for the right words for his next request. "Order me a pizza."

"Gotta go." I hang up.

———

"YO! FINN!" Lincoln greets me with a smile from the other side of the bar when I sink down on a barstool.

Lincoln collects bills off the bar on his way toward me. He hasn't worked at Twisted Fox long and recently joined our circle of friends. He's Archer's brother, and he was recently released from federal prison.

Their father had started doing shady shit with the family business. While Archer left to avoid trouble, Lincoln stayed, attempting to turn his dad straight. When the feds showed up, Lincoln had refused to feed them information about his father, which led him to being charged with crimes.

When he was released, Archer hired him to bartend here. Then, Cassidy was going through her own trouble, and now, they're dating. Lincoln recently asked Cassidy to move in with him, but after Grace revealed she was pregnant, Cassidy told Lincoln she couldn't leave her without a roommate.

The memory of Faith asking me about moving in with Grace

smacks into me. Grace hasn't brought it up since our dinner, so I'm not sure how she feels about it. Since Cassidy refused to leave Grace without a roommate, Lincoln practically lives there now too.

"What can I get you?" Lincoln asks.

I drum my fingers along the bar. "A Coors is good."

It's the first time I've actually had someone serve me here. Normally, I walk behind the bar, snag what I want, and pay for it.

Turning, he grabs a bottle from the fridge, pops off the cap, and slides it to me. "How's the new job? Miss us yet?"

I chuckle. "The new job is going well. It's different, but I'm getting used to it."

"Luxury Imports is a good-ass dealership. I bought cars from there before my life fell apart."

I'm convinced Lincoln isn't normal as he laughs. Even though he went to prison for a crime he technically hadn't committed, only witnessed and hadn't snitched, he doesn't have a chip on his shoulder that I'd definitely have. Sometimes, I'm jealous of how well he handles the shit that's gone bad in the past.

He leans back on his heels and shoves his hands into his pockets. "If I ever decide to trade it in on something new, I'll holler at you."

I smile. "Thanks, man."

I sold my third car today, and when I added the commission I'd receive, I nearly fell out of my chair. It's more than I'd make in a month working anywhere else. The amount some people spend on cars baffles me. Hell, I could buy a house with that kind of money.

Some of my coworkers have lightened up their asshole attitudes—most likely after somehow finding out that I'm the father of his sister-in-law's baby.

Did Brian tell them that?

I'm sure they talk a lot of shit behind my back, though. Assholes just don't want to get fired. Not that I'd ask Brian to can a guy for not liking me.

Lincoln slaps his palm along the bar. "You're actually just the person I wanted to talk to."

I take a swig of my beer. "What's up?"

He shoves his hand through his short black hair. "Cass might kill me for telling you this, but ..." He pauses, looking from each side of the bar, double-checking she's not here to kick his ass. "She's pregnant."

I wait to read his reaction before replying.

Is this good or bad news to him?

From the shit-eating grin on his face and the way he's practically bouncing on his toes, I'm going with good news.

I smile. "Congrats, man."

He chuckles. "There must be something in that townhouse's water or some roommate ovaries wanting to get knocked up at the same time."

He taps his fingers along the bar. "And that's why I want to talk to you."

I hold my hands out in a jokingly innocent gesture. "It wasn't me, I swear."

Leaning across the bar, he pushes my shoulder. "Real funny, jackass."

He stares at me, unblinking. "A two-bedroom townhouse isn't going to work unless the babies want their nursery in the living room."

"Okay," I slowly drawl the word out.

"Grace told Cass that her sister mentioned you moving in with her."

"Okay," I repeat in the same tone as before.

He frowns that I'm not feeding his conversation yet before perking up his shoulders. "Well, buddy, now comes the time when you help everyone out and become Grace's new roommate."

I stiffen in my chair.

"We have an empty penthouse after Archer and Georgia moved out. Before, I didn't mind staying at the townhouse. Grace is cool, but now, I'd like some room to start a family. We won't move out until Grace has another roommate, and she mentioned to Cassidy there was talk of you doing that. Is it something you're really considering?"

I cover my face with my hand. "Looks like I'd better talk to Grace."

———

IT TURNS OUT, Lincoln asking me to take their roommate position was perfect timing.

After I left Twisted Fox, my dad's landlord, Roger, called, notifying me that my dad wouldn't leave. Unbeknownst to me, he'd evicted my father months ago, and he was done with allowing him to squat at his rental, free of charge.

Muttering every curse in the book, I got into my car.

Thirty minutes later, I'm pulling into the driveway of the rental my father apparently isn't paying for. He's on the lawn, arguing with Roger … and next to them stand two police officers.

Great.

This isn't the first time I've dealt with the police regarding my father. I'm sure it won't be the last either.

All eyes are on me as I step out of my car.

"You called him, you son of a bitch?" my dad snarls to Roger before flipping him the bird with both hands.

Roger, a thin man with balding hair, pushes up his thin-framed glasses. "What was I supposed to do, John? You won't leave!"

My father stomps his foot like a third grader who lost the kickball game. "This is between us." He swings his arm out. "Yet you called the police and my son."

"The neighbors called the police because you were throwing stuff out the front door and threatening to beat me up," Roger deadpans.

My temples throb as I join the group. "Dad, leave him alone. It was his last resort. This is your fault for not paying your rent."

He should be grateful Roger has put up with him this long.

"Thank you." Roger exhales a long breath.

I nod, a hint of sympathy in my eyes. My dad is a lot to handle and never makes life easy on anyone. He's a landlord's nightmare, and he can't keep a place to save his life. When I was growing up, we moved at least three times a year, jumping place to place, dodging landlords.

I turn to Roger, ignoring my father's outburst behind me. "Where do we go from here?" My mouth turns dry in regret as I pull out my wallet. "How much does he owe?"

My father's shit-talking stops. He sees a way out now, another scheme not to have to pay his rent and have me cover for him—*again*.

"He's three months behind," Roger replies with a shake of his head.

"Two months, motherfucker!" my dad yells to my back.

"Three months," Roger states. "He kept promising to have the money to pay the back rent, but then I realized that wasn't happening. That's when I delivered an eviction notice a month ago, and he still won't leave."

"Three months … so six grand?" I ask.

Roger nods. "If you don't count late fees."

"Can I pay it?" I'll have to dip into my savings, but I don't know what else to do.

Roger shuffles his feet against the grass. "Don't worry about that. It's his responsibility, not yours. Even if he paid every cent he owes, he can't move back in. I won't deal with him anymore, and I rented it to another tenant. I already have to deal with him trashing the place— cigarette burns and stains on the carpet, holes in the walls, and the bedroom door is somehow missing."

"It's not that bad!" my dad yells, stepping closer to Roger and thrusting his finger in his face. "And I'd better get my goddamn deposit back."

I grab the collar of my dad's shirt and jerk him back before the cops do. "Go pack your shit, and let's go."

"Screw that!" Spit flies from my dad's mouth as he speaks. "My TV is in there! My bed! I ain't letting him sell that."

"No one is taking your shit," I say, raising my voice. "We'll get it moved either to my place or a storage unit."

My dad smirks at Roger. "Damn straight, we will. Don't be putting your hands on my things."

I pinch the bridge of my nose. "Dad, get your ass in your car and drive to my place unless you want to be sleeping on the street tonight." I turn to Roger. "I'll arrange for his shit to be picked up."

With a slew of curses, he does as I said, slamming his door and glaring at us.

"I'm sorry, Roger. I'll mail you a check for the back rent," I tell the middle-aged man before turning to the officers. "Thanks for coming out."

Jesse, the chief of police who's dealt with my father one too many times, tugs at his ear. "As rude as this sounds, I hope this is the last time I see your father."

"Same," I say.

"Maybe him finding a place out of town will help him stay out of trouble," he continues. "Get him away from the bad crowd he hangs out with. If he goes to jail again, he might be in there a while."

"I'll see what I can do."

Jesse slaps me on the back. "Be safe, and good luck, Finn."

———

I STEP OUTSIDE to my patio and call Grace. As much as I want to talk face-to-face, I'm keeping an eye on my dad until he calms his ass down.

There's a sense of relief that I didn't have to give Roger six thousand dollars but then came the predicament of finding my dad somewhere to stay. His credit is terrible, so it'll be a struggle to find someone to rent to him, especially if they reach out to past landlords for references.

My only options are to throw him out on the street, drop him off at a homeless shelter, or make my apartment his homeless shelter. Since I'd feel like an ass going with either of the first two, I choose the last. The problem is, we'd last maybe ten minutes living together before a fight erupted. I can let him stay there, and since Lincoln told me he and Cassidy were game for crashing at the penthouse, I can see if I can stay there until I find a new place for my father.

Let's pray that my dad doesn't fuck my place up like he did the others.

The first person I call is Lincoln, telling him that I need somewhere to crash and asking if he and Cassidy were cool to sleep at the penthouse for a few days. Cassidy is with him, and they say they're fine with it.

My next call goes to Grace.

"Hello?" she answers.

"Hey." I plop down on a patio chair, crossing my ankles in front of me. "How are you feeling?" It's the first question I always ask now.

"Pregnant," she replies with a laugh. "But not too bad. I just devoured ten Oreos, so that always helps."

"Oreos always save the day." I chuckle and scratch my cheek.

Asking for favors isn't something I'm good at, nor is it something I do on the regular. At times, I have an ego issue. Not the type of egotistical guy who has a big head on his shoulders and thinks he's the shit. I hide behind a false ego so people don't see my struggle.

"And you?" she asks, breaking me away from my thoughts.

"It was okay." I choose against telling her about my dad nightmare and scuff my shoes against the concrete. "Can I ask you a favor? And you can say no if you're not cool with it."

"Of course. You can always ask me for anything."

I puff out a breath. "Remember how Faith suggested I stay with you?"

"I remember my overbearing sister asking this, yes." She laughs.

"My dad needs somewhere to stay, and I offered him my apartment. Since I have a one-bedroom and Cass said I could take her bed, are you okay with me staying a few nights until we find him somewhere else?"

"My house is always open to you," Grace says with no hesitation.

———

WALKING IN THE LIVING ROOM, I find my dad slouched on the couch, chomping on barbecue potato chips with his dirty tennis shoes propped up on the glass coffee table.

"You need to restock the kitchen," he says, holding up the bag. "Too many healthy options for a man like me."

"You can go to the grocery store if you don't like what I have." I stand in front of him and cross my arms. "You ready to explain why you haven't been paying your rent?"

He wipes his chip-greasy hands onto his jeans. "That's none of your business."

"When you're evicted and crashing at my place, it sure is."

Not that I'll get the truth.

I'm sure he'll feed me some bullshit excuse.

"It's not easy, paying bills," he replies, cracking his knuckles. "I struggle."

This is the part where I used to feel bad for him.

Now, I know he's a liar.

"How are you struggling if you don't pay the bills that are supposedly the reason you're struggling?"

He only shrugs, pops a chip in his mouth, and loudly munches on it.

"You get plenty of money from your Social Security—enough to pay your bills."

I stare at my father—a man I've embarrassingly never looked up to. As the years have passed, his appearance has deteriorated. In my teens, he was a drunk, but all the liquor and drug use has taken a toll on him. He's lanky, his cheeks are sunken, and his clothes are baggy. His hair—with a large receding hairline—is oily.

I collapse onto the couch. "Dad, do you want to get some help?"

As usual, he snarls at my question. "I don't need nothing from anyone."

I hold out my hand. "Dad—"

"No!" he screams, shoving the bag of chips onto the couch. "I ain't having this conversation with you."

I wouldn't consider my father a junkie, but I could be wrong. He isn't high every time I see him, but it's getting worse each time. But there's no denying that he does his fair share of using.

With a groan, he pulls himself to his feet. "I need to shower."

———

"DON'T MESS ANYTHING UP," I tell my father.

Even though I've lived in the same apartment for years, I do a quick scan of the living room, taking in every inch of it. I rented a one-bedroom so people wouldn't attempt to move in with me.

No one wants to rest their head on a couch every night.

Call it an asshole move, but us living together would result in nothing but endless fights. He'd have wanted to take the easy road—live with me, not pay a penny, and blow his money on bullshit. My plan was for him to finance himself, although that didn't seem to work out. Now, he's here, in my one-bedroom apartment, while I'm finding somewhere else to crash.

It's small, but I've made the place nice, made it mine ... with Grace's help. Hell, she made most of the selections. We'd go shopping, and she'd pick shit out.

The floors are a dark hardwood and the walls beige. A deep-set taupe leather sectional is in the middle of the living room with matching coffee and end tables. A black shag rug sits in the middle of the living room. A few framed photos are on the tables—all with Grace and me, or my friends and me. There's a small kitchen with a four-seater table. I don't spend much time here because I like to stay out, stay busy.

"Oh, don't you worry." My dad smirks. "I'll take good care of the place."

There was no controlling his smile when I told him he could crash at the apartment *for two weeks* and I'd stay somewhere else. He never asked where I'd stay or if it'd cost me anything. All he cared about was his ass being covered.

I'll still need to check on him regularly to ensure he doesn't have visitors or fuck my shit up.

Earlier, I packed up all the crap I didn't want him touching and stuffed it into the trunk of my car. Grabbing my bag, I throw it over my shoulder, give him one last warning, and tell him to call me if he needs anything before leaving and making my way to Grace's.

CHAPTER EIGHTEEN

Grace

FINN MOVING IN IS a blessing in disguise.

I had no reservations about telling Finn yes when he asked to stay at the townhouse. With Lincoln and Cassidy working at night more, I'll feel protected with him here. The downside is my fear of him discovering my secret. So far, throughout the years, I've done well with hiding it, but the more people around means the higher my risk is of being exposed.

Georgia and Lola know. Cassidy and Lincoln have their suspicions, but I've always brushed off any concern. With Finn knowing me so well, with him caring about me so deeply, I'm uncertain if he'll allow any *brushing off*.

Finn has a way of cracking open the shell I've kept glued together for so long.

He's a man who can read me as if we shared the same brain. He knows when something is wrong, even when I try to hide it. He knows when something is deeper than what I'm letting on. There's no doubt in my mind that Finn is my soul mate.

The soul mate I can't have.

I've also never lived with a man before.

Finn texted me five minutes ago to let me know he's headed my way.

Snatching my phone from my bathroom vanity, I call Faith.

"What if Finn staying here is a mistake?" I ask. "I didn't consider what would happen if I had an episode."

"Grace," Faith says my name with sympathy and understanding. "You've done well with them the past few years, and last time, you didn't freak out. You called me. Having Finn there will most likely help with them. Like Brian does with me."

"If he finds out, it'll be mortifying," I croak, sitting on the closed toilet seat.

"Let's say he does. I bet you a new Gucci bag he won't judge you for it."

"He won't judge me to my face, but he could think I'm strange." I wrinkle my nose. "And nope with betting you another bag. You always win."

She laughs. "And you know I'll for sure win this one."

"Yeah, yeah, yeah," I mutter.

"Everything will be fine."

I slide off the toilet at the knock on my front door. "He's here. Pray for me."

"Quit overthinking and have fun with your fake baby daddy. If you need anything, I'm only one call away.

"Oh my God, you're crazy, and I'm sure you're happy that you're getting your way with this."

"Absolutely I am. Thank you, Finn's dad. Give me the address, and I'll send a fruit basket."

BEING ALONE with Finn isn't out of the ordinary.

Him temporarily living with me? That's a different story.

It's not that I don't feel comfortable around him. I'm just uncertain of where this will take us. We've been dipping our toes into such new territory lately—fake dating, him playing my baby daddy, now us staying together. This has been a month of twists and turns.

A sense of disappointment hits me when he walks through the front door with only a duffel bag thrown over his shoulder. He packed light as though this is only temporary and he's scared of asking for too much. I wasn't expecting a moving truck, but a duffel bag seems too fleeting. Deep in my heart, I already know it'll hurt when he returns to his place.

He swings the bag off his shoulder and grips the strap. "I'm going to toss this in Cassidy's room."

I nod with a smile and head into the kitchen for a glass of water.

Finn meets me. "I really appreciate you letting me stay here."

"Always," I reply.

"Does this mean I get the roommate hot chocolate you girls always talk about?"

Georgia and I started the *roomie hot chocolate* when we first moved in together. We created the perfect spiked hot chocolate recipe and drank them from mugs with our faces on them. When she moved out and Cassidy moved in, I got a mug for her, and that was our drink we made once a week. As a joke, we bought Lincoln one when he started staying with us on the regular.

"I can make you one," I tell him. "And a virgin for yours truly."

"Shit, I need to quit forgetting you can't drink."

"Geesh, you say that like I'm an alcoholic or something."

He jerks his head back, and his shoulders stiffen at my comment. "Nah, I know alcoholics, and that's not you." Gone is the playfulness he had.

Finn doesn't show his emotional side often. He's a pro at maintaining the *cool and fun guy* image, but like me, sometimes, the things we want to hide the most shine through the cracks.

Even though it's never been brought up, I'm certain there is alcoholism or addiction in his family. He never drinks more than two beers, I've never seen him drunk, and he's the closest with the one friend in our group who doesn't drink.

As bad as I've wanted to poke at Finn's head until I picked everything out, I need to wait until he's ready to tell me—that he fully wants to open himself up and release what pains him.

"What if we skip the drink and have a roomie pizza instead?" I suggest, tilting my head to the side and meeting his gaze.

His shoulders slump as if a weight has been lifted. "Pizza sounds damn good."

Since neither of us wants to fix a pizza, we order one. I change out of my maxi dress into sweats and join Finn in the living room, taking the opposite side of the couch from him.

"I meant what I said, Grace. I'm here for you if you need anything. You name it, and I'm there. You never have to do anything alone."

For a moment, he's rendered me speechless. Finn has always been helpful, always told me he's here for me, no matter what, but this goes deeper than before. He's laying it out there—that he's not only there for me but also my baby. There's nothing Finn would refuse me.

That's not me bragging.

It's me knowing that I've never been in love with a man, and I will never love a man as I do him. Even if I searched high and low, Finn has a heart that no one else has—one filled with forgiveness, which is more than I deserve.

We eat pizza. We watch Netflix.

When I go to bed, my nerves spiral.

Please let this be a normal night for me.

CHAPTER NINETEEN

Finn

THERE'S A SCREAM.

A loud, piercing scream.

I jump out of bed and sprint out of the bedroom.

Rushing down the hall, I follow the second scream to Grace's bedroom. Wiggling the doorknob, I find it locked.

"Grace!" I shout, pounding on the door in a panic. "Grace! Open up!"

The screaming stops.

My hands are shaking as I draw in deep breaths. The doorknob moves, and Grace flings the door open. A dim light in her bedroom allows me to see the expression on her beautiful face.

It's fear.

Torment.

Expressions I've never witnessed coming from her.

A tear runs down her cheek.

"Are you okay?" My voice is harder than it should be, but I'm fucking scared.

She's staring straight ahead, but it's like she can't see me.

Staring into nothing.

I snap my fingers in front of her.

She blinks as if powering back on and stares at me blankly.

I slip by her, barging into the bedroom to see if there's anyone I need to kill.

"A nightmare," she chokes out. "I had a nightmare."

Whipping around, I watch the recognition dawn on her face of what happened. She takes slow steps to her bed and sits on the edge. I do another sweep of her room and verify the closet and bathroom are empty. I don't want to seem overbearing, but I've never heard someone yell like that over a nightmare.

After confirming I'm not about to kick someone's ass, I sit down next to her, leaving a few inches between us. Her hand is pressed to her chest, and her eyes are brimmed with tears. Her breathing is ragged, and she works hard to control it.

I wait until she calms.

Wait until she looks at me.

But she only does the first.

Reaching out, I tenderly take her hand. "Are the nightmares a normal thing ... or is it because I'm here?" My body turns rigid with tension as I await her response.

I shut my eyes, and it hits me. All the times that Georgia and Cassidy said they couldn't leave Grace alone. Her hating the dark and staying at her parents' whenever they worked late.

I always took it as a woman not wanting to stay home alone— which is understandable. Especially since Georgia's form of a good time is murder documentaries.

"I wouldn't say normal ..." She shrugs, forcing herself to appear nonchalant. "I get them when I'm stressed."

My pounding heart relaxes when she half-turns to face me.

At least it's something.

Better than her staring at the damn wall.

"It's not you being here, I promise," she says, her face pale. "They just happen sometimes."

I nod, another question popping up inside my head. "Do you always sleep with your door locked?"

"It's something I've done since my teens and not because I'm uncomfortable with you here."

"Are you okay? You want me to grab you water? Anything?"

She shakes her head. "I'm okay."

"I'm right down the hall." I point toward the door.

Her face grows paler.

I change course, slightly stuttering as I struggle to find the right words. "If you're not up for going back to bed, we can watch a movie?"

"You work early in the morning."

"Babe, I'm used to staying up late and surviving on limited sleep. If you need me awake, I'm awake."

She quietly exhales. "A movie sounds good."

She climbs back under her comforter, and I take the space beside her, not getting underneath the covers. Instead of a movie, she turns on a show we've seen countless times. As she slowly falls asleep, I'm hit with a wave of uncertainty.

Do I return to my bedroom?

I can't lock the door behind me.

Instead of leaving her, I stay next to her—on top of the blankets— and fall asleep, hoping she doesn't freak out in the morning.

———

"I'M KIND OF EMBARRASSED," Grace tells me the next morning.

The sun shining through her curtains woke me early, before her, and I tiptoed to my bedroom before she woke up. I showered, got dressed, and was in the kitchen, waiting for her.

Her face appears refreshed as if she got a full eight hours when she appears. Her hair is thrown back into a braid, and her baby bump is starting to show through her dress. I've never dated or been with a pregnant woman, but I find a baby bump on Grace to be sexy as hell.

"Nah." I take a sip of my coffee. "We all have nightmares. I had them bad as a kid because my father found it normal to watch horror movies with me while I was growing up. I get it."

The only difference is, Grace wasn't scared of the bogeyman, or

Jason, or Freddy Krueger. The terror on her face alerted me that it was deeper than your typical nightmare.

A blush stings her cheeks. "Thank you for being there for me."

"I told you, if you need me, I'm there."

No matter what.

CHAPTER TWENTY

Grace

I'M a pregnant woman walking into the city's hottest nightclub.

Something I never anticipated happening.

I expect judgmental stares, but thankfully, no one seems to notice.

Since my baby bump is starting to show, I went with a loose-fitting maxi dress and sandals tonight. Not that the dress is out of the ordinary. Comfortable is my style. My friends have labeled my style as *sophisticated flower child.*

Colorful strobe lights and loud music blare through the crowded club. Finn and I maneuver through the bodies hand in hand. We pass a group of people yelling at each other over the music and stop at the VIP section. The bouncer jerks his head toward Finn and allows us entry.

We don't go clubbing often, but since it's Lola's birthday, we all made an exception. Normally, we tend to hang out at someone's house or go to dinner, only really going for a night out if it's someone's birthday or we have something big to celebrate. I'm grateful Lola got us a table so we can hang out. I hate bumping into bodies while holding a conversation, and I have the rhythm of a three-year-old jamming to "Old Town Road," so the dance floor is out of the question.

Riding with Finn is common for me on nights like this. I prefer leaving early, and he never minds taking me home when I'm ready. Not that my friends wouldn't, but I hate being the buzzkill of the party.

Our friends are seated around the booth except for Lola and Georgia, who are semi-dancing in the corner. Purses, glasses, bottles of liquor, and a bucket of ice are scattered along the table.

"There's the baby daddy and baby mama," Lincoln says when we come into view.

"Grace!" Lola shouts, stumbling toward us. "My bestie carrying my future godchild. Thank you for being here!"

"Um, excuse you," Georgia says from behind her. "I'm the future godmother."

Lola wrinkles her nose. "We can *all* be a godparent." Her speech is slightly slurred.

The birthday girl doesn't get drunk often. Silas is sober, so she tends not to drink much. Not that Silas would care if she did. He's always up for clubbing. No one knows *why* he doesn't drink, but I don't think it's addiction.

Georgia shrugs. "I'll accept that."

Georgia, sporting a sequined crop top and jeans, squeezes into the spot next to Archer. Her boyfriend appears as happy to be clubbing as I do visiting my OB/GYN.

"Happy Birthday," I greet Lola, dropping Finn's hand to hug her.

Everyone is relaxed in their space. Jamie and Cohen are next to each other, and Jamie is showing him something on her phone. Their attendance is surprising. With the two kids—one being a baby—and Jamie's crazy hours in the ER, they don't get out much. Georgia and Archer are snuggled together, her leg over thigh. Lincoln has his arm thrown over Cassidy's shoulders while she sips on water. Maliki and Sierra, our friends who live in Blue Beech, are laughing with drinks in their hands. Maliki once hung out with us more, but he returned to his hometown to take over his father's bar. Sierra is Cassidy's older sister and the one who helped her get a job at Twisted Fox. Silas, the only one not on the couch, is sprawled out on a chair next to everyone as if he's the king of the party.

Finn helps me onto the couch before sinking into the space next to me on the end.

I gape at Lola. "I haven't seen you this wasted since college."

"I've *never* seen her this wasted, period," Silas says. He spoke to me, but his eyes warily stay on Lola. He hasn't been as loud or as playful as he usually is tonight.

"Agreed." Georgia nods next to me. "Did something happen today?"

Lola shakes her head, her eyes heavy-lidded. "It's my birthday. I was gifted a complimentary bottle from the club since I'm the owner's alcohol rep. He also sent over some bubblegum shooters." She motions to the tray of shooters, snags one, and knocks it back.

The birthday girl definitely looks gorgeous in her short black dress and red stiletto pumps. Her dark hair is straight and parted down the middle, a rhinestone pin clipped to the side. I've always considered my style boring compared to her edginess. Her style changes from day to day, and she can get away with it.

Silas runs his hand through his dark hair in frustration. "I'll be sure to inform Phil you're cut off."

Lola rolls her eyes. "Buzzkill."

"This is weird," I tell Finn underneath my breath.

"Them at odds?" he asks.

"They never argue."

Our waitress interrupts us to take more drink orders.

"Just a water?" I ask Finn when he tells the waiter he'll have a seltzer water like me.

He grins down at me. "I figured you should have a sober buddy."

I sneakily point to Cassidy. "She's not drinking either, and the past few times I've seen her, she's been ordering the same drinks as me. I wonder if she's prego."

He shrugs. "It might be good to have a pregnancy buddy."

I give myself a mental reminder to ask. It can't happen here, and I need to figure out the best way to go about it. You always hear of those women who ask someone when they're due, only to find out they're not actually pregnant. I'd be mortified.

"My best friend." Lola's voice drags me away from our

conversation. She topples into Silas's lap, sitting sideways, and wraps her arms around his neck.

This type of flirting is normal for them. Unlike Finn and me, they've never held back their desire for the other. Although they swear they've never acted on it. They find it normal, *as friends*, to sit on each other's laps, dance together, and share a bed.

At times, I wish I could be as brave as her. To flirt with Finn and not be scared of judgment or rejection.

Lola tips her head down, her dark hair becoming a curtain around their faces. I covet the confidence she has. The girl gives no fucks.

My hand clamps over my mouth when she shifts and straddles him.

"Holy shit," Georgia mutters at the same time Finn says, "That's a new one."

Cohen leans in. "I've never seen it go that far between them."

All eyes are on them. Lola whispers in Silas's ear. Sierra, the closest to them, scoots in closer to eavesdrop.

"Are they about to bang right there?" Lincoln asks when Lola grinds into Silas's lap.

"Nah," Archer states matter-of-factly. "Those two play mind games with each other." He dances his fingers over Georgia's thigh. "Remember when we used to do that shit, babe?"

Georgia tilts her head to the side. "Mind games wasn't straddling and grinding against you."

"This won't end well," Finn says. "She's drunk, and Silas is annoyed."

I steer my attention back to tonight's entertainment. Silas's shoulders are rigid, and his jaw is clenched. He's anchored his hands to Lola's hips, halting her from grinding more as they converse. The serious expression on his face tells me to look away, but I can't. I gasp when Lola grips Silas's hand and drags it down to her thigh.

Silas abruptly stands, his face hot with a fury I've never witnessed from him, causing Lola to drop onto the floor.

"Goddammit, Lola," he huffs, a wince spreading across his whole face, and he raises his voice. "Drink some water because you're being a sloppy fucking drunk." As soon as the words leave his mouth, regret flashes across his face.

Everyone is silent, watching this play out.

"Come on." He puts his hand out to help her up, but she pushes it away.

Lola's eyes water as she pulls herself to her feet. "No, I don't want your help."

"I'm sorry." His voice breaks.

"I think you should go." She adjusts her dress and folds her arms over her stomach while failing to meet anyone's gaze. "That's what I want from you for my birthday. To leave." This is the most vulnerable I've ever seen Lola.

"Fine." Silas pinches the bridge of his nose. "I'll go."

Just as he turns to walk away, we hear," Well, well, look what we have here," come from a voice I don't recognize.

I shift in my seat and find a man I've never seen before standing at the head of the table, running his hands together. Two guys stand behind him, a few inches back, like they're his right-hand men. He's tall with dark hair and a clean-shaven face. Even though he's not wearing an expensive suit and tie, his casual clothes are just as pricey as what they would cost.

"Uh-oh," Finn says. "This night might get worse than it already was."

"What do you mean?" I ask without glancing at him.

The guy rubs his hands together. "Silas fucking Malone."

Silas slowly turns to face the mystery man and icily stares him down. He steps to the side to block off Lola from the guy's view.

The man moves in closer and strokes his jaw. "I haven't seen you in forever. You act as if your family doesn't exist."

"I'm a busy man," Silas says, his tone challenging.

"Busy, huh?" he scoffs, scanning our area and taking in the surroundings. "Enough time for a birthday party though, huh? Who's the birthday someone?"

Lola steps around Silas. "Me."

The man runs his tongue over his lips. "Goddamn, the birthday girl is hot." He delivers a cocky smile while holding out his hand to her. "I'm Trent, Silas's brother."

"Stepbrother," Silas corrects with a snarl. "No blood relation. Thank fucking God."

"Oh, come on, brother," Trent mocks. "Let's forget about the past. How about this? Let's share a drink. We can go to my table—which is larger and surrounded by NBA and NFL players and other high-profile people—or stay here."

Silas works his jaw. "Nah, we're good. Go hang out with your high-profile friends and beat feet."

Trent doesn't pay Silas a glance. Lola has all of his attention. "At least let me buy the birthday girl a drink."

"She's had enough to drink," Silas snaps, popping his knuckles.

Archer hauls himself to his feet, joining Silas, and Lincoln does the same. Trent chuckles at Silas now having his right-hand men.

Lola chews on her lower lip. "I wouldn't mind a birthday Sprite, though. I don't want to be hungover tomorrow."

"I think you've already crossed that line," Silas says.

Trent snaps his fingers. "A birthday Sprite it is." He does a sweeping gesture toward the table. "Any of these guys your boyfriend?"

His eyes level on Silas, no doubt knowing his reaction to Trent's flirtation will be a sign that Silas likes her.

Lola doesn't cast one glance toward Silas before answering, "Nope."

Silas curses under his breath and wipes his forehead with the back of his arm.

This isn't Lola.

She's not spiteful.

She'd never want to purposely hurt Silas.

What is going on with them?

I can't blame her, though. She has to be hurting from Silas's rejection. She's prideful, someone not typically turned down. If I was coming down from the rejection of a lifetime, of a man practically dumping me on the floor, I'd take that Sprite offered by a dreamy man.

Our waitress comes scrambling toward us, nearly tripping on her heels, holding a tray of drinks. "Sorry! I got caught up at a table."

"Totally fine," I say, taking my seltzer water and handing Finn his.

She turns and halts when she notices Trent. "Hey, Trent. Can I get you something?" She giggles.

"Nah, I'm good, Abby." He wiggles his fingers toward Lola, causing Abby to frown. "I'm going to escort the birthday girl to the bar, get her a drink, and we can talk more privately."

He holds out his elbow, and Lola is smart to scurry forward. Her action puts more space between Trent and Silas, possibly preventing a fight.

Silas starts to follow them, but Archer snags his elbow to pull him back.

"Unless you plan on making things right with Lola this minute, sit your ass down," Archer grinds out. "You just humiliated the girl in front of everyone on her fucking birthday. Don't do it a second time."

"Let him get her a drink while you think about your weird asshole actions," Georgia chimes in.

Silas slumps down into his chair. A man who always exudes confidence appears as if he took a beatdown.

"What the hell was that about?" Cohen asks. "Why would you do that shit to Lola?"

Even though they're friends who respect the bro code, they have no problem calling each other out when they're in the wrong.

"I'm so confused," I mutter.

"We all are," Cassidy says, not bothering to lower her voice so Silas doesn't hear. "Lola was looking at Silas with stars and horniness in her eyes. Instead of nicely turning her down, he pushed her off his lap." She shakes her head. "That has to do something to a girl's ego. Especially when Silas acts like he's in love with her."

"Acts like?" Finn snorts. "Silas *is* in love with her."

"I hate that motherfucker," Silas says out of nowhere. "I'm doing everything not to storm down there and beat his ass."

"Why do you hate him?" Jamie asks softly.

Silas taps his foot. "He's shady as fuck."

"He's shady as fuck because he's really shady as fuck or he's shady as fuck because he's flirting with Lola?" Lincoln asks.

"Both." Silas grimaces.

"Are you going to finally admit you two have hooked up?" Georgia asks, always one to ask for gossip.

Silas stares at his tapping foot. "Nah, we've never had sex."

"But have you *hooked up*?" Sierra clarifies.

Silas stays quiet.

"How about this?" Finn says. "Grow some balls and go apologize and tell Lola how you feel."

Silas's eyes are sharp when he stares at Finn. "I could say the same shit to you, brother."

I freeze.

Finn hunches forward. "Don't take your anger out on me, man."

Silas points at me. "Grace wouldn't be pregnant with another man's baby had you grown some balls."

I jerk my head back. As I clutch my stomach, my heartbeat turns sluggish. My thoughts cloud as if I'd drunk as much as Lola.

Silas has never acted like this before.

Finn jumps to his feet and bares his teeth. "Watch your goddamn mouth."

"Does the truth hurt?" Silas asks, his stare on Finn intense.

They're in a standoff, only inches apart, while everyone gawks at them. Within seconds, Archer is back on his feet, prepared to intervene in yet another altercation.

Finn wipes the edge of his mouth, and his tone turns more scathing. "Like you're doing with Lola? Instead, she's going to hook up with your stepbrother."

Silas rears his fist back, but Archer stops him.

"Whoa," Georgia says. "We all know Lola isn't hooking up with anyone tonight."

I grip Finn's wrist, not only to stop him but also for assistance to stand. "This is not the place. Let's go."

Silas pays a glance at me, and his face drops as if he sees the humiliation on mine. "Shit, Grace. I'm sorry." Regret ripples through his eyes. "I was pissed and—"

"It's fine." I run my hands up and down my arms. "I just …" I'm holding in tears. "It's time for us to go."

Silas folds his hands together and bows his head. "Really, Grace—"

I stop him again. "You're sorry. Okay. I get it."

If we don't leave in a minute, I'm going to break down.

Without another word, Silas turns and storms off.

Finn grips my hand tighter than he ever has. "Someone, go talk to Silas because it damn sure won't be me tonight. We'll talk to you guys later."

People hug me good-bye, telling me not to take Silas's words to heart. The mood is somber. Something like this has never happened in our group. Sure, there are disagreements. Georgia and Archer hated each other for months, but nothing like this.

Even though our friends have joked about Finn and me liking each other, it's always been done in humor.

Never in anger.

Never has it sounded so bold and in our faces.

It was a verbal smack of truth straight to the heart.

Silas was right. If Finn *and I*—not just him—had stopped being scared, maybe I wouldn't be pregnant with another man's baby. Even with the pregnancy, even with us faking it, still, neither one of us has told each other our true feelings.

Our steps are rushed as we leave the club.

As I sit in his passenger seat, I open my mouth … then shut it … then open it. No words come to me—except for Silas's that keep running through my mind. Finn tightly grips the steering wheel and is focused on the road. It's a quiet ride, the only sound the pop station playing quietly on the radio.

"I'm sorry," I whisper into the darkness of the car when he parks in the driveway.

Even though I'm unsure of what exactly I'm apologizing for, I'm sorry for a multitude of things.

Not opening up my heart to Finn when I should've.

Getting pregnant by Gavin.

Asking Finn to sacrifice so much because of a decision I made.

Not telling off Silas for his hurtful words.

There's so much I wish I could take back.

I play with the strap of my bag. "Obviously, Silas was in the wrong for what he said—"

"Nah," Finn interrupts, resentment in his tone. "Silas was right."

"What?" I sputter, freezing.

"He was a dick about it—that's for sure. But that doesn't mean he was wrong." He shuts off the car and jerks the keys out. "I should've told you my feelings years ago."

My breathing restricts as tingles rush up my chest. "What are you talking about?"

He shifts to face me, and I wish the darkness didn't block out his face. "I'm talking about how I've been too chickenshit to admit that my heart beats for you, Grace. That it nearly broke me when I found out you were pregnant … and it wasn't with my baby."

Silence fills the car as I digest what he just said.

Take in every word of his confession.

Words I've wanted to hear for so long, but it almost feels like it's too late now.

CHAPTER TWENTY-ONE

Finn

THIS MIGHT NOT BE the ideal place to finally confess my feelings, but it needed to be said. Holding it in for so long had been a mistake.

Grace getting pregnant should've been a hard enough smack in the face, but I was stupid. What shoved me over the line? Seeing the heartache on Silas's face when Lola walked off with Trent. Another push in the right direction was Silas setting my ass straight. His words were harsh but much needed. It was time I stopped pretending, or I'd be the next man watching the woman he loved leave with another man.

It might be too late to change Grace being pregnant, but I can change her not being mine.

Grace is quiet.

Is her silence good? Bad?

Did my honesty scare her?

"Want to go inside?" I unsnap my seat belt. "I hate not being able to see you."

Turning on the overhead light is an option but still not enough. I want to see every expression that crosses Grace's face when I lay out my truths to her.

"Yes," she whispers into the darkness. "Let's go inside."

I gulp a mouthful of air before stepping out of my car. Grace does the same, and we meet where her walkway starts. I rest my palm on the curve of her back as we walk up the porch steps and into the house. The door clicks behind us, and I follow her into the living room, flipping on the lights.

Grace turns and focuses her eyes on me in expectation. There's no going back now. I can't say what I said and then chicken out. I zero in on her, admiring how beautiful the woman I'm in love with is. Her strawberry-blond hair is in some type of French twist, exposing her radiant face. A light-pink shimmer is glossed over her lips, making me want to taste it.

Grace is everything I want but what I don't deserve.

That's what my head has always told me.

I was stupid for listening to it.

Why did I think I don't deserve her?

I don't come from money. Grace gives no fucks about that.

I don't have a fancy-ass college degree. Grace has never judged me for it.

I don't come from her world. Grace has never said she wants differently.

Not once has Grace given me a reason to believe I'm not good enough for her, so why am I holding myself back? I'm tired of being scared—because I am good enough, damn it.

I'm a good man who's taken care of himself when no one else would.

I'm a helping hand to anyone, even those who don't deserve it.

When the day comes, I'll do anything for Grace's baby.

"Grace." My voice hitches with emotion when I say her name.

I advance a step, bringing myself closer to her. She needs to see the honesty in my eyes—a testament that she's everything I'll ever want. I can hear my heart thrumming in my chest from the combination of my fear and excitement.

I'm going to spill my heart out to her.

This could result in rejection.

A lost friendship.

But it needs to be done.

If Grace turns me down, I'll still be her friend.

Still be a call away for anything she needs.

We make eye contact, and I scramble for the right words.

I can't fuck this up.

Grace stares at me, unsure of where I'm going with this.

If I'll say what I need to say.

Hell, I'm playing this by ear.

Thirty minutes ago, I was sitting in a club, having no idea this would happen.

Reaching out, I cup her face with both my hands. "I'm in love with you."

I don't want to waste time with bullshit words.

I'm not good with them.

Knowing me, I'd fuck them up.

What's a better way to explain yourself to someone than to say those words?

I love you.

It says so much.

She squints at me, fluttering her eyelashes while processing what I said. "What?" Her voice is shaky.

My body relaxes as I repeat myself, "I'm in love with you."

I stroke her cheek with my thumb.

My truth is finally released.

Her chin trembles underneath my hands. "I love you too, Finn."

I'd dreamed about this moment happening countless times. It went differently. The excitement I'd hoped for was nonexistent. She said the words I'd been dying to hear, but they were said with the enthusiasm of someone finding out their vacation had been canceled.

There's no excitement.

Yet it's also not rejection.

It's … indifference?

My throat constricts, and I pull away as if my touch were no longer welcome. The heaviness of reality consumes me.

Grace winces, her eyes squeezing shut at the loss of me. "I'm sure this isn't the reaction you expected."

I step back. "I'm not sure what I expected."

Her eyes are watery when she opens them. "Finn," she says my name as if it pains her. "This has everything to do with me and nothing to do with you."

The high I felt for vomiting out my truth crumbles.

I rub my chin with one hand. "I think us admitting we're in love with each other has something to do with me."

Her face is expressionless. "If this were months ago, it'd be different."

"How?"

"I'm pregnant!" she shrieks, gesturing to her belly. "With another man's baby. That changes everything."

"You think I give a shit about that?" I rush out before allowing myself to polish my response. I pound my hand against my chest. "That changes nothing. I don't love you any less. I'm telling you I love you as you are—*everything* you are. I'm done playing pretend. I want this"—I indicate between us—"to be real. I want to spend the rest of my life with you."

She gawks at me, her mouth hanging open.

I lose a breath when she steps closer, stands on her tiptoes, and presses her lips against mine.

Everything happens so fast.

I curl my arm around her waist and drag her close.

Now that I have her, I'm never letting her go.

"Grace," I whisper against her soft lips, "you have no idea how long I've wanted this. To be able to do this."

It's my turn to kiss her.

Our kiss starts out impulsive.

It turns hot.

Hungry.

Desperate.

I slip my tongue between her lips and into her mouth, and the taste of strawberry lip gloss hits me. Grace sighs as our lips caress each other's. Our mouths stay connected as I walk us to the couch. I fall back onto it and pull her onto my lap. My dick immediately hardens when she straddles me. I grip her hips and bite into her lower lip before raining kisses down her jaw and neck.

Goose bumps pop up along her soft skin in the wake of my lips. My excitement explodes when she shudders at my touch. Bunching up her dress to her hips, I shove my hands underneath it, no longer able to hold back the urge to touch her.

To touch her the ways I've wanted to for years.

She rocks against me and whispers, "More."

My eyes widen, as I'm momentarily shocked, and I give her what she wants.

More.

Using a single finger, I slip her panties to the side and dip my finger inside.

"Shit, baby," I hiss. "You're soaked."

"For you," she says, encircling her arms around my neck. "Just for you."

To help me, she tilts her waist back, and I slide my finger between her folds.

I've never been so turned on in my life.

She writhes above me and gasps when I thrust a finger inside her.

Her pussy is a tight wall against my single finger.

Will she be comfortable taking my cock?

I halt, stopping myself at the thought.

I'm going too fast.

She loses a breath and stares at me, wide-eyed, when I slowly draw my finger out of her. My chest heaves in and out, and I drop my head back, resting it against the cushion.

"Shit, Grace," I groan. "I'm sorry."

"Why are you sorry?" she slowly asks. "Why'd you stop?"

I raise my head to meet her gaze. "I don't want to rush this with you. I didn't tell you I loved you to sleep with you."

She needs to know my intentions for baring myself to her wasn't to have sex.

I rest my hand on her shaky thigh.

"Is it because I'm pregnant?"

Her question shocks me into silence.

I've never slept with a pregnant woman before. Not because I find them unattractive. But this is Grace. I want her any way I can have her.

Before I can say she's lost her mind and her pregnancy has nothing to do with me stopping us, she whispers, "I know I'm bigger. A pregnant body might not exactly be a turn-on … especially with it not being your baby."

My chest seizes tight. I hate when she points that out.

"I understand, Finn," she adds in a strained voice.

"What?" I pull back and stare at her, stunned, and soften my voice. "Baby, my attraction to you is not the issue. It will *never* be the issue." I tilt my hips up, grinding my erection between her thighs. "Feel how hard my cock is for you? I just don't want to rush it."

"But—"

I press my finger against her lips. "Let me prove it to you." I grind against her again. "Show you how much I've wanted to have you for years. How I've wanted to take you, all cute and polite, and dirty you up in bed. You have no idea how bad I've wanted to make you mine, fuck you the way I know you should be fucked, and never let you go."

My voice is raspy after my confession.

Some words I meant to say.

Some I didn't.

Maybe she wasn't ready to hear all that yet.

"Do it," she says, challenging me. "Make me yours. Prove you want me like this."

Pushing my hands between us, I tighten my hold on her ass to lift her. She wraps her legs around my waist as I stand and head to her bedroom. As hot as messing around on the couch sounds, I want her in a bed. I need ample room to show her she's everything to me.

I flip the light on, carefully set her on her feet, and sit on the edge of the bed. I drink her in as she stares at me in curiosity.

Crossing my arms, I lower my voice. "Strip for me. Show me that gorgeous body I've lusted over for years."

CHAPTER TWENTY-TWO

Grace

FINN'S WORDS light a fire inside me.

I'm a vanilla girl.

I've only had sex with vanilla men.

Straight to missionary type of men.

I'd bet my car Finn isn't a vanilla, *straight to missionary* man.

A man asking me to strip is new.

If it were any other man asking, I'd be timid.

Uncertain.

But this is Finn.

And the way he's eyeing me like a snack gives me a boost of confidence.

He wants me to strip for him?

I'll strip for him.

My breathing is ragged as I step out of my dress. Without thinking, I wrap my hands around my stomach, hiding myself.

"All of you, Grace," Finn demands. "Every single inch."

I drop my arms, unsnap my bra, and my breasts burst free.

"Shit," he mutters.

I stand tall, wearing only panties, a sense of pride shooting through my veins. I don't bother covering my breasts because I know his next command would've told me not to. Finn licks his lips, his stare sweeping up and down my body in appreciation.

"You are the sexiest woman I've ever seen." He falls back onto his elbows, holding himself up. "Now, let me see that pretty pussy of yours."

I nearly fall back a step at his words.

I rub my thighs together, feeling the stickiness of my arousal, and run a finger between my legs before slowly pushing my panties down.

"You're soaked for me, aren't you?" he croaks out.

I smirk. "Possibly."

Two can play this teasing game, buddy.

My eyes sweep straight to him as my panties fall to the carpet, and I kick them off my feet.

He rises, no longer on his elbows, and his back is straight. "And you thought I wouldn't find this the sexiest damn thing ever?" His breathing turns ragged. "You are breathtakingly beautiful." He crooks his finger, signaling for me to come closer.

I erase the distance between us, and he raises my leg onto the bed. I shudder as he strokes the inside of my thigh.

"I love this body of yours"—he plants a soft kiss to my growing belly—"every inch of you, and I'm going to show that appreciation by worshipping your pussy." He widens the space between my legs, dragging his hand up and down my thigh. "Can I taste you, Grace?"

"Yes," I half gasp, half moan.

"That's my girl."

Standing, he carefully pushes me onto the bed and climbs over me. I relax into my mattress, ready for whatever he's willing to give me. Goose bumps coat my skin when he slips a hand up my thigh before settling himself between my ankles.

He spreads my legs wide, putting me on full display for him.

Another first time for me.

Call it the pregnancy hormones.

Call it being with Finn.

But for the first time in my years of having sex, I've never felt so comfortable with someone.

Finn lowers his head and stares between my legs, as if he were studying for a test. His head falls forward, and he takes my clit between his lips, gently sucking on it. "I'm going to make you feel so good, baby."

"Oh my God," I mutter, tingles shooting up my spine.

With no warning, he dips his head lower and strokes the length of his tongue between my lower lips. My back hitches off the bed as a burst of pleasure shatters through me.

It's only the first lick, and I'm already a goner.

I grip the back of his neck, holding him down. "More, *please*."

He chuckles. "Oh, I'm going to have fun with you."

I grin.

No more vanilla sex for this girl.

Finn is awakening sexual urges I've never had before.

I've never been a fan of oral sex because it's never been a fun time. It's an annoying attempt where men fake making an effort to make you orgasm but never actually reach the finish line.

Finn?

He's putting in all the effort.

He gets an A+++++ for the things he's doing with his tongue.

He adds his fingers.

Sucks on my clit.

I writhe on the sheets and moan his name.

The same way I have when I've fingered myself, thinking about him, but this is so much better than anything I could've ever imagined. I move into his touch, grinding my core against his face, and I'm shocked he's not gasping for air at how tight I'm holding him. I want him there forever. A warm wave of pleasure hits me, shooting through my veins and lighting me on fire.

Finn groans against my clit as I ride out the wave of my orgasm.

My Finn-induced orgasm.

The best damn orgasm of my life.

"Holy freaking crap," I gasp. "I'm going to ask you if you think I'm attractive every day if that's what you do to prove me otherwise." I'm not sure how much he understands since I'm saying the words through heavy puffs of air.

He chuckles—it's deep and raw. He pulls back and swipes his

tongue over his wet lips—wet from my getting off on his face. I expect his next steps to be rolling off the bed, scurrying to the bathroom, and rinsing out his mouth.

That move was a Gavin regular.

I should've known Finn is nothing like Gavin.

I love the feel of his body weight as he moves up my body and slaps a kiss to my lips.

He lingers for a moment, sliding his tongue between my lips. "Don't you taste good?"

I'm not exactly sure what *good* vagina tastes like, and I can't taste much, so I nod and mutter, "Mm-hmm."

He collapses onto his back and catches his breath. "That is definitely a top ten best moment of my life."

"Oh, really?" I turn on my side and prop myself up with my elbow. Looking down, I meet his eyes. They're tired but lust-filled. "What's number one on that list?"

Without one moment of hesitation, he answers, "Hearing you say you love me."

I didn't expect that.

Sure, other men have said they loved me.

But not for a second do I doubt Finn's love for me.

This is the moment I realize that even though I've said those words to other men, I've never meant them. My heart had never filled with so much emotion like it did with Finn when those three words slipped past my lips.

I stare down at him with half-lidded eyes. "That's mine too."

He grins and taps his fingers along his lips.

I slide closer to him, and he clutches the back of my neck to bring me closer. Our kiss is slow, sensual, and when I pull back, something catches my eyes.

Finn's erection underneath his jeans.

My mouth waters, wanting to taste him just as bad as he did me.

"Can I add another top ten to mine?"

He raises a brow at the same time I climb over him.

I seat myself at his knees and run my hand along the outline of his cock. "Let me return the favor."

He groans as I take both hands and slide them up and down each side of his dick.

Excitement zips through me.

Like with men performing oral on me, I've never been a fan of sucking cock before.

At this moment, there's nothing more I want than to see Finn take his dick out and feed it between my lips.

"I want to taste you," I say, practically begging.

Finn starts to rise. "Grace, you don't have to."

I lean forward, remembering I'm naked for the first time as my boobs rub against the roughness of his jeans. "I *want* to." Smiling, I press my palm to his chest and shove him down.

I hate that my hands shake as I unbuckle his jeans. It's not that I'm nervous or that I don't want to. I'm excited that this is finally happening. I want to see all of Finn and show him I can pleasure him just as good as he pleasures me.

Well, I don't think my skills will ever match up to his.

The man has a talented tongue.

Finn tilts up his hips, helping me push down his jeans. I don't bother pulling them all the way off, and they stay bunched up around his ankles.

His cock stands at full attention. It's bigger than I anticipated, bigger than any cock I've seen. That's even including the porn Lola sent me the links to when I was in a dry spell. Since I teach my students measurements, I know he's *at least* a good six inches.

The man's cock is half a darn full ruler size.

I gulp, unsure of how well I can take in his length.

Finn grips the bottom of his cock. "Do whatever you feel comfortable with, babe. I don't expect you to deep-throat, swallow, whatever. This cock is yours to do with as you please."

I clasp my hand over his. "I want to do what you like. Show me."

He slips his hand off his cock before covering mine with it. With his eyes on me, he waits until I meet his stare before using both our hands to jerk him off. When we reach the head, he twists our hands, and we lose eye contact as he drops his head back and groans.

"You good on your own?" he rasps out.

I nod.

His hand disappears, leaving me on my own, and Finn props himself up onto his elbows, giving himself a perfect view of me about to suck his cock. I do one last stroke before lowering my head and licking the tip.

"Yes," he groans.

I open my mouth wide, and in my head, I replay the porn I watched, remembering how the woman hollowed her cheeks out as she sucked. My lips curl around his cock as I give him the best blow job I've ever given in my life. Slobber slides down my lips and onto my chin, hitting the sheets.

"Grace," Finn moans. "Just like that, baby."

His hand goes to my head the same way I did with him—only he's gentle, slowly guiding me into sucking him just as he likes it. Lowering my hand, I play with his balls, squeezing them. His knees lock up, tightening the room I have between them.

"I'm coming," he warns, grabbing the base of his dick as if ready to stop it while waiting for my reaction.

"In my mouth," I say against his cock, unsure whether he can understand me. To be clear, I give him a thumbs-up, and he chuckles at the same time his cum spurts into my mouth.

Finn relaxes against the sheets. "And that's made it to the top ten list."

I laugh, a red blush creeping up my cheeks.

I'm a bit shy but also proud of myself.

I did that. I made him come that hard.

After we catch our breaths, Finn kisses me softly before helping me out of bed. He scurries to his bathroom while I brush my teeth. As I'm finishing up, he joins me in the bathroom, and nervousness hits me.

Is he sleeping with me tonight?

I don't want to assume something, but surely, if a man had his face between my legs, he'd at least want to stay to sleep off the exhaustion of pleasuring me?

I want him in my bed.

To stay with me tonight … and every night.

As I'm lost in thought, Finn comes up behind me and circles his arms around my waist.

"Can I stay with you tonight?" he softly asks in my ear.

I reach up and clutch the top of his arm. "Yes, and you never have to question the answer to that again."

As I snuggle into his arms, I sleep through the night.

No nightmares.

Only a dream … of Finn being with me forever, of him being a father figure to my child, and of us having more children.

———

"I DON'T KNOW how I'm supposed to see my friends with a straight face."

Finn and I are standing in the kitchen. I'm drinking orange juice and him coffee. Even though we crossed friendship lines last night, it hasn't been awkward this morning. It's comfortable, as if waking up in each other's arms was what our future had been destined to be.

Finn winks at me. "Why's that?" The smirk on his face confirms he knows exactly why.

I bring my cup to my lips, smiling and speaking inside it, "You gave me the best orgasm of my life. I'm going to be walking around with orgasmed-out stars in my eyes for the next month."

He stands taller, pride on his face. "Let's not forget your skills either." He whistles. "I struggled not to come in seconds."

Pride settles through me at the compliment of pleasuring him like that. I've never felt so sexy, so skilled, as Finn makes me. Never has a man made me feel more attractive—with the weight gain, pregnant belly, and all.

I set my cup on the counter and swallow, remembering how he tasted inside my mouth. It's something I want to have over and over again. I read that pregnant women are horny a lot, but I've never wanted to taste, to kiss, to be with a man as badly as I do with Finn.

"Those words aren't going to help me keep a straight face, mister." I wiggle my finger in his direction.

He leans against the counter with his legs slightly open. "All you have to do is spend the morning questioning Lola about her and Silas."

"Lola won't mutter a word about it. You know how private she is."

"You find anything out, you share the gossip."

I shake my head. "If she says not to, I can't break girl code."

He places his hand to his chest and gasps. "Not even for ..." He briefly pauses and furrows his brows. "Your guy best friend?"

I frown. "Is that what you are still? My guy best friend?"

He fixes his deep stare on me. "I'd love to say boyfriend, but I don't want to assume anything. I'm afraid of jumping too fast and scaring you, Grace."

"Us together doesn't scare me." My words are rushed out.

"You want to be mine then?" He strokes his jaw while waiting for my answer.

"I want to be your everything."

He narrows the gap between us, grips my waist, and lifts me onto the counter. "You've been my everything for years."

———

"FIRST THINGS FIRST," Georgia announces when the waitress returns with our drink orders—lemonade for Cassidy and me and mimosas for everyone else. "Lola, we need to know what the hell happened last night."

It's a tradition for us girls to go out for our birthdays and then do a brunch the day after. Brunch is where we hand over gifts and gossip. Lola chose a small bistro that makes the best sandwiches, and the weather is nice enough for us to sit outside. Not too hot, yet not too cold. We're seated around a table, ready for food and gossip.

Lola, sporting oversize black sunglasses, shakes her head. "First things first. I'm hungover, and I'll talk about anything but that."

"Come on," Georgia says, the only one having the guts to question Lola. "What pissed off Silas so much that he acted how he did?"

Since Cassidy and Jamie are new to the group, they don't push the friendship boundaries as much as Georgia does with everyone. For some reason, my short, sarcastic friend can pull the truth out of anyone. Although Lola is a tough nut to crack.

"I've never seen him like that," I add. "He threw you off his lap."

I'm certain my comment will cause Lola to come to Silas's defense. Even with whatever happened to them last night, she's always his biggest supporter.

Lola snatches her mimosa. She wraps her fingers around the glass, her long black nails on display. "Silas doesn't like it when I drink that much." She shrugs as if we'd believe her half-assed answer.

"There's no way he was that mad over you having a few drinks," Georgia deadpans next to her. "Not to mention, you looked like you wanted to jump his bones."

"It was actually hot," Cassidy inputs. "Until the whole dropping you on your ass part."

Lola winces at the reminder. "Sorry, but I'd prefer not to talk about my best friend rejecting me. It was dumb on my part, smart on his."

Silas and Lola are two of a kind. They share a *give no fucks* attitude and are fun. We'll give last night a *get-out-of-jail-free* card for their bizarre behavior. We all insist they hook up on the down-low, but they deny it. Last night makes me rethink that notion.

"What about his stepbrother?" Jamie asks, letting Lola off the hook. "You two looked chummy."

Lola sighs dramatically. "He's nice. We exchanged numbers. He walked me to Lincoln's car, where he and Cass took my drunken ass home." She throws Cassidy an appreciative nod.

"He was a gentleman," Cassidy adds. "With how Silas described him, I expected him to be a jackass. While we waited for Lincoln's car, he chatted with us. I think Silas was jealous of him buying Lola a drink."

"Is it weird, though?" I ask, hoping I don't sound like a Debbie Downer. "With him being Silas's stepbrother?"

Lola licks her red lips. "They're not close. Their parents didn't start dating until their senior year of high school, and they never hung out. Silas's mother left his father for Trent's dad. I understand Silas not being a fan, but Trent had nothing to do with what his dad did. According to Trent, Silas has hated him since the day they met."

"As bad as it sounds, I get his anger," Sierra says. "I was pissed when I found out my father had an affair and secret child. I took it out on my brother's girlfriend for a while since she had something to do with it."

Lola nods. "My father was the king of affairs. It's why I don't trust men."

"Since Lola won't share anything, let's move on to Grace and Finn," Georgia says, causing everyone's attention to flash to me. "Finn looked ready to kill Silas for what he said about you getting pregnant because Finn was a wuss."

My straw squeaks as I move it in and out of my cup. "I'm happy he did. It knocked sense into Finn." A smile spreads across my lips at thoughts of being with Finn last night.

On my drive to brunch, I devised different stories to explain how our night went. With all of Lola's drama, I wasn't sure if Finn and I would come up. I should've known if Lola stayed quiet, I'd be the next in line.

Georgia gapes at me. "What?"

"Now, this is a much better conversation." Lola leans back in her chair and sucks on the orange from her drink. "Did you fuck?" She's never one ot beat around the bush or worry about her words.

I play with my hands in my lap. "We didn't … have sex. Just messed around."

"First base?" Georgia asks. "Second base?"

A collection of amused stares is pinned on me.

"What base is tongues?" I relax in my chair.

It's a relief to finally say that Finn and I share the same feelings out loud. These are my friends, and they'd never judge me. There isn't one person at the table who doesn't show a sign of excitement. Even Lola's hungover ass is grinning.

"How was it?" Cassidy asks.

My smile is so wide that my teeth are showing. "It was amazing. I could spend the rest of my life having him … go downtown on me."

"Cheers to that!" Georgia says.

Everyone raises their glasses and clinks them against each other's.

"Does that mean you're dating now?" Sierra asks.

"I don't know." My shoulder slump, and I lose the grin I've worn all day. "His feelings for me might change after the baby is born. I'm going to get fat—"

"Shut the hell up with that attitude," Lola interrupts. "Finn worships you. He isn't going anywhere."

CHAPTER TWENTY-THREE

Finn

AFTER GRACE LEAVES, I shower, grab the baby book from her nightstand, and stride into the kitchen to make myself a lunch. With a plated turkey sandwich in hand, I venture to the living room and make myself comfortable on the couch. Taking a bite, I start educating myself on all things pregnancy and baby. I want to be able to help Grace with whatever she needs.

I try to block out what'll happen when the baby is born. Before last night, I was sure I'd never be able to have her. Now? I have more hope of that not happening.

My baby education is interrupted when my phone chimes with a text.

Silas: Can we talk?

I expected him to reach out to me today. Silas is a good dude, and we've never had issues. His dickhead behavior last night was out of the ordinary.

Me: If it's about last night, I get it.

Silas: Are you with Grace?

Me: Nah, she's at the birthday brunch.

Seconds later, my phone rings.

Silas.

"I was an asshole last night," he says when I answer. "I wish I could blame it on the alcohol, but that's obviously not the case."

"Nah, dude." I set my sandwich down and transfer the plate to the coffee table. "I'm buying you dinner for helping me get my head out of my ass."

"Does that mean you finally told Grace how you feel?"

"Sure did," I reply with a nod.

"How'd that work out?" His tone is layered with confidence.

"Pretty damn good." I stretch out on the couch, a dopey smile on my face.

"I'm happy for you, man." He chuckles. "Looks like you do owe me dinner."

"Now, it's time for you and Lola to do the same." It's ballsy of me to bring up Lola after what happened last night. "You're the last couple in our group who needs to get their shit together."

Our group started out as individuals, and everyone has started coupling up.

"Lola and I are ... more complicated than Grace and you," he says irritably.

I shut my eyes, hating that I need to make this point to him. "Trent was hitting on her. You need to make your move before she gives him a chance."

He scoffs. "Lola isn't that fucking stupid."

I mock his scoff. "Do you remember what you did last night?"

Silence.

I can almost picture him grinding his jaw.

He needs to be hit with the truth.

"You dropped her on her ass on her birthday," I state. "She walked off with Trent. We both know it wasn't only a friendly gesture from Trent."

"I have to go. I'll talk to you later, man."

He ends the call.

———

AS BAD AS I hate not being at the bar, I'm beginning to enjoy my job at the dealership.

My bank account also likes it.

My coworkers are starting to come around, and there's a sense of deep pride every time I sell a car. I loved my job at the Twisted Fox, but it's almost like I hit an achievement each time someone thanks me for helping them get their dream ride.

Another plus?

The dealership is close to Grace's school, and our lunch breaks are at the same time.

"Hi, Finn!" A bright smile crosses over Rachelle's face when I enter the school's office. "You brought Grace and the baby lunch. So cute!"

The more Grace's belly grows, the more questions she gets. Me bringing her lunch regularly has led some of her coworkers, including Rachelle, to assume I'm the father. I have no problem with those assumptions. Like them though, I'm curious as to who the father is. Anytime the topic is brought up, Grace shuts down. She's already going through enough, so I'm scared to push her. There's also the deep pit in my stomach when I think of learning the truth. From the few details she's told me about him, I already want to kick the motherfucker's ass. If I find out who he is and run into him, it might cause issues.

"Another visit?"

My gaze moves from Rachelle to find Principal Asshole strolling toward me. He stops behind Rachelle, his fingers gripping the back of her chair, and icily stares at me. Thrusting out his chin, he crosses his arms.

I return his glare. The weird-ass motherfucker keeps creeping up every time I'm here as if he were watching the parking lot. I want to hop over the counter and ask what his problem is, but I can't. That could result in the end of lunch visits with Grace. I'm sure fighting the principal is a straight road to being banned from the school.

Holding up the bag of boxed chef salads, I smile. "Grace loves her Freddy's salads."

"I'm well aware," Asshole grits out.

The fuck is that supposed to mean?

His response rubs me the wrong way, but I act like it doesn't.

Don't let him know his words affect you.

Rachelle smiles again—this one not as genuine as before. "You know where her room is, Finn. Enjoy your lunch." She's catching on to his weird sudden appearances too.

"I suggest limiting your visits," Asshole says, glowering at me. "You're becoming a distraction to my female employees."

Ah, there it is.

Jealousy.

Not only that, but his creepy factor also keeps moving up notches.

His female employees?

Rachelle gasps, her face paling.

He curls his upper lip and glowers at Rachelle. "That includes you."

Not wanting this to go further, I turn and shake my head.

"You're one weird-ass dude," I mutter under my breath. Without waiting to find out if he heard me, I yank the door open and leave the office.

The scent of cafeteria food is in the air, and a kid yells, "Hey! I'm the line leader," before shoving another away.

Grace's classroom is at the end of the hall, and I tuck the bag of food underneath my elbow as I approach it. The door is open, and I tap my knuckle against it, lightly knocking.

Grace is standing on a chair, taping a poster to the wall. When each corner is secured, she turns to look at me from over her shoulder.

"Hey," she greets, sliding the tape into her pocket.

Advancing into her classroom, I drop our food and drinks onto a desk and help her down from the chair.

"You need to be careful doing that," I say, squeezing her hand tight before releasing it and smacking a kiss to her lips. "Don't they have ladders for that here?"

She pulls the tape from her pocket and drops it into her desk drawer. "Yes, but I hate hunting them down. A chair does just as good of a job."

"Did something happen between you and the principal?"

I curse myself for asking that so soon. I planned to approach the conversation while we ate, throwing it out there as small talk.

Grace lowers her gaze, her tone turning flustered. "Why … why do you ask?"

"The way he reacts to seeing me isn't …" I search for the right word to use without sounding too much like a dick. "It's not normal."

Jealousy.

That's what the man exudes whenever he sees me.

"Uh …" Grace bites into her lower lip. "Kind of."

"Is he …?" I stop, allowing my words to trail off, unable to say them out loud.

"He is," she says, her voice quiet and shaky.

My chest tightens. I turn my head to the side and tightly shut my eyes, digesting the news. "Oh, wow." It takes a moment before my stare returns to her. "I guess that finally answers the question of who the father is."

"It does," Grace whispers, her hands clutching her stomach. "Unfortunately."

"Fucking asshole." I grit my teeth and want to throw the food across the room. "I want to beat his ass."

My mind scrambles with what Grace told me about him being married and keeping it from her. *What a dumbass.*

"Trust me." She cringes. "I want to kick his ass every day I see him."

"Wow." I slide onto a student's chair, the connected desk tight at my stomach. "It's going to be hard not to kill him when I'm here."

This new revelation won't stop me from visiting Grace.

I was worried about being a dick before, but now that I know what he did to Grace, there's no more Mr. Nice Guy. If he says something smart, I might not be able to touch him with my hands, but I'll give him a verbal beatdown like no other. He'll know never to mess with Grace.

"Look on the bright side," Grace says. "Had he not done what he did, maybe we wouldn't be together like we are now."

"Or maybe you wouldn't be pregnant by the cheating dick. Eventually, we would've dragged our heads out of our asses."

Grace flinches at my response, all the color draining from her face.

"Shit, sorry." I roughly drag a hand through my hair, tugging at the ends to cause myself pain—an attempt to forget about Principal Asshole. I can't let my anger get the best of me in front of Grace. It'll only make her feel worse about the situation.

I snatch the bag from the desk and start dragging out the contents. My appetite is gone, and the sight of the food makes my stomach curl. I snap off the lid and hand Grace's salad to her. I don't even bother with mine. I gesture to her to sit down, and she warily does.

"How did it start between you and him?" I ask, standing in front of her desk.

Grace unwraps a plastic fork. "Having this conversation while in the same building as him isn't a good idea."

I snap my fingers. "Good point. Speaking of being in the same building, you think you can do this every day? What about when you have the baby?"

"I don't love being around him, but I also won't give him the satisfaction of pushing me out of my job. I was here first." She grabs her drink and uses it to point to the door. "He can go."

"If he messes with you, tell me. Tell someone. It seems he doesn't like the idea of you being with anyone else."

That's an understatement. Dude goes into creep mode.

"It's because he still wants to be with me." She drops her fork at her confession—a sign that she didn't plan on disclosing that information.

I raise a brow, and my lungs constrict. "What?"

"He wants me to wait for him until he can leave his wife."

"Are you …?" I glance at the door, watching it as if he'll appear there. "You're not considering that, are you?"

"What?" she shrieks. "Absolutely not. I want to be with you, Finn. *Only you.*"

I swear, when I take another glance at the door, someone scurries away from it.

———

"DO ME A FAVOR?" I slide out a barstool and plop down on it.

Since it's early, Silas is the only one working the bar. Not many people go for a drink straight after work. It's something I've never done. I used to work until the wee hours of the morning, and the act always reminded me of my father.

When he actually held a job, he'd reward himself with a drink— well, *drinks*—afterward.

Silas wipes his hands with a rag while strolling over to me and throws it over his shoulder. "Yeah?"

I wrap my feet around the stool legs, already feeling dizzy before drinking an ounce of liquor. "Pour me a drink."

He nods, smiling quizzically. "I got you."

Turning on his heels, he sings along with the music playing in the background. He chooses a bottle of vodka—the most expensive one Twisted Fox carries—and pours me a double.

Grace had plans with Faith after work. Not wanting to be alone, I drove to Twisted Fox. A drink will help clear my head. It was difficult, focusing on work after discovering Grace works with the guy who knocked her up. Not only that but he also wants to be with her. I shudder at the thought of her falling victim to his games again. Grace is strong, but the guy sounds like a master manipulator. It'd kill me to lose Grace to him.

He could leave his wife and ask Grace to be one big, happy family.

I finally have all I want in my hands, and today proved how easy it can slip away.

"You look like shit," Silas says, smacking a square napkin in front of me and setting my drink on top of it.

"I feel like shit." I knock back the vodka, and it burns down my throat.

He cocks his head. "What's up?"

"I met the guy who got Grace pregnant." Even after the vodka, my throat goes dry.

"Oh fuck. Who?"

I tap my fingers along my chin.

Does anyone else know who the dad is?

Will that break our trust?

Just like Silas won't tell us anything about him and Lola, if I confide in him about Grace, he'll remain tight-lipped.

"It's a guy who works at the school," I reply, pinching the bridge of my nose.

Silas studies me for a moment. "You've been thinking about them being around each other almost daily?"

"That ... among other things."

"Don't worry about it. Grace has been in love with you for years, man."

"Nothing is ever permanent, though." I sigh, hating that I'm being this negative man. "Even when there's love, relationships don't always work out."

I rest my elbows on the table. I came to the bar to chat with the bartender, like one of those drunks who lives at bars. Now that I've said the words out loud, I no longer want to talk about it.

"And you and Lola?" I ask. "Any updates on her and Trent?"

Silas presses his fist to his mouth as if settling himself down from those names being said together. "She hasn't said a word to me, but from what I heard, they exchanged numbers." He shakes his head. "Lola is talking with Trent. Grace works with an ex. And we thought being friends with girls we liked was gonna be easy."

CHAPTER TWENTY-FOUR

Grace

"I WENT ON A DATE WITH TRENT," Lola tells Georgia and me.

"What?" I shriek. "How could you do that to Silas?"

Lola's face tightens, and she sucks in what sounds like an irritated breath. "Do what to Silas? He made it clear how he felt for me on my birthday."

I'm not sure if Lola is talking to—*dating*—Trent to get back at Silas for his behavior at the club or if she genuinely likes him. We're all best friends who share secrets, but Lola is the private one of the group. She provides the bare minimum about her life. Our friends haven't gotten together since the club, so I haven't witnessed how Silas and Lola are now. When we texted earlier, she told me they were fine.

"Have you talked to him about it?" I might as well be the one who dives into questions. She can't get that mad at a pregnant woman.

Lola shakes her head. "Barely. He texted and apologized that night. I told him it was no big deal, and I was over it."

"But you're not over it," I deadpan.

"I'm definitely not over it." She rests her elbows on the table, the bangles around her wrist making a noise as they hit the table. A painful expression crosses her features. "Maybe this is the end of Silas and me."

Her statement startles me. That's a big deal.

"Yeah, right," Georgia says, leaning back in her stool. "You and Silas are two peas in a pod."

Lola drums her nails along her glass. "He's been distant lately." She flips her ebony hair over her shoulder before hunching forward. Her head drops—an attempt to hide the hurt flashing along her face.

I cringe. Lola has saved me from uncomfortable conversations countless times. It's time I do the same for her.

"Finn knows who my baby daddy is," I cry out.

All *Lola and Silas* talk are overrun by my confession. During Lola's birthday brunch, I shared the mess that was my relationship with Gavin.

"He knows about Principal Jackass?" Georgia asks before snarling. "I can't stand that asshole."

"That makes two of us," I grumble. "He keeps saying he wants to be with me."

I haven't told Finn about the many visits Gavin has paid to my classroom to tell me he was leaving his wife so we could be together. I don't entertain the idea and always tell him I don't care. He could leave his wife tonight, and I'd still want nothing to do with him.

Once a cheater, always a cheater in my book.

People can change—I'm well aware. But this man hid an entire marriage and family from me. He talks about his wife as if he has no respect for her, which is further proven by the cheating. I'd never trust Gavin, and he disgusts me. I hate that I ever allowed him to touch me.

The only man I want in my life, in my baby's life, is Finn.

———

"YOU OKAY?" Finn asks from across the table. "Is it morning sickness? Should we add doughnuts to the list of shit that makes you nauseous?"

"God, no," I grumble, wiping frosting from the edge of my mouth. "Thou shall not take a pregnant woman's doughnuts unless they want a pregnant woman's foot up their ass."

Since moving in, Finn declared himself the master of breakfast. It was a meal he typically didn't have, so he's tried everything. He either makes me breakfast or takes me out. The breakfast process has been a lot of trial and error.

He made eggs. They made me nauseous.

Oatmeal? Baby isn't a fan.

Bacon? Good ole bacon? I ran to the bathroom and puked.

Meat and dairy have become a thing of my non-pregnant past.

Now, all I want are foods dipped in ranch or taco sauce. I'm shocked I haven't dipped this Long John into some ranch yet.

Even with my love of doughnuts, I'm surprised I'm not sick. Not because they're gross. Nor is it because the baby isn't a fan. It's because today is an exciting one.

No more will I say *the baby*.

It'll be *he* or *she*.

Today, I'll find out the sex of my baby.

There's always a rush of pent-up excitement when I think about it.

Nervous jitters—but good nervous jitters.

Then, that happiness balloon bursts.

It'll be a good day but also a lonely one.

I'll have no one next to me at the appointment to share the good news with. No one holding my hand as we stare at the screen with anticipation. I'll be solo, a single mother.

Today's news will change my life.

Faith offered to join me, but it's parents' day at Raven's school. I'd feel terrible if Faith missed that because of me. I haven't broken the news to my parents yet, so my mother tagging along isn't an option either. I could ask one of my friends, but they're busy. There's also a twinge of embarrassment for bringing your best friend with you. It's as if they'd immediately know no one else was in the picture.

I also haven't asked them because I've been trying to build up the nerve to ask the man sitting across from me.

I shouldn't be nervous. The man has had his tongue between my legs, and his cock has been in my mouth.

Why am I scared of asking him to come with me to a doctor's appointment?

Finn has spent every night in my bed since the night of Lola's birthday party. We've snuggled, made out, and progressed to third base, but we haven't slept together yet. The first time we hooked up, we were a mix of emotions, of desire and lust. Now, it's as if one of us is afraid of crossing that line. When it comes, there'll be no going back. Sex is more final, and ever since I became pregnant, I've seen it as more of something that you only do out of love.

I shove the last bite of doughnut into my mouth and wash it down with apple juice. Not a good combination, but my pregnant appetite would have apple juice with every meal if possible.

"I, uh …" I struggle to find the right words.

Finn sets his coffee to the side to provide me his full attention.

"Whatever it is, hit me." He rubs his hands together.

"I have a doctor's appointment today." I stare at him, unfocused, not wanting to see him as clearly in case he turns me down. "I'm going to find out the sex of the baby."

"Who's going with you?" His face hardens when I shake my head. "No one?"

I gulp. "No one."

"Wrong." He leans in close. "I'm going with you." He quickly presses a kiss to the tip of my nose.

That's the thing with Finn.

If he knows someone needs something, he's there.

Yes, we might be dating, but that doesn't mean he's obligated to go. He could've easily blamed it on work, especially since it'll be last minute.

With no hesitation, Finn said he'd be there.

Another event where Finn steps up and does Gavin's job.

Another action that'll pull me closer to him even though I know in the end, he'll leave. Finn is a thirty-year-old man who's never talked positively about commitment. When baby talk comes up with our friends, he always shakes his head and says he doesn't think it's for him.

Does that mean my baby and I won't be for him either?

It's one thing to hang out with the pregnant girl and another when there's a screaming newborn in the next room.

CHAPTER TWENTY-FIVE

Finn

RIGHT NOW, I'm like a damn toddler on Christmas morning.

Not that I've ever believed in Santa.

When I was at the old age of five, my father told me Santa was fake and wanted to make it clear that any gift I received was from him, period. Dick wanted to take all the credit ... even for the ones I received from different charity organizations.

I've been brimming in excitement all day. Hell, I'm shocked I haven't broken out in dance. For what seems like the hundredth time today, I check my watch. As soon as the time that I've been waiting for hits, I jump up from my chair.

I high-five Brian before leaving and getting in my car to pick up Grace for her appointment.

Today will be another addition to my top ten list.

Grace asked me to be there with her for this appointment. She's handing over a trust not easily given. She could've asked one of the girls to accompany her, but I was her pick. That feels damn good.

I blare my music, singing along with the song, and drive to Grace's school. When I pull into the parking lot, I spot her standing at the entrance. Her attention is on the children running around the playground. As I get closer, she turns, and her face practically glows when her eyes meet mine. I grin, and my heart fucking brightens at the reminder of where we're going.

The fact I'm experiencing this with her is the best high I'll ever get.

I pull over to the curb, and she gets in before I have the chance to jump out and open the door for her.

She shyly tucks a strand of hair behind her ear. "Hey."

"Hey, babe." I cup her cheeks between my hands and brush my lips against hers. "You ready to do this?"

She eagerly nods and buckles her seat belt. "I am *so* ready."

———

THE DOCTOR'S office is on the second floor of a small medical building.

Elevator music plays in the waiting room while Grace and I sit side by side. My knee is bouncing up and down to the beat while we wait for her name to be called. Two other couples and a woman are in the waiting room. One couple is going back and forth about baby names, the other a grocery list, while the woman is on her phone. No one is paying attention to us, but in the back of my mind, I wonder if they think I'm the father of Grace's baby.

With a light laugh, she rests her hand on my thigh, calming it. "I think you're more nervous than I am."

I swallow. "I think you might be right."

She starts to reply, but a nurse interrupts, "Grace Mitchell."

We stand, and I ball up my fist, stopping myself from grabbing Grace's hand. This isn't something normal for us, and I'm not sure what to do. We've held hands aplenty, but for some reason, this moment feels different.

I stand to the side as the nurse takes Grace's weight and blood pressure before leading us into a room. Grace sits on the exam table while answering the nurse's questions. As soon as the nurse leaves, I scoot my chair as close to Grace as possible. Before we can make conversation, my gaze whips to the door at the sound of a knock.

"Come in," Grace calls out.

The ultrasound tech walks in with an eager smile. "Hi, guys! My name is Sylvia, and I'll be doing your ultrasound. Today's the day we'll learn the sex of the baby. Is that something you'd like to know?"

Grace tucks a curl of hair behind her ear. "I'm so ready for it."

Grace's attitude toward being pregnant is changing. At first, it was shock and almost dread of keeping the secret and feeling alone. As time has passed, she's been growing more comfortable with the idea of becoming a mother. Some days, she pulls up her shirt to show off how fast her belly is growing. She recites excerpts of the baby books she's been reading. It's no longer fear. It's excitement. Sure, I see the nervousness in her eyes at times, but that never beats out how breathtaking it is to watch her face light up while she talks about having a baby.

As far as the sex, she hasn't told me what she wants. Our friends have asked a few times, but she always tells them it doesn't matter to her. No matter what, I know the baby will be loved by Grace like no other.

The redheaded tech's attention turns to me.

"This is Finn," Grace bursts out as if feeling the need to define who I am.

She pauses, her mouth opening, and I can see the wheels turning in her head as to what to introduce me as.

I straighten in my chair. "I'm the father."

CHAPTER TWENTY-SIX

Grace

"IT'S A GIRL!" Finn shouts again when we get into his car. He grabs my face and kisses me. "We're having a girl!"

It's been an emotional day.

Before leaving the school, Gavin questioned where I was going.

To which I told him none of his damn business.

Finn then introduced himself as the father of my baby.

I nearly collapsed when he did, but it created a moment of relief.

And we found out the sex.

"A girl," I squeal against his lips.

As the last word leaves my mouth, I feel his smile drop against it. He pulls away and grimaces as if he'd been slapped in the face.

With wide eyes, he says, "I mean ... you're having a girl." All excitement in his tone has vanished.

Each word said with sadness.

His face is unreadable.

But I know what he's thinking.

Why he corrected himself.

We're not having a girl. I am.

This isn't his baby.

As fun as it's been to pretend, reality is here.

Her father is a man I despise—one inferior to the one next to me.

Her father isn't the one who nearly jumped out of his seat in excitement when the tech delivered the good news. It tears me up that I did this to my baby. I should've been smarter about who I slept with, but in the end, I'll never regret having her.

Is the timing wrong? Yes.

Is it with the wrong person? Yes.

But how can I regret something I already love so much?

I could ask Finn to step up, but it's unfair to put that weight on him. We've only been dating a short time, and this is the first serious relationship he's ever been in. Everything is great now, but throw in the responsibilities of a newborn later, and he might realize it's not what he wants.

Finn clears his throat and shakes his head as he braces his hands against the steering wheel. "Sorry, I guess I got in a little over my head." He squeezes his eyes shut. "I don't know what that little girl will be to me, Grace."

I hunch my shoulders forward and sit in silence.

"I just don't want to get attached." He withdraws his hands from the steering wheel, and they fall limp in his lap.

I swallow, struggling for words.

This is a Finn I've never seen before—a broken, confused man.

All because of me.

I caused this.

My ribs suddenly feel too tight as my heart hammers against it.

"I don't want to get too attached," Finn says, staring ahead. "And then lose everything."

Tears pool in my eyes. "I'm sorry I put you in this position." I shrink into my seat. "It was unfair and selfish of me to do so. I'm truly sorry. If I could take it back, I would."

He whips his attention to me, his face twisting in betrayal. "Take back our relationship? The time we've spent together?" He gestures between us. "I'm confused and hurt that you said you'd take *back* what the hell we've created here." His lower lip trembles. "I'm already confused because I'm falling so hard for you, growing so attached to not only you but also to the little one who'll soon be in this world."

I stare at him with intent. "What ... what are you saying?"

"I'm saying that I want to be just as much in her world as yours." His statement is said with complete certainty.

"You say that now, but what about when she's born?" My chest hitches. "It'll be different ... overwhelming. It's a lot to ask of someone. What if you wake up in the morning and decide you no longer want that responsibility?"

"That won't happen," he rushes out.

"Your life can change. You could meet someone else—"

He stills. "Meet someone? Like another woman?"

I nod, sniffling back tears as my chin trembles.

"Fuck that," he enunciates each word. "I don't want *another woman*. Have you seen me open up myself with another woman like I have with you? Hell, I moved in with you." He smacks his hands together with each point he makes. "I'm here for you through your pregnancy because it's *you*. I don't want another woman. My feelings, my *love*, for you and the baby will never change."

"Finn," I sigh, taking his hand, "I'm just scared. I don't want to lose you."

And after years of hiding behind our feelings, our friendship, Finn and I are finally letting everything come to light. No longer can we hold anything in because it might lead us to losing each other.

He squeezes my hand before cupping the back of my head and pulling me into him. "I'm all in, Grace. I want everything with you— marriage, kids, all of it. There will never be anyone else but you."

CHAPTER TWENTY-SEVEN

Finn

"YOU READY TO MEET THE PARENTS?" Brian asks while I'm on break.

I blow out an upward breath. "I wouldn't say that."

He chuckles. "Trust me, they sound more intimidating than what they are. Sure, they're strict, but once you get to know them, they're cool."

"Maybe for you." I gulp. "You fit in with them."

Brian raises a brow. "What do you mean?"

"You have a good job." I count the reasons on my fingers. "Come from money. College-educated." I thrust my thumb into my chest. "Me? I threw people out of bars and come from the slums."

He flaps his hand, dismissing my words. "You're not just a guy who threw drunk people out of bars. You're more than that, man. You're a good dude. That matters more than anything. Don't sell yourself short, Finn. I didn't think you were like that."

Good point.

I've never been self-deprecating.

But with Grace, it's always been the issue.

She's so damn perfect.

There will never be a day I won't question if I deserve her.

"If all else fails, I'll text you a list of her mom's favorite wines," Brian adds. "Her dad likes golf."

I throw my head back. "Good thing I don't know shit about golf."

"Google it." He flicks his finger toward the computer in front of him. "But don't mention my man, Tiger Woods."

"Why?"

"Her mom hates him after the whole cheating scandal."

"Wine, golf, but not Tiger." I snap my fingers. "Got it. Any other pointers?"

"Just stay calm and keep it cool."

"Easier said than done."

———

IF THERE'S anything that can cheer me up, it's coming home to Grace.

When I walk into the living room, she's lounging on the couch with her pregnancy pillow. Her hair is wrapped into a high ponytail, her face makeup-free, and she's wearing her fluffy purple robe.

"Hey there," she says, shooting me a flirtatious smile.

I return the smile while moving deeper into the room and toss my keys on the coffee table. "How was your day?"

This.

It feels so domesticated.

Like something you'd see on a damn Disney sitcom.

"Good." She yawns. "Except my feet are killing me. I thought about cutting them off a few times while the kids were at recess."

"How about I make you dinner?" I wink. "And give my babe a little foot massage."

She throws her arms back. "A foot massage. A vagina massage. I'll take all the massages."

Grace and I haven't progressed more in the hookup department. I finger her and eat her out. She jacks me off and sucks my cock. My dick hasn't been inside her yet, but I want to wait until she's ready.

Honestly, until *we're* ready.

Once we pass that mark, it'll break me if I lose her.

Knowing what it's like, being inside her, and then her leaving would kill me.

I make grilled chicken and veggies, massage every inch of her, and then she falls asleep in my arms.

———

"YOU READY FOR TOMORROW?" Grace asks.

We're in bed, a show playing in the background, but neither of us is watching. Our minds are focused on tomorrow.

I blow out a deep breath, sinking my head deeper into my pillow. "As ready as I'll ever be."

Too bad I haven't had practice for this. My dumbass never deemed it necessary in the thirty years of my life to prepare myself for meeting the parents. Eventually, I should've known the day would come when I met someone I wanted to get serious with.

From what I've learned about her parents, they're strict but not assholes. They helped with Georgia while Cohen was busting his ass to provide for her and never judged them. They also raised Grace, who is the kindest damn soul I know.

I bet if they had to choose the perfect boyfriend for Grace in a lineup, it damn sure wouldn't be me, though.

Here I go with the self-pity bullshit.

I'm glad we're finally getting this over with.

Not only do I have the stress of meeting the parents, but Grace is also going to tell them she's pregnant. I have to then lie and say I'm the father. A point against me becoming their favorite person by knocking their daughter up out of wedlock. I'm already starting off on the wrong foot, and I need to work harder to make a good first impression.

Grace turns to her side, propping her chin on my bare chest while peering up at me. "They're going to love you, Finn."

I tilt my head back. "Let us pray."

She chuckles, slapping my stomach. "You know, we've never talked about your family before. What are they like?"

My stomach knots at the dreaded family question.

Yet another reason why I avoid meeting the parents.

They might ask about my family, and my life goal is to avoid that topic as much as possible.

I keep my head back, unable to look at her. "There's nothing to talk about."

She drums her fingers along my stomach. "Finn, all I know about your childhood is you're an only child. That's it. I know nothing about your parents."

Sweat builds along my hairline.

I could easily lie. I've done it before. Make up some happy story about some single dad and happily ever after bullshit. But this is Grace, and I refuse to lie to her. That's why instead of lying, I've always dodged the conversation.

No more of that.

No more hiding.

Grace knows me better than anyone and would never judge me for something I couldn't control. She'll never look down on me for my father's ways.

I stare at the ceiling and reach down to run my hand through her hair. "My mom died when I was four."

"I'm so sorry, Finn," she says, her voice soothing. "How did she die?"

"Drug overdose." My answer comes out strangled. "I don't remember much about her."

Sometimes, I hate myself for not remembering anything. The only recollection I have of my mother is from pictures my dad had before getting drunk one night and burning them.

"And your dad?" There's no change in her tone.

The moment of truth.

For the both of us.

What I'm about to say is something I've never said out loud.

My muscles tighten, causing my jaw to hurt. "I'm waiting for the day I get the call that he's dead from an overdose."

I choke back the emotions from my admission as it sends a wave of nausea through me.

The bed shifts as Grace scoots up and grips my chin, moving it slightly so we're eye to eye.

She caresses my jaw. "Wow, I had no idea. I feel bad that I haven't been there for you to talk about it with."

I shake my head. "It's not exactly something to brag about, so I keep it to myself."

She lowers her hand, capturing mine in it, and laces our fingers. "Thank you for telling me that. I love learning more about you, and whenever you're ready to open up about anything else, I'm here."

And that's why I knew it was safe for me to tell Grace this.

Other people might push for more—for every damn detail—but Grace waits, allowing me to do it on my time.

I raise a brow. "That doesn't scare you away?"

She shakes her head. "Of course not." She squeezes my hand. "Finn, you can't control the family you were born into. All you can control is the direction you've taken your life from there. You? You're not an addict, you don't make reckless decisions, and you are a good man, a hard worker, and an amazing boyfriend."

Boyfriend.

Heat radiates into my chest at that one word.

That one word switches up my mood, evaporating the dread of talking about my family into something better.

No matter what happens, it feels damn good to say that Grace Mitchell is my motherfucking girlfriend, and I'm never letting her go. No, if I can have it my way, Grace Mitchell will be my motherfucking wife.

CHAPTER TWENTY-EIGHT

Grace

SCREW the people who said you get used to morning sickness.

I hope you get splinters in your feet.

If there was anything in this world I could damn to hell, it'd be morning sickness.

Scooting away from the toilet, I slouch against the wall and wipe my mouth.

"Again?" Finn asks, walking into the bathroom.

"Again." I swipe away sweat from my cheek.

He kneels down in front of me, bare-chested and wearing only gym shorts. "If I could, I'd trade places with you in a heartbeat."

He leans in to kiss me, but I swat him away.

"Vomit breath," I say, cringing.

He chuckles before planting a kiss on my forehead. "I'd still kiss you, vomit breath and all."

"I sincerely suggest you see a professional for making that comment."

He stands. "You want me to make you breakfast?"

I raise a brow. "A baby-friendly vodka smoothie?" A grin spreads across my vomit lips. "I'll let you add kale to make it fun and healthy."

"Eggs and bacon, coming right up."

I grab the towel I was using to wipe my forehead and throw it at him as he starts to leave the room. "That isn't the support the baby books suggest!"

I'm sure the baby isn't the only one to blame for the nausea.

My nerves are on overdrive about telling my parents today.

On top of that, I'll be lying to them about who Finn is.

Well, halfway lying.

I'll tell them I love him—truth.

That we're dating—another truth.

That I plan to be with him as long as I can—fact.

That he's the one who knocked me up—big, fat lie.

I shouldn't be as worried as I am. It's not like my parents will disown me.

They'll just be *disappointed*.

Disappointment is worse than anything.

It's them saying they had better expectations for me.

He turns to look at me, bracing the doorframe with his hand. "It won't be that bad, babe. I'll be by your side all day."

———

THIS HAS BEEN the longest I've gone without seeing my parents.

Not even when I was in college was it this long.

I probably would've tried for longer had my mother not left a voicemail, threatening to show up at my house and work if I didn't attend family dinner today. I'm surprised it took her this long. I went from seeing them every week to being a no-show for months. They have to know something is up. The question is, what do they think it is?

Wiping my sweaty hand down my dress, I cast a curious glance at Finn when he drives up the long driveway to my parents' house.

"Wow," Finn comments, staring at the two-story white-bricked home. "This is a nice place." His gaze casts to me. "Have you lived here your entire life?"

I shake my head. "We moved here in my teens, and I moved out after college."

My mind wanders to where we lived before and how I preferred it. The fireplace was warmer. The living room cozier. The pantry and my bedroom larger. I wanted to live there forever, but then it became tainted—nothing but a reminder of what'd happened there. So, we ran away to this home, hoping it'd become our new favorite.

"You ready for this?"

Finn tenderly brushing my arm drags me out of my thoughts.

"I am," I lie, unbuckling my seat belt and gripping the door handle.

Finn is already nervous. Me telling him how anxious I am would only make it worse for him. We get out of the car, and he meets me at my door, taking my hand in his. With every step we take up the walkway, I second-guess myself. When we reach my mother's flower bed, scattered with roses and tulips, I halt, taking a moment to prepare myself.

At least it's only pretending about one thing.

Not a relationship.

The sweet scent of my mother's favorite cherry candle welcomes us. As if they knew we were here, my parents are waiting for us in the foyer. Dropping Finn's hand, I curl my arms around my stomach to hide it. I chose a loose-fitting dress for today, but that doesn't mean I'm not apprehensive about my growing belly. I'm not showing *that* much, but there's a baby bump you can't miss if you pay close attention.

My mother, her hair color the same as mine but shorter, stands in front of us, wearing an emerald dress with gemstone earrings. Her gaze is scrutinizing as if her brain is working to find out why I've been dodging them. I fail to meet her eyes and swiftly move them to my father. He's a tall man, on the skinny side, and his face is unreadable—as per usual.

He's not looking at me. No, his gaze is focused on Finn—full of concern and caution.

I chew on my lower lip, wishing I'd mentioned Finn would be with me. I'd stupidly left out I was bringing a plus-one.

Needing to take the lead on this one, I exhale a deep breath. "Mom. Dad." I drop one of my hands to motion to Finn. "This is

Finn. My … boyfriend. Finn, these are my parents, Tyra and Gregory."

It's Finn's turn to be scrutinized by my mother. She's assessing him as she does her clients. Finn dressed for the occasion—a black button-up shirt, dark jeans—and his hair is freshly cut.

I clear my throat, dragging my mom back into the conversation.

She shoots Finn a polite smile. "It's nice to meet you, Finn." Her eyes briefly move to my stomach, as if she knows, but everyone turns to the door when it swings open.

The sun beams through the doorway as Raven sprints into the house, one of her sandals flying off in the process.

"Grandma! Grandpa! We're here!" she shouts, nearly tripping as she hugs my father's legs. "And we brought cherry cobbler! Mommy lied and told Daddy she made it, but we really picked it up from the bakery."

I cover my mouth to mask my snort.

Finn chuckles.

"Hey!" Faith says as she and Brian join us. "We need to work on your snitching, kid."

I squeeze my belly, grateful for their appearance, saving me from the possible awkward moment of my mother asking questions I don't want to answer. I have yet to decide how I'll break the news. Finn asked me on the drive here, but I told him I was still working on it.

"It might be best for you to fill me in, though," Finn commented.

"I'll send you a text," I told him.

"What?" he stuttered. "We're going to discuss the plan via text in front of them?"

We went back and forth until he agreed to just wing it.

Last night, I'd thought I had the perfect plan—tell them right before leaving and then make a dash to my car. It would stop a face-to-face conversation. Everyone knows there isn't a more stressful conversation than one in person.

Give me a phone call.

A text.

Easy-peasy.

Looking someone in the eyes while speaking about something sensitive?

Hard stuff.

To master that plan, I first have to sit through dinner and manage to keep my mouth shut.

———

"NO WINE?"

I nearly drop my glass at my mother's question.

We just sat down for dinner, and I declined my mother's offer for a glass of wine. Her eyes widened when I said I was sticking with water for tonight. Like with my friends, that's a sure sign something is off. My mom would've definitely expected at least a glass from me, given I just brought a new man home.

Everyone's eyes are on me.

This is the moment I realize I suck at secrets.

"I'm pregnant."

All I hear is my mother's glass shattering to the tiles.

CHAPTER TWENTY-NINE

Finn

I TOLD Grace it was a mistake not to have a Telling Them You're Pregnant plan, but she said she wouldn't know until the time came. Us deciding on a strategy would've stopped the slight armpit rings hidden by the dark color of my shirt and would've stopped the ache in my throat that's been there since we got into my car.

Knowing Grace, I was certain she couldn't hold in the news all night until we left.

I at least thought she'd make it past dinner.

My heart gallops in my chest. It's been doing that since the moment I walked into the Mitchells' home.

Not only because I was meeting them for the first time.

Scratch that. I was only meeting *her mom* for the first time.

I was certain her dad recognized me—just what I'd been afraid of.

I've fucked up in my life, but every mistake I've made, I learned from.

I've changed.

But no matter what, I'm my father's son.

And that motherfucking sucks.

Brian scoots out his chair and grabs the glass from the floor.

"It's fine," Tyra rushes out, stopping him. "Just leave it."

Her voice is shaky. Her face pales.

Everyone, even Raven, is quiet, waiting on her parents' reaction.

Brian ignores her request, snags the shattered pieces, and places them on the table. He pours her another glass. Tyra grabs it, chugs down the wine, and pours herself another.

Moving my attention from her, I focus on Gregory.

He clears his throat. "I take it, you're the father?" Like before, his face is unreadable.

Does anyone ever know what this man is thinking?

No.

That's probably why he's so good at his job.

"I sure hope so," Tyra cries out, gaping at me.

Grace pays me a quick glance and nods. "He is."

I wonder how well they know their daughter.

There's more than nervousness in Grace's tone.

She's not a good liar, and had I not known the situation, I'd have known she was lying.

I lower my hand under the table and capture hers, giving it a squeeze of assurance that I have her back, no matter what.

We've got this.

"I am," I repeat, my voice clear and controlled.

Tyra's gaze whips to Faith. "Did you know your sister was pregnant?"

"Yes," Faith says with a shrug. "I think it's amazing." She motions toward me with her wineglass. "Finn is a good guy, and I think they'll make great parents."

I am a big Faith fan.

She and Brian are good people.

Tyra gasps. Obviously, she has a flair for the dramatic.

She stares at Faith, stunned. "You knew and didn't tell us?"

Faith lifts the glass to her lips and says into it, "Not my news to tell."

"Does that mean Aunt Grace has a baby in her belly?" Raven asks, chomping on a dinner roll.

"It sure does," Faith replies.

Raven jumps out of her seat. "Can I see?"

Faith catches her arm before Raven passes her. "I don't think so. Aunt Grace will show you her belly another time."

Raven pouts while returning to her seat. "You promise, Aunt Grace?"

Grace's lower lip trembles as she nods. "Yes."

The herb-roasted chicken gets neglected as a result of the news.

The questions start.

All coming from Tyra and none from Gregory.

He throws in comments, but no drilling comes from him.

I wish I could climb into his brain and figure out what the fuck he's thinking.

We tell them we started dating a few months ago.

The pregnancy wasn't planned.

I plan on being there for her.

Tyra questions if we're getting married, but luckily, Faith asks a question to detour us away from that conversation. When Tyra tries to go back to the subject, Grace tells her we're focused on the baby at the moment. I gulp, wanting to tell them that I'd marry Grace tomorrow if she'd have me. But Grace is taking the lead, and I'm only speaking when absolutely necessary.

We explain how we've been friends for years.

By the time dinner is over, I'm exhausted.

Tyra seems more comfortable now that she's better informed. In fact, she seems excited about having another grandchild.

Tyra asks Grace and Faith to help her in the kitchen, and I use that moment to go to the bathroom. I'm in need of a moment alone before my head explodes. On my way back to the dining room, I admire the home, passing expensive artwork, a curved staircase, and a billiard room.

"Finn."

I turn suddenly at the sound of my name to find Gregory standing inches from me. He shoves his hands into the pockets of his black slacks, and unease lines his features as we stare each other down.

His staredown isn't one of intimidation.

It's more along the lines of wanting to know what the fuck I'm planning to do with his daughter.

"Let's talk." A harsh sigh leaves him before he jerks his head toward an open door.

I nod. "All right."

Shit is about to get awkward real quick.

I follow him into an office filled with dark bookshelves lined with law books. He circles the massive desk, rolls out an executive chair, and sits—his posture near perfect. Clasping his hands together, he rests them onto the desk.

"Have a seat," he demands.

I ease into the chair, doing my best to match his posture and not slouch. I wait for his interrogation ... or threats to stay the fuck away from his daughter. Although the chance of him scaring me away from her will be harder in his eyes because he's under the impression his daughter is having a baby with me.

"Does Grace know about your past?" he sternly asks.

That's the question I've been terrified of.

The reason I took so long to take my relationship further with Grace.

I didn't want her to know about my past.

I told her about my family, but what her father knows? It's deeper. It's humiliating.

But she does deserve to know.

"She doesn't," I reply, hating the hint of shame in my voice from keeping this from her. It's embarrassing that I haven't been as open and honest with her as I should've been.

"I figured so." He expels a long breath, and his eyes are serious when they level on me. "Finn, I'm well aware that people make mistakes. Every day, I look at people's mistakes and decide the consequences of them. Their future is in my hands. For as long as I've been a judge, I pride myself on reading people well. I'm pro second chance because people learn, and as bad as it seems, some are given shitty cards in their game of life. When they're young, it can take a minute to figure out the best way to play them. Along the journey, they might break the law." He hesitates and holds up a finger. "Sometimes, good people break the law because they don't want to starve or for their families to go without." His voice turns low and even. "The day you walked into my courtroom, I knew it was because of the cards you'd been handed. You weren't some punk kid breaking the law for fun. You were a *survivor*. The second time, I'll admit, I wasn't happy about it, but there was something in my gut that told me to give you another chance—that you weren't some hardened criminal who'd do wrong in society. You had a bad family—no offense—and you needed to escape their ways."

My brain flashes back to those times I saw him in the courtroom. I was fourteen and fifteen, scared out of my motherfucking mind over what would happen. I didn't want to go to juvie, but I also needed food. My pride wouldn't let me ask others for help—not to eat, not for school supplies, not for basic necessities. So, I shoplifted the shit I needed because I saw that as a better option in my immature eyes. I stopped the petty crimes after Judge Mitchell—aka Gregory, aka Grace's father—told me that was my last chance.

"I know your family," he continues. "I was aware of the household you were growing up in. And frankly, I was relieved you were only shoplifting, not robbing homes, doing drugs, or harming others." He shakes his head and scoffs, "You were barely a teen, stealing food, cough medicine, and ibuprofen."

I shut my eyes at the memory. I was so sick. I called my dad for hours, only for him to tell me to stick a cold washcloth on my forehead and take some ibuprofen. When I told him we didn't have any, he told me *tough shit* and to sleep off my fever. I was miserable, so I shoved on my boots and walked a half-mile to the local convenience store, not giving a shit about being busted because even if I got arrested, the jail had to have some damn medicine.

Gregory taps his desk, a wrinkle creasing along his forehead in concentration. "After that final warning, I never saw you in my courtroom again. I did, however, see you bagging groceries at the market six months later. It made me proud that I'd seen you were a good kid and not thrown you to the wolves." He smiles for the first time tonight; it's a timid one, as he's still wary of my role in his daughter's life. "My Grace, she's understanding." He snorts. "Way more understanding than most. Be honest with her. She deserves to know the past of the man she's having a child with."

I do the first thing that comes to mind.

I salute him. "Yes, sir."

And then I feel like a fucking idiot for doing so.

Do people in their circle salute each other?

His smile widens, not making me feel so much like a dumbass.

Then, his lips press into a thin line. "And don't break her heart."

I lift my head high and wait until his eyes meet mine before answering, "I won't."

If there's any certainty I have in life, it's that.

I'll never hurt Grace Mitchell.

"If it's worth anything, I think you'll be an amazing father."

That statement.

It's as if he'd just told me I won the lottery.

That I'd have happiness for the rest of my life.

"You'll be an amazing father."

It's everything I've ever wanted to hear because it's everything I've always been terrified of. I don't have a good dad. Neither did my dad. Bad dads run in my DNA, and I've always worried about whether I'd break that curse.

I gratefully bow my head. "Thank you."

He gives me a strong, decisive nod before standing. "I'm here if you need anything. Brian has seemed to already taken a liking to you. Anything Grace, the baby, or *you* need, don't hesitate to come to us. My biggest priority has always been my family, and it seems you've now joined it."

Nearly speechless, I repeat, "Thank you."

He stares at me in expectation. "On another note, do you plan to marry her?"

CHAPTER THIRTY

Grace

"TONIGHT DIDN'T GO AS bad as I'd expected," I tell Finn when we get home.

But it also didn't go as well as I'd hoped.

My mother's reaction was dramatic, to say the least.

Which is weird because she tends to be the most levelheaded person I know. I guess not seeing your daughter in months and then learning she was randomly knocked up might lead a parent to that sort of reaction.

He nods. "It didn't."

"You want to tell me what my father said in his office?"

After I was done helping my mom in the kitchen, Finn was nowhere to be found. When I asked Brian where he was, he said my father had stopped him on his way back from the bathroom and that they were in his office. My father is a fair man, but he's also not one to beat around the bush. He speaks his mind and reads people well, considering that's his job. Whatever they talked about in that office, I hope to God it doesn't scare Finn away.

It's not like Finn is required to stay if it does.

It's times like this that I remember he's not the father and he isn't obligated to be here.

Finn's back straightens before he releases a deep breath and sits on the couch. "We need to talk." He pats the space next to him with a fixed look of concentration on his face.

Oh God.

Here it comes.

There wasn't much conversation on the ride home. We laughed about Raven's request to see my belly, not reading the room whatsoever.

The nervousness I had earlier returns with a vengeance.

I take slow steps to the couch and carefully sit down. Out of recent habit, my hand rests against my stomach. Finn gently smiles when he notices my movement before placing his hand over mine. We sit like this for a moment—our hands over the reason our relationship has changed, the reason our lives will change.

Finn clears his throat. "Today isn't the first time I've met your father."

I grow quiet, chewing the inside of my cheek before saying, "Okay?"

Where is he going with this?

Does he mean they met at the grocery store?

Did my dad find out we were hanging out and confront him?

Finn rubs his eyebrow. "I got into some trouble, and your dad was my judge."

"Oh …" My voice wavers with just that one word. "And what kind of trouble did you get into?"

His hand doesn't leave my belly. "When I was a minor, I did stupid shit. Shit I'm not proud of."

"Can you define *shit you're not proud of*?"

What does one define as stupid shit when breaking the law?

Punching someone?

Stealing?

Or killing?

"Shoplifting. Petty theft. I stole things I needed to survive because no one else had provided them for me."

My shoulders relax at his answer.

I know Finn hasn't had it easy. Not only from the admission about his parents last night. He's made random comments about his life. Unlike some of our friends, he doesn't talk about his parents. But also, like others, like Cohen and Georgia, he seems to agree with them when conversations of having terrible parents come up. I've heard stories of Finn coming from nothing and rising above it. And if my father had been worried Finn would be a threat to me, he'd have kicked his ass out of his house.

"Finn," I whisper, stopping until I have all this attention. "I'd never judge you for that. You had a crappy childhood and had to do things you're not proud of." My mouth turns dry at my next question. "Did he give you jail time?"

"Nah." Finn shakes his head. "He let me off the hook both times."

I smile. "That means he thought you were a good kid."

"I guess so." He pulls his hand away and turns on the cushion to face me. "Are you sure you want your baby around someone like that? Who's been in trouble with the law?"

I hold back from telling him his question is stupid.

Maybe it's dumb to me, but from the distraught look in Finn's eyes, it's something that scares him. Losing me—losing *us*—terrifies the man sitting next to me with tears nearly in his eyes.

I speak softly, "Finn, I wouldn't want any other man to be with us."

CHAPTER THIRTY-ONE

Finn

I FALL down on the couch and replay Grace's words through my head.

I grin.

Reveling in them.

Pushing them so deep into my brain in hopes that they'll stay there forever.

I sweep my gaze to her. Affection glows in them.

I want this woman.

Physically—because damn, my dick gets hard when I just look at her. *And* it is hard.

But not just in that way.

I want her emotionally.

And I want her *forever*.

"Grace," I say her name like a demand.

I'm not sure who goes for it first, but one moment, we're side by side on the couch, and the next, our lips are connected. Our kiss is intense and intimate. Shifting, I grip her hips, positioning her on her back, and crawl over her. The couch is small, and there isn't much room, but that won't stop me from touching my girl. I have one foot on the floor, and my other knee is pushed into the couch cushion. We don't break our kiss, and I groan when Grace rotates her hips, pushing her core up against me. Thrusting my tongue into her mouth, I claim her as we dry-hump on the couch.

My heart races as I push up her dress, lift my hand, and play with the string of her panties with one finger.

"Baby," I whisper against her lips, "you're soaked."

Her panties are the wettest they've ever been. Her pussy is ready for me.

My heart races. We've messed around some, but never have we had anything this emotionally charged. I've touched her, tasted her, but we haven't crossed any lines beyond that. Tonight, shit's changed. We're baring our all to each other, sharing a connection deeper than friendship and hooking up. We've said the *I love you*, but now, we're exposing our true selves. The deeper we fall into each other, the deeper that love grows.

All the issues I had been worried would push Grace away did the opposite. I told her my past, and she only wanted me more. I've made it clear I want her to be my future. Her parents accepted her pregnancy *and me*. There's nothing that can hold us back any longer. It's as if we were waiting for the pieces to come together before passing the final line of intimacy.

Pulling back, I gently caress her jaw. "I love you, Grace. I love you more than I've ever loved anyone in my life." No one will ever mean as much to me as she does. "It's always been you."

Her eyes widen, and we stare at each other, nearly in a trance.

Her breathing quickens, and when I peek down, her chest is heaving in and out.

Reaching out, she runs her hand over my neck before gripping the back of it. "Then make love to me."

"Are you going to give me all of you?" I bury my face in the curve of her neck. "Are you mine?"

"Yes," she whispers, shivering as I suck on her neck. "Always."

Yes.

Always.

I fall back, sliding off her, and bring myself to my feet. Holding out my hand, I help her up. As much as I'd like to make this sexier—

throw her over my shoulder or some shit like that—I don't want to hurt her. I lead her to the bedroom, and as soon as I turn on the lights, my lips return to hers. I walk her to the bed and tenderly lay her down on her back.

Desire rushes through me, and I'd love to make this quick. To pull off her panties and shove inside her, giving it to her hard and rough. But that's not how I want my first time with Grace to be. It needs to be special, memorable, and better for her than for me.

Grace stares at me, licking her lips, as I unbutton my shirt and toss it over my shoulder. The chill of the room smacks into my back as I lower myself over her. My dick twitches under my pants the moment it makes the slightest brush against Grace's body.

Dear God, don't let me nut this early. Please.

I moan when she urgently attempts to bend forward, but it's not easy for her.

Frustrated, she falls back and frowns. "Take off your pants *right now*. I would, but this prego body doesn't make it easy for me to rip off your clothes."

I chuckle. "I guess I can do the job for you." With a smirk, I waste no time in giving in to her demand. Popping my zipper open, I slightly climb off her in order to kick them, along with my boxer briefs, off. My cock springs forward, aching for her, and she gasps.

I stroke it. "Is this what you want?"

I never thought I'd be talking to Grace like this or jerking myself off as Grace wriggles underneath me, licking her lips. Her eyes are glued to my hand moving up and down my cock, as if it's the best thing she's ever watched.

"You want me to fuck you with this?"

She nods, and it shocks the shit out of me when she says, "If you don't *right now*, then I'm going to stick my own fingers in my panties and get myself off."

"We can't have that, can we?" I wink, dropping my hand from my cock and moving back up her body. Planting a soft kiss to her lips, I flick down the straps of her dress, lowering them, and drag it down her body before tossing it the same way I did with my clothes.

My mouth waters at the sight of her wearing only a bra and

panties. Dropping my head between her thighs, I suck her clit over her panties. She arches her back, gasping, and unsnaps her bra at the same time. Giving her one final flick of my tongue, I peel her panties down her legs. I fall back to take a good look at the woman I love.

Her breathing is deep. Her breasts bounce with every movement of the chest. Her belly moves the same way.

Before thinking, I kiss her stomach, rubbing my hand over it, and say, "You are so fucking gorgeous."

Her eyes shut, and her shoulders relax.

Lowering my hand, I run a finger through her wet slit. "I can't wait to fuck you, baby. It's going to feel so good."

She squirms underneath me. "Then get to it. *Fuck me*, Finn."

And with those dirty words that rarely leave Grace's mouth, I make one hard thrust inside her. She releases a loud moan, her back moving higher than it was when I sucked on her clit. Bracing myself, I collapse my body over hers, holding myself up with a hand on each side of her head. I still inside her and tell myself to slow down. I change positions, rotating my hips from side to side, hoping to hit every sensitive spot inside her. Her nails dig into my arms, deeper and deeper every time I rock inside her. Her pussy is so tight, so wet, and so fucking amazing.

My cock has never been in a pussy this wet and tight.

Then I freeze.

Fuck!

She stops, staring at me in confusion.

"I'm not wearing a condom," I breathe out.

I've never barebacked anyone before. It's not that she can get pregnant, but I don't know what she's comfortable with.

She points at her belly. "Not like I can get knocked up again."

"I'm clean," I confirm. "Never had sex without a condom ... and it's been a while."

"Same," she whispers. "I got tested as soon as I found out about Gavin."

With those words, I return to making love to her.

Slowly sliding in and out of the woman I love.

She tilts her hips up, meeting me thrust for thrust until it's no longer slow and sensual.

It's fast, hungry, and raw.

"Swear to God, Grace"—I peer down at her, sweat building along my forehead—"after this, I will give it to you so slow."

She smiles. "Good, but now, I want it harder." She pushes her waist up, circling her hips so her clit rubs against my groin, and moans. "Get me off. *Please.*"

Our moans, our heavy breathing, fill the room.

It's a struggle, but I wait until she's gasping my name below me, until her knees buckle up and she gets off, before I come inside her.

CHAPTER THIRTY-TWO

Grace

I FALL BACK against the sheets in exhaustion.

It's been a weekend of sex.

Missionary.

Doggy.

Me on top—my first time thirty minutes ago.

In our bed.

On the couch.

In the shower—which was difficult for a pregnant woman, but Finn seemed to situate us perfectly. It's a plus, having a strong man. Gavin's skinny ass would've never been able to hold me up while also thrusting inside me.

Unlike getting rid of morning sickness, the rumors about horniness when you're pregnant are true. I've never wanted sex—never wanted intimacy—as much as I do with Finn. I've never experienced a happiness like this before, and I've never felt safer in his arms.

And now, we finished morning sex.

Early as heck in the morning sex.

Finn woke me up with his head between my legs, and then we ended our romp with his cock between them.

"I think this is the only time I'll like mornings," Finn says, catching his breath.

"Glad I could change that for you." I yawn and groan at the same time. "And you're keeping me up quite late and changing that for me."

"That's because you're irresistible, babe."

———

I'VE NEVER CONSIDERED STABBING anyone.

Until now.

"Good morning," Gavin says with a mischievous smirk as he walks into my classroom.

I cast a glance at the scissors chilling in my pen holder.

Could I say it was an accident?

I could stab him somewhere that'd leave no permanent damage, like his foot or something. His foot would be nice because then the jackass couldn't stroll into my classroom, looking like the smug jerk he is. All I know is his presence here will ruin my happiness of what this weekend gave me. I can't let that happen.

Ignoring him and the stabby urge, I grab my phone and pretend to text.

"Oh, come on." He inches farther into my classroom. "Can't you show a little more excitement to see me?"

"I'm not excited to see you," I deadpan. "In fact, it'd make me very excited if you turned and left, and I never had to see you again. That'd make my day."

He tsks. "I remember when you liked me. Our conversations went so much better."

"Then I learned you were a cheating scumbag," I chirp.

"How's our baby?"

His question sends fire through my veins.

My phone falls from my hand and onto my desk.

He receives the reaction he wanted.

It's been weeks since he's mentioned the baby. I hoped he would find me ignoring him an easy escape from taking responsibility for what he'd done to not only me but also to his wife and children.

What would be a better outcome for hiding you'd cheated and knocked a woman up than the other woman not being able to stand the sight of you now?

"You need to get out of my room," I grind out. My gaze flicks back to the scissors.

"No can do." He arrogantly lifts his chin. "I'll be sitting in and watching you teach today. Make sure you're doing your job."

I ignore him in an attempt to get him to leave.

"Who's the guy who keeps visiting you?"

I grip the edge of my desk and push my chair out. "That's none of your business."

He gives me a spiteful smile. "As the father of your child, I think it is."

"You know what? I'll leave." I stand and do my best to storm out of the classroom, although my pace is on the slower side, given my pregnancy.

Passing the teachers' lounge, I make a right to Georgia's office and knock on the door. As much as I want to confide in Finn about Gavin's taunting, it'll lead to nothing but trouble. If Finn finds out Gavin is messing with me, he'll kick his ass.

Without waiting for an answer and hoping she isn't busy, I open the door and burst into her office. I'm out of breath—both from the baby weight and scurrying away from Gavin as fast as I could. I need to take a seat.

"Good morning, babe," Georgia says, not even affected by my sudden entry. "I have to say, the baby bump is looking hot on you, Mama."

I sink back in a chair, sitting in front of the desk she's perched behind. I'm still getting used to seeing my free-spirited friend—former boutique and part-time bar employee—have a behind-the-desk job. She started working here—taking the place of the retired school counselor—not too long ago, and I couldn't be happier. There's nothing better than working with your best friend.

I frown down at my belly. "I feel ... unhot."

The high of my weekend has been shot down to ashes, thanks to Gavin.

"Wrong, and I'm positive Finn would state otherwise." She tosses a stack of papers away from her and tightens one of her two buns on the top of her head. "How are you two doing, by the way?"

I texted Georgia the night I told my parents about the pregnancy —post amazing sex with Finn. I told her it went well, but that was all she got before Finn was ready for round two.

Affection spreads through me at the mention of Finn. It erases a smidgen of the anger Gavin dragged out of me this morning.

"We're good," I reply. "I was scared things would change after he met my parents, but it's only gotten better." I refrain from telling her that Finn had already met my father. I'm not sure who all knows about Finn's juvenile run-ins with the law, but I won't be the one to ever tell them.

Her eyebrows squish together. "Then why do you look like they canceled Snickers bars?"

My head pounds. "Gavin paid me a visit in my classroom."

"Ugh, is the bastard still giving you a hard time?"

I reluctantly nod. "I pray he gets fired every day."

"Report him."

"And say what?" I throw up my arms in defeat. "I didn't know he was married and slept with him?"

"No. You tell them he's practically harassing you."

I swallow down my fear of having to take it that far. "He'll get bored of me. I'm just waiting it out."

"No one can get bored of you, babe, so I wouldn't count on that happening." She takes a sip of her iced coffee. "You need to stick it to the man where it hurts. Report him or … I don't know … tell his wife what a piece of shit he is."

She—along with Cassidy, Lola, and Sierra—have told me to tell his wife. It's the right thing to do, and I'd want my husband's mistress to come to me. Confrontation makes me nauseous, and I try to prevent it at all costs. If I went to his wife, I'd be going head-to-head with her because she'd ask questions that I'd have to answer. And who knows if she'd even believe me?

"If you don't want to tell her, I'll tell her." Georgia shrugs. "I'll mention that there are rumors that he's been having an affair with another woman. I won't even say it's someone who works here."

Georgia is always the one who comes up with the wild plans—ones that usually lead straight to trouble.

"No, that's not necessary." I run my hand over the few wrinkles in my floral dress. "I'll wait it out."

I stand at the sound of the bell, and we make plans to meet for lunch before I return to my classroom.

———

"YOU HOMEWRECKING WHORE."

I tense in my chair at the shrill voice screaming those words. At the same time I lift my head, a woman comes barreling into my classroom —her waddle-walk similar to mine.

Even though it's only the second time I've seen her, I know who she is. I'd recognize her from across the grocery store because the first time I laid eyes on her, she introduced herself as Gavin's wife to everyone in the office. That's also the day when I refrained from introducing myself as Gavin's mistress ... and the day I broke things off with him.

I jump at the sound of my classroom door slamming shut as she stares at me with murderous eyes.

Her orange maxi dress sways from side to side as she grows closer. "You've been fucking my husband behind my back."

From her appearance, you wouldn't think words like that would fall from her lips in public—that she wouldn't make a scene at her husband's place of employment. She's nearly the opposite of me. Curvy—with a breast size I would kill for. Her black hair is cut into a bob, hitting the curve of her shoulders. Briefly, I wonder what Gavin's other mistresses looked like because I'm almost certain there are/have been others.

Swallowing hard, I hold up my hands, palms facing her. "Whoa, I'm not screwing your husband."

She thrusts the phone in her hand in my direction. "That's not what the texts between you and him say. I looked through his phone!"

When I stand, she gasps at the sight of my belly. "I had no idea Gavin was married. As soon as I found out, I broke things off."

She blinks at me. "How do you not know when someone is married?"

I sigh. "It seems your husband was as good at hiding that he was married as he was at cheating on you. The man lies, and I want nothing to do with him."

"And the baby?" She gestures to my stomach. "It's his?"

I turn quiet, refusing to look at her.

"Wow." She seethes, her lips forming a thin line. "It is."

"I don't want anything from him," I rush out, my cheeks burning. "To be honest, I'd prefer if he were out of the picture."

Maybe she'll make that happen. If I caught my husband having an affair in the workplace, I wouldn't be comfortable with him keeping that job with her.

"You'd prefer him to be out of your life?" she snarks. "Real nice, considering you ruined our marriage."

"I ruined nothing," I bite out. "As I said, I had no idea he was married until the first day you came into the school."

She's not digesting my words. Her outrage overtakes any reasoning she has. Her confronting me isn't an attempt to get answers. She needs someone to take her anger out on.

"Stay away from my husband," she demands, spit flying from her mouth.

Before I tell her that's what I've been trying to do but he isn't making it easy, she charges out of the room. I release a breath of relief … until her next show happens.

"That's right, people!" she screams in the hallway. "The woman who teaches in that room slept with my husband!"

My knees buckle, and I grip the edge of my desk to stop myself from crumpling to the floor.

Why is she doing this to me?

Does she not believe I didn't know?

If she read through Gavin's texts, she'd have seen the endless times I asked him to leave me alone.

When I confronted him for being married.

When I called him a liar.

Sick of the all-around bullshit, I push my shoulders back, lift my chin, and leave the room. My colleagues are standing in the hall, their classroom doors open, and kids' voices filter out each one of them. Humiliation rises up my cheeks, but I do a decent job of hiding it while I dodge their questions and charge toward Gavin's office. As I pass his wife, who seems to be shocked that I showed my face, I flip her off.

Georgia is standing outside his door. "You want me to kill him? I can make it look like an accident."

"No," I bite out. "That'll stop me from doing it myself."

Without knocking, I open his door and gasp. Gavin's office is destroyed—shattered picture frames on the floor, décor pieces lying next to them, a crooked painting clinging to life on the wall. The desk has been cleared of all its contents as if everything was pushed to the floor in one angry swipe.

"You got her wrath, too, it appears," Gavin says, sitting with slouched shoulders.

"Nice office," Georgia says from behind me. "I'd call this décor style *something that assholes deserve*."

I shoot Georgia a look over my shoulder. "Can you give us a moment?"

She nods. "If you need anything, I'll be outside the door … and most definitely not listening."

"Yeah, okay," I say sarcastically, knowing her ear will most likely be against the door, listening to every single word.

I've never seen Gavin like this. He's not used to being on the other side of the provocation. He's used to being the one in control, and he's lost that. His Adam's apple bobs, and sweat has built up along his hairline. He stares at me vacantly, as if he's lost all thought process. His actions finally came back to bite him in the ass—in the worst way possible. He could lose his job for this.

"I admitted everything," Gavin says as soon as I shut the door, forcing his words through clenched teeth. "Vivica knows about us and the baby."

"So does everyone in the school," I grit out. "She announced it in the hallway."

"Fuck," he hisses, slamming his fist on the desk.

I do another scan of the room. "Did you admit it to her ... or were you caught?"

His jaw twitches. "Does it fucking matter?"

I stay quiet.

"I forgot my phone at home, and she went through it. She came here, confronted me, and I was honest with her. I should've done it before. She deserved to know I was unfaithful and no longer in love with her." His tone turns serious yet softens some. "I love *you*, Grace. I want *you*."

I glare at him. "You've lost your marbles if you think I'd ever be with you." I cross my arms and kick my foot out. "I wish I'd never met you. Now, all my coworkers know what happened." As I blink away tears, it's a struggle to keep my voice stable. "I'm taking the rest of the day off. Find someone to cover me for the mess you caused."

He reaches out toward me. "Grace—"

"I'm taking a personal day!" I shout, turning around and whipping the door open. I nearly fall into Georgia when I step out.

She flips Gavin off before turning her attention to me. "Want me to take a personal day with you? I'm totally down."

"No," I sigh. "You'd probably be his last priority to find a cover." There could be students who need her today.

"True." She hugs me while we walk out. "I'll be over as soon as I get off. And don't you worry. I'll set anyone straight who talks shit here, and I need to hunt down his crazy wife, so she'll shut the fuck up."

Oh God.

I forgot about her.

"Thanks, babe." I avoid Rachelle's gaze, scurrying out before she asks any questions.

As soon as I get in my car, the tears come.

I'm sobbing, my nose snotty, when I call Finn.

"What's wrong, baby?" he rushes out in panic.

I break down and tell him the situation.

"That motherfucker," he snarls. "I'm leaving work now. Do you want me to pick you up from the school?"

"No." I sniffle. "I'll meet you at home."

———

FINN IS WAITING for me on the porch. As soon as I pull into the driveway, he jumps down the steps and hurries to me.

"Baby," he says, wrapping his arms around me the moment I step out. "It'll be okay."

Will it, though?

Everyone at the school knows.

People will talk.

I could lose my job just as easily as Gavin could.

My parents will ask why.

And word will spread.

Shoot, they could know by the end of the day, given how many people they talk to.

Finn holds my hand as we walk into the townhouse and carefully helps me onto the couch. He waits until I get comfortable, helping me put a pillow behind my back, and then paces in front of me.

"I'm going to kill that asshole," he grinds out, clenching his fists.

I pull my hair into a ponytail. "Finn, I don't want you to get in any trouble. Hopefully, he quits."

He halts and looks at me in concern. "What if he doesn't?"

My shoulders slump. "Maybe I'll quit. His wife shouted from the rooftops that I slept with her husband without even clarifying that I'd had no idea he was a damn husband!" I'm nearly screaming at the end of my statement.

"Whatever you want to do, you have my support," he says before falling to his knees and taking my hand.

———

FINN TOOK MY MIND—WELL, *attempted* to take my mind—off what had happened today with pizza and ice cream. I could sleep for days and not forget what happened. Heck, they could try hypnotizing me, and it'd still be lodged in my brain. It's the most embarrassing moment in my life. Nothing will ever top that.

It was almost like something out of a movie—where the angry wife stomps through the workplace, confronting her cheating husband and his mistress. The only problem is, it's my real life ... and I had no idea about her. It sucks that she didn't blare out the entire story. Heck, I'm sure if she did a poll, most people would say they had no idea Gavin was married until the day she came in and introduced herself.

I wonder if that's why she made it known he was married when she got into town. It could've happened in the past, and she wanted to stop it before it did again.

My attention moves from the TV when my phone beeps with a text. I chew into my lower lip, contemplating on whether to check it. Gavin has been texting nonstop. So have my coworkers. Knowing it's for the best, I ignore it.

"Georgia texted me since she figured you're avoiding your phone," Finn says.

He holds out his phone to me, and I read her text.

Georgia: Grace, how are you?

I hit the reply button.

Me: Okay, I guess. Given the situation.

Georgia: I set bitches straight all day. They know what a pig Gavin is and how he lied to you.

Me: Don't do anything stupid and get yourself fired.

Georgia: If that happens, we'll start a school together. Gavin is the one who needs to be fired.

Me: You can't get fired for sleeping with someone.

Georgia: Conflict of interest. He's your superior. He's been harassing you. And who knows? You might not be the only one he's done it to.

Me: I hope he hasn't.

Georgia: I'll keep my ears open. Love you.

Me: Love you too.

I slump against the cushions.

Then I feel it.

Sitting straight up, I place my hand on my belly and squeal. For a moment, all my dread morphs into excitement. I wave Finn over, and he arches a brow.

"The baby!" I screech. "She just kicked." It was a slight movement, nothing too strong, but my baby is moving. In the back of my mind, I'd like to think it's her giving me a sign that everything will be okay. A reminder that it doesn't matter because I have her.

He grins. "Really?"

Grabbing his hand, I place it next to mine on my stomach. My heart beats rapidly as we wait in anticipation for another kick.

We both flinch when she kicks again.

"Hi, baby," I whisper, rubbing my stomach.

Finn beams up at me.

"We're so ready to have you here with us."

Finn falls to his knees and kisses my stomach. "We can't wait to meet you."

And just like that, my baby has already made a terrible day better.

———

WHEN FINN GETS INTO BED, I climb on top of him.

He's killed all my insecurities for being pregnant. No man has ever made me feel as beautiful as he does.

"Mmm," he groans, moving the sheet out of the way to make me more comfortable. "I like this."

He lifts me off him enough to push his shorts down, exposing his thick cock. My mouth waters. I've never been a highly sexual person, never one to talk dirty or tell someone I want them, but I love being this way with Finn.

Reaching out, his strong hand cups the back of my neck, pulling me down to his mouth. As we kiss, his hand slides down my back to my ass, cupping it while also dragging me into his erection. I love kissing this man, and I love kissing while grinding against him even more. He slips my panties to the side, causing me to buck forward, and slides a thick finger in and out of me. As I'm rocking my hips, he digs his hand into my waist to stop me and then impales me with his hard cock. I grind into him, finding the perfect position, and Finn allows me to set the rhythm. As I grow closer, my blood pressure rising, I bounce on top of him. Bending at the waist, he cups my swollen breasts, pushes them together, and drags them to his mouth. His tongue goes from one nipple to the other, back and forth, until I'm grinding so hard against him that I know I'll be sore tomorrow.

An intense burst of pleasure blasts through me, and I cry out his name before collapsing onto his chest.

"That's it, baby," Finn grunts. "I love when you come all over my cock."

I lie limp against him as he starts fucking me—really fucking me. Anchoring his hands to my hips, he holds them down while pounding into me. I struggle to catch my breath and dig my nails into his arms until he's the one moaning my name. His body shakes, and he cups my head as he joins me post-orgasm.

———

AFTER I RODE Finn until I could no longer move, he carefully helped me off him, kissed me, and rolled out of bed. Seconds later, he returns with a wet washcloth to clean me up. It's one of my favorite things he does after sex. No one knows how to take better care of me than Finn.

After he's finished, he tosses the washcloth into the dirty laundry, grabs me a water bottle from the kitchen, and slides back into bed with me. He's so different than other men I've been with. I'm realizing now what Georgia meant all the times she said it was different when you had sex with *a real man*. None of the guys I was with before Finn were anything like this. They normally cared about their orgasms above mine and never made sure I was comfortable or cleaned up after. They typically rolled over and told me good night. Not that I've had many sexual partners since I don't like people knowing my secret.

I move to my side, staring at him, and lightly brush my fingers along the tattooed quote on his side.

It's his favorite Stephen King quote from *The Dark Tower* series. When I asked why he got it, he told me that it's the only book series he's read through and the realest quote he's ever read. I never thought too much into it, but as he revealed his past to me, I understand. Finn has gone without love for most of his life. Sure, our friends are there for him, but he's never had someone care about him more than themselves or have someone's life be consumed with their feelings for him.

That's me.

I want to show Finn that love can beat out the hate he had while growing up.

I want to prove to him it doesn't have to be destructive, though.

Our love can bring us both happiness.

CHAPTER THIRTY-THREE

Finn

THIS GAVIN MOTHERFUCKER had better count his days.

Had I not been trying to be a better man for Grace—and not wanting her to get fired from her job—I'd have already been in his office, punching his face in. He texted Grace nonstop, and she wouldn't let me reply. He said he was in love with her, would fight for their baby, and would make sure he had his parental rights.

His baby.

Fuck that motherfucker.

My throat grew thick as she read the texts to me. As much as I think Grace wouldn't go back to that asshole, the nerves are still there.

What if I lose them?

What if Grace decides she wants her baby to have a real family and that I'm no longer needed?

I shudder, pissed at myself for having those thoughts. But now that I have Grace, I'm terrified to lose her.

When Grace falls asleep, I slide out of bed and plod into the kitchen for a drink. My plan was to get a glass of water, but I opt for whiskey instead. I expel long breaths between gulps before pouring myself another while collapsing onto a chair at the table. I'm not sure how long I sit there, playing those texts back through my mind as if it were a song stuck on repeat.

I have everything I've ever wanted.

Now, there's a threat that could take it all away.

I can't lose Grace.

CHAPTER THIRTY-FOUR

Grace

I REFUSE to sit back and let Gavin ruin my job.

Not only do these pregnancy hormones make me break out in tears over a damn Pampers commercial, but they also bring out the anger inside me as well. Gavin needs to be the one to go. Not me. I love this job, this school, the staff—minus him—and I'm not giving it up.

Georgia texted me this morning and said Gavin took a sick day.

Thank God.

I don't want to face him yet.

The teachers' lounge turns dead silent when I walk in. Rachelle drops her bagel. The gym teacher spits out his water. The librarian nudges another teacher and signals toward me.

Georgia is behind me, always having my back. She even threatened to accidentally spill her iced coffee on someone if they said something rude.

I tend to be the shy girl and never get into confrontations. I'm the quiet one in our group of friends, but I'm done with being quiet. This is a situation I have to be loud about. I have to stick up for myself and tell people the truth.

I get straight to the point. "Did Principal Long tell any of you he was married before his wife moved here?"

People shake their heads.

Others look around the room as our coworkers answer.

"The first day he was here, he wasn't wearing a wedding ring," one girl chimes in. "Laura and I checked because we thought he was hot. When Laura asked if he was available, he smirked and never said anything else."

"Same here." A girl raises her hand. "I was shocked when I found out he was married. We joked about him having a double life."

If only I'd been a part of that conversation.

"He even told me he was on some dating website," a guy added. "When I told him I was married, he told me he was sorry."

"Ew," Georgia says.

Hearing them say this is a relief. People will believe me.

I stand up straight as if I'm about to deliver an important speech. "He told me he was single." Even though that's all I planned to say, I continue, needing them to know I'm not a shitty homewrecker, "He was staying in a temporary small condo and had no evidence of a family. We decided to keep our relationship private in fear of being the talk of the school, not because we were having an affair."

There.

They can choose to trust me or not.

But that's my truth, and if anyone knows me, they know I'm not a liar.

"We get it, girl," Rachelle says. "No judgment here. After all the lies he told, after the way he reacted to that other man visiting you, I'm on your side."

―――――

SOMETIMES, I forget Finn isn't the actual father of my unborn child.

Like today, as we're leaving our birthing class and stopping at Twisted Fox for dinner.

Finn is the perfect labor practice partner. He performs our breathing exercises like a pro.

Everyone greets us as if we were celebrities when we walk into the bar. With all the drama, appointments, and planning for the baby, we haven't spent as much time here as usual. Not to mention, Finn now works full-time at the dealership. We're both usually exhausted when we get home from work. Hopefully, when everything dies down, we can visit more.

When we sit down, my mind wanders.

Will Finn be with me in the delivery room?

If not, these classes are pointless.

Will anyone be in there with me?

I can ask my mom and Faith. They wouldn't say no. I'm sure Georgia and Lola would also be there for me if I needed them. As much as I love them, I feel as if I've gone through this journey with Finn more than anyone. He's the one who holds my hair back when I'm puking. The one who taped one of the ultrasound pictures onto his car dashboard.

"Everything okay?" Finn asks, staring at me from across the table —most likely picking up on my mood change.

"Yeah," I quickly reply.

"Babe," he deadpans, "I know when something is wrong, and *something is wrong.*"

I don't want to have this conversation here.

I need to figure out the best way to approach it before we have it, period.

I rub my stomach. "I think the pregnancy nerves are getting to me."

"Anything I can do to help?"

That's Finn.

What can he do to help?

"Hey, guys!" Cassidy says, appearing at our table in her waitress outfit with a pen and notepad in her hand. "What can I grab you?"

I order a grilled cheese and lemonade. Finn orders wings and a water. Cassidy salutes us and skips off to her next table—a group of guys sporting college sports gear.

Finn leans in, resting his elbows on the table, and taps my head. "What's going on in there, baby?"

I gulp, wishing Cassidy had dropped off my lemonade already. "I'm wondering what it'll be like in labor."

"Are you nervous?"

I nod repeatedly. "Definitely nervous."

He smirks, pulling back to smack his hand against his chest in pride. "I mean, you do have the best goddamn birthing coach in the world. I'm expected to *tap in.*"

"I can't believe you just referred to being in the delivery room as *tapping in.*"

"As I told you before, I'm here for whatever you need. A shoulder to cry on during *Vampire Diaries*, hands to rub your sore feet, setting up the nursery, there with you when the baby is born. I'm all yours. In fact, it'd be an honor to be there with you in the room … if you'll have me."

I grin wildly. "I'd absolutely love that."

Cassidy drops off our drinks, and minutes later, Silas and Georgia join us. They want all the baby updates. Georgia asks Finn if he's ready for the baby to come as if he really were the father. It seems our friends are on the same thought process as I am.

It's us.

Me and Finn doing this together.

I need to stop thinking otherwise.

I need to stop worrying about everything falling apart.

Becoming a mess.

Only that's exactly what happens.

CHAPTER THIRTY-FIVE

Finn

MY LOUD-ASS RINGTONE shakes me out of my sleep.

Nearly knocking down everything on the nightstand, I quickly grab my phone and silence it, not wanting to wake Grace. There's no stopping the frown from forming when I see the name flashing across the screen. He'll keep calling until I answer, especially when it's this late.

Calls this late are never a good thing.

Like I told Grace, I'm always on pins and needles, waiting for the call to hear I no longer have a father. He might not be the best father, but he's my father, goddammit. Albeit a shitty one, he's the only family member I had growing up. My grandparents nor his siblings wanted anything to do with us. My mother was gone. We were all each other had. My father could've given me up when he and my mother couldn't provide for me. He could've said *fuck that* to having a child and sent me to foster care, but he didn't.

I'll forever be grateful for that, so maybe that's why I answer when I shouldn't.

Why I give him money when I shouldn't.

Why I stupidly see him doing his fucking job as a father as a favor to me.

Like I owe him for my life when he's the one who chose to bring me into it.

Pulling on a pair of gym shorts, I silence the phone when it rings again and rush into the living room. Just as I'm about to call him back, my phone rings again.

"Hello?" I answer in a harsh whisper.

"Finn," my father barks out, "I'm stranded, and I need a ride home."

"Stranded?" I hiss, stumbling toward the laundry room and picking up a dirty tee. I sniff it, finding it satisfactory, and slip it on. The least amount of movements to wake up Grace, the better. "How are you stranded somewhere? You have a car."

"I hitched a ride with some old friends to catch up with buddies from high school. Good ole times, you know?"

"Can whoever you rode with take you home?"

"I can't find one ... and the other is wasted off his ass." He snort-laughs as if it's the funniest shit he's heard all night.

"I'll call you a taxi or Uber."

"I ain't getting in no Uber and getting murdered!" he drunkenly screeches. "You want to be planning my funeral, kid?"

I snatch my keys, shove my feet into my shoes, and turn off the alarm. "Send me the address, and I'll pick you up."

———

THERE'S NOT a doubt in my mind that it's a drug house I'm pulling up to.

Snatching my phone from the cupholder, I call my dad, but he doesn't answer. I curse before calling him again. No answer. Sitting in my car, I debate on leaving his ungrateful ass, but knowing I'd probably have to return later, I get out of the car. Old '80s rock blares from the house as I walk inside, a cloud of smoke hitting me in the face. Places like this always make me anxious. The police could show up at any time and think I'm involved with whatever bullshit is happening here.

This isn't the first time I've had to pick him up from a hellhole like this. I've made it clear to my father that he's not to call me for bail money if he gets arrested. I blink a few times, clearing my vision, and continue walking until I arrive in the living room. A crowd of people, my dad among them, are sitting in the living room, drinking ... and doing other illegal shit.

"In my car *now*," I yell to my father. "You have thirty goddamn seconds to get your ass up, or you won't have a ride home. You can stay in this dump."

"Hey, man," a guy sporting circular glasses cries out. "That's fucking rude."

I ignore the man and keep my eyes on my father.

"My son, always the buzzkill," he says, pulling himself up from the couch with a beer in his hand. "Always tryna tell me what to do, like he's my parent."

"If you acted like the parent, I wouldn't have to." My blood pressure rises with every word that leaves my mouth.

This shit can't happen when the baby is born.

I won't keep enabling my father.

No more.

"You shut it," he yells. "I was your father when no one else was there to take care of you."

Oh fuck. Here comes the emotional drunk.

I grab the back of his shirt, jerking him forward, and push him outside. "You're mistaken. I took care of you. Who kept food in the house? Me. Who made sure I had everything I needed for school? Me. Who paid when the landlord came knocking on the door for late rent? Me."

He stumbles forward and turns to look at me, snarling, "You shut your mouth! I sacrificed a lot for you too."

I point at my car. "Get your ass in there before I make you walk home."

He screams profanities while stomping to the car and slams the door shut. When I slide into the driver's side, I shake my head in frustration. The ride back to my apartment is quiet. He's still crashing there, and since I've been so busy, I haven't pushed the issue for him to move out. I check on him regularly, and as far as I can tell, he hasn't been doing stupid shit inside it.

"Thanks for the ride," he grumbles, shooting me a quick glance of what looks like … gratitude?

That's a first.

I nod and wait until he disappears inside the apartment before fishing my phone from my pocket. My stomach twists when I see the messages, one after the other after the other. Eight texts from Grace, asking me to call her and where I am, and ten calls. Hitting her name, I put my phone on speaker and race home.

No answer.

I call again.

No answer.

I call Faith next.

"Grace!" I yell into the speaker when Faith answers. "I had to run an errand. She called and texted me a shit ton of times, and now, she's not answering."

"Where are you?" Faith's voice is panicked, making me grow more alarmed alongside her.

"On my way home." I speed around a car, hearing them blare their horn behind me, and hurriedly beat a yellow light before it turns red. I hear rustling in the background.

"She's probably freaking out," Faith mutters, and I'm not sure if it's something she wanted me to hear.

"What?" I yell. "Why would she be freaking out?"

Because I'm gone?

Because I left in the middle of the night?

I know her ex was a cheater, so maybe she thinks I left to be with another woman?

Faith blows out a ragged breath. "It's a long story. Just hurry up and get there."

"I'm working on it," I grind out, tightening my hold on the steering wheel.

Luckily, it doesn't take long before I'm pulling back into the driveway. I jump out of my car and sprint toward the house. I'm yelling

Grace's name as I burst inside. Every light in the house is on, shining bright. When I turn the corner and hit the living room, I find Grace pacing back and forth. Her body is shaking, and when she turns to look at me, her face is red. Tears run down her splotchy cheeks. She's staring at me, but her eyes are blank, vacant, as if she's almost in a trance.

I bolt toward her and yell her name. Her hands are shaking when I grab them to stop her. She freezes, blinking at me, but doesn't say a word. Every muscle in her body trembles as I hold her, and her crying breaks out into sobs.

Pulling her against my chest, I hold her tight. "Calm down, baby. What happened?"

"They …"

My body tightens at that one word, and I pull away.

"They came in and tried to hurt her!" she shrills, painfully staring at me before retreating backward.

"Came where?" I scope out our surroundings, searching for someone. When Grace doesn't reply, I stalk out of the living room and down the hallway. "Are they in here? Did they leave? Did you call the goddamn cops?"

All I see is red as I charge through the house, frantically checking the kitchen, bedrooms, bathrooms, closets for someone but find nothing.

Grace is muttering, "No," under her breath as she follows me.

I whip around and snap my fingers in front of her face. She blinks at me as if struggling to process what's happening.

"I shot them," she rambles before hysterically repeating, "I shot them," over and over again.

She's hysterical. I struggle to find words. Struggle to figure out what the hell to do.

"You shot someone?" I ask, attempting to calm my voice in hopes that it'll calm her. "Where are they?" My eyes widen. "Where the hell did you even get a gun?" My gaze stupidly darts around the room again, just in case I missed a dead body lying around here somewhere.

"Grace!"

With Grace still in my hold, I turn us to find Faith rushing into the townhome. Her hand flies to her mouth as she takes in Grace's appearance.

"What is going on?" I scream, my voice shaking. "She said she fucking shot someone!"

Faith stumbles toward us but still remains a few inches away. "She's having an episode."

My heart pounds against my chest as confusion overwhelms me. "An episode?"

CHAPTER THIRTY-SIX

Grace

I'M SITTING cross-legged on the couch where Finn and Faith walked me to and sat me down. Finn is on his knees in front of me. My eyesight is blurry as I stare at him, fighting to focus on his gorgeous face, but it's a struggle. He's speaking, snapping his fingers in front of my face. I open my mouth, but no words form.

I fixate on Finn in distress. His skin is bunched around his eyes as he speaks to me. My ears are ringing, and I can't hear him or read his lips.

I'm burning up, my body temperature feeling close to a fever. Torment overcomes me before I suddenly jerk out of my daze. When I bounce back into reality, I cringe, wishing I could sink into the cushions and disappear. As I focus on the room, those around me realize I've returned to the real world. Finn flings his arms around my shoulders and pulls me into his chest, shielding me.

"Baby," he whispers as I fall limp in his hold. "Talk to me."

Staring over his shoulder, I cast a glance to Faith and nod.

"Thank God," she breathes out. She hastily steps forward before stopping. Normally, this is the part when she grabs me, hugging me tight like Finn is.

Finn knew what I needed.

Just like Faith knows.

I've had attacks in front of others before.

Georgia, who called my parents and did her best to console me. Luckily, with us being friends for so long, she was aware.

My parents, who know how to handle me.

And an ex, who lost his shit and told me I was crazy. He's most likely the one who gave me anxiety about my issues coming to light.

I don't want to be *crazy*. I don't want to be afraid of the dark anymore.

I cry into Finn's shoulder, soaking his shirt, but he doesn't flinch. Faith sits next to me and rubs my shoulder in tiny circles.

I should feel stupid. I normally do.

Stupid, crazy, and frightened.

But at this moment, I don't.

I feel loved. Understood. Safe.

The only sounds in the room are my sobs as I break down and Faith saying, "It'll be okay."

I'm unsure of how much time passes as we sit like this—me clinging on to Finn like he's my lifeline and Faith sitting beside me, comforting me, like always. They both allow me to release the fear I'm experiencing while they shelter me from panicking further. My crying calms, and hiccups replace the tears.

The humiliation I had ceases as I realize the people around me won't judge me. They love me—every quirk, flaw, and fear. When I pull away from Finn, his focus doesn't leave my face. His wide eyes study me, inspecting every inch of me as if he's searching for answers he's too scared to ask.

"Grace, honey." My sister's words come out slow and cautious.

I flick away tears with my hand and look over at her.

She clasps her hand over mine—a silent question, asking if I'm okay.

"I'm good now," I croak out. "I'm good now."

Finn, who seemed almost speechless, finally says, "Is there anything I can do?"

"No." I sniffle. "You guys being here is all I need."

These types of situations aren't easy.

Dating someone like me is difficult.

I'm more than what's on the outside. My webs are weaved thick to keep things hidden.

I can't sleep alone at night.

I'm practically afraid of the dark.

I don't trust people.

I'm a hot mess, but I mask it well.

"Do you want me to stay?" Faith asks.

I shake my head. "No. I'm okay."

Finn is here.

Faith squeezes my hand. "You sure?"

"I'm sure." I gulp and look at Finn. "I just want to go to bed and sleep this off."

"All right," Finn says.

Faith stands at the same time Finn helps me up from the couch. She hugs me tight, kisses me on the cheek, and tells me to call her if I need anything.

I wait until she leaves, surprised my body isn't trembling.

Will Finn ask questions now that we're alone?

"Can you just take me to bed, and we'll talk tomorrow?" I ask before he gets a chance to interrogate me on my freak-out.

Finn nods. "Of course."

As he walks us to the bedroom, I'm squeezing his hand so tight that I'm surprised I don't cut off circulation. He flips on the light as if knowing that's what I need and tightly tucks me into bed. Without a word and without bothering to turn off the light, he slips into bed beside me and drags me to his chest.

"I got you," he whispers into my ear. "I'm here."

I shut my eyes, positive I'll be fighting sleep all night.

I'm wrong.

Being in Finn's arms is the relaxant I need.

I fall asleep moments later.

———

THE NEXT DAY, I call off of work, go back to sleep, and don't wake up until I'm no longer exhausted.

Last night mentally drained me.

That stress isn't good for me or the baby.

I wanted to break down and cry again when Finn told me he called in too. Knowing my sister, she told Brian about last night. He'd have no issue with giving Finn time off to be with me. I'm grateful Faith found someone who understands the trauma we went through. Throughout their relationship, he's always been her helping hand. Her savior.

I'm sipping on the fruit smoothie Finn made me and lounging on the couch. The news plays on the TV, but I'm numb to whatever the anchor is saying. All my brain is processing is how I'll need to explain myself to Finn. After what happened last night, it can't be pushed underneath the rug. I wanted to hide it from him for as long as I could, but I know it's finally time. Like Brian is for Faith, Finn can be my savior.

Finn sits next to me. His smoothie is greener than mine. He makes fun of my smoothies and how I only add four spinach leaves but refer to them as *green smoothies* sometimes.

"It's better than eating a cheeseburger," is my argument.

So throw in all the fruits and give me something yummy.

"Whenever you're ready to talk, I'm here," Finn tells me.

My thoughts rush back to when Faith told me she confided in Brian about what had happened to us. She drank nearly a bottle of wine to prepare herself and cried the entire time. He held her, and in the end, she said it was the best thing she'd ever done. She no longer had to hide behind her fears, as we'd done for years. Now, she's happily married with a daughter, and she can sleep without a night-light. No more nightmares. No more flashbacks. I want that too.

In order to get that, I have to put on my big-girl panties like Faith did and open myself up. Unfortunately, I can't chug a bottle of wine. *A smoothie it is.* Maybe I should throw a Kit Kat in with it—you know, for stress-relief purposes.

I sit cross-legged—my favorite position for talking about uncomfortable situations. It's almost like I'm in my own anxiety ball.

This needs to be done.
I trust Finn enough to confide in him.
I love him.

Snagging the remote from the coffee table, I turn off the TV. Shifting to face him, I blow out a raspy breath. Noticing the change in mood, Finn settles his smoothie on the end table next to him and provides me with his full attention.

Before I bare myself to him, I take in the sight of him. His eyes are tired. The few times I woke up last night, Finn was awake. Exhaustion registered on his face when he kissed me good morning and helped me into the shower. Last night seemed to mentally suck him dry as well.

I hug myself, and though it's a struggle, I meet Finn's eyes. Other than the police and my parents, Georgia is the only person I've revealed my skeletons to. Lola knows bits and pieces, but not the entire story.

"When I was thirteen, two men broke into our house," I start, wetting my lips. "My parents were at some charity event that Faith and I had begged them to stay home from. The guys were family members of a criminal my father had given a harsh but deserving sentence to. The men came for retribution—to pay my father back for not giving their brother only a slap on the wrist." My body suddenly feels ten times heavier. "I was in my bedroom upstairs when Faith screamed. I ran out and looked over the stairwell, seeing them pinning Faith down. They told her she was going to pay for what my father had done. In fear, I ran to my parents' bedroom and grabbed the gun from my father's nightstand. I sprinted down the stairs … and they were …" I gulp, and the tears I begged to stay away appear. "They were about to rape her. I yelled for them to stop or I'd blow their heads off. The man laughed and lunged for the gun, so I shot him."

Finn is quiet, watching me with intent.

I breathe in deeply before slowly exhaling. "I figured shooting the guy would stop the man on top of Faith, but it only seemed to anger him more. She was lying there, crying and screaming, so … I shot him in the back. He fell limply on Faith's body, causing her to scream louder. She shoved him off her and slid across the floor before gaining the ability to walk. She scrambled away from him and into my arms. She yelled at me to call 911, but all I could do was stare at the guy squirming on the floor. Tears were in his eyes. I knew I should help him, but I was so angry. Faith ran into the living room to grab her phone as I watched the men I had just shot, lying there and bleeding, without helping them. My counselor said I was frozen in trauma, but after all these years, I'm still not sure why I didn't try to help them.

I scrub a hand over my wet face. "The guy who was on top of Faith wound up dying. The other had surgery and lived." My chest tightens as if it were strangling the words out of me. "I killed someone, Finn, and what happened that night haunts me. I have nightmares, replaying them barging into our home. I'm scared of being home alone at night. I live in constant fear of it happening again."

It made the news, and my parents moved us to Anchor Ridge, a few towns over, so we weren't the talk of the neighborhood. There were mixed emotions on what'd happened—some people praised us for sticking up for ourselves while others were angry a thirteen-year-old knew how to shoot a man. They called my father irresponsible for having loaded weapons in the house. Little did they know, he'd taken us to gun safety classes, almost as if he knew there was a risk it'd happen with his job.

I'm in tears by the time I'm finished. "I don't want to be this way … to be broken." I press my hand to my chest. "I'm about to be a mother. It'll be my job to protect my baby, so I need to stop being scared."

"Last night," Finn says in a low tone, "what happened?"

"I woke up, and you being gone must've triggered something in me."

He slowly scoots closer, waiting for me to tell him it's okay to do so. I sluggishly nod, and he pulls me onto his lap. Like last night, he holds me close and allows me to release my hurt against his chest. When I drag myself away, a gentle smile is on his face.

He plays with a strand of my hair, twirling it around his thick finger. "You're always safe with me, baby." He dips his chin slightly. "My father needed a ride home, and I didn't want to wake you. It won't happen again." He drops a kiss onto my lips, then my nose, and then my forehead. "Thank you for telling me this. It means everything to me."

CHAPTER THIRTY-SEVEN

GRACE

Grace

"IT'S ABOUT GODDAMN TIME," Silas says when Finn and I walk into Lincoln's penthouse, holding hands.

"Another couple," Lincoln adds with a smirk. "Four down." He casts a glance at Silas. "One to go."

Silas flips him off.

The reactions aren't surprising. Not all of our friends knew about Finn's and my change in relationship, although I'm sure they already assumed with us living together. But we haven't been around as much, given the current drama, my pregnancy, and him no longer working at Twisted Fox.

The girls knew after finding out what happened with Gavin's wife. They were adamant about coming over for a girls' night. They asked questions. Questions I couldn't lie about.

It's been a long week. There's been an ease in my nerves since Gavin took a leave from work—most likely waiting for talk of his wife's actions to die down. Even though I set everyone straight, I've steered clear of the teachers' lounge.

According to Georgia, after I left on the day Gavin's wife confronted me, Gavin charged out of his office in search of his wife after finding out that she hadn't left. He led her out of the building, threatening to call the police with every step if she didn't listen.

I haven't decided what I'll do if he comes back. Finn said he'd support me if I quit, but I love teaching too much. I pray that Gavin stays gone until my maternity leave, and then I'll decide from there.

"I'm really happy for you," Georgia says, perking up next to me.

"Remember how we'd bet who'd get pregnant first?" Lola asks.

Georgia laughs, pointing at her. "And we all said it'd be you."

"Pfft," Cassidy says. "You thought *Lola*, the commitment-phobe, would be the first?"

"We damn sure didn't think it'd be Grace," Georgia argues. "And I wasn't about to jinx myself in high school."

I laugh. "Me neither. That's why we voted on Lola."

Lola delivers a red-lipped smile. "Come to think of it, I don't know why we didn't put our money on Grace. She's always loved kids."

"Now, who's the next to get pregnant?" Jamie bounces a cooing Isabella, her baby, on her knee. "Two down—me and Grace."

"Uh …" Cassidy hesitates before slowly holding up her hand. "That'd be me." She inhales a quick breath before continuing. "Well … not next since I already am."

All our attention swings to her.

"I'm sorry," she rushes out, staring at me. "I've kept quiet because I didn't want to outshine your moment. I wanted to try to find the right time to tell you … and I guess this is the right time."

I squeal, "Really?"

She nods. "Like you, I was totally shocked."

I frown but then immediately correct myself, hating that she thought announcing her pregnancy would ruin any moment of mine. I get it, though. She's told me plenty of stories about the competitiveness in the sorority she was in before getting expelled from college.

"I guess that makes three down," Georgia says, scooting down the couch to hug Cassidy.

"Congrats, girl." Lola blows her a kiss. "We're going to have a shit ton of baby shopping to do."

Snapping my fingers, I gesture for Georgia to help me. She jumps up from the couch, grabs my elbow, and pulls me to my feet.

Taking the few steps to Cassidy, I hug her tight. "I'm so happy for you, babe."

It's nice to have someone going on this journey with me.

She hugs me back. "Thank you. I swear, after taking the test, I understood your panic. I was freaking the hell out."

When I pull away, I take the seat next to her. "What did Lincoln say?"

"Another reason I was nervous. Our relationship is kind of new, but he's ecstatic." A relaxed grin spreads across her face. "I also wanted to talk to you about the living situation. The townhome is a two-bedroom, and you'll need a nursery. The penthouse is a two-bedroom, and we'll need a nursery. If you're okay with it, the townhouse is all yours. Jamie agrees too."

CHAPTER THIRTY-EIGHT

Finn

"IF GEORGIA KEEPS DRAGGING me to baby showers, I'm going to make her ass have my baby real soon," Archer grunts, leaning back in his chair.

He chose the worst timing for his comment because as soon as the words leave his mouth, Georgia passes us.

She comes to a halt. "News flash, babe: baby showers are for *everyone*." She licks her lips. "And I love the baby talk. We can practice when we get home tonight."

He throws his head back. "You'd better keep that promise."

She saunters closer, tips her head down, and smacks a kiss to Archer's lips.

Today is Grace's baby shower, and it's being held at Faith's house. The girls have been hard at work, making it perfect for Grace. It looks like a damn flamingo blew up in here with all the pink. Grace told her parents she wanted to keep it small, but there are still at least fifty people here hanging out in the backyard.

I've met Grace's grandparents, aunts, uncles, cousins, and countless other people I've forgotten the names of. Every move I make, I'm stopped and introduced as Grace's boyfriend and the father of her child. I get asked how long we've dated, when I plan to pop the question, and if I'm ready to be a father. I've repeated the same story so many goddamn times that it's hard for even me to remember it's a lie.

I'm not the baby's father.

But I want to be her father.

The dust from Gavin has started to settle. The asshole is still on leave with another principal filling in for him. The day after Cassidy moved out of the townhouse, Grace and I went shopping for the nursery. She sat on the floor, setting up her shower registry online while I painted the walls yellow and assembled the furniture.

I chuckle. "I love how she always sets you straight."

"Oh, fuck off," Archer groans. "Don't act like Grace isn't the same with you."

"Speaking of Grace, it seems like you've done a kick-ass job of convincing people you're the dad," Lincoln says, grabbing his beer and taking a long draw. "Our plan has worked."

"Yeah," Cohen says. "Do you plan to step up … permanently?"

I gulp back my water and search the yard for Grace before replying. She's at a table with the girls, her parents, and her grandmother. She throws her head back, laughing, her tight braids falling along her shoulders. She lights up, her smile bright. I love seeing her this way, especially after everything she's gone through. She's wearing a white dress that shows off her belly with the pearl necklace I bought her for her birthday last year.

Every day when I wake up, my goal is to make Grace's day better than the last.

"If she'll have me, yes," I finally answer. "The dad is an asshole. Grace and I are together. I've been by her side, not him, and we plan to raise her together."

We've talked about it countless times. When we sit on the bed, feeling her stomach, waiting for the baby to kick. When we're on the couch, our favorite show playing in the background, listening to the baby's heartbeat with the machine we bought. I've gone to every doctor's appointment since the ultrasound and all her labor classes.

Cohen slaps me on the back. "I'm happy for you, brother. I've known Grace since she and Georgia became best friends. I've never seen her as happy with someone as she is with you."

"Cheers to our relationships and babies!" Lincoln says, holding up his beer.

"I'll cheers to babies because you're my friends, but fuck no to a relationship cheers," Silas mutters.

"Way to put a damper on a good day," Lincoln comments.

"Don't mind him," Archer says, waving his hand through the air. "He's pissed Lola is dating his brother."

"First off, he's not my brother," Silas corrects. "And second, she's not dating him. They went out to dinner. I told her not to. She's not listening to me." He says the last sentence with a twisted snarl.

Archer levels his eyes on Silas. "Man, unless you stop bullshitting and date her, she'll continue not to listen to you."

Our conversation is interrupted by Grace's mom yelling that it's time to cut the cake.

"Finn!" she says, calling me over with a wave of her hand. "Come on!"

Standing, I walk to the front of the yard and meet Grace at a long table. A three-layer pink cake sits alongside endless desserts—again, all pink. We stand at the head of it, on display, and I kiss Grace without even thinking about the crowd.

Everyone applauds, and when I pull away, a flush runs up her cheeks.

"I'm pretty sure the inside of that cake will be pink," Grace whispers to me.

I raise a brow. "Let's see, shall we?"

She grips the cake slicer, and my hand cradles hers.

Just as we're about to slice the cake, there's a loud clapping, followed by a deep, taunting voice saying, "Sorry for running late."

Terror flashes in Grace's eyes, and mine blaze with fury as Gavin strolls through the yard as if he owns the place. She drops the cake cutter, and it tumbles to the ground.

Gavin stands tall and smirks while staring straight at me. "I know it looks bad for the father, but traffic was a bitch."

CHAPTER THIRTY-NINE

Grace

THIS CAN'T BE HAPPENING.

Gavin makes a beeline in my direction, and my anxiety worsens the closer he gets. The smirk on his face confirms he's not here to do the right thing. He's here looking for trouble. This is about to be a god-awful mess. He walks as if he were leading a parade, and this is one big show.

My grandmother's wrinkled hand flies to her chest as she gasps.

My mother's drink drops from her hand at the same speed my heart feels like it's dropping from my chest.

My father says, "What the hell?"

"I'm going to kill that motherfucker," Finn growls.

People speak around me—some in hushed voices, some stating their concern loud enough that I can hear.

What the heck do I do?

I look at Finn, who appears to be on the same thinking page as me. He can charge across the yard and beat up Gavin, but that'd make him look bad in front of my family and friends. I gaze furtively around the yard, and everyone's attention is on the shit show about to start.

"Why is he here?" Finn seethes, his nostrils flaring.

"I-I have no idea," I stutter.

As far as I knew, Gavin was still on leave. He hasn't texted or called in weeks. Someone even mentioned they heard his wife was making them move back to their hometown.

Gavin turns in a circle before pointing at Finn. "This guy here, he's a fraud." He gestures to the crowd. "They are deceiving all of you. I am Grace's baby's father, but Grace got mad at me. Now, this guy is stepping in. But I'm going to fight for my baby."

Finn must lose all patience because this is the moment he charges toward Gavin. He gets one punch in, causing Gavin to stumble back before Archer snags Finn around the waist and pulls him back. Considering Finn's and Gavin's size difference, Gavin is stupid to taunt Finn. He'd better feel lucky that Archer stopped them.

I stand frozen in place, unsure of what to do.

"You need to leave," Archer warns Gavin, still holding Finn back.

Gavin wipes the blood off his lip. "I'm not going anywhere until Grace tells the truth."

"You have thirty seconds to turn your ass around, or I'm letting him get another punch in."

Everyone awaits Gavin's next move since he's the star of the show.

I'm brought into a hug, and I cast a glance at Georgia as she takes me into her hold. My sister comes along the other side, doing the same thing. Lola, Cassidy, and Jamie join us. Behind Finn are Cohen, Silas, Brian, and Lincoln. Gavin would be stupid not to leave because the sight of all of them together, pissed off, is terrifying.

"If he doesn't listen to Archer, I am taking this cake and throwing it at his head," Georgia says. "I'll buy you another one."

"Then I'm kicking him in the balls," Lola says.

"And I'll pour my drink over his head," Faith adds.

Gavin and Finn face off, glaring at each other, and Gavin doesn't budge.

Brian steps in, walking in front of Archer to speak to Gavin. "Look, this is my home. I'm asking you to leave. Otherwise, I'll call the police and have them escort you off my property." Brian fishes his phone from his pocket and holds it up. "I'm sure a police report would prevent you from securing any job in your field in the future. Think about that."

Reality dawns on Gavin as if that thought never crossed his dumbass brain.

He jerks his head toward me. "You need to tell them the truth because, in the end, I'll be there for you and the baby."

I pull away from my friends and bolt in Gavin's direction. Finn tries to stop me as I circle around them to get into his face, but I swat him away.

"Don't you get it, Gavin?" My tone is consumed with anguish, and my heart shudders in my chest as my tears come. "I want nothing to do with you." I swing my arm toward Finn. "This man here, he was the one who picked up all the responsibility you didn't."

Talking comes from everyone again at my confession.

"He was there for me at my appointments," I continue. "He's already providing for the baby, buying everything she'll need—"

"She?" Gavin's eyes widen, and he flinches while retreating a step. "You're having a girl?"

I ignore his question and go on, hoping my words sink in, and he never comes back. "He takes care of me, and goddammit, he's not married!"

That's when the reaction from the crowd goes ballistic in shock. I've never felt as on display in my life.

Gavin cowers, and his eyes bore into mine. "When he leaves you— because you know he will—you'll regret pushing me out of your life."

"Not fucking happening," Finn scoffs.

"He's not like you and me," Gavin says. "A man like that doesn't go for sweet girls, Grace, baby. You'll bore him, and he'll run off with someone else."

"You motherfucker!" Finn breaks from Archer, but Brian scurries to stand in front of Gavin, protecting him from a beatdown.

"Whatever happens, happens." I play it off as if his words didn't hurt me, but my chin trembles and more tears appear. "I'd rather be a single mom than be with you."

Brian pushes Gavin back. "The cops"—another push—"will be here any minute"—another push—"so go."

Gavin solemnly nods, finally getting the hint, and he turns and walks away.

Finn rushes to my side and pulls me against his chest.

"Get me out of here," I say, finally allowing the tears to break free.

"I got you."

He cradles my head into his chest as he walks me into Faith's house. We pass a few people sitting in the dining room, and he takes me upstairs to their open guest bedroom. He shuts the door, carefully sits me on the bed, and falls to his knees, so our faces are level with each other's.

My chin quivers as he stares at me with pain in his eyes.

"Baby," he croaks out, nearly in tears himself, "I am so sorry."

I run my hands through his soft hair. "That wasn't your fault."

It was mine.

I'm the one who allowed Gavin into my life.

Who slept with him.

How did he even know where to find me?

The details of my baby shower?

"When something painful happens to you, it hurts me too," Finn says, taking my hand in his. "And all that bullshit he said about me getting bored with you? That'll never happen."

My hands fall when he leans forward to press his lips to mine.

"I love you, Grace, and we'll figure this out."

Our attention turns away from each other at a knock on the door. It slowly opens, and my mother and Faith stand in the doorway. My mother's eyes are red and glistening with tears as she scurries into the bedroom.

"Oh, honey," she cries out, falling onto her knees next to Finn. "Is that true? What that asshole said?"

I can't help but chuckle at her reference to Gavin.

I nod. "It's true. We started dating, but then I found out he was married."

My mom sighs.

"I told him it was over, but then later, I found out I was pregnant," I confide. "I thought I'd have to do it alone, but Finn stepped up." I cast a glance at Finn. "We're in love, and we plan to raise the baby together."

"We will," Finn says. "I don't care if we have to fight him tooth and nail in court."

"We'll figure out a way for that to happen," Faith says. "You have a family who works in law."

I wipe my eyes. "What am I supposed to do about everyone out there? I can't go back out. I'm humiliated."

It'll be rude, but there's no way I can face everyone after what Gavin did. I'm already going to be the gossip for the next year and considered a joke. I lied to everyone about who the father of my baby is. Then he, the biological father, showed up and turned out to be a giant asshole, and while I confronted him, I aired that he was married.

Oh, what a baby shower to remember.

CHAPTER FORTY

Finn

I HOLD my head high as I thank everyone for coming after telling Grace I'd take care of the people at the baby shower. I'm embarrassed as fuck, but I can't imagine the humiliation she's going through. A few ask questions before leaving, to which I give them quick one-worded answers. Others thank me for being there for Grace. No one has said anything negative … to my face, at least. I'm sure there will be tons of talk about this later.

I have a shit ton of stuff to figure out.

How did Gavin find out about Grace's baby shower?

How can I get him to leave us the fuck alone?

Brian helps me see people out while the girls are with Grace.

"Thank you."

I glance over to see Gregory stopping next to me.

I raise a brow. "What?"

"Thank you." He holds out his hand, and I shake it. "I was worried about you and my daughter—not going to lie. Tyra and I thought it was too fast. We were upset we'd never met you … well, met you as our daughter's boyfriend. It was strange to us, but we didn't know to think otherwise. What you did for Grace, being that hand for her to hold, means a lot to me. I'm sure playing the part was largely so Grace didn't disappoint us. As far as I see it, you're the father. A father is more than genes. A father is someone who will do anything for his child, who is there for them through thick and thin, and that, Finn, is you. I'm honored to have you as part of our family."

Their acceptance means so much to me. There's only one thing holding Grace and me back from being a family, and I need to correct that.

————

IT WASN'T hard to find Gavin's address.

I just asked Georgia, the detective. All she needs is the internet, and she can find anything about anyone in minutes. Pulling up to the two-story home he recently moved into with his wife, I think twice if this is the right plan. It could result in doing more harm than good, but I need to take my chances. If there's a way I can get Gavin out of the picture, I'll take it. If it ends up going bad, I'll deal with the consequences.

Exhaling a deep breath, I step out of my car and stroll up the walkway. Three days have passed since the baby shower disaster, and Grace and I have worked on devising a plan to get rid of Gavin.

The door is answered within minutes after I ring the doorbell, and a dark-haired pregnant woman stands in front of me.

I lean back on my heels. "I'm looking for Gavin."

She tilts her head to the side. "Who are you?"

"I'm a friend."

"Gavin doesn't have friends here." She shakes her head. "Well ... male friends."

I can't stop myself from snarling at her response. "Look, I need to talk to him. Is he home?"

She doesn't move.

Since being vague isn't working, I go for lying next. "It's about his job."

Her shoulders straighten. "What about it?"

"Vivica, that's Grace's boyfriend."

Vivica whips around, and Gavin stands a few feet away from her, his eyes narrowed in my direction. She goes to slam the door in my face, but I dart my hand out to stop her.

I lower my voice. "I promise, this is only to help you. Hear me out."

Gavin doesn't say a word, just delivers a dirty look as I walk in. I can't decipher whether he is only allowing this to keep from pissing off his wife or if he's truly interested in why I'm here. We pass two kids playing in the living room, and Vivica asks them to go play in their bedrooms.

Gavin stands straight, clasping his hands in front of him. "To what do we owe the pleasure, Finn?"

"I want you to stay away from Grace," I demand.

"What are you talking about?" Vivica asks. "He told me he hasn't talked to her since he took his leave."

"That's a lie." I scratch my head and put all my attention on Vivica. "He showed up at her baby shower, causing a scene and telling everyone he was going to fight for his rights as the baby's father."

Vivica takes a step forward. "Excuse me?" She whips back to glare at Gavin. "Is this true?"

"I ..." Gavin stutters for the right words. "We were in an argument ... and I was ... just trying to figure out what to do."

"How did you even know where her shower was?" I ask.

He shrugs. "I still talk to a few teachers, and they overheard Grace and Georgia discussing it. They also invited some coworkers, and I got my hands on an invite."

"You bastard!" Vivica slaps Gavin across the face, doing the work I wish I could, but I'm trying to stay out of trouble. "You promised me you'd stay away from her! You swore to quit pulling this stuff and finally be faithful." She rubs her stomach. "We're having another baby, for Christ's sake!" she cries out. "You're destroying our family."

"I'm sorry!" Gavin croaks. "I'm trying to do better. I promise."

"You showing up at my girlfriend's baby shower isn't trying to do better," I argue. "It's you doing worse." I step forward. "You want to make things right with your wife ... with your family? Leave mine alone."

"Is she okay with that?" Vivica asks. "She doesn't expect anything from Gavin?"

I shake my head. "Not one damn thing."

"Looks like yet another lie," Vivica says, words directed at Gavin. "You told me she is suing you for child support and won't let you get out of this."

"Not true." My attention is also on Gavin as I pull out the envelope from my back pocket. "I can make it easy for you to fix your marriage." I open the envelope and slap the papers against his chest. "Here are papers to sign over any rights you'd have to Grace's baby. We will pay you ten thousand dollars to get you the fuck out of our hair." My gaze swings to Vivica. "We won't ask you for a dime, and you won't have to worry about any extra baby-mama drama."

Being the kick-ass attorney she is, Faith drew up papers and went through all the legalities with us on possible scenarios to get Gavin out of the picture. Grace's parents offered the ten thousand in hopes it'd convince Gavin further. I'm grateful as fuck for everything they're doing for us.

Vivica snatches the papers and quickly scans them before shoving them into Gavin's chest the same way I had. "Sign the papers, Gavin, or I'll have my attorney draw up divorce papers tomorrow."

Conflict covers Gavin's face. I'm not sure how the guy is as a father, but as a husband, he's a piece of shit.

Will he be willing to say good-bye to his child?

All he seems to care about are games of manipulation. He's most likely using being the father as an excuse to get Grace back because not once has he asked about the baby's well-being.

"Think of what you could do with ten grand," I say, going with my next strategy. "That's a lot of money."

"He'll do it," Vivica bursts out, grabbing a pen from her purse on the entryway table. She smacks Gavin's cheeks a few times as if to wake him up and hands him the pen.

He slowly grabs it. She rifles through the pages until she gets to the last one and pounds her finger against the dotted line. With a sad nod, Gavin signs ... and I nearly fall down in relief.

———

ONE MORE STOP.

One more stop until I can go home to my girl.

I wasn't sure if I'd go through with it. It's a stretch, and it could disappoint me if it doesn't work out. But since I'm on a roll, I might as well keep going until everything is lined up.

I take the steps up to my apartment two at a time. My dad and I have only talked a few times since the night Grace had her nightmare. I've been so busy with figuring shit out with us and helping to get the townhome baby ready. He hasn't asked me for money—*shocker*. Worry hits me when I open the door. I never know what I'll walk into with my father, so I'm expecting a trashed place and an even more trashed father.

The TV is on, and when I walk into the living room, a man is sitting on the couch, sipping on a Pepsi.

"Who the fuck are you?"

I made it clear to my father that I didn't want any of his friends inside my apartment. He can take that shit somewhere else because the last thing I want to worry about is drugs here or people stealing my shit.

The guy smiles up at me. "I'm Darryl." His voice is friendly, not slurred—a first for one of my dad's friends. He's also not high ... and he's dressed in clean clothes.

What the hell is going on here?

"Where's my father?" I grit out.

The guy might not be high, but I'm still suspicious.

"In the shower." Darryl places his Pepsi on a coaster on the coffee table.

I scratch my head. "Why are you here?"

"Your father is riding with me to our meeting and seems to be running late. I told him to take his time, and he told me I could wait in here."

My head spins. "Meeting? Meeting for what?"

His face falls. "He still hasn't told you?"

"Hasn't told me what?"

"I think it's best you have that conversation with him."

With perfect timing, my father walks out of the bedroom, buttoning up his shirt.

He smiles. "Oh, hey, son. I see you've met Darryl."

I raise my brows. "I have, and he said you're going to some *meeting*?"

Darryl stands. "I'll wait outside. Give you two some privacy to talk."

I rub the back of my neck.

What the fuck is going on?

What kind of meetings would my dad be attending?

I inspect my dad, taking in his kempt appearance. He's put on weight and is obviously freshly showered. His words were clear.

He stands inches from me, crossing and then uncrossing his arms. "I'm attending meetings ... addiction support groups ... to help me sober up. Darryl is my sponsor."

"To help you sober up ... or are you sober?"

He gleams with pride. "I've been sober seven days now. I know it's not much, but it's a start."

I've never felt so much damn pride in my life. "Seriously?"

He nods, his smile filled with just as much pride. "Yes, son."

I smile, yet it's still reserved. "That's fucking awesome, Dad. I'm so proud of you."

He's never done this before. Anytime I've mentioned him getting help or seeing a therapist, he's always insisted he doesn't need help ... that those people don't know what they're talking about.

"What made you decide to do this?" I ask, retreating a step.

"You. My life. Seeing the disgust you had when you picked me up at that house." He gestures to my apartment. "Seeing how living in a nice place can be. I went to the bar, and Archer wouldn't tell me where your new job was." His face falls. "That hurt ... but what really hurt was when I was leaving. Someone stopped and congratulated me on becoming a grandfather soon." His chest hitches. "I had no idea, and as I sat in my car, angry at first, then I burst into tears. That's when it finally hit me. Why would you want someone like me around your baby? I was a piece-of-shit father to you and was still acting irresponsibly. I sat there for an hour, thinking about being a grandfather, and my heart lit up, son. It was like a sign of me needing to get my shit together, so I can be a good grandfather."

Whoa.

This isn't what I expected.

I came here to tell my father he could stay in the apartment but that he would need to find work and get himself some help. I was on the fence about whether to disclose the baby information to him.

"I'm proud of you." His voice chokes up. "Now, it's time for you to be proud of me. For my grandchild to be proud of me. Please give me a second chance to show you that I can be a better person."

I'm shaking all over, and I shut my eyes.

It's what I wanted from him all along while I was growing up. I was always sad that I wasn't special enough to push him in that direction. It makes me fucking ecstatic that my baby is that important to him to finally take the initiative.

"It's a girl," I state, a wave of heat hitting me as my eyes grow teary. "We're having a baby girl."

"I'm so happy for you, son."

And for the first time, my father and I hug.

CHAPTER FORTY-ONE

Grace

GAVIN IS GONE.

The week after the baby shower incident, I was informed my coworkers had signed a petition asking for him to be fired. Since some of my coworkers had been at the shower, they wrote letters to the school board, demanding his temporary replacement become his permanent one. The school board listened, and bye-bye, Gavin.

He's gone from my work. He signed over his parental rights. I blocked his number. My life should be Gavin-free now.

Good riddance.

The school day has ended, and there's a spark back in my step—a slow step, given the baby seems to be growing like a weed these days.

I peer up from my desk at a knock on the door to find a nervous Vivica.

Just when I thought I was Gavin-free.

"Hear out," Vivica says in one breath.

"How about I show you out?" I counter, gripping my pen so tight that I'm waiting for it to break in half.

"I won't take much of your time," she pleads.

"What do you want?" I uneasily glance around the room, waiting for Gavin to appear … or something.

Who even let her in?

After the show she put on, she should have been banned from stepping foot into this school. Not only that but her husband was also just fired.

She grimaces. "I want to apologize."

I hold my hand up, warding her off from coming closer. "No need."

She holds her belly, which is bigger than mine. She looks ready to give birth at any moment. "That's not my character. I've never done something like that before—not even with Gavin's other mistresses. Maybe it was the pregnancy hormones ... I don't know. Something just snapped inside me."

"I have pregnancy hormones too," I deadpan, not trying to sound like a bitch yet not being overly nice because what she did wasn't cool. "And I found out the father of my child was married, and then he proceeded to practically harass me. Not once did I ever consider treating someone like that, especially someone who hadn't done anything. If you had read my text exchanges with Gavin, you would've seen that I asked him to stop texting, to stop calling, because he was married. No one knew about you until the first day you showed up."

She recoils at my words, but they needed to be said.

I take a steeling breath. "You deserve someone better than him, Vivica. I hope you realize that for the sake of yourself ... and the sake of your family."

Her face tenses. "You know nothing about my personal life. I came here to apologize. I did. Thank you for getting those papers drawn up and the money. I believe that you didn't know, and I appreciate you ending the affair when you found out. Now, we're just looking for the next step. It seems everywhere we go, my husband can't keep his dick in his pants." The last statement is said with a snarl. "I wish you luck, Grace."

"You too, Vivica."

She's sure as hell going to need more than luck.

Maybe a frying pan to whack Gavin over the head and knock some sense into him.

When she disappears through the door, I grab my bag and go home to a man who can keep his dick in his pants.

To Finn.

The man I love.

CHAPTER FORTY-TWO

Finn

"I'LL NEVER GET ENOUGH of you," I say to Grace as I kiss up her thigh.

She woke up crampy and nauseous and called off work. I did the same to cater to her. I made her favorite meal and gave her a massage … which led to now—my face inches from her pussy and my mouth watering. If all else fails, an orgasm always makes my girl feel better.

Before devouring her, I plant a quick kiss on her belly—one of my favorite things to do. The due date is close. The baby bag is packed and at the door. A car seat is strapped into each of our cars. We're ready for our little one to come. At least, we think we are. Neither one of us knows what to expect. Sure, we've read the baby books, attended classes, and been given advice from our friends. But I don't think any of those one hundred percent prepare you for having a baby. I told Grace we'll learn as we go, we don't have to be perfect, and we will make an amazing team.

"Another go at inducing labor?" Grace asks, laughing while staring down at me.

We've had sex—lots and lots of sex—and blame it on attempting to induce labor.

The real reason, though, is we love being intimate with each other. Holding hands, kissing, sex, whatever it is, I love it with Grace.

Her thighs shake at my first lick up her slit. I love how sensitive she is to me. Squirming underneath me, she moans my name as I softly circle her clit with my thumb and navigate my tongue in and out of her. As she gasps and when I know she's getting close, I shove two fingers inside her, working her the way she loves to be worked. In our months of dating, I've learned what Grace likes … and what she looks like when she's about to orgasm.

I quicken my pace, slamming my fingers in and out of her, and she begs for more.

My attention moves away from her thighs to her eyes when she clutches my wrist.

"I need you inside me," she begs. "I need more."

"Come on my tongue, and then I'll give you this cock," I demand, raising my mouth to suck on her clit while finger-fucking her. "And then I'll come inside you."

My words set her on fire, and seconds later, her back arches. I devour her, loving the way her pussy tightens against my fingers, and my cock jerks in my pants, knowing he's next in line. Drawing back, I crawl off the bed, unbutton my pants, and slide them down my legs.

"Uh … Finn," Grace says as I pull my shirt over my head.

I toss it across the room. "Yeah, baby?"

She points at where I just was. "I think my water just broke."

CHAPTER FORTY-THREE

Grace

MILLIE ANGELINE DUKE.

My daughter.

Our daughter.

I love that she has Finn's last name. With my family's expertise in law, they were able to get that done for us. Finn is her father, and I wouldn't want it any other way.

I'd asked him to take a few days to think about it before agreeing to it. It's a big deal—an eighteen-year commitment. But Finn said he's all in—forever.

I'm exhausted, and I've attempted to rest as the nurses have told me to do. The ten hours of labor was hard on me—mentally and physically—but I forgot all about that when they handed me my beautiful little girl. Six pounds and four ounces of perfection were finally mine to hold after talking to her through my skin for so long. I was terrified of motherhood, but now, I want nothing more than to be the perfect mother to my little girl.

I cried. Finn cried. Faith cried. Millie cried.

The delivery room was one giant sob-fest.

While Faith had been a good source of mental support in the

room, Finn was my right-hand man. The best partner a pregnant woman could have.

He accepted my verbal abuse.

"You eat that cheeseburger in front of me, and you'll never eat one again."

"Tell me it's easy to push again, and I'm pushing you out that window."

The poor guy held my hand while I practically ripped his off while crying out in pain. But he'd never walked away, never looked at me any different.

I'm also sure whatever he saw the doctor working with down in my nether regions wasn't a pretty sight. I'd be surprised if he wants to put his face down there again.

RIP, oral orgasms.

The baby classes had paid off. Finn was my comfort blanket while I gave birth. He knew what to say and do to keep me going. He had been my comfort blanket during my entire pregnancy really. I'm not sure if I could've done it without him.

Finn sits in the chair next to me, cradling Millie in his arms. As I lay my head back, my mind wanders to the day we decided to pretend. I couldn't have known it would be the best thing I'd ever done. It was always supposed to be Finn.

He was always supposed to be my lover, the father of my child—and from the comments he keeps making, my husband. He's brought up marriage more times than I can count, but I told him that we needed to have our baby first, and then wedding talk could start. Heat radiates through my chest at the thought of being his wife.

"She's beautiful," Finn says, his gaze sliding away from Millie to me. "Just like her mother." He runs his finger along her face. "She has your eyes."

That heat turns ice-cold. I wish I could do what he just did. I'd love to examine Millie and point out every similarity she has to Finn, but I can't. I hate that dread crawls up my throat and ruins this happy moment. Millie won't resemble Finn because she's not his. It's a tough pill to swallow and one I'll have to digest myself. It'd kill me to ever bring it up to Finn.

Biologically, he might not be Millie's father.

But in every other way, he is.

There's a knock on the door, and as soon as I call, "Come in," it flies open.

"Where is my goddaughter?" Georgia sings before holding up a gift bag. "I have presents on presents on presents to give her."

Lola nudges her with her elbow. "I think you mean, *my* goddaughter."

They've been arguing over who the godmother will be for weeks now. Each of them bringing me sweets to sway me in their favor.

I laugh. "How many times have I said that you're both the godmothers?"

"Is that a thing?" Georgia asks. "Can there be two? And if there's two, who's number one?" She sets the bag down on the small couch in the corner. "If so, I'm number one."

A line forms behind the girls. It feels good, having my friends here. Georgia texted an hour ago, making sure I was ready for people, and I replied that I was. I want the people I care about to meet my little one.

Cassidy waddles in and looks straight at me. "Don't tell me any horror stories, please. Lincoln has made me watch birthing pregnancy videos, and I'm terrified."

Finn chuckles. "Prepare yourself for war, Lincoln."

"Hardy-har-har," I grumble.

Georgia is the first to ask to hold Millie because she's Georgia, and she always has to be the first in line. Nervously, I tell her to take a seat as if she were a child holding a new puppy, and I instruct Finn to carefully place her in Georgia's arms. I give Georgia directions on how to hold her, to protect her head—nearly everything the nurses said to me. I'm going to tell anyone else who asks to hold her the same. It's only been two days, and I know I'll do anything to protect my little girl.

There are so many things I can't wait for—to take her home, to change her diapers regularly (weird, I know), and to give her as much love as I can.

I think back to how this day might have been if it had been Gavin with me here and shudder. I'd have kicked him out of the room. The next thought that swims through my brain is having to do it alone without Finn. The thought nearly pulls tears from my eyes. Millie deserves the perfect family, and that's what we'll give her.

Not a half-assed dad.

A family to love her, to want her, to put her first.

I'll never worry about the issues Vivica has to worry about. Finn would never cheat, never turn his back on us, and never put himself before his family. I have a good man.

By the time everyone leaves, I'm exhausted. That doesn't stop me from cradling my daughter to my chest as I doze off to sleep. This is my new life, and I can't wait for the journey it takes me on.

EPILOGUE

Finn

"THAT'S the hottest thing I've ever laid eyes on."

My gaze sweeps over to Grace sitting on the bed. "Huh?"

She gestures to Millie in my arms. "You, shirtless, sexy, wearing gray sweats while holding our baby." She licks her lips. "I always thought you were hot, but this is like an orgasm." She pouts. "The only orgasm I'll have for a minute."

I chuckle. "Now, do you understand all those times I told you that motherhood looks sexy as fuck on you?"

"Yeah, yeah, yeah," she mutters. "You told me how sexy I was when I was like a stuffed turkey."

Tonight is Millie's first day home. Our friends wanted to throw a welcome-home party, of course, but we told them to wait until the weekend. Not only do Grace and I need time to adjust, but so does Millie. Even after such a short time, I love this little girl. Grace allowing me into their lives is a fucking blessing I'll never take for granted.

I inspect her in my arms. She's so tiny but already weighs down my heart. She yawns, her tongue sticking out, before shutting her eyes again. I tiptoe to her bassinet, kiss her forehead, and carefully lay her down, making sure she's lying exactly how we were instructed she needed to be. As I climb back into bed with Grace, I think about having more babies with her.

No matter what, Millie will always be my daughter. When I confided in Cohen about taking on the rights as her father, he asked if I'd ever tell Millie the truth about her biological father. I gulp, thinking about when that day would possibly come. It's hard to know the future, but I hope I never have to disclose that information to her. Grace and I made a pact; albeit some might think it's selfish of us, as far as Millie will ever know, I'm her dad.

I pull Grace into my arms. "How are you feeling, baby?"

"Exhausted but happy ..." She sighs. "Content. You?"

"The happiest I've ever been."

Grace and I took the long route in our relationship, but the greatest things often take time, right? Like fine wine, it only gets better. For years, we chased the dream of a relationship but never fully jumped in. It's been a marathon, but I'm glad I never stopped chasing her, happy I never gave up.

We're done chasing each other.

Chasing our feelings.

We've caught the love of our lives.

And now, we're a family.

I hope you enjoyed Finn and Grace's story! There's so much more in the Twisted Fox series with other characters getting their own HEA. All books can be read as standalones. I'd love for you to join me for Silas and Lola's story, Last Round!

Last Round

CHAPTER ONE

Silas

"REMEMBER that time you switched his mom's name to his side chick's in his phone, and he ended up sending her nudes instead?"

Something about listening to conversations in bars is intoxicating.

I absorb it like the mixed drinks I create.

People perch on heavy stools and slur their darkest secrets.

Admit their drunken truths.

It's different tonight. I'm not listening to an intoxicated soul pour their heart out. It's three women wedged toward the end of the bar, debating on who had the pettiest ex revenge.

I observe them, pretending to dry a martini glass, and replay the last retaliation in my mind.

He sent nudes to his mom instead of his side chick.

I shudder. I'd jump off a goddamn cliff if I accidentally sexted my mother, let alone sent her a dick selfie.

Yet another reason I steer clear of relationships.

No girlfriend, no revenge.

I learned that lesson in high school when a two-week fling declared her love for me and then keyed my car after I broke up with her. That shit is for the birds.

I set down the glass and grab another. I've never seen them in the three weeks I've bartended at Luna Bar, but that's not unusual. It's a busy bar with different faces coming and going, depending on whatever event the bar is throwing—fight nights, ladies' nights, or bar crawls.

Luna Bar isn't a dreary bar with dimmed lights and classic country tunes blaring from a jukebox. The lights are bright, and the music genre falls somewhere between Hank Williams and Imagine Dragons, so I can hear them decently.

The clock hasn't struck midnight, so plastered coeds aren't packing the place yet. Being the kick-ass employee I am, I ignore customers waving me over with drink requests. I can't tear my eyes away from them.

More specifically, I can't stop staring at *her.*

There are three of them, but I've fastened my focus on the woman who'd swapped the names. We'll call her Name Swapper. She's a dark-haired beauty—a nameless, shit-stirring woman who screams trouble.

But me? I live for fucking trouble.

Stroking my jaw, I admire her sitting perfect-postured on her stool while sipping on a cotton candy–colored cocktail. Her tongue wraps around the tip of the red straw—the same color as her lips— with each drink. Every so often, she fiddles with her straight hair that's as dark as the sky will be when I clock out tonight, and the strands fall to each side of her cleavage. Her skin tone is one people lie out in the sun for hours to achieve, but I'd bet tonight's tips that it's natural.

I've worked at bars long enough to guess people's ages. I'm usually right on the money on who's carrying a fake, who recently hit legal drinking age, and who is decades older than me. My guess is she's in her early twenties.

When admiring her from afar isn't pleasing enough, I approach them. Their conversation ceases as they wait for me to explain myself.

I point at Name Swapper and deliver a confident smile. "You win. I'll be sure to hide my phone when we're at your place later."

The strawberry-blonde next to her gasps.

The brunette to her right scoffs.

Name Swapper stares at me, unimpressed, and settles her half-full glass onto the sticky bar. Her voice is bored when she says, "What makes you think I'd be interested in you *or* your phone?"

I ignore the racket around me, rest my elbow on the bar, and invade her personal space like an asshole. "How about you give me your number? I'll be sure *you're* the only woman receiving my dick pics."

I should be ashamed of myself for the weak-ass pickup line, but hey, time is limited. The bar will soon grow overcrowded, and my chance to shoot my shot with her will be severed. It's rare for me to hit on women in the workplace. I very much believe in the phrase *don't shit where you eat.* I've witnessed too many coworkers hook up with customers, only to deal with the wrath of them showing up to start drama later.

Hard pass on that shit.

But something about this woman is different. A sense that she won't look for me later or expect anything the next morning.

She stares at me, silent and smirking.

I raise a brow. "You single?"

"No fuckboys with side chicks at the moment." She plays with her straw, still feigning boredom, but that smirk tells me she's enjoying this game.

"Good news for me then." I snap my fingers, pull my phone from my pocket, and shake it in the air. "I do need to put your number in since it seems you can't be trusted around phones."

"Cocky." She squints in concentration and bites the corner of her plump lip. "Cocky is my type, so what the hell?"

Score.

My grin matches the same one I sported the night I lost my virginity to Miranda Smith in the back seat of my dad's old BMW. Good-slash-embarrassing times. At least now, I last a hell of a lot longer than I did at fifteen.

She recites her number, and I type it into my phone. With her attitude, I predicted she'd put up more of a challenge and not hand her number over like loose change.

"And your name?" I ask when finished.

"Lola."

"Nice to meet you, Lola." I slide the phone back into my pocket. "I'm Silas."

She gestures toward my pocket. "I don't reply to texts, FYI. Call or don't bother."

Weird.

That's the first time I've heard someone say they prefer calls to texts. Hell, I'd rather receive a text than a call any day. You call me, and I'll let it ring fifty times until it goes to voicemail.

I snap my fingers. "I'll be sure to call then, sweetheart."

She rolls her eyes at my sentiment.

This woman is unreadable. One moment, she's acting as if she wants to jab a straw through my eyes, and the next, she's giving me her number.

"Yo! Bartender!" A customer pounds his heavy hand on the bar. "Quit trying to get laid! We need drinks!"

Lola shifts in her stool to look at him. The frat boy waves his arms in the air, anxiously seeking my attention.

She points at him. "You'd better go do your job before they fire you."

"Fuck him." I shrug with confidence I shouldn't have about being unemployed. "What can I get *you?*"

They simultaneously hold up their drinks.

"He already served us." Lola signals to Cohen, the other bartender on duty. He's also my boss.

I slightly frown before nodding. "Let me know when you're ready for your next round."

I wink and walk away even though I'd prefer to stay and chat with her.

Have to play hard to get and all.

I also need to do my job.

I make the frat douchebag and his friends Long Island iced teas and roll my eyes at their lack of tip before strolling toward Cohen. He hired me after I was fired from my last bartending gig. I'd worked at Club Layla a year before I mistakenly slept with a shot girl … who was also the owner's niece. We'd agreed it would be a one-time thing and there'd be no commitments, but she didn't keep her end of the deal.

Again, don't shit where you eat.

"The three chicks in the corner," I say to Cohen, signaling toward them. "Let me make their drinks from now on. I might break my *no hooking up with customers* rule with her."

The beer he's filling overflows and spills onto the bar. He quickly jerks the glass away and grabs a towel, and regret pours through me. Telling your boss you plan to sleep with a customer is a stupid move.

Cohen wipes up the mess before saying, "Which unfortunate woman is this?" His face is unreadable, unsure about whether he's pissed or amused at my statement.

I discreetly point at Lola. "The mouthy, dark-haired one."

He snorts, snatches a glass, and repours the beer. "Yeah, that hookup won't be her. I'd choose someone else ... or just worry about your job."

"Why?" I pinch the bridge of my nose. "Is she your girl?"

"That's a big *fuck no*." He hands over the beer and cups my shoulder, turning me to face them. "The one on the right is my baby sister, who you by no means want to hook up with. The other two are her best friends."

Phew. At least Lola isn't his sister.

I can't afford to lose this job.

Well, I can, but I don't want to.

"Shit, sorry, man. I had no idea."

"As long as it isn't my sister, I don't give a shit who you pick up." He shrugs and signals a *give me a sec* motion to a customer. "You said the dark-haired girl gave you her number?"

I nod.

"Friendly advice: don't call her."

"What? Why?" I scoff. "You in love with her?"

A deep laugh rumbles from his chest. "On second thought, call her. Give it a chance."

When I peer back over to the three, they're staring at us. Lola sends me a flirty smile and waves.

"Is this some trick?"

"Nah." Cohen shakes his head. "Lola's a good girl ... has a *great* phone voice. Call and ask her out. I think you two would be good together." He jerks his chin toward the waiting crowd. "Now, get your ass to work."

I spend the rest of my night pouring beers, mixing endless drinks, and handing out shots. My opportunities to speak to Lola fade, and she leaves before I get the chance.

At least I have her number.

———

I YAWN three times in a row while parking my car in the garage. It took us twenty minutes to get everyone out of the bar, and then cleanup took another hour.

I kill the engine and walk into my house with Lola on my mind, like it strangely has been all night. I'm typically not a man who stresses over a woman. I'd rather cook rice grains one by one than form an emotional attachment with someone. I tried once—the relationship thing, not the rice—and learned my lesson when it ended in disaster.

As I kick off my shoes, I wonder what calling her would be like. I wasn't the only guy who hit on her tonight. I counted at least five. Five assholes I wanted to sucker punch for doing the same thing I'd done. To get back at them, I overcharged them for their drinks.

It was an asshole move.

Sue me.

Why was I the lucky bastard to score her number?

What made me so goddamn special?

And why do I find her so goddamn special that I've been fixated on her since I stepped behind the bar?

Maybe it was her disinterest in me.

That she was immune to my charm.

Calling Lola might be stupid, it might kick me in the ass later, but I hope it'll be worth it.

———

A RESULT of working all night is sleeping all day.

My parents didn't raise me on the belief of a typical nine-to-five workday. I was taught to work every minute of every day. If you weren't working, you were lazy. My father, Grady Malone, was a workaholic who expected the same from me. I grew up envisioning that as my future, but that mindset changed when disaster hit.

Now, I bartend a few nights a week and host club parties. That provides enough money not to have a life wrapped around working a job I hate.

I open the French doors that lead out to my patio, relax on an outdoor lounge chair, and kick up my feet before calling Lola.

It rings four times.

My back straightens when a deep, masculine voice answers.

The fuck?

Is this her dad?

Brother? Boyfriend?

"Is"—I scratch my head—"Lola there?"

It's like I'm twelve and calling a chick's house phone before cell phones were a thing.

"Motherfucker," the guy hisses into the phone. "She did it again!"

"Uh ... did what?"

He blows out a ragged breath. "I'm Callum, Lola's ex. She thinks it's funny to give my number to the men who ask for hers. It's her revenge, reminding me it was a mistake to cheat on her."

Well played, Name Swapper.

Little does she know, her little trick only makes me want her more.

———

I WALK INTO THE BAR, grab a dirty rag, and sling it at Cohen. "You're an asshole."

The towel lands on his shoulder, and he flicks it off, watching it fall onto the linoleum floor.

"You called her, didn't you?"

"I called *someone* who sure as fuck wasn't Lola." I mock his voice and mimic his stance from the other night. "Lola's a good girl ... has a *great* phone voice. Call and ask her out."

"You brought it on yourself, man."

"How? For asking for her number?"

"For being an idiot. Did you honestly think a smart-ass like her would hand over her number that easily?"

I didn't, but I allowed my ego to get in the way and tell me it was my charm that had sealed the deal.

"When is she coming in again?"

"That's none of your business."

I rub at my tired eyes. "As an employee, I should know who's visiting this establishment."

"As your boss, I think you should worry about being an employee and less about weekend hookups."

Our conversation stops when the door opens. It's only three o'clock, so the lunch rush is gone, and the dinner rush hasn't arrived yet.

The door slams shut behind Finn, the bar's bouncer, and he strolls toward us.

"Silas! My dude!" He circles behind the bar and slaps Cohen on the back while keeping his attention on me. "Barbecue tomorrow at Cohen's place. It's his birthday, so don't forget his gift."

Cohen frowns at the word *birthday*. "I don't want gifts."

As a single father, Cohen prefers to do everything himself and never asks for favors. I once offered him and his son free baseball tickets to a game I couldn't attend. He wouldn't take the tickets until I accepted money for them.

"I'll be sure to get you a shitty present for the terrible advice you gave me," I tell Cohen.

Finn shakes his head. "Nah, get him a Pornhub gift card. The dude doesn't get laid much, so he needs good content for his spank bank."

I raise a brow. "They sell Pornhub gift cards?"

Cohen smacks the back of Finn's head, and he winces. "You're uninvited, fucker."

I've heard of Cohen's barbecues before, but I haven't attended one. I've always been good at keeping a distance from others.

An idea hits me, and I perk up.

"Will Lola be there?"

Finn blinks at me. "You know Lola?"

Cohen laughs. "He was lucky enough to get her number."

Finn crookedly grins. "Wait a minute. You got the pleasure of speaking with Callum?"

"Sure did," I mutter.

"Dude, I'd stop there," Finn warns. "Lola would tear you apart and then spit you out."

I eye Cohen, ignoring Finn. "Will she be there?"

He nods. "Oh, she'll be there, but I can't promise she won't kick your ass."

"Challenge accepted."

CHAPTER TWO

Lola

CALLS from your exes carry two different emotions:

Anger that you're no longer together.

Sadness because you're, well, no longer together.

Calls with my ex are an alternative to the standard. Callum is angry, but not because we're no longer together.

"What did I tell you about giving out my number?" he hisses through the phone.

Revenge is best served in the form of receiving calls from the men who hit on the girl you'd cheated on.

"Whoops." I laugh, not bothering to hide my enjoyment of his irritation. "I must've gotten our numbers mixed up again."

"Admit it," he says, and I can imagine the smug smile he's sporting. "You do it because you miss me."

Men and their egos—always thinking revenge is because we still love them.

"Negative." I open my car door, settle my bag into the passenger seat, and balance my phone between my ear and shoulder as I get in the driver's side. "I do it because I'm bored, and you deserve it."

"Bullshit. You still think about me."

"You're right. I think about you when I reflect on how it was to have a shit boyfriend. Have a good day, and I'll be sure to send more phone calls your way." I end the call, toss my phone down next to my bag, and push my black sunglasses up my nose.

Some might consider giving his number out petty. It is. But I don't care because Callum deserves it.

Let me paint the beautiful scene of dating Callum.

Imagine having sex with your boyfriend and him not caring about your big O. Then the asshole has the audacity to pull out, release on your stomach, and smear it across your skin—as if his jizz is a damn gift. He then rolls off the bed and says, "Gotta go clean up, babe." Like *he's* the one with cum on his belly.

As I lay there, brooding over how sticky and gross sperm was, his phone beeped with a text.

Then beeped again.

And again.

Then it rang.

I make no apologies for my nosiness—it could've been an emergency, you know? I grabbed his phone to find a text from *Brittany: Blonde from Club Mania.*

Like an idiot, his passcode was his birthday, so it didn't take a rocket scientist to unlock it.

Brittany: Blonde from Club Mania had texted, asking if he missed licking her vagina … and then sent a close-up picture of said vagina he'd allegedly lapped up.

I scrolled through their past messages to learn they'd licked each other several times while he and I were together.

I proceeded to do what any sane person would. I grabbed his favorite—very expensive and dry-clean-only—shirt to clean his cum off me, pulled my lace panties up my legs, slipped my dress on, and left without a word, certain I'd figure out the best revenge for him later. He texted after his shower, discovering his bed was empty, and I replied that he should spill his cum on someone else because it would no longer be his pleasure to do so on me.

I thought of my revenge the next day while visiting my granny in the nursing home when a guy asked for my number. A guy I'd never be interested in because he'd helped his grandmother cheat during bingo, which caused my grandmother to lose. Knowing I couldn't associate myself with another cheater, I came up with the bright idea of giving him Callum's number.

That was a month ago, and since then, it's become my new go-to.

Ten outta ten, ladies.

Highly recommend it.

———

BARBECUES AT COHEN'S are my favorite.

I'm not much of a barbecue girl per *se*—considering I'd burn down the entire block if I attempted to even light a grill—but I enjoy *attending* them. I get to sit outside with the girls and munch on calorie-ridden snacks while Cohen grills. It's something we've done since high school.

Cars are packed on Cohen's driveway, so I park on the curb. I step out of my black Porsche and grab his birthday gift—a bottle of Johnnie Walker Blue Label. With him being a bartender and my family owning one of the top liquor distribution companies in the Midwest, we appreciate quality alcohol.

The sun beams down on me as I walk up the drive and then step through the creaky wood gate that leads into the backyard. The air smells of fresh-cut grass, and I make my way toward the round table where everyone is seated. The usual gang is here—my best friends, Georgia and Grace, along with Cohen and Finn. Who isn't usually here is the extra person seated next to Finn.

It's *him.*

Silas.

The guy I gave the wrong number to at the bar.

And the one who most likely called said number, given Callum's call earlier.

Cohen stands at the grill, flipping burgers. The others are wrapped in deep conversation, clueless to my arrival, but not Silas. He's sitting tall in the chair that directly faces the entrance to the backyard. He levels his gaze on me as though he's been anxiously awaiting my arrival.

The shit-eating grin on his face confirms he's not as shocked to see me as I am him. He doesn't appear as angry as I'd expect from someone who was given the wrong number. He knew I'd be here and came with one goal—to mess with my head, not rip it off. If he were that upset about my wrong-number game, Cohen never would've allowed him to come.

I keep a straight face, tighten my hold on the gift bag, and pull my shoulders back before strutting toward them.

Two can play this game, buddy.

I'll also be kicking Cohen's traitorous ass.

Silas's smile grows more arrogant with every step I take toward him.

Today is the first time I've had to face one of my wrong-number victims.

I didn't have to worry about the nursing-home cheater because, luckily, my grandma quit bingo, stating, "That bitch Thelma always wins."

The few others were random men at bars.

"Look who's finally arrived!" Silas shouts, dramatically slapping his knee like my grandfather does when he sees a grandchild walk in, and then stands. "It's Callum."

As much as I wish I didn't, I freeze at him calling me Callum.

Oh, this asshole.

He'll be lucky if he leaves this barbecue alive … or at least with two working legs. He could easily live with only one kneecap … and surely, taking out one leg isn't much prison time.

Shaking away my thoughts of bodily injury, I keep my chin up and stroll forward. Drinking Silas in, I hate that he's exactly the type of man I find attractive. Six-plus feet so that there's still a significant height difference when I wear heels. Thick hair, the color resembling the top-shelf whiskeys I sell to clients on the regular. It's long on the top and shorter on the sides with a slight flip in the front. The black button-up, rolled at the elbows, that he wore at the bar is replaced with a simple black tee. Just like I love wearing black, I find it incredibly attractive when men do too.

That night, I spotted him the moment he walked behind the bar. Unfortunately, I'd sworn off guys after my breakup with Callum. I'm not made for relationships. The first few times I'd cracked open my heart, it'd resulted in nothing but letdowns. The way my love life is looking, I'll be the future Thelma—alone in the nursing home and cheating during bingo.

Another reason I knew Silas was off-limits was his job. Cohen has recounted endless bartender stories—how they're in that line of work for the thrill of the nightlife. They have no issues going home with random women like it's their reward after a long night's work.

I shake my head, getting myself together, and walk toward them. All eyes have turned to me as everyone awaits my response when I reach them.

I ignore Silas and glare at Cohen. "Really? You invited him?" I hold up the gift he no longer deserves. "I'm taking this back. No expensive liquor for traitors."

"Technically, Finn invited him," Cohen corrects before pointing his spatula toward Asshole Bartender. "Silas is cool. You two need to talk out your wrong-number differences."

I flip Cohen the bird while still refusing to glance at Silas.

Finn, smirking wide and proud of providing today's entertainment, signals back and forth between Silas and me. "How did you two meet?"

I roll my eyes at Finn's terrible job of playing clueless. He definitely knows.

"She gave me her number at the bar," Silas answers smugly.

My gaze flashes to him as he takes the few steps separating us. I inhale the rich scent of his cologne. It's familiar and expensive … and my favorite. There's something attractive about a man who wears a strong cologne—a sign that he enjoys being in charge.

"Either the music was too loud or I'm losing my hearing because I heard her name wrong," he continues, his focus solely on me as he holds out his hand. "It's good to see you again, Callum."

I narrow my eyes at him and swat away his hand. "Funny, jackass."

"Aunt Lola said a bad word!" Noah, Cohen's son, shouts before crawling out from underneath the table like an ant who's been waiting for a crumb to drop.

Shit, I hate when he hides down there.

For some strange reason, Noah plays with his toys under the table. Georgia said it's because he likes to listen to grown-up conversations. I now agree with that statement.

"Sorry, Noah," I say, feeling the need to explain myself to a kid who has to be reminded not to eat his boogers. "It was an accident."

He nods, accepting my apology, and runs over to Cohen, asking for a juice box.

I walk around Silas to find a chair, bumping my shoulder into his. Throwing my head back, I groan when I discover the only empty chair is between Georgia and Silas.

Did he set that up too?

It wouldn't surprise me after he came here and put on a show. I contemplate grabbing the chair and dragging it to another spot, but that'd prove his little game is working. I can't have that. While he scoots out his chair and sits, I drop my gift onto the small bench where the others are. I sit down to his right, smacking my elbow against the side of his head, and turn my back to him. He lets out an *oomph*.

"Thanks for the heads-up," I hiss to Georgia.

She lifts her phone from the table. "Check your phone for the fifteen text messages I sent."

"Shit," I mutter, sliding my hand into my crossbody and realizing I left my phone in the car.

"Sorry," she whispers. "I had no idea he was coming. I was surprised too."

I frown, but before I get the chance to reply, Silas taps my shoulder. I peer back at him.

"Did you fall from heaven?" he asks, and I wait for a cheesy comment to follow. "Because so did Satan ... and I think you might be him."

My mouth falls open.

Not what I expected.

I narrow my eyes at him. "Um, that's rude."

"I'm rude?" He scratches the five o'clock shadow along his sharp jawline. "What kind of evil person comes up with an idea like that?"

"I think you mean, what kind of *genius* comes up with an idea like that?" Georgia, the CEO of snooping on conversations, says.

That's my girl.

Silas doesn't even pay her a glance. He leans closer to me and lowers his deep voice. "How are you doing today, fake number-giver? Ruin any other guy's dreams of finding love?"

"Nope." I shake my head. "You were my latest victim."

He chuckles. "I should've known it was a trick when you said to call. Texting is always the way to go." He's amused, almost impressed.

"No, I still think calling is better," I say with honesty. "It's more intimate. Texting is so easy … you can't read emotions or lies through texting."

"Too bad for you we'll never get a chance to have a phone call. I don't talk to people who are Satan's sidekick."

"Yet you're talking to me right now."

"Yes, to get your advice on staying out of hell since it seems you have all the inside information."

"You can start by not hitting on random women every night at work." I finally turn in my chair to face him and ignore the attention on us.

That night at the bar, I was aware of his eavesdropping. When he asked for my number, I debated on whether to give it to him. Since it was the first time in a while I'd been interested in a guy, I was tempted. But my intuition stepped in to tell me he was bad news and most likely had a call log full of Brittany: Blonde from Club Manias in it. I observed him as he worked, witnessing woman after woman hit on him while he flirted back.

No, thank you on that.

I was surprised Cohen vouched for him being a good guy. Cohen is picky over who he brings around Noah and us. If he'd thought Silas was a weirdo, he'd have never let him come today.

Silas scoffs, "You were the first woman whose number I asked for at Luna Bar. Consider that flattering."

I mock his scoff. "Yeah, right."

"Ask Cohen. The last thing I need is some random hookup showing up at my job. I have a strict *no hooking up* policy at work."

I raise a brow. "Does that mean you're celibate then?"

He chuckles. "Why, yes, my darling, that's exactly what it means."

"I believe the people who claim the earth is flat more than that."

"How about this?" He strokes his jaw. "Let's start over. You can tell me why your parents named a beautiful girl like you Callum. If their goal was to steer men away from you, it wasn't necessary since you're evil. And I'll tell you why it was a mistake, giving me the wrong number."

"*Fine.* Since Cohen invited you, I'll believe you're a halfway-decent person."

"A whole-way decent person. Now, tell me your *real* name."

"Lola. I didn't lie about that."

"Your *full* name." His dark eyes study me.

"Why?"

He shrugs. "Just curious."

"What makes you think I'd give you my full name when I wouldn't give you my number?"

"Good point." He snaps his fingers. "I wouldn't believe you anyway."

"It's Lola Delgado." I suddenly feel the urge to prove him wrong. "Exactly what I told you at the bar. I'm not a liar."

He eyes me skeptically. "You gave me the wrong number."

"Believe me or don't. I don't care either way."

"It's just hard to trust the Princess of Darkness."

"Is Silas *your* real name?"

"Sure is. You see, I'm an honest person."

Georgia laughs. "I think this guy might actually give Lola a run for her money. That's a first."

"You know ..." Silas says, obnoxiously smiling while ignoring everyone else—even Noah zooming around the yard, his arms in the air, proclaiming to be an airplane. "If your goal is to make your ex jealous, I have better ways of doing so."

"Perfect!" I exclaim with overemphasized enthusiasm. "Let me give you his address. I forgot my favorite sweater there and would love to get it back. It's black ... super cute. Would you mind grabbing it for me? It was pretty expensive."

"Black sweater. Got it. Anything else? Your anger management books? Nice pills? A way to remove the stick up your ass?"

Oh, wow, he definitely deserves a busted kneecap.

As bad as it sounds, arguing with him is fun. It's nice to talk to someone with a similar sense of humor.

I rest my elbows on the arms of the chair. "If it makes you feel any better, my ex called and yelled at me."

"Sweetheart, I don't give two fucks about your ex. He probably deserved it. You should've just pulled that game on another guy and given me the real one because I'm much more deserving."

"I'm not sleeping with you … if that's what you think you're *deserving* of."

He snorts. "My wanting to sleep with you and the offer to do so are gone. Knowing you, you'd go all praying mantis on me and bite my head off afterward … or Lorena Bobbitt me."

CHAPTER THREE

Silas

"FOOD IS READY!" Cohen shouts, interrupting my discussion with Lola.

My stomach growls, but I couldn't give two shits about a cheeseburger. I'd rather keep talking to Lola and learn the hints she provides about herself between the sarcasm and insults. I've never had so much interest in someone before. It scares yet excites me that for the first time in years, that sense of craving to know someone has returned.

If Lola hadn't attended, I'm not sure I would've come today. Even though I have endless *acquaintances*, I don't have many people I consider good friends. I keep people at a distance, which usually surprises others because I'm a jokester and easy to talk to.

Lola and I are the last people to rise and make our way to the picnic table covered with food—burgers, hot dogs, chips, a large chopped salad, and desserts out the ass. Lola goes first, placing a burger onto her plate—no bun and instead wrapped in lettuce. She grabs a bag of barbecue chips and scoops a beer from the cooler. I do the same, copying her selections but choose a water instead of beer.

Georgia snorts when she glances from Lola's plate to mine. "I see the both of you are current bread haters."

Lola peeks at my plate and blows out a noisy breath. "Really?"

"I wondered why you were copying my meal." I smirk before bringing the burger to my lips and biting off a chunk.

She rolls her eyes and reaches toward my plate.

Uncertain of her next move, I swiftly slide it out of her reach. "Nuh-uh. I don't trust you around my food."

She rolls those wide brown eyes. "Oh God, are you going to make a comment like that every time we're around each other?"

"Are you saying we'll see each other again? An invite? Do I get to go to your birthday party?"

"As long as you bring an amazing gift."

"Noted. When is your birthday?"

"June twenty-third. The best day of the year."

I drop my burger, the fear of that one bite making its way back up my stomach, and a chill runs through me.

"What?" She blinks, cocking her head. "Is that your birthday too?"

"Nah." I shake my head while also hoping to shake away the memories. I clear my throat before continuing, "I tend to steer clear of Cancers. They're usually trouble."

"Look at you, a man who knows his horoscopes."

I nod, hating that while it's a good day for her, it's fucking tainted for me.

Maybe that's a sign Lola isn't the best person to be around.

All she'd be is a reminder of my past.

"Dad! My hot dog is all gone!" Noah yells from the kiddie table inches from us, intruding my grim thoughts. "Time for a yummy cupcake!"

"Really?" Cohen replies, staring at the ground.

I follow Cohen's gaze and see Noah's hot dog, now covered with grass, next to the table.

"He technically isn't lying," Georgia says.

"No, he is lying," Cohen says, his voice stern and parent-like. "What did I tell you about fibbing, Noah?"

"That it'll make my tongue fall out," Noah replies with a frown before sticking out his tongue. His eyes grow wide. "Oh no! Is it going to fall out? I can't eat any cupcakes then!"

Lola shifts in her chair to look at Noah. "You get three lies before it does. So, you'd better choose them wisely."

"Really, Lola?" Cohen asks.

"What?" She shrugs. "The kid is going to know *you're* lying if it doesn't fall out now. I'm actually saving your ass."

"Aunt Lola said ass!" Noah says, pointing at her.

"Listen, kid, I was just sticking up for you," Lola replies before dramatically staring up at the sky. "God, take the boy's tongue away."

Noah smacks his hand over his mouth. "No!"

Cohen stands. "I'm going to make you another hot dog. You eat it or no cupcakes for a week."

"Fine," Noah mutters, crossing his arms and pouting.

"Cancers also have a potty mouth," I whisper to Lola, leaning into her. "I wonder what else that mouth does."

"Talks shit." She grabs a chip and nibbles at the edge of it. "Eats guys like you for breakfast."

My thoughts of her birthday crumble as we return to our game of jest.

"Looks like no cupcakes for you either, liar." I smirk. "Are you going to return the question and ask what my mouth does?"

She grins wildly. "Fails to give women orgasms?"

I slide my finger over my bottom lip. "Too bad for you, you'll never get the luxury of finding that out."

"And too bad for you, you'll never get the luxury of going anywhere near my vagina."

"I didn't know demons had vaginas."

Her smile doesn't falter. It only grows.

"You two do know my kid repeats everything he hears?" Cohen interjects, spoiling our fun. "The less he hears *the word,* the better."

It seems anytime Lola and I get wrapped up in conversation, everyone around us fades.

Relaxing into my chair, I tune in to the surrounding exchanges to learn about everyone. I shut my eyes, fighting away recollections of when I had something similar. Maybe this is what I need—friendship again. I told myself I didn't deserve it, but this group makes me reconsider that punishment I set upon myself.

———

"ARE you going to give me your real number yet?" I ask Lola as we eat birthday cupcakes. "Or will it be your priest's … therapist's … attorney's? I'm almost certain you have all three on speed dial."

I don't want her number to hook up with her now. I want it because A.) it won't make me feel like too much of a schmuck, and B.) I want to see her again.

Lola laughs, wiping frosting from the side of her lip. "I can provide you with all three if you'd like?"

I lick my finger before reaching out and sweeping the tip over the frosting she missed. She sucks in a breath, and I grin, proud of myself for obtaining that reaction from her. When I pull away, she snatches her drink and chugs it as if wanting to wash away the response her body gave me.

"Are you still in love with your ex?" I ask.

"Am I in love with a cheating prick? That'd be a negative." She grins. "I just enjoy a good revenge and need a little entertainment for the rainy days."

"How about you let me be the entertainment on those rainy days?"

"Fine. You give me *your* number, and when I have a rainy day, I'll *think* about calling. But I'll most likely depend on Netflix."

When she pulls out her phone, clad in a bright neon-green case, I beam while reciting numbers.

"Call. Don't text." I grin and can't wait until she calls because she'll be the one getting the surprise this time.

CHAPTER FOUR

Lola

"NOW THAT BUSINESS is taken care of, when are you free for me to take you out?"

I deliver the generic smile I regularly do when this happens. "It's against company policy to date clients."

The man grins, unfazed by my response—unsurprisingly—and runs a hand down his expensive black suit. He's a guy who thinks the rules don't apply to him even though I'm sure he has a similar policy at his company.

Vince Billings owns the largest chain of liquor stores in Iowa and has ordered his liquor from 21st Amendment—my family's business—for years. I acquired their account last year. Initially, I worked with his son, who is my age, but then Vince came to the office one day and saw me. He immediately switched the contact information to himself.

Vince is nice—don't get me wrong—and good-looking for a man my father's age. Other than him asking me out, he hasn't given off any creep vibes. His invitation would thrill most women.

But me? I vowed never to date a client.

Or a man in power, like him, who sees rules as speed bumps, not roadblocks.

My grandfather, Robert Delgado, founded 21st Amendment

decades ago. It's now a wholesale liquor distribution company whose clientele spans over fifteen states. My father, Robert Delgado II, was promoted to president ten years ago, and soon, he'll pass the company down to my brother, Robby, and me.

Growing up around the business, I've witnessed men with authority have no problem breaking marriage vows for other lovers.

I guess my distrust started when I was sixteen, newly licensed, and skipped school to surprise my father at his office. His secretary attempting to stop me should have been a sign to abort mission. Instead, I was the one surprised when I burst into his office and found a woman half his age blowing him. Not only did I want to acid-wash my eyes, but I was also furious. His immediate response was to push her to the floor, buckle his pants, and bribe me to keep it a secret. I got a new Audi … and then tattled to my mother the next day.

That was when our family relocated from the city to a small Iowa town an hour away. My mother saw Anchor Ridge, Iowa, as a fresh start and a way to restrain my father from cheating. Her grand plan failed.

My father was caught with another mistress not too long after—not by me, thank God. My mother divorced him, and I refused to speak to him for six months. After forced therapy together, I understood the divorce was for the best. They were happier apart, and the reality is, some people aren't made for marriage.

Now, my mother is happily married to a faithful man, and my father's still unhappily chasing his next screw. So, I blame him, along with the few fuckboys I've attempted to date, for ruining my trust in the male species.

Vince laughs, shoving his hands into his pockets. "I spend enough money with 21st Amendment for them to overlook that. Trust me."

I shyly smile, hoping to appear almost clueless. "I don't want to lose my job."

My father wouldn't fire me, but if I start dating clients who share the same birth year as him, he'd question whether I was responsible enough to run 21st Amendment when he retires. With all his affairs, not one has been with someone involved in the company. He's not a fan of mixing business with pleasure.

Vince plays with a bottle of a new and overpriced tequila that's all the rage with millennials. "How about this? If you lose your job, I'll match your salary without you even lifting a finger."

No, thank you on the sugar-daddy offer.

I check my watch. "Oh shoot, I'm running late for my next appointment."

He chuckles. "Ah, I get the hint, Lola."

I stay quiet.

He motions toward the table. "The same time in two weeks?"

"I'll schedule you in."

"Give me more of these products. Campus liquor stores sell this trendy shit like it's candy. The coeds see it on social media and will pay anything to post a selfie with it."

"Will do." I salute him. "I'll make a list and have it ready."

"You're the best. And let me know if you change your mind and want to go to dinner … a movie … hell, I'll even take you on a vacation if you want."

"I'll keep that in mind."

———

THE FIRST THING I do when I get home from work is take off my heels. As much as I love my black Jimmy Choos, they're a bitch to stand in all day.

But with heels comes power.

With power comes higher sales.

Some say I had it easy.

That nepotism gave me my position.

Yes, I got my job because my family owns the company, but I've also proven my worth there. My sales numbers exceed others every month. I don't sit in the office and call potential clients. No, I go to businesses and convince them why we're the distributor for them. Then when I acquire the customer, I upsell them.

It also helps that most of my clients are men—liquor store, bar, and club owners. I don't mind doing a little flirting to get them to buy an eighty-dollar bottle of vodka instead of a twenty.

All's fair in the love of sales and marketing.

I trek to my bedroom, change into sweats and a tee, and unlock my phone to order takeout. Just as I'm opening the app, my phone rings.

Georgia.

"Hey, babe," I answer at the same time my stomach growls.

"You. Me. Grace. Drinks tonight."

"It's not girls' night."

We have a weekly mandatory girls' night.

"Yeah … and? We don't only get together on girls' nights."

"I know." I yawn. "I changed into comfy clothes and was about to order food and call it a night."

"Lame," she sings out. "Let's go out. Eat bad food. Then we can call it a night."

"Fine," I groan. "But I'm not dressing up, so pick somewhere chill."

"That makes two of us. Wear sweats. Wear jeans. Wear a onesie. I'll pick you up. Drinks and dinner are on me."

I change into leggings and a sweatshirt, throw my hair into a ponytail, and wait for Georgia to pick me up.

Georgia and Grace have been my best friends since I moved to Anchor Ridge in high school. I was the new girl at their school. We met at a party, where I witnessed Grace turn a guy down. He gave her a hard time, so I stood up for her. After that, we became inseparable, forming our best-friend trio. I don't know what I'd do without them.

We come from different backgrounds, and our personalities are diverse, but I could never see myself without them in my life. I'm private yet mouthy and sarcastic while Georgia is in your face and loud. Grace is quiet, soft-spoken, the girl-next-door type. Our differences balance each other out.

———

"SERIOUSLY?" I ask when Georgia pulls into Luna Bar's parking lot.

She whips into a space, shifts the car into park, and peers over at me. "What?"

I've never had an issue with Luna Bar. We've hung out in what I'd consider the mid-grade bar a few times. Cohen always discounts our food and liquor, and there's a sense of security with him watching over us. But after the Silas situation, I'm not sure how seeing him will be. Since he works at Luna, I should've thought twice before giving him a fake number. After our conversation the other day, there's no doubt he'll give me shit if he's working tonight.

I hold back the urge to ask Georgia if he is. She'll think I'm interested.

"Oh, nothing," I mutter. "I just thought we'd mix it up tonight."

"You said casual, and this is pretty casual."

Fingers crossed that Silas isn't working tonight.

Too bad, deep down, I'm secretly hoping he is.

CHAPTER FIVE

Silas

I GRIN cheesier than I should when Lola plops down on a stool at the bar. Like last time, I ignore customers and head directly to her. "Aw, babe. You came to see your boy."

Screw tips.

I'd rather hang out with her.

The desire to sleep with her is now off the table. I want to keep it strictly platonic. Not only do I not want her to hate me, but I'm also a little scared of her being around my dick. She might chop it off or some shit.

Thou shall not risk your manhood for crazy chicks, even if you think they'd be an amazing lay.

Grace and Georgia take the seats on each side of her. They were cool at the barbecue, much nicer than Name Swapper. Grace is a bit shy, and her striped dress fits her personality. Georgia is quite the smart-ass but not as evil as Lola and reminds me of a damn flower child every time I see her.

But I have no desire toward them—only Lola. I guess evil is my type. I'd be the first to die in a horror movie. I'd go straight to the scrial killer if she had dark hair, a glare that I found sexy as fuck, and a body that put an hourglass to shame.

That excitement rises at the realization she's sitting on my side of the bar, not Cohen's. Technically, there aren't any available stools on Cohen's side, but I won't allow that detail to ruin my Lola high. I'd bet tonight's tips that she could ask any dude to give up his stool for her, and he would.

She laughs at my greeting. "You wish."

I nod toward her messy ponytail and casual outfit. "I see you dressed up for the occasion too."

That comment results in her flipping me off.

The night we met, she was in a short black dress.

She wore black shorts, a crop top, and wedges at the barbecue.

And tonight, even in her baggy sweatshirt and tangled hair, she's just as gorgeous.

I motion toward Cohen, who's busy shaking a martini. "Why are you not sitting over there then?"

"Faster drinks. We figured fewer people would be on this side of the bar." She bites into the corner of her plump lip. "Word is, you make watered-down margaritas, and Noah could mix up better drinks than you. I'm steering clear of that, and I'll have a simple glass of wine. Surely, you can't mess that up."

"An order of hot wings and onion rings for each of us too," Georgia adds, draping her purse along the back of her stool. "We're starving, and Lola gets meaner when she's hungry. You've been forewarned."

"First off," I say, pointing at Lola, "I'm frightened of a meaner version of you. Second, even though I've concluded that you three are monsters, I will not allow wings and onion rings to be served alongside wine." I shudder at the horrific combination. "Wings and onion rings go well with margaritas. I'll prove your drink slander wrong."

Lola shrugs. "Fine, but don't let us down."

"I've never been known to let a woman down." I wink.

Georgia scoffs, "Pickup lines that lame won't work on her. Do better than that. Assholes are Lola's kink."

Grace nods in agreement.

"Yep," Lola says. "Cutesy isn't my thing."

I smirk. "Lucky for you, I'm not cutesy, sweetheart."

"Sweetheart is a cutesy sentiment," she fires back.

"Fine, I'll make your pain-in-the-ass self a drink. How's that for cutesy?"

"Doing better."

I walk away to start their drinks. It's a weeknight, so we're slower. Slower means fewer tips but more time to bullshit with Lola.

You can't have the best of both worlds.

I use every skill I learned during bartending school to make their margaritas and spend more time on them than I should. Hell, I didn't try this hard when I made last year's Super Bowl MVP a drink.

There are a few secrets to creating the perfect margarita: chill the glass for five minutes, use fresh lime juice—none of that imitation shit —and always add top-shelf silver tequila. To spruce it up, I add strawberry, grapefruit, and basil.

Pride rolls through me as I hand them over, giving Lola hers first. I stand in anticipation, waiting for her to taste it.

She takes a slow sip, shuts one eye as if in deep concentration, and then takes another. Licking her lips, she says, "Not too bad."

"Not too bad?" I make a *chef's kiss* gesture. "It's perfection."

"Aw," Lola says mockingly, her eyes meeting mine in amusement. "Does that upset your ego?"

"It does actually because there are two things I'm known for—my drinks and making women come back for more."

She scrunches up her face. "Cheesy and cutesy. Ew."

I chuckle, facing my palms toward her. "Sorry, sorry."

"Dude, she isn't going to sleep with you!" an overweight and balding man across the bar shouts. "We need another round, *and* my wife is up for a threesome if you want to get laid."

Grace, who just took her first drink of my delicious margarita, spits it out at the man's remark. "Did he really say that?"

Lola snorts, jerking her head toward the man, now joined by his thin, red-haired wife, and they're making out. "If you can't sleep with me, might as well bang a middle-aged couple."

"Piss off," I grumble. "That just shows how many people want me." I hook a thumb toward myself.

"A man wants to watch you fuck his wife." She chews on the tip of her red nail, hiding a smile. "That won't make me jealous."

"Eh, I'm declining their offer, *but* if you ever reconcile with Callum, I'm up for it. He can watch the two of us together."

She dramatically gags. "You just stated two things that will never happen."

"Your loss, Name Swapper." I slap the bar. "Now, I'll be back to hear you admit that's the best drink you've ever had. Onion rings and wings, coming right up."

———

"JUST SAY YOU CAN'T GO," Georgia tells Lola. "Blame it on cramps. The flu. The universe is in retrograde."

I pause mid-pour, ready to eavesdrop on my next Lola conversation. It seems to be a new hobby of mine. Not one of the conversations I've snooped on of hers has been boring. I help a customer, peek a glance at Lola, pour a drink, sneak a stare at Lola. She coincides with every job duty tonight.

They've devoured their food, and for someone only mildly impressed with my margarita, Lola sure had no problem ordering another round.

Lola groans. "He'll make some speech about being present if I want to be in charge someday." She knocks back the remainder of her margarita.

Grace sighs, sliding her straw in and out of her glass. "Let's brainstorm on excuses for you to bail."

"The only excuses I have are death or hospitalization." Lola throws her head back before jerking it up suddenly, as if a thought hit her. She playfully smacks Grace's shoulder. "Break my foot. Use the stool."

"What?" Grace gapes at her. "You want me to cause bodily harm to get you out of a work social?"

Georgia shakes her head. "That wouldn't work. He'd tell her to grab crutches and not be late."

Deciding it's my time to shine, I finish the drink I was making, pass it to the customer, and walk to them. "What are you trying to dodge?"

"Nothing," Lola answers, waving me away.

I stay put. "I'm the king of dodging shit." I press a hand to my chest. "Tell me what it is, and I'll give you an escape plan."

Lola half-shrugs. "Just some stupid work thing."

I crack a smile. "I'm sure being the Princess of Darkness is a hard job."

She snatches her napkin and tosses it at me. "Funny."

"What's the deal?" Propping my elbows onto the bar, I lean into her space. "Why don't you want to go? Do they make you grow horns during the initiation into hell? I'd probably want to skip out on that day too."

She grins, half-shrugging. "If that were the case, I'd go so that I could find a demon to haunt you."

"Please make sure she's hot." Tingles shoot up my neck as I move in closer, taking in the sweet smell of her perfume. It's sexy and bold, just like her. "What's so bad about it?"

"It always ends up being a big couples thing." Lola frowns before slapping both of her friends' arms. "And these two have other plans because they're bad friends at the moment."

"Call Callum," I suggest. "You have his number memorized … or I can do it for you? We've chatted before. We'll exchange Lola horror stories."

"He'll be there," Lola says. "And most likely with some random date he found the night before."

"Whoa, you work with your ex?" I guess I'm the only one with the *don't shit where you eat* rule.

Lola massages her temples. "Unfortunately."

"Rookie mistake, Lola." I shake my head as if I were her coach and she just lost a game. "Rookie mistake."

She scowls at me. "Like you haven't slept with anyone you work with."

Just like she wants to dodge that event, I avoid that comment and don't answer.

I slide my elbows off the bar and stand straight. "I'll go with you. I'll be your date."

Lola blinks at me. "What?"

I'm as surprised as she is at my date offer. I'm not a man who meets coworkers, families, friends, any of that shit. It's not like I'd ever see them again, so it's pointless.

Georgia perks up in excitement as if she were five and it was Christmas. "That would stick it to Callum."

I snap my fingers, unsure of why I'm not telling them I was only kidding. "Awesome point."

Lola eyes me suspiciously.

My gaze doesn't leave hers. "I make for a great fake date, I promise."

"Is this something you've done before?" Lola clips a loose strand of hair behind her ear while eyeing me in uncertainty. "You seem pretty confident in yourself."

"I usually charge for my services"—I pause and fake bow—"but for you, I'll make an exception."

She stares at me deep as if attempting to read my mind. "You're crazy."

"Just offering my services. Take it or leave it. It's up to you." I smirk at her and walk away.

CHAPTER SIX

Lola

I'M CONSIDERING HAVING a man pretend to be my boyfriend.

What is wrong with me?

A responsible adult would suck it up and go solo, but I've never been a fan of my father's work events. And it's not that I can't get a date. I don't want one.

Dating apps, Snapchat, and website after website offering ninety-day trials to find your perfect match or your money back have made dating a nightmare. If Silas is comfortable with playing pretend boyfriend, why not? He's fun, and he won't try to date me afterward.

I nearly fell off my stool when he suggested the idea. After taming my shock, I pulled myself together and played it cool. In the back of my mind, I knew I'd take him up on his offer.

I pick up my phone to text him but remember what he told me.

Call. Don't text.

Giving me a taste of my own medicine.

It rings twice before a boasting voice answers, "Anger Management Hotline. How may I assist you today?"

I'm quiet for a moment, replaying the words in my mind.

"Hello?" the man says. "Is someone there, or are you in the process of sucker punching a guy, breaking a poor man's heart, or kicking puppies?"

I laugh. "Is that the best you've got?"

Props to Silas for attempting to alter his voice, but there's no erasing the cockiness that bleeds through it.

"What was that?" he asks, unfazed by my calling him out. "You need to schedule another appointment since you canceled your last one to attend your weekly visit to the underworld?"

"First off, I'd kick *you* before I ever kicked a puppy."

He breaks character, his tone returning to normal. "Good to know you'd protect an animal over me."

"You're not as cute. Sorry, not sorry."

"There you go, battering another heart."

"Keep talking shit, and I'll batter your balls next." I sit down on one of the overpriced leather dining room chairs I purchased with my first bonus check, rip off my strawberry yogurt lid, and shove a bite into my mouth.

"I take it you're calling to ask me out on an apology date? *Or* is this you requesting me to be your eye candy to your work event?"

I can imagine the smug expression on his face. "Eye candy? More like desperation candy. You're the Peeps of sweets."

"Keep telling yourself that, sweetheart. *And* Peeps is the number one–selling Easter candy, by the way."

"I'm not even going to waste my time fact-checking that because Peeps could grant immortality with just one taste, and I still wouldn't eat them." I'm mid-bite when something dawns on me. "Wait. How did you know I was calling? I never gave you my real number."

"Thank you for providing the reminder that you gave me some schmuck's number, who you kicked to the curb, instead of yours."

"You're welcome." I crack a smile before licking my spoon clean. "I figured you needed some entertainment."

"Cohen gave me your number."

I move the phone from one ear to the other. "That little shit."

"Technically, he's a half-shit. He only gave me the first three numbers and then told me it was my job to figure out the rest. When you called, the first three matched up, and I took a guess that it was you."

"What if it wasn't me?"

"I guess I'd have had to spend my day talking someone through an anger issue. I think I have a soothing voice. Don't you agree?"

"Nope. The cockiness triggers a migraine with me every time."

"You know what's good for migraines?"

"Not talking to you?"

"Orgasms." He emphasizes each syllable of that word. "That is an area of expertise I excel in. They used to call me Orgasm Rx."

I cover my face and hold in a laugh. "I'm seriously reconsidering this whole fake-date idea."

"When and where do I need to pick you up?" He clicks his tongue against the roof of his mouth. "Is there a certain route I need to take to the gateways of hell?"

"I think you mispronounced *heaven.*"

"And I think you mispronounced, *Thank you, Silas. I'm so happy you'll bless me with your time and presence.*"

I finish my yogurt, toss the empty container into the trash, and stroll into my living room. "Thank you, Silas. I'm writing an editorial the next day on what it's like to go out with a dude with an ego the size of the ocean. I appreciate you giving me plenty of material to work with."

"Aw." He chuckles. "My little number-changing rebel is writing a diary entry about me."

I scoff, "You wish."

"On the plus side, it'll give me another opportunity to talk to Callum. I have a list of things to ask him. The first being, how can I avoid dying when I'm around you?"

"That's it. I'm bailing."

"Nah, we have a hot date. Send me the details and your address, and I'll see you then. Catch you later, Princess of Darkness."

He ends the call.

What did I get myself into?

CHAPTER SEVEN

Silas

FAKING a relationship isn't a hobby of mine.

I've never done it.

I'm not sure how I got myself into this mess.

Lola.

That's how.

I'm not a relationship guy.

I tried it once, and it decayed the life I'd always known.

It ruined others' lives too.

All because I thought I knew what love was, thought I could pull off some *Romeo and Juliet* shit. Over the years, I've grown up and learned that love is merely an infatuation with someone you want. Sometimes, that infatuation can survive marriage, children, and the mundane of life. Others see love as a shiny, new toy, but then the desire slowly wears off. They cheat and fall out of love, and everyone around you suffers. Then it's off to the next obsession. Love is a fantasy that I want nothing to do with.

Lola and I are almost strangers, and I have no idea why the fake-date idea popped into my head. I allowed it to drop to my lips and spill from them. She'd pulled me into her web from the moment I overheard her and her fellow psychos talk about the demise of their ex-boyfriends.

GPS announces I've arrived at my location, and I park my car in front of the one-story townhome with a manicured lawn. The bright red door is fitting for the owner, but I expected a black home that looked straight out of a horror movie.

I hesitate before stepping out of my Audi, unsure if I should text her and say I'm here. Or if I should walk to the door, date-style … even though today is sure as fuck not a date.

I enjoy out-of-the-box shit like this. Call it a field trip, if you will.

"Ah, fuck it," I grumble.

It's Lola I'm picking up. She won't assume it's a date if I go to her door. I'm also curious what the inside of her place looks like. Waiting until a spandex shorts–wearing woman passes us with her petite, dressed-up dog, I head toward the front door, passing a black Porsche on the way up the drive. My knuckles meet the red paint on her door when I knock, and I take a step back, waiting for her to answer.

"Damn, you look hot," I say when the door swings open and Lola stands in front of me.

A black dress hugs her hourglass shape, and her black heels are the tallest I've seen her sport. She texted me last night to remind me of the dress code, so I pulled out the suit I'd worn only a few times from the back of my closet.

I step forward and walk in, not waiting for an invite.

"Come on in," she grumbles, moving to the side to allow me better access.

The open floor plan of her home provides me with a hint of Lola's life—the plush white couch that few would dare to have in their home, for fear of staining. Three red paintings hangon the living room wall. The place is so clean that it looks almost unlived in.

I slip my hands into the pockets of my black pants. "You ready to do this?"

She shoves her phone into her bag. "Nope."

"We can ditch and do something better?"

"I wish," she groans, her shoulders slumping. "My father would kill me."

"Father?" I cock my head. "I thought this was a work event?"

Meeting the parents isn't what I expected tonight. If I'd known that was the case, I'd have called in sick to tonight's festivities. Acting like her boyfriend around her coworkers is one thing, but around her family? Nah, that produces more difficulty and effort. I'm great at pretending. I've done it nearly the past decade of my life, but it's not easy to act like you're dating a woman without doing the shit couples do—kiss, hold hands, look at each other with stars in your eyes. Lola would probably castrate me if I tried to kiss her.

"My father works at the company." She snatches her keys from the hook hanging on the wall.

"Works at the company … or *owns* the company?" I'm uncertain why this thought creeps into my mind. Maybe because there's no way an entry-level employee could afford this home and the car sitting in the driveway.

"Um … owns."

"What company?"

"It's 21st Amendment."

"The alcohol distribution company?"

"The one and only."

Impressive.

Anyone involved in the liquor business knows 21st Amendment is one of the best you can go with. They supply alcohol for the biggest clubs, liquor stores, and bars in the state.

"What do you do there?"

"Sales."

I smile, mentally picturing her showing off her products. Hell, if she came to Luna Bar and I oversaw orders, I'd purchase whatever she told me to.

She sighs. "You ready to play the lying game?"

"Definitely, but we need to get our stories straight on the way. It's necessary to know how evil my date is."

She holds up a finger. "Fake date."

"Fake date." I nod.

We leave her house, silently walking side by side, and her heels make a *click-click* against the pavement. She doesn't argue about me driving. The sweet smell of her perfume overtakes the evergreen air freshener hanging from my rearview mirror.

I plug the address into my GPS and hit her with questions as soon as I shift the car into drive. "Favorite food?"

Lola buckles her seat belt and relaxes into the seat. "This is a business party. Why do you need to know my favorite food?"

"What if I'm asked personal questions?" I tap my fingers along the steering wheel. "You want me to tell them I only fuck you on the regular but know nothing about you?"

She shrugs. "Sounds like a good plan to me."

"Cool." I turn at a light and merge with traffic. "I can't wait to tell your father that." I cast a quick glance at her, raising a brow. "Should I go into explicit detail … try to sell him on the idea that I fuck your brains out?"

"Funny." She stretches out her legs and moves her head side to side as if stretching it too. "Um … you can say hummus if you're asked?"

"Bullshit. No one's favorite food is fucking hummus. Try again, Satan. I'd have pictured your response to be more along the lines of *the broken hearts of men* or *the poisonous apple given to Adam.*"

She crosses her arms, unaware that it accentuates her cleavage, and I lick my lips. "I'll retract that statement and say it's your head if you keep talking shit because I'm going to bite it off."

"Kinky … I like it."

She snorts. "If you say hummus, my father will believe you."

"If I say hummus, your father will never believe I've wined and dined you, making me a shit boyfriend. Now, hit me with something believable." I'm not about to pretend to be a bad boyfriend. I want to be the best damn fake boyfriend ever.

"Strawberry cheesecake."

"That's more like it."

"Glad my favorite food is now more to your liking." Her response bleeds sarcasm.

As much as I want to pay her a glance, I keep my eyes on the road. Responsible driver over here. "You going to ask what mine is?"

"Nope. I figured I'd make it up as we went."

"So … if someone asks you that, what will you say?"

"Hummus," she quips with no delay.

"Oh, fuck off," I say around a laugh.

She returns the laugh while pulling a tube of lipstick from her Louis Vuitton bag. "You asked."

"All right, all right. Favorite sex position." I hope she doesn't shove my face into the steering wheel for that question, but messing with her is fun. A pretend boyfriend doesn't need to know that tidbit of information.

She doesn't shove my face into the steering wheel, but she does push my shoulder. "None of your business."

"Ah, that's my favorite too. It really hits the G-spot. Girls crave it."

Pulling down the visor, she refreshes her lipstick and smacks her lips together when she's finished. "You wouldn't know what a G-spot was if it smacked you in the face."

"Your type of man?"

"One who doesn't talk as much as you."

"Hey now." I reach out and tap her thigh. "Be nice to the guy doing you a favor. Otherwise, we can call Callum. You two can make up, and I'll drive home."

"Ugh, fine," she groans. "I will provide all the intel you need to my life. I'm just nervous to see him."

"You still have feelings for him?" I frown, hating the idea of that.

"No, I'm nervous because I want to kick him in the balls, and my father would kill me for assaulting one of his employees." She sighs and stares straight ahead. "And for some reason, I want to know why he cheated."

She's nearing the line of vulnerability with me, and I don't want to run for the hills. I want to drag more of it out of her.

"He did it because he's a cheating bastard who can't keep it in his pants," I state matter-of-factly. "It had everything to do with him and nothing to do with you."

She sends me a skeptical glance. "How are you so certain?"

I grip the steering wheel. "Because any man in his right mind would be stupid to betray your trust, to play a dangerous game that'd leave him without you. Callum is an idiot. That's why he did what he did. Sometimes, it takes men losing something to realize they made a mistake."

She stares at me, impressed. "Look at you, all wise guy. Who would've thought you could come up with something like that?"

"That's why we're playing the *get to know you* game, Name Swapper. You'll find out I'm cool as hell and a better man than the one who played you."

"Shockingly, I'm starting to like this Silas you're giving me."

I grin at the compliment as if it were the equivalent of hitting the lottery. "Wait until I play the boyfriend role. You'll fucking love me."

———

VALET PARKING IS a bonus we don't talk about enough. Probably because it's always a lazy and unnecessary perk. You don't have to search for a spot or walk whatever distance to your destination.

A kid I went to school with argued with a man over a parking spot once. The fight escalated, and my classmate shot the man. He's now serving time for attempted murder. Not only did he lose his spot but his dinner reservation was also canceled.

He sacrificed freedom and a filet over a parking spot.

Fucking idiot.

I toss my keys to the valet and dash to Lola's side to beat the valet from opening her door. Tonight's job is to be the chivalrous and well-mannered boyfriend. She stands, running her hands down her dress, and I hold my elbow toward her. She peers at me in surprise before slipping her arm around it, and we walk into the century-old building.

Tonight's event is being held at Lady Emporium, a deserted library that the state had planned to tear down until a developer stepped in and purchased the rickety building. He remodeled, loaded cash into it, and now, people pay top dollar to hold their parties, weddings, and proms there.

I've bartended and attended events at Lady Emporium, but there's always something new to appreciate here. The high ceilings, crystal chandeliers dangling from them, and expensive marble beneath our feet. The ballroom is crowded with people, huddled in their little cliques, extending every age range.

No wonder Lola didn't want to come solo.

"Lola." A man stands in front of us, blocking our path, and eyes Lola with deep regret. He's tall, slender, and dressed in a stiff suit.

Lola clears her throat and tightens her elbow hold on me. "Callum."

Ah, so this is the lovely Callum.

Had she given it a few minutes before saying his name, I might've picked up on the familiarity of his voice.

His gaze cuts to me before snapping back to her—no doubt an attempt to act like I'm not a threat to him. *Act* being the key word. I know when a man is jealous of another. Even though I shouldn't be, I'm the same with Lola. I can only imagine how territorial I'd turn if we slept together, dated, and then I lost her.

His lips tighten. "We need to talk."

"Hard pass," Lola replies.

"Come on." He presses his hands into a pleading gesture. "You owe me that."

I arch a brow and hold back the urge to tell him she doesn't owe him shit. But I know Lola, and she has a spine as strong as a diamond. The revenge stories I've heard from her prove she won't need any help with putting Callum in his place.

"I don't owe you a goddamn thing." Her voice is powerful and firm as if she were presenting a million-dollar deal. "You lost the right to talk to me when you cheated."

"Please," he begs. "Let me explain."

"No," is her only response.

His eyes widen at the realization she won't fall into the trap of his ways, so he turns his attention my way. "I see you've already replaced me, huh? You didn't seem like the type who'd automatically jump into another man's bed."

And as strong as Lola is, now's my time to step in.

"Whoa," I say, breaking our connection to pull Lola slightly behind me. "Don't talk to her like that."

He's not helping me be the perfect fake boyfriend. If we end up fighting within five minutes of arriving, that'd be the ultimate fail.

Callum thrusts out his chest so hard that it's almost comical. "Or what?"

Lola was smart for leaving this idiot. She's just as smart when she cups my elbow and tugs me back from stepping toward Callum.

"He's wasted," Lola says, "if you can't tell by the smell of his breath. Ignore him, and we'll move on to speaking to someone who isn't an asshole."

"If you don't want to talk here, can we do it another time?" Callum asks, shooting a woman a dirty look when she runs into his shoulder. "We can do coffee, dinner, whatever you want." Desperation fills his voice and face, but I don't feel sorry for him. He chose to cheat and end their relationship.

Lola peers away from him as if she's lost all interest she ever had. "I'm good."

"Why do you give my number to random guys then?" He scrubs his hand over his reddened face. "It's further proof you miss me."

"Or I'm just a spiteful bitch." Lola raises a brow, not even caring that she just referred to herself as a bitch. She takes my hand. "I need to go find my father … you know, *your boss*. He could easily create an excuse to fire you if you kept talking like this to his daughter."

"That's some bullshit," Callum grumbles.

"Don't worry. I won't say anything as long as you leave me alone." Lola turns away, so she's no longer facing him and he's talking to her side. "We're broken up. I'll stop giving your number out. It's over."

"I'll see you around, babe." His voice wavers with the last word.

Lola cracks a smile. "Not if I can help it."

I smirk, jerking my chin up at Callum as we pass him, and squeeze Lola's hand. I ignore people as we make our way through the crowd. "I'm surprised he didn't fire Callum when you broke up."

"He never knew we were dating. I kept it a secret." She comes to a halt. "And you're about to meet the boss."

"How did we meet?" I rush out, realizing we didn't discuss the important details on the drive here.

"Make up something off the top of your head, and I'll agree." She shoots me a quick look. "Don't make it something sexual."

"In front of your father? Gross."

We haven't even reached the ten-minute mark, and I've already met the ex and now the father. I wasn't prepared to be bombarded like this straight from the get-go. Hell, I didn't even know that her father would be present until she told me when I picked her up, and I couldn't bail then.

The man walks with wide steps and approaches us with ease. Lola stands tall, matching his posture, and I understand where she got her perfect one from.

"Lola," he says, a gleam in his eyes when he reaches us.

She breaks away from me to hug him and kiss his cheek.

"You look nice, honey," he says when they part, and then his gaze flashes to me. "And who is this?"

"This is ..." Lola pauses, searching for the correct way to label us.

"Her date," I answer for her, holding out my hand.

He shakes it, his grip strong. "Robert Delgado II."

"Silas Malone. It's nice to meet you, sir."

Lola raises a brow at my saying *sir*.

He smiles. "This is the first time Lola has brought a date. You must be special to her."

"Yes, sir. I think she's falling in love." I cringe when Lola's heel meets my shin.

Robert chuckles at her response. "Come on. We have an incredible lineup of spirits tonight. We'll have a drink and get to know each other."

It takes all my strength not to tell them I have an emergency and need to leave. Since I don't want to embarrass Lola, I push forward and follow them, maneuvering around people holding loud conversations while sipping on champagne and cocktails. Compliments and hellos are thrown to Robert every few minutes.

Robert stops at a four-person table, and just as I pull Lola's chair out for her, a blond woman around Lola's age joins us.

"Hey, honey." Her tone is full of pep—the kind they always give the preppy girls in movies. She runs her hand along Robert's shoulder and then down his arm before enveloping his hand. "I thought you ran off on me."

Robert smacks a kiss to her cheek. "Of course not, baby."

Lola's eyes harden in their direction as she settles into her seat. I run my hand along her shoulder—like what Blondie did to Robert, only not as desperate.

"Hey, Lola," Blondie says in almost a squeal. Her eyes widen when she sees me taking the chair next to Lola. "Who's your friend?"

I wave. "I'm Silas."

The woman presses her hand to her deep cleavage. "I'm Kelli, Robert's girlfriend."

Robert stands proud at the statement—no doubt loving having an attractive and young woman at his side.

Lola settles her elbow onto the table, turns her head, and covers her mouth as if holding words in.

I smile, making sure it's not overly friendly so Lola doesn't kick my ass for it later. "It's nice to meet you." I'd look like a straight prick in front of Robert if I reacted how Lola was and didn't say a word to her.

"You too," Kelli says as Robert pulls out her chair, and they sit.

Robert rubs his hands together. "I have a rare whiskey coming our way."

As if on cue, a server stops at our table with a tray of drinks in crystal glasses. She carefully starts placing the glasses in front of us.

"I'll just have a water," I say, stopping her when she comes to me.

Her gaze pings from me to Robert, clueless on what to do.

Robert shakes his head. "Have one drink with us. I promise it'll be worth it." He holds up his glass. "This is five hundred a bottle."

"I'm driving tonight, and I want to make sure your daughter gets home safe."

I smile at him. If Robert argues, it'll make him look like an asshole now. I used to dread this part when I went out. People would stare at me in shock and throw out question after question about why I didn't drink. I'm a bartender, a regular at clubs, and I fit the image of a party guy.

"It's a relief you worry about my daughter's safety," Robert says, smiling before his eyes meet Lola's. "I like him. How long have you two been dating?"

CHAPTER EIGHT

Lola

THERE ARE two reasons I don't bring men around my father:

I haven't had a boyfriend serious enough for him to meet.

He works too much and has hardly been around since my mother divorced him.

Shock accompanied my father's arrival when he saw Silas. He and my mother have been bringing up marriage more lately as if trying to find out where my future is headed. Now that my father assumes I have a boyfriend, he'll ask about Silas, so I'll have to create a breakup story.

I shift in my seat. "Not long."

"Yeah," Silas says with a nod.

"I'll be back with your water," the server tells Silas.

The night is full of conversation with no quiet gaps at our table. I don't say much, but my father says plenty. Kelli throws in remarks here and there, a smile on her injection-filled lips. I tend to tolerate my father's women, but I'm not a Kelli fan. She mistakenly talked shit about my mother in front of me, and we haven't gotten along since. It's not like she'll last long anyway.

Everyone at the table stared at Silas, dazed, when he declined the whiskey. I had grown up around liquor, and I can taste quality with one sip. Any other bartender would never turn down a whiskey like this. Some would consider it a once-in-a-lifetime opportunity because it's not something you can buy in stores. You have to know someone who knows someone to get it.

I'm thankful that Silas keeps my father entertained with conversation so I don't have to do the job. The smartest thing I did tonight was have him come.

————

"HOW DID I DO TONIGHT, Name Swapper?" Silas asks as we pull out of Lady Emporium's parking lot.

An overplayed song drones in the background of the car. It's after ten o'clock. Later than I wanted to stay and earlier than my father wanted me to leave.

I stretch out my legs and yawn. "Surprisingly, you did a great job. You might want to take up a career in fake dating."

If I were to ever bring a real boyfriend around my father, I'd hope his and Silas's mannerisms and behavior were similar. By the end of the night, my father loved him, the coworkers he introduced Silas to found it easy to chat with him, and Kelli eyed him as if ready to seduce him the moment my father kicked her to the curb.

When I'd answered my door at the beginning of the night, I had been impressed at the view of him standing there. I'd told him to dress somewhat formal, and he had taken my direction seriously. His black suit fit as if God had approved every stitch to its perfection.

"Nah, it's too stressful." He stops at a red light and places his hand over his heart. "I try to live an honest man's life, Lola."

"That's nice to know," I say around another yawn.

We make small talk on the drive back to my house. He asks what it's like, working at 21st Amendment, and I drill him on bartending life.

"Are you not a drinker?" I ask.

He sighs as if this is a regular conversation for him. "Nope."

"If you don't mind me asking, why?"

Saying *if you don't mind me asking* is stupid. I already asked him if he was a drinker. That pretty much is the opening to asking questions. Since I'm a private person, I don't usually dive into people's personal business.

His attention stays on the road. "It's not my thing."

"But you're a bartender," I state like *duh*. "No wonder people say your drinks suck."

That was actually a rumor I made up that night at the bar. Cohen had mentioned Silas was one of the top bartenders at Luna Bar. I just enjoy giving him a hard time about it.

"You, of all people, should know my drinks don't suck." He hits the blinker and turns onto my road. "Drinking is not required of bartenders. We just need to know what mixes well together." He stops in front of my house, shifts the car into park, and unbuckles his seat belt. "I'll walk you in."

I clamp my mouth shut. Even though I want to ask twenty more questions, I can tell he doesn't want to talk about it any longer. I wouldn't want someone I'd only met a few times—fake date or not—to intrude on my life like that.

I dart my arm out, stopping him from opening his door. "You don't have to do that. Tonight wasn't a real date."

He takes my hand, squeezes it, and returns it to my lap. "This fake date is a gentleman, so I'm walking you up. I won't try to make out with you—even if you asked me. You, my favorite devil, are no longer a woman I want to sleep with."

I suck in a breath of rejection and fidget with the chain of my purse. "What do you want to do with me then?"

Why does him saying he no longer wants to sleep with me have my heart thudding dully in my chest?

My stomach clenches as nausea hits me.

"A friend," he clearly states, opening his door. "I want us to be friends." He stops and peers back at me. "I'd love for you to want that too."

"Of course." I force a smile, my eyes meeting his friendly ones. "Friends."

He walks me to my door, and before he leaves, I give him a little wave.

And that short conversation cements my relationship with Silas. My *friendship* with him.

———

RELEASING A DEEP SIGH, I rest my back against the door and drop my purse onto the floor when I walk into my townhome.

I flip on a light and then press my hand to the wall, balancing myself to remove one strappy heel and then the other. Though it's unusual for me to leave stuff around my home—I'm a type A—I step over them and trudge down the hallway toward my bedroom.

I bought the open-concept townhome a year ago. My parents provided the down payment after I graduated from college, but I'm responsible for everything else. The fluffy white carpet feels comforting against my bare feet as I move through the room. The interior is nearly monochrome—mainly black and white with pops of color spread along the home. There's also a lack of patterns—all the pillows, furniture, and décor stick to solid colors.

It's a one-bedroom—what my parents told Robby and me they'd provide each of us until we needed something larger. I think it was their plan to prevent us from having roommates. My father has made it clear that he only sees them as distractions—even though the man apparently doesn't consider throwing events and sipping on expensive alcohol with his flavor of the month isn't.

I step out of my dress when I land in my bedroom and am slipping on a lace teddy when Georgia calls.

"How was the big date?" she asks as soon as I answer.

"It was *not* a date," I reply, pulling down the comforter and fluffing out my pillow.

"Fine. How was your *fake* date?"

"It was fun."

"Is he there with you now?"

"Um, no. Home all alone."

Unfortunately.

Had Silas not made the whole *I want us to be friends* speech, there was a possibility I'd have asked him to come in. Not even for sex, just to hang out for a while longer.

"Did he try to come in for a nightcap?"

"Surprisingly, no." I head toward the bathroom to brush my teeth and do my eighteen-step skincare routine. "He said he no longer wants to sleep with me and instead wants to be my friend."

"Hmm …" She pauses, thinking. "He'd be a nice addition to our friend group. I like him, and Cohen seems to think he's a good guy."

I shrug. "Fine with me."

"Grace has Finn. You'll have Silas. It's time for me to find myself a guy bestie."

"You have your brother."

"Eh, so not the same." She goes quiet for a moment, and her voice lowers. "Noah, buddy, I told you, it's past your bedtime." She sighs. "I have to figure out a way to bribe the kid back to bed. Call me tomorrow, okay? We can do lunch and chat. Love ya."

"Love you too." I end the call after hearing her tell Noah he can have a candy bar if he promises not to tell his dad.

A half hour later, I'm back in my bedroom and plugging my phone into the charger. As I slip into the chilly sheets, my phone beeps with a text.

Silas: I enjoyed our fake date. Good night, my little devil.

Smiling wide, I immediately reply.

Me: Thank you for coming, my little fake date.

His response is just as quick.

Silas: I'd prefer a better nickname than that boring-ass one.

Me: MINE IS THE DEVIL!

Silas: Devil suits you. Fake Date isn't flattering enough for me. We're going to be so much more than that. Brainstorm tonight and let me know in the morning. I just wanted to say good night.

Me: Good night … my soon-to-be nicknamed friend.

Silas: *kissy face emoji*

This is something unexpected.

I didn't think this would happen.

When I got ready for the event tonight, I thought it could go one of three ways.

1. Silas wouldn't show.
2. It'd end up in disaster.
3. He'd try to sleep with me at the end of the night.

None of those happened.

Instead, it only turned into so much more.

It made me want to know more about this man, give him more of me, and have a few more *fake* dates.

I slap a hand over my forehead.

This man might ruin my hard-ass persona I have going on here.

He also might ruin me.

CHAPTER NINE

Silas

Two Years Later

"HEY THERE, BIG SHOT," Lola shouts over the music, pressing her lips to my cheek and stopping at my table. "This place is packed."

I grin, pride beaming through me, and kiss the top of her hair. "The turnout is amazing."

Wrapping my arms around her, I squeeze her side. She's my biggest cheerleader and the support system I never knew I needed. The night we met forever changed my life for the better, and I can't imagine not having her around. It'd be a boring and depressed life without Lola.

Cohen finally got his dream—owning a bar. He and Archer, a guy who worked with us, partnered up to start Twisted Fox—a small-town bar in Anchor Ridge, Iowa. He worked his ass off to get the place ready. The girls helped with the design and decorating. I volunteered to kick off the place with a night to be remembered grand opening.

I enjoy bartending, but I love throwing events more. I told the guys I'd bartend part-time at Twisted Fox, so I could be involved with everyone. They immediately offered Finn the bouncer position, and he gladly accepted.

Twisted Fox might be smaller than what I'm used to, but I put in more work with the opening than I have with large clubs with thousands of partygoers. I have *friends in high places* connections, and it's easy for me to ask influencers to post where they're hanging out for the night. They post, and the people will follow, hoping for their chance to see the influencers and to also hang out where *the cool people* do. Social media is the key to marketing these days.

What was once an old diner has been remodeled. There's a large bar, TVs on every wall, and sports memorabilia Cohen picked up on the days he went to the flea market. It's something he and Noah like to do together.

Lola squeezes my arm. "I'm going to go tell the guys congrats. This is so exciting!"

I raise a brow. "Don't act like you didn't play a large part."

She spent hours and sleepless nights with Grace and Georgia here. That's something I've loved since I slid into being in this group of friends. They are die-hard ride or dies. If you need something, they're there. If someone needs help, they'll spend every minute doing it. It's an entire network of people who you know will always have your back.

"Dude, is that your girlfriend?" Eric, a guy recently drafted into the NBA, asks. His question is directed toward me, but his eyes are on Lola as she makes her way through the crowd, swinging her hips with every step.

"Nah," I reply, shaking my head. "Best friend."

Eric's teammate shakes his head. "How can you be best friends with someone that hot and not want more?"

It's a frequent question sent my way. Lola is gorgeous—exactly what drew me to her. And the more we become friends, the more beautiful she gets to me. Even if she doesn't try, eyes follow her in desire everywhere we go. Just like I made sure the bar's opening was perfect, Lola made sure she looked fucking perfect to celebrate it.

A short dress that flares out at her thighs shows off her toned tan legs. Her black hair is down but clipped back on each side, keeping it out of her eyes.

I rub my chin. "I don't date."

"Not even *her*?" Eric asks, gripping his beer bottle around the neck. "Man, I say that, too, but I'd break that rule in a heartbeat for her."

"If I dated her, I'd fuck it up and lose her." I scrub a hand over my face, the reality of that smacking into me. It's something I remind myself of every day.

Even though I get along with everyone in the group, Lola is my person. We click. We're there for each other anytime it's needed—whether it's taking care of the other when one of us has the flu, being the first one in line when the other has reached a new life achievement, or just having someone at our side. She's the first person I call anytime I have good news.

Always.

That's why Lola is my best friend, and we can never be anything more.

————

"YOU DID IT, GUYS," I say around a yawn.

It's been a successful night. The Twisted Fox grand opening went great. We fucking killed it, and with Cohen and Archer running it, I know the bar will be successful. Everyone is gone, and for the past hour, we've said we need to get the place cleaned up and then go home to get some sleep. But instead, we've been sitting here, bullshitting and having our own private celebration for our friends' achievement.

Cohen has always been the patriarch of our friend group, and Archer recently joined us. Although I don't think it's something he'd planned on doing. He's a loner—prime example: he's behind the bar, doing shit, while we've all been sitting around, talking. The past few months he's worked with us, opening the bar, he and Georgia have bickered like two kids on the playground. Archer is a man who doesn't say much, but most of his words are talking shit to her.

No one knows why they hate each other—well, none of us guys. The girls act like they do, and while Lola and I are close, she refuses to gossip about her friends.

"*We* did it," Cohen corrects. "Twisted Fox wouldn't be here if it wasn't for everyone's help. I appreciate it so much."

Finn smirks, holding up his beer. "Does that mean free alcohol for life?"

"No," Archer grunts. "You can have an employee discount on food, though."

"Always the rude one," Georgia comments, shaking her head.

He shoots her a deep glare, and she shrugs.

Lola leans into me, resting her head on my shoulder. "I love the entertainment they provide."

I slide my fingers through her thick locks. "I have a feeling we're going to get so much more of it too."

"We're a team," Grace says, perched up in her stool. "A family. We'll always have each other's backs."

CHAPTER TEN

Lola

THINGS I'LL DO before getting in another relationship:

Chew leather.

Fight a cobra, blindfolded.

Swallow a dozen wasps.

I slump onto my couch and tug my phone from my jacket pocket. Just as I'm about to text the girls *Code Red*, I stop, remembering they have plans tonight. Georgia has a shift at the boutique, and Grace is at dinner with her parents.

Silas invited me to dinner with him tonight, but I stupidly declined because I had a date. A ridiculous date where the guy took me to a dinner with his friends … and his ex. His ex was a nightmare, making comments and giving me the stink eye all night. I'm almost positive I caught her friend confiscating her knife, so she didn't do anything stupid. After she called me a dumb whore and the guy not standing up for me, I booked an Uber and hightailed it out of there. It wasn't a night for a stabbing.

Maybe tomorrow, after I've had a little more vodka.

Or if I could be the one doing the stabbing.

The guy didn't attempt to stop me from leaving.

One of his friends did follow me out and apologized, asking me to come back in.

Like that was going to happen.

So, now, I'm home, unstabbed and annoyed.

That's the last time I find a guy on a dating app. I'd steered clear of them for so long, but a coworker found the love of her life on one, so I thought, *Why not?*

To make my shitty night better, I grab my phone and text Silas.

Me: May Day! May Day! Root beer floats, stat.

My *May Day* texts are always different. Sometimes, it's root beer floats or tacos, milkshakes, sushi, pizza—whatever my frustrated heart desires.

My phone rings.

"Fucking May Day *again?*" Silas asks, yelling over the loud noise in his background.

"Yep." I sigh. "Again." Another sigh—this one more dramatic.

"Fine, I guess I'll bail on this orgy I was about to have so you can hang out with a *real* man."

"I'm slapping you in the face for lying about participating in an orgy when I'm sure you're at Twisted Fox with the guys. And as for the *real man* comment, only guys with small cocks refer to themselves that way."

He chuckles. "I'm looking forward to it. Let me kick all these people out of my bed. Be there in fifteen." He doesn't hang up fast enough for me not to overhear him telling the guys he has to go.

While waiting for Silas, I change into sweats and one of his tees that I stole from him during a trip a few months ago. He keeps asking for it back, but he should know once I confiscate an item of clothing from him, it belongs to me.

Possession is nine-tenths of the law, people.

Right on time, there's a knock on my door, and Silas walks in with a grocery bag, the handles tangled around his wrist.

I eyeball him, my lips curling into a smile, and gesture to his clothing. "You really look like a man who was about to orgy it on." I step closer and slap his stomach.

"Jesus," he hisses, his knees buckling, but he quickly steadies himself. "The fuck was that for?"

I play with the door handle. "I told you I was slapping you."

"I thought you were only shit-talking," he mutters before lifting his arms. "I've got the goods ... and the goods will be on the floor in a minute if you don't move your sexy ass out of the way."

I step back, allowing him to slide between me and the doorway, and we make a beeline toward the kitchen. His sneakers squeak with each step he takes across the bamboo flooring. Settling the bags on the counter, he pulls out a tub of vanilla ice cream and a two-liter of root beer. I open a cabinet, pluck two glasses, and place them next to him.

"Tell Silas what happened," he says, dragging the ice cream lid off the container.

"Ugh," I say while gathering two spoons and the scooper.

"Was it better or worse than the guy who invited you over, stocked his fridge full of food, and then told you to make him dinner?" He scoops out perfect ice cream globes and drops them into the glasses.

"Oh my God, I totally forgot about that little prick." I grip the two-liter, twist open the lid, and pour it over the ice cream, watching the bubbles dance at the top of our glasses. "I texted you to have bail money handy in case I poisoned the food I didn't end up making."

"Didn't he say he did it because he wanted to see how you'd be as a housewife?"

I nod. "And I told him I'd be a black widow."

"You have to give the guy some credit, though." He tosses the scooper into the sink and pushes the ice cream into the freezer. "That took some balls."

"Balls I was close to cutting off and frying in a skillet for his dinner."

"Balls are balls, baby doll."

With our glasses in our hands, we migrate to my living room, popping a squat on the couch. I dunk my spoon into my glass, scoop up ice cream and root beer, and shove it into my mouth.

"Mmm," I moan into my spoon.

"Are you ever going to tell me why you keep going out with these assholes?" he asks, settling back against a pillow. "You don't even like to date."

"Are you ever going to tell me why you don't drink?"

I inhale a short gasp, dropping my spoon into the glass, and it's as if everything stops. Looking away from him, I direct my gaze to my lap. Those words weren't supposed to tumble from my lips. They were supposed to remain suppressed in my mind and never be released in the open around him.

I haven't mentioned Silas's sobriety like that since our fake date years ago. At first, I was concerned he had a problem, but as time passed, I've learned that's not the case. Silas is private about his sobriety for a reason, and it'd be selfish of me to pester him for what that reason is. Some people want to conceal why they make the decisions they do, and I respect that.

I hope he'll tell me one day, but I don't push him.

Our friends also asked, and like me, after he blew us off the first time, they retreated. We might be nosy, but we're also respectful toward each other—except for Archer and Georgia.

That's why my brain is processing how I managed to allow myself to go there tonight. I had *one* vodka tonic at dinner, so it wasn't a drunken question.

Silas clears his throat, and I tilt my head up, staring at him with apologetic eyes.

"It's not my thing," he replies, scratching his shoulder with the handle of his clean spoon. He hasn't dipped into his float yet. "I like to be in control … something you can't do when you're drunk." His words are restrained as he recites his answer like a prepared speech.

"Have you ever been drunk before?" I ask, putting my foot in my mouth again. My throat tickles as I wait for him to either tell me or change the subject.

His Adam's apple bobs. "Yes."

"So, what changed?" I've already opened the can, so might as well see how much I can yank out. "Did you have a bad experience? Piss yourself in front of the popular girls?" A forced laugh rolls up my throat.

He eyes me suspiciously. "I grew up. Decided it wasn't for me."

"But being around drunk people is?"

"We want what we can't have." He winces—a sign he didn't mean to tell me that. Shock flashes across his face like a burn.

"Can't have?"

He repeatedly shakes his head, his shoulders tightening. "I didn't mean it like that." Shoving his spoon into the float, he moves it around, the sound familiar to someone stirring their morning coffee. "Tell me about how your date went wrong." He squeezes his eyes shut and continues to play with his drink.

"It was awkward," I reply, that same sense returning. "He invited me to a dinner for his friend's birthday but never warned me that I'd be meeting his friends twenty minutes after meeting him."

Silas loosens his shoulders, and his body begins to relax. "Sounds bad but not terrible. Were his friends weird?"

"His friends were nice, but his ex, not so much."

"He brought his ex?"

"He didn't *bring* her, but they have the same circle of friends. He knew she'd be there and still invited me. Probably thinking it'd make her jealous."

He settles his glass on a coaster on the coffee table, the ice cream melting. "You need to stop dating losers. None of them are worthy of you."

A weight forms in my chest—a heavy burden of the truth that I love when my best friend says stuff like that to me when he shouldn't. When it only complicates things further.

Silas and I joke around about dating other people, but we never go into deep details, and we most definitely don't discuss hooking up with anyone else. We're human, and just because we can't form an emotional connection with someone doesn't mean we don't want intimacy—even if only for a night. I don't expect Silas to keep his dick in his pants since we're only friends, just like he doesn't expect me to keep my vagina under lock and key.

I scoot closer to him, afraid my question changed tonight. He's acting—*faking*—like he's the same Silas, but his muscles are tight, and he's looking everywhere but at me. I need to rewind to where I didn't slide into a territory I had known I shouldn't.

"One of these days, I'm going to find me a normal guy who takes me on normal dates," I say, forcing some pep in my tone.

His gaze slowly returns to me. "Doubt it."

"I'd better."

"Why?"

"I'd prefer not to be alone for the rest of my life, thank you."

"You'll have me."

"I don't want to be *romantically* alone, so unless you plan on marrying and screwing me for the rest of your life, then I still need someone."

We're falling back into the old Lola and Silas, and that brief awkwardness is dissolving.

"You want to get married someday? I thought you hated marriage?"

"I don't *hate it* … I just have a hard time believing in it."

"Because of your father?"

I nod and shove another bite into my mouth. He knows about my father's infidelities, just as I know about his mother's. We've confided in each other that it's hard to believe in people and relationships after we've seen the ones closest to us become toxic.

"Damn Robert Delgado," he mutters with a chuckle. "Always fucking everything up."

I lick my spoon clean and point at him with it. "Uh-oh, you'd better not let him hear you say that. He loves you."

Silas has attended countless work events with me since our fake date. We told my father we decided we were better as friends. He was skeptical at first, but with how many years have passed, he finally believes us. Or at least, he says he does, but he still mentions Silas anytime I tell someone I'm single.

I set my glass to the side, shift, and face him, crossing my legs. "Would we change if I got into a serious relationship?"

Anxiety swirls through me at the question—at the thought of losing him.

He grimaces, his back straightening. "I hope not but probably. All I ever want is for you to be happy, Lola. If you get into a relationship, as much as I'd hate for that to happen, we'll adjust and stay friends."

"You know, some guys wouldn't be comfortable with their girlfriend having a guy best friend."

"Then I'd hope you'd kick them to the curb because I'd pick you over a woman any day. If they couldn't accept our friendship, which is a large part of my life, that's not accepting me. You're too special for me to lose."

"You think you'll ever find someone you'll eventually want to be with?"

He draws in a deep breath, and his dark brows furrow. "Even if I did, I don't know if I could open myself up to them like they'd want. I don't have enough heart to give someone a chunk of it. Nor do I think I have enough hands to accept someone giving me theirs. I don't think I'd be as careful with it as I should."

Silas's relationship logic is hard to understand because he's such a good man.

Any girl would be lucky to have him, so why does he think he'd be better off alone?

I haven't seen him toy with women's emotions or promise them something he couldn't provide.

There are two explanations of why someone fears love:

1. They've witnessed heartbreak from others.
2. They've experienced heartbreak themselves.

My tone is hesitant, the words nearly choked out, when I ask, "Have you ever been in love?"

He flinches, staring at me uneasily. "What?"

"Have you ever been in love?" I repeat. "Do you hate it because it's something you've experienced that didn't work out?"

"Love is for fools, Lola," he replies with a huff.

"All right, were *you* one of those fools who fell in love?"

He blows out a long breath. "Once ... I thought I was."

My mouth falls open, a knot forming in my stomach.

Years of friendship, and we've never ventured into this talk before.

"Who was the girl?" I rush out, wanting to get every piece of him he's willing to give before he returns to hiding his secrets.

I also already hate the girl before he's even given me details. She made Silas resentful of love, and from the change in his demeanor at my question, whatever happened really affected him.

He looks away from me, peering straight ahead to nothing. "That's not important."

"Oh, come on. We're best friends." I slap his leg—an attempt to appear playful, but it only creates more tension.

He stares at me with vulnerable eyes, but I can see he's trying to fight it. "It was in high school. It wasn't a big deal."

I jump when he suddenly reaches forward and snatches the remote from the table. His action causes our glasses to shake, and one of them nearly falls off the coaster. He snags it before my white rug is stained and levels it, giving it a second to make sure it's staying.

He flips on the TV. "I'm not talking about this."

This is the first time Silas has acted like this.

To where I've seen something that affects him this deeply.

There was once a time when this man who doesn't believe in love found love.

And whatever he experienced ruined him for anyone in his future … even me.

CHAPTER ELEVEN

Silas

LOLA'S QUESTIONS haunt me on my drive home.

Have I ever been in love?

It's a question I can't answer because I don't know.

Years ago, I thought I was, but what did I know at eighteen? I still had a curfew, was applying to colleges, and was a disrespectful prick.

How did I know what love was when I didn't even know who I was yet?

Even if it was what people call *real love*, I don't deserve to have it now.

I'm not a man for love.

I'm a man who destroys the faith you ever had in it.

That's why I don't take it … don't ask for it … don't want it.

A woman's heart is safer in the hands of someone else.

It was a dagger to the heart as I listened to Lola talk about eventually getting married. The cut was deep, and it hurt, but it's what's best for her. I wouldn't wish a lonely, miserable life on anyone, although I dread the day that comes. Whoever that someone is won't deserve her.

My feelings toward Lola confuse the shit out of me. She's my best friend, but sometimes, my selfish heart craves more. Sometimes, when

I look at her, my mind wanders—a mental torture of trying out love again with her—but I fight those feelings.

It's not right for us.

It'd taint our friendship, our lives, and hell, everyone around us too.

No disrespect, but fuck love.

Fuck love for ruining my life and locking my heart up in a steel cage.

And fuck situations where you end up wanting more with your best friend.

But just like I've stayed away from liquor, I'm strong-willed, and I have the power not to let anything go further with Lola. We will always be friends—nothing more.

I'm a good actor. It's easy to be the fun guy who throws parties and lives life to the fullest. I'm so fucking fake.

I don't have a life to live to the fullest.

I don't deserve it.

I don't deserve to get wasted, to drink with my friends, to feel the high of liquor.

I don't deserve a lifetime of happiness ... and that's why I'll never get it.

———

I GROAN when I see my father's name flash across the phone screen. It's a jackass move, but we don't always see eye to eye.

"Hello?" I answer.

"You sound like you just woke up," he says, his voice loud.

"I work nights."

"You didn't RSVP to Janet's birthday party."

Janet was my father's mistress. During my senior year of high school, he left my mother to be with her. My mother, embarrassed by my father's actions, left town to stay with her family in Colorado. I didn't want to leave my senior year of school, so I stayed with my father. A month later, he married Janet, and she moved into our home with her son, Trent.

I move my phone from one ear to the other. "Will Trent be there?"

I hated Trent from the first time my father introduced us, and the hatred grew worse when he transferred to my high school. I've let go of my resentment toward Janet, but that'll never happen with Trent. Months after he moved in, he did something unspeakable. That grudge will always be there.

He hesitates before answering, "Yes." His tone tells me he briefly considered lying.

"Then no." Unlike him, I don't hesitate.

"Silas. It's been *years*. Don't you think it's time to move on?"

I grit my teeth, hating that he was brought up this early in my day. He's like a thunderstorm during a special event—no matter what, he ruins the entire thing.

"Time doesn't erase what happened." I clear my throat, shutting my eyes, hoping the memories don't pop through. "It won't fix what he did."

His voice deepens. "He's your brother."

"Stepbrother. There's no shared blood. Even if there were, it wouldn't make a difference."

"What am I supposed to do then? Tell Janet you can't come because you're still upset with her son?"

"Upset?" I force my words through clenched teeth. "He didn't steal the last Oreo from the pantry, Dad. He ruined not only my life but others' lives too. I'm not just upset with him. I despise him."

"That's not true, nor is it fair to pin that on him. You were all teenagers."

"We were old enough to know better."

"It seems we need to make separate plans." He pauses and releases a deep breath. "Again."

"Sorry," I grumble.

"If you were sorry, you'd stop holding this grudge."

"I'm sorry that you and Janet are stuck in the middle of this. I'm *not* sorry for never wanting to see the asshole again."

There's a moment of silence. This is a regular conversation between us. It's hard for him and Janet to deal with having children who can't stand each other. But that's Trent's fault, not mine. Regardless, I'd never tell anyone to choose sides. All I ask is for her to celebrate shit with us separately and keep that bastard away from me.

You know that saying, Your life can change at any moment?

My life is proof of that.

A proven tale that it's the truth.

In the span of ten minutes, everything I thought was pure in my life was taken from me.

In such a short time, I lost my life and myself.

CHAPTER TWELVE

Silas

High School—Senior Year

I'D NEVER SEEN a dead person before.

And quite frankly, I wish that were still the truth.

I could've gone my entire life without witnessing it—the splatters of blood, the smoke mixing with the darkness of the night, and the car alarm screaming as if it were signaling for help on its own.

I gulp, my breathing ragged, my hands shaking, as I stare down at them. My head spins as I attempt to calm it down, unsure of what to do, as sirens blare in the distance. They grow louder and louder, closer and closer, as my heart rams against my rib cage, as if it wanted to burst out and observe the scene itself.

Soon, others will join me.

They'll survey the scene as the alarm rings through their ears.

Will they blame it on me?

Will they slap handcuffs around my wrists and say what a rotten bastard I am?

Or will people feel sorry for me, but I'll still live with the guilt for the rest of my life?

My body throbs, and as much as I want to act tough, sobs break through my façade.

Police cars, a fire truck, and an ambulance swerve around me, circling me in and giving me no chance to escape even if I wanted to. But they ignore me, one firefighter pushing me down onto the pavement as he rushes toward the burning car. They ignore my Camaro, still running but in park with the driver's door thrown open.

"I'm sorry," I whisper, not having the strength to pull myself to my feet. "I'm so fucking sorry."

Pain and guilt tighten around my neck like a noose.

Some will say it's my fault, but was it?

I didn't hit their car.

I was only on the road, speeding around the turns, to stop them.

To protect them.

But I failed.

CHAPTER THIRTEEN

Lola

"HOW LONG HAVE you known about them?" Silas asks, giving me the stink eye.

We're sitting in Cohen's backyard, the sun setting in front of us. Today was Cohen and his girlfriend, Jamie's, gender reveal party. And boy, was it eventful.

They found out they were having a baby girl. *Yay!*

Then Cohen discovered Archer and Georgia had slept together. *Not yay!*

It was once, years ago, before they knew who each other was, but they'd kept it from him—for understandable reasons. They'd been doing a great job of hiding it until Georgia started flirting with Archer's brother, Lincoln, and all hell broke loose. What was supposed to be a friendly little party has turned into a shit show.

Good times.

Never a dull moment in this circle of friends.

Grace and I were the only ones who knew about them sleeping together, and it was supposed to stay that way. Silas endlessly questioned me on why they hated each other, but I always acted clueless. I love the guy, but I would never break Georgia's trust.

But maybe it'll bring the two of them to finally admit they have feelings for each other. Although Archer will have some groveling to do after what he pulled the morning after they slept together.

"Oh, please," I reply with a snort. "Anyone with a brain knew there was history between them. I'm surprised it took this long to come out."

Silas flicks his finger against the table. "Those two are in love with each other. They'll be dating by the end of the year."

"Isn't it strange how two people who hate each other can also be in love?" I sigh. "Maybe that's what I need."

Silas stops his finger, peering at me and raising a brow. "Huh?"

"To fall in love with someone I hate."

"Do you even hate anyone?"

"Yes." I nod. "Paul Lemmings. In fifth grade, the asshole pulled my hair and called my dog ugly." I tap my chin. "Oh! And Britney Spears' father."

"Tell me I'm not going to have to stop you from hunting down Paul Lemmings in hopes of falling in love with him."

"Maybe." A playful smile passes over my lips. "Maybe he can pull my hair a different way now."

"Shut your damn mouth." He confiscates the glass of red wine in my hand. "No more for you, young lady."

I laugh. "If Archer, the brooding jerk, can convince someone to fall in love with him, there's hope for us all." I gesture toward him. "Even you."

He stares ahead. "Nah, I don't think so."

"You know, every time I bring up relationships around you, you act like they're the male version of menstrual cramps."

"Never had menstrual cramps, but I'm sure with what I've heard, it is."

"*But*"—I stretch that word out—"let's say you did get into a relationship. What's your type, Silas Malone?"

Nearly a year has passed since I asked Silas if he'd ever been in love. Since his reaction was so out of character, I've steered clear of the conversation until tonight.

He plays with my wineglass, moving it in circles, and the wine splashes against the rim. "That's an irrelevant question because it'll never happen."

"This is a what-if game. It doesn't mean it'll happen."

He sets my glass down, reclines in his chair, and crosses his arms behind his neck. "You don't want to know, trust me."

"Oh my God!" I swing my arm out to smack his chest. "Is it some weird kink? Like axillism?"

He drops his arms, and they fall slack onto his lap. "The fuck is axillism?"

"It's when someone likes to have sex with people's armpits."

His mouth falls open as if he's about to speak, and then he shuts it and holds his finger up as he comes up with the right words. When he does, they leave his lips slowly. "You think my type is … *armpits*? Like body odor is a turn-on for me?"

"Hey, buddy. You're the one who said body odor, not me."

"Please, for the love of God, tell me you made up that word."

"Nope. My brother had this friend who showed us armpit porn once. He explained it to us *in detail*." I shudder, remembering how fascinated he seemed by it. *No offense to his fellow axillism peeps, though.* "It's a real thing."

"To clear the record, my type is not armpits."

"Good to know. Then *what is* your type?"

Turning his head, he stares at me, eyes wide. "You."

This time, it's my mouth dropping. "What?" That one word comes out in six stutters.

"Don't act so shocked, Devilina."

I'm keeping my composure, but *holy shit*. Warmth infuses my body.

Get your shit together, Lola.

I smile confidently. "You like me. How cute." Throwing my head back, I dramatically speak up to the sky. "I'm Silas's type, God. Did you hear that?"

He playfully cups the back of my head and tips it back down. "Whoa, hold up. Let me clarify. Someone *like you*."

"Meaning me, sucker." I snatch my wine, chug it, slide out of my chair, and jump to my feet as if I'd just been called down on *The Price is Right.* "I mean, it doesn't exactly surprise me, considering I'm cool as hell. Some might even say I'm semi-attractive."

Since my dumbass didn't consider wine and jumping don't go well together, I wobble, and before I fall into the table, Silas pulls me onto his lap. Our faces—*our lips*—are only inches apart when I raise my head. I get a hint of the mint gum he was chewing earlier, and that, along with him, sobers me up. I didn't expect him to say that, and even though this isn't the first time I've sat on his lap, it's never been this intimate. It's not something we've ever done alone—always around friends and *always* playful. This, right here, is the opposite of that.

I'm not the only one who is shocked. Just like I didn't expect him to say that, I don't think he expected to either. It dropped from his lips so effortlessly, though, as if it'd been locked up for years and finally just broke from its cage. It seemed as if hurling the truth at me almost pained him.

There have been times I've thought about what a different relationship with Silas would be like. But then those thoughts go crashing down. Silas has been clear that attempting any relationship with him would be like giving written consent for him to crush your heart, injure it, and then hand it back with an *I told you so* look on his face.

I clear my throat and rest my elbow on his shoulder. "It appears we're alike because you're also my type. I mean ... not you, but someone *like you*." I mock the voice he used when telling me that.

He's no longer playful, not with the pained expression on his face when he looks at me. "If that were the case, then why'd you give me a fake number when we met?"

I wince at the memory of me turning him down. "I didn't know you."

Even though he's quiet, I take in his change of breathing as well—a sign that I'm not the only one who's nervous about discussing this.

"I thought you were a fuckboy," I state, going forward. "A guy who only wanted to get in my panties."

He starts to talk, most likely to deny it, but I talk over him.

"Which I wasn't mad about because it was who you were: a player wanting a quick screw. Then I saw you at Cohen's, and we clicked and became best friends. And, hey, consider yourself lucky because my friendship slots are very limited. But as for what we were talking about, my type is someone who wants a relationship as strong and fun as we have."

He fixes his stare on me, and I can hear the movement of his chest heaving in and out. He grips my waist and slowly moves me, so my back is against the arm of the chair, and I'm not so much on him. It's almost like a rejection—that we were too close and we needed space.

"But there are plenty of ways you're not my type," I say, quickly recovering from looking like a fool.

He scratches his head. "Hmm? How?"

"You don't want a relationship."

He nods. "I'd be a boyfriend from hell. You know … where you're from."

"Oh, please. I see the front you put on." I lean back against the arm more, slightly raising my chest, and Silas's eyes drop to my cleavage. "There's so much more to you than the whole player persona you put on."

His eyes don't stay on my chest long, and he diverts his attention to me. He's looking at me, but it's half-assed—not fully there as if his eyes are on me but his mind is somewhere else.

"Bad guys don't attend parties and act like fake boyfriends," I go on. "They don't show up with snacks when a girl is sad, and they most definitely don't know said woman's take-out orders by heart." I dig my nails into his shoulder. "That kind of man—I hate to tell you—is made for relationships."

If my words hit him, he doesn't offer a reaction to it.

His face is blank. "You're the only woman I do that with. Ask me Georgia's take-out order, and I'd be clueless."

"Exactly! That's why you're *my type.*"

His eyes finally meet mine, deep-set, drinking me in like I'm liquor —a drink that's off-limits to him. He clears his throat as if clearing his mind, and his words are raspy when he says, "Maybe once upon a time, I could have been that guy for you, but now? Babe, it'd never happen." He squeezes my thigh. "I'll never be your prince in shining armor. I'd be the one who broke you so hard that it'd be impossible for you to be rescued by someone else. You'd never want that fairy-tale love because I'd have broken every dream you had in it."

There's a finality in his voice with each word, and it causes the hair on my arms to stand. He speaks as if he truly believes he'd be the villain in any story.

Well, little does he know, I love villains.

"I'm the Devil's spawn, remember? I don't want fairy tales. I'd gladly take a broken man, a man hiding in the darkness, who feels as if he's not worthy. You know me well enough to know I don't and will never look for a Prince Charming. I'd rather have the dragon who sets fire to anyone who tries to get to me."

"I'd set *you* on fire and leave you to burn. Trust me when I say I'm toxic."

Cupping his strong chin, I jerk him closer to me. "Why do you talk about yourself like that? Why do you think you're so fucked up?"

I know plenty of people I'd consider fucked up. He is not one of those people.

Broken? Definitely.

Fucked up? Definitely not.

He's this gorgeous man who's had something tragic happen to him —something that threw a curveball, destroying any hope he had for being someone's lover.

"I don't think I'm fucked up. I *know* I am." His body trembles beneath mine—every damn part of him. His lips. His arms. His legs.

"No, Silas, you're not," I whisper, settling my hand on his thigh— the one my ass isn't halfway on. "You just went through something."

"I'm fucked up, and me wanting to kiss you right now proves that more."

I hold in a breath.

"Would I want to slide my hands through your hair and devour your mouth with mine?" he says it so low I can barely hear it.

But I heard it, and my body is reacting to every word he said.

What he said lights me up in ways I've never felt before.

"Then do it," I say boldly without giving myself the time to consider what his reaction to my statement might be.

He presses a finger to my lips like he knows he can't cross that line, but he needs to touch my lips in some way, and bows his head. "It'd be the kiss of death to our friendship."

My lips slowly part, and as I speak, his finger glides down my chin. "Or the start of something new."

Licking his lips, he cups my face tight as if it were the shield holding him back. Then he drops his hand, as if he's lost the restraint, and curls his hand around the back of my neck, pulling my face closer to his.

I gulp, inhaling a breath.

Then the sound of a door slamming shut rings through the air.

Silas pulls back.

I gasp.

Cohen comes stomping through the backyard like a kid whose party got ruined … because, well, it sorta did.

And now, he just ruined mine.

Silas scoots the chair back, grips my waist, and slides out from under me. As he does this, his waist—*his erection*—brushes against the back of my thigh, stealing my breath. His eyes shoot to me in fear, and I look from one side of the yard to the other, so I don't push him back down and straddle him.

Silas moves faster and plops down in my abandoned chair—the chair I probably should've stayed my happy ass in—and he grips the arms of the chair as if trying to talk himself down. He won't even look at me.

"All right," Cohen says when he reaches us. He's so absorbed in his predicament that he doesn't notice how awkward Silas and I are acting. "Which one of you knew about my sister and Archer?"

"Not this guy," Silas says before immediately pointing at me, his fun-guy front returning. "There's your culprit right there."

I glare at him for throwing me under the bus.

He ignores me, so Cohen is the next victim of my glare.

"Look, Archer didn't know who Georgia was, and vice versa."

"Then what happened? When did it happen?"

"Before you introduced them, and if you want to know more, ask Georgia. It's her story, not mine. But for now, the secret stays here." I tap the side of my head, wishing I could do it to Silas, only a little harder.

Maybe it'll knock some sense into me too.

I went into Cohen's backyard, knowing Silas was my best friend.

Now, I'm more confused about our relationship than ever.

CHAPTER FOURTEEN

Silas

IF I HAD to compare myself to any animal, I'd say I was a chameleon. I'm able to blend myself in with whatever environment I'm thrown into.

I only allow people to see what I want them to see. I'm seen as a people person, the jokester, the one who never takes anything seriously. But it's all an act. No one, other than my family, knows the real me and the burdens I hide deep within my soul.

I toss my shit across the bathroom floor and step into the shower, the hot water burning as it slides down my skin.

What the fuck was that with Lola tonight?

Sure, we flirt with each other, but our conversations have never turned so intimate.

Thinking about her and her words, I lower my hand, wrap it around my cock, and stroke myself. There's so much I find attractive about Lola … so much I love about her. Not only physically but also her attitude, her personality, and the way she plays hard while also having a heart of gold.

We're the same but opposite.

She acts tough but is soft.

I act normal but am really rough on the inside.

Lola has never gotten so real with me like she did tonight.

I stroke myself faster, the buildup growing stronger, and when I release, it's her name I moan. Since we met, anytime I jack off, I always think about her.

I step out of the shower, wipe off my face, and shake off my hair.

Cohen interrupting us was a sign that we need to be careful—that whatever ideas we have cluttering our friendship need to be laid to rest.

————

I CLENCH my jaw while reading the text.

Trent: Want to grab a drink? Talk about shit before my mother's party?

I fight with myself on how to respond. I hate when he reaches out. I decline, and then he looks like the good guy who tried.

He's not the good guy.

Like me, he's the villain.

I'd never voluntarily sit down and have a drink with him. The few times we've been around each other at family occasions, he attempts conversation, but I can't stand the sight of him. When he transferred to my school, we had almost a rivalry. I hated his mother for breaking apart my parents' marriage. He hated my father because he was the reason he had to move schools his senior year.

Then the party happened.

He did something no one can take back—all because he's a selfish bastard who doesn't care about anyone but himself. He didn't have to do what he did that night. His beef was only with me, and he should've left the others out of it. His decision ruined everyone's lives … except his because the asshole acts like it never happened, like he didn't create tragedy.

Instead of replying, I delete his text, hoping to forget he even exists.

CHAPTER FIFTEEN

Lola

"AND THEN THERE WERE TWO," I tell Silas, plopping down on the couch and patting the empty space next to me.

He takes a sip of his water before sitting. "Because the others scurried off to their bedrooms to most likely bang."

"Bitches," I grumble. "How dare they."

We're at Archer and Lincoln's grandparents' lake house, which is about two hours from Anchor Ridge, with Archer, Georgia, and Lincoln's girlfriend, Cassidy. We ordered pizza and hung out. Then it was time for the couples to ditch us. Georgia was the first to fake a yawn, telling us she and Archer were going to bed. Shortly after, Lincoln and Cassidy did the same.

Silas snatches the remote. "What's your movie of choice for tonight?"

I shrug. "You pick."

He shakes his head. "Nuh-uh. Last time I picked, all you did was comment on how unrealistic every scene was."

"The guy jumped off a bajillion-story window, landed on his feet, and then ran as fast as the car he was chasing." I throw out my arm. "If you think that's realistic, we need to get that brain of yours checked."

"It's an *action* movie. That's what they do."

"You know what I do? I call bullshit on that."

He drops his head back. "Exactly why I told you to pick what we're watching. No Hallmark shit, though."

"When—and I stress, *when*—have I ever picked Hallmark?"

Silas opens his mouth, most likely to make some ridiculous comment, but stops when a moan comes from down the hallway. His gaze shoots straight to me, and I slap a hand over my mouth to hold in my laughter but fail.

"Oh my God," I choke out between laughs. "Two of them are totally hooking up."

Silas places his hand to his ear as if trying to get a better listen. "Who do you think it is?"

"Georgia," I say with certainty. "That girl has a loud mouth, even if she tries to be quiet."

Silas rests his hand on the arm of the couch. "Should I go tell them to keep it down?"

I rub my nose. "I'd feel terrible, ruining their ... mood."

"They're ruining our mood, though." He gestures toward the TV. "We can't watch a movie when there's porn playing in the background."

"We can turn the volume up." I stare at him timidly. "This is also Archer's place. Is it cool to tell people not to bang in their own house?"

Technically, it's his grandparents' but same difference.

Silas rubs his hand over the leg of his sweats. "We'll just crank up the volume." He hands me the remote. "Pick a movie."

This is the first time we've ever been in a situation like this. Not much time has passed since our friends started coupling up. They also used to be less in our faces about it, but I guess those days are over. When Georgia invited me to come, I made sure Silas was coming so I wouldn't be the odd one out.

Now, I think sitting here with the background noise of sex might be more awkward. And just when I think it can't get weirder, there's action coming from Lincoln's room.

"Jesus, fuck," Silas hisses, scrubbing a hand over his face before gesturing toward the remote. "Pick something, pronto, please."

I flip through the different Netflix options and decide on a suspense movie. That will make both of us happy—Silas gets a little bit of action, and I get a little bit of mystery. Win-win.

Before hitting play, I snag the blanket folded over the end of the couch, prop a pillow up, and make myself comfortable. Silas doesn't care when I rest my feet on his lap.

"Blanket?" I ask. "I *guess* I'll share."

He shakes his head. "I'm good."

The couples are still at it, and it gets worse when we hear the echoes of what I'm sure is a bed hitting the wall, reverberating through the house.

Thump-thump-thump.

I fake gag. "All right, I'm about ten seconds from changing my mind on telling the porn stars to relax. There are people trying to live sexless lives over here."

Silas chuckles. "Play the movie. It'll drown them out."

The movie starts, and not even five minutes in, a sex scene begins.

It's been a while since I've hooked up with anyone, and now, sex is all that's happening around me. Silas and I refuse to look at each other. We've watched movies with sex scenes before but never when also surrounded by people having sex, never when we're hearing moans and groans and beds shaking and intimacy.

The man—a main character—is banging a flight attendant hard in the back of a private plane. And I mean, *she's most likely going to be sporting some bruises and she might not be able to walk off the plane* kind of screwing.

It was dumb of me to choose an R-rated movie. I should've thought ahead. I figured there'd be some violence, some blood, but I didn't consider there'd be soft-core porn.

I stare at the screen, nearly bug-eyed as my breath catches in my throat.

This could be us.

Having sex.

Me throwing my head back as he pleasured me.

No, no, no.

Bad Lola.

It's affecting Silas too. He shifts on the couch, adjusting his pants, and hits my foot in the process, as if he forgot it was there. I lick my lips at the outline of his hardening cock through his sweats. The view and feel of it against the edge of my foot is mesmerizing.

I can't exactly smack my face to rid of the thoughts, so I suck in a deep breath and decide to go about this a different way.

"I'm going to call this one out as unrealistic too," I comment, my voice raspy. "There is no way a man makes a woman come that quick. No way."

Silas's gaze darts to me, but he doesn't utter a word. Our eyes meet, and I should divert my attention because I have a feeling that I'm staring at him in a similar way. His breathing is heavy, and he rests his arm over his waist, shielding my view of how aroused he is. My tongue darts out, licking my lips, and I have to fight the urge to lower my hand and dip them into my panties.

We're not supposed to want each other like this.

It isn't what our friendship allows.

I want my best friend in ways I shouldn't.

"We could do it one time," I say.

"What?"

"Hook up." I pray that he doesn't turn me down. "Just once because we're both obviously … turned on."

He stares at me, stunned. "You're turned on?"

I shoot him a *really* look.

"I can leave the room if you want to take care of that."

I deliver that same *really* look as before, slowly dragging my foot over his lap and rubbing it over his erection. My chest is heavy, and I'm practically panting. He shudders underneath me, and I can feel my pulse against my throat.

We both want this.

"This is dangerous," he mutters as the room grows hot.

Or maybe it's just me.

"It is," I whisper.

He carefully moves my feet off his lap and bends my knees. I stay quiet when he starts to get up. Gulping, I wait for it—the rejection— for him to leave the room because at least one of us is thinking rationally.

But he doesn't stand.

Instead, he settles himself on his knees next to me. I maneuver, so I'm on my side, staring down at him. Stretching forward, he caresses my cheek. I tremble when his fingertips slip down to between my lips. I stop myself from opening wider, from sucking on his finger, scared that might be too much.

He peers down at me with hooded eyes in what appears to be admiration. "Are you sure about this?"

I urgently nod. "Positive."

Briefly, though, those thoughts hit me.

Is this selfish?

To put our friendship on the line for one night? One time?

Tipping his head down, he briefly kisses me. I open my mouth, allowing him entrance, and he sucks on the end of my tongue before pulling away. I curl my hand around his neck, attempting to bring him back, but he doesn't allow it.

But right now, in the emptiness of this room, with the background of passion playing around us, I want him more than ever.

Every inch of my body craves him.

And if I sink my hand deep into my heart and drag out the contents, the truth of how I feel will be thrown out for all to see. I've craved Silas for so long, but I've been afraid to admit it. Admitting your feelings for someone could lead to rejection and embarrassment.

And once I admitted it to myself, how was I supposed to not look at him and hope for more?

He rests his hand on the waist of my sleep shorts, his finger toying with the loop of the tied strings. All it would take is him untying the strings, and we'd be opening a door we've kept closed for so long.

And when he does, everything changes.

"Rise up a little for me," he demands.

I do as I was told, and he jerks my shorts down. I peer down to find Silas's gaze leveled on my black lace panties. He wastes no time, as if he knows how desperate I am, before he slips my panties to the side. Moving closer, nearly halfway hovering over me, he jerks one of my legs up.

And without warning, he slides two fingers inside me.

They fill me perfectly. His thumb presses against my clit—not gentle, but not too rough. He plays with it while slipping his fingers in and out of me. He's focused on his fingers, not taking a break to look at my face, as if this is his life's biggest goal. I writhe underneath him, growing breathless, and his breathing comes out ragged.

I'm staring at him as he works me with full concentration as if he needs his performance to be perfect, and then my back is arching, and I'm moaning his name. It's quiet, only for our ears—unlike my friends. Our little secret means hushed moans.

It's quick, like I shut my eyes for a few seconds and then it's over. As I'm catching my breath, Silas stands, pulling at the bottom of his tee with the same fingers he had inside me.

"Do you want me to …?" I burst the words out, my brain only halfway functioning, and point at the bulge in his pants.

He shakes his head, standing tall. "Tonight was about you."

I do a circle motion with my hand toward his cock. "But what about *you*?"

"Tonight was about you," he repeats, his voice firm, and he jerks his thumb over his shoulder. "Do you want something from the kitchen? I'm going to grab a water."

"No," I say, my voice trembling. "I'm okay."

I watch him turn, giving me his back, as my heart batters against my chest, telling me to call him back. Silas isn't the first man who's pleasured me … but he's the first guy who's ever made me feel a passion like that by only fingering me.

And now, he's shut down.

He made me orgasm and then mentally left.

Our relationship has changed.

Whether it's good or bad, I'm unsure.

All I know is, we'll never be *just friends* any longer.

Silas is scared of ruining our friendship.

But is he more scared of being in love with me than losing me?

CHAPTER SIXTEEN

Silas

WHEN I MAKE it to the kitchen, I throw open the fridge door and frantically grab a water.

What were you thinking?

You weren't supposed to touch her.

You were supposed to keep your relationship platonic.

Lola is more than just a friend.

She's my world.

And now, I might lose her.

I chug the water, open the fridge for another, and gulp that one down too. Jerking a chair out, I slump down onto it, dropping my head between my open legs.

"What did I do?" I whisper to myself, my voice cracking.

I'm not sure how long I sit in the kitchen, reminding myself what a mistake I just made. It was a spur-of-the-moment thing, and the way Lola was rubbing my cock and licking her lips had already gotten me riled up.

"We could do it one time."

Those words were my undoing.

I force myself out of the chair and sluggishly return to the living room. The sounds of our friends' lovemaking have dissipated. The only noise is the movie Lola picked. I shouldn't have allowed that. I should've scrolled through the shows and found the most PG-rated one I could.

Lola is facing me, her eyes shut, her hand resting underneath her cheek as she sleeps. A rush of relief leaves me because I have time to work out what I'm going to say before I have to face her again.

This can't happen again.

We need to stop it before it gets too deep.

I'm going to fight like hell to make sure nothing changes with Lola after what happened tonight.

Hopefully, this wasn't a life-changing mistake.

I need to get out of here.

CHAPTER SEVENTEEN

Lola

IT'S silent when I wake up alone with a blanket tucked around my body—most likely Silas's doing. Rising, I move my neck from side to side, working out the crick I already feel coming. The silence tells me Silas is most likely gone.

After giving me an amazing orgasm, when he said he was getting a water from the kitchen, I didn't expect him to be there nearly all night, as if he were pumping the water from the well in there. Had I known he'd scurry off, scared, I'd have run to the guest bedroom and at least been comfortable in my sleep of shame.

When did he leave?

Why did he leave?

Did last night ruin us?

Yawning, I snatch my phone from the coffee table and find a text from the couch evacuator.

Silas: Had an emergency. Archer said you can ride home with them.

What the fuck?

I clench my hand around my phone.

There's nothing like being ditched by the man who fingered you last night.

The text was sent six hours ago—one a.m.

What an ass.

Silas could've easily woken me up and told me since he somehow communicated with Archer to take me home.

Shivering, I wrap the blanket tighter around me and reply, unsure of how long it'll take him to see my text since it's early. He drove two hours home late at night, and Silas isn't an early riser.

Me: You could've woken me up and told me.

His response comes moments later, shocking me.

Silas: Sorry. You looked so peaceful, sleeping. I would've felt like an asshole.

Yeah, bullshit. He's not getting out of this that easy.

Me: I wouldn't have been mad.

My message goes through, and my fingers hover over the screen as I chew on the edge of my lip. It needs to be brought up, and I have a feeling he won't do it.

Me: After that orgasm, you could've woken me up every hour of the night, and I wouldn't have said a damn thing.

Three bubbles form on the screen. Then disappear. Then form again. I jump when my phone beeps with his message.

Silas: I've told you for years that I have mad skills.

At least he's being playful.

That has to count for something, right?

————

BY THE TIME the others join me in the kitchen, I'm showered, dressed, and searching for something decent to drink.

"Archer, you're rich. You need to invest in an espresso machine here. If there's no Starbucks, you have to make up for it somehow," I say, leaning back against the cabinets and frowning at the hot muck in my cup.

"I've been telling him that," Georgia says, skipping down the stairs and slapping Archer's stomach. "I don't even know how to work a normal coffee maker. Everyone drinks iced coffee now."

"Not me," Lincoln says. "I'm not picky about my coffee."

"That's because you got used to that prison coffee," Cassidy says, running her hand through her straight blond hair. "I don't know how you haven't gone back to your Starbucks ways."

Lincoln shrugs. "Don't knock it until you try it."

I raise a brow. "Prison or shit coffee?"

"Eh"—Lincoln smirks—"both."

"Let's hit the road and grab some decent coffee … and a McMuffin," Georgia says.

"Sounds good to me," I mutter, ready to get out of here as fast as I can.

Even though no one said anything, I saw the curious eyes when they didn't see Silas. I'm sure Archer told Georgia I was riding with them, and since Lincoln and Cassidy are somewhat newer to the group, they don't get deep into our business. Silas said he had an emergency, so that's all I'll say if they ask.

———

JUST AS I'M shoving the last bite of my McMuffin into my mouth, I get another text from Silas.

Silas: You make it home okay?

I debate on whether to answer him, so I set my phone down and sing out about how my loneliness is killing me with Georgia to our favorite Britney jam. Silas bailed on me in the middle of the night, so he can wait for a response.

———

AN HOUR LATER, I strip off my clothes, throw them in the laundry basket, and step into the shower. Tipping my head back, I allow the water to sprinkle down my face as I think about last night.

It changed my friendship with Silas.

When I get out, I finally reply to him.

Me: Nope. I'm currently walking home because someone left me stranded.

He replies to me minutes later when I'm trudging into the kitchen.

Silas: Funny, you pain in the ass. I made sure Archer could take you home before I left.

Me: You woke him up but not me?

He didn't wake me up because he knew he'd have to face me after making me orgasm. One thing I hadn't discovered about Silas before is that he's a chickenshit.

Silas: I didn't want to piss you off. Him? I don't really care if I do.

Me: Why'd you bail?

Silas: I had some family shit come up that I needed to take care of. Sorry.

I don't believe him, but I'm also not in the mood to call him out for the second time today.

CHAPTER EIGHTEEN

Silas

EVEN THOUGH I'M concerned it might be awkward, I smile when Lola walks toward the bar at Twisted Fox. It's the first time we've seen each other since the lake house.

That was a week ago, and it's rare for us to go that long without seeing each other. We also haven't talked to each other as much as we used to. I'm blaming it on us both being busy with work so that I don't have to meet the reality that we caused this distance between us—Lola saying only one time and me going through with it.

"Hey you," I greet when she tugs a stool back and plops onto it.

"Hey, ditcher," she replies with a playful smile.

I chuckle, shaking my head. "Always a pain in my ass."

So far, not as awkward as I feared.

She shrugs, tossing her dark hair over her shoulder. "Better to be a pain in the ass than someone who bails on their friend in the middle of the night."

All right, so she's choosing awkward for tonight actually.

"Oh, come on," I groan, throwing my head back. "I told you, it was an emergency."

"What was the emergency then?"

"It was a family thing. My mom needed something." I slam my eyes shut, hating that I just lied to her.

I left because of myself. My hands shook as I covered up Lola, grabbed my keys, charged to my car, and left the lake house. After driving around for hours, contemplating whether to go back, I went home. Not that I got any sleep.

Once, I ran to the bathroom, worried that I'd puke because my anxiety was so goddamn high. Another minute, I sat at the edge of my bed, my palm against my chest as my heart raced.

"I'll make it up to you." I grab a square white bar napkin and drop it in front of her. "I promise."

She taps her black nails against the bar. "I take gifts, food, or cash."

I smile at her remark, and it puts me a little more at ease. But no matter what, we both know what happened. I knelt beside her, helped her push down her shorts, and pressed my fingers inside her warmth. I stroked her and played with her clit until she came apart below me. And it is a memory that I'll never forget.

Lola grunts when a woman shoves herself between Lola and the man sitting next to her. She turns, glaring at the woman, and jerks her shoulder back, slightly hitting the rude woman, who's paying her no mind.

"Hey, hottie," the woman around Lola's age greets, and Lola snorts at her little name for me. "Can I get a sex on the beach?"

The woman tries to straighten herself out, but there isn't room, and Lola isn't moving for her.

I salute her, trying not to laugh at Lola mean-mugging the girl. "I got you."

"And your number," she adds.

"No, you can't." Lola answers for me, her voice sharp. "He'll get you your ridiculous drink, and then you can go on your way."

I retreat a step, shocked at Lola's words, and the woman shifts to look at her.

"Are you his girlfriend?" she snarls.

Lola hesitates, her eyes squinting. "I'm his boss, and he can't give his number to thirsty customers."

"I can only give thirsty customers drinks," I say with a nod of confirmation.

I've never given a woman my number in front of Lola, no matter where it is. And she's returned the favor.

"Whatever," the woman grumbles, her flirty voice now hard. "I'll just take the drink then."

She steps back, moving around Lola and between an open stool and a burly man, who calls her sweetheart and asks if she wants him to buy her drink. I quickly make the drink, some of the OJ splashing as I finish it off, and hand it to her. She delivers a look as dirty as the one Lola gave her, snatches it from me, throws some cash down, and leaves —no tip included.

Damn, that sure took a quick turn.

I open the drawer, shove the cash in, and return to Lola. "I love it when you get all territorial."

She laughs, now chewing on her nail. "Don't act like you're not the same with me."

"I do it to protect you." I gesture to the bar. "Are you not hanging with the girls tonight?"

"Nope. Grace has been weird lately—absent and secretive. Georgia is forcing Archer to go shopping. So, I came to see Cassidy."

I curl my hands around my mouth. "Bullshit."

She flips me off.

I rest my elbows on the bar, on each side of her, and lean in closer. "You came to see me, your favorite person in the world."

She rolls her eyes. "Whatever." She groans. "I need a drink to keep my mind off this douchebag at work."

My muscles tighten, and my back straightens. "Whose ass do I need to kick?"

"No one's." She cringes. "Some guy at work is giving me a hard time and trying to turn everyone against me by telling them I'm given the easy-to-close and bigwig clients because of who my dad is. In reality, I'm given the harder clients because I'm better at closing the deals."

I snarl and give myself a reminder to have her point him out the next time I attend a work event with her. "Who cares what him or what a few people think? Your dad knows what you're capable of, and that's all that matters."

"I know. It just sucks, having people talk shit about you." Her shoulders slump. "Especially when it's not true."

I brush my hand over hers but pull away when she trembles at my touch. "Tell me what I can do to make it better."

Her attention is pinned to her hand as if she can still feel my touch there. "Make me the best damn drink you can … and don't let me yell at any girls who hit on you."

Is this how it's always going to be now?

Are the simple touches we once had—which were playful and we didn't read too much into them—finished? Do we have to be careful, be nervous, with the way we are around each other now? Do we have to change the friendship we once had?

CHAPTER NINETEEN

Lola

WHEN I WALK into Twisted Fox with Georgia, Cassidy, and Grace, I spot Silas at our favorite table waving us over. Since our talk at the bar, our relationship has returned to normalcy—for the most part. We act like the incident at the lake house never happened. It's better for our friendship that way. Plus, it's not like we haven't had hookups that didn't result in relationships. Ours should be the same way.

Silas kisses my forehead when I reach him, stands, and jerks the stool out for me to sit next to him.

Georgia plops down and dances in her stool as she slaps her hand on the bar. "All right, give me your margarita orders."

"Strawberry," I say.

"Make that two strawberries," Cassidy adds.

"Just a water for me," Grace replies in a soft voice.

All eyes direct to Grace.

"No margarita?" Georgia asks, raising a brow.

Not only are margaritas Grace's favorite, but she also looks stressed. She's a teacher, so I usually blame it on being around crazy children all day, but it's something deeper. I don't want to ask in front of everyone because I tend to pry into people's personal business privately.

"I wish." Grace slaps a hand over her mouth, shutting her eyes as if she let out a secret she hadn't intended to. She lowers her hand and tone at the same time. "I work in the morning."

She and Georgia both work at an elementary school. Georgia is the school counselor, and Grace is a teacher.

Raising my wrist, I peer down at my watch. "Babe, you look like you've had a hell of a day. Have a drink, scarf down some greasy bar food, and don't give a shit about calories. Consider it a serotonin booster." I wink at her. "Trust me, I'm a pro at this stuff."

Grace drops her hand underneath the table, resting it on her stomach. "Maybe another time."

"Whoa," Silas says. "You knocked up or something?"

The table turns quiet as if Silas released a secret he wasn't supposed to. Well, everyone, except for Cassidy, who breaks out into coughs. If she were actually choking, I'd swat Silas to give her the Heimlich. But that's not why she's coughing. It's to hide the truth she knows about what's going on with Grace.

And from Silas's question, my guess is, there's a bun in Grace's oven.

Grace chews on her bottom lip, not yet denying it. Grace doesn't lie because she's terrible at it. Girl gives herself away in minutes. No matter what, you immediately know.

She fidgets with her hands as everyone awaits her secret.

Then she slowly nods and shuts her eyes.

I stare at her, unblinking, while everyone else has their own reactions.

"Who's the father?" Finn asks, and my eyes shoot to him. There's a deep cut of pain not only in his voice but also evident on his face.

Finn is in love with Grace. Grace is in love with Finn.

I had no idea Grace was dating someone, and she isn't the type for random hookups. I'd expect a pregnancy announcement from Georgia or Cassidy, sure, but not Grace.

I thought Silas and I had some friendship turmoil brewing. Grace's pregnancy just beat that out. If there's a baby daddy in the picture, that man might push Finn out of Grace's life. It's the same concern I've had with Silas if one of us gets into a serious relationship.

Grace clears her throat. "I don't want to talk about that."

Our friends start throwing out questions, and Grace's face twists in unease. The poor girl appears freaked out enough about being pregnant. The last thing she needs is to be interrogated when she can't even have a drop of liquor.

I hold up my hand to stop them. "She'll talk about it when she's ready." I send Finn a *shut it* look.

"Do your parents know?" Georgia asks as if she needs just one question to appease her for the night.

"Not yet," Grace croaks out.

Grace's parents are strict—not asshole strict, but more *we expected better out of you* strict. Her parents are pretty much perfect, so Grace can't call them hypocrites for wanting that out of their children.

My parents? They have no right to question my ways when my dad humps anything with a vagina. At least his infidelity gives me an excuse not to be a golden child.

Georgia grabs Grace's hand and squeezes it. "Do you want me to go with you when you tell them? I mean, I'm down for being a second mom."

This is why our friendship works so well. While I'm good at sticking up for my friends and telling people to shut up, Georgia is the positive and comforting friend. Those traits are probably what made Archer fall in love with her. He was a broken man, fighting an internal war with himself, and she helped him through it.

Grace doesn't look back at Finn. She tells us she doesn't have a plan and doesn't know what she's doing yet since she just recently found out. The bar isn't the place to make her dive into what secrets she has. Grace needs privacy right now.

When I sneak a peek at Silas, I find him staring at Finn in concern —most likely having the same worry for him that I'm having for Grace. They'll both need support systems through this new development in their lives.

For years—longer than Silas and me—Grace and Finn have run away from their feelings in fear of losing each other. But now, it seems almost too late for them.

Grace is having another man's baby.

Finn looks like he no longer has a beating heart.

My chest hurts because I'm scared this might be my future with Silas.

———

I DRANK one too many margaritas tonight.

In my defense, so did Georgia.

"You okay?" Silas asks when he parks in front of my house.

I rode to Twisted Fox with Georgia, but since we decided to take a trip to Tipsy Town, Archer drove her home, and Silas is my ride.

I'm not drunk. I can say my ABCs. I know my birthday. I'm not seeing triple. I just had a little too much. I rest my head against the headrest and think about Grace and what she's going through. She has us, but I still can't imagine the fear and loneliness inside her.

If her baby daddy were a decent guy, we'd have already met him. She would've had more enthusiasm because Grace is one of the most positive people I know. She always sees the light at the end of the tunnel. Whoever the father is, it's someone she doesn't want it to be. And from the way she looked at Finn, my guess is, she wishes it were him.

I know Silas's question meant to be more along the lines of, *Tell me you're not about to puke in my car*, but that's not what's on my mind.

"Do you ever get lonely?" I ask.

He shifts to look at me, the dim light above us providing the only illumination in the car, but he doesn't answer.

"Because sometimes, I do."

Silas strokes his jaw. "Sometimes ... but when it happens, I call you."

A hint of a smile forms on my lips. "Same."

My emotional side rarely makes an appearance in the outside world. I keep that bitch hostage most of the time because I don't want people to ever see me as weak. For years, I watched my mother sit in the kitchen and cry after my father was caught cheating again. I'd stand in the hallway, peeking around the corner, as she begged him to stop. She was broken and sad, explaining that to him between sobs.

But even with all that pleading, my father couldn't commit to her. She threw out every emotion she felt, but nothing changed. All he saw was a woman he could walk all over, and all I saw was that emotions made you look weak. On the outside, my mother was a strong woman. You'd never know she was breaking behind closed doors.

She was lonely—I saw it in her eyes every morning after my father stayed out late. I'd hear her crying at night, masking her whimpers into a tissue. And as much as I hated it, when I snuck around and stared at her, I knew I'd never allow that to be me.

I love my mother, and her going through that hell made me decide I never would. No one, except myself, would ever break me with their actions.

The car goes silent, the outside traffic the only noise around us.

Silas jerks his chin toward my house. "Do you want me to come in and keep you company?"

I shake my head. "No, I'm okay."

"You sure?"

"Positive."

I gulp. *Hide those emotions.*

"Lola." Reaching out, he cups my chin and strokes it, the action giving me goose bumps. "You call me anytime you feel lonely, do you hear me? I'll be there for you, no matter what."

I nod, and for some reason, my chin trembles in his hold. "I know."

And I do know that. If I call, Silas is always there.

His hand leaves my chin to stroke my jawline. "You know you're the most important person in my life, right?"

"I know." My words are barely audible.

"You know that I love you?"

I nod again, unable to form words.

"That means, you'll never be alone. *Never.*" He puts so much stress on his last word, making it heavy, making it a fact. "I'm sure seeing Grace and Finn tonight has you worried about us. It crossed my mind too. But they're not us. Even something like that couldn't break our bond. You're the best thing in my life."

I wrap my hand around the wrist of his hand stroking my face—not to stop him, but to keep his touch there.

He smacks a loud kiss on my forehead. "Let's get you inside."

My heart drops into my stomach when he pulls away. He turns, stepping out of the car, and I do the same.

His hand rests on the arch of my back as we walk to my front door. "You sure you don't want me to come in?"

I shake my head, fetching my keys from my purse. "I work in the morning. You probably need to talk to Finn tonight and make sure he's okay."

He squeezes my waist. "Call me if you need anything."

I feel like my mother as I cringe when he pulls away. "Okay."

"Love you." He places a kiss on my cheek, only inches from my lips.

I turn my back to him, unlocking my door, and he stands there, making sure I'm safely inside before leaving. After shutting the door, I rest my back against it, the wood cold against my bare shoulders. As much as I don't want it to, as much as it surprises me, a single tear falls down my cheek.

It's the alcohol.

It has to be—because this isn't me.

Or is it?

I've never had to show my emotions because I've never been close to losing someone I care so deeply for, never feared how empty my life would be without them.

That dread, that desperation, is now close to bleeding through me.

I want a bond like Cohen has with Jamie, like Archer and Georgia, and Lincoln and Cassidy. And seeing Grace and Finn reminded me that might never happen with the only person I think it could.

But why?

Each one of them had difficult journeys but pushed their way through them because their love for the other was worth it. Cohen hated Jamie and her family for years, and she's his baby mama's sister. Georgia and Archer had a bad beginning, but they're making up for it now. And Lincoln is a felon, dating a woman with family in law enforcement. Maybe my mother's pleas weren't enough for my father, and her love wasn't enough to keep him, but my friends are examples that, sometimes, love is enough.

They chose each other, chose their hearts and happiness.

They opened themselves up, their broken and dark parts.

Can Silas and I do the same?

Or will one of us be my mother, pleading for something the other will never give?

CHAPTER TWENTY

Silas

LOLA'S WORDS haunt me as I walk back to my car. Shrinking into my seat, I replay them in my head.

She has no idea how lonely I get.

No one does.

I rest my head against the steering wheel. I'm lonely, but I do everything in my power to blanket that loneliness—hang out with my friends, *Lola*, and work nonstop. It doesn't work all the time, though. When the loneliness does creep through, I allow it to eat at me because I deserve it.

Lola is changing. It could be our friends coupling up and starting lives together. It could be Finn's reaction to Grace's news tonight. Eventually, Lola will want that too.

TWISTED FOX IS STILL OPEN, and I dodge people on my way to the bar. I fall on a stool in the corner and give myself a moment to reflect on tonight and what it means for our group.

As soon as the last customer leaves, Finn races behind the bar, snatches a bottle of whiskey, and pours himself a double. After draining it, he slams it down on the bar, and I'm shocked the thing doesn't shatter.

I join him, slapping his back. "You good, man?"

It's a dumb question because it's obvious he isn't, but I wasn't sure how to approach the situation.

"All good." To wash away his lie, he pours another drink.

I steal the bottle from him. "Don't bullshit me."

"Would you be pissed if you found out Lola was pregnant?"

I look away, hoping he doesn't see how that statement affects me. "I don't know."

"Bullshit. You would."

I sigh. "Let me drive you home."

Instead of replying, he swipes the bottle back and takes a long chug. It's nearly empty when he hands it back.

"Let's go," he says, wiping his mouth with the back of his arm.

Like with Lola, our ride is quiet. He spends most of it on his phone, frantically texting, and my guess is, he's texting Grace. After dropping him off, I drive to the one place I shouldn't. I call myself an idiot when I park my car and sit there, knowing I won't have the guts to get out.

I go here when I need a reminder that I don't deserve the good life.

Lola is lonely, and the reality of my friendship not being enough of what she needs frightens me to the core. I'm going to lose her just like I lost the reason I can't step out of my car.

———

"I'VE MISSED YOU, HONEY," my mother says, her voice musical while staring at me from the other side of the table at her favorite restaurant.

I clutch the menu and smile at her. "I've missed you too."

I love my mother. Mona Malone—she kept the last name because she said it had a certain ring to it—is the strongest woman I know. After my father left, she allowed herself a year to mourn their marriage, then she returned to Anchor Ridge and moved on with her life. She and my father are cordial to each other, and she's forgiven but not forgotten what he and Janet did.

She clasps her hands in front of her, resting them on the white tablecloth. "What have you been up to?"

"Not much. Working." I shrug. "The usual."

"Girlfriend?" It's a question she always asks.

I cringe. "You know there will never be a girlfriend."

I hoped the topic wouldn't come up, but each time, she tends to find a way to weave it into the conversation. If I didn't love her so much, I'd bail every time for that very reason. I already know what's coming next.

"Silas, honey," she starts, "I know what happened all those years ago was tragic and devastating, but eventually, you'll need to accept it and move on."

I wince at her words. I don't know why since it's always the same speech.

Reaching out, she rests her hand over mine. "You deserve happiness regardless of what you tell yourself. What happened wasn't your fault." She sighs. "I just want my son back."

I abruptly pull away, staring at her blankly. "You lost that son years ago."

There's hope in her eyes. "But we can bring him back."

I stay quiet.

"I talked to your father. He said Trent has been reaching out to make things right between you." She's so mellow, so calm, while my heart is racing in my chest.

"Trent can kiss my ass," I bite out.

"Silas—"

"Don't *Silas* me," I interrupt before unraveling my napkin and smoothing it out onto my lap. "Let's talk about something else."

The server cuts into our conversation when she takes our order, and we move on to a lighter chat—one that doesn't have my stomach curling, threatening to puke up lunch. Something that doesn't remind me of the mistakes I once made.

———

"HOW WAS LUNCH WITH YOUR MOM?" Lola asks over the phone.

"Not bad," I reply, scratching my cheek.

Not bad after she stopped trying to lecture me.

"Did you get that chicken dish I'd told you to try?"

"Yeah, and it was meh."

"Ugh, you need better taste buds."

I chuckle. "What did you do today?"

"I started narrowing down what to do for my birthday. You know, the best day of the year."

My chest caves in, and I force myself to sound excited. "Oh yeah … what are you thinking you want to do?"

Either Lola doesn't catch on to the dread in my voice or she chooses to ignore it. "One of my clients offered me a table at Sixes. It's been a while since we've been there, so I figured, why not?"

"Hmm."

"And you'd better be there this year."

"I will." An ache forms in the back of my throat.

"I'm serious, Silas. No bailing, do you hear me?"

"I hear you."

Today has been nothing but somber reminders of my past. First my mother and now Lola—even though Lola has no idea why. Every year, this happens, and every year, I wish I could ask Lola to change her birthday. No matter how hard I try, I can't bring myself to be in a celebratory mood. So, I don't show.

It's the only time we've had issues in our friendship.

Her birthday.

I'm always a no-show. I make up for it later, and it's not like I purposely lie. I plan to go, I hype myself up, but when it comes time to leave, I can't step out my front door. It's too hard.

"Promise me," she says, breaking me away from my thoughts. "Promise me you won't ditch me on my birthday."

"I promise as long as nothing comes up."

"Oh, bullshit. I don't want any excuses. You know when my birthday is every year, yet no matter what day of the week it falls on, you go MIA. I'm always there for your birthday and make sure it's special for you."

Forgetting her birthday isn't the issue.

It's the only day of the year that I dread.

———

"IF JAMIE and I can make it with two little ones at home, your no-kid-having ass can too," Cohen says, sternly staring at me from across the bar.

"What's the deal with Lola's birthday anyway?" Finn asks. "You never miss anyone's but hers."

"Will you be there?" I ask him, hoping he'll say no because Grace is pregnant, which will pull the attention away from me.

Finn nods.

So, everyone but me will be in attendance. *Fuck my life.*

I kick my feet against the stool legs. "How's it going with Grace?"

"It's weird, having a girl roommate," Finn says. "It'll take some adjusting, but I'm happy to be there for her."

"*There for her* is an understatement," Lincoln says. "My man is understanding the damn assignment of playing baby daddy."

Not surprisingly, we found out Grace's baby daddy is a married piece of shit. Oh, a married, *also expecting a baby on the way with his wife* piece of shit. Grace wants nothing to do with him, but she also didn't want to tell people she got pregnant by a taken man. To help with her problem, we came up with a plan—Finn will act like her baby daddy. He was reluctant at first, given it's a weird job, but he agreed to it, knowing it'd help Grace.

He also agreed to move in with Grace to make it more believable. Cassidy gave him her bedroom and is staying at Lincoln's penthouse.

Finn shrugs. "I want to be there for Grace any way I can."

I shut my eyes, wishing I could be the same for Lola every single damn day of the year.

"And the new job?" Cohen asks.

"Yeah, traitor," Lincoln says, tossing a beer cap at Finn, "how's the new job?"

"It's different." Finn runs his hand over his stressed face. "The hours have taken some getting used to as well as not being here and hanging out with you assholes."

Grace's brother-in-law owns a luxury car dealership and offered Finn a job, so he could be more available to Grace. Finn was reluctant to take it, worried that Cohen and Archer would be upset with him for leaving them, but they couldn't have been happier for him. At the dealership, he'll make more money and have better benefits. At the end of the day, we always want our friends to do their best and be happy.

After an hour of hanging out at the bar, Finn leaves to be with Grace. Cohen and Lincoln linger to their side of the bar for their shifts. And Archer, who maybe said five words while we hung out, stops me before I leave.

"The war going on in your head," he says out of the blue, "let Lola drag you out of it before you lose her. You'd better show up at the party because if you keep bailing, she'll stop inviting. Your invite will go to another man. Remember that." He slaps me on the shoulder. "Don't fuck it up."

Without waiting for a reply, he turns around and walks toward the Employees Only door.

Not fucking it up is easier said than done.

CHAPTER TWENTY-ONE

Lola

SILAS IS the most dependable person I know.

Except for on my birthday.

I almost didn't invite him this year, so I wouldn't get my hopes up. I've questioned him numerous times on why he seems to have an issue with my birthday, but he says it's nothing. He promises to show, but then he goes MIA every year.

"Do you think Silas will show tonight?" Georgia asks, eyeing a black dress before returning it to the rack at the boutique we're shopping in.

"Who knows?" I grumble, shrugging to play it off like I couldn't care less. Fingers crossed that I look convincing. "He said he would, but if he doesn't show, then he doesn't."

My stomach knots. Worrying about Silas showing up for my birthday has been a nonstop thought.

She gives me a disapproving frown. "There you go again."

I twirl a strand of hair around my finger. "What again?"

"Acting like you don't care if he's a no-show."

"Silas doesn't owe me anything." The words hurt as they come out of my mouth.

"Except he's one of your best friends—behind me, of course. He can't bail on your birthday with no explanation again. It's weird and rude."

"Sometimes, people have stuff that comes up."

"Every single year?"

I turn away from her, pretending to focus on a rack of lingerie. "Maybe he's not a birthday kind of guy."

"He shows up for everyone else's birthdays, just not yours."

She steps to my side and grabs my hand to stop me. "Sorry, babe. I'm not trying to be a downer, but it sucks to see you sad on your birthday when he bails. If he doesn't show this year, he'd better explain himself this time."

I nod, digesting her words, but I'm unsure of how my reaction will be if he doesn't. At least I chose a place where I could drink this year.

Georgia means well, but I hate hearing it. I try to tell myself that Silas doesn't owe me anything. He's not my boyfriend or lover, so I can't get angry with him. I don't expect people to show up to my party. I told Grace and Finn they could skip it with everything they have going on.

"What about this one?" I hear Georgia say around a gasp, and I realize she left my side. When I shift to look at her two racks away from me, she's holding up a short red dress.

"Hello, birthday dress," I say, staring it down.

"Now, off to find some shoes," Georgia says, perking up at my approval of her choice.

I find the perfect pair of strapless black heels and then stop at the salon for a blowout.

Don't feel sorry for yourself, Lola.

It's not cute, and it doesn't go with your new dress.

———

BIRTHDAYS ARE a big deal to me.

Yes, I'm one of those girls.

Judge me all you want.

It's not about the gifts or the attention. It's how I was raised.

For as long as I can remember, my family has always gone all out for birthdays. No matter what anyone has going on, we always make sure to celebrate. I had lunch with my mother and Robby earlier today. Tomorrow morning, I'll have brunch with the girls.

"There's the birthday girl," Harry, Sixes' club owner, shouts, throwing out his arms when he sees me.

I rode to the club with Lincoln and Cassidy since they live the closest to me. I almost asked Silas for a ride, but the last thing I wanted on my birthday was to wait around, only for him not to show, like a bad '90s flick where the cool guy asks the girl to prom as a joke and ditches her. With perfect timing, Georgia, Archer, Cohen, and Jamie pulled up to the valet behind us. We waited for Maliki and Sierra, our friends from Blue Beech—a town a few counties over—and then went inside.

Harry waves us forward in a follow-me gesture. I grab Georgia's hand, and we form a human chain, careful not to lose anyone while filing through people. Harry leads us up wide stairs and gestures to the security guard to move to the side, giving us entry into the VIP section.

"We have birthday-girl shooters and bottles coming your way," Harry says as a server approaches us, staying at his side. He jerks his thumb toward her. "This is Abby. She's your server for tonight. Abby, whatever she orders is on the house."

Abby eagerly nods, pulling at her sequined skirt that she's paired with a crop top, the bar's logo in the center. "I'll take good care of them."

The bouncer strolls over to Harry, whispering in his ear, and he tells us to have a good time. Abby asks which drinks I'd prefer and says she'll be back.

As soon as she leaves, everyone takes their seats. I check my phone, hoping to find something from Silas, but nothing. He texted me *Happy Birthday* this morning and had breakfast and flowers delivered. When I asked if he'd be here, he replied with a simple, *Of course.* I almost called him but didn't want to look desperate. That was six hours ago, and as much as I want to, I have too much pride to ask again.

If he shows, he shows. If he doesn't, then I'll act like it doesn't affect me. I've given up trying to figure out why my birthday is such a burden to him.

Abby returns with a bottle of Grey Goose, cocktail shooters, and mixers. I grab the vodka, unscrew the lid, and drink it straight. It burns, like acid falling down my throat, and I nearly gag. I haven't had straight vodka in years.

"Jesus, Lols," Georgia says. "I know it's your birthday, but you might want to calm it down. The night is still young."

"The night is still young, but I'm not getting any younger." I hold up the bottle. "Might as well live it up now."

Loud club music plays around us, but it's not so in your face in the VIP area, so we can still hear each other speak. I'm not sure if that's a good or bad thing tonight. Maybe I need some chaos to drown out my thoughts of spending yet another birthday without Silas.

"If Silas doesn't show up, it's not going to be pretty," Georgia attempts to whisper to Archer, but since Georgia can't exactly whisper, I hear her.

I check my phone again.

Nothing.

That calls for a cocktail shooter. It's tastier than the vodka, so I take another. Every time I stupidly look at my phone, I take another shot.

This is what happens when I get my hopes up even though I said I wouldn't. As I'm taking my whatever number shot, I stop in my tracks.

Silas is walking toward us, sluggishly inching toward the table, with intent on his face. His powerful figure stands out among the lingering people, and I can nearly hear the echo of my heart as I bolt toward him.

He's here.

Too bad he's not as happy to see me as I am him.

CHAPTER TWENTY-TWO

Silas

THREE HUNDRED AND sixty-four days of the year, I live a normal day-to-day life. I have no problem with rolling out of bed, leaving my house, and acting like an adult.

But there's one day that I can't, when I can barely function. When every time I attempt to do my mundane actions, I'm hit with the memories. In fear of them, I don't want to get out of bed. And that day just so happens to fall on Lola's birthday. Not going to lie, I've even considered asking her to change her birthday before. I'm that desperate to steer clear of it. It's scribbled out of my calendar in bright-red permanent marker. It's my personal doomsday.

My head is already throbbing when I walk into Sixes. If I had it my way, I'd be at my house, ignoring everyone and waiting for this day to end. But Archer's words smacked some sense into me. If I keep this up, I'll lose Lola. We're already treading into those dangerous waters. My absence would just pull us deeper into it. I can't let that happen.

Curse words leave my mouth, low and barely audible, as I make my way toward our friends. I ran into Harry as soon as I walked in, and since I knew him from throwing events at his club, he pointed me in their direction. My mouth is dry even though I chugged a bottle of water before exiting my car and tossing my keys to the valet. Tonight will be the hardest night I've had to pretend.

Lola's gaze meets mine. She grins as if I'm the birthday present she's been waiting for. Seeing her this happy is why I dragged myself out of my misery and came to the club. Like one of those people who darts toward their loved ones at the airport, she jumps into my arms. I capture her around the waist, holding her up, and her hair drops into my face.

"You actually came!" Her voice is slurred, and alcohol lingers from her red lips as she peers down at me.

I carefully set her on her feet, taking in how stunning she looks in her red dress and heels. "I actually came."

"I didn't think you would." Her face softens. "I figured it'd be another year of Silas ditching me and then apologizing for it tomorrow."

"I'm here." I kiss the top of her head, knowing my words will be limited tonight.

"Thank you." Her words are nearly a whisper—a sharp contrast to the slur she gave me earlier.

She snatches my hand, erasing the distance between our friends and us, and their expressions are filled with approval when I join them.

Damn, it feels good not to be a letdown this year.

"How much have you had to drink?" I ask Lola, squeezing her hand.

She spins to face me and holds up her thumb and pointer finger, leaving some space between them. "Just a teensy-weensy bit."

"What's a *teensy-weensy* bit?" I raise a brow while jerking my head toward the table covered in liquor bottles. "An entire bottle?"

"I'm not sure." She shrugs. "I figured if I got drunk, I wouldn't think about you ditching me."

Her words sting, and I drop my head in shame. She's this drunk because of what I did in the past.

Is this how she looked every year when she realized I was a no-show?

This isn't Lola. She doesn't wear her heart on her sleeve like some of our other friends. A crowbar is needed to crack her open to even draw out shards of obscured pieces. I've also never seen her this drunk. Sure, I've heard stories of her wild college days with the girls, but nowadays, she always stops after a few drinks. She said she got that out of her system.

And even though I shouldn't be, I'm annoyed with her behavior. Almost pissed.

"He actually came," Georgia tells Archer, attempting to keep her voice down, but as usual, she doesn't.

I brace a hand around Lola's waist before she topples over and point at her. "She's drunk as hell."

Archer nods. "That she is."

"I've never seen her like this."

Lola is now talking to Maliki about different liquors he needs to start carrying at his bar, Down Home Pub.

"Blame yourself for that," Archer says, never caring to filter his words.

I huff. "You're blaming me for her being plastered? Maybe blame yourself for not stopping her."

"No," Georgia says, answering for her boyfriend. "We're blaming you for playing head games with her all these years. She drank because she figured you wouldn't show. It's as simple as that."

Lola, now done with her conversation with Maliki, separates herself from me. "Let's dance." She holds out her hand toward Georgia.

I scrub a hand over my face. "Or let's find you some water."

"I choose dancing," she chirps, not even considering my idea.

"How about you choose not to drink anymore?" I almost feel like her father. "You were worried I wouldn't make it, and I get it, but I'm here now. You don't have to act like this."

She winces as if I slapped her in the face and grabs Georgia's hand. "We're dancing."

Georgia allows her to pull her up from the couch, and they hold hands while walking away from us, dancing to the beat of the music. I scrub a hand over my face, wishing I hadn't come.

"Nice going." I fall back into a chair next to Archer and glare at him. "You could've stopped her from chugging liquor like it was water."

Archer shrugs his broad shoulders. "Not my circus, not my monkeys."

My glare deepens. "No, she's just your girlfriend's best friend."

"It's her birthday. I'm not going to play babysitter. Let her enjoy herself."

"There's the baby daddy and baby mama," Lincoln calls out.

Our conversation ends, all attention cutting to Grace and Finn strolling in our direction. Even though Finn said he was coming, I wasn't sure if Grace would. Which was stupid because the girls are always there for each other.

"Grace!" Lola shouts, stopping her dancing to stumble toward them. "My bestie carrying my future godchild. Thank you for being here!"

"Um, excuse you," Georgia says from behind her. "I'm the future godmother."

Lola wrinkles her nose. "We can *all* be a godparent."

Georgia shrugs. "I'll accept that."

"Happy birthday," Grace says, hugging Lola before Finn guides her to the couch. They sit down at the end of it, making themselves comfortable.

"I haven't seen you this wasted since college," Grace says, her eyes on Lola.

"I've *never* seen her this wasted, period," I add. Even though I'm replying to Grace's comment, I'm studying Lola.

"Agreed." Georgia nods. "Did something happen today?"

Georgia knows why Lola drank so much, so I don't know if her question is a cover, so other people don't know. My guess is, it is.

Unlike me staring at her, Lola hasn't glanced in my direction since Grace and Finn arrived.

"It's my birthday. I was gifted a complimentary bottle from the club since I'm the owner's alcohol rep. He also sent over some bubblegum shooters." Lola motions to the tray of shooters, then snags one and knocks it back.

I run a hand through my hair in frustration. "I'll be sure to tell Harry you're cut off."

"Hey, guys. Can I get you anything else?" the server says, interrupting the birthday shit show.

Grace and Finn order what Lola should be ordering—seltzer water.

I consider leaving. I can apologize to Lola when I'm not a depressed dick and she's sober.

I start to stand, but Lola saying, "My best friend," causes me to freeze.

She collapses onto my lap, the weight of her a sudden shock, and sits sideways. Her breathing is ragged as she wraps her arms around my neck.

I inhale her sweet perfume, almost getting as drunk on it as Lola is, and my mind races. This isn't the first time she's sat on my lap, but it is the first time since I fingered her on the couch. If it were beforehand and if she wasn't drunk off her ass, I would find it normal.

She tips her head down, and her black hair curtains our faces as if giving us privacy from everyone. I groan, hating that my dick hardens when she shifts to straddle me. Just like all her other actions tonight, the expression covering her face isn't one I'm used to. This is a different woman with different emotions and a different mindset tonight.

"I want to fuck you," she whispers into my ear. Unlike earlier, her words aren't slurred. They're clear as if she hadn't had one sip of liquor.

There's no hint of humor in her voice.

None of our usual playfulness.

I shut my eyes, a pain squeezing at my heart. "You're drunk."

"And?" She slowly slides against me, rubbing her core against my erection, and I groan. "We can leave and finish where we left off at the cabin. This time, I can touch you, tease you, *fuck you*."

Every muscle in my body tightens.

This can't be fucking happening.

This isn't the time or the place to have a conversation like this.

This isn't the time or the place for me to have to stand my ground and most likely have to be a dick to her on her birthday.

She's making a fool of herself. A fool out of me because whatever I do, it will be a show in front of our friends. I can allow her to dry-hump me, which she kinda, sorta is. I can leave with her and have sex with her. Or I can kick her off my lap.

I shut my eyes, growing more and more turned on at the feel of her body against mine. My cock aches, calling me a dumbass at the idea of turning her down. It's been a minute since I've had sex.

"Lola," I grind out, "this isn't the place."

"Then let's leave," she breathes out. "Get out of here. No one will care. They'll probably be happy for us."

My head is spinning. I clamp my hands around her waist, halting her from grinding, thinking it'll solve the problem.

Lola snatches my wrist, plucking it off her waist, and drags it down to her thigh.

And that's when I do something stupid. Without thinking, I abruptly stand.

And Lola drops to the floor.

CHAPTER TWENTY-THREE

Lola

I'VE NEVER BEEN this humiliated in my life.

As I'm on the floor, staring at Silas in shock, I think about my mother. All those times I saw her as weak, as ridiculous, for begging my father to be with her.

I'm my mother.

I finally understand her pain.

Our situations are different, yes, because my father married her. Promised her until death do they part. But Silas swore to never hurt me, and he did.

On my birthday.

In front of all our friends.

Embarrassment hits me from every angle. I was nearly dry-humping him in public. He dropped me on my ass. It was the alcohol's fault to begin with along with my emotions and the lack of eating since I hadn't had an appetite. The thought of Silas not coming made me disgusted at the thought of food.

My gaze is pinned on him, my eyes watery, and my dress is damp from a vodka glass that dumped over in what I'll always refer to as *the fall of my ass*. Hurt and tears are in my eyes. Unreadable emotions are in his. If he didn't want me in his lap, he could've moved me off more casually … carefully … not as if I were a dirty T-shirt being tossed on the floor after a long day at work.

"Goddammit, Lola," he says around a huff before raising his voice. "Drink some water because you're being a sloppy fucking drunk." As soon as the words leave his mouth, regret flashes across his face.

Everyone's eyes are on us.

He's never talked to me like that.

Then it's almost like what happened just dawned on him.

"Come on." He reaches out, holding out his hand, but I swat it away.

"No, I don't want your help." I sniffle, blinking back tears, and pull myself to my feet. With how tipsy I am, I'm surprised I'm able to. My head spins, my world turning upside down, and the noise around us fades away.

"I'm sorry," Silas croaks.

"I think you should go," I demand.

He was the first person I wanted here, and now, he's the last person I want to see.

I adjust my dress, failing to look at anyone, and fold my arms over my stomach. "That's what I want from you for my birthday. To leave." This is the most broken I've ever felt in my life.

"Fine." Silas pinches the bridge of his nose. "I'll go."

We stare at each other. He looks at me as if begging me to change my mind about asking him to leave … and I want to. I'm holding in sobs when he turns to walk away.

"Well, well, look what we have here," a man calls out.

Silas freezes, and I look forward and see a guy standing in front of us. He's staring straight at Silas while running his hands together. Two men stand behind him, but I quickly dart my gaze back to the man who called Silas's name. He's tall, clean-shaven, and attractive.

"Silas fucking Malone," the guy says, his tone a mixture of excitement and cockiness.

Silas stares him down, his glare colder than he looked when I was practically dry-humping him. He steps in front of me, blocking the man's view of me.

The guy strokes his jaw while coming closer. "I haven't seen you in forever. You act like your family doesn't exist."

Whoa.

Who is this man?

Is he related to Silas?

It dawns on me that I've never met anyone from Silas's family.

"I'm a busy man," Silas says, his voice full of warning.

"Busy, huh?" The guy does a once-over of our friends and scoffs. "Enough time for a birthday party, though, huh? Who's the birthday someone?"

This is where I can get my revenge on Silas.

He obviously doesn't want this guy to see me.

I walk around Silas, revealing myself, and all this commotion sobers me up. Holding up my hand, I say, "Me."

"Goddamn, the birthday girl is hot." Cocky Boy extends his hand, staring at me instead of Silas now. "I'm Trent, Silas's brother."

"Stepbrother," Silas corrects with a snarl. "No blood relation. Thank fucking God."

"Oh, come on, brother," Trent says. "Let's forget about the past. How about this? Let's share a drink. We can go to my table—which is larger and surrounded by NBA and NFL players and other high-profile people—or stay here."

Silas works his jaw. "Nah, we're good. Go hang out with your high-profile friends and beat feet."

"At least let me buy the birthday girl a drink," Trent says.

"She's had enough," Silas snaps, popping his knuckles.

Archer and Lincoln stand and join Silas, and Trent chuckles.

"I wouldn't mind a birthday Sprite," I say, chewing on my lower lip. "I don't want to be hungover tomorrow." I cringe at the thought of consuming anything containing alcohol. I cringe more at the thought of turning around and facing everyone after what Silas just did.

"I think you've already crossed that line," Silas snarls.

Trent snaps his fingers. "A birthday Sprite it is." He does a sweeping gesture toward the table. "Any of these guys your boyfriend?"

His eyes fasten on Silas as if he wonders if it's him and that's the only one he cares about.

"Nope," I quickly say, not bothering to look at Silas.

Screw that.

He did what he did, so I'm not going to worry about how he feels about me being around Trent. Plus, the faster I can get away from here, the better.

Silas curses under his breath and wipes his forehead with the back of his arm.

If Silas hadn't done what he did, I'd have turned Trent down. Hell, I'd have turned any guy down. But now, all I want to do is escape. His rejection killed me.

Before I grab Trent's hand, Abby scurries toward us, holding a tray of glasses. "Sorry! I got caught up at a table." She hands Finn and Grace their drinks, and when she sees Trent, her face brightens, and she giggles. "Hey, Trent. Can I get you something?"

"Nah, I'm good, Abby." Trent gestures to me, and Abby frowns. "I'm going to escort the birthday girl to the bar and get her a drink, so we can talk more privately."

He drops his hand, and this time, he holds out his elbow. I put mine through the open space, connecting us. We walk away, and I don't glance back at Silas once.

Call me a bitch.

Call me whatever.

But at this point, I don't care.

CHAPTER TWENTY-FOUR

Silas

I GO to follow Lola and Trent because, well, fuck that shit, but Archer snags my elbow, pulling me back.

"Unless you plan on making things right with Lola this minute, sit your ass down," he practically snarls. "You just humiliated the girl in front of everyone on her fucking birthday. Don't do it a second time."

I wince at his words, fire burning through me. I'm pissed at Trent for showing up and speaking to me. I'm pissed at Lola for leaving with him. I'm pissed at myself for my behavior.

"Let him get her a drink while you think about your weird asshole actions," Georgia adds, looking like she wants to rip my head off as much as I want to do to Trent's.

She's protective of her friends—as they all are. I've witnessed her kick guys in the shin for less.

I plop down on the chair—the same one where Lola told me she wanted to fuck me. The same one where I turned her down and embarrassed her. I want to stand up and kick it, punch it, do something. As I sit there, I inhale deep breaths in hopes that it calms my racing heart.

This is my punishment for coming tonight, for thinking I could get away with having a good time. Nothing good ever comes out of this day. Not only did Lola and I have a disaster, but Trent, out of all people, also had to show up. My past keeps coming back to haunt me.

Instead of being as miserable as I am about this day, he's now hanging out with Lola, saving her from me—the big, bad best friend who embarrassed her. I dropped her off my lap—one of the worst things I could've possibly done—but I didn't know what else to do. And I hadn't thought before standing.

I slump my shoulders, opening my legs, and drop my head between them.

I'm losing my best friend because I can't get over my past.

"What the hell was that about?" Cohen asks, causing me to raise my head. "Why would you do that shit to Lola?"

I'm asking myself the same question, buddy.

"I'm so confused," I mutter.

"We all are," Cassidy says. "Lola was looking at Silas with stars and horniness in her eyes. Instead of nicely turning her down, he pushed her off his lap." She shakes her head. "That has to do something to a girl's ego. Especially when Silas acts like he's in love with her."

"Acts like?" Finn snorts. "Silas *is* in love with her."

They're talking about me now as if I weren't even here. As bad as I want to tell them to shut up, all that's on my mind is Lola and what I did.

"I hate that motherfucker," I hiss, balling up my fists. "I'm doing everything I can not to storm down there and beat his ass."

"Why do you hate him?" Jamie asks, her voice careful and soft. As a doctor, she's used to handling tough situations.

I tap my foot. "He's shady as fuck."

Always has been.

Always will be.

I will never trust Trent.

He can't be trusted with secrets, with friends, with people's lives.

He can't be trusted with Lola.

"He's shady as fuck because he's really shady as fuck, or he's shady as fuck because he's flirting with Lola?" Lincoln asks.

"Both." I grimace, hating their names being said together.

"Are you going to finally admit you two have hooked up?" Georgia asks.

I stare at my tapping foot—an action to stop me from jumping up and beating Trent's ass. "Nah, we've never had sex."

That's the truth. Georgia asked if we've hooked up, and I said we've never had sex. It's not lying.

"But have you *hooked up?*" Sierra clarifies.

I stay quiet. I'd never say anything about what happened the night at the lake unless Lola said it was okay. But then I don't know if I would want people to know because it'd make our friends give us hell about being together.

"How about this?" Finn states with confidence. "Grow some balls and go apologize and tell Lola how you feel."

My face burns, a slash of anger crawling through me, and I glare at Finn. "I could say the same shit to you, brother."

He doesn't have room to talk. He's loved Grace for years, and he hasn't done anything about it. Finn is as terrified of losing Grace as I am with Lola.

"Don't take your anger out on me, man," Finn snaps, hunching forward.

I stand and point at Grace. I shouldn't say the words, but they blurt out from my loose lips. "Grace wouldn't be pregnant with another man's baby had you grown some balls."

My stomach churns. I said that to get back at Finn, but I stupidly hadn't thought about how it'd affect Grace.

Finn bares his teeth as if he's ready to beat my ass. "Watch your goddamn mouth."

At this point, a fight sounds good to me.

I need this.

Someone to take my anger out on ... my hurt ... my regret.

It shouldn't be a friend, though.

I stare at Finn with hard eyes. "Does the truth hurt?"

Everyone watches us, glaring at me as if they want to kick my ass.

Archer stands, preparing to jump in if he has to.

Finn wipes the edge of his mouth. "Like you're doing with Lola. Instead, she's going to hook up with your stepbrother."

Oh, fuck no.

Those words should've never left his mouth.

I rear my fist back, but before it can make contact with Finn's face, Archer pulls me away the same way he did when I tried to stop Lola. He shoots me a warning glare.

"Whoa," Georgia says when Archer has the situation handled. "We all know Lola isn't hooking up with anyone tonight."

Grace grabs Finn's wrist, stopping him from standing to beat my ass. "This is not the place. Let's go."

I slam my eyes shut, the sound of Grace's voice causing more guilt to build inside me. "Shit, Grace. I'm sorry. I was pissed and—"

"It's fine," she rushes out, but I can tell it's not. "I just … it's time for us to go."

I fold my hands together and bow my head. "Really, Grace—"

She talks over me. "You're sorry. Okay. I get it."

Her lower lip trembles, making me hate myself more. Add Grace to another person I humiliated tonight. I'm not even drunk, and I'm acting like an imbecile. Instead of creating more damage, I turn around and walk away. On my way out the door, as I pass the bar, I hesitate.

Maybe it's time for me to break my sobriety.

Maybe it's time I started numbing myself.

CHAPTER TWENTY-FIVE

Lola

"THE BIRTHDAY GIRL doesn't look like she's having a good time," Trent says as the bartender hands over our Sprites.

Yes, he also ordered a Sprite.

"She is most definitely not," I reply, circling my straw through my drink.

He runs his hand over his smooth cheek. "Who pissed you off?"

I wave off his question. "It doesn't matter."

He shifts to face me. "It was Silas, wasn't it?"

I take a sip of my drink.

"Let me make up for whatever he did."

Gripping his Sprite with one hand, he holds the other out to me. I grab it, and we mosey through the crowd toward the subdued section of the bar, where two-top tables are scattered throughout and the music is softer. I've never been in this area of the club, but I've heard about it. It's for the VIPs of the VIPs who like the club but prefer to be on the tamer side of things. It's quite contradicting to go to a club but not want the club experience.

I retreat a step, our hands still clasped, as I flit my gaze over the section. "Are we allowed to be here?"

Maybe I'll ask Harry for a table here next time.

Who am I kidding? I will never celebrate a birthday here again.

Trent offers a reassuring smile. "I didn't reserve a table, but it's okay. I know Harry." He motions toward the other side of the club, close to where my table is. "I was with my friends over there, but you look like you'd rather drink swamp water than socialize. I figured we could drink our Sprites and chat. Sober you up. Get you away from whatever has you upset."

My friends won't mind if I take a minute for myself, away from everyone. I don't want to be around Silas, and I don't know if he's gone.

He leads me to a table near the back of the room, grabs my Sprite, and places our drinks on the table before pulling out a stool for me.

Trent is attractive—tall, dark-haired, and handsome. Not as handsome as Silas, but it was no surprise that Abby was nearly drooling when she saw him. Not only does he look good, but he's also made me feel comfortable tonight.

"Why does Silas hate your guts?" I ask, sitting down and hoping my question takes the attention off me.

Trent scoots his chair closer to mine before plopping down. "His dad left his mom for mine. It was a messy situation, and as stepsiblings, we didn't get along because of it. We were immature teenage boys. I let it go. Silas hasn't."

Silas has mentioned his father leaving his mother, but he never said anything about a stepbrother.

"Have you tried speaking to him privately?"

Trent nods. "All the time. I've invited him to meet up, have coffee, talk, anything, but he won't. He even refuses to attend family events if I'll be there."

"Oh."

That doesn't sound like Silas, and I don't want to talk bad about him, especially not knowing the entire story. But no matter what, my loyalty remains with Silas—even if I want to punch him right now.

Trent pats my hand, catching on to my silence. "Enough about him. Let's talk about *you*."

"Well … it's my birthday."

My brain isn't exactly on its A game right now. I took too many shots, fought with my best friend, and am now with a man said best friend hates.

I'm tipsy.

Okay, maybe a little beyond tipsy.

I can't drive home, but I can recite my full name.

"I got that part, babe." Trent chuckles. "What do you do?"

Simple question. My gool ole drunken brain can also answer that.

Props to me.

"Alcohol sales."

"Oh, cool." He grips his glass and taps his fingers against it. "What company?"

"It's 21st Amendment."

I'm usually more cautious about telling someone where I work, but Trent is Silas's stepbrother. And even though Silas isn't a fan, so far, Trent has been nothing but nice to me. I'm thankful he came to our table and rescued me.

"That's awesome. I have a few friends who order from 21st Amendment."

"What about you? What do you do? Tell me about yourself."

"I work for an athletic talent agency. We represent and find deals for athletes."

"Oh. That's cool."

He pauses, a moment of silence passing. "Did you and Silas ever date?"

"Nope," I quip.

Please don't ask if we've hooked up.

I don't know if my inebriated brain can figure out the best way to lie.

He nods. "I just don't want to touch something that's his."

My head snaps up. "I'm not someone's property."

"Shit, that's not how I meant it." He grimaces. "I don't want to ask you out if you and he have been together."

I shake my head. "We're friends."

Silas made it clear we're nothing.

So, nothing is what we'll be.

Trent blows out a long breath. "How can I make the birthday girl smile?"

I smile timidly. "You're already helping."

He grins. "Glad I'm doing my job."

We talk for over an hour.

About our jobs, families, hobbies.

He enjoys cooking. I don't. So, he offers to cook for me sometime.

We're both homebodies and only go out for special occasions.

Silas isn't brought up again.

Trent seems nice, so why is Silas holding a grudge?

I'll need to ask him when I'm done kicking his ass. Even though what he did was wrong, I'll let him explain. If he wants to make up for what he did tonight, he needs to tell me what his problem is with my birthday.

When it's time to call it a night, Trent walks me back to my friends. Silas, Grace, and Finn are the only ones gone while the others are chatting. I don't ask where Silas is because I don't want them to know his behavior hurt me as deep as it did.

Trent walks me out of the club with the others and waits outside for the valet to bring our rides. He has no problem with introducing himself and making conversation with everyone.

Before I get into Lincoln's car, he asks for my number.

And I give it to him.

I HAVEN'T HAD a hangover this intense since college.

I do a once-over of the room I'm in. It's Archer's old bedroom. Technically, it's still his current bedroom, but he and Georgia rarely sleep here. Archer owns the penthouse, and after Lincoln was released from prison, he moved in with him. Not too long ago, Archer surprised Georgia and bought a house she'd liked. Now, Cassidy and Lincoln stay here since Finn is crashing in Cassidy's old bedroom. It's all one big roommate web.

Me? I'm not a roommate kind of person.

I enjoy my space too much.

I'm here because Cassidy said she was in no way allowing me to go home alone last night. She mentioned something along the lines of choking on my vomit even though I told her I wasn't near that drunken stage. I argued for a good five minutes until I gave in because I was too exhausted to care at that point. All I wanted was a comfy bed, water, and a toothbrush—and thankfully, they had a spare one.

As I stretch in the bed, my head throbbing, flashbacks of last night worsen my headache. Silas made it the worst birthday I've ever had. I don't know what's going on with our friendship, but it's changing. At first, I wasn't sure if it was good or bad, but after the whole lap drop, it was bad.

My mouth is dry as I reach across the bed and collect my phone from the nightstand. I shrink back against the pillow as I scan the texts on my screen. Georgia. Grace. My mother. Trent. *Silas.*

My body feels heavy as I open his text first. He sent it last night, after I went to bed.

Silas: I'm sorry. So fucking sorry.

His message seems so … dead … nothing like our usual texts. I normally wake up to *good morning* texts from him, not apology ones. I haven't felt this lonely, this forgotten, in years.

I ignore Silas's text, answer my friends, and then open Trent's message last.

Trent: Good morning. I hope your hangover isn't too bad this morning.

His message brightens my mood.

I immediately reply.

Me: I'm never drinking again.

Trent: We've all said that before.

Me: True, but this time, I really mean it.

Trent: Let's go out and have a birthday redo since yours wasn't as great as you'd wanted.

Me: I'd like that.

———

THE FIRST THING I order at brunch is a mimosa—my whole *never drinking again* plan long gone.

Do I need a mimosa with this hangover?

Definitely not.

Everyone else does the same, except for Grace and Cassidy, who opt for a lemonade.

Our birthday-brunch tradition started in high school. It began with milkshakes, and then we graduated to mimosas once we could drink. Jamie, Cassidy, and Sierra have joined in as well. I chose a small bistro, and since the sun is shining and the humidity is tolerable, we're sitting outside.

"First things first," Georgia says after the server hands over our drinks. She plays with the straw in her hand, and it's like the drink gives her the confidence she needs to start her questions. "Lola, we need to know what the hell happened last night."

I push my oversize black sunglasses up my nose. "First things first. I'm hungover, and I'll talk about anything but that."

"Come on," Georgia groans. "What pissed off Silas so much that he acted how he did?"

"I've never seen him like that," Grace says. "He threw you off his lap."

I grab my mimosa. "Silas doesn't like it when I drink that much."

I shrug, hoping they believe that lie. Silas has never encouraged me to be sober.

"There's no way he was that mad over you having a few drinks," Georgia argues. "Not to mention, you looked like you wanted to jump his bones."

"It was actually hot," Cassidy adds. "Until the whole *dropping you on your ass* part."

I wince, remembering it so clearly. "Sorry, but I'd prefer not to talk about my best friend rejecting me. It was dumb on my part, smart on his."

"What about his stepbrother?" Jamie asks. "You two looked chummy."

"He's nice," I reply. "We exchanged numbers. He walked me to

Lincoln's car, and then he and Cass took my drunken ass home." I give Cass an appreciative nod.

"He was a gentleman," Cassidy says. "With how Silas described him, I expected him to be a jackass. While we waited for Lincoln's car, he chatted with us. I think Silas was jealous of him buying Lola a drink."

Everyone seemed to like Trent, and he didn't give off any douchebag vibes when he wasn't around Silas. Maybe they bring out the worst in each other.

"Is it weird, though?" Grace asks. "With him being Silas's stepbrother?"

"They're not close," I answer. "Their parents didn't start dating until their senior year of high school, and they never hung out. Silas's dad left his mother for Trent's mom. I understand Silas not being a fan, but Trent had nothing to do with what his mom did. According to Trent, Silas has hated him since the day they met."

"As bad as it sounds, I get his anger," Sierra says. "I was pissed when I found out my father had an affair and secret child. I took it out on my brother's girlfriend for a while since she had something to do with it."

I nod. "My father was the king of affairs. It's why I don't trust men."

"Since Lola won't share anything, let's move on to Grace and Finn," Georgia says, and I smile at the subject change. "Finn looked ready to kill Silas for what he said about you getting pregnant because Finn was a wuss."

When I woke up this morning, Cassidy filled me in on what had happened after I left and how Silas and Finn argued.

I guess Silas decided it was asshole day.

Grace blushes as she plays with her straw. "I'm happy he did. It knocked sense into Finn." A slow smile builds along her face.

Georgia gapes at her. "What?"

"Now, this is a much better conversation." I lean back in my chair and suck on the orange from my drink. "Did you fuck?" *Sorry, not sorry for my straightforwardness.*

"We didn't … have sex …" She trails off as if searching for the right words. "Just messed around."

"First base?" Georgia asks. "Second base?"

Everyone happily stares at Grace.

It's about damn time they got together.

"What base is tongues?" Grace asks, always my somewhat-innocent friend … who also got knocked up by the principal … so she doesn't seem as innocent as she once did.

There isn't one person at the table who doesn't show a sign of excitement.

"How was it?" Cassidy asks.

"It was amazing," Grace replies, looking on top of the world. "I could spend the rest of my life having him … go downtown on me."

"Cheers to that!" Georgia says.

Everyone raises their glass and clinks them together.

"Does that mean you're dating now?" Sierra asks.

"I don't know." Grace's smile somewhat drops. "His feelings for me might change after the baby is born. I'm going to get fat—"

"Shut the hell up with that attitude," I interrupt, hating that she's feeling insecure about that. "Finn worships you. He isn't going anywhere."

Now, if only Silas were the same.

More of my friends dating each other.

Silas and I are the only ones left in our circle who aren't getting together.

One by one, they're finding men who are into them.

And day by day, Silas and I are only growing more and more apart.

Our happily ever after isn't with each other. Just our friends ever after.

And everyone, myself included, needs to start accepting that truth.

CHAPTER TWENTY-SIX

Silas

I WAKE up on the couch, my muscles sore, and regret immediately hits me.

My behavior was out of line last night.

With Lola. With my friends. With everyone.

Finn should've kicked my ass. I would've deserved it.

I slept in until midafternoon and wince at the countless texts on my phone.

Most from my friends.

Not one from Lola even though I texted and apologized to her last night.

She's the first person I text.

Me: Please answer me. Want to get dinner? Hang out tonight? Let me make up for my asshole behavior.

Five minutes pass without a reply.

Closing out of her text, I hit Finn's name.

Me: Can we talk?

Unlike with Lola, my phone immediately beeps with a response from him.

Finn: If it's about last night, I get it.

I blow out a breath of relief. Finn probably gets it because he's gone through the same battle with figuring out where things are in his relationship with Grace. He's also protective over her. I saw his reaction, the hurt on his face, when he found out Grace was pregnant with another guy's baby. It hurt him like no other. Watching Lola walk away with Trent out of all people matched the same hurt he'd felt.

Me: Are you with Grace?

I need to apologize to her too.

But I also need to talk to Finn alone.

Finn: Nah, she's at the birthday brunch.

Oh yeah, their annual birthday brunch.

Hopefully, Lola is at least enjoying herself there. Although she's probably experiencing one hell of a hangover.

I hit Finn's name to call him.

"I was an asshole last night," I say as soon as he answers. "I wish I could blame it on the alcohol, but that's obviously not the case."

"Nah, dude," he replies. "I'm buying you dinner for helping me get my head out of my ass."

Even though I'm having a day from hell, a flicker of a smile presses against my lips. "Does that mean you finally told Grace how you feel?"

"Sure did."

At least one good thing came out of last night.

Sometimes, you just need a jackass to point out the truth.

And I was that jackass.

"How'd that work out?"

"Pretty damn good."

"I'm happy for you, man." I chuckle. "Looks like you do owe me dinner."

"Now, it's time for you and Lola to do the same. You're the last couple in our group who needs to get their shit together."

"Lola and I are … more complicated than Grace and you."

"Trent was hitting on her. You need to make your move before she gives him a chance." Finn knows some about Trent because he's been with me other times when I've run into him.

I scoff, my stomach filling with dread, "Lola isn't that fucking stupid."

No way will she fall for his bullshit.

He mocks my scoff. "Do you remember what you did last night?"

I stay silent for a moment.

"You dropped her on her ass on her birthday," he says as if I don't fucking remember. "She walked off with Trent. We both know it wasn't only a friendly gesture from Trent."

"I have to go. I'll talk to you later, man."

I end the call.

As if with perfect timing, as soon as I hang up, another call comes through.

Trent.

That motherfucking jackass.

I hit Ignore and throw my phone across the room.

I scrub my hand over my face.

I need to talk to Lola.

I need to apologize.

Before I lose her.

CHAPTER TWENTY-SEVEN

Lola

I'VE IGNORED Silas all weekend. I need time and space to get my thoughts in order and am second-guessing everything about our friendship.

I cracked open a chunk of myself for Silas. He knows about my family, my father's affairs, my failures. But him? I'm learning he didn't reciprocate. He only told me the basics while keeping anything deep hidden. He never told me about Trent, about their high school rivalry, or that his father had an affair with Trent's mom. I never expected him to give me his life story, but being someone's best friend means sharing your life and experiences with them.

Was I a bad friend for not asking?

But it's not like I could read his mind and know his childhood hadn't been as peachy as he played it out to be. The only characteristic Silas has that maybe things weren't perfect is his sobriety. When I asked if alcoholism ran in his family, he told me no and that his parents barely drank.

I pause my *Desperate Housewives* episode when the doorbell rings and get up to answer it. Looking through the peephole, I find Silas on the other side, shifting from one foot to the other.

I grip the door handle when it rings again. My hand is sweaty as I slowly turn it and then pull away.

"Lola," Silas calls from the other side. "I'm fucking sorry, okay? Just let me explain myself."

Another knock.

Another plea from him to open the door.

I stare at him, one eye shut, and the small hole isn't providing as much view as I want.

His voice breaks, nearly pleading, on his third, "I'm sorry."

That is what breaks me.

I never wanted this to happen to our relationship.

The spinning has returned, and I answer the door before changing my mind.

"Thank you," he breathes out when I do. Sweat has built up along his forehead, and his eyes are red.

"Hey," I say while avoiding eye contact.

If I look at him, if our eyes meet, I might break.

I've kept myself together to avoid bursting into tears. With how my heart is sinking, I'm not sure if I'll be able to keep it that way. I'm shocked I've made it this long without crumbling. I credit it to the tough exterior I always put on. It helps when you always fake you're okay.

My mom sweeps back into my thoughts.

Then it wanders to Silas.

He's faking it. I'm sure of it.

I was blind to it before, but after last night, after faking it myself, it's become clear that he's broken in ways that many people aren't.

I sniffle and turn my back to him, hoping that I can compose myself while walking into my living room. He follows, his footsteps heavy and loud on our short journey.

Silence lingers in the air. There's none of our usual cracking jokes or arguing over what movie we'll watch. All that playfulness has shriveled up and died. I'm angry about what happened last night, about his secrets, about why he can't open up to me. There's no pretending today.

We sit on opposite ends of the couch. There's never been so much distance between us. Snatching a pillow, I pull it into my lap, hugging it to my stomach as if I were a young girl and this was my favorite stuffed animal, and I just woke up from a nightmare.

I don't speak.

He said he wanted to explain himself, so that's what I'm allowing him to do.

Neither one of us has looked at the other.

As I peek at him, I catch him massaging his temples.

"How pissed are you at me?" he finally asks.

Something in me snaps. Instead of telling him how pissed I am, I'm going to show him. He deserves to witness the pain and humiliation that have been my sidekicks since the club.

I shift to face him, to stare him down, so he can see the pain on my face. "Gee, I don't know, Silas." Heat spreads across my face like a blanket. "Tell me how pissed you'd be if I threw you off my lap in public *on your birthday!*"

I expect him to look away, but he doesn't. His tired and worrisome eyes are settled on me.

When he speaks again, his words are strangled. "Do you remember what you said that night?"

"I wasn't *that* drunk."

"So, you remember asking me to fuck you?"

It's a struggle not to wince, not to pull back and react to his words. I could lie and say no, but I want him to know I remember every single thing he said and did. I remember and will always remember everything that happened last night. From what each shot tasted like to the excitement I had when he arrived and then to the despair I felt when he stood up, and I slid off his lap.

Do I regret asking him to fuck me? Absolutely.

I wish I'd never said those words, wish I'd never climbed onto his lap, wish he never knew that I'd gladly take a relationship with him that exceeds more than friendship. But it happened, and there's no taking it back.

"I do." I clear my throat, and my voice is hoarse. "I apologize for that. I wasn't thinking clearly, but it doesn't excuse what you did."

"I'm sorry," he croaks, rubbing at his watery eyes. "I reacted without thinking."

There's heartbreak and regret on his face. I'm sure mine shows something similar. Our bond had been so strong, so deep, and one night snapped it into something that feels almost forced now. It's like we never knew each other.

He's sorry. His apology is genuine. I've seen fake apologies. My father handed them out like candy to my mother.

I soften my voice. "You could've done it differently, though. You could have moved me, carried me somewhere else so we could talk, anything other than what you did." I try to swallow back the tears that match my mother's when she heard those fake apologies. "You completely humiliated me, and more than that, you hurt me."

"I was already trying to survive the night before I even got to the club." He squeezes his eyes shut as if being hit with a memory. "When you climbed onto my lap, I wasn't thinking clearly."

"Why?" I whisper. "Why is my birthday such a problem for you?"

"It's not your birthday that's the problem."

"Then what is it?"

His shoulders move as he roughly shakes his head. "It doesn't matter."

I drop the pillow from my hold, tossing it to the floor, and scoot in closer to him. "It does matter." I slap my hand against my chest. "Why won't you open up to me? We're supposed to be best friends and know so much about each other, but I didn't even know you had a brother."

Our eye contact shatters when he turns his head to stare ahead at the paused television screen. "We're best friends, but if I told you everything about me, you wouldn't want to be my friend any longer."

I flinch, and my response comes out in a stutter. "What?"

He rubs his hand over his tortured face, and it's halfway covered when he peers back at me. "Can we please … I'm begging you … talk about something other than this?" When our eyes meet, his are filled with sorrow, and he gives me the same broken, "*Please*," that convinced me to open the door.

Shutting my mouth, I stay quiet while contemplating what to do. We need to talk about this because if we don't, it'll only cause more tension. Nothing good comes out of running from conversations that need to be said. Unspoken words lead to broken relationships.

He grips the couch, not giving me a chance to say something, and raises himself to his feet. "I'm going to go."

He's leaving.

Walking away.

Not even giving us a chance to break down our feelings from last night.

You're just like your mother, Lola.

Loving a broken man.

"Trent asked me out," I blurt as if I'm trying to even the score with him leaving.

He stops in his tracks, his shoulders pulling forward. "All right then. Learn he's an asshole yourself."

My words didn't cause him to break down and deliver the truth to me. He only shakes his head, staring down at the floor, and heads toward the door.

Before he leaves, he turns to look at me. "You're my best friend. I love you in ways I've never loved anyone else. Don't ever forget that."

He gives me no moment to digest his words, to take them in again, before he hurries out of my house as if he'd committed a crime and the getaway car was waiting.

If he loves me in ways he's never loved anyone else, why won't he give me more than what he gives everyone else?

As soon as the door clicks shut, the tears pour down my cheeks as if they were at the surface, waiting to find out Silas's next move.

He chose the cold shoulder.

Silas is choosing to break us.

I'm scared our relationship is on its last round, and we're going to lose.

CHAPTER TWENTY-EIGHT

Silas

LOLA WENT on a date with Trent.

It could've been some random guy, but no, it had to be him. I don't know where they went, how it went, and I don't want to know. The thought of them together haunts me. Finn broke the news. He didn't do it to be a dick. He did it to knock some sense into me. I've already lost two people who meant the world to me, and now, I'll lose Lola.

Lola and I went from talking nearly daily to checking up on each other every few days since the night I left her house. A few times, I've almost texted and asked if she was hanging out with Trent to get back at me, but I always stop myself. Lola isn't spiteful like that.

She's changing. *We're* changing.

Tonight will be the first time I'll see her since I showed up at Lola's place after her birthday. Lincoln and Cassidy are throwing a get-together at their place, and everyone will be there. As much as I don't feel like socializing, I need to see Lola.

———

LOLA IS ALREADY THERE when I arrive at their place, sitting on the leather sectional in the living room. Jamie, Georgia, and Cassidy are with her, and they're chatting away. Georgia's hand gestures, waving through the air, tells me they're talking about something she considers dramatic.

If it wasn't for the birthday disaster, Lola and I would have ridden here together. There are so many what-ifs that could've gone differently on her birthday. I could've gone about rejecting her in a different way. I could've not shown, and she'd never have met Trent. That night was just a complete nightmare.

I say hi to the room, waving at them, but fasten my gaze on Lola. She stares at me, her eyes tired as if she hasn't been sleeping well either. I hesitate, wondering if I should go to her, but the guarded expression on her face stops me from doing so. Not wanting to put her on the spot, I slip past them and meet the guys in the kitchen.

"Sup, chickenshit," Lincoln says when he sees me.

There's no question as to why he called me that. Other than at the bar, I haven't been around my friends much since Lola's birthday, but when they do see me, none of them have a problem with calling me out.

Cohen shakes his head and lifts his beer. "I second the chickenshit and raise you a dumbass."

"Fuck off," I say, shooting them both the finger.

"We're just trying to help you out," Lincoln says.

Grace and Finn walking through the front door interrupts our conversation, and I exhale a breath, happy at the opportunity to take the attention off me. They're holding hands and sporting bright smiles.

"It's about goddamn time," I call out, cupping my hands around my mouth.

"Another couple," Lincoln adds with a smirk. "Four down." He casts a glance at me. "One to go if you quit being a dumbass."

I flip him off again.

At their arrival, the guys and I venture into the living room as Grace sits down. She's smiling, but there's a hint of exhaustion on her face. The other day, Finn mentioned the pregnancy has taken a toll on her energy. Luckily, she has him, and he's making sure she doesn't have to lift a finger.

Georgia squirms next to her. "I'm really happy for you."

"Remember how we bet on who'd get pregnant first?" Lola asks.

I smile, realizing how bad I missed her voice.

Georgia laughs and points at Lola. "And we all said it'd be you."

Whoa. Didn't expect that.

If I had my guess, Grace would've been the first. She's a teacher, and she likes kids.

"Pfft," Cassidy says. "You thought *Lola*, the commitment-phobe, would be the first?"

I rest my back against the wall, shutting my eyes, and imagine a pregnant Lola. She'd be a gorgeous, glowing mom-to-be.

"We damn sure didn't think it'd be Grace," Georgia argues. "And I wasn't about to jinx myself in high school."

Grace laughs. "Me neither. That's why we voted on Lola."

Lola delivers a red-lipped smile. "Come to think of it, I don't know why we didn't put our money on Grace. She's always loved kids."

"Now, who's the next to get pregnant?" Jamie bounces a cooing Isabella, her baby, on her knee. "Two down—me and Grace."

"Uh …" Cassidy hesitates before slowly holding up her hand. "That'd be me." She inhales a quick breath before continuing, "Well … not next since I already am."

Everyone's attention flashes to her. Mine is quick, a simple glimpse, and then my eyes return to Lola, studying her. She's all smiles for her friend.

"I'm sorry," Cassidy tells Grace. "I've kept quiet because I didn't want to outshine your moment. I wanted to try to find the right time to tell you … and I guess this is the right time."

Grace squeals, all the tiredness on her face fading. "Really?"

Cassidy eagerly nods, her blond ponytail bobbing in the air. "Like you, I was totally shocked."

"I guess that makes it three down," Georgia says, scooting down the couch to hug Cassidy.

"Congrats, girl." Lola blows her a kiss. "We're going to have a shit ton of baby shopping to do."

I take the two steps to Lincoln, smacking his stomach. "Why didn't you tell me, asshole?"

He looks like he's on top of the world. "I've been waiting for when she was ready. If I had it my way, I'd have hung fucking flyers all over the bar and streets."

He winks at me before joining Cassidy, wrapping his arms around her from the back and kissing her neck. She squirms, throwing her head back and laughing into his cheek.

I tune them out, staring at Lola in concern, as my mind drifts to the night we found out about Grace's pregnancy. That was the night Lola told me she was lonely. I clench my teeth at the thought of Trent making her *less* lonely.

———

LOLA RODE with Georgia and Archer to Lincoln's, so I asked to drive her home at the end of the night. We need to talk, and I miss being alone with her.

Dammit, I just fucking missed her.

It's like I'm missing a piece of me—an organ I could survive without, but it'd make my life easier if it were still there, like a lung, a kidney, a limb.

She didn't immediately jump for joy. She paused, hesitation on her face, but then nodded and said, "Okay."

"How are you doing?" I ask, focusing on the road ahead of us.

"Good." She plays with the strap of her purse. "Busy with work."

I nod, sneaking a quick glance. "You okay after Cassidy's announcement?"

She tilts her head. "Yes. Why?"

"When I took you home the night after Grace told everyone about her pregnancy, you were happy for her but told me you felt lonely at times." I clear my throat. "Do you feel the same tonight?"

"I'm happy for Cassidy."

"But are *you* happy?"

"I have a good life, good friends, and a good family. For the most part, I'm happy. As far as lonely-wise, I'm not sure how I feel anymore.

For so long, I believed I was wired differently. I refused to see a relationship as something that could brighten my life because I was scared that it'd end up as nothing but my mother and father's. But maybe I just needed that time to figure myself out." She lowers her voice. "I don't want to be alone for the rest of my life … don't want to be *single*."

"I get that."

And I do.

At times, I look around my empty home, knowing it'll never be filled with more. No children running around like Cohen's. No lovemaking like at Archer's. No holidays with presents sprawled around the living room floor while my child shows me all the cool shit Santa brought him. I've thought about having it—*smiled* while thinking it—but then I snap myself together.

The inside of the car turns quiet as I digest Lola's words. My turn signal has never sounded so loud as I veer onto her street. I brake, putting the car into park, and bow my head, wishing I had the right words to assure her she'll never be lonely because I'll always be at her side. But as far as her not wanting to be single, that's something I can't provide.

"Eventually, you'll find the right one, and she'll capture your heart." Emotion overflows her voice.

"Trust me," I say around a raspy laugh, "I don't have much heart to keep myself going, let alone to give someone a part of it."

"That's such a bullshit excuse."

I refuse to look at her. "No, it's not."

"You could …" Her voice turns pained. "You could try to give your heart to me. I promise, I can work with even a sliver of it." There's a hint of hope in her voice at her last words as if she's been waiting to get that out and she's proud of herself for doing it.

"And what, Lola?" My reaction is embarrassing. The coldness in my tone is out of line. "Take *a sliver* of yours, only to destroy it later? I refuse to do that to you."

"We can have a happily ever after just like our friends if you'd just quit thinking so negatively about yourself." That hope dissipates. "You've never hurt me in the years that we've been friends."

"Exactly. *Friends* being the key word."

"You're in love with me." She says it with certainty, with agony, yet with fear. "I know it. You know it. Everyone knows it."

I wince at her words—at the truth. "I do love you."

"In what *way* do you love me?" She says the words, but it's as if she needs the confirmation from me—for me to tell her exactly the love I have for her zipping through my veins, as if she were embedded inside me.

I'm thankful for the darkness surrounding us, happy that it's here to cover the lies I'm about to feed her. "As a friend." My heart putters in my chest, this time reminding me that what I say will change our entire dynamic. "I'm sorry, Lola, but I can't be anything more than your friend. That's all I can give you. If you're looking for love, I hope you find it."

"What broke you?" she whispers. "*Who* broke you?"

I give her silence. A refusal to answer. A refusal to crack myself open and pull out the answers, my secrets, my darkness. Lola wants to take a chance at love. If I were the person she took that leap with, she'd learn that our love would be so like her parents'. I'd break her as much as her father did her mother.

Unlike her selfish father, I refuse to do that.

"All right then." She grips the door handle.

Reaching out, I touch her arm, stopping her. "I love you, Lola."

"Just not enough to do something about it."

CHAPTER TWENTY-NINE

Lola

"SO, THE BABY SHOWER WAS A DISASTER," Trent says from across the table when I finish telling him my story.

"Literally like something out of a movie," I reply.

"Or out of Grace's worst nightmare."

Georgia, Grace's sister, and I threw Grace an amazing baby shower. Everything was going well—minus Silas and me hardly talking once he found out I went to dinner with Trent—until Grace's *real* baby daddy showed up. He made the announcement to everyone that Grace and Finn were faking it.

The thing the asshole didn't know was that maybe they lied about who the biological father was, but Finn has been more of a partner to Grace than him. Grace and Finn love each other, and as far as Finn sees it, he's the baby's father.

He's the one who's been there for her throughout the pregnancy— the doctor appointments, setting up the nursery, parenting classes, being an emotional partner for Grace. Not the douchebag who hid his marriage, his children, and that his wife was also pregnant.

Finn was also there for Grace when the douchebag's wife went to Grace's work and made a scene. It was all a mess and put her through emotional hell. It took some damage control on Finn's and Grace's sister's part, but they've managed to control the idiot now.

This morning, I'm having a coffee date with Trent at the local coffee shop before we go to work. We've gone out a few times. The first was a dinner. Then we attended an Italian festival, where I ate enough food to keep full for days. And this is our third coffee date before work. Trent is fun, carefree, and easy to talk to. At first, I was worried that he'd asked me out to get back at Silas, but he hasn't mentioned him once. Then I thought he'd asked me out in hopes of hooking up, but we haven't had sex or gone any further than a simple good-night kiss.

Trent raises his coffee. "Can I interest you in an event that isn't a disaster?"

I raise a brow. "What's that?"

"My mother and stepfather throw this annual charity event to help the local homeless shelter. Want to be my plus-one?" He playfully smiles. "I promise you, there will be no secret baby mamas of mine showing up and making a scene."

"Ah, man." I dramatically frown. "That sounds way too boring for my liking."

"A little normalcy helps balance out the drama."

I shake my iced coffee. "Oh boy, is this meeting the parents?"

Trent chuckles, shaking his head. "I promise, it won't be uncomfortable. It always has a large turnout, so you won't be put on the spot."

"Will Silas be there?" I pluck a chunk of my banana bread off and drop it into my mouth, hating that I asked that before committing. I don't want to show up and catch Silas off guard.

Trent shakes his head. "Silas doesn't attend anything family-related. If he knows I'll be there, he's a no-show. It seems he only attends events with you and your friends, not us." He directs his gaze downward, and he quickly scrubs a hand over his face.

He's also usually a no-show on my birthdays too.

I frown. "That's sad."

I hate that for him, but as I think about it, I believe Trent. Silas hardly talks about his family.

"We've tried everything," Trent continues. "I've apologized for my wrongs, but he can't seem to get past it."

"Get past what? Some ridiculous teenage rivalry?"

"He hasn't told you about Sienna?"

Sienna?

I straighten in my chair and shake my head.

"Figures."

"Who is Sienna?"

"That's his story to tell. Not mine." He takes the last swig of his coffee and slowly swallows it down, his Adam's apple bobbing in the process.

"But if it involves you, why can't you tell me?"

"I only played a small part."

"I hate when people do that—give you a crumb of something but not provide more."

He blows out a breath. "I told someone what Silas was doing behind his back."

"That's why he hates you so much?"

"That's why." He checks his phone. "We'd better get going. Don't want to be late for work."

I have a feeling there's more to the story than that.

———

"MEETING THE FAM?" Georgia practically shrieks. "Um, that's a pretty big deal."

I roll my eyes. "Quit being dramatic. It's some charity-banquet thing."

She turns her gaze to Archer. "Is it a big deal for a guy to invite a girl to go to some charity-banquet thing where the family will also be?"

Archer shrugs, pulling himself up from the couch. "I wouldn't know. You pretty much showed up to all my shit, uninvited."

She throws a pillow at him. "Shut up. You loved it."

"Will Silas be there?" Archer asks.

I shake my head. "Trent said no."

He raises a brow. "How does *Trent* know Silas's agenda?"

"He doesn't show up to anything family-related."

"Can Trent get a plus-two?" Georgia asks. "If Silas does show and it turns into chaos, I need a front row seat."

"What *you need* to do is have my baby since it seems all our friends are getting to be dads but me," Archer says.

"Then *you need* to get to work on a nursery."

He throws his arms up. "I'm not building a nursery before you even get pregnant."

Georgia grins. "You know I like to be prepared." She shifts to me. "Just like you'd better prepare yourself in case you walk into some family drama."

———

I DEBATED on whether to cancel with Trent.

Back and forth like a teeter-totter.

My head spinning as if I were on a Tilt-A-Whirl.

I enjoy spending time with him. Go figure, the one other guy I click with has to be the stepbrother of the only man who's ever truly known me. No, it couldn't be a random man. Leave it to me to get wrapped up in a mess like this.

I have no idea where things will go with Trent, but as someone who's gone on some terrible dates, Trent has by far been the best in years.

At the end of the day, I said yes. If Silas wants to live his life in misery, if he wants to keep me at a distance, then that's his choice. And I'll turn in the other direction to find myself happiness. At least, that's what I tell myself as I clasp the strap of my stiletto around my ankle.

———

"WOW, THIS PLACE IS NICE," I say, staring out the window, admiring Trent's parents' home.

The driveway is large enough to be considered a parking lot, and it's crowded with cars. With so many people here, Trent was right—I won't be put on the spot.

Trent stops at the valet—the three of them dressed in black suits with funky polka-dot ties—and hands his keys over.

Something I've never understood is how exactly these types of parties work. Tens of thousands of dollars are spent to throw an affair like this, but why not just donate that money? Do they make more in donations than what the party costs? Or do they consider it a write-off?

My father holds charity events for work sometimes but definitely on a smaller scale: donate fifty dollars and wear jeans to work for the month or donate to be entered into a raffle for an extra vacation week. Something that always ties in with work.

Trent takes my hand, holding it tight, and leads me toward the door, where two men—same ties as the valets—are holding trays of champagne with fake smiles.

"Your parents sure know how to throw a party," I comment.

"My mom likes to go all out." Trent grabs two champagne flutes and hands one to me. "You should've seen my birthday parties, growing up. Craziness and way overboard."

I smile. "Are you a big birthday person too?"

He squeezes my hand. "I love birthdays. Blame it on my father."

"Same. Silas hates them."

I slam my mouth shut, wishing I hadn't brought him up. I planned for it to be a Silas-free night—free of speaking about him and thinking of him. I'd have given him a chance, been willing to leave every other man alone, if that was what he wanted. But he didn't. He told me no, turned me down as if he hadn't been sending mixed signals our entire friendship.

Trent ignores my Silas comment. "Your birthday? What day is it again?" He squints as if trying to remember the date of when we met.

We squeeze around a couple of people arguing over who donated the most money tonight.

"June twenty-third."

Trent freezes, causing me to stumble ahead of him, and I grip the handle of the flute tight, relieved I didn't spill it all over my dress. And even though I told myself I wouldn't think of Silas, his reaction reminds me of how Silas reacts anytime my birthday is mentioned.

"Do you ..." A prickle sweeps up my neck. "Do you know someone else with that birthday? Does that date mean something?"

Trent drops my hand, and just as I think he's going to pull away, he curls it around my waist. "Nope."

Trent is a sucky liar.

Classical music, played by an orchestra, fills the room. This is much fancier than some charity raffle I'm used to. I knew Silas had money, came from money, but nothing like this.

"There's my stepdad and mom." Trent points toward a crowd of people, not exactly singling anyone out.

His hand rests on the indent of my back while we head toward them. The group breaks apart, splitting in different directions.

"Trent," a man says when we approach them, smiling, deep laugh lines forming around his mouth. "I'm glad you made it, son. And I see you brought a date with you." His tone is inviting, cheerful.

I wouldn't think this was a man who had left his wife for his mistress.

This is Silas's dad.

After years of friendship with Silas, I'm finally meeting his father but not with him.

I stare at him, taking in the familiar features he and Silas share. The shape of their faces, their hair color, the way their cheeks lift when they smile.

I hold out my hand, returning the smile. "I'm Lola."

His hold is light, not businessman-like, when he shakes it. "Grady Malone. It's nice to meet you. Thank you for coming."

"Oh, wow. She's gorgeous," a woman says, appearing at Grady's side. She presses her hand to her chest before lightly brushing my arm. "I'm Janet, Trent's mother."

I smile and introduce myself to her.

"One request: you need to improve your nonalcoholic beverages at parties if you want me to come."

And just like I know his features, I know his voice.

It stands out in every room, in every crowd, around anyone.

I stiffen and do a double take as Silas steps to his father's side. I hold in a breath, watching him narrow his eyes at Trent before glaring at me.

CHAPTER THIRTY

Silas

THE ONE TIME.

The one time I show up to an event to appease my father, it turns out to be a bigger nightmare than I imagined. Just like the night of Lola's birthday, I didn't want to come. I need to learn my lesson that when I get a sense of dread while walking into something, I should turn and abort mission.

The reason I kept walking?

My grandmother called and begged me to come—something she hadn't done in years. The last time was my grandfather's funeral, which I attended. She only asks when it means a lot to her because she knows it's hard on me. I couldn't say no to her. I also didn't have anything else to do, so I figured I'd go and at least be able to see my grandmother. If Trent did show, I could dodge him. *Or* tell him to stay away from Lola.

Lola is rapidly blinking as if attempting to process that she's not imagining me. Trent's rubbing his forehead, his shoulders tight. My father glances between us, curiosity in his eyes.

"Oh, hey, Silas," Lola finally says. "I didn't know you'd be here."

My father signals back and forth between Lola and me. "You two know each other?"

Lola nods. "We're friends."

"That's how Lola and I met," Trent says as if wanting to save Lola from the awkwardness. His arm is casually draped around her waist, causing me to snarl. "I ran into them at a club, and Lola and I hit it off."

"Lola," my father repeats the name as if it's finally dawning on him. "This is *the* Lola?"

Lola has been brought up in our dinners before when my father asks how I'm spending my time since I hardly visit my family. His brows are furrowed as he stares at Lola, and it's not like I can lie and say no with Lola standing right there. Lola appears as if she'd prefer I'd say no—the color gone from her face as she averts her gaze from everyone.

I tap my foot, trying to stop myself from walking away from everyone. "It is."

My father angles his concentration on me, a look of understanding on his face.

My thoughts are racing. To stop focusing on Trent's hand on Lola, I glance from one side of the room to the other, back and forth, as if searching for a lost person in the sea of overdressed people.

"I'm going to go say hi to someone," I lie before turning on my heels and walking away from them.

I place the glass on a random table and storm up the stairs to my old bedroom. Slumping onto the edge of the bed, I rub at my throbbing temples, the image of Lola and Trent together burning through my brain.

I need a minute.

A minute to prepare to see them together again.

Or I could just leave.

No one would expect anything different from the son who caused chaos in the community.

Resting my palms against the bed, I brace my fingers against the black duvet and pull myself to my feet.

If this is a game Trent is playing, I won't let him win.

I'm staying to make sure Lola is okay, to keep an eye on her—and to also torture myself. I move down the stairs at a slow pace and keep

my head down until I'm close to where Lola and Trent are talking to
my father and the man he founded the charity with.

I crack my knuckles, watching them, and jerk back at my father's
voice.

"You're in love with her," he says, stepping to my side. "Which is
why I'm lost as to why she's here with Trent and not you."

"Like she said, we're friends," I mutter.

"I'm familiar with wanting someone thinking you can't have them.
I know what it looks and feels like."

"Don't." I glare at him. "Lola and I are nothing like you and
Janet."

"I know, I know." He sighs. "You'll lose her to him if you don't get
your head out of your ass."

I avoid eye contact with him and stare directly at the couple. "Are
you telling me to go steal Trent's date?"

"Is it stealing if she's already yours?"

"I thought you wanted Trent and me to make amends?"

"I do, but I also want you to be happy."

"And I want her to be happy, but that won't be with me," I say
before walking away.

I stand to the side, watching them from afar. A few people stop
and say hello. It annoys me because they're taking my attention off
Lola. Everyone views me differently here. In my new life, in my circle
of friends, I'm the life of the party. But in this world? I'm the kid who
created tragedy.

"Trent said you usually don't attend this stuff," Lola says, stepping
up next to me. "Otherwise, I wouldn't have come."

My mood softens when I look at her. Her dark hair is down in
loose curls. Her cocktail dress is different than her usual style—a light
pink, shimmering with butterflies. I smile, remembering another time
she wore it. It was a work event, and I told her as much as I loved her
wild, dark side, it was nice to see her sweetened up.

She punched me in the gut and asked, "How was that for sweet?"

We shared a hotel room that night, sleeping in separate beds, but
those were the days when shit wasn't weird between us.

"I don't, and tonight is a reminder of why it's smart not to."

My mouth is dry. I stare at the champagne glass in her hand, watching the bubbles dance together. Even though I don't drink, something would be damn good right now to help erase seeing them together. I start to ask her where her little date is but stop myself.

The less I see her with Trent, the better.

Her lips open into a smile as if attempting to cheer me up. "Your family seems nice. I'm glad I got to meet them."

I can't stop myself from scoffing. "I'm glad Trent did that for you because I couldn't."

"Wait," she snaps, holding her palm toward me. "Are you angry with me for coming?"

I cross my arms. "You don't think it's fucked up that he brought you here, knowing you're *my* friend?"

She stares at me in disbelief. "No one thought you were coming, and considering I'm *your friend*, shouldn't you be happy to see me?"

I drown everyone out and focus on just the two of us.

"I'd be happy to see you if you weren't out there, playing around with a man I despise."

"Is everything okay here?"

With the worst timing ever, Trent reaches us like he was watching and made his way over at the sight of my anger. I hate being angry with Lola and her being angry with me. It rarely happened in the past, and now, it seems like we can't escape that cloud lingering over our friendship.

"Everything would be okay if you left," I bite out, my nostrils flaring and every muscle in my body tensing.

"Whoa," Trent says, stepping closer to Lola. "No one thought you'd be here. Lola is your friend. Why do you care if she's here?"

It's as if he and Lola rehearsed that statement on the ride here, just in case I showed.

My pulse speeds, my heart pounding, and I raise my voice. "I care because you're using her to get back at me."

"Get back at you?" Trent yells, his upper lip snarling. "I didn't even know you'd be here, asshole."

My brain isn't processing what I'm saying, and I swing my attention to Lola. "You're both doing this to get back at me."

"Excuse me?" Lola asks, retreating a step from me.

"Dude, talk shit to me all you want, but leave her out of this," Trent demands, and the way he goes to Lola, blocking me from her, is so familiar to what I did at the club.

He thinks he needs to protect her from me?

From me?

Her goddamn best friend?

The man who's looked out for her for years and always been by her side?

"Lola didn't do anything but accept an invite," Trent goes on, and Lola peeks over his shoulder at me, her face brimming with embarrassment as people around us watch.

Trent stares at me, stone-faced, waiting for my next move.

I point over his shoulder to Lola. "She'll be another woman you ruin, just like the last one I cared about."

"Oh, you want to go back to that?" Trent says, loosening his tie, and I do the same. "You always seem to forget the part you played in it too." He steps forward, our faces inches away from each other. "You seem to forget that she questioned how you felt the same way Lola does."

"Trent," Janet yells from a distance.

"Silas!" screams my father, stomping in our direction, aware a fight is about to ensue.

The anger I felt for him that night returns like a bad nightmare.

Before anyone can stop us, I swing my arm back and punch Trent in the jaw, knocking him back a few steps.

CHAPTER THIRTY-ONE

Lola

I'VE NEVER SEEN Silas like this.

Sure, he's been angry before. He's punched a few guys for grabbing my ass or disrespecting me, but this? This is much deeper. Silas punches him, his face filled with so much fury it's as if he wanted to kill Trent.

Seconds after being punched, Trent snaps back, wiping the blood dripping from his nose and onto the expensive rug underneath them, and lunges back at Silas. Silas grunts when he's pushed into the wall, and a full-on fight ensues. Silas scores another jab to Trent's face, and Trent responds by drilling his fist into Silas's eye.

Finally, a group of men successfully breaks them apart.

I avert my eyes to the rug, staring at the blood, knowing that everyone thinks the fight is my fault. But then I quickly raise my chin. *I won't act like this affects me.*

It's not my fault these two are having some pissing contest. Something deeper brought on the war between Silas and Trent.

Three men stand between Silas and Trent, ready as if waiting for one of them to start round two. Trent is blocked from my view, so all I see is Silas. His face is burning, and he wipes his arm along his face to collect the blood before he rips his suit jacket off his arms and throws it onto the floor. Blood falls, staining his white button-up, but all he does is stare straight ahead as if he has tunnel vision and only sees Trent.

"Just wait," Silas says. "I'm going to kill you. It's what you deserve."

A light whimpering sounds from behind me, and I turn to find Janet. She meets my gaze, giving me an apologetic nod, and tenderly cups my shoulder.

Trent huffs, raising his voice so Silas can hear him. "It's what I deserve?"

Guys yell as Trent circles around them to get back to Silas, but he holds up his arms as if saying he means no harm.

Trent thrusts his finger in Silas's direction. "Do you not remember what happened that night? Do you remember *who* went upstairs with Sienna? Because it sure wasn't me. Sienna is dead because of the secret you two hid."

"Fuck you," Silas screams, and I swear his voice is so powerful that the sparkling chandelier vibrates from it.

"Enough," Janet yells, moving around me and stalking toward them. "Both of you!" She swings her arms in the air. "Enough!"

Silas stands straight, his chest heaving in and out so deeply that I'm shocked he's not hyperventilating.

I rush to his side, frantically grabbing his arm. "Calm down. *Please*. Let's go talk."

Janet shoots me an appreciative head nod.

"You have no idea who he is." Silas seethes, baring his teeth. "You shouldn't have come. I shouldn't have come. We don't belong here."

He grabs my drink, chugs the remainder of the appletini, and throws it onto the floor. The sound of glass shattering echoes through the silence of the room.

"I'm out of here," he says before squeezing past me and pushing his way through the people who are watching—slack-jawed, bug-eyed, and hands covering their mouths.

I don't realize tears are running down my cheeks until I no longer see him.

CHAPTER THIRTY-TWO

Silas

I HADN'T HAD a single sip of alcohol since I was eighteen.

That changed tonight.

And as I charge into Twisted Fox, it's about to be more than the sip I had of Lola's nasty-ass apple-something. Whoever my stepmother hired to bartend needs to be fired ASAP.

I ignore hellos, ignore those who try to make conversation and ask why I'm a bloody mess, and head straight for the bar.

Pointing at Lincoln, I say, "Vodka. Make it a double."

Lincoln freezes, taking in my appearance. "Good one. What the fuck happened to you?"

"I'm not kidding," I grind out, licking caked blood from the corner of my lip.

"Dude, in case you forgot, you don't drink." He says it as if I'd just come out of a coma and asked who I was.

I clench my fists, noticing the broken skin on my knuckles, covered in Trent's blood …and possibly mine as well. "I drink now."

"Not happening. I won't be the one responsible for breaking your sobriety. You're upset about something, so sit your ass down, and we can talk about it."

Ignoring him and his request, I storm behind the bar and snag a bottle before he gets the chance to stop me. "You don't want to serve me? I'll do it my damn self then."

Customers gasp as I twist off the cap, drop it onto the ground, turn the bottle up, and lift it to my lips. Even though I finished off Lola's drink, straight vodka is nothing like a watered-down martini. It hits me harder, nearly knocking me on my ass, and I stumble back against the liquor shelves.

Just like that, in a matter of seconds, after years of saying no, I broke my vow. I stomped on the one thing I'd said would stay with me for the rest of my life.

The liquor burns, going down, but it's a sweet burn, a satisfying one, a reassurance that I'll forget everything about tonight.

"Jesus," Lincoln hisses, spinning on his toes and yelling for Cassidy as she walks by, not noticing the shit show I've started.

She whips around. "What's up?"

Lincoln jerks his head toward me as I take another swig. "We have a problem."

"Yes," she says, drawing the word out. "I'll get Cohen …" Her voice lowers. "And call Lola."

"Don't bother calling Lola," I yell, playing with the bottle. "She's with Trent, meeting our parents."

Cassidy freezes, no longer going to get Cohen, and Lincoln does the same before a customer calls out, "Enough of the pretty-boy dramatics. I need a drink."

I hold up the vodka and take a gulp in a *there ya go* gesture.

Cassidy scurries off, disappearing down the Employee Only hallway, and I take another desperately needed drink.

Lincoln ignores the customer and keeps his attention on me. "Man, I know you're upset about Lola, but you're going to regret this when you're in the right state of mind." He shakes his head in frustration, and his words slowly leave his mouth as if he's not sure I'll process them if he says them any faster. "Put the bottle down, have a seat, and we can talk."

I wave off his Dr. Phil speech. "Nah, I'm good. I don't want to talk about anything."

"Too damn late," Cohen says harshly, appearing out of damn

nowhere. Taking me off guard, he steals the bottle from me. "My office. Right now."

"Piss off," I grumble. This time, it's me taking him off guard as I re-collect the one thing that can help me leave behind thoughts of Lola and Trent. In fear of him stealing it back, I take another swig of the vodka.

"Jesus fucking Christ," Cohen mutters before glancing back at Cassidy. "Call Lola."

Why are they saying, call Lola?

Like she isn't on a date with another man at the moment.

Fuck it. Let them call her and ruin it.

"Lola," I whisper her name into the bottle before taking another swig.

Was it a mistake, hiding pieces of myself from her?

I'm unraveling, the darkness seeping through those openings, showing my friends who I really am. They don't know the real Silas— the one who struggles with who he is and is ashamed of the things he's done.

Standing there, gripping the bottle as if it were my lifeline, I draw in deep breaths as if I don't know if the next one will come.

Cohen grabs my elbow, jerking me away from the shelves, and Lincoln grabs my free elbow.

"Watch the bar, babe," Lincoln tells Cassidy, and she gives him a thumbs-up, worry lining her features.

I'm overpowered as they walk me through the bar, people pointing at me and talking about my swollen eye. I'm talking shit, telling them to mind their business, as I'm shoved down the Employees Only hallway. Just as we're passing Archer's office, the door swings open, and he appears in front of us.

He eyes me, raising a brow, taking in my beat-up appearance, a bottle hanging from my fingers. "The fuck is wrong with him?"

"Lola," Cohen answers, pushing me into his office while curses leave his mouth.

He and Lincoln roughly sit me down in a chair while Archer slams the door shut behind us.

"Shocker," he grumbles.

Pulling away, Cohen slams his hand on his desk, causing shit to rattle and papers to slide off. "Jesus, why do I always have to deal with your guys' relationship issues here?" he groans. "I'm about to ban all of you from this damn bar."

"I never thought he'd be a depressed drinker," Archer comments, shaking his head in disapproval. "It makes sense, though."

I slump down in the chair, my head spinning, regret hitting me as hard as the vodka. Surprisingly, no one attempts to take the bottle from me again. They watch me as if I were a child playing with a dangerous object they were scared to take away because it'd provoke me further.

CHAPTER THIRTY-THREE

Lola

I HURRIEDLY WIPE tears from my eyes as Trent darts toward me. "I need—" I'm struggling to catch my breath. "I need a break ... need to get away from these ..." I motion toward the nosy crowd. "Everyone."

Trent nods, his lip busted, and takes my hand. He holds it tight as if he's reassuring me that everything will be okay, that he'll protect me the best way he can. Our pace is frantic, and I nearly stumble up the stairs he leads me up. We rush down a hallway and into a bedroom with bare walls and a strawberry smell—one of those plug-in scents.

When Trent releases me from his hold, I stare at my hand, fastening my gaze on the blood.

Whose blood is it?

Trent's?

Silas's?

Both of theirs?

A light across the room flips on, showing off the attached bathroom, and Trent rifles through the drawers. He turns on the faucet, wetting a washcloth, and slowly treks back to me. I'm shaking as he carefully guides me onto the bed. Dropping to his knees, he takes my hand, flipping it over, and starts cleaning off the blood.

"No," I stutter, sniffling as I attempt to grab the washcloth from him. "You're the one covered in blood."

He chuckles—an attempt to appear lighthearted, but it's forced and phony. "That wasn't the first time Silas and I have fought. After what happened tonight, it might not be the last either."

"That doesn't make it right," I mutter when he grabs my other hand. "I'm not the one bleeding."

"And I'm not the one who just had to endure the embarrassment of that."

"That wasn't your fault. Silas was—"

"He was hurting," Trent says for me as if he doesn't want me to think negatively of the man who just started a fight with him.

Should I have gone after Silas?

Yes.

The moment he finished my drink, I should've stopped him. But I was shocked, frozen on my feet, when Silas stormed out of the party. Had I tried to chase after him, I'd have face-planted and endured further embarrassment.

When Trent finishes and there's not a speck of blood on me, he allows me to clean his face. He winces as I carefully remove the evidence of his earlier brawl. He already has a fat lip, and a bruise is forming under his eye. When I'm finished, I stand, walk to the bathroom, and deposit the washcloth into the sink.

As I return, I find Trent on the floor, his back against the bed, and his head is bowed. "I'm sorry. If I had any idea that would happen, I wouldn't have invited you."

"I shouldn't have come," I whisper, sliding down next to him, our thighs touching as we stretch out our legs.

I need to talk to Silas, but right now, I'm so angry with him. He embarrassed me again, and at this point, I'm not sure how much more I can take. If Silas doesn't open himself up to me, if he doesn't explain why he's had this sudden shift in his character, we might not be friends any longer.

"Do you want me to take you home?" Trent asks.

"I think that's a good idea."

He stands before helping me to my feet. "Do you want a change of clothes? I'm sure I have some old high school clothes that will fit you somewhere in here."

"This was your room?"

He nods. "It looked cooler when I lived here, I promise."

I smile, grateful for him trying to make light of our situation and not as weird. "Sure."

As he opens a drawer, my phone rings. I fetch it from my bag to see Cassidy's name flashing across the screen.

I quickly answer. "Hello?"

"You need to come to Twisted Fox, like, right now." Her sentence almost sounds like one word because she says them so fast. "Silas is here."

I press a palm to my heart, thankful he's in good hands. "Thank God."

"He's here, *drinking.*"

"Oh my God."

"Exactly what everyone here thinks. If you can, please get here ASAP."

"I might be the last person he wants to see right now, but I'm on my way." I look at Trent. "I need you to take me to Twisted Fox. It's a bar not far from here."

"I know where it's at. Let's go."

I don't bother changing clothes. If I need to calm Silas, I doubt me showing up in Trent's old high school gear would help the situation.

———

"WILL you tell me what's going on?" Trent asks fifteen minutes into the ride.

We snuck down the back stairwell and into the garage, and Trent snagged the keys to his Grady's BMW—he said he wouldn't mind. I shrugged. It sounded better than having to wait for the valet to bring Trent's car around.

"Silas is there and upset, so they asked me to come." I withhold the information that Silas is drinking.

He nods. "You're a good friend to him."

"Contrary to what you've seen recently, he's a good friend to me."

He peers over at me. "Is that all you two are? Just friends?"

"That's all." I try my hardest to sound confident in my words even though it's the last thing I feel about our friendship.

He nods again. "Even with our issues, Silas is a good guy. He went through some tough shit in high school, and it seems he might never fully recover from it."

He keeps telling me the same thing—Silas went through something tragic in high school—but it's driving me crazy that no one will elaborate.

"Why doesn't he drink?"

"I'm not sure. My guess is, he's punishing himself."

"Do you have something to do with that?"

"I had a part in what destroyed him, but even if he thinks so, it wasn't all my fault."

Cassidy texts again, asking if I'm coming, and I tell her yes before asking her to keep me updated if things get worse. I texted Silas a few times, but he hasn't replied.

When we pull up to Twisted Fox, I'm ready to jump out of the car and see Silas. He might've hurt me, but I need to make sure he's okay. He's drinking—something he's never done, upset or not.

Clutching the door handle, I peer at Trent when he steers into a parking spot. "Thank you for the ride. I can have one of my friends take me home."

He unbuckles his seat belt. "I'll walk you in."

I hold out my hand. "That might not be a good idea."

He shakes his head and opens his door. "Neither is letting you walk into whatever you're about to walk into alone."

"My friends are here."

He steps out, not saying another word, and I do the same. Together, we walk into Twisted Fox, and I'm unsure of what we're about to discover. My heartbeat turns sluggish as I scan the bar, frantically searching for him with Trent on my heels.

"He's in Cohen's office," Cassidy says when she sees me before her eyes shoot to Trent, and she raises a brow. "Not a good idea."

I shrug. "Neither is Silas drinking."

Cassidy's comment doesn't change Trent's mind about tagging along, and I storm toward Cohen's office. The door is closed, but I don't bother knocking before swinging it open. I gasp, taking in the sight of a drunk Silas hunched over in a chair as if he's in time-out.

Silas's hand is tightly gripped around a vodka bottle, and his eyes are bloodshot as they slowly travel to me. I'm unsure if it's from drinking or crying, considering it appears he's done his fair share of both. He hasn't cleaned himself up, so he's still sporting blood on his face and white shirt.

"You motherfucker," Silas snarls.

I stiffen, shocked he'd talk to me like that, but then I follow his gaze over my shoulder to Trent standing behind me.

Silas's attention swings back to me. "Not only are you going on dates with him, but now, you're also bringing him here?"

Trent steps to my side. "She needed a ride here to take care of you, dumbass. You've already ruined our night, so there's no coming here to have fun."

"Hey, man," Archer says in warning to Trent.

Silas stands, shifting his body back and forth to catch his balance, and I'm surprised our friends aren't helping him.

No, wait, I'm not.

They're going to make Silas deal with the consequences of how he's acting tonight. Silas isn't wasted. He can still stand on his own, and his words aren't slurred, but it's also been a while since he drank. He's more angry than anything.

He blinks rapidly while focusing on me. As he does that, Archer swipes the bottle from his hold, causing Silas to glare at him. Archer shrugs because he couldn't care less about Silas's anger.

"You brought her here, huh?" Silas scoffs. "*Now,* you care about people's well-being? You sure didn't care about Sienna's."

I wince at her name, wishing I knew who she was.

Trent blows out an exasperated breath. "We were in goddamn high school! Quit blaming it all on me because you're too scared to realize you played a bigger part than I did. I did something shitty, yes, but I'm not responsible for their deaths. Neither of us is. Kenny is who we should blame. He's the one who killed Sienna."

Kenny?

Who the fuck is Kenny?

Now, we have a Kenny thrown in with a Sienna that I know nothing about.

My attention is moving back and forth between the two, trying to process their conversation and take in every word I can, searching for clues between each one of them.

"Don't say their names," Silas yells.

Trent shakes his head. "No one told you to sleep with her."

"Fuck you!" Silas screams, and I'm sure everyone in the bar heard him.

"No one told you to race after them either," Trent continues as if he wants to rub salt in the wound. "You made that decision."

CHAPTER THIRTY-FOUR

Silas

TRENT'S WORDS are a knife to my gut, twisting the memories and truth into every muscle and vein.

I try not to blame Kenny for what happened.

How can you think bad of your dead best friend?

I swallow down Trent's words.

Swallow down the truth.

I made the mistake of getting caught with Sienna, of secretly hooking up with her, but Trent made the mistake of ratting us out. Even if he didn't know what would happen, I'll never forgive him for it.

He took Sienna from me.

And now, he's taking Lola.

No one here, other than Trent, knows what happened that night—what changed me. And I hoped to keep it that way.

Of course, he's fucked that plan up too.

Cohen stands, staring at Trent. "It might be time for you to go before it makes the situation worse."

Trent nods, looking away from me to Lola. "You're a good person." He motions toward me. "He's poison. Don't let him drag you down with him. It'll only end up with you being hurt."

"Oh, fuck off," I yell, my pulse speeding as I tremble, fighting to control my anger. "The only person who's poison is *you.*"

Trent ignores me, as if I no longer exist to him, and stares at Lola. "Are you sure you're good? I can wait out in the car until you figure this out."

"She's fine," Lincoln says. "Trust me, we got her."

Trent nods. "Call or text me when you get home, okay?"

"Okay," Lola whispers.

I clench my fist, hating that he's speaking to her, that he's acting protective—like he cares about her as much as I do. I should be in that position, not him.

He goes to kiss her cheek but then suddenly stops, realizing the bad timing.

How strong are their feelings for each other?

Stronger than ours?

No way. Lola and I have years of history.

Trent could never match that.

But he does have something I don't—the ability to be in a relationship.

After what happened, everyone blamed me.

Not him.

I was the one caught with her.

Trent doesn't say another word before turning around and leaving.

"What the hell is wrong with you?" Lola screams at me before grabbing the bottle of liquor from Archer's hand. "Why did you do this? This isn't you!"

My throat tightens, and my words are strangled as I say, "Maybe you never knew the real me."

CHAPTER THIRTY-FIVE

Lola

"MAYBE YOU NEVER KNEW THE real me."

I want to collapse and sob at Silas's words because they're the truth. I don't know the true Silas, but in my defense, he only allowed me to know what he wanted. He gave me the lighthearted Silas—the one who wore a smile as a daily uniform and hid his secrets so deep that it was as if it were a second skin.

My best friend—the man, albeit he's being a total jackass at the moment, I wanted to spend the rest of my life with—just said I don't know the real him. The guilt is strong right now.

Cohen and Archer are staring at me for answers as if I'll know what to do about the drunken Silas standing in front of us. Even though my heart is tugging to comfort him, my anger also has me frozen in place as I think about my birthday, for the stunt he pulled at the party, and for pulling away from me. This Silas—the one who's finally coming to light—his main job seems to be hurting me.

Is this the Silas he's been scared to show?

That he's this bitter man, doused with resentment?

His breathing is rushed, nearly coming out in pants, and with each exhale, the liquor on his breath becomes more potent. He'll regret his actions in the morning.

"Silas," I whisper, forcing myself forward, closer to him. "Why don't we go talk in private?"

"No." His tone is clipped, his answer short, concise, and harsh. "Trent was right. I'm no good for you. Even though he isn't either, he might not be as fucked up as I am. Hell, he seems like he's doing just fine, even after what he did."

"What did he do?" I yell, the power to keep my voice low gone.

He shakes his head violently. "There's a reason I don't drink, why I can't see you on your birthday, or commit."

"*Please*," I beg. "Let's talk in private."

If he doesn't want to explain it in front of Archer and Cohen, I get that, but he needs to with me.

"I'm good." His eyes are blank, unreadable, and I groan when he stalks out of Cohen's office—too fast for anyone to stop him. Storming down the hallway, he pushes the exit door open and walks out into the darkness.

Cohen, Archer, Lincoln, and I crowd into the hallway, and when Cohen goes to follow, I throw my arm out to stop him.

I pat his shoulder. "I got this."

Cohen's eyebrows draw together. "He's in pretty rough shape."

"Which is why I need to be the one to talk to him."

If there's anyone who can help even just a little, it's me. They might not think so because he's so angry with me, because I showed up with Trent, but even with the issues we're going through, my bond with him will never break.

"Whatever you do, don't you dare get in the car with him," Archer demands.

I nod. "I won't."

It's chilly when I step out, and the guys stand at the open door as if they were watching their firstborn attend her first prom, their eyes glued to me. I shiver at the breeze and see Silas turn the corner of the building toward the parking lot. Even though it's a struggle with my heels, I speed up my pace.

Damn heels.

I would've taken Trent up on his *change of clothes* offer if I had known I'd be playing chase tonight.

"You can't drive," I yell out into the night.

Silas freezes as if my words were a barricade in his path and stares back at me over his shoulder. I can see his face from a distance, somewhat clear, because the parking lot lights are bright—something Archer and Cohen required when they were installed.

"I'd never drink and drive," he sneers. "Not after what happened."

He flinches. Those words weren't supposed to make the journey out of his mouth and into the public, not supposed to come out around me. I add them to my mental notes, to the words Silas and Trent have provided that I've begun piecing together while trying to figure out what could've happened in my head.

There was a girl involved: Sienna, who's now deceased.

A guy: Kenny.

Something happened with drinking and driving.

And Silas blames himself.

Was he drinking and driving?

Is that why he doesn't drink?

No. I can't wrap my head around that.

Wouldn't he be in jail?

That's a manslaughter charge.

Cohen would've known when he looked up his background check upon hiring, so that can't be it.

Then what is it?

"Go back inside, Lola," he yells, scuffing the toe of his shoe into the ground. "It's dark, and this is a bar. It's not safe for you."

I cross my arms and continue in his direction. "If you're out here, then I'm out here."

He turns and returns to walking, but his pace is slow, allowing me to catch up with him while also not making it obvious. He's not stumbling, he doesn't appear too wasted, but I'm sure we look childish. If someone were to drive by, they'd assume we were a drunk couple arguing, but I don't care. I'm not leaving Silas alone and hurting like this.

Maybe that's why he's kept his past buried for so long.

He didn't have someone to help fight those demons with him.

If only he'd tell me, if only he'd open himself up, I'd be there at his side the rest of the way.

He peeks down at my shoes when I reach him. "Your feet are going to kill in the morning. I don't want to get a text with you blaming me for that."

"Does that mean you plan to talk to me tomorrow? Or will you be too hungover?" I frown at his lack of answer as he stares ahead into the night. "Or you might be dead since you're walking in the opposite direction of your house that's *twenty miles* from here."

Coming to a halt, causing me to nearly trip, he bends down. I stare down at him as he unties his shoes and takes them off.

With a shoe in each hand, he holds them out to me. "Put these on."

I stare at them with wide eyes. "Huh?"

"Put my shoes on." He shoves the shoes closer. "If you must follow me, I don't want your feet to hurt."

"Thank you," I whisper.

He takes my hand and helps me sit on the curb. I thought he wanted to escape me, but here he is, waiting for me to change my shoes. I ignore the thought of my dress getting dirty, unstrap my heels, and replace them with his shoes. I tie them as tight as I can, but they're still too big.

I'm about to look more childish with my Ronald McDonald shoes, but I'll make do.

He stares down at me, despair in his eyes, before assisting me to my feet. I sigh when he takes my heels. Without a word, we return to our walking. As bad as I want to question him, there's a possibility that doing so might cause him to close up and tell me to go back inside.

A bright light forms behind us, and a car slows down, going at our pace.

The window rolls down, revealing Cohen.

"Look, guys," he calls out from the driver's side, "let me drive you home, and you can talk about this in the morning."

I nod, hoping Silas agrees so we can take Cohen up on his offer.

Silas shakes his head, his shoulders slumped, my heels smacking against his leg. "Take Lola home, but I'm good." He peers over at me with wet eyes. "Get in Cohen's car."

I cross my arms. "Nope. If you're staying, then I am."

"Jesus," Cohen hisses. "Talk it out and text me when you're ready for a ride. I'll wait in the parking lot."

He pulls away, and as bad as my feet are already killing me, I refuse to go. This man needs to be assured that no matter what war he's battling emotionally, I'm there for him. He's okay. *We're* okay. At least, we're on the verge of being okay.

Is this my fault?

My stomach churns.

Did me being with Trent trigger something inside him?

Does my happiness cause Silas's darkness?

I considered Silas to be one of my best friends, but I was dumb.

Grace and Georgia are my best friends. We don't share romantic feelings. I don't want to hand them my heart and go to sleep in their arms.

I want all of that with Silas.

Silas isn't my best friend. He's my everything.

I'm unsure of how much time has passed when I finally say, "Are you ready to tell me what drove you to drink tonight?"

CHAPTER THIRTY-SIX

Silas

"ARE you ready to tell me what drove you to drink tonight?"

Chills run up my spine at Lola's question. I kick my toes against the small rocks along the sidewalk, feeling them jam through my sock and into my toe.

There's so much that drove me to the bottle tonight, but I focus on one.

"I can't stand seeing you with him."

We stop as if we were in a movie and needed a dramatic pause to amplify our emotions. I've wanted to say that for so long, so my confession deserves a minute since it's taken too many to tell her that.

"Silas," she whispers, shifting us until we're facing each other. Her face is just as broken as my heart feels, as if she's mourning the downfall of our friendship as much as I am.

I'm exhausted. Hopeless. Fucking shattered.

My voice shakes as I continue, "I thought I'd be okay, seeing you with someone else, but seeing you with him, out of all people, it rips me apart, and that's why I drank."

"I'm sorry," she says, slowly reaching out to rub my shoulder.

I've never been vulnerable with anyone.

Only Lola.

She makes me want to be a better man.

She makes me want to be more than this damaged man who cuts out anyone if they get too close.

When I took my first drink tonight, I hated myself. Hated myself for breaking the pact I'd made so long ago, hated myself for the pain on Lola's face as I made a scene, and I was embarrassed at the humiliation on my family's face. As I sat in Cohen's office, waiting for Lola to arrive as if she were picking her child up from the principal's office, my mind focused on the last time I'd turned to the bottle, the last time I'd used it too much to numb me.

Her birthday is what triggered me.

Triggered this to come out.

On her birthday, that's when the depression, sadness, and regret always kick in. But I usually give myself the day to soak in my pity. This year, I didn't in fear of disappointing Lola again.

"Now, please, for the love of God, let Cohen take you home." I squeeze my eyes shut, her touch a calming effect—almost as strong as the vodka.

"I told you," she says softly, "I'm not going until you do."

"*Please*. I need some time." My lips tremble. The fear of breaking down in front of her is strangling me. "I won't do anything stupid, I promise."

"Can you take that time in Cohen's office? Anywhere but out here?" She sniffles, and I know she's just as close to crumbling as I am. Mascara blotches sit underneath her eyes, and her face is red and puffy.

"I promise, I'll be okay." I pull my phone from my pocket and call Cohen. When he picks up, I say, "Lola is ready to go home."

"Got it," Cohen replies, and I hang up.

"Silas—" Lola starts.

"We're not having this conversation here … like this." Dropping her shoes onto the ground, I take her face in my hands as she still rests her fingers on my shoulder and cup her cheeks as if I might never see her again. "We will, though. I promise. I will break down and tell you because I don't want to lose you. I will give you every piece of me if it means you're still in my life."

Tears fall down her cheeks, hitting my thumbs, and I choke back my own emotions. Just as she opens her mouth to reply, Cohen pulls up.

"Please," I beg with sorrow in my voice. "Get in that car, and I swear, I'll be fine."

"Lincoln is over there," Cohen says as if reading our minds even though we're hunched together, our voices low. "He'll keep an eye on him."

I frown that I've been assigned a babysitter, but I get it. I'd do the same if my friends were falling apart, so it makes sense they'd do it for me.

I rub my thumb over Lola's cheek and catch her tears before slowly pulling away.

"At least text me tonight," Lola says, our faces only inches apart. "If you don't, I'm getting in my car and driving here. Do you hear me?"

I slowly nod. "I hear you."

She kisses my cheek, her lips so close to the edge of my lips, and my shoulders slump.

"Here." As she pulls away, she bends down, untying my shoes.

I shake my head, stopping her. "Keep them."

"You're barefoot."

"Consider it an insurance policy that I'm not going to shut you out."

"Okay," she whispers.

I help her into Cohen's car, not paying him a glance, and when she pulls away, I sink down onto the curb. Shutting my eyes, I allow the memories of what happened that night to surface. I sit there, in my own regret, wishing I'd been a smarter man back then.

CHAPTER THIRTY-SEVEN

Lola

"GIVE HIM TIME," Cohen says on the drive to my house.

If this wasn't Cohen, I'd struggle to mask my tears, but he'd never judge me.

"I don't know what to do anymore," I say with a sniffle. "I'm just ... so confused. And I feel selfish that I never realized Silas was suffering through this internal hell. I'm a bad friend for not catching on to it."

"Don't. I've known Silas for longer than you, and I had no idea. He was good at playing the part."

"Until he couldn't any longer."

"Until he was afraid of losing you." His voice is soft, calming, but also sure of himself.

I sigh, my throat tightening at the thought. "He'll never lose me."

"We know that. The problem is, he doesn't."

"I'm in love with him." My last word comes out in a sob, and I cover my mouth. I'm not sure if it's to stop my tears or that I'm shocked. Because for the first time, I've allowed myself to reveal my feelings for Silas.

Even though I'm saying it to the wrong person, it feels good to finally release it. To speak my truth.

"I know. We all know. *Silas* knows."

I peer at Cohen. "Just because someone knows you love them, that doesn't mean they have to love you back."

"He tries to hide it, but there's no doubt in anyone's minds that he doesn't love you. He's scared, and sometimes, it takes us seeing our worst nightmare to figure out what we want in life. His worst nightmare was seeing you with someone else, so you being with Trent was the push that he needed to get out of it."

"Is that ..." I play with my hands in my lap. "Is that how you felt with Jamie? That you were going to lose her?"

He nods. "The same with the other guys. It made us wake up. Silas is getting there."

When we pull up to my house, I find Trent sitting on my front porch steps.

I pull in a heavy breath, unsure of what to do.

"You want me to talk to him?" Cohen asks, shifting the car into park.

I shake my head. "No, I got this."

I'm the one who started hanging out with Trent, so I need to be the one to figure it out with him.

"I'll be sure Silas gets home safe. You two are going to be okay, Lola."

"Thank you." I tip my head down. "Give the kiddos a kiss for me."

"I will. Think about what you want, okay? Not what anyone else wants, only *you*."

I nod and step out of his car.

Trent stands as I approach him, and he runs a hand through his thick hair. "I hope you don't find this weird. I was going to wait a little longer, and if you didn't show up, I would have gone home. I was just worried about you."

I give him a gentle smile. "I'm okay. Thank you. I appreciate you checking, and I'm sorry tonight turned into a mess."

He shakes his head, holding up a hand. "Don't apologize. You had nothing to do with what happened tonight. That was a long time coming, and you just got shoved into the middle of it. I'm sorry for my role in it." He pushes his hands into his pockets, and I notice he hasn't changed out of his bloody shirt either. "What happened when I left?"

"Silas and I talked for a minute, but he asked for space, so Cohen brought me home."

"You want me to stay, keep you company?" He stops and rushes out his next words. "I'll sleep on the couch."

I press my hand to his chest, knowing that this will probably be the last time Trent and I have a face-to-face conversation. Guilt coils in me for bringing him in the middle of Silas's and my problems.

"Thanks for the offer," I whisper, "but I'm okay."

"I understand." He stares at me, his face brimming with concern. "You said Silas and you were just friends. Is that the truth?"

I can't look him in the eye. "I don't know."

"I think you do, but you're scared of it." He brushes his lips against my cheek before stepping to the side, allowing me better access to my front door. "Good night, Lola." He waits until I walk in before leaving.

———

THE TEARS RELEASE as soon as the door shuts behind me, and I slouch back against it, allowing my emotions to overcome me. I plod to my bedroom, checking my phone with every step, praying for something from Silas.

It's not even midnight, yet this feels like the longest day of my life. I get ready for bed and change into my pajamas, and just as I'm about to leave Silas's shoes on the floor, I tuck them underneath my arms instead. I keep them there as I slide into bed, and as gross as it seems —especially since I don't even allow dirty clothes near my bed—I situate them next to me, hugging them to my chest. I need something related to him to comfort me.

I keep my phone in my hand, gripped tight as if it were my lifeline. I check my messages in case I missed something from him and slump my shoulders when I see I haven't. Scrolling through our text messages, past the ones before my birthday, I read our history—our past of how we once were.

Two weeks ago:

Silas: Rise and shine to my favorite girl! I'm on my way with your fave breakfast, so get your cute ass out of bed.

One month ago:

Me: Tinder is gross. Vomit.

Silas: That's because you haven't swiped right on my profile.

Me: I swiped left as soon as I could once I read your profile that said, "Lola has my heart." I thought you were talking about another woman you were hung up on.

Silas: Nah, there's only one Lola who'll ever have my heart.

Me: It might not be the smartest to make that known on Tinder.

Silas: Why? They need to know you're my girl before everything.

I swipe away tears, missing us, and take in every word of the happiness we once had. My sob-fest is interrupted when my phone rings, and as much as I love Georgia, my tears come out harder when I see her name instead of Silas's.

I clear my throat, snap my fingers in front of my face, and shake my head—all attempts not to sound as broken as I feel. I'm not the girl who gets swept up in her emotions, and before all this happened, I stupidly believed I wasn't the girl who'd cry over a broken heart.

"Hello?" I'm proud of how strong my voice sounds.

"Hi," Georgia says—no chirp, all seriousness. "Archer told me what happened. I'm about to leave now, and I should be there in about ten minutes."

"You don't have to do that. Stay home. It's late."

"I want to be there for you."

"I appreciate that, and thank you." I sigh. "I think I just need a moment to myself."

"Okay, call, and I'll be right over if you need me," she says softly before briefly pausing. "You love him, don't you?"

"I do." I lose what little control I had.

She releases a long breath. "Swear to God, there's just something about brokenhearted men that get us every time."

"Yes, and then they break our hearts."

"Not always. Sometimes, they grow hearts."

CHAPTER THIRTY-EIGHT

Silas

"GO AND MAKE THINGS RIGHT," Cohen says, stern and parent-like, when we pull up in front of Lola's house.

It's late, but I texted to make sure she was okay with me coming over.

After she'd left Twisted Fox, I'd stayed outside for a good hour, pitying myself. Lincoln silently stood in the distance, waiting for me to get myself together until I'd called Cohen and told him I was ready to talk to Lola.

Cohen didn't lecture me on the drive. All he said was, he was here if I needed to talk. That's Cohen—the only father in the group and the father to the group.

Today has been a shit show. I finally snapped—the deep-seated emotions I'd controlled for so long had become uncontrollable, fighting their way into my new world. I hate myself for the pain I caused everyone, including my father, Janet, and my grandmother, for my actions at the charity event. And my friends for my behavior at Twisted Fox. None of them deserved any of that.

But especially Lola—for her birthday, the party.

I've been pushing the person who means the most to me the

farthest away. I need to apologize for how stupid I've been acting the past few weeks.

I miss her.

Miss us.

Even though she's expecting me, my heart pounds when I knock on her door, not knowing what to expect. The door swings open, and she stands before me, wearing one of my old tees and pajama shorts. Her face is clear of the makeup stains she had earlier, and her hair is in a messy ponytail. Unlike me, she's pulled herself together. Even with all that, her eyes are still puffy, still red, and I know that's because of my actions.

"Hi," she says shyly, touching her cheeks as if making sure her tears are gone.

"Hi," I say in response. I don't want to say the wrong thing. I want to make things right with Lola, so I need to be careful.

I turn briefly and wave at Cohen, telling him all is good—that Lola didn't slam the door in my face. He rolls down his window, gives me a thumbs-up, and drives off.

If only I had the confidence he has in me.

"First things first," Lola says, waving me inside. "We need to get you cleaned up."

I step inside, slow, my body tight.

"I can't believe you haven't changed out of this bloody shirt." She peeks down at my feet. "At least you found some shoes."

I scratch my head. "Cohen had a spare pair in his trunk."

This isn't Lola and me.

We're never like this—so hesitant with our words, so careful with every move we make, for fear it'll upset the other.

She takes my hand, and I lace our fingers together, holding her tight, as if I never want to let go, never want to lose her. I shuffle my feet as she leads me through the house and into her master bathroom. Her bathroom smells like her—like the citrus shampoo she uses and her perfume.

Gripping my shoulders, she settles me onto the lid of the toilet seat. She waits, making sure I'm stable, before pulling away and grabbing supplies from her drawers. I focus on her as she opens the cabinet for her first-aid kit. Shame rocks through me. After all the embarrassment I caused her, she's still here for me.

"I'm sorry," I say, my voice shaking.

When she drops to her knees, our eyes meet. I painfully stare at her in desperation, praying she sees the apology over this beat-up face of mine.

If she does, she doesn't tell me. She grabs my chin, supporting it in her hand, and inspects my face while hers is unreadable. I'm not sure if it's that way because she's over my shit or if she's trying to hide from me. She's given me her all so many times, told me how she felt, and I turned my back on her. Maybe she's done with handing me something so precious, only for it to be stomped on.

She situates her supplies at her feet, and I wince when she starts cleaning my face even though I deserve the pain. She's deep in concentration as if desperate to remove all evidence of what occurred tonight. I treated her terribly, and now, she's taking care of me.

"What's going on, Silas?" she finally asks, her voice as difficult to read as her face.

I stare at her, leveling my breathing, and I lick a remnant of blood she missed from my lip. "I don't know."

I came here to explain myself, and that's all I'm giving her?

That won't do with Lola.

Just like me, it's difficult for her to find the right words. In front of her is a man who has been so involved in her life and is now pulling away. I don't blame her for doing the same.

She stares at me, her face pain-stricken. "You don't know …" Her voice becomes shaky. "Or you don't want to tell me?"

I'm going to lose the woman I love if I don't crack myself open and hand her the section of me that only she can fix. She will walk away, tired of my shit, as if she has no choice. She'll take the sliver of happiness I have with her. I'll crumble more with every waking day.

That's why, as I sit in the bathroom, her nursing me from a fight with a man who threatened to take her from me, I sit in anguish, conflicted with myself on what my next move should be.

To open myself up and find love.

Or to shut down and be lonely.

Those are my only two options in this life with her.

Fuck that. Losing her isn't an option.

I will unlock every secret and open every door that is me to keep her.

"I'm struggling," I whisper.

She has no idea how even those two words were a war to get out.

Please, God, help me get through this battle.

Help me keep her.

Her eyes are tired as they meet my despaired ones. She runs a single finger over my busted lip. "With what?" Her tone is soft and soothing—a side of Lola no one else sees. A side of her I haven't seen until tonight.

I relax into her touch, take a deep breath, and do something I never thought I would. "With my feelings for you."

And with those five words, our entire relationship is about to change.

Whether it's good or bad, I'm unsure.

Her finger freezes in the middle of my lip. "What do you mean?"

Don't have a change of heart.

Tell her, dumbass.

Tell her who you really are.

The things you've done.

My heart rattles in my chest, as if nervous to give itself away, but I force myself through it. "In high school, I made a terrible mistake that cost two people their lives."

I've gained her full attention, but she doesn't say a word, as if terrified I'll stop if she does.

I rest my hand over hers, not only because I'm scared of her pulling away but also because her skin against mine will give me the push that I need to get through this.

I gulp.

And do it again.

And again.

And she waits with patience, never once pushing me.

"I can't get over it. Their deaths are why I don't date, why I don't drink, and why I can't go out on your birthday."

"Silas, I'm not understanding." She cups her hand over mine, the one that's resting on hers. "Please tell me."

I nod, squeezing my eyes shut, and for the first time ever, I tell someone exactly what happened.

CHAPTER THIRTY-NINE

Silas

High School: Senior Year

SNEAKING AROUND with someone is a pain in the ass.

Especially when it's around your best friend's back.

Sienna and I have been hiding our relationship from everyone—including her twin brother, Kenny—for months. We didn't mean for it to happen, and when it did, we said it'd only be one time. But one time wasn't enough, so we swore it'd only be two. Then two wasn't enough, and I wanted to be around her every second of the day. Which is hard when you're hiding your relationship.

But lately, anytime she brings up going public, I insist we need more time. Kenny is protective of her, and so are her parents. Given my reputation of being a *player*, they'd force her to stay away from me. It's better to be together in secret than not to be together at all.

Tonight, we're at a friend's party. Kenny is grounded, and we've been drinking, so Sienna's and my inhibitions are lowered. We're not being as careful as we typically are. Not only have I been touching her all night but I'm also attempting to make up for arguing last night. She asked if we were going to prom, and I hesitated, knowing it was more complicated than a simple *let's go to prom together*.

But now, she seems to be over our fight—until the next time she gets unhappy.

I'm gripping her hand as we hurry up the stairs, and she giggles when we enter a bedroom. Her mouth is on mine as soon as I click the lock on the door. I love kissing her, I love tasting the strawberry bubblegum she always chews, and I love wrapping my hands in her curly hair.

She raises her arms as I pull her shirt over her head, and I toss it onto the floor while leading her to the bed. As I hover over her, I tickle her waist, causing her to giggle more.

"I love being with you," I say against her lips before sticking my tongue between them.

As I start kissing her neck, she pulls me back.

She strokes my shoulder. "What are we, Silas?"

I raise a brow. "What do you mean?"

It's a stupid question because I know what she means, but it gives me more time to come up with an answer.

"I hate feeling like a secret," she whispers, looking away from me.

I move a curl away from her eyes. "You're not a secret, babe."

"Then tell Kenny. Stop being scared."

The erection I had is starting to shrivel from the conversation I hate more than anything.

I level myself onto my elbow to meet her eyes. "I'm not scared. I just know it'll cause issues. With him, with your parents, with my parents. Your parents look at you like you're innocent, and I'm the *playboy*," I say the word in their mocking voice. "Once they find out we're dating, once they find out we're having sex, all hell will break loose. Your parents might not even let us see each other. I don't want that. That's what I'm afraid of. I'm afraid of the truth making me lose you."

She shuts her eyes. "Do you love me?"

I'm quiet.

"Silas," she stresses. "Do you love me?"

I'm eighteen. Do I even know what love is?

Instead of answering, I kiss her hard, my tongue diving into her mouth, not giving her the chance to continue our conversation. I slide my lips to her ear, nibbling on the skin behind it, knowing it's her sensitive spot. She melts underneath me, and long gone is the *what are we* talk.

When I move my lips to her mouth, she moans into mine. I slide my hand up her skirt—slow and careful because even though she isn't the first woman I've been with, she's the one I want to please more than anything. She's soaking for me, and I think back to the night she gave me her virginity. Moving her panties to the side, I slowly press a finger into her warmth, loving that she's always ready for me.

That we're always ready for each other.

I've hooked up with other girls before, but I've never felt such a pull to them—never wanted to please them, be with them, never craved them as much as I do Sienna. Even though we haven't gone public, she's still mine, and I'm still hers. I've been committed to her in every way—not even thought about touching another girl.

She lifts, dragging my shirt over my head, and I'm unbuckling my pants when the door is kicked open.

One second, I'm on top of Sienna, and the next, I'm being dragged off the bed. Chaos erupts, and my head spins as I'm thrown to the ground, two sets of feet kicking me. As I pull myself up and push them off me, I look forward, look for Sienna, but my view of her is cut off by people.

I attempt to push through them but am held back by the two guys who kicked me.

"Get your fucking shirt on, and let's go," Kenny yells to Sienna.

With all my power, I grit my teeth and elbow each guy, causing them to let go of me.

Fucking traitors.

"Don't you dare talk to her like that," I seethe, getting a quick glimpse of Sienna as she holds the sheet to her chest and reaches for her shirt.

I cringe at the embarrassment on her face, wanting nothing more than to tuck her in my arms and protect her from it.

My nostrils flare as I turn my attention to the crowd, hoping to direct their attention away from her to me. "All you motherfuckers! Get out!"

"Out of all the chicks you could've messed with, you chose her?" Kenny screams, clenching his fists. "My sister isn't one of your stupid whores!"

"We were going to tell you," Sienna sobs, tugging her shirt on.

Kenny snatches her wrist and drags her out of the room.

Anger roars inside me, and I fight my way through the crowd, following Kenny and Sienna while yelling their names.

People scream at me, calling me names, asking how I could betray my friend like that. Being Kenny's friend for so long, I know how he gets when he's angry, how he doesn't ask questions before he goes crazy.

"Let her go, or I swear to God, I'll knock you out." I jump over the staircase, growing closer, and that's when I see Kenny slap Trent on the back.

"Thanks for the heads-up, man," he says while on his way out the door.

They disappear through the front door, and Trent smirks at me. Grabbing the collar of his polo, I slam Trent against the wall. A picture falls to the floor and shatters.

"What the fuck did you do?" I scream in his face, spit flying onto his cheek.

Trent laughs. "I just let the truth come out."

"I'll deal with you later," I snarl, letting him go and sprinting outside.

Kenny is across the yard, shoving Sienna into his Mustang, and it's still a struggle to work my way through the crowd. He peels out, his wheels spinning before driving off.

How many people are fucking here?

I can't run fast enough to keep up with a car, so I jerk my keys from my pocket, sprint to my Camaro, and drive. I don't see them, don't see their taillights in the darkness, but I trust my instincts and drive toward their house. When I finally catch up with them, Kenny is speeding around a sharp curve.

He doesn't make it around that curve.

Brakes squeal, and the car flips before sliding to the side of the road, flames shooting from the car. I feel like my life is flashing before my eyes. And even though it's not my life being taken, I'm losing the person who was my life. I cover my ears, the car alarm screaming into the empty air as I sprint toward the wrecked Mustang.

I never told Sienna I loved her because I was scared.

June twenty-third will haunt me for the rest of my life.

CHAPTER FORTY

Lola

MY VIEW of Silas is blurry from my tears, and I slide my hand up, touching his cheek. Slowly, I swipe away the tears that have fallen down his splotchy red cheek.

I've cried during movies.

Cried while reading books.

But nothing has ever shattered me like Silas's story as I witness the raw pain, seeing this broken man before me.

In the span of one night, I've met parts of Silas I never knew existed. The angry side. The sad side. And now, the heartbroken and torn side. I once viewed this man as flawless, as perfect, as not having a care in the world. I never knew he carried this heavy weight of history on his shoulders. Not only did he lose people he loved, but he also witnessed them losing their life. He saw the very thing that killed them and could do nothing to stop it.

Something like that breaks a person.

I don't know how he's been strong, how he's hidden from it all these years. I get the secrets, the reason he held it in—because he was terrified of losing us. But what Silas doesn't know is that it'd have only helped us understand him, to be there for him and hold his hand along the way.

Rising on my knees, I pull him into my chest, cradling his head, and allow him to hide himself. I'm an emotional shield, giving him privacy to let go, to release the pain he's been keeping inside. I hold him tight, tears streaming down my face as he sobs against me, as he drains his hurt and hands it to me, giving me what I've been asking for all along. And I'm fulfilling the promise I gave him—that I'll always be there, no matter what.

This is the man I'm in love with.

Broken, not broken.

Happy or soaking my shirt with his tears.

He's my everything.

And now, I can give him what he needs to heal from this.

We sit there, and I lose track of time. Even as my knees go sore against the tiled floor, I'm willing to sit here all night if it's what he needs. When he pulls back, his face is almost lifeless, as if he's given all he can give for the night. As much as I want to know more, to dig out every detail, he looks exhausted enough.

I kiss the tip of my thumb and trace it along his mouth before pressing it to his lips. His shoulders curl over his chest, his entire body shaking. He inhales deep breaths, calming himself. He offers a pained stare, no longer hiding from me, and his eyes glisten from his hurt.

Sliding my hand down, I slowly unbutton his shirt, and as I undo each one, I massage the now-exposed skin with the same thumb I touched his lips with. He's silent, still, tears swimming in his eyes. After dragging the shirt off his shoulders, I ball it up in my hands and toss it behind me. I drop my hands, fingering the hem of my shirt, and peel off my tee—*his* tee that I stole one night.

I'm standing in front of him, wearing only a sports bra, as my chest heaves in and out.

"Here," I say, unsure if my word is even audible through my tears. "Put this on."

He shakes his head but grabs it, and I take a step back when he stands.

"No, I like seeing you in it."

I shiver when he reaches out, pulls me closer, and slides his chilly hands up and down my arms before slowly lifting them. I sigh at the loss of his touch as he pulls at the neck of the shirt and carefully slips it back over my head.

"DOA," he says, his voice clearer than it has been all night. He stares above my head, toward my shower, as he speaks. "That's what the paramedics said as I stood there and watched them carry their burned bodies out of the car." He draws in a breath. "Everyone blamed me. I was the reason Kenny was so pissed. I was the one who got into my car and chased them." His tears land in my hair. "When I got home, I found Trent sitting on the porch. My friends later told me that Trent messaged Kenny that I was upstairs with Sienna. All Trent said was that he was sorry, and if he could take it back, he would. I told him he was the one who deserved to be dead ... and then he said no one would be dead if it wasn't for me. And even though his words hurt like a bitch, they were the truth."

"He was wrong. They were all wrong." I press my hand to his chest, over his heart, and feel his frantic pulse.

"If I'd never touched Sienna, if we'd never gotten caught, they'd still be alive."

"You were teenagers in love. Her brother's recklessness is what caused their deaths. I know there's guilt, but you don't need to wear the burden of it being your fault. You tried to stop him, tried to stop it from happening."

"I was banned from their funerals." His voice hardens with that statement.

"They needed to find someone to blame because their son, the one who was responsible, was gone. Them needing someone else to blame in their grieving was unfair to you."

His lips move to my ear, and goose bumps cover my arms. "Now, do you see why I think I'm no good for you? Look what happened to the last girl I loved. She's dead, Lola." His voice breaks, hurt ricocheting with every word. It's as if he believes his confession might cause me to walk away from him. "I don't deserve you for what I did."

"Stop punishing yourself." I cup his neck, dragging his head closer to mine, and it's me now whispering in his ear. "You deserve happiness just as much as I do ... just as much as anyone. No matter what, I'll always be at your side. I'll always be your friend."

He flinches, pulling back as if I'd slapped him. "I hate that word."

"What?"

"Friend." Desperation is on his face. "I'm fighting with myself, Lola. Even though I say I don't deserve you, I also don't want to lose you."

I sniffle. "I don't want to lose you."

"I'm in love with you."

I stare at him, wide-eyed, words catching in my throat.

"I'm in love with you, and I wanted you to understand why I am the way I am. What I just told you is why I've been fucking terrified of crossing any lines with you. I can't do that anymore. I came here, risking our friendship, to tell you I'm as lonely as you told me you are. When Sienna asked me if I loved her, I was scared to believe that love was real because I didn't know what it was. But with you, I know exactly what it is because it's how I feel about you. Words can't explain the emotions I feel when I'm with you, the happiness, the fact that I never want to be with anyone else. It's love."

I'm quiet, still scrambling for words, as my head spins.

Taking my hand, he walks me into my bedroom and sits me on the bed. Dropping to his knees, the same way I did with him in the bathroom, he cups my neck, drawing me close to him.

"I'm sorry," he says through quivering breaths, "for the pain that I caused. But I'm not sorry for opening myself up to you, for giving you all of myself. You have me, Lola. All of me—my anguish, my fears, my past, and my nightmares—because I know I'm in good hands. But you also have my heart, my soul, my everything … because you're my everything."

CHAPTER FORTY-ONE

Silas

HAVE you ever had something happen that makes you feel a thousand pounds lighter?

Told someone something that was way overdue?

I'm showing Lola all my weaknesses, but I'm also giving her all my strengths.

That balances itself out, right?

She can have this broken man, and in exchange for taking him, she can also have his heart.

Is that considered a fair deal?

Everything that's happened in my life—the good, the bad—has led me to Lola. She is the woman who was sent to heal this brokenness inside me, just like I'm there to show her real love—that a man can stay committed, that he can give a woman his heart unconditionally and never make her feel lonely.

Without Lola, I'm not sure where I'd be, but I know it'd be somewhere low.

Unhappy.

Drowning in my pity.

With Sienna, I was young and dumb, but I know right from wrong now. My biggest regret from my past is not telling Sienna that I loved her. She died, uncertain of my feelings. She died, not knowing if the man she loved, loved her back. I failed Sienna, failed to keep her safe, and I've learned that lesson. I've grown, and I won't make that mistake again. I refuse to allow another woman I love question my feelings for her.

I was scared to tell Lola, scared of losing her, but just like with Sienna, if I hadn't told her my true feelings, I'd have lost her.

Lola's tears have returned as she bows her head and stares at me, her eyes gentle yet also confused. "Will this ruin us?"

"Possibly." I'm giving her all the honesty I have inside me. "But it could also make us the happiest we've ever been. I just need to know you feel the same way."

I release her when she nods, wanting a better view of her face, of her eyes so I can see the truth in them. I hold in a desperate breath, a life-changing breath, and wait for her to tell me what the next road in my life will be.

Her hands are shaking, her lower lip trembling, and then slowly, her face somewhat relaxes. "I love you. With all my heart. With everything that I am."

She's spilling her heart out as much as I am mine. And even though I'm reminded of the pain from my past, even though I'm angry with myself for drinking and taking my sadness out on her, hearing those words shines a light over all of that.

My and Lola's relationship has been based on timing. We weren't meant to be together romantically years ago. Neither of us was ready for something that strong. Had we tried, I'd have broken her heart … if she'd even been ready to give it out. We needed that time, those years to find out who we were and what we wanted in life. Our friendship allowed us to build the foundation that constructed our love.

I don't regret the time it took us to get here, don't wish this had happened sooner because I was a different man back then.

A man undeserving of her.

A man who wasn't ready to face his demons.

Us becoming friends to lovers is how our story was always meant to be.

Us being side by side in our journeys without expectations is what we needed.

And now, our story has reached the end of its friendship and the beginning of more—what all this time has been preparing us for.

I didn't love Lola the minute I saw her.

There was no love at first sight for either of us.

But now, there's love with every glance at each other, love with every conversation we share, and love every time we touch.

And just like I fought like hell not to fall in love with her, it's now time I fight like hell not to lose her.

She runs her hands through my hair. It's soothing, relaxing. "Now, you need to get some sleep."

I nod. "Sleep sounds amazing."

She wraps her arms around my neck. "I've missed you."

Our eyes meet.

And there's no hesitation before our lips do the same.

It's slow. Intimate. And worth all the years we waited.

CHAPTER FORTY-TWO

Lola

POURING your heart out to someone can be exhausting.

We're mentally and emotionally drained and in dire need of rest.

Especially Silas. He got into a punching match with Trent, drank, walked down a dark street for an hour, and then came here to reveal his truths, his inner demons, to me.

But I have a feeling we'll sleep better tonight than we have in weeks.

Rest easier.

Now that the weight is off our shoulders.

The truth is out.

When Silas notices his shoes in my bed, he points at them, raising a brow. I tell him not to ask and toss my pillow at him. I hand him a pair of old gym shorts I stole from him, and then we get into bed.

I turn on my side to stare at him. It's surreal, different yet familiar at the same time. We've loved each other as friends for years, but now, we're opening our hearts for a deeper connection.

"Come here," he says around a yawn, dragging me into his side while he's on his back.

I cuddle against him. He stares down at me, his eyes heavy, and I can't believe he hasn't passed out yet. His eyes shut and then open back up.

He kisses my forehead, mutters a quiet, "Good night," and doesn't make it a few seconds before drifting to sleep.

I do the same not even minutes after.

———

WE SLEEP IN LATE.

The rest much needed.

I'm still spooning his side when I wake up, my head resting against his chest, and I can hear his heartbeat. It's different than last night— relaxed, calm, not frantic. As I slowly pull away, I cringe when I see the drool I've left as evidence of my being there.

Um, gross.

I stare at him, uncertain of what to do, and wonder if he'll wake if I clean it.

"It's not the first time you've drooled on me," he whispers.

I draw back, startled at his voice, and I cast my gaze on him. He has one eye open, focused on me, and yawns.

I smack his chest. "How the hell did you know what I was thinking?"

"I was watching you."

I shove my hair behind an ear. "With one eye?"

"Yes, I can only halfway take the sunlight in your room." He grins up at me. "You're a drooler. It's cute."

"I'm *so* not a drooler." I wipe up the evidence of the drool with the back of my hand. "You're a snorer."

"Hey now, I never said I didn't *like* your drool. It's like a trinket of you being here, a memento that I had you close enough to drool on me."

To change the conversation of me apparently being a drool monster, I reach out and trace my hand along his jawline. "How are you feeling? Hungover?"

I love how we can touch each other like this now.

Be so intimate.

He rubs his forehead with two fingers. "I forgot how bad hangovers suck. I don't miss this shit."

"What made you stop drinking before?"

I'm treading into dangerous territory. He opened himself up last night, gave me pieces of him, and I don't want him to think I'm asking for more too soon. We might've reached a new space in our relationship, but it's fresh. Like twelve hours fresh.

He opens the other eye, and sorrow flashes in them as he adjusts his gaze on me.

"You don't have to tell me," I rush out. "I don't want to push you."

I start dragging my hand from his face, but he clasps my wrist to stop me and lowers it to his chest, on his heart—the same spot where my head was sleeping ... and my drool decorated.

His skin is warm, and his heartbeat picks up. It's not as relaxed as it was when I woke, but it's not almost leaping from his chest like last night.

He shakes his head, fighting back tears. "I was banned from their funeral, but I went anyway. I sat in the parking lot with a half-gallon of cheap vodka and got drunk. It was stupid, but I was so fucking hurt that not only did I lose them, but everyone was also pointing the finger at me. Saying I killed them. Their cousin came out and threatened to kick my ass if I didn't leave. I told him to go ahead. But instead of physically fighting me, he broke me down with his words, saying I didn't deserve to numb myself with liquor and needed to suffer for what I'd done. My parents showed up, forced me into their car, but their cousin's words haunted me on the drive back. When I got home, I grabbed all the liquor I had stashed in my room, flushed it, and vowed to never drink again. I kept that vow until last night."

"I'm sorry what I did made you break your sobriety."

I lose my touch on him as he rises, pulling me up with him. He rests his back on his headboard while pulling me to my knees so that we're facing.

He strokes my cheek, and I quiver. "It's not your fault. It's mine. For the first time in years, I felt like I needed to numb myself."

"From what?" I gulp. Guilt consumes me, but his touch relaxes me. "Wanting me?"

"Yes."

"Did it work?"

"I wouldn't have shown up here if it had. I could never drink away my feelings for you. They're so deep that they're untouchable. You're inside me, Lola. A part of me that there's no getting rid of. Last night, even when I tried to drink you away, it didn't work. All it did was make me realize that if I didn't man up, I'd lose you." His hand freezes on my cheek, and he doesn't break eye contact with me. "I never want that to happen."

He's surrendering his secrets to me.

His feelings.

Everything that is him.

"I'm not going anywhere." I drag his hand to my lips and kiss his palm. "I'm all yours."

He smiles.

"But I need something from you."

"What's that?"

"Tell me if something isn't easy for you ... like my birthday. You can't give me you and then pull away later out of fear that it'll upset me."

He nods. "I promise you."

"No one ever said falling for your best friend was easy."

He lightly chuckles, pulling me closer until I'm nearly sitting on his lap. "It's actually harder."

"I don't know about that. We skipped a lot of steps. We already know so much about each other. Already comfortable."

"We can do this now." He presses his lips to mine, and this time, it's my heart pounding. "And this." His hand disappears under the sheet, and he caresses my thigh, playing with the hem of my shorts.

I stop him when he goes for another kiss. "I have morning breath."

He cups the back of my neck. "Yeah, and I don't give a fuck about that."

"I do." I laugh. "I need to shower."

He groans, and as I slide off him, the hint of an erection presses against my leg. I grin, loving that I have that effect on him. I'm surprised when he follows me.

"Guess what," he says.

I peer back at him from over my shoulder. "What?"

"I'm in need of a shower too." He comes up behind me, tickling my waist, and I double over, laughing. "Want to clean me up again?"

I escape his hold and head toward the bathroom, swaying my hips from side to side, my intent to make his erection unbearable. The tiles are chilly underneath my bare feet as I collect the trash and the first-aid kit from the floor, turn on the water, and grab a towel from the closet. I can feel his eyes pinned on me, but I act like I don't notice.

"You going to grab me a towel too" he asks, his voice raspy.

I peek a playful glance at him. "Why?"

"Lola," he groans, and his tone turns pleading. "Can I please join you for a shower?"

I turn on my heel, pointing at him with the towel. "You can wait your turn."

"What?" he stutters.

"Did you think I wouldn't get back at you for dropping me on my ass at the club?" I smirk and brush my hand along his arm as I walk past him. "I'm showering. If you want to watch me while you wait your turn, be my guest."

"What?" he repeats, as if he's struggling to process my words.

I strip off my shirt. "You can watch me shower or go back to bed and wait until I'm finished."

He gestures to his waist, to the outline of his bulge. And as much as I want to see it, I give myself a pep talk to hold my ground.

"Are you trying to torture me?"

Yes. Yes, I am.

"Call it a consequence for your actions." I wiggle out of my shorts, tugging them down my legs with my panties, take off my bra, and step into the shower.

The door is glass, giving him a straight view of me, and I tip my head back, water droplets falling down my bare chest.

Trying my hardest not to make it obvious, I sneak a peek at him.

He leans back against the vanity, his arms crossed, his gaze latched on to me. "Am I allowed to … what are the rules here?"

I smile. "The only rule is, you can't touch me."

He removes his shirt, dropping it to the floor. "Oh, I can easily join you in the shower without touching you."

"Correction: you can do anything but touch *or join me.* Other than that, do what you please."

"I always said you were the damn devil."

"The devil always gets her payback."

CHAPTER FORTY-THREE

Silas

FROM THE MOMENT I met Lola, I knew she loved a good revenge.

Now, I'm on the other end of that.

And it sucks.

I'm intoxicated as I watch the hottest show I've ever seen.

Lola's wet body. Water dripping down her perfect curves. Plump breasts that I'd give a kidney to have my mouth on.

I watch her, fixated, and my dick grows harder and harder.

She lathers shampoo into her hair, paying me no mind, as if torturing men like this is something she does on the regular. Tipping her head back, she rinses it from her hair, and releases a slow moan while grabbing the conditioner. While conditioning her hair, she peeks over at me for my reaction.

I tighten my fists—an attempt to stop myself from pushing down my shorts and stroking my cock while she rinses her hair again. If Lola wants to play games, I'll tap in, stopping her from seeing how bad I'm aching to touch her.

Teasing me seems to be Lola's favorite foreplay.

I'll have to remember that … and then give her a piece of her own medicine.

I have a feeling Lola and I will have plenty of push and pull, of teasing, and it's exactly what I expected being with her would be like.

"You doing okay over there?" she asks, trying to sound as innocent as possible.

"I'm good," I croak. "Just a normal day in the office. Nothing new I haven't experienced in a bathroom."

I shut up.

Not the smartest thing to say, dumbass.

You want her to allow you to join her in the shower, pleasure her in the shower, not drown you in it.

"Oh, really?" She spills body wash onto a loofah. "You've watched other women shower before?"

"Fuck no. Only you."

"I don't believe you." She glides her hand between her breasts, slowly cleaning herself with the loofah. "I'll be getting you back for that as well."

"Bullshit," I groan, my knees feeling weak, and grip the edge of the vanity to hold myself up.

She covers every inch of herself with soap, and the sweet scent of her body wash drifts through the room. The steam of the shower fogs the glass and interferes with my view of her.

"I'm trying …" I stop, catching up with my breathing. "I'm trying to be a gentleman over here."

But you're making it really fucking hard. The same with my dick.

I groan when the shower door opens, and Lola steps out, water dripping from every inch of her perfect body. As much as I'm trying to be the gentleman I said I was, I can't stop myself from slipping my gaze down her body. I lick my lips, my breathing a mixed pattern of shallow yet quick, as she leaves the water running.

"And now," she says with a twinkle in her eye, "it's time to stop being one."

I take one long stride toward her, circle my arms around her waist, and glide her back into the shower. The water is hot as I press her against the shower wall. She gasps, a mischievous smile on her face.

When I place a hand to each side of her head, her eyes meet mine as I slowly lower my mouth to hers.

"I still have morning breath," she says, inches from my mouth.

"And I still don't give a fuck."

It seems almost dramatic.

In slow motion.

As our lips connect.

She opens her mouth, morning-breath thoughts long gone, and thrusts her tongue into my mouth.

This isn't our first kiss, but it's our first passionate one.

Our first mouth-devouring, *I need you right now* kiss.

The kind of kiss I craved to share with her.

The one I never thought would happen.

She sucks on the end of my tongue as her hands frantically push down my shorts, and they pool at my feet. Grabbing my ass, her nails digging into my skin, she draws me closer to her. The moment my bare cock hits her thigh, she moans. I move my lips to her neck, lapping up the water as I rain kisses along it.

"Wrap your legs around me," I say, unsure if the words sound demanding or shaky as they leave my mouth.

She hooks her leg around my thigh, and I carefully open the shower door. As I carry her out of the shower, she quickly turns it off, and I deposit her on the vanity. I make sure she's stable and drop to my knees, fully ready to worship every inch of her.

I spread her legs open, the space perfect for me to fit between, and caress her thighs. She shivers, her face burning with desire as her eyes meet mine.

"This okay?" I whisper.

She grins, tipping her hips so that they're closer to my face. "Let's consider it an apology for what you did at the club."

"Oh, babe, this is just the start of the apology." I kiss each of her thighs, slow and precise. My gaze drifts back and forth from her face to her pretty pussy, soaking the view of her turned on in both places.

When I take my first lick, I smile against her slit, and she shivers above me. I give her my tongue, lapping her up, and don't add my fingers until she moans. With two fingers, I slowly stroke her before adding another, curling my fingers inside her warmth as I gently suck on her clit.

I start a game, just like she did with me.

I slide my hand out of her pussy and then slowly play with her clit.

I stop playing with her clit and return to pleasuring her with three fingers.

I could eat her out for every meal and still never be fully satisfied.

She rocks her hips, getting closer, her moans growing louder, and she grips the back of my neck, pinning my head between her legs, not letting go until she's arching her back and her legs are shaking.

I don't stop as she comes into my mouth.

No, I wrap my arms around her thighs, dragging her quivering thighs closer, and devour her harder. Suck her clit faster.

She wanted to play games.

I'm not showing her any mercy as she pants above me, asking for more yet also saying she can't take any more.

When I'm fully satisfied that she's fully satisfied, I stand, licking my lips, lapping up every taste of her that I can.

"Remember when I said I wanted you to fuck me at the club?" she says through ragged breaths.

I nod, sliding my body between her legs, and brush her wet hair from her face.

"I want you to fuck me."

"You sure you're ready?"

"Absolutely." She points at the drawer below us. "Condoms are in there."

My hands are nearly shaking as I pull one out, rip it open with my teeth, and roll it onto my cock. I don't have to stroke myself, don't have to get myself hard, because my dick is throbbing to feel her, throbbing to feel what my tongue did as it dived into her pussy.

My head spins as I align my cock with her entrance, curl my arms around her waist, and slowly sink into her.

I do what Lola asked me to do at the club.

I do what I've dreamed of doing.

I do what I want to spend the rest of my life doing.

And even though we're wet, even though it's messy, there's never been anything more satisfying than being inside the woman I love, to watch my cock move in and out of her, owning her in ways I never thought that I would.

Angling my head down, I nip at her lips before fully kissing her, our tongues dancing together. Her ass is nearly off the vanity as our hips move faster, and she meets me thrust for thrust, moan for moan. When she's close, she shoves her face into my neck, and I groan when her teeth sink into my skin as she comes undone.

Waves of pleasure push through me harder than I'm thrusting into her, and I don't make it two more pumps until I'm exploding into the condom, feeling on top of the world.

CHAPTER FORTY-FOUR

Lola

OUR SEX MIGHT'VE BEEN the hottest sex I've ever had, but now, we're a wet, freezing mess.

Silas and I had sex.

Holy shit.

When last night's craziness happened, I thought our friendship was doomed.

We went from fighting to crying to fucking.

I'll take it.

Only next time, none of the first two and more of the last.

"We're so dumb," I mutter, attempting to get my pulse under control as he carefully eases the condom off his cock and tosses it into the trash.

On his way back to me, he snags my towel from the hook. Sitting on the counter, I lick my lips while taking in the gorgeous sight of him. With everything that happened earlier—his lips and fingers between my legs—it was impossible to think about anything else.

Sure, I've seen him shirtless plenty of times—each time a turn-on but me acting like it wasn't—but now, I can admire all of him. And I'm thoroughly impressed.

I study him, water dripping from his body but him not caring, as if I might be quizzed on every inch of him later. My gaze drops to his cock—thick, long, a slight curve to it, and the biggest I've ever been with before. Thank God I was incredibly turned on and wet. Otherwise, I'd have had an issue with letting him go as deep as he did, allowing him to give it to me as good as he did.

Our sex was passionate.

Steamy.

Everything I'd imagined it'd be with him.

"Huh?" he asks, opening the towel to dry me off.

"We're so stupid," I repeat, my eyes still on his cock but losing the view when he steps closer to me.

He grimaces, and his words are rushed. "I'm sorry. I didn't mean for our first time to be on the bathroom counter. One thing led to another—"

I press my finger to his lips to stop his words. "It was perfect. Was it short and sloppy? Yes. But I loved it."

He frowns. "Short? I mean, it'd been a minute since I'd had sex, but I wouldn't say it was *short*."

I laugh. "I didn't mean it *that* way. It was everything I'd hoped, and if you had drawn it out, if you hadn't been thrusting into me so hard, I probably would have complained because I was so desperate for your cock and an orgasm. Just like you, it'd been a while since I'd been with anyone."

He smirks, drying me off, lowering the towel and sliding it between my thighs. "Been a while, huh?"

I sigh breathlessly when he spreads my thighs wider and gently rubs the towel over my clit. "I appreciate you trying, and I don't want to hurt your feelings, but three orgasms in a row isn't going to happen."

"Oh, really?" he asks in challenge.

Suppressing a moan, I nod. "Really."

He's careful as he caresses my sensitive nub, and his breathing turns ragged as he stares down at where he's playing with me. "Since it's been a while what have you been doing to get yourself off?"

"What have *you* been doing?"

"Jacking off to thoughts of you."

Heat radiates through my chest at his response. "You're lying."

"I'm not." His voice is level, calm, as he dips the towel between my folds. "I thought of all the things I'd do to you if I ever got the chance."

God, that's so hot.

I tilt my waist up to meet his touch, almost frantic for it.

"Did you ever think of me when you touched yourself?"

"A girl never masturbates and tells."

I grind against the towel, and with his free hand, he cups my ass, bringing me to the edge of the vanity.

He chuckles, his lips hovering over mine. "How many fingers did you push inside yourself when you thought about me?"

I stay silent and groan when he drops the towel.

"Was it this many?"

My back arches, and I nearly come off the vanity when he slides his long fingers inside me.

He easily finds my G-spot, as if it were something he did on the regular. His eyes are wild yet also concentrated as they meet mine.

Using his free hand, he catches my chin between his thumb and forefinger. "Is this about to be a third orgasm, baby?"

"I ..." I'm struggling to find the word to answer him, struggling to focus on anything but his fingers working me so precisely, so skilled.

"You what?"

"I think so," I rasp—at least, I think I do.

He chuckles. "Who's the only one who can give you this many orgasms?"

"You," I manage to moan out.

His face burns with desire as he pleasures me—so good, so deep, so perfect. "And who's the one you think about when you finger this pretty little pussy?"

"You," I sputter, sweat forming along my forehead, my bathroom suddenly feeling like it's a hundred degrees.

"That's right. Always me."

I gasp at the feel of his erection brushing against my leg as he works me.

The thought of having him in my mouth excites me.

I'm fucking his hand.

Wanting more but not wanting him to stop to give me more.

I'll get this third orgasm and then drop to my knees and suck him.

The thrill of doing that sends a ping of excitement through my veins.

I want this man—emotionally, physically, in every way he'll give me.

And with just his fingers inside me, his thumb on my clit, I fall apart.

He catches me as I collapse into his arms. I tuck my face into his chest, drawing in deep breaths, until he tilts my head up to look at him.

"I love watching you lose it at my touch," he grits out. "I love *you*."

I grin a cheesy, bright grin that's never crossed my face before.

An orgasmed grin.

A *this is the happiest day of my life* grin.

"I love you." I lick his cheek before pressing my lips to his. "Now, it's your turn to shower."

"You going to join me?"

"Absolutely."

As soon as we get into the shower, I drop to my knees and take his thick cock into my mouth. He gathers my hair in his hand, gripping me tight, and I expect him to direct me on how he wants it. Instead, he lets me set the pace, allows me to suck him in a way I feel comfortable.

I do.

Fast.

Then deep.

And I don't stop until he comes in my mouth.

————

"HOW SHOULD WE TELL OUR FRIENDS?" Silas asks.

We're orgasmed out.

We ordered takeout.

Now, we're snuggled on the couch with Netflix playing in the background, but instead of watching a show, all we've done is talk. He's sprawled on his back, and I'm on my stomach, resting my chin on his chest to get a good view of him. Our legs are tangled together, and my body is halfway on his.

We're back to being the old Silas and Lola, talking about anything and everything. But now, we have a bonus of venturing into territories we never did, roads that weren't open before.

He explained why it was hard for him to go out on my birthday. My stomach curled as I thought about all the times I'd texted, only to be ignored, and how he always had to lie to me. I remembered how angry I'd been at the club and how I couldn't piece together why he looked so pained. In the back of my mind, I always thought it was me.

He told me about Sienna, about Kenny, about his troubles with Trent.

I loved the playful Silas, the friendly Silas, the one who never had a care in the world.

But this one?

That love is deeper now.

So deep that it can never be pulled out of me.

I can't wait for what our future has in store for us.

I smirk, tapping my fingers along his cheek. "My vote is, we just start making out in front of them."

He throws his head back, laughing. "Swear to God, you come up with the craziest shit. I wish I could crack open that brain of yours, my little name-swapping devil."

"Hey, we have to keep it entertaining, spice it up from the other ways our friends have done it."

Us making out would be the least of their worries after last night. I woke up to multiple texts from our friends, both the girls and guys, asking if I was okay, if I'd talked to Silas, if he was okay. I texted them back, saying we were fine, that he was here, and I'd talk to them about things later. The guys said good luck, and the girls sent me their love. Silas also had texts from everyone.

"Oh, I think I've kept it entertaining enough for how I acted last night." His lips press tight into a grimace. "They're going to have a shit ton of questions, and I have a lot of apologizing to do to them and my parents."

I caress his cheek, hating the sudden pain in his eyes. "Everyone figures it was because I was with Trent."

Reaching out, he grabs me from under my armpits, moving me until I'm straddling him.

He pushes my hair from my face and runs his hand through it. "I'm not blaming you for my childish behavior."

I relax into his touch. "It's fine. Once we tell them we worked it out, they'll be happy. Trust me." I laugh, stroking his hand in my hair. "Like, literally, *worked it out.*"

He cracks a smile, twisting a strand of my hair around his finger. "Is this how it'll be, dating you? Dirty comments and sexual innuendos?"

I rest my palms on his chest, giving him my weight. "Is that any different from when we were friends?"

"Yes, now, we can follow through with them."

I squeal when he playfully squeezes my waist and run my hand through his hair. "I'm serious, though. Blame it on me. I know they're our friends, but if you don't feel comfortable telling them, don't. They're concerned because they care about you."

He blows out a heavy breath. "I'll talk to them."

I need a plan on what to tell our friends, but for right now, I have no problem with blaming it on Trent and me. If and when Silas is ready to talk about his past, then I'll be open about it too. I have his back until then.

"We're really doing this, huh?" Silas asks.

I raise a brow. "What do you mean?"

"We're really going to be together?"

My heart speeds just at those words, at the mention of us being together. "As long as you're serious, then yes. I can't have us start, and then you go back on it. If you have any hesitation, let me know now. It won't change our friendship."

"There is no question. This is what I want, Lola. You're what I've always wanted."

CHAPTER FORTY-FIVE

Silas

"HEY, MAN," Cohen shouts when I stroll into Lincoln's penthouse.

The other guys—Finn, Lincoln, and Maliki—all call their own form of greetings.

Three days have passed since I acted a fool at Twisted Fox, and I haven't been back since. They texted me, making sure I was okay, but I needed time to clear my head before going out again. I've spent all my free time with Lola—either crashing at her place or her at mine.

And even with spending so much time together, we can't get enough of each other. We wake up in each other's arms every morning and go to bed together every night. We have electrifying sex nearly everywhere.

In our beds. The shower. Random furniture. On the floor.

It's like we just discovered sex.

Or discovered sex with the right person.

Lincoln invited me over for poker night, and I know there will be questions on why I turned into a different person that night. None of them have given me any strange looks as I move into the penthouse and find the living room couch shoved into a corner, a poker table in its place.

"I ordered pizza," Archer says, tossing his phone onto the kitchen island. "Should be here in about ten minutes."

When I walk into the kitchen, I notice the lack of alcohol lying out. Usually, on poker nights, the guys have drinks. My guess is, that's intentional … because of me.

Finn updates us on Grace and the pregnancy. I hate the shit they had to go through with Grace's baby daddy, but I'm glad they got it sorted out. The guy signed over his rights, and Finn plans to be the father when the baby is born. Finn is a good guy and didn't deserve the shit I said to him on Lola's birthday.

Then Lincoln questions him on what to expect with Cassidy's pregnancy. Maliki and Archer then argue over whether Georgia or Sierra will get pregnant first. Maliki already has a daughter from another relationship, but he'd like to have another with Sierra.

After devouring the pizza, it's time to play some poker. I'm not a great poker player, and we usually lose to Lincoln—apparently, you get a lot of practice playing cards in prison.

As soon as we sit, I start my apology, cringing inwardly at what I did. "I want to say sorry for my dumbass behavior lately." I pay each of them a remorseful glance. "What I did was messed up."

Cohen, sitting in the chair next to me, slaps my back. "We've known you long enough to know that's not you."

"Yeah," Lincoln says, shuffling the cards. "We've all had bad days … gone through some dark times."

Finn nods, smiling at me. "We just want to be there for you. If you need anything, call … text … show up. Whatever."

I nod as each one speaks. "I appreciate that, guys."

Not only would I feel lost without Lola, but it'd hurt to lose my friends too. The girls and guys. They came into my life when I needed them the most, and they've provided me with some of my brightest times. And even though I haven't been the best person to be around, they still invited me tonight.

"Do you want to talk about it?" Maliki asks, taking a drink of water.

Do I?

Or should I blame it on Lola, like she said I could?

Do I keep hiding from the truth?

No.

It's time I stop hiding.

I massage the back of my neck, giving myself a silent pep talk. "I dated a girl in high school who passed away ... the same day as Lola's birthday."

"That explains it," Lincoln says under his breath.

My head buzzes as I continue, "It always hits me pretty hard around that time, and I guess, this year ... it was worse for me."

"Worse because you went to Lola's birthday party?" Cohen asks at the same time Finn asks, "Because she was with Trent?"

"Both," I say with no delay.

The mention of that night causes my mind to drift to thoughts of Trent and Lola. I know they went out a few times, but I haven't asked her any questions. I don't want to know. It wouldn't be fair for me to ask her if they did anything, hooked up ... or for me to be upset with her over it. If I hadn't acted how I did, they'd never have even talked or exchanged numbers.

"Are you and Lola good now?" Archer asks.

"We're good." I scratch my cheek. "Working everything out."

"I'm happy to hear that," Maliki says. "We've been waiting for you to get your head out of your ass and wife her up before another lucky bastard did. But I have to warn you, the smart-ass ones are always the hardest to handle."

Maliki's girlfriend, Sierra, reminds me of Lola in some ways—loud, doesn't give a shit, and does what she wants.

I chuckle. "I've handled Lola enough to know how she is."

"We all have a past," Archer says, surprising me since the dude hardly talks. "I struggled for a while, but then Georgia came into my life—"

"Georgia *pushed* her way into your life, giving you no opportunities to run," Finn says with a laugh.

"Pretty much," Cohen says. "My sister has a way of doing that."

"She might've been a pain in my ass, but she helped me through it," Archer continues. "There's something about having someone by your side that makes your struggles easier to get through."

"Hear, hear," Cohen says.

We all cheers with our waters.

They don't ask more questions, only make it clear that if I need anything, they have my back.

We play five rounds of poker.

I win once.

And then I go home to my girl.

———

"HOW HAVE YOU BEEN?" Trent asks as he stands next to me.

Tonight is the first time we've seen each other since the night of the charity event—when I punched him.

Two days after, I texted him a quick, *Sorry for punching you*, after Lola insisted it was the civil thing to do.

I groaned but did it even though I can't stand him. But she was right. I shouldn't have punched him.

I'm here, at one of my grandmother's dinners, as part of my apology for my behavior that night. I sent my grandmother flowers. Lola and I took my father and Janet to dinner—Lola being introduced as *my* date this time. That felt damn good. My grandmother asked for one more thing as part of my apology—to attend one of her dinners. Thank fuck she also extended that invite to Lola, so she could come with me.

I brought Lola, and Trent brought a date too. That helped it not be as awkward. Dinner went well, no punches were thrown, and we managed to put our differences aside for our family. My grandmother took Lola and Sylvie, Trent's date, on a tour of her new flower garden, leaving the two of us alone.

That was either a good decision or a stupid one.

We can make small talk or work out our differences.

Or we could fight again.

"Good," I reply, watching my grandmother point out flowers to Lola.

He tips his head toward them. "I'm glad you and Lola worked it out."

I shoot him a skeptical look. "Are you?"

"I'm not going to lie and say I didn't like her." He brings his drink to his mouth but doesn't take a sip. "But after that night, I knew I didn't stand a chance. Lola sent me a pity text the next morning and said she couldn't see me anymore."

I can't stop myself from smiling at his last statement—at him backing off, but her also making it clear she'd never be his. "I see you moved on quickly, though."

He chuckles. "Sylvie and I are friends who go to shit together when we don't have dates."

"Lola and I did the same thing for years." I crack a smile at the memory, watching Lola throw her head back and laugh at something my grandmother said.

Now, we no longer have to pretend.

Janet already took me aside when I went on a bathroom break to tell me how happy she was that Lola and I found each other and that I'd better not mess it up and lose her. Her eyes watered when I told her Lola knew everything and still loved me.

Trent blows out a harsh breath and drains his drink, and out of nowhere, he says, "She was with me too."

My gaze flashes to him. "Lola?"

"Sienna," he immediately corrects. "Sorry, should've done better at clarifying that."

I furrow my brow. "You and Sienna had a thing?"

He nods, staring straight ahead, as if reliving the memory. "On and off."

"When?"

"Right when I moved to your school, Sienna and I started talking. Then after you two started your secret relationship, she blew me off. But the night before the party, she texted me, mad at you. We met up at the park, and she swore she was done with you and sick of being a secret. But then I saw you and her walk upstairs. It pissed me off, so I texted Kenny. I had no idea he'd do what he did." He squeezes his eyes shut. "Their deaths fucked with my head, too, and it took me some time to work through it because even though you think I didn't care, I knew I had some blame."

It makes sense. Anytime Trent saw Sienna and me together at school, his attitude always got worse when we got home that day. He'd start fights in front of her, but I always thought it was because he hated me.

And as I stare ahead, watching my grandmother and Lola, watching Lola talk with Sylvie, I realize that maybe I'll be okay. I'll never forget about Sienna or Kenny, never forget the role I had in their deaths, but each day, I'm healing from the emotional wounds I've suffered from it.

Even after, with all the confusion of Sienna and me, deep down, I hope she knew I loved her. I hope she knew, as I chased them, I tried to save her.

I clear my throat. "That night was just mistake after mistake."

"Agreed." He holds out his hand. "Truce?"

I hesitate before shaking it. "Truce."

Love causes people to do spiteful things.

It makes us act before thinking.

Trent and I will never be best friends.

We'll never have poker nights or hang out solo.

Maybe years down the road, that'll change.

But for now, since we're both healing from our mistakes, we can be better men.

CHAPTER FORTY-SIX

Lola

"I CAN'T BELIEVE Grace had her baby," I squeal from Silas's passenger seat.

Silas hangs a right into the hospital parking lot and searches for a spot. "You can't believe it? She was pregnant. It was inevitable."

"Shush." I smack his arm. "You know what I mean. It seems so real now. Like, she had a baby come out of her, and now, that baby is out in the world to have Grace as a mom." I relax in my seat. "Grace will be an amazing mom."

I'm so happy for her and Finn—that they found their way to happiness. Even though Finn isn't the biological father, he's stepped up in every way a father should. He loves Grace and that baby girl as if she were his own. He's texted us picture after picture, over the moon to finally be able to hold her. They have so much heart, and I know baby Millie will be loved.

"I'm thrilled they worked it out," Silas says while parking.

I clasp my hand over his. "Just like us."

We might've been the last of our friends to make it official, but we were one of the firsts to fall in love. We just needed our timing to be perfect, and timing is a hell of a thing. Silas had some growing to do, some demons to fight, and I had to convince my heart it was okay to be put on the line. I trust Silas with my heart, with my everything. And one day, maybe that'll be us, sending picture after picture of our baby.

Silas leans across the console, taking my chin in his hand, and smacks a kiss to my lips. "Just like us."

I love that we can do that anytime now—that we can kiss, touch, make love without questioning if it'll change our dynamic. Our friendship, our relationship, our love have grown so much stronger. We're discovering so much about each other, falling in love so much deeper, and I can't imagine him not being by my side as I go through life.

All the fear of handing him my heart, only for our relationship to end up like my parents', is long gone. He'd never hurt me, never look for someone who wasn't me, and I trust him more than anyone.

And the sex?

Holy hell. It's amazing.

The man hardly touches me, and I come apart.

We're in a normal relationship. Him hanging out with my family. Me with his. Our families hanging out together. We've even been around Trent a few times, who said he was happy we finally pulled our heads out of our asses. I thanked him for being what Silas needed to take a stand and fix himself. Otherwise, we would've fallen apart as friends and never had the chance to be together.

I grab my gift—well, *gifts* because I tend to go overboard.

Silas and I walk hand in hand into the hospital, and when we step into the elevator, he looks at me with intent. "Do you think you'll ever want to have babies"—he pauses, as if nervous—"with me? Together?"

I hit the floor button. "Well, I don't know who else I'd have them with."

He chuckles. "You know what I mean."

"If you're game, then I'm totally game," I answer with no delay. It's something I've never said, but apparently, it's something my brain knows I want.

His face lights up. "That's a very romantic response from you."

I shrug. "Look, the only romance we need is in the bedroom … where we can do said baby-making."

"You'd be an amazing mother." He takes a step back, resting his chin in his palm. "If it's a girl, she'd probably have a smart mouth like you, and we'll be in trouble."

"And if he's anything like his daddy, he'll be just as troublesome as you. But also, a little heartthrob."

He grins wildly, takes a step closer, and wraps his arms around my waist. "I love this."

I settle my palm on his chest and peer up at him. "What?"

"Talking about our future kids." He rests his forehead against mine. "Our future."

The elevator dings, the door opening, and we hurriedly step apart. An older nurse stands in front of us.

"Oh, don't you two worry," she says with a wave of her hand. "You're not the first couple who's made out in the elevator on the way up here." She shakes her head, a large smile on her lips. "Something about visiting babies makes people want to have babies."

For the first time in years, I grow flustered and quickly shake my head. "We weren't making out."

"Oh, honey, but you were about to." The woman winks.

"She's not lying," Silas whispers into my ear, and I nudge him with my elbow before we step out.

The nurse's smile doesn't waver as she takes our spot. As we walk toward the heavy doors of the maternity unit, we find Georgia, Archer, Lincoln, and Cassidy standing near the waiting area, talking.

Cassidy rubs her belly as if she's as close to bursting herself. She's the first to notice, and she waves us over. "We're making bets on who's next to have a baby."

"Um, you," I answer, pointing at her belly.

She smiles. "Let me rephrase. Who will be the next to announce a pregnancy?"

"Like you guys did in high school, I bet on Lola," Lincoln says.

I motion toward Archer and Georgia. "Um, they've been together way longer and are *engaged*."

"How long you've been with someone doesn't dictate how ovaries work," Cassidy says, resting her palm on Lincoln's shoulder and giving him some of her weight. "Archer and Georgia have been together longer than Lincoln and me."

"True," Georgia cuts in. "I guess it's really a matter of whether Archer's or Silas's sperm is faster."

"Really, babe?" Archer asks, shaking his head.

"Jesus, I'm terrified of a little Georgia," Lincoln mutters.

I cock my head. "But not of a little Archer?"

Silas smirks. "Nah, a baby Archer will just sulk in the corner."

Archer flips him off.

"I vote Silas and Lola," Cassidy says. "Something just tells me."

"I vote me and Georgia," Archer says with a shrug. "Maybe that'll manifest, and it'll happen."

"Same." Georgia wraps her small arm around his muscular one. "I like betting for myself."

Silas shoots me a glance. "Should we do the same then? Bet for ourselves?"

I nod. "Yep."

Everyone gawks at us for a moment. Georgia and Archer are engaged and have talked about a family. Archer is ready to be a father anytime. But Silas and I haven't mentioned anything like this to our friends.

"Speaking of babies," Georgia says. "Let's go meet the new addition to our family." She claps her hands, nearly jumping for joy.

I smile. While I'm happy for Grace and Finn, I don't allow my emotions to bleed out as much as Georgia. That girl doesn't wear her heart on her sleeve. She wears it as a damn badge.

We stroll down the hall, Silas's hand finding mine again. As soon as Georgia knocks, Grace calls for us to come in. We walk in, sanitize our hands, and see Grace in the hospital bed. Finn is next to her with Millie in his arms.

"Where is my goddaughter?" Georgia sings before holding up a gift bag. "I have presents on presents on presents to give her."

I nudge her with my elbow. "I think you mean, *my* goddaughter."

Grace laughs. "How many times have I said that you're both the godmothers?"

"Is that a thing?" Georgia asks. "Can there be two? And if there are two, who's number one? If so, I'm number one."

I playfully roll my eyes as we settle our gifts onto the small couch where others sit. Millie is going to be one spoiled girl.

Cassidy waddles in behind us, Lincoln resting his hand on her back, and she looks directly at Grace. "Don't tell me any horror stories, please. Lincoln has made me watch birthing pregnancy videos, and I'm terrified."

Finn chuckles. "Prepare yourself for war, Lincoln."

Georgia is the first to hold Millie, and I'm sure had someone tried before, she'd have pushed them to the side. Grace is nervous as Finn carefully settles her into her arms as if he's sad to even let her go.

Finn has always been a good man.

But Finn as a father? It's indescribable.

It's an entirely different level.

Silas sits by my side as I hold Millie. "She's awfully wrinkly for being so young."

Finn shoves his shoulder. "Jealous you're not as cute as her?"

"Her wrinkles are adorable," I say, tracing her tiny forehead with the tip of my finger.

Silas leans into me. "I wonder how wrinkly our baby will be."

I laugh, shaking my head. "I'm sure after that comment, she'll have her fair share of them."

As I hold Millie, my thoughts drift to the night I told Silas I was lonely. My heart needed something, but I was clueless about what that was exactly. As I look around, that question is answered.

It's this.

Friends. Family. Love.

It's seeing Grace having a baby and me wanting the same. It's glancing at Georgia's engagement ring and seeing me doing the same with one Silas picked out.

People can grow up in dysfunctional homes, witness toxic relationships, but if they find the right person, it'll give them hope. Silas gave me that. And I want to give that to our children ... with a man who's currently discussing baby wrinkles.

AND GETTING to the baby-making is what we do when we get back to my place.

We're undressed in minutes. I squeal when Silas grabs my ass, hoisting me up, and I wrap my legs around his waist. His cock is hard, and I rub against his erection as he carries me to the bedroom.

"Can we work on winning that bet?" he asks before slamming his mouth onto mine.

Panting into his mouth, I say, "Absolutely."

He tosses me onto the bed, and before I can catch a breath, he's peeling off my pants and panties. Without bothering with his, he spreads my thighs, making room for himself.

He licks me.

Sucks me.

Finger-fucks me.

Until I'm falling apart beneath him.

There has never been a man who's cared about my orgasm more than Silas.

Hell, he even cares about it more than I do.

As I catch my breath, coming down, my heart still beating wildly, Silas strips off his clothes. I shove him onto his back and straddle him. Just as quick as he had his head between my legs, I tease him at my entrance before lowering myself fully on his hard cock.

I freeze.

Even though we talked about baby-making, it doesn't mean it has to happen right now.

Me? I'd be totally fine with it.

And even though Silas said he wants to win that bet, I don't move.

"You're not wearing a condom," I whisper, settling my hands on his chest to hold myself up.

He stares up at me, unblinking. "Are you okay with that?"

I slowly nod.

"Then so am I." He grips my waist and grinds into me. "This is about to be the best sex of my life."

For the first time ever, we have sex without a condom.

It feels more intimate.

Closer.

I ride his cock, switching from slow to fast to rough to soft.

Wanting to draw it out for as long as I can.

"Fuck," he moans, swiping my hair from my face and pulling my head down to kiss me. "You give it to me so good, baby."

It doesn't take long until I gasp his name and then collapse against him. He grips my hips tighter, driving into me until it's time for him to moan out my name in release.

CHAPTER FORTY-SEVEN

Silas

I WAS NEVER a fan of weddings until I found someone I wanted to marry. In fact, I only attended two weddings before today—my father and Janet's, and my mother and her new husband's. The first one, I was forced to attend, and I sulked in the back row and spit spitballs at the back of Trent's head.

Today has been nice. Georgia and Archer had a small, intimate ceremony in Hawaii—which I was game for because a vacation with Lola sounded like a damn good time. A vacation with *all* our friends since all of us were able to attend.

Call it rude, but during the ceremony, I paid more attention to Lola. I imagined marrying her, of me standing where Archer was and her walking down the aisle. We'd say our *I do*s and live happily ever after. It sounds cheesy, but hey, when you know, you know.

Cohen walked Georgia down the aisle, and Archer attempted to hide his misty eyes as he stared at her.

Archer had been right when he told me to get my shit together as I debated on whether to attend Lola's birthday. Not that the advice was good timing, given the disaster that happened, but his words stuck with me. Georgia had changed his life and helped him heal from the past. Lola has done the same for me.

"Is your stomach still upset, baby?" I ask around a yawn as we walk into the hotel room.

The reception was fun, but Lola hardly ate, only drank sparkling water, and whispered she was nauseous as she saw the newlyweds cut their cake.

"It's a little better," she says around a stressed sigh, reaching for the back of her dress.

I stop her, helping her with her dress, and massage her tense shoulders as the beige bridesmaid dress pools at her feet.

Tipping her head back, she relaxes at my touch.

Sweeping her soft hair off her shoulder, I slowly rain kisses along her neck before whispering in her ear, "Do you want me to order you something from room service to help with the nausea? Or run to the store?"

She shakes her head, her voice timid as she says, "I'm okay."

"Do you think it's the flu? Jet lag?"

"Um ..." She draws the word out for what seems like a minute.

I freeze, my heart falling into my stomach even though I have no idea what it is yet. "What?"

"I think it might be ..." She pauses, turning to face me, and chews on her plump lower lip.

My eyes widen as I go into panic mode.

Is she sick?

Cancer?

Done with my ass?

"A baby," she whispers.

"What?" I stutter out again, my heart now in ultimate panic mode.

"A baby," she says clearly as if she's practiced it in the mirror a few times.

We haven't talked about a baby since the hospital, but we also haven't been careful. When we want to have sex, we have sex, not giving a care in the world about protection. Hell, I don't know if there's even any in either of our homes—even though I wouldn't consider my home mine anymore since I sleep at Lola's nearly every night.

"I missed my period. I've googled pregnancy symptoms, and I

talked to Grace about it." She shivers, goose bumps popping along her arms. "What I'm feeling, what's happening with my body, is similar to what she experienced."

I clasp her hand, settle her onto the bed, and grab her pajamas from the suitcase. I unstrap her shoes, tossing them to the side, and slide the tank over her head. I fall at her feet to slip her shorts on.

"Have you taken a test?"

She shakes her head. "No ... not yet. I thought I'd give it more time. It could be stress from the trip, helping with the wedding, something. But my body seems off, and I haven't had my PMS phase either."

"We need to get a test."

She stops me from standing, resting her hand on my chest and playing with my shirt buttons. "What are your thoughts about this, Silas? How will you feel if it's positive?"

"Baby"—I soften my voice and grab her hand, running my thumb between hers and her pointer finger—"I want everything with you." I raise her hand and bring it to my lips. "Do you want me to go get a test?"

"It's late."

"There's a store in the lobby." I kiss her hand, then her forehead, and then her mouth—drawing that one out longer, tasting the small slice of strawberry cake she had before saying she couldn't eat another bite or she'd vomit. "If they don't have one there, I'll catch an Uber. Otherwise, I'll be up all night, thinking about it."

"Okay." She blows out a breath. "I'd tag along, but I'm so tired. I don't know if I would make it to the lobby."

"I got this, baby."

I pull back the blankets and tuck her in before walking out of the room. I don't find a pregnancy test on-site in the hotel, so I take a quick trip to a convenience store that has them. When I return to the hotel room, Lola is sleeping. As much as I want her to take it, to find out at this very moment, she looks so peaceful.

Instead, I place it on my nightstand and undress. Careful not to wake her, I snuggle to her side, spooning her to me, and grin.

I wanted Lola the moment I saw her at the bar, but I never

thought it was possible. Finding love again was never on my radar, but here we are, in love. Everything good I thought would never happen has.

Anticipation spirals through me.

A baby.

I might be a father.

If it's negative, that'll be fine.

It's not our time.

My and Lola's relationship has always been about timing.

Maybe it's our time for a baby.

———

"SORRY," Lola says the following morning, flipping onto her back in bed to peer up at me. "I fell asleep on you."

I grin at her. "You had a long day and needed the rest." I bow my head to kiss her. "Good morning. How are you feeling?"

Even though the bed was comfortable as fuck, I hardly slept. It was like I was a kid waiting for Santa. All I could think about was the news we'd find out this morning. But I won't rush her to take the test. It'll be when she's ready.

"Tired, but better now that I broke the possible new development in our lives to you …" She trails off, rubbing her hand through her hair. "Did you get the test?"

I nod. "I did, but you can wait until you're ready to take it."

Her eyes are wide, concern in them. "How would you feel if it's positive?"

"Damn good."

"And negative?"

"I won't lie and say a little disappointed because I got my hopes up, but I'd have the woman I love, so still, damn good."

She reaches up and caresses my face. "You're the best thing to ever happen to me, you know that?"

"Trust me, I know the feeling because you're what saved me." I rest my forehead against hers. "You're what gave me life again."

We lie there for minutes, our breathing heavy.

We know that when she takes that test, our lives might change.

———

"YOU GO LOOK at it because I can't," Lola says, tapping her foot, staring at the bathroom door like a monster is going to come out.

She took the test, and the stick is in the bathroom, lying on the counter, front and center. The star of the show. The most precious item we have in this room.

I brace my hand on her leg to stop her foot. "Why don't we look at it together?"

"Why don't you just do what I said?"

I chuckle. "There's my girl coming out."

I don't take her words as an insult because she's been a nervous wreck all morning. She fidgeted and dropped the stick five times before peeing on it.

I drum my fingers along her thigh. "You really want me to do it without you?"

"Yes," she groans. "Ugh, I don't know."

"We can wait for as long as you want." I scrunch my brows. "They don't time out, do they? Like we have ten minutes before it goes away?"

"How would I know?" she shrieks. "I've never taken a pregnancy test before!"

"Really? There's never been a time you thought—"

"Nope. I always used a condom, except for you, took birth control, prayed to the pregnant gods."

"Oh, but what about with me?" I sit up straighter as if I'd just been served an award.

She grins. "With you, I told the pregnancy gods to do with me what they will."

I kiss her forehead. "I love you. Let's see what the pregnancy gods have blessed you with."

"Love you too," she whispers before squeezing my hand and slowly standing while releasing a slow breath. "Let's do this."

It's a short walk to the bathroom, and her hand is sweaty as it grips mine. My chest swells with hope when we grab the test with shaking hands. Our eyes meet, our focus solely on the other as if trying to read what's on the other's mind.

I drop a quick peck to her head. "You ready?"

Her hand, her chin, her body are trembling. "Ready."

We count down from three, and as soon as we look at the stick, the bathroom goes silent.

I blink at it, focused. "I'm pretty sure that means positive."

We should've read the directions.

"I'm pretty sure you're right," she replies.

It takes a moment for the news to dawn on us.

"Holy shit," Lola finally yelps. "I'm fucking pregnant."

Her eyes are wide as they look at me, and my entire body relaxes.

"Baby!" I yell, not caring if everyone in the hotel hears me. *Let the whole damn world know.* "We're having a baby!"

She jumps into my arms, the stick still in her hand, and I don't give a shit as it hits my neck. Just like Archer, I attempt to hide my tears, but it doesn't happen.

I'm going to be a father.

Call *The Guinness World Records* because I'm the happiest damn man alive.

CHAPTER FORTY-EIGHT

Silas

I WOKE with a sense of determination today.

Got out of bed—a rarity on this particular day.

A smile on my face—the first time in years.

It's Lola's birthday, and I'm going to give her the best damn birthday she's ever had. It's wild that a year has passed since the club disaster. It's also wild that we're having a baby.

We took all the tests in the box that day.

Then when we got home, we took more.

Then went to the doctor.

It was confirmed.

We're having a baby, and I couldn't be happier.

But before tonight's festivities, there's something I need to do.

I'd come here when I was depressed, when guilt was eating me alive, but now, I'm here to cleanse myself, to help myself heal. Lola offered to come with me, but it's something I need to do on my own. She's helped me move on so much, but this final step needs to be done by me.

I'll always have guilt over what happened with Sienna and Kenny.

Always know that I played a part in their deaths.

But I also know that I tried to protect her and stop them.

The morning air is sticky yet chilly as I step out of my car and walk through the cemetery entrance. I've sat outside the gates countless times, but today is the first time I've gained the guts to walk through them.

I know where their gravestones are because I watched the funeral from afar. I watched their family break down, people hold their mother up as they were lowered into the ground.

I'm not sure what I'll do when I get there since I didn't plan anything out, not knowing if I'd go through with it.

They're buried side by side, sharing one headstone.

Sienna and Kenny Jenkins
Taken too soon and will always be remembered.

THEIR FACES FLASH through my mind, memories of the times we shared together coming next, and I squeeze my eyes shut.

When I open them, I stare at the headstone, taking in every curve and slant of their names, and whisper, "I'm sorry."

I'm sad.

Yet I'm also angry with Kenny for putting Sienna in danger and killing her.

I stand there, unsure of how much time has passed.

As I'm about to leave, a timid, soft-spoken voice says, "I'm sorry."

It's nearly the same way I said it that night at the crash scene— guilt mixed with sadness and anger.

Looking over my shoulder, I see their mother behind me. I hold in a breath, waiting for her to tell me to get the hell out of here.

"I'm sorry," she repeats, her eyes on me, not the headstone.

I rub my hands down my pant legs at the realization that she's talking to me.

This is the woman who told me she wished I'd rot in hell for what I'd done, who told anyone who would listen that I was the boy who'd killed her children, who'd taken advantage of their daughter. She ran my name through the dirt, even tried to sue me for wrongful death until my father agreed to pay them a settlement and keep it out of the courts. Mary Jenkins despised my existence.

And now, I have no idea what she'll do about me being here.

She can't sue me for being at a cemetery, but she can scream at me, smack me.

Is she apologizing because she's about to kill me or for the way she put a teenage boy through hell?

I gawk at her as she pulls her sweater tight around her body and steps next to me.

Silence passes between us until she says, "I'm sorry," again.

I stare at the headstone as if it had the answer for what's happening. "What do you mean?"

"I'm sorry for blaming you." Her eyes water as she shifts to face me. "You were a high school kid, and there we were, blaming you." She shakes her head. "We wanted to find someone to blame, but after time passed, after therapy, I realized you were the same age as Kenny. I asked myself how I'd feel if someone treated him like that had he been in the same situation. Kenny was the one who had forced Sienna into his car. He was the one who had driven recklessly, but it was hard to accept one of our babies had caused the death of the other one."

I came here, expecting to find peace with Sienna and Kenny.

I didn't expect to get it with their mother as well.

Would I have felt differently, not allowed the guilt to eat me as much, if they hadn't treated me the way they did?

There's no going back to know that answer.

And what happened, happened.

I blink at their headstone. "I understand."

She hesitates before slowly reaching out, putting her hand on my shoulder. "I hope you've found happiness now. I hope we didn't break you too much."

Her face is red when I finally direct my gaze to her. And a bit of warmth, of hope, spreads through me.

I offer her a polite smile. "I'm going to be a father."

I shut my mouth immediately after.

Shit.

Her children will never have that luxury. She'll never have the chance to be a grandmother.

"Congratulations." Her tone is genuine—no animosity coming from her at my news. "I wish you and your family the best. And I mean that, truly, from my heart."

———

MY FIRST TEAR falls when I get into my car to leave the cemetery, and I sink into my seat before smiling.

"I did it," I whisper.

I worked up the nerve to walk into that cemetery.

And Mary worked up the nerve to speak to me, to apologize.

Everything takes time.

———

"IS THERE a way to put more chocolate on this?" Lola asks, sitting next to me, holding a plate with a slice of birthday cake on it. "Or hot sauce? That actually sounds amazing."

"That sounds like the most disgusting thing I've ever heard," Archer mutters. "I don't know if I can hang out with anyone that weird."

"Just wait," Finn comments, shooting his attention to Archer. "Georgia will have the weirdest pregnancy cravings too."

"Nah, all my girl wants are burritos from Le Mesa. Swear to God, I almost asked if I could buy stock in the business since we order takeout from there so much."

"Le Mesa does have some killer food, though," I say.

It's a regular spot for us to hang out when we have Taco Tuesdays.

It's crazy how much our life has changed. Here we are, having a birthday, where everyone is either pregnant or already a parent. Cassidy had their baby girl, Emma, and she and Lincoln have been on top of the world. She and Grace have been a giant help to Lola with any questions she has regarding pregnancy and birth. The guys have also been the same way with me.

Then Georgia and Sierra broke the news that they were expecting.

It's like getting pregnant runs in the water at Twisted Fox.

I caught on to the nervousness of everyone, worried I'd bail on Lola's party tonight. Even after Lola said we could stay in a hundred times so things wouldn't be hard on me, I felt fine, like I was a different man. So, I told her we'd do something simple, go to dinner, but instead, we drove to Cohen and Jamie's, where everyone was waiting for us.

They yelled, "Surprise," as soon as we walked in, and Lola gave me her angry pregnancy glare because she hates surprises.

But seconds later, she was smiling and laughing.

I peek over at the woman I love, thinking about how far we've come.

My gaze falls to her belly, taking in the bump, and I grin.

I did it. Created a life I love. Attended her birthday without dread.

This is my life.

Something I thought I'd never have.

I've made it to happiness.

We've made it to happiness.

And so have our friends.

———

"GOD, I've been wanting to do this all night," Lola says around a moan, her hands eagerly unzipping my pants. She places a quick kiss on my bulge over my jeans before roughly pulling them down.

Pregnant Lola is horny-as-fuck Lola.

We had plenty of sex before, but it's on a different level now. Not that I have an issue with it. I loved seeing Lola naked, thought it was the best sight in the world, but Lola naked and pregnant?

Holy shit.

My cock gets hard anytime I think of it.

There's the excitement that she's mine, that we're having a family and made it this far. We've discussed marriage but decided to take it slow because of how marriage has scared us in the past. Although I know I'd never do anything to fuck up a life with Lola—to hurt the person I love and committed myself to, like our parents did.

Lola also said she wasn't walking down the aisle while pregnant, but I have a ring for her for when the timing feels right. It's waiting—something I had custom-made that fits her in every way.

Chills climb up my spine when her lips wrap around my cock with no warning, and she sucks the tip before taking my entire length into her mouth. She doesn't gag while deep-throating me, only moans when I hit the back of her throat. I grip her hair, keeping a hold on her but allowing her to decide the pace. As I grow closer, I can't stop myself from tilting my hips up, feeding her more and more of my hard cock before pulling her head away from my lap.

"Time for you to fuck me now," I grind out.

She grins, her eyes bright, while climbing onto my lap and falling on my cock, pre-cum already dripping from the tip. She rides me rough and fast as I play with her nipples before reaching down to her belly, slowly rubbing it. It doesn't take long until she falls apart above me, collapsing against my chest, although it's harder now for her to do than it was before.

A few pumps later, and I'm throwing my head back, clenching my jaw, and busting inside her.

She rests her palms on my chest, and I lean forward to kiss her.

"I love you," she whispers against my lips. "Thank you for loving me"—she laughs, pointing at her belly—"and for impregnating me."

"Anytime, baby." I laugh. "I love you."

EPILOGUE

Lola

Twelve Years Later

"DO you remember when our lives were sane?" I ask the girls. "We had silence, freedom, no whining about losing iPads."

"Babe," Georgia deadpans, "our lives were never sane."

"Saner than this." I motion toward the kids running around the yard, yelling at each other, a few throwing balls while talking shit, like their fathers do. I stop to cup my hand around my mouth and yell, "Amelia! Don't you dare throw that drink on Jax."

Twelve years have passed since I found out I was pregnant, but it seems like an eternity. We have families, marriages, SUVs, and soccer practice schedules. Hell, Grace even convinced me to join the PTA.

Zero out of ten.

Still trying to find a way to bail myself out of that one.

I might be a mom, but I'm a cool mom, okay?

Silas and I married eight years ago when the timing was perfect. Even though we knew we wanted to spend the rest of our lives together, we had so much happening with being new parents and our jobs that we wanted to wait. Silas's mother, of course, insisted on the wedding planning and went all out. Silas even asked Trent to be one of his groomsmen since they'd started working on their relationship for the sake of his family. Amelia also likes playing with Trent's daughter.

Now, our circle, which was once a small group of friends, has grown.

Silas and I have Amelia.

Georgia and Archer ended up with twins—a girl and a boy.

We still beat them on the whole *who will get prego first* bet. Although she found out a couple of weeks later, so it wasn't by much.

Finn and Grace had a girl to give Millie a little sister.

Cassidy and Lincoln have two—a boy and a girl.

Jamie and Cohen added another to their family.

Sierra and Maliki have Jax.

Jax, for some reason, doesn't get along with my daughter.

Amelia, for some reason, has kicked him in the balls one too many times.

As everyone started to get busier, it became harder for Cohen and Archer to work as much. So, they asked Lincoln, Silas, and Finn if they wanted to become part owners of Twisted Fox. The guys were ecstatic, and Silas immediately jumped on the opportunity. Then I became the president of 21st Amendment after my father stepped down until I realized I didn't want to work as much either. So, I demoted myself and gave my position to Robby.

"Mom! He deserves to have the drink spilled on him!" Amelia yells. "And a kick between the legs!"

"Who?" Georgia asks, looking around the yard.

Amelia comes stomping toward us with Jax at her heels. "Jaxson! He's the biggest jerk in the world."

"Hey," Jax says, crossing his arms and glaring at Amelia. "Don't get mad at me because I'm better at everything than you are."

"You're not better at anything than her," Theo, Cohen and Jamie's son, tells Jax.

Jax flips him off, resulting in Sierra jumping out of her chair and scolding him. "Dude, mind your business!"

Amelia stomps her feet and raises her knee as if she's ready to give Jax a good kick. "Don't tell him to mind his business."

"Seriously, Jax," Sierra groans. "You are just like your father."

Jax smirks. "You're married to him, so is that supposed to be a bad thing?"

Even though we shouldn't, everyone at the table either laughs or smiles since we're obviously very mature. The guys join us to find out what the commotion is about.

"Sorry, babe, but he got you there," Maliki says, coming up behind his son. He throws his arms up when Sierra glares at him. "I'm just saying."

Georgia signals back and forth between Amelia and Jax. "Those two are going to get married one day. I'll put my money on it right now."

"Can we please not talk about marrying my daughter off?" Silas says. "Those two hate each other."

"*And?*" Georgia asks. "Archer and I hated each other. Shoot, Maliki kept kicking Sierra out of his bar, and now, they're married."

Jax's green eyes widen as he gawks at Maliki. "You kicked Mom out of your bar?"

"You hated Mom?" Roman, Georgia's son, asks Archer at the same time.

"Can I kick Jax out of Daddy's bar?" Amelia asks, swatting her dark hair—the same color as mine—out of her eyes while glaring at Jax.

Silas shakes his head. "Sure, honey." He turns his attention to Maliki. "My daughter isn't going to marry a kid who sticks gum in her hair."

Georgia clicks her tongue against the roof of her mouth. "Just wait and see."

"Babe," Silas says, glancing at me, "tell them you're only supposed to fall in love with your best friend."

"Amelia is my best friend," Theo says, narrowing his eyes at Jax. "Does that mean we're going to fall in love?"

"That means, it's time for you boys to mind your business and quit talking about falling in love with my kid," Silas says, and I crack up.

Silas comes up behind me, resting his hand on my back before caressing my neck. "Remember when I found out we were having a girl, and I say she'd be a little firecracker?"

I laugh, staring up at him, a bright smile on my face. "Oh, she's definitely our little firecracker."

Silas and I might've been the last to get our happily ever after.

To admit we loved each other.

But sometimes, the last round means everything.

READ THE ENTIRE TWISTED FOX SERIES

BOOKS BY CHARITY FERRELL

TWISTED FOX SERIES

(each book can be read as a standalone)

Stirred

Shaken

Straight Up

Chaser

Last Round

BLUE BEECH SERIES

(each book can be read as a standalone)

Just A Fling

Just One Night

Just Exes

Just Neighbors

Just Roommates

Just Friends

STANDALONES

Bad For You

Beneath Our Faults

Pop Rock

Pretty and Reckless

Revive Me

Wild Thoughts

RISKY DUET

Risky

Worth The Risk

ABOUT THE AUTHOR

Charity Ferrell is a USA Today and Wall Street Journal bestselling author of the Twisted Fox and Blue Beech series. She resides in Indianapolis, Indiana with her fiancé and two fur babies. She loves writing about broken people finding love while adding humor and heartbreak along with it. Angst is her happy place.

When she's not writing, she's making a Starbucks run, shopping online, or spending time with her family.

Subscribe to my Newsletter here
www.charityferrell.com

 CPSIA information can be obtained
at www.ICGtesting.com
Printed in the USA
LVHW110008010622
720183LV00021B/198